Other Books by S. M. Stirling

Praise for *The Protector's War*

"[A] vivid portrait of a world gone insane. . . . It also has human warmth and courage. . . . It is full of bloody action, exposition that expands character, and telling detail that makes it all seem very real. . . . *The Protector's War* is grim and infused with a sense of hopeless dread. It is the determination of its major characters to create a safe and loving world that makes the book so affecting."   —*Statesman Journal* (Salem, OR)

"Against a colorful, action-filled background, Stirling shows characters who've solved the problems of immediate personal survival and can now focus on their legacies."
—David Drake, author of *The Way to Glory*

"Without a doubt. [*The Protector's War*] will raise the bar for alternate universe fiction and shows all of S. M. Stirling's hallmark ability to tell a stirring tale with vivid characters."
—John Ringo, *New York Times* bestselling author of *Ghost*

"An exemplary specimen of the postapocalyptic tale. That SF subgenre has to blend hope with ashes, nostalgia for the old, dead civilization with excitement about building a new one, adventure with reflection, lost technology with its replacements, and outmoded expectations with new paradigms dictated by the circumstances. All this Stirling does, with panache, insight and ingenuity. He alternates massive, thrilling set pieces that are impeccably crafted—pirate attacks at sea, ambushes by bandits, a charge of feral British hippos—with quieter chapters that examine core human issues such as responsibility, love, justice, jealousy, camaraderie, and spirituality. The blend is very effective. Just as your heart is racing fit to burst, you get a break."   —*Science Fiction Weekly*

"Villains of the darkest hue are matched by average men and women grown into heroes of Arthurian stature and complexity. The action streaks across the page like an avenging blade. . . . When you're finished reading, you'll beg him for more."   —John Birmingham, author of *Designated Targets*

"The characters are distinct and clearly drawn, with a lovely sense of humor. . . . Very readable."   —*SFRevu*

"Consistent excitement and dramatic tension . . . a marvelous adventure and a strong entry in an improving trilogy. The new characters and overseas settings are an immense asset, in that we finally see the global scope of the Change. Thus, there's even greater depth to the overall story."   —*SF Reviews*

continued

THE PROTECTOR'S WAR

S. M. STIRLING

A ROC BOOK

ROC

Published by New American Library, a division of
Penguin Group (USA) Inc., 375 Hudson Street,
New York, New York 10014, USA
Penguin Group (Canada), 90 Eglinton Avenue East, Suite 700, Toronto,
Ontario M4P 2Y3, Canada (a division of Pearson Penguin Canada Inc.)
Penguin Books Ltd., 80 Strand, London WC2R 0RL, England
Penguin Ireland, 25 St. Stephen's Green, Dublin 2,
Ireland (a division of Penguin Books Ltd.)
Penguin Group (Australia), 250 Camberwell Road, Camberwell, Victoria 3124,
Australia (a division of Pearson Australia Group Pty. Ltd.)
Penguin Books India Pvt. Ltd., 11 Community Centre, Panchsheel Park,
New Delhi - 110 017, India
Penguin Group (NZ), cnr Airborne and Rosedale Roads, Albany,
Auckland 1310, New Zealand (a division of Pearson New Zealand Ltd.)
Penguin Books (South Africa) (Pty.) Ltd., 24 Sturdee Avenue,
Rosebank, Johannesburg 2196, South Africa

Penguin Books Ltd., Registered Offices:
80 Strand, London WC2R 0RL, England

Published by Roc, an imprint of New American Library, a division of Penguin
Group (USA) Inc. Previously published in a Roc hardcover edition.

First Roc Mass Market Printing, September 2006
10 9 8 7 6 5 4 3 2 1

Copyright © S. M. Stirling, 2006
Map courtesy of Ms. Kier Salmon
All rights reserved

ROC REGISTERED TRADEMARK—MARCA REGISTRADA

Printed in the United States of America

To my nephew,
Gregory Taconi-Moore.
Long life, health, many tubas.

ACKNOWLEDGMENTS

Thanks to Wayne Throop, a valiant laborer in the handwavium mines and the unobtanium smelter, for help with technical explanations; to Harry Turtledove, for a Monty Pythonesque remark that gave me a flash of inspiration (or at least that's what *I* call it) and some excellent advice on how to integrate a subplot; to John Whitbourn (author of the excellent *Downslord* series and much else) and Steve Brady, for help with dialects; to Steve Brady again, for going all around Robin Hood's barn, or at least Bedfordshire and Buckinghamshire, helping with research; to Kier Salmon, for once again helping with the beautiful complexities of the Old Religion; to Don Ware, for information on Brownsville, which appears—somewhat fictionalized—in the book; to Melinda Snodgrass, Daniel Abraham, Emily Mah, Terry England, George R. R. Martin, and Walter Jon Williams of Critical Mass, for help and advice. And thanks to Dominic Duncan, of the Santa Fe Best Buy, for rescuing this book from a total hard-disk failure!

Special thanks to Heather Alexander, bard and balladeer, for permission to use the lyrics from her beautiful songs, which can be—and should be!—ordered at www.heatherlands.com. Run, do not walk, to do so.

Thanks to Arthur Conan Doyle, Leslie Anne Barringer, Rafael Sabatini and a long and honorable list of tellers of tales, of knights and banners and derring-do. I try my poor best to follow in the hoofprints of their destriers.

All mistakes, infelicities and errors are of course my own.

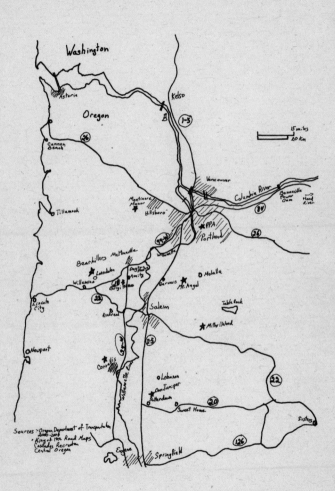

CHAPTER ONE

Woburn Abbey/Aspley Wood/Rasta Bob's Farm
Bedfordshire/Buckinghamshire, England
August 12th, 2006 AD—Change Year Eight

I've been here before, John Hordle suddenly realized, his
thumb moving over the leather that covered the grip of his
bow.

The moon was up, and it glittered on the ruffled surface
of the water to his left, where swans and ducks slept or
swam lazily. But there was still little light under the three
tall yews and the big oak; the night around him was still
save for night birds, the *whoo-whit* of tawny owls and the
screech of the barn type. Seven armed men lay grimly
silent behind brush and waist-high grass, watching the
great country house a quarter mile to the northeast. Candles and lantern lights flickered and blinked out behind the
windows as the servants and garrison sought their beds.
The pale limestone of it still glowed in the light of moon
and stars.

*When was that? Before the Change, of course, but when?
In summer, I think.*

Woburn Abbey was old; it began as a great Cistercian
monastery, in the year when the first Plantagenet was
crowned King of England. Henry VIII hung the last abbot
from an oak tree on the monastery grounds when he broke
with Rome and declared himself head of the Church, and
granted the estate to a favorite of his named John Russell.
The fortunes of the Russell family waxed and waned with

those of the English aristocracy and England herself. In the palmy years of the eighteenth century the fifth duke rebuilt the country house in Palladian magnificence and surrounded it with a pleasance—deer park and gardens covering five square miles—very convenient with London only thirty miles to the south. In 1953 the eleventh duke had opened it to the paying public, complete with golf course, pub, guided tours and antique shop—and avoided the forced sales which so many of his peers suffered after the Second World War.

Came on a day-trip, I did, drove up the M1. After I enlisted, but before I did the SAS selection . . . August of 1996, ten years ago to the month. Me first leave . . . who was the girl? Blond all over, she was, I remember that for certain. And she giggled.

In England the Change had struck in the early hours of the morning on March 18, 1998: the owner's family and Woburn's staff had only begun to realize what the failure of electricity and motors and explosives meant when the first spray of refugees from Milton Keynes and Luton arrived in the area two days later. The last duke's heir set up emergency quarters in the buildings and in tents in the great park, doing his best to organize supplies and sanitation. That ended when the last of the deer were eaten or escaped; by then most of the animals in the attached Safari Park had been released, before the keepers realized that even lion and timber wolves, tiger and rhino were edible when the other choice was death.

Shortly thereafter the hordes fleeing north from London met those from the midland cities moving south, and the great dying was well under way. A cannibal gang from the south side of Milton Keynes used the buildings as a headquarters for a time, roasting the meat of their catches in the fireplaces over blazes fed by the Regency furniture, rutting in the beds where Victoria and Albert had slept, and sitting beneath the Canalettos and Rembrandts to crack thighbones for the marrow with Venetian-glass paperweights. They turned on each other when prey grew scarce, and the last died of typhus on Christmas Day of 1998, shivering and comatose and alone.

Mary Sowley, that was her name. Bugger me blind if it wasn't ten years ago to the day. *We drove through Safari Park and looked at the bloody lions and didn't that get her motor going . . . She married that commuter in Essex, the one with fuzzy dice hanging from his rearview mirror. God alone knows where the poor bitch left her bones. Hope it was quick.*

Bicycle-borne scouts from the Isle of Wight scoured Bedfordshire in the spring of 1999; the smaller island off the south coast of the greater had kept two hundred thousand alive in the wreckage of a world, but resettling the British mainland was urgent. Their primary concern was to see where a useful crop of volunteer wheat could be reaped from fields unharvested the previous year and find the tools to do it, but on instructions from new-crowned King Charles III they made a stop at Woburn and a cursory attempt to board up windows and close doors as well, to protect the pictures and porcelain within. By the summer of Change Year Eight the estate was on the northeastern-most fringe of the recolonized zone, a royal garrison post in the commandery of Whipsnade.

There's some who'd say it's stupid to think about girls just before the hitting starts. Sam Aylward had, for example; but then Samkin was the sort who polished bullet casings in his spare time to cut down on the chance of a jam. *I wonder where old Sam ended up? He was abroad somewhere on the day of the Change.*

It was now nearly a decade later, and even past midnight John Hordle was sweating beneath his chain-mail shirt and underpadding. Insects buzzed and burrowed and bit amid the mysterious rustles and clicks of any forest at night—though these days that could include the movements of large carnivores with intent to harm.

Men are more dangerous, he thought whimsically. *They'll go for your throat when they* aren't *hungry.*

He could smell the intense yeasty smell of the dirt scuffed up beneath him as he crawled into position where grass and thistles stood tall. Training could let you move soundlessly; it didn't make you any lighter, and John Hordle had reached seven inches over six feet when he turned twenty in the year of the Change. He'd never been fat, but the only time he'd been under two hundred fifty pounds was that winter and spring, when the rations on the Isle of Wight had gotten just short of starvation amid hard labor and wet chill.

A soundless alert went among the men of his squad as boots tramped through the night, tense expectancy as a pair of sentries made their rounds between the raiding party and its target, tramping along the low ridge between the water and the house.

Vicious SIDs, he thought, motionless but acutely conscious of the speeding of the blood beating in his ears. *Or Varangians, as Sir Nigel prefers. More dignified, I suppose.*

The armor of the big men who paced by was enameled a dull matte green; they wore steel breast- and backplates, mail sleeves and leggings, and rounded sallet helmets with flares to protect the neck. That color didn't reflect much, but moonlight still glinted on steel—the honed edges of broad ax blades. Those were long-hafted weapons meant to be swung two-handed; the trademark of their unit.

"Hun er sviska!" one said, murmuring and shaping the air with his free hand. Which meant, roughly: *What a stunner!*

Special Icelandic Detachment, right enough, Hordle thought.

He'd picked up a little of the language—mostly in bed and from girls—since the islander refugee immigrants poured in during the second and third Change Years.

Same as King Charles, when he threw over Camilla and took up with Hallgerda. Mind, I don't blame him. Those legs!

The other guard chuckled and nodded: *"Hun heldur áfram og áfram."* That translated as: *She goes on and on!*

His left hand closed slowly on the grip of his longbow; there was an arrow on the string and four more were laid out in front of him, points and fletchings blackened with soot. One of the SIDs flipped his ax down from his shoulder and began a casual practice routine with it, spinning it in his hands and switching from right-hand leading to left on the fly—far from easy, and risky with an unshielded edge. It made an unpleasant *fweeept* sound as it cut the air in blurring arcs and circles.

Go on, Njal, Hordle thought, willing them to notice nothing. *Back to your nice cozy room and take a nap ...*

The Woburn Abbey garrison was a thirty-man platoon of the Special Icelandic Detachment—SID—First Heavy Infantry Battalion, according to report. King Charles didn't want regulars guarding a prisoner who'd been as popular with the troops as Sir Nigel Loring. That was why they'd moved him here, as well, rather than keeping the baronet under house arrest on his own commandery of Tilford Manor in Hampshire; too many of the folk there had been men of his own, or refugees he'd seen through the Dying Time on the Isle of Wight and led to settle their new lands. But Bedfordshire had only been colonized the last four years, and that, lightly; most of the dwellers were relocates from the Scottish islands and from Iceland and the Faeroes. They'd spent years working for others before they could accumulate tools and seed and stock to set up on their own, and they'd come this far north because the good land farther south was already claimed. And they were still much more likely to be unquestioning in their support of the royalist government than the native English.

Gratitude's a wonderful thing, Hordle thought sourly, as his chest moved in a slow, regular rhythm and his eyes flicked back and forth in a face darkened with burnt cork. *Too bad Charlie didn't stay grateful to Sir Nigel for getting him out of Sandringham and down to Wight.*

He'd been with the SAS—Special Air Service—detachment Nigel Loring took to rescue the heir to the crown from the Norfolk estate a week after the Change; the Household Cavalry had taken the queen out of London directly, in full Tin Bellies fig and using their sabers more than once on the mobs.

Perhaps if she'd lived Charles wouldn't have gotten so strange ... Or if any of the politicians had made it ... The last messenger out of London had said Blair was on his way, but he'd never arrived.

If ifs and buts were candied nuts, everyone would have lived through the Change, Hordle thought.

A clank sounded from behind him. Ice rippled through the sweat on his skin; the sound had been faint, very faint, but it was worse than a snapped twig—nothing else on earth sounded quite like metal on metal. The two SIDs stopped.

"Who goes there?" one of them called, his English accented but fluent. He reached for the horn slung at his belt. "Show yourself! This is a prohibited zone!"

"Oh, you conscientious keen-eared shite," Hordle sighed.

He drew the hundred-fifty-pound longbow's string to the ear with a slight grunt of effort as he rose to one knee; the SID he aimed for had just enough time to put his lips to the horn's mouthpiece before the arrow slashed through the intervening twenty feet. A sharp metallic *tunk!* sounded as the punch-shaped arrowhead struck the center of the guardsman's breastplate and sank nearly to the feathers, with the head and a red-dripping foot of shaft sticking out of his back.

The horn gave a strangled blat that sprayed a mist of blood into the air, looking black in the moonlight and turning his yellow beard dark. He toppled backward with a clank. Two more bows snapped in the same instant: one shaft went wide, but the other slammed into the second Icelander's nose. It had been shot uphill, from a kneeling position, and it angled upward through his brain and cracked out the rear of his skull, knocking the helmet off, spinning. The body shook in a moment's spastic reflex on the ground, rattling and rustling the armor as bootheels drummed on the turf.

Hordle was on his feet and moving before the helmet came to rest on the sheep-cropped grass. He ran crouching into the open, grabbed both bodies by their throats and dragged the two men and their gear back to the shelter of the brush at a quick, wary walk. There was blood on his left hand as he dropped them and sank down again beside his bow. He washed palm and fingers clean with water from his canteen, and reached under the hem of his mail shirt to wipe it off on the gambeson. It wouldn't do to have his hands sticky or slippery.

They waited silently, watching and listening. No sound of alarm came from the great Palladian manor ahead, a glimmer of pale limestone in the moonlit night. He nodded as Alleyne Loring came up beside him, going down on one knee. The young officer was twenty-eight, Hordle's age almost to a day. The pub that Hordle's father ran, the Pied Merlin, was less than half a mile from Tilford Manor, and they'd grown up as neighbors and playmates before the Change and served together since.

Alleyne wore an officer's harness armored in plate cap-a-pie, from steel shoes to bevoir and visored sallet. He slid the visor up along the curved surface of the helm as he used his binoculars to scan the overgrown parkland between them and the entrance. It had been scattered trees and deer-grazed grassland before the Change, but even after the abbey was reoccupied there had been no labor to spare for ornamental work—the garrison here lived from its own fields and herds, with a little help from nearby farmers. There hadn't been enough stock to keep the vegetation down either, until the last year or two. Bushes gleamed with beads of dew, and the grass was better than waist-high in places.

"All right," the younger Loring said softly. "That gives us fifteen minutes until they notice. Go!"

He drew the long double-edged sword at his waist and led the way at a run, moving with practiced agility despite the sixty pounds of alloy-steel protection, an extra sword and a heater-type shield slung over his back. The six archers who followed were more lightly armored: open-faced helms, chain-mail tunics, sword and buckler. Hordle kept an arrow on the string and grinned in a rictus of tension, they'd be visible now from the upper stories of the building—to anyone unblinded by artificial light who knew what to look for.

"Who dares, wins," he muttered to himself. "Or gets royally banged about if things go south."

Nigel Loring woke in darkness. He lay for a moment letting his eyes adjust, ears straining for the sound he'd heard. Had it been his imagination? A fragment of a dream—a dream of combat, before the Change or after it? God knew his life had provided plenty of material for nightmares, starting with Oman back in the seventies.

No. That was something. Perhaps an animal on the grounds, or a guard stumbling in the darkness, but something. Something real.

Maude Loring stirred beside him in the big four-poster bed. "What is it, dear?" she asked.

"Shhh," he said, straining to hear again.

Nothing, but there was a tension in the air. He put out a hand in the darkness and touched her shoulder. Then he swung his feet to the floor and padded over to the window. They were in the Covent Garden suite—bedroom, dressing room and bathroom, the latter restored to limited functioning. The same engineers who'd set up the wind-pump system to give the house running water had put a grid of steel bars over the window, mortising the ends into the stone. That was a rather soft local limestone; Sir Nigel had determined in the first days of his captivity here that he could get the frame out, with a few hours' unobserved work and some tools. He'd filched a knife and could have improvised a chisel from it, but the guards were quite alert—two below the window all night, and a pair at the doors—all stolid types who pretended they couldn't speak English or follow his halting Icelandic.

The bars were thick and close placed, allowing a hand to go through but not an elbow, but they didn't totally destroy the view, and the windows themselves were half-open on this warm summer's night. His eyes weren't the best—he'd needed corrective contacts since an RPG drove grit into them in a wadi in Dhofar—but seeing was as much a matter of knowing how to pay attention as sheer input. He looked down the long stretch of grassland across the park to the west, and saw moonlight glinting on the Basin Pond and the dark bulk of the Abbot Oak— where Abbot Hobbes had been hung in 1538. His hands tightened on the steel as he saw movement south of there, dark figures flitting towards the building. Not the roving patrol the Varangians kept up here, either. There were far too many of them; he estimated at least four or possibly half a dozen, but they moved so quickly and skillfully it was hard to be certain.

"Maude," he said softly, turning to see her sitting up and alert, her white face framed in dark hair. "Something's happening. We'd best take precautions."

She nodded briskly, swung out of bed and began to dress. They had had twenty-two years together before the Change and eight since, and neither needed many words to know the other's mind. He quickly slipped into his colonel's undress uniform—that was the post-Change version, designed to be worn under armor or as fatigues, tough and practical and with grommets of chain mail under the armpits, to cover the weak spots in a suit of plate. This set was clean, but there were stains from blood and sweat and the rust that wore off even the best-kept armor. His wife looked a question at him as he felt behind the frame of an eighteenth-century painting of a London scene and took out the dinner knife. He'd palmed it when the Varangians had arrested them at table with the king at Highgrove and brought them here. It had been filed down to a point and given a respectable edge over the last two weeks, and she'd carefully braided and tied unraveled fabric from the bottom of an Oriental rug onto the grip so that it wouldn't slip in his hand.

He slipped the blade up the right sleeve of his jacket. She dressed then herself, in riding breeches and tweed jacket—they were allowed exercise, though always separately and under heavy guard. King Charles had made their confinement comfortable enough, probably the result of guilt and reluctance. Queen Hallgerda hadn't managed to talk him into throwing the pair into a dungeon or sending them to the headsman's ax—not quite yet.

But she will do it, given enough time to convince him it's for the good of the realm. Damn the woman!

"What do you suppose is happening?" Maude said calmly.

"Not quite sure, old girl, but I think it's a rescue attempt," he said, his voice equally serene.

Although I feel more nervous than I have in thirty years, he thought. *It's a trifle different when the wife's along too.*

"I don't suppose . . ." Maude said.

Sir Nigel shook his head. "If His Majesty was going to give us the chop for asking about Parliament and elections and lifting the Emergency Powers Act once too often, the Varangians would handle it without needing to sneak about through the shrubbery. Light the candle, please. If it's friends come to call, we should make sure they know we're in. Then give me a spot of help with the furniture."

She nodded calmly; he felt a stab of pride as she picked up a lighter and flicked it alive, then went around the room touching the flame to candlewicks and the rapeseed-oil lanterns, as calmly as if they were back home at Tilford. Mellow golden light filled the room, touching the chinoiserie of the wallpaper, the pictures and mirrors in their ornate frames, and the pale plaster scrollwork medallions on the ceiling. It was a melancholy sight, in its way; the detritus of a thrice-lost world, the elegant symmetries of the Age of Reason filtered through the Age of Steam and his own twentieth century. The current situation was more suited to an older, darker period—the Wars of the Roses, perhaps, or even the stony roads of Merlin's time.

A few seconds sufficed to force a mixture of wood splinters and candle wax into the keyhole; then he shoved wedges made from shims worked out of the interiors of tables and settees under the doors. Together they dragged a massive desk over and tipped it up against the frame, lodging the edge against the pediment above and bracing smaller items in the remaining space. It had all been planned in advance, of course, against the chance they would need it.

"That should hold them for a little while," he said, as a shout from the other side asked what they were doing.

Maude nodded, she was a strong-featured woman of fifty, two years younger than he, and three inches taller than his own five foot five. It went unspoken between them that the Varangian commander almost certainly had orders to see that they didn't survive any rescue attempt.

"If you could detach this table leg for me, darling?" she asked politely.

He nodded, braced a foot against the frame and

wrenched the mahogany loose, working it back and forth so that the pegs wouldn't squeal when they broke. Sir Nigel was a small man, but nobody who'd seen him exert himself thought he was weak. Maude smiled and hefted the curved hardwood.

"Makes me nostalgic, rather." At his glance and raised eyebrow, she explained: "About the size and weight of the hockey stick I used back at Cheltenham as a girl."

She took a good grip on it and waited; Sir Nigel took the opportunity to use the splendid bathroom one last time. He'd rather have had his armor with him, but unlike a suit of plate, the cloth uniform did have a button-up fly, and a functioning loo wasn't all that common these days. He might as well have one last chance at decent English plumbing.

As he returned a horn sounded, dunting and snarling in the night—not the brass instrument the regular forces used, but the oxhorn trumpet the Special Icelandic Detachment affected. The clash of steel sounded, rapidly coming closer, and men's voices shouting—and then a few screaming in pain.

Nigel Loring smiled slightly. "And they wouldn't tell us where Alleyne was," he said dryly, feeling another glow of pride—for his son, this time.

"I rather think we know, now," she said.

"Right on schedule," Alleyne Loring said. "Good old Major Buttesthorn."

They approached the great Georgian country house from the west. The long stretch of grass was being used to graze the garrison's horses and working oxen since the Basin Pond provided a natural watering point, and large dark shapes shied and moved aside as they trotted forward. A sudden clash of steel sounded faintly from over Woburn Abbey's high roof, and then the snarl of a signal horn. Hordle grinned more widely. The SIDs' families were quartered in one of the two big outbuildings behind the main house, the South Court, and the cover there was much better for a clandestine approach. The diversionary attack was going in right as planned—with maximum noise and plenty of fire arrows. *That* ought to keep the day watch at home; with luck, some of the ones on night duty would hurry back.

But not all of them—and if the rescue party wanted Sir Nigel and Lady Maude out alive, they had to move quickly. For that matter, the garrison commander would probably send a detachment out here as soon as he collected his wits. Hit them fast when they weren't looking, and put the boot in hard while they were still wondering about the first time. . . .

"That's the window," Alleyne said, pointing.

"Just like the drawings, sir," Hordle said.

The abbey was built like a giant uneven H, with the short arms and the Corinthian facade in the middle of the connecting arm facing west, and the longer east-facing ones enclosing a court open in that direction. The rooms faced west, and the candlelit window was sixty feet up and a hundred distant from where the storming party halted.

Hordle took a blunt-headed arrow from his quiver; it had a small slip of paper fastened to it with a bit of elastic. He drew carefully, well under full extension, and shot. The arrow hissed away, and an instant later he was rewarded with a tinkle of breaking glass.

The arrow smashed the windowpane and flicked across the room to dent the plaster. Nigel Loring winced slightly at how narrowly it had missed a painting by Nebot; his wife was already unfastening the message.

" 'Stand clear and pick up the string from the next,' " she read. "But dear, we can't climb down even if they *do* have a rope attached. The bars . . ."

Whhhptt.

The first shot hit the bars and bounced back. The second landed in the room trailing a thin cord, and Maude Loring began to haul it in hand over hand, a pile of it growing at her feet.

"Sir Nigel!" a voice called from the hall outside their suite. "Please to open the door, immediately!"

He didn't bother to reply. Seconds later the first ax hit the outside door of their suite.

"Keep going!" he barked to his wife, and went to stand beside the doorway.

Through the piled furniture he could see the panels begin to splinter; a two-handed war ax made short work of anything not built to military specifications. The dry splintery scent of old wood filled the air, followed by the *glug-glug-glug* sound of Icelandic—in this case panting curses between grunts of effort. Loring flipped the knife down into his hand and into a thumb-on-pommel grip—good for a short-range stab—then risked a glance over his shoulder.

The heavy rope had come up at the end of Maude's cord—two of them, in fact, both woven-wire cable. One was the top of a Jacob's ladder, and she was a little red-faced with effort before she clipped that to the bar nearest the left side of the window. The other had a ring clip swagged onto the end. She fastened it to the center bar, made sure that the thin cord that prevented it from falling back was still tied to a chair, and stepped back.

"Encourage them to hurry, my dear," he called, and turned back to his own task—making sure the Varangians didn't break through too soon.

"You chaps! *Do* hurry—we're in a spot of bother here!"

He heard her voice crying out into the darkness, and then the first axhead came all the way through the panels of the door. It withdrew, and took a yard-wide chunk of the battered wood with it. A gauntleted hand groped through to feel for the knob and lock. Sir Nigel had anticipated that, and left a pathway he could use; he slid forward and stabbed backhanded, his arm moving with the flicking precision of a praying mantis. Stainless steel stabbed through buff leather and flesh and bone, and he barely managed to withdraw it in time as the guardsman wrenched his arm back with a scream.

One, he thought. *Out of this fight, if not crippled.*

There was no great army of men here; less than thirty. The entire Special Icelandic Detachment numbered only three hundred, and it was a quarter of the ration strength of the British army as of Change Year Eight—and the troops all spent the majority of their time laboring on public works or doing police duties or working to feed themselves. More wasn't necessary when the whole of mainland Britain held only six hundred thousand dwellers.

Immigrants included, he thought, poised, as the axes thundered again. *Well, they're just doing their duty as they see it.*

"Right," John Hordle said. "Let's clear the way!"

They tallied on to the main cable, Hordle and Alleyne at the front—the younger Loring was only six feet and built like a leopard rather than a tiger, but strong as whipcord with it.

"Remember, *stop* pulling the moment it comes free!" Alleyne said sharply. "If we pull the precursor cord loose, we'll have to run another up."

Hordle took a deep breath and called: *"Heave!"*

Seven strong men surged backward against the cable with hissing grunts of effort, driving against their heels as if this were a tug-of-war game at a village fair. Steel squealed against rock; he could feel the bar bending as the cable went rigid, and then there was a sudden release of tension as it broke free. They all threw themselves forward at once, and Hordle blew out his cheeks in a gasp of relief as he saw Maude Loring's hand come through the remaining bars, hauling up the cable and setting it on the next of the steel cylinders. The first fell, bent into a shallow U, clattering and clanging as it dropped on the pavement below the window.

"Ready . . . *heave!*"

This one came more easily; they knew the strain needed, and knew they could deliver it. A man could get through already; one more and it would be easy. Lady Maude looked over her shoulder as she refastened the loop.

Then she called, urgently: "They're in the room!"

"I'm coming, Mother!" Alleyne shouted, dashing for the ladder.

"Christ!" Hordle shouted; they'd need another bar out before *he* could get through, for certain! And the Lorings couldn't climb out, either, not with SIDs in the same room. They had to get some blades in there, to throw the SIDs back on their heels and give the Lorings time to break contact. So . . .

"Heave, you bastards!"

Maude shouted out the window: "They're in the room!" and snatched up her table leg.

Some corner of Nigel Loring's mind wished desperately for a sword. Three Varangians were crowded into the entrance, hampering each other—but not enough that a man with a converted table knife had much of a chance against three armored killers. Two of them set their shoulders against the desk and the other furniture that blocked their way and started rocking it back by sheer brute strength; the third punched the top of his ax at Loring's face like a pool cue, an effective stroke when you didn't have room for a chop—five pounds of steel would crush your facial bones in with unpleasant finality. The Varangian expected Sir Nigel to leap back; they knew he was agile enough. That would give the axman space to push his way into the drawing room, drive Nigel into a corner and demolish him.

Instead he jerked his head just enough aside to let the pell of the ax go by; blood started from his cheek as the grazing steel kissed him, a burning coldness. Then he slid forward again with that dancer's grace, his left hand gripping the ax and pulling it to one side, the knife in his other whipping across in a backhand slash at the other man's eyes. The guardsman bellowed in alarm and snatched his head aside in turn, saving his eyes at the price of taking a nasty cut that opened his face to the bone along one cheek, and relaxing his hold on the ax as he did.

Sir Nigel's hand clamped down on it at once and pulled sharply; he stabbed backhand with the knife once more, and the ax came free as his opponent twisted once more to avoid the point. It hit the shoulder joint of the back and breast and snapped with a musical *tunnnggg* sound; then the Varangian did something sensible: smashed one gauntleted fist at Nigel's face, and used the other to draw the short sword hung at his waist. Sir Nigel skipped back-

ward away from the gutting stroke of the man's upward
stab.

The mass of furniture overturned with a roar, scattering
itself across the room in a bouncing, crackling tide. The two
Varangians who'd pushed the barricade out of the way
stumbled forward, puffing and off-balance for an instant.
Nigel saw that, but there was nothing he could do about it.
His own panting reminded him forcefully that he was fifty-
two this coming September—in superb condition for a
man his age, but still a good three decades older than his
immediate opponent—and air burned like thin fire in his
lungs. He could smell the acrid odor of his own sweat as it
ran down his cheeks and shone through the thinning gray-
blond hair on his scalp.

The Varangian was enraged by the slash that had nearly
taken his eyes. It streamed blood into his red beard across
a face contorted in fury, he stood eight inches taller than
the Englishman, and seemed to have arms longer than an
ape's as they wove with sword and dagger advanced. Sir
Nigel hefted the ax; it was heavier and longer than he liked
in a weapon but he gripped it expertly with his left hand at
the outer end of the helve and his right, feet spread and at
right angles—which might have been a mistake. The
guardsman's blue eyes went a little wider as he recognized
hold and stance, and he made no move to attack. He didn't
have to. In a few seconds his comrades would be on Loring, and it would end in a flurry of ax strokes impossible to
counter.

"St. George for England!" Loring shouted, and attacked.

His first move was a feint, a lizard-quick punch with the
head of the ax. That brought the Varangian blades up to
block. Stepping in, he delivered the real blow—an overhead loop that turned into a cut at the neck, hands sliding
together down to the end of the haft. The other man began
a sidestep and block to deflect it, but at that instant Maude
Loring's chair leg cracked into his elbow. The chain mail
there probably saved the bone from breaking, but the two-
handed blow on the sacral nerve still made his hand fly
open by reflex, and the dagger in it went flying. His wild
stab with the short sword left him open, and the ax in Sir

Nigel's hands fell on his shoulder with a sound like a black-smith's hammer.

The Varangian toppled backward with a sound that was half curse and half scream of shock and pain; the broad curved cutting edge of the ax had gone through the metal of his breastplate, just deeply enough to sever his collar-bone. Torn steel gripped the blade tightly enough to pull Nigel forward; he released the haft of the ax perforce. Movement caught the corner of his eye, to the right—

A figure in dark green armor squeezed through the win-dow. It was a complete suit of plate—officer's or lancer's gear—and there was the face so much like his, below the raised visor. Alleyne Loring was grinning as he reached over his shoulder to flip a longsword through the air, then dropped a shield to the ground and skidded it over with a push of one foot.

Sir Nigel raised his hand as the weapon spun towards him; the leather-wrapped hilt smacked into it with a com-forting solidity, and he had a yard of double-edged, cut-and-thrust blade in his fist. It was his own, intimately familiar from eight years of practice and battle. He snatched up the heater-shaped shield as well; it had the five Loring roses on its face, and a diagonally set loop and grip on the rear. He slid his arm in from the lower left, took the bar at the upper right corner tightly and brought that fist up under his chin *just so*. . . . He had the shield up under his eyes and the sword poised while the two hale Varangians hesitated. Another figure climbed and wiggled through the window, cursing the tightness—a man huge and familiar, grinning as well as he took his archer's buckler in his left hand and drew the great hand-and-a-half sword slung by his side with the other.

Little John Hordle, Nigel thought, grinning back. *Well, the card's full and the dance may begin in earnest!*

More Varangians crowded through the shattered door, bearing axes and the spike-blade-hook menace of a guis-arme on its six-foot shaft. There was a moment of silence as the three Englishmen stared at their foes—silence save for the moaning of the wounded man crawling out the door among his comrade's feet—and then it began. An ax swung at Nigel; he stepped into the stroke, sloping his shield to glance the battering impact away at an angle, stabbing around it at a face.

Steel rang on metal, thudded against wood; breath sounded harsh as men stamped and shoved and thrust through the great candlelit drawing room. Over it a roar of battle cries:

"Konung Karl! Konung Karl!"

"A Loring! A Loring!"

"St. George for England!"

"Ettu skit Engelendingur!"

Hordle's wild-bull bellow joined the cries as his heavy sword cracked into the shaft of an ax and through it and into a face: *"Die, you sodding SID bastard!"*

Then the guisarme hooked over the edge of his shield, hauling him forward and off-balance, leaving him open to the wielder's partner. The Varangian poised his ax to kill, but an arrow went by, close enough to brush the fletching against Sir Nigel's neck. It buried itself in the Varangian's face, slanting past his nose and coming out the angle of his jaw, breaking most of the teeth on that side of his face in the process. Nigel killed the man behind the guisarme by reflex, a swift twisting thrust to the neck, then turned his head to see someone kneeling in the window with his bow in his hands. He recognized the narrow dark face: Mick Badding, from his old SAS company.

"Get out! The horses are here and the SIDs are coming round!" the man shouted.

Seconds later the last two Varangians were out of the room, dragging a third between them by the arms. They'd left two dead behind them, and chances were they'd be back soon enough. Or they'd simply hold the corridor and then come around to cut off the rescue party outside the window.

"Time to depart indeed," Sir Nigel said. "Maude, if you'll go first—"

He looked around, then made a small choked sound. The sword fell from his hand, clattering on the floor. Maude Loring was lying there herself, clutching at her side. Nigel and Alleyne went to their knees on either side of her, looking incredulously at the wound in her side. From the broad slit that her fingers tried to hold closed, Nigel guessed that the point of the short sword had gone in under her floating rib. Judging from the amount of blood that flowed through those fingers and spread a stain on the carpet, skill or chance had wrenched the knife-edged weapon around in the wound, cutting into her kidney or several of the great veins.

Father and son shared a single appalled look. Both knew from experience precisely what that particular injury meant: death, not long delayed. A pre-Change trauma unit might have been able to keep her alive, if she were in it *now*. All the surgeons in the Changed world couldn't save her, with a miracle thrown in.

"Maude . . ." he croaked, unbelieving.

Her face had been clenched against the scream that would distract him from the life-and-death focus of combat. Now it relaxed, and the hand against her side did too. He clamped the wound with his own, but the blood tide was ebbing even as he did. Her eyes moved from his face to Alleyne's; she tried to say something, then shuddered and went still.

"Maude . . ."

Time ceased to move. Words went by, without meaning until a voice shouted in his ear: "Sir! Colonel, there's no *time*. We have to move *now*."

That seemed to start his mind working again, after a fashion. *Men have died to free you. Your son's here— Maude's son. You have to move* now. He reached out and shook the younger man across from him by the side of his helmet until the armor rattled on him.

"Alleyne!" he snapped. "Pull yourself together, man!"

His son obeyed with an effort that made him shudder, but his eyes slid down towards Maude's harsh features again, now relaxed and somehow younger.

"Put her here," Sir Nigel said gently, standing beside a couch.

The body had the boneless flaccidity of the newly dead. Nigel closed her eyes and held them for a second, then stood and scrubbed his left hand across his face, forcing a deep breath into his lungs. Hordle and Badding were throwing the wrecked furniture into the doorway again; then the big NCO smashed a lamp on it. Flame splashed up from it as the glass oil reservoir shattered. It roared higher as several others joined it.

"Sir," Badding said. "Out."

"You first—"

"Sir, don't play silly buggers with us now. Your lady's dead and beyond help. You're what we *came* here for!"

The man's dark-bearded pug features were twisted with concern; Badding, Nigel remembered, had a wife and three children and a farm near Tilford, and a young sister he'd brought through the Change. He nodded, picked up the shield and sword, went to the window and swung himself out. The impulse simply to let fall was strong. Instead he made himself put hands and feet to the ladder. Too many were depending on him.

"I am *so* sorry, Nigel," Major Buttesthorn said. "So very sorry."

"Fortunes of war, Oliver," Sir Nigel said, in a voice that forbade condolences, even from an old friend.

They were stopped in a deep hollow in the Aspley Woods, northwest of Woburn Manor, surrounded by feral rhododendron and waist-high bracken. Those hills were densely forested with oak and beech and ash, ancients two centuries old and towering a hundred feet above them in a canopy that allowed only a rare glimpse of starlight above, the moon having set. The small, almost flameless fire was enough to make tea—or rather the herbal substitute that went by that name these days. He could smell the slightly acrid scent of it over the scent of damp leafmold as he checked automatically for red-ant nests before sitting.

One of the soldiers thrust a thick mug into his hands; he sipped automatically at the hot brew, heavy with beet sugar to hide the taste. In the distance a wolf howled over the nighted hills—some distant part of Loring's mind told him it was one of the packs descended from the escapees released by the keepers of Woburn Safari Park and Whipsnade, the country extension of London Zoo near here. The rest of him felt at one with the cold, lonely sobbing that echoed through the night, fierce and solitary.

Get a grip, Nigel, he scolded himself. *And wolves are very social.*

"And thank you, Oliver," he said aloud. Raising his voice slightly: "Thank you all. I know you've taken a very great risk."

There was a murmur, but not much talk; they were too close to possible pursuit, even if their back scouting had shown the remaining Varangians preoccupied with putting out fires and sending off messengers rather than actively following the raiding party. And beyond that, traditional English reserve seemed to be making a comeback in the Changed world—something he rather approved of, along with a good many other things.

Everyone crouched and reached for weapons when a rustling went through the woods like heavy careless feet in the dried leaves, then relaxed when John Hordle chuckled.

"Badger," he said. "Does sound like a man bludging about, eh?"

Buttesthorn sat near Nigel. "Do you want us to take care of the Varangians who're left?" he said, his voice soft and careful, as if the other man were fragile or explosive or both. "We'll be going back that way . . . might actually be safer with no witnesses, don't you know . . ."

Nigel shook his head. His son was standing guard out in the darkness; out where there was nobody to see his face. Nigel envied him. It was as if his own mind were a compass needle; every few seconds it seemed to slip out of his grasp and turn back towards the sentence *Maude is dead.* Each impact hit him with the same force.

"No," Nigel said, surprised at the calmness of his own voice. "It's no use, Oliver. In a fight like that, you strike out at anyone who's going for you. The man probably didn't even know who he was stabbing, just that someone had hit him on the elbow and *he* was about to be struck with a very large ax. This isn't about personal vengeance. And you wouldn't have the advantage of surprise, anyway. Say what you will of them, the Varangians are stout fighters and in a stand-up battle there aren't enough with you to overrun them."

Oliver Buttesthorn bowed his head. Loring went on: "Besides, you're going to be needed here, Oliver. I can't stay, not unless I'm prepared to start a civil war. Which I am not—and besides, we would lose."

"It may come to that," the other officer said.

"And it may not. And in a few years, if it *does* come to that, perhaps you *won't* lose. But I would, if I tried it now. You can't harvest a field before it's ripe."

His smile was slight and painful as he sat with his back against a fallen log, but Buttesthorn's brows went up. The other man was about Loring's age and only a few inches taller; he would have been fat save for the ruthless standards of their regiment before the Change and hard living and harder travel and fighting afterward. Instead he was built like a balding, red-faced fireplug.

"Just thinking," Loring said. It helped a little, to keep his mind on impersonal things. "It's a great pity Charles has become so . . . eccentric."

One of the enlisted men in the background muttered something that sounded like *Gone bloody barking mad, you mean?*

"He was splendid, those first few years; well, he did know all that organic farming bit, which was frightfully useful. The Emergency Powers decrees were essential, at first. And then the other things . . . I was quite enthused when he abolished that metric nonsense and brought back the old weights and measures."

"And pounds, shillings and pence! If only it had stopped there," Buttesthorn said. "I blame Queen Hallgerda for encouraging him."

Loring shrugged. "That's how she and her relatives have elbowed themselves into power," he said. "By backing up his, ah, whims. And one can see why they were resentful; far too many people expected all the Icelanders to stay farmhands forever, just because they arrived hungry and destitute. Still, her faction's alienating more and more people of all backgrounds. The king may be . . . strange, but his sons are both very likely young men."

"Unless Hallgerda Long-Legs has them done away with in favor of her own brood," Oliver said grimly. "His Majesty may be mad, but by God it's certain he's not impotent or infertile. Three already!"

"Well, old chap, that's why you need to keep a careful eye out and make preparations," Nigel Loring said, finishing the so-called tea. "And keep up the pressure finally to call a real Parliament. Now you must get going, old friend, and so must I."

"That's the farm, sir," John Hordle said not long after dawn.

A chorus of *pink . . . pink . . . pink . . .* came from blackbirds their passage had disturbed; the twittering of robins and the long liquid trilling of song thrushes wove through it. With some part of himself that wasn't numb, Nigel Loring reminded himself that he should listen carefully; he'd left England many times before, but this was likely to be the last parting. Riding east from Aspley Woods, down the escarpment and then back northwestward across sandy heath with the cool smell of dew-wet heather crushed beneath a horse's hooves . . . there wouldn't be much more of that, if they made good their escape.

He nodded and halted his horse with an imperceptible shift of balance and the slightest touch on the reins; that wasn't an easy trick to learn, in the heavy war saddle and a full suit of plate. Compared to the way he'd learned to ride—in the slight English saddle, and then foxhunting—it had felt like being strapped into an upright coffin. But he'd picked up the knack rather thoroughly.

Even an old dog can learn the odd new trick, he thought, shading his eyes with his hand and peering northeastward against the dawn, the visored sallet helm slung to his saddlebow.

The farmer had probably taken up the land here because there was a tax-and-rent reduction for those willing to be first in such places, isolated and dangerous, and the ten-foot-high fence of angle iron and barbed wire that surrounded the houses was supporting evidence. This was the very northernmost edge of cultivation; in fact, there wasn't another active farm for half a mile, and the old A5130 had been hacked back into barely passable state to reach the narrow lane that led to the homestead. North of here the road was simply a linear mound of thornbush twenty feet high.

The largest building in the little cluster of habitation was a long, low-slung, whitewashed cottage with a thatched roof and small square-paned windows; several centuries old from the look of it and the size of the oaks and beeches in the garden—which included a lawn ornament in the shape of a four-foot black rooster half hidden in tall shaggy grass. Four other cottages stood nearby in a rough row along an old laneway, ranging from a tiny half-timbered affair to a modern two-story probably built in the 1960s. They'd all been reroofed with thatch—probably because if you grew long-stemmed wheat it was easier to use the straw than find fresh slate or tile. Besides which, it was officially encouraged.

Early as it was, the farm's folk seemed hard at work. He uncased his binoculars and looked; smoke rose in slow drifting columns from the tall brick chimneys that pierced the roofs, and he saw a woman in overalls and Wellingtons leading a horse towards a cluster of barns and a pond a hundred yards south. The space around the barns held a comfortable litter of tools—a two-furrow riding plow, a set of disk harrows and a tipping hay rake. Two more women hoed in an acre-sized stretch of vegetable garden, and an indeterminate teenager walking back towards the farmstead from the barns had a yoke over the shoulders and buckets of milk on either end. A brown-skinned girl child of eight or so in a shapeless wool frock fed chickens that clustered and gobbled about her feet with grain held in her apron. Another who might have been her sister save that she was pink and blond guarded a clutch of toddlers with the aid of a nondescript collie. Everyone was breeding enthusiastically these days, but from the numbers there must be at least three married couples here. The smell was of turned earth wet with the morning, smoke and manure and baking bread.

He could hear the rising-falling moan of a wool spinning

wheel from the small cottage, joined by the rhythmic *thump . . . thump . . .* of a loom. A post-Change metal wind pump whirled merrily to fill a tank set in an earthen mound. Forty or fifty acres of cultivation surrounded the steading, in fields edged by hedges new or newly trimmed back; sheep and cattle grazed on pastures whose origin as a golf course was barely visible. Stooked sheaves of wheat and barley stood in neat tripods and children with slings sent a flock of thieving black rooks up from them. Other fields held harvested flax in windrows, potatoes, turnips, beets and a young orchard that was just coming into bearing, with apples glowing red among the leaves.

The cleared land was an island, though. Beyond it was wilderness. The hedge around the field further north where the men labored at clearance was typical—it had sprouted twenty feet high or better, a wall of hawthorn and bramble, and the hawthorn had spread further horizontally both ways, covering the old farm lane and sloping out into the field from all four sides as well. The faster-growing bramble intertwined with it and went on ahead, reaching out nearly to the center of the field, each cane starting a new plant where it dipped and touched the ground. It hadn't reached the center of what had been an open space yet; that was merely chest high with dock and nettle. Most of the land was a tangle taller than a man, with bramble canes ranging from pencil-thick to thumb-thick coiling between each other in a mass of thorns and tough wood and dense green leaves hiding it all. It was thick with birds as well, their voices louder than he'd ever heard on an August day before the Change, and with insects and small game. Rabbits burst out and fled in hysterical bounds as the dense scrub was chopped down.

His skin itched just looking at it; bramble thorns broke off beneath your skin, and often the result was infection and septicemia. Most of lowland Britain was like this now—big patches even in the south and a continuous mass of it from the frontier of settlement here to East Lothian in Scotland—save for pre-Change forest and moor. Plenty of saplings were already sprouting through the ground cover—oak and beech, ash and alder—but it would be generations before the king trees grew tall enough to close the canopy and shade out the scrub.

"You're certain of them?" Nigel asked, tilting his head towards the men in the field.

Both Hordle and his son nodded.

"Hordle introduced us," Alleyne said. "Brief acquaintance, but I agree with him. That means taking the farmer's men on his word, but they haven't turned us in yet, eh? And he did give us some very useful pointers on Newport Pagnell. He's hunted that far north a few times."

Hordle continued: "You didn't have much to do with Bob, sir; he mustered out to take up the farm about the time we got back from that mission in France, four years ago. But I've known him a good long while now, since before the Change. I, mmm, warned him to volunteer for escort duty back when we took the queen out of London, and recommended him, like. Warned him to get the missus and his boy in the convoy as well. He vouches for his folk; one of them's an Icelander, but he's got no use for the queen's party. And we need fresh horses and supplies."

Nigel nodded agreement. He and Alleyne couldn't ride their war mounts in full harness for long—that wore the beasts out, and they might need trained reflexes and best speed before they reached the coast. The same held for his son, and Hordle's weight was a trial for anything he rode in any event. Eight years wasn't long to breed up a horse herd, and they were still scarce despite imports from friendly Ulster.

He took a firmer grip on his lance, his hand on the shaft and the butt resting in the ring welded to his right stirrup. The shield slung over his back clattered as he rode along the cleared lane until the farmhouse was hidden from view, then down towards the men working in the field ahead.

A broad strip had already been chopped free of brush near the dirt roadway, and the gate had been hacked out of a mountain of vegetation covering it. The cleared land looked as if giant moles had been at work, holes pocking the deep brown boulder-clay soil where the roots of the bramble bushes and blackthorns had been ripped out.

Every so often in the cleared space there was a great heap of brushwood twice man-height, and a few smoking circles of ash showed what would be done once the cuttings had dried enough to burn. A little farther out the farmer and two helpers were chopping at the heavy tangle with bill-hook and ax and machete, piling it in mounds then tearing out roots and an arm-thick stump with a wheeled machine whose steel tines were pulled by four oxen.

Hard work, that, Loring thought. *More difficult every year.*

The three men turned at the sound of hooves, quickly snatching up weapons—two longbows, which the law now said every adult had to keep and practice with, and a bill-hook that would slash through men as easily as tough thornwood. The area to the north of here wasn't quite clear of human life; a few thousand feral outlaws still haunted it, even after plague spots like Milton Keynes were burned out. The Brushwood Men probably weren't technically cannibals these days, but they weren't really human anymore, either, and it would be little consolation to their victims that the raid was for food stores and tools rather than long pig.

The men at work relaxed when they saw the horses and harness, and eased further when they were close enough to see faces. All three wore tough cord trousers, boots and knee-length linen smocks, the classic smock frock of the English rustic. The last men to wear them as daily routine outside plays and pageants had been dying of old age about the time Nigel Loring's great-grandfather used his head to stop a 7mm bullet from a Boer Mauser at Spion Kop. Two years ago an order had gone out from Highgrove to "encourage" the making and wearing of the archaic garments in every Commandery.

The king had thought it would introduce an element of tradition and continuity into the countryside. Nigel didn't think the effect in front of him was quite what Charles had had in mind . . .

" 'Ullo, Bob," Hordle called, as they rode into speaking distance. "Told you I'd be dropping by with some friends."

"Hey, mon, I see yuh," the farmer replied. "Little John

an' he friends always welcome at Jamaica Farm. I don' forget who get we out of London."

He was black—not exactly a startling sight even these days, but rare; there hadn't been all that much of a New Commonwealth immigrant presence on the Isle of Wight, nor on Man and Anglesey and Arran and Orkney. The yawny-drawly Caribbean accent was strong in his deep bass voice, turning it soft and pleasant. Standing side-by-side, his head would have been a few inches below Hordle's, which made him merely tall instead of towering, and he was strongly built, corded muscle moving under the sweat-slick ebony skin on his forearms.

The dreadlocks do *rather clash with the smock frock,* Nigel thought fleetingly. *So does that gold hoop earring.*

An equally big blue-eyed man leaned on a long-hafted billhook. He—Nigel blinked—had a leather rugby goalie's helmet on his head, set with a pair of bull horns above his ears and tufts of his white-blond hair sticking through the straps. Beside him a lean redhead set his bow down and looked dourly at the three riders; he wore a Scots bonnet and by his weathered face was nearer forty than thirty, the oldest of the three by most of a decade.

"Nice pinnie you've got on there, Bob," Hordle said, grinning and nodding at the smock frocks. "Fetching, it is. Though maybe it'd look a bit daintier with some flowers embroidered about the edge? And a lace collar?"

"Dese dress de *national* dress," Bob replied. "King Charlie, he say it get we in touch wit' our English roots. Mon, English roots be strong!"

He pointed to where his machete rested, amid a tangle of arching brambles taller than a mounted man's head. "Dese, dey got canes grow t'ree inches a *day,* and grow new roots where da hell dey touching; you leave one *bit* of root, dey grow up again. And we out of weed killer—use de last from Wyevale Garden Centre, two, t'ree year ago. Feeling de English roots more and more on Jamaica Farm."

"Oach, aye, indeed," the redhead said. "And it is often on Skye I felt the hankering for just such a smock frock as this, so English I was. Archie MacDonald, at yer sairvice, sair."

His voice had a soft West Highland lilt, almost Irish save for the rolled R's.

"Já," Gunnar Halldorsson put in, naming himself as well. "Me too. Studying marine engineering in Reykjavik, sometimes I felt naked without a smock." His thick-fingered hand tented the coarse linen away from his body. "In memory of my great-great-great-great-great-great-grandmother carried off by Vikings in the year 900, ha? So, the hat too." He flicked thumb and forefinger against one of the bull horns.

Bob fished in his pockets and came out with a cigarette made from a twist of paper, snapping open his lighter.

"The smocks, I don' make no trouble, I say, fine. Easy to make and clean. The 'thatch on every roof' order, it don' bother me—thatch on me Jamaica Farm to start wit' anyway. But when decree straight from Highgrove say we have to learn de *morris dancing . . .*" He took a long drag on the short, fat smoke. "Then I say to de king, 'Charlie, mon, you kiss my fine royal Rasta ass!' "

"And when *my* land is cleared, he can kiss mine," the Icelander said, grinning. "Remember, we start on it this year."

"And on mine," the Scot reminded him. "In the meantime, t'waur better we get these gentlemen under cover. The old south barn, until sunset; that'll rest the horses, the which will do them hairm."

The barn had been one of the outbuildings of Wavendon Manor; the rather undistinguished manor house itself had burned not long after the Change. The floor below was loose-box stabling, now holding their mounts, and an open space where lay a horse-powered threshing machine—remade to ancient patterns since the Change—disassembled for maintenance after the recently completed harvest. Chickens and turkeys wandered in to peck at odd grains on the floor; families of swallows flitted through the openings under the eaves, to and from their mud-built nests.

The second floor held mountains of loose hay over rafters and an open slatwork of boards, and the fugitives had bedded down in the middle of it, invisible unless someone climbed up the ladder and poked around with considerable determination. The hay made a deep soft bed, sweet-smelling with clover, well-cured and hardly prickly at all; the loft was dark and warm, with slits of hot light moving through the gloom. From where he'd set his horse blanket he could see out between the boards towards the farmyard, and with only a little movement over the edge of the hay down into the ground floor.

Sir Nigel long ago acquired the soldier's ability to sleep whenever he had the opportunity, in circumstances far less comfortable than this. When he awoke it was an hour past noon, and his hand was already on the wire-and-leather-wrapped hilt of his sword as he sat up. The bright metal came free of the sheath with a hiss of steel on wood and leather greased with graphite and neat's-foot oil. Alleyne was already awake and armed. The bleak lines newly graven in his son's face made Nigel wince slightly; losing one's mother was hard enough in the natural run of things ...

Then the younger Loring shook his head slightly and nodded towards the ladder. Hordle woke on his own a moment later, his soft rasping snore cutting off instantly as he reached for the great hand-and-a-half blade that lay beside him.

Nigel looked through the fringe of hay. A girl was climbing the ladder with a large basket over one arm. She was the one he'd seen feeding the poultry, and was rather obviously the farmer's daughter, with skin the color of milky tea and dark hair that tumbled in loose curls beneath a kerchief. The eight-year-old's head came over the edge of the piled hay as she climbed the ladder and stepped off onto the lath flooring of the loft. The solemn eyes went a little wider as she saw the three longswords in the hands of the men who crouched there, and she gave a little *eek!*

Then she smiled in delight as they slid the blades back into their sheaths, obviously entranced with the *secret importance* of it all.

"Hello, sir," she said to Nigel, holding out the basket and dipping her head to the others. "I've brought you sommat for dinner. Me mum said I should stay and bring back the basket when you're finished." A pause. "It's like Flora Macdonald and the Young Pretender!"

Well, Archie MacDonald's been talking, Nigel thought, smiling. *I hope she doesn't expect me to wear a dress as a disguise.*

"Thank you very much, my dear," he said. "What's your name?"

Her accent was a curious mix of Caribbean and broad Yorkshire; at a guess her mother had been born in Leeds or Bradford, from generations of factory workers. And there was something else there as well, a singsong lilt Nigel had noticed among many of the youngest post-Change generation, doubtless the product of the mixing-pot southern England had become. He rose and then went down on one knee to take the wicker basket with its checked cloth cover.

"Di," she whispered, looking down shyly. "Diana Bramble, Sir Nigel."

Probably named after St. Diana, Nigel thought, amused; the king's first wife had grown still more popular in retrospect. *Of course, compared to Camilla, and still more to Queen Hallgerda . . .*

The girl's wondering eyes went from his lined and weathered face to Alleyne's blond, fine-featured handsomeness to Hordle's great red ham of a countenance. "And you're Little John and Alleyne, aren't you?"

"Err . . ." *The man may be trustworthy, but he hasn't much sense of security. Still, I suppose it's impossible to keep secrets in a place like this—trying would simply make everyone curious.* "Err . . . yes, Miss Bramble, we are," Alleyne replied.

"Do you know the king, sir?" she asked suddenly.

Nigel's eyebrows went up. "I do, young mistress," he said. "We've worked together since the Change."

"Is't he really a bad man? I mean . . . he's tha *king.*"

Hordle snorted, and whispered sotto voce. "No, he's the soul of Christian charity, and we're running away from him because *we're* a roit wicked bunch of frighteners."

Nigel frowned at him and spoke gravely: "No, but he's . . .

ah . . . been under a great deal of strain, and I'm afraid it's made him . . . strange."

"You mean 'e's gone raving bonkers, like Archie's Uncle Willie?" she said inquiringly, then went on: "Uncle Willie talks to people who aren't there, and cries *a lot.*"

Hordle gave a shout of laughter, strangled off into a snort, and Alleyne chuckled despite himself.

"His Majesty's a bit strange, this last little while," Nigel told the girl. "And he's made some bad decisions because there are people around him who tell him what he wants to hear, instead of what's true."

She nodded. "Bad people like that there wicked queen," she said.

Nigel forbore comment; as far as he'd been able to tell Queen Hallgerda *was* wicked, if being ruthlessly ambitious and power hungry counted—and unlike some, he didn't think her admittedly rather stunning looks and undoubted charm made up for it. Doubtless if she'd stayed a junior clerical employee at a fish-processing plant on Heimaey off Iceland's west coast it wouldn't have mattered much. With a kingdom to play for, it became a matter of life and death.

Maude's death, he thought grimly, and then schooled his features before the child was frightened. *Dealing with our dear queen is the only thing that might tempt me to stay . . . no, not worth more destruction.*

Di sighed. "I'd like to see the court, and Winchester. It moost be bee-yootiful."

Her eyes were wide at the thought of the metropolis. Nigel smiled; Winchester was the capital these days, and had all of ten thousand people year-round, the largest city in the British Isles after Cork. That was just enough to keep the eighteenth-century core of the cathedral town from falling completely to ruin. To this child and her generation, whose horizons were bound by the farm and the enclosing wilderness and the little hamlet of Wavendon to the west where she went to church on Sundays and school in the winter months, Winchester was what London had been to him. Only far more distant and unobtainable—a trip there a wistful daydream rather than an hour or two on a train or in a car.

"Perhaps you will take a trip there, one day," Nigel said.

Another solemn nod, then she looked at him more closely, and at Alleyne. "Dad says you're a hero, for standing up to the king," she said, and he blushed. Then she frowned. "But you don't look like a hero. You're too old, and you're going bald. You look like a daddy. *He*"—she pointed at the younger Loring—"*He* looks like a *real* hero. Right dreamy, he is. Laak t'old pictures."

Nigel laughed outright at that, and Hordle turned redder than ever as he suppressed a bellow of mirth. The younger Loring brushed hay from his tousled yellow hair and smoothed his mustache in furtive embarrassment.

"Thank you," he said. "But he is my daddy, and he's far more of a hero than I. Let's have our dinner, shall we?"

The basket contained a pair of farm-style loaves, stone-ground whole meal baked that morning and still a little warm, butter out of the churn, two roasted chickens, their skins golden brown and crisp, potatoes done in their skins and a salad of fresh greens and tomatoes, a seasonal delicacy nowadays. Diana Bramble said a brief grace; John Hordle converted his reach for a leg into a vague gesture and clasped his hands as she spoke, then compensated by spinning lurid tales of Alleyne Loring's heroism—mostly true, if highly colored—until Diana gazed at the young man with a worshipfulness that doubtless made him hideously self-conscious. They finished with cheese-and-apple tarts and clotted cream; then the girl packed the plates and cutlery back in the basket with care and went to the ladder.

" 'Bye, Little John!" she said. "I've got to go and do my jobs now. Carding and spinning." She made a face, and then a little curtsy. "*Bo*ring! 'Bye, sirs."

"What a charming young miss," Nigel said. *We always wished we'd had a daughter as well,* he thought, and sighed slightly.

"Reminds me of my sister's kids," Hordle agreed, yawning.

"I'll take first watch, then," Nigel said, and grinned at his son. "*You've* made a conquest, it seems. Dreamy, indeed!"

Alleyne snorted and they settled down again, but it was he who first lifted his head a few minutes later. "Hooves," he said.

Young ears, his father thought, and said aloud: "How many?"

"Half a dozen, at a guess, one more or less. Hordle?"

"Horses it is, sir. Not likely to be the neighbors dropping in for a cuppa, either, is it?"

Tension crackled through the loft. They looked at each other and began preparing with silent speed, the two Lorings helping each other into their complex harness as Hordle pulled on his padded tunic and the chain shirt over it. The great muscles in his arms coiled and bunched as he strung his longbow, and then he slipped the leather-and-steel guards on his forearms and counted the arrows in his quiver. They left the helmets for last; it would take only a few seconds, and they needed every fraction of sight and hearing to avoid having to use the gear at all.

"Thirty-nine," the bowman said quietly, his sausage-thick fingers deft on the feathered shafts.

"I don't want any of Bramble's people hurt," Nigel said in the same tone, but with a snap of command in it. "For any reason whatsoever. That's clear?"

The other men both nodded. By then the hooves were clear to the older man as well, a dull hollow clopping on the dirt and broken pavement of the A5130. Alleyne wormed through the hay to put his eye to a knothole, moving cautiously to spare the laths under them—there were sixty pounds of steel on him now, in addition to his own whipcord hundred seventy-five.

"Half a dozen and a packhorse," he whispered. "Just turning onto the lane to the farm. They're hobelars."

That meant mounted infantry archers, like the bulk of the regular army, equipped as Hordle was. Six made a section, the smallest unit; adding two mounted men-at-arms made it a lance. Nigel caught sight of them an instant later, jogging their mounts up the laneway, turning east at the dogleg that led past the pond and barns. A woman was there, the farmer's wife, a solid figure with a long rake in her hands and her brown hair done up in a bun under a wide-brimmed straw hat—real wheat straw, with a frayed edge.

She turned for an instant and shouted in purest West Riding, confirming Nigel's guess: "Di! Roon and fetch yer dad!" Then she went on to the soldiers: "Don't water yer 'orses there, lads. There's flax in t'pond, we just put it in ter ret and it's reet mucky, ba 'eck. Cum on oop t' t'ouse and use trough in t'yard instead, t'gate's open. There's soom apple tarts left over from dinner, if ye'd laak, and a jug of cold cider too, 'appen."

That brought delighted smiles to the fresh-faced young men; one thing that hadn't changed was that army field rations were fit to gag a stoat. Nigel Loring realized with a start that only the section leader had been old enough to shave when the Change came—in fact, it looked as if most of them hadn't had their voices break by that day eight and a half years ago. They seemed younger than their years to him as well, despite the weather-beaten skins of outdoorsmen.

"It's a kindly thought, Mrs. Bramble," the section leader said. " 'Tis a hard late camp we'll hae tha night."

His patrol were all dust caked, with sweat runnels through the brown dirt on their faces, and their horses looked worn as well; the mounts wore leather barding on their chests and leather socks strapped to their fetlocks, but they'd still suffered the odd scratch.

Nigel was close enough to hear him well. The accent was Scots, but not the gentle lilt of a Highlander; he'd pronounced the *ght* in "thought" with an almost guttural sound, not a simple hard T, and "night" as *ni'cht*. An Orkneyman, at a guess, and from somewhere remote like Westray at that, with bright blue eyes and a close-cropped black beard that had the white line of a scar through it. There was a corporal's chevron riveted to the sleeve of his mail shirt. The men took off their helmets at his waving gesture and swung down, leading the beasts over to the metal trough, joking with three girls only a bit younger than themselves who came out of the farmhouse kitchen bearing the promised food and drink. One Junoesque blonde had a tray of mugs and a stoppered jug, and two freckled redheads carried heaped plates of tarts.

Gunnar's sister and Archie's daughters, I'd say, Nigel thought.

"Drink water first, y' daft boogers," the section leader snapped. The men obeyed, most dumping a helmetful over their heads as well. "And one mug each, nae more. We've work tae do and it's eight hours before sunset." He held up a gauntleted fist. "Any man drunk on duty weil ansur tae my little friend here."

Then to the girls, in a quite different tone, reaching for the pastries: "Thank *you,* young misses. Ah'll cheust tak a nave-fil."

Nigel found himself nodding in approval as the patrol watered their horses and applied salve to their hides; the men hadn't even had to be told to see to their mounts before themselves, and their equipment was as neat as you could expect when working this overgrown country—the green-enameled metal of the mail shirts gleamed with a thin film of oil, and the fletchings on the arrows that jutted over each man's right shoulder were tight and even. There was a charge he recognized on the bucklers slung from their belts, too: the royal arms quartered with a chevron argent, three roses gules.

Tony Knolles's men, Nigel Loring thought. The family was distantly related to his. *Oh, bugger, as Hordle would put it.*

He'd worked with Knolles before the Change, mostly counterterrorist work in south Ulster in the 1980s, and since the Change as well; the last he'd heard of him was that he commanded a company of the Guard working out of the forward base at Stowe. If he'd heard news of the escape he would have moved quickly and decisively—efficiently to boot.

He's entirely too competent. So is this corporal, on a smaller scale. And Knolles isn't nearly so disenchanted with the king as I, either.

The rest of the farm's folk came up as the soldiers rested and ate and sipped appreciatively at their cider. That was natural enough as well, a visit being a change in the routine, but it put his teeth on edge—the more who spoke, the more chance of someone letting an unguarded word slip.

"Good day to you, Artie, mon," Bob said when he emerged from the long cottage, wiping a napkin across his mouth, evidently just finishing dinner. He slapped the corporal on the shoulder. "Tanks again for de harvest work."

The corporal shrugged. "We're under orders tae he'lp whaur we can, Bob," he said.

"Yuh still pick me Jamaica Farm to help. Gudrun!" he called, and the blond young woman looked up from chatting with one of the hobelars. "Ninyam an' bockle for dese good men, good and plenty."

"Yuh here lookin' for Brushwood Men?" the farmer went on as she hurried away to pack food and drink. "Or de dam' leopard? Duppy ting take me *sheep*, mon."

"Nae." The corporal's mouth shut like a steel trap. "Fugitives, under warrant o' proscription frae the Crown. Two—Sair Nigel Loring, and his son, Alleyne. There's serious charges, ye ken, agin them and any who harbor 'em."

He went on to give a description. Bob Bramble mimed surprise; it would have been excessive in someone less given to the flamboyant.

"Me hear 'bout him prisoned at Woburn," Bramble said, rubbing at his chin and letting the creole accent grow stronger. "No hear 'bout him es-caaap-ing. Bad business. Me noh quite undastan. Sir Nigel, he good mon, I always hear."

The corporal's face was expressionless—perhaps a little too stiff—but Nigel thought he caught uneasy looks on some of the archers behind him, and outright scowls from the farm folk. Then his heart skipped a beat as little Diana Bramble stamped out to confront the section leader.

"Sir Nigel *is* a good man!" she said shrilly, shaking a finger up at the Orkneyman's face, ignoring his bulk and armor. "You've got no bloody business going around hunting heroes like they was foxes! I wish Sir Nigel and Alleyne were here so they could take their swords and *cut you up*! You . . . you *loathly bugger*!"

"Diana!" her mother said, reprovingly. "Watch your tongue, my girl!"

The noncom snorted and scowled, turning away and making a brushing gesture with one hand, as at an annoying fly. Diana's diatribe escalated into a wordless howl and she kicked the soldier—neatly, in the sensitive part of the shin just above his riding boot. She was wearing heavy brogue-style shoes, and there was real conviction behind the hack she gave him.

"So there!" she shouted, then turned and ran.

"Ye cheeky peedie whalp!" the noncom shouted, and nearly fell over as he made a grab for her.

The Orkney accent was suddenly thicker than oatmeal as he hopped in the dust and horse apples of the farmyard, holding his knee. Then he controlled his temper with a visible effort, and stamped the boot down again at the sound of a subdued snicker from behind him. When he whirled to look at his men they braced to attention, motionless except for one still chewing on an apple tart.

"Are you a cow, then, that ye're chewing a cud, Jones, you daft taffie!" he snapped. "Search the farm! High and low! We've orders," he went on half apologetically, turning back to Bramble. "We'll just tak a keek aboot . . ."

One of the farm folk was an older man, the oldest Nigel had seen on Bob's holding; lean, gray and messy-untidy in a way the others weren't despite plain clothes and hard outdoor work. Now he ambled forward and grabbed the corporal by the shoulders.

"You're sairching?" he said. "For Doris? Have you seen Doris, then? Have you word of her? *Have* you?"

"Oh—"

The corporal bit back something pungent, and didn't quite stiff-arm the older man away; far too many folk who'd lived through the terrible years were a bit wandered in their wits, and it was convention to treat them gently. The graybeard still burst into tears as he staggered back, and Archie MacDonald jumped forward to lead him away as he called more and more loudly for Doris, whoever she was. People milled about talking and gesturing, and the

corporal of the detachment looked for a moment as if he'd
like to cry himself.

"Get searchin', I said!" he half screamed, and stamped
away towards the house. "They twa're armed and dangerous, remember! Stay in touch and sing out if you see
them."

One of his men stayed to hold the horses. The others
split up hurriedly, clapping their helmets on, drawing their
swords and taking their bucklers in their left hands. Nigel
moved back from the wall with slow, gentle care and
caught the eyes of the others, looking over towards the ladder. He and Alleyne moved towards it, their shields ready
on their left arms. Hordle came behind them, an arrow on
his string, waiting on one knee with his torso bent, ready to
rise and shoot; his face had the hard blankness of an oak
board. The big man's friendly smile could make you forget
what he was like in action . . .

There's no problem unless someone comes up here, Nigel
thought. *If they do . . .*

Hordle would take out the one who discovered them,
then jump down and put a shaft through the corporal and
get the horses running. He and Alleyne would have to hunt
down the rest—though a longbow *would* penetrate even
good plate if it hit precisely right, chances were they could
overwhelm the patrol if needs must. And they *must* not let
any escape to carry word . . .

The thought of cutting down honest English soldiers
made his stomach twist, but bringing him in now would give
Queen Hallgerda's party at court too much extra leverage.
Losing him for good would cost that crew dearly in pres-
tige—and make people less afraid, which they couldn't afford, not being much loved even by their own folk.

The silence stretched as a soldier walked in through the
big double doors. The dimness within was near darkness to
eyes fresh from open sunlight, and he tripped and cursed
and staggered as he ran into the disassembled threshing
machine, windmilling his sword out—you could give yourself a nasty cut if you fell with one in your hand.

"Sod me if I like this above 'alf," he muttered as he recovered his balance. "If Nigel Loring's a traitor, I'm fuck-

ing Queen Hallgerda." He stabbed the sword into a small pile of burlap sacks, then flicked open a big plywood bin of raw wool still in the fleece. "Not in there, are you then? Christ, what an effing waste of time!"

He looked around, blinking, then went over to the loose-box. Nigel made a conscious effort to control his breathing, ready to step into the open space, hang by his hands and drop the remaining distance to the dirt floor. He'd drop the sword first, and it would be waiting point-down and hilt-up in the dirt . . .

"You're a big fellow, aren't you?" the soldier said to Pommers, taking something out of the small canvas haversack on his belt. "Here, 'ave a taste. Better you than that brass-arsed Jock."

That was probably a carrot, or perhaps an apple; the big gelding crunched enthusiastically, and then whuffled around the soldier in the hopes of something more. Alleyne's black was less friendly, turning from the other end of the box to cock a suspicious eye at the stranger.

"You're both big fellows, eh?" the man said thoughtfully.

He started to look up to the hayloft, then cleared his throat and hitched his belt. "Nobody here, Corporal!" he said cheerfully as he walked out. Then he did look up, and slowly and deliberately winked. "Except enough gear to break your neck if you're not right careful."

John Hordle eased off on the draw of his great yellow bow. His hazel eyes were coldly intent as they followed the man out into the bright sunlight. So were Nigel's as the patrol reassembled. Gudrun came out with two burlap sacks that bulged promisingly; even more promisingly, one clinked like a stoneware jug tapping against something, and the soldier who strapped it over the packsaddle of the baggage beast smacked his lips. The patrol mounted again and put their mounts up to a canter as they left.

"Well, did me hear anyone say *stop workin'*?" Bob said, when they'd passed out of sight, bound south.

The little crowd began to disperse. The master of the farm grabbed one ten-year-old by the arm—his son, from the looks.

"Anasi, you run quick-quick, climb de big oak. Back

when dey out of yuh sight. Gudrun, a load fo de guests. Archie—"

"Think we should move the schedule up, sir?" Hordle said, as the talk drew away from their hiding place.

Alleyne looked at his father. Nigel nodded. "Definitely. I don't think that man who searched the barn will talk— but I *know* Tony Knolles will smell a rat. He's the one whose team finally tracked down Sean Donnelly."

Alleyne's eyebrows went up. "He was in charge of that personally?"

"Very personally," Nigel said grimly. "Donnelly walked into what he thought was a safe house in Dundalk, just over the Irish border. And there Tony Knolles was waiting, with a sharpened spade—quieter than a gun, you see, didn't want the Garda forced to take notice. Buried young Sean and two of his cell in the garden that night and flitted off, nobody the wiser."

Hordle snorted. "Good for the shrubbery—probably the first time the Provo bastards were any use. But I see what you mean, sir. We'd best scarper."

"We had to be careful how much we cleared," Hordle said. "All we had time for, sir, and we couldn't be conspicuous about it, either."

"You only had a week to prepare," Nigel Loring said, leading the horse out of the narrow laneway.

It had been a country road for a thousand years before the Change, the Lower End Road from Wavendon to Salford. Nature had reclaimed it since, ripping up the two lanes of tarmac with sprouting seedlings, convolvulus vines with their pink-throated white flowers, and the inevitable bramble; the hawthorn from the roadside hedges had nearly met in the middle, turning the road into a stretch of brush forty feet across and twenty high.

The old SAS men and their helpers had cleared just enough to let horses pass in single file, down the center where the vegetation was weakest. Sir Nigel had trouble with the twelve-foot length of his lance, holding it horizontally by the balance more often than not. The burden wore at his arm. It was hot in the green gloom, and above the leaves it was another bright warm day. It was a relief to finally break through as they came into open country where a little wind could leak through the joints in his armor. The field ahead had enough sheer size to keep bramble vines from overrunning everything. They dismounted to hack an overgrown gate free. Nigel paused, panting, as they finally cut the last of the vine and shrub cane free of the wood and hauled it open. He and Alleyne had done most of the work; a suit of plate did have the advantage of making you more or less immune to thorns.

"MacDonald, you take the spare mounts on to the fox covert there," Nigel said, pointing across the tall grass and weeds.

"M1's just down the cutting after, sair," the Scot agreed. "I'll be checking the way's clear, then."

John Hordle looked southwest, frowning; he popped a blackberry into his mouth with purple-stained fingers, dumped the rest out of his helmet and clapped it on.

"Thought I heard something, sir, and now I'm sure," he said, as he strung his bow with a twist and wrench. "Don't think the SIDs could have caught us. Didn't look as if they were going to make any pursuit at all. Those hobelars who searched the farm?"

"There's three lances of the Guard based out of Stowe, regulars," Alleyne said. "If Knolles has them all out searching like those, he'll be riding back and forth between the parties. You think he'd smell a rat, Father?"

"Without a doubt," Nigel said. "But this isn't the only path he'd have to secure. It could be a diversion—and Tony would think of that. He has a tricky mind, and he likes to make very sure of all the possibilities."

"Then they'll split up for sure, sir," Hordle said. "If they really want to catch us, they'll split six ways and cover every track we could take."

"Captain Knolles *will* press the search hard, whatever his men think," Nigel said.

He looked right, into the field that rose slowly to the roadway cutting and a plantation of beech trees three hundred yards ahead.

"I'm afraid Major Buttesthorn and his men spent a lot of effort making their way clear for them," he said.

"What shall we do, sir?" Hordle asked.

"That rather depends on how many of them there are," Nigel said crisply.

Pity it takes a fight to bring me out of my funk, he thought. *But that's how God made me.*

"Let's go . . . but not too quickly. The M1's just over that rise, and if they get on our trail there, it's a straight race. We cannot afford that. Better to meet them here."

They pressed on through the gate, leading their mounts. Nigel was glad MacDonald had gone on ahead; no doubt the Scot was a brave man, but he preferred to depend on those whose qualities he knew thoroughly. They could hear the sound of hooves now, coming through the narrow way hacked behind them, shod hooves pounding on the broken pavement of the road. The three of them rode up the long gentle slope ahead; it hadn't been overgrown with bramble or blackthorn, but the grass was up to the horses' bellies, starred with a few of the season's last bloodred poppies and with nettle fortunately past the stinging stage. They rode slowly, birds and small game darting out of the grass before their horses' hooves—rabbits, a lithe foot-long stoat dragging a dead rabbit of its own, a pair of little muntjac deer that ran into the beechwood ahead and then barked frantically.

"There they come!" Hordle called.

"Halt," Nigel said crisply. "We want them to come on."

He shaded his eyes with his hand and peered. "Ah, a demilance. They did split up to follow the possible trails—the other two are probably hacking their way through the bramble thickets even as we speak. And yes, it's Knolles himself."

A lance was the term for two armored horsemen and six hobelars; a demilance was half that. He saw them file through the ruined field gate, and reached down to his saddlebow for his binoculars. Knolles's face was unmistakable—harsh with its great hook nose crossed by a scar—as was his red shield with its silver chevron and the roses on it. And he was looking back through his own field glasses, visor up.

Nigel returned the glasses to their leather-lined steel case, set his sallet helmet on his head and fastened it, brought his own shield across from his back and dipped his lance to the distant figure; beside him Alleyne did the same. Knolles nodded, then waved his longbowmen on; the odds were four to three, but three of his had missile weapons. Nigel could hear the men's voices crying out, faint and shrill as the archers below dismounted and spread out in front of their commander, trotting forward through the waist-high grass with arrows on their strings. Hordle dismounted likewise, a savage grin on his face as he bent to tear off a clump of grass and then tossed it up to test the breeze.

"It's uphill just a bit, and the wind's in their faces," he said. "The bloody fools've forgotten I can overshoot them by fifty yards."

"Do your best, Sergeant," Nigel said.

The first of the Guard archers stopped and bent his bow. The snap of the bowstring was faint at this distance; that would be a long shot under any circumstances. The arrow twinkled as it spun uphill, and then they could hear the faint hissing of its passage just before it thumped into the earth and disappeared in the long grass ten feet from Hordle.

"That's Jack Graham," he said absently. "Good man to have a beer and a bit of a yarn with. Arms like a gorilla, he has, for all he's under six feet—good shot, Jack, and it's the last you'll make until next spring."

. He drew the great yellow bow and shot. "Over!" he swore.

Downrange the stocky broad-shouldered man in his green-enameled chain-mail shirt and green uniform threw himself down with a yell as the long shaft hissed malignantly over his head. He shot back, two shafts in quick succession; the last one nearly reached Hordle's feet.

"All rightie then, I gave you an extra two," Hordle muttered, and shot again.

This time the arrow went home, through the other man's right shoulder. He fell, then sprang up, dancing with rage and shaking his left fist before crumpling again; the curses came faint and far against the wind.

"Well, that's what you get for bloody shooting at me!" Hordle shouted, laughing, and reached for another shaft. The remaining pair of archers would be in range in a moment, and the odds were now even.

"Wait," Nigel Loring said. Hordle looked over his shoulder. "Put your handkerchief on this."

He sloped his lance, dropping the long diamond-shaped head by the tall archer's shoulder, and held it there while Hordle stuck the scrap of off-white linen on the sharp point. Then he raised it again and waved it back and forth to catch the other officer's eye; he could hear Knolles's voice call the archers back immediately, and the Guard commander trotted forward to meet him as he sent his horse out into the middle of the field. They halted at lance-length apart, their visors raised; the wind murmured through the long grass and the woods behind, the thick brush ahead to the west. The warhorses mouthed their bits, tossed heads and stamped forefeet in challenge as they sensed their riders' tension and throttled anger. Nobody could hear what the men said through that susurrus of white noise.

"You're under arrest, Colonel Loring," Anthony Knolles said. "And you've added firing on the forces of the Crown to the tally of charges!"

Nigel felt himself smile; it was even genuine, which hadn't happened often since his wife died. He'd always liked Knolles, who was an entirely honest man—and who had a mind as savagely straightforward as an ax blade. Nothing could turn him from his duty but death—and even then one would be well advised to cut his head off to make sure—but he didn't handle conflicting duties well.

"Not under arrest quite yet, Tony," he said. "And you haven't lost any men yet, either—good men the country needs. I've a proposition for you, old boy."

"You'll return with me, and name your accomplices," Knolles said. "Besides those two, that is."

"I'm most assuredly not going to give you any names," Nigel said serenely. "Here's what I will do. We'll run a course here and now. You beat me, and I'll surrender myself; you let my companions go—they're planning on leaving the country in any event. If I beat you, you let us all go and I promise on my word as an officer and a gentleman—and a Loring—that I'll leave England as well—'abjure the realm,' to use the terminology His Majesty prefers. We won't go to Ulster or the mainland colonies or Gibraltar, either, of course—nowhere in Europe, in fact. The king will have heard the last of the Lorings."

His face went tight. "Except for Maude, of course. His Varangians have ensured that *she* stays."

Knolles blinked at the savagery of Loring's momentary expression and winced slighty. "How on earth are you going to leave Europe?" he asked. "Where else is there to go? Norland—"

"Is part of Europe. Come now, Tony. You didn't think I was going up the M1 just to join the Brushwood Men, did you? And of course I can't tell you the details or destination, because you'd have to report it and the king might try to stop me."

"I have definitive orders," Knolles said.

Nigel smiled. "You had very *emphatic* orders from the politicians not to cross the border that time in South Armagh, Tony," he said. " 'Eighty-five, wasn't it? We didn't pay much attention then, either of us."

A smile struggled to break through the other man's craggy features for a moment, then he shook his head.

"You always were stubborn . . . I have to bring you back, Nigel. You know that." He sighed. "You should have accepted the governorship of Gibraltar when they offered it you last spring. You'd have got a gong with it, too."

"Which would have put me conveniently out of the way until I retired," he said dryly.

"I cannot simply let you go!"

"No. You *can* try to personally capture me, Tony. As I said, if you win, you return with your mission accomplished. If not . . . well, you can honestly say you did your best and took losses in the trying."

"You're better at this King Arthur business than I,

Nigel, and you know it," Knolles said. "I still feel like an actor waving this stick about, sometimes. Don't you?"

"Not recently. More sporting than guns, what? And you *have* knocked me off my horse in practice bouts, you know."

"Not as often as the reverse," Knolles grunted sourly.

"You *could* bring me back," Nigel pointed out. "And without endangering any of your men. It was pure luck that shaft didn't go through your archer's throat. There aren't so many Englishmen left we can afford to waste them—or their sons and daughters yet unborn."

Knolles looked over his shoulder; his men were grouped around their wounded comrade.

And you know they're not enthusiastic about this, Loring thought. *They're good soldiers, they'll do as they're told, but you can't make them like it.*

"Very well, Sir Nigel," Knolles said formally. "There aren't many men whose bare word I'd take, but you're one."

"Thank you, Tony," Loring said. "And Tony? Whatever happens, look after the princes."

Knolles's face changed slightly; backing the king didn't mean he liked the new queen any too well.

"Here? Or up on the M1?" he said. "No rabbit burrows there."

"We can check before we run the course. The footing's better for the horses on grass than on tarmac and I'd prefer to come off on dirt, if I'm going to come off at all."

Knolles nodded assent and turned his horse. Sir Nigel did the same, riding two hundred yards along the side of the low slope at a slow walk, checking the ground for rabbit burrows and foxholes beneath the yard-high growth of grass and thistles. At the end of it the horse turned in its own length at the pressure of his thighs, superbly trained and willing. He felt a pang of absurd loss; not only was he going to have to part with it soon, but it would be spending the rest of its life pulling plows and harrows on Rasta Bob's farm. Doubtless well-treated, but . . . he ran a gauntleted palm down the smooth hard curve of the yellow gelding's neck.

Four hundred yards away Anthony Knolles was a tiny figure of steel and menace on his big black warmblood. Nigel bared his teeth; now he could stop being responsible and rational, and *hit* someone. He'd been wanting to do that very badly for a day and a half now.

With identical gestures they reached up to snap their visors shut; the world darkened, sight limited to the long narrow slit ahead. He squeezed his thighs, and Pommers broke into a walk, a trot, a canter . . . and then a hard hand gallop. Nigel braced his feet in the long stirrups, brought the shield around under his eyes, the lance down—held loosely at this stage. Hooves thundered, throwing divots of turf and brown earth high under the uncaring blue arch of the sky. The world shrank down to two bright lance heads and a shield marked with a silver wedge.

Two and a half tons of horseflesh, human bone and muscle and steel armor hurtled at each other. He slanted the lance across Pommers's neck, clenching his legs against the horse, locking himself into the high-cantled saddle.

And I don't much care whether I live or die, he knew. *Alleyne and Hordle escape in either event. If Maude's waiting for me . . . and if there's nothing beyond . . . then sleep.*

Suddenly the other armored lancer was *close.* Loring clenched his legs and leaned forward, the lance tight under his arm, the point unwavering. At the very last instant his knees pressed, and the yellow horse swerved slightly, leaning away. Loring's lance head stayed glued to its target, the narrow spot where the bevoir laced to the breastplate . . .

Crannng! Then *crack!* like a miniature roll of thunder as the tough ashwood of a lance shaft broke.

Nigel Loring swayed drunkenly in the saddle at the massive impact hammering on his shield and smashing his hips backward against the cantle; the curved sheet metal shed most of it, cunningly held to glance the point, but it was enough to tear him half out of the saddle and lose one stirrup; the warhorse itself staggered and nearly fell. The taste of iron and copper filled his mouth as his head snapped violently forward and back, rattling his brain in the skull and cutting his lips against his own teeth. He threw aside the broken stub of the lance before he realized what had happened to his opponent.

Knolles's black horse galloped on. Loring sprang down from the saddle, fell flat on his face, levered himself erect and staggered over to the spot where the other man lay fallen. For a moment he thought he was dead—gone gray-pale, with blood flowing from nose and mouth and one ear. The helmet was gone completely, the laces burst by the terrible leverage when Loring's lance head caught it under the bevoir. One of the captain's archers dashed up and fell on his knees on Knolles's other side, dabbing at his face with a square of linen soaked from a canteen.

"Oh, hell. Oh, bloody hell, sir, you shouldn't have done it—"

Knolles's eyes fluttered open; they were green, and wandered vaguely for a moment. Then he turned his head to spit blood and what was probably a bit of tooth, and the archer gently raised his head to let him drink from the canteen. He spat the first of that out, tinged pink, then drank thirstily and moved feet and hands and fingers to check that they still functioned.

"Glad you're all right, old chap," Loring said; the relief was genuine, a warm surge that melted some sliver of the glacier within.

"All right? You nearly tore my ruddy head off, Nigel!" Knolles said, then winced in pain at his own voice. "I think you've broken my collarbone, too, damnit. This isn't nearly as much fun as doing it with blunted practice lances, is it?"

Nigel put a hand gently on the battered armor of the other's shoulder. "The harness will hold it until you get to a doctor," he said. "And we're even for Armagh, eh, what?"

"*I* have to explain this to His Majesty," Knolles grumbled.

"Your collarbone will argue for you," Loring said. "And Tony . . . I meant it about looking out for the princes."

He rose, feeling a stab in his back and a ringing in his ears. *I really am getting a little old for this,* he thought. *It was hard enough to learn a whole new way of war in my forties.*

The pain seemed to make him feel better, somehow. Alleyne came up, leading Pommers by the reins. "Do you need a hand mounting, Father?" he said, as Knolles's men carried him away.

"You insolent pup . . . of course I do, boy!"

Hordle came up and made a stirrup of his hands, lifting with gently irresistible strength as Nigel swung into the saddle again with a grunt.

"That was a joy to be'old, sir," he said. "Fe, fi, fo, fum, bang in the oc-u-lari-um!"

Nigel snorted. "We're not out of England yet," he said. "It's a long wet way to the Wash, and longer still to . . . wherever we're going."

Alleyne looked around. "I know we have to do it," he said. "Still, leaving England forever . . ."

"Better than looking over our shoulders at Osborne House," Nigel said stoutly. "And there's nothing more English than leaving England and finding land elsewhere."

CHAPTER TWO

Larsdalen, Willamette Valley, Oregon
March 17th, 2007 AD—Change Year Nine
Gunpowder Day

"Sometimes you have to break heads," Michael Havel said.

"To be sure, Mike, that's the way of it in this wicked world," Juniper Mackenzie replied.

She gave him an urchin grin, and tossed back curls whose bright copper glinted in the fresh morning sun. More of the lilt and burble of her mother's people crept into her voice as she went on: "But I'll be pointing out once more that it's cheaper to break them open from the *inside*. And they're of more use afterward that way, sure. We'll find ways to tweak his nose, never fear, but this grand alliance you've been wanting won't happen soon."

Havel gave a snort of unwilling laughter. "Ah, the hell with it, Juney, I'd rather subvert the bastard than kill his grunts too. I just don't know if we *can*. Anyway, we've been talking politics for days. Now I've got some gunpowder to test."

The other visiting dignitaries formed up, in no particular order: Abbot Dmowski from Mt. Angel in his brown Benedictine robe; a group of self-appointed SCA nobility from just east of there; Finney and Jones from the Corvallis Faculty Senate a raggle-taggle of the smaller communities. He sighed and put on the helmet he'd carried tucked under one arm; it was a plain steel bowl with a riveted nasal strip in front, hinged cheek guards and a leather-lined chain-mail aventail behind to protect the neck. *This* particular one had a tanned bear's head mounted on it, the snarling muzzle shading his eyes.

His wife, Signe, came up on his right side, ignoring Juniper's friendly nod. She flicked at the capelike fall of fur that spread back from the bear head, to settle it on his mailed shoulders. Even though he'd killed the bear himself—with a spear, right after the Change—he still felt mildly ridiculous wearing it; it had been Signe's younger sister, Astrid Larsson, who came up with the idea.

The first of her crimes against common sense, he grumbled inwardly. *But not the last.*

The crowd below cheered at the sight of the ceremonial helm, and started chanting; some drew swords and waved them in the air to the beat of the words.

"Lord Bear! Lord Bear! Lord Bear!"

"You deserve it, O Lord Bear," Signe Havel said, smiling at his tightly controlled embarrassment. "And so do I—I was shooting arrows into it while you shish kebabed its liver, remember? Sort of our first date ..."

"I remember it better than I like," he said, with a smile that drew up one corner of his mouth.

He touched a finger to the scar that ran up across his forehead from the corner of his left eye, remembering the hoarse roaring that sprayed blood and saliva in his face, the blurring slap of the great paw and the glancing touch of one claw tip, agony and black unconsciousness coming up to strike him like the ground itself.

Just an inch closer, and there'd've gone my face and eyes.

"Let's get on with it," he went on, his voice a little rougher, letting his left hand fall back to its natural position on the hilt of his backsword.

She put on a helmet that sported a crest of yellow horse-hair from brow to nape, almost the same color as her own wheat blond mane. An attendant handed her a small metal tray with half a dozen smoldering pine splints on it, and they stepped out. The skirts of their knee-length chain hauberks clashed musically against the steel splints of their shin guards, and the plate of the vambraces on their forearms met with a dull *tink* as they linked hands, his right to her left.

Their path led down the broad staircase that led from the upper garden to the great lawn where the ceremony would be held, between banks of Excel early lilac already showing a froth of lavender blossom. Militia with sixteen-foot pikes lined the route, their mail shirts and kettle helmets polished for dignity's sake. The crowd was hundreds strong and good-natured, cheering as they saw the leaders, ready for the barbeque and games and entertainments that would follow throughout the day—it seemed a little odd that they'd turned the memorial day of humanity's worst disaster into a holiday, but things had turned out that way. It was a brilliant spring morning, the air washed to crystal by yesterday's rain, and cool.

Around sixty, he thought. *Perfect.*

The flower banks nearer the house were just starting to bloom—sheets of crocus gold and blue, rhododendrons like cool fire in white and pink and purple around the tall oaks—he caught faint wafts of their scent, and the smell of crushed grass was strong and sweet, stronger than that of massed, indifferently clean humans or the occasional tang of livestock and their by-products. You could see clear across the Valley from up here in the Eola Hills, right over to the snow-peaks of the Cascades floating blue-and-white against the horizon, but the sunlight still had a trace of winter's pale glaze. If you distilled *spring* and poured it over a landscape like spray from a mountain river, this would be it.

All the same he was already sweating under the armor. Over the last nine years he'd gotten so used to its heat and constriction and weight he scarcely noticed it anymore unless something called it to his attention; the gear he'd carried as a marine back in the early nineties had been much heavier, and awkward to boot.

Trouble is, I'm being *reminded.*

Juniper Mackenzie looked indecently comfortable in her tartan kilt and saffron-dyed shirt of homespun linsey-woolsey, a brooch holding her plaid at the shoulder, a flat Scots bonnet on her head with a raven feather in a clasp shaped into the antlers-and-crescent-moon sigil of the clan. The Chief of the Mackenzies was eight inches shorter than his five-eleven, a slender woman, perhaps a year or two older than Havel's midthirties. She had the long, sharp-boned, triangular face that often went with Scots-Irish ancestry, softened by an expression that seemed to bubble laughter even at rest. She'd told him once that the pale freckled complexion, green eyes and fox red mane were from her mother, who'd been Irish plain and simple—born and raised on Achill Island off the west coast at that.

She smells better than I do, too, he thought: soap, clean female flesh, an herbal hair wash of some sort and a hint of woodsmoke. *Better than Signe right now too, for that matter.*

Even with the leader's luxury of more than one gambeson—so that they could be switched off and washed occasionally—you never really got the old-socks-and-locker-room smell out of the thick quilting you wore under armor. Mingled with horse sweat soaked into leather and the oil you rubbed on the metal of the armor to keep it free of rust, it was the smell of a trade: the trade of war in the Changed world.

He walked to the center of the stretch of grass; sheep kept it cropped now, not so neatly as it had been when this was a rich man's toy, Ken Larsson's summer place. The others dropped back; the troopers who stood to keep a circle cleared here were from the Bearkiller A-lister elite, armored as he was, their long single-edged swords drawn and points touching the grass before them. Sunlight flashed and glittered and broke from the honed edges as they flourished them upright in salute.

He approached the brass bowl that stood on a stone plinth; it was heaped with a gritty gray-black powder. A hush fell over the crowd, broken by the susurrus of breath, the voices of children running around on the fringes, somewhere the neigh of a horse. Birds went loud overhead—honking geese, tundra swans, V's of ducks heading north—and a red-tailed hawk's voice sounded an arrogant *skree-skree-skree.*

Signe offered her tray of pine splints. Havel took one

and waved it through the air until flame crackled, sending a scent of burning resin into the air along with a trail of black smoke.

Then he tossed it neatly into the bowl of gunpowder.

Fumphsssssss . . .

The powder burned slowly, black smoke drifting downwind with a stink of scorched sulfur. The flame flickered sullen red; an occasional burst of sparks made people skip back when clumps were tossed out of the bowl like spatters from hot cooking oil. There was none of the volcanic *woosh* it would have produced before the Change; the sharp fireworks smell was about the only familiar thing involved. When the sullen fire died, nothing was left but a lump of black ash; a gust of wind swept it out in feathery bits to scatter across grass and clothes and faces.

"Well, *shit*," Mike Havel murmured softly under his breath.

They did this every year on the anniversary of the Change, just to make formally and publicly sure that it hadn't reversed itself; it had grown into something of a public holiday, too—more in the nature of a wake than a celebration in the strict sense, but boisterous enough for all that.

The watching crowd sighed. Some of the adults—men and women who'd *been* adult that March day nine years ago—burst into tears; many more looked as if they'd *like* to cry. The children and youngsters were just excited at the official beginning of the holiday; to them the time before the Change was fading memories, or tales of wonders.

Though by now we wouldn't get the old world back even if the Change reversed itself, he thought grimly. *Too many dead, too much wrecked and burned. And would we dare depend on those machines again, if we knew the whole thing could be taken away in an instant?*

He felt a sudden surge of rage—at whoever, Whoever, or whatever had kicked the work of ages into wreck, and at the sheer unfairness of not even knowing *why*. Then he pushed the feeling aside with a practiced effort of will; brooding on it was a short route to madness. That hadn't killed as many as hunger and the plagues, but it came a close third, and a lot of the people still breathing weren't what you could call tightly wrapped.

"Sorry, no guns or cars or TV, folks," he said, making his voice cheerful. "Not this ninth year of the Change, at least. But a pancake breakfast we can still manage. Let's go!"

"You're supposed to eat it, my heart, not smear it all over your face," Juniper Mackenzie said to her son; she spoke in Gaelic, as she often did with him, something to keep her mother's language alive a little longer.

Alive in Oregon, at least, she thought. *On the other side of the world . . . who knows?*

She suspected and hoped Ireland had done better than most places, uncrowded as it was and protected by the sea. And Achill Island . . . it was likely lonely places in the Gaeltacht had done better still than Dublin, but who could tell for certain?

"Was it your face you put in the dish, instead of your fork? What would the Mother-of-All say, to see you wasting it so?" she went on, plying the cloth as the boy wiggled and squirmed.

She was only half serious as she wiped sticky butter and syrup from around Rudi Mackenzie's mouth, but the serious half was there too. Nobody who'd lived through the Dying Time right after the Change would ever be entirely casual about food again; plague had taken millions, fighting there had been in plenty, but sheer raw starvation had killed the most. Some survivors were gluttons when they could be, more were compulsive hoarders, but hardly anyone took where the next meal was coming from lightly. Nobody decent took the *work* involved in producing food now lightly, either.

"The Lady? She'd laugh an' tell me to lick my fingers," Rudi said, also *an Gaeilge,* and did so.

Then he grinned an eight-year-old's grin at her, and stuck out his tongue. "So there."

"I expect She would," Juniper said. "And yes, you can go play."

The boy's smile grew dazzling, and Juniper felt her heart turn over as he threw his arms around her neck.

"Graim thu, maime!"

"I love you too, son of my heart. Scoot!"

Most of the Willamette communities had envoys sitting along the high table. There was her friend Luther Finney, a whipcord-tough old man who'd been a farmer near the town of Corvallis and still was—and sat on the University Council as well, since the ag faculty of Oregon's Moo U had ended up taking over that area. Captain Jones of the university's militia, too. The abbot of the warrior monks of Mt. Angel was wearing armor under his black Benedictine robe—presumably to mortify the flesh; they'd gotten rather strange there. Nobody from farther north than that; the abbey's lands were a thumb poked into the territories of the Portland Protective Association, and Lord Protector Norman Arminger was no man's friend.

A scattering were from the smaller groups south of the empty zone around the ruins of Eugene; some of those were Witch folk like her clan, and had taken to imitating Mackenzie customs, or taken them and run with them, often to embarrassing lengths—the leaders of the McClintocks were not only dressed in kilts, but in the wraparound Great Kilt rather than the more practical tailored *feilebeag* style her folk wore. Some others were the saner type of survivalist, of which southern Oregon had had many, some just survivors. There was even a kibbutz.

Juniper and her party were sitting at the center of the upper table, near Mike Havel and his folk. The Bearkillers were hosts here, and the Mackenzies honored guests and allies—which was good, but a bit awkward in one respect . . .

Well, shit, this is a problem, Mike Havel thought, watching the boy run. *Oh, is it ever a problem.*

He had to hide a grin as Rudi's mother tousled his hair before he jumped off the bench and dashed shouting to join an impromptu soccer game not far from where the trestle tables stood on the great lawn, bare feet flashing and kilt flying—that and a Care Bears T-shirt were all he was wearing; most had a broader comfort range with temperatures these days.

He had something of her pale coloring, though there was as much gold as red in the hair that fell in ringlets to his shoulders, and his eyes were gray-green. Feet and hands promised he'd have a tall man's height when he got his growth; right now he was all arms and legs. He was already agile as a young collie, though, vaulting across a friend's back and cartwheeling from sheer exuberance. Even in youth his face had a promise of jewel-cut handsomeness, square-jawed and straight-nosed, and a trace of the exotic—high cheekbones, a tilt to his eyes. Those were the legacy of Havel's blood, east-Karelian Finn mingled with Norse and Swede and a dash of Ojibwa; he'd run into Juniper while he was scouting the Willamette that spring and she was out of her home territory over in the Cascade foothills with a small party doing the same thing. Only for three days, but it had been intense, starting with a stiff fight with a cannibal band and moving on to . . .

Well, to screwing our brains out beneath the pines for one glorious night. Damn, how was I to know she'd get pregnant? The whole thing was real odd, almost like a dream.

That she *had* gotten pregnant was the problem, this last little while. Turn the boy's bright hair raven dark and he was his father's spitting image, minus a quarter century—his actual blood father, not Juniper's handfasted husband Rudy, who'd died with so many others when the Change hit precisely nine years ago, caught in an airplane taking off from Eugene's airport. Young Rudi had been born nine months later, but this year it was finally unmistakably clear that he'd been conceived some time after Rudy Starn's life ended in flame.

I can't really regret fathering him. His inward grin grew wider as he applied himself to the breakfast. *It was a hell of a lot of fun, to begin with. And he's a great kid, and it looks like Juney's making a good job of raising him.*

Wistfully: *I wish I could see him more often, show him stuff . . . being a father is a lot more enjoyable than I thought it would be, but Christ Jesus, they grow fast!*

His twin daughters, Mary and Ritva—named for his mother and his father's mother—had brought out a soccer ball, and the kids started kicking it around in a whooping impromptu game that swarmed over the lawns. It didn't much resemble a pre-Change match, starting with the forty-odd kids of various ages playing, moving on from there to the hound dogs joining in and culminating with a fair bit of grabbing and tackling. The twins had a particularly wicked method: one of them would drop, curled up into a ball, in front of someone's shins and the other would accidentally-on-purpose run full-tilt into their backs. They were identical—snub-nosed, with straw blond braids and cornflower blue eyes that slanted like his—and young Rudi went flying head over heels. The pair of them were only a few months younger, and they proceeded to pin him to the turf in a laughing tangle. All three were good-natured as tussling puppies but still exhibited half-learned judoka holds.

"You know, back before the Change, some schools thought playing dodgeball during recess encouraged too much aggressiveness," Havel said with a grin, nodding towards the scrimmage.

Most of the others at the high table laughed with him; a large percentage had children of the same age range. Not many people past their prime had lived through the first year after the Change, and the leaders were mostly in their thirties, like him. Even Abbot Dmowski, fortysomething and fiercely celibate, smiled in a lean way; he was an uncle, according to the intel reports.

The only one not smiling was Signe Havel.

Ooops, Mike thought. *Perhaps not the most tactful remark.*

With their faces close together, the parentage of the three was quite obvious; so were the maternal admixtures, with the originals sitting so close together, and people must be noticing—and Signe Havel had a much better eye for the little nuances of social interaction than he did.

Falling over your own large feet again, Havel thought.

He could see Signe Havel turn her head and follow Rudi with her eyes—and those eyes narrow, anger the hotter for her suspicion not being *quite* certain.

"OK," he murmured in her ear, leaning close. "But this

ain't the time or place to discuss things. And it isn't the kid's fault, anyway."

"No, it's yours," Signe said—but she kept her voice equally low.

It's too bad, Juniper Mackenzie thought as the younger woman turned to glare at her. *And we were good friends before she realized. Perhaps Mike and I should have told her; it's not as if I wanted to take the man from her, or there was anything between us after that one night but friendship. I wanted to. Well, done is done.*

In self-defense she loaded her plate with buckwheat pancakes studded with dried blueberries, slathered on applesauce and butter, added bacon on the side, and poured herself a big glass of rich Jersey milk. Then she dug in, making small talk with her neighbors. She'd learned acting skills as a traveling musician before the Change, and more since; being a leader was mostly keeping up a show.

Signe Havel—nee Larsson—was a Nordic beauty in her midtwenties, tall and sleekly curved, her hair a golden fall and her features perfection, save for a slight nick in the straight nose and a corresponding scar on her cheek—and the small blue mark of an A-lister between her brows. Besides her own twin girls playing with the pack, a two-year-old son sat in a high chair not far away with a nanny in attendance. She was younger than Juniper by just over a decade, but a power in the land nonetheless. Larsdalen had been her family's country home before the Change; her brother Eric was Mike's right-hand man and her father Kenneth his close advisor.

"Well, it's off to the clachan we'll be going, then," Juniper said cheerfully, pushing the plate away after she mopped it with a piece of pancake and swallowed that. "It's been grand guesting here, Mike, and meeting you ladies and gentlemen again, but there's much to do at home."

Mike frowned in disappointment and his wife hid a smile.

Mike, you are a darling man, strong and handsome as the dawn, and clever in a heavy-footed male way, and I wouldn't regret that lovely night even if it hadn't given me Rudi . . . but it's surprised I am Signe hasn't knifed you . . . yet, Juniper thought, and went on aloud, wiping her fingers on the napkin: "Ah, there's some good in every turn of fate. Now calories are what keep you alive, not what make you fat."

"We all have things to talk about," Mike said, waving a hand to the others at the head table. "We're not finished yet, Juney."

You've gotten used to telling people what to do, Mike, she didn't say aloud. *Now when you have to persuade them you should remember there's a time to talk, and a time to stop hammering and let the arguments filter through on their own.*

"We've had three days of talk and we've all agreed to wait and see," Juniper replied.

Much to your displeasure, Mike, and a bit to mine, but the Corvallis people aren't coming 'round this month; I think Abbot Dmowski scared them green with his talk of a Crusade to crush Evil, not to mention his anathemas against Arminger's own pet pope.

Aloud: "The Protector's not going to attack tomorrow, is he now?"

Unwillingly, Mike Havel shook his head. "Nah, he's too cautious," he said. "But——"

"But we Mackenzies need to prepare for Ostara."

That argument was true——the spring equinox festival came very soon——and had the additional merit of being religious and hence unanswerable. Good-byes were made, horses rounded up——so was a protesting Rudi——and the Mackenzies mounted, a double-twelve of them not including her son on his pony.

Mom? her daughter signed.

My heart? Juniper replied.

Eilir Mackenzie had been born long before the Change; fourteen years before, to be precise, and on the day of Ostara, the festival of the vernal equinox in the Old Religion. Not that that had meant anything to the teenaged single mother Juniper had been then; she'd been a nominal Catholic then, and only started to study the Craft after the fight to keep her child. That hadn't been made any easier by the daughter being deaf.

Now she's twenty-three herself! Juniper thought, bemused. *Well, twenty-three in four days. How swift the Wheel spins!*

Astrid wants to come along, Eilir signed. *And Reuben—it's Ranger business. That OK?*

Juniper hid a sigh. The two girls had come up with the Dunedain Rangers the year after the Change, and she'd thought it an excuse to playact with their friends—an equivalent of the Scouts. Maybe it had been, then, but they hadn't grown out of it. She looked over the heads of the crowd and raised a brow to Mike; he nodded. Astrid Larsson was his sister-in-law, for all that she'd been adopted as an honorary Mackenzie years ago, and Reuben one of his people.

Eilir waited, taller than her mother and black-haired, but with the same green eyes, straight-featured face and pale freckled skin; slender and strong, able to outrun a deer and ride like Epona Herself and dance the night through. Back in high school *her* blood father had been Juniper's first lover, if you could call him that—the backseat of a Toyota had been involved, just the once. He'd turned out to be a faithless fink as well, but at least Eilir had gotten the good points of his splendid athlete's body and his charm, with a lot more character; Juniper flattered herself she'd supplied some of that.

To be sure, Juniper went on. *I'll be as glad of Astrid's company as any of her friends, and Reuben is a good lad.*

Astrid had spent a good part of her time among the Mackenzies these past nine years, and she *was* a dear, and much admired by the younger generation. Also wild and . . . not crazy, but perhaps touched by a Power more mischievous than kind.

Juniper's hands went on: *But she'll have to stay a few weeks, maybe a month. Rangers or no, they can't come back across the Valley alone. It'll have to wait until we drive that horse herd over, and it's not in from the Bend country yet.*

Eilir grinned. *No problemo, Supremely Autocratic Clan Chieftain Mom. She wants to be there for the Circle on Os-*

tara too. And then we could go up to Mithrilwood for a while, get in some hunting and Rangering around.

Juniper nodded, and gave a final wave to the Larsdalen folk. Then she made the Invoking sign—a pentagram, drawn in the air from the top point down—before she chanted:

> *"Lord and Lady, bless this journey*
> *Keep it safe to wandering's end;*
> *Yours in parting and in meeting—*
> *Guard loves and hearth as home we wend."*

The rest of her riders and a fair number of the bystanders joined in with the final "Blessed be." The youth beside her had the pole of the Mackenzie banner socketed into a cup welded on his left stirrup, proudly holding the ashwood flagstaff as the green-and-silver horns-and-moon flag snapped in the cool spring breeze. He unslung his cow-horn trumpet from the saddlebow with the other hand and blew into the silver mouthpiece: *Huuuu-huuuu-huuuuu!*

Folk shouted farewells as the horses' hooves beat out a grinding clop on the old crushed shell and new gravel of the long driveway. Juniper looked over her shoulder for a moment; Mike raised his hand in salute and turned.

Looking that way, the big yellow-brick house with its white pillars didn't seem very different from the time before the Change when it had been a Portland industrialist's toy—set at the head of a long east-facing valley in the Eola Hills, gracious with a century's mellowing amid gardens and lawns and giant trees.

It was when you turned and looked down the broad V of the valley that you returned to the Changed world with a vengeance. The Bearkillers hadn't been idle since they got here towards the end of the first Change Year, nor the folk they gathered around them. There were buildings flanking the roadway; the original manager's house and sheds and barns, and others ranging from the rawly new to seven or eight years old. Some were log-cabin style, in squared timber; if there was one thing you weren't going to run short of in western Oregon, it was *logs*. Others were frame, disassembled and reerected here. Digging an earth dam and berms turned part of the creek into a pond; below it a waterwheel turned to power sawmill and gristmill. Next were the big storage warehouses and grain elevator, the rows of workshops, then the cottages, and the low-slung barracks, last, closest to the fortifications.

A steep-sided earthwork thirty feet high and twenty thick spanned the valley's cut. The Bearkillers were pushing it up the hills on either side and along the summit of the steep scarp in back of the house, and now a thick stone curtain wall stood atop it—big rocks set in concrete mortar hiding a framework of steel I-beams, with more cement plastered over the surface until it was fairly smooth, albeit patchy where the sides of the bigger boulders showed. A massive stone blockhouse sat over the cleft where the roadway went though the middle of the berm. Four round towers of the same construction flanked the gatehouse, crenellations showing at their tops like teeth bared at heaven; nothing else broke their exteriors except narrow arrow slits, and more towers walked down the wall to either side at hundred-yard intervals. A tall flagpole on one of the gate towers flaunted the brown-and-red banner of the Bearkillers. A militia squad guarded the open gates, farmers and laborers and craftsfolk in kettle helmets and tunics of boiled leather or chain mail doing their obligatory service, polearms or crossbows in hand.

Their mounted leader was in the more elaborate harness of an A-lister—the Bearkiller elite force—and there was a crisp lordliness in the gesture he made to the troops.

"To the Mackenzie—salute!"

His squad lined the road and crashed the ironshod butts of pike and halberd and glaive down on the pavement. The leaves of the inner gate were pulled back to either side—massive doors of welded steel beams running on tracks set into the concrete of the roadway.

Juniper led her people into the echoing gate tunnel, under the chill shadow of the massive stone. As she rode, she looked up at the murder holes above, where boiling oil or water, flaming gasoline or hard-driven bolts could be showered down at need; and at the fangs of the twin portcullis that could be tripped to drop and seal the passageway off.

You could call Mike Havel a hard man, but not a bad one; he and his friends were capable, rather—and realists. But you *could* say they were businesslike to a daunting degree, which was mostly a good thing, and had saved her life and others' many times, but . . .

There was still a hulking brutal strength to the stonework; when she looked at it the ancient ballads she'd sung for so many years came flooding back, with a grimness added to their words by hard personal experience since the Change. You could hear the roaring shouts and the screams, the wickering flight of arrows and the ugly cleaver sound of steel in flesh, smell the burning.

"My, and haven't we come a long way in nine short years," she murmured, as they rode out into the bright sunshine and the rolling vineyards beyond the earthwork, their hooves beating hollow on the planks of the drawbridge.

It's a good thing that there's no more copyright, Mike Havel thought. *Astrid would be going to the big house for all the places she ripped off the details for this, not on a visit to her friends'.*

This ceremony was much more private than the testing of the gunpowder, although it also involved a circle of watchers standing with swords drawn. It was on the rear patio behind the big house, with all the registered A-list members not on inescapable duty standing in serried, armored ranks on either side of the broad pathway that led to the old swimming pool. Otherwise only the apprentice candidates were present. There were seven this time—inductions were held every few months—all sternly controlling their excitement, all between eighteen and twenty-one, and showing the effects of a night spent sleepless and fasting. They were in the full kit of the Bearkiller elite, except for the helmet and blade.

Havel stood beside the brazier where the iron heated, near a trestle that bore seven swords; the light crinkle of sound from the charcoal could be heard clearly; the only other sounds were the sough of the wind and an occasional chinking rustle from two hundred ninety-one chain hauberks.

Not that I've got any objection to ceremonies. Any force needs them, like uniforms and flags and medals and songs. The Corps had some great ones ... well, people have already died for the Bearkillers. All it takes is time to add majesty, I suppose. To these kids it's the biggest deal there is. Let's make it perfect for them.

The military apprentices approached. Will Hutton stepped out to bar their path, resting the point of his backsword against the breast of the first; he was a wiry man well into his forties, with blunt features and skin the color of old oiled walnut wood and tight-curled graying hair, the drawling Texan rasp still strong in his voice.

"Who comes?" the second-in-command of the Bearkillers asked. "And why?"

"Military apprentice Patrick Mallory, sir," the young man answered clearly. "I come to claim membership in the Outfit's A-list."

"Have you passed all the tests of arms and skill and character?"

"Sir, I have."

Hutton raised his voice: "Is there any Brother or Sister of the A-list who knows why Patrick Mallory, military apprentice, should not seek enrollment? Speak now, or hold your peace ever after."

Silence stretched. Hutton lowered his blade and stepped aside. "Pass, then."

The A-lister-to-be strode on past into the circle, his boots clacking on the flagstones, and came to a halt at arm's length in front of Havel and saluted; he was a broad-shouldered young man of medium height, eyes and hair an unremarkable brown, skin pale with the long gray skies of winter.

Havel answered the gesture and reached aside to pick up the sword resting across the trestle, standing with the steel across the leather palms of his gauntlets.

"This is a sword," he said. "An ax can chop wood; with a bow or a lance you can hunt; knives were the first of all tools. The sword is a thing men make solely for the killing of their own kind; and those who don't carry them can still die on their blades. Only an honorable man can be trusted with it. What is honor, Apprentice Mallory?"

"Honor is the debt we owe to ourselves, Lord Bear. Honor is duty fulfilled."

"If you take the sword you take death: in the end, your own death, as well as your enemy's. What is duty, next to death?"

The reply came proudly: "Duty is heavier than a mountain. Death is lighter than a feather."

"You take this sword as token of the support and respect our community gives its defenders. The price is your oath to do justice, to uphold our laws, to put your own flesh between your land and people and war's desolation. Are you ready to take that oath?"

"I am, and to fulfill the oath with my life's blood."

"Do you swear to stand by every Brother and Sister of the oath, holding them dearer than a parent, dearer than children?"

"I do, unto death."

Havel reached forward and slid the sword into the empty scabbard at the other's waist, and went on: "Kneel."

The apprentice went down on one knee and held out his hands with the palms pressed together. Havel took them between his own and looked down into the fearless young lion eyes as he listened to the apprentice's words: "Until the sea floods the earth and the sky falls, or the Change is undone, or death releases me, I will keep faith and life and truth with the Bearkillers' lord; in peace or war, following all orders under the law we have made."

"And I will keep faith with you likewise," Havel said. "Let neither of us fail, at our peril. Now accept the mark that seals you to the Brotherhood."

He released the boy's hands and reached for the wooden handle of the thin iron resting in the white-hot charcoal. Mallory's face was unflinching as he touched the brand between his eyebrows; there was a sharp hiss and scent of burning. Signe stepped forward with a quick dab of an herbal ointment for the burn. Despite the pain, there was an enormous grin breaking through the solemnity as Mallory stood.

Havel struck forearms with him, outside and inside, then pulled him into a quick embrace and turned, one arm around the young man's shoulders.

"Brothers and Sisters, I give you Brother Patrick Mallory, enrolled on the A-list of the Bearkillers! So witness earth—so witness sky!"

"By Earth, by Sky—Brother Mallory!"

Metal-backed gauntlets punched into the afternoon air as near three hundred voices roared the name.

"Take your place in the ranks, Brother Mallory. We have the work of the Outfit to do." Mallory walked to the rear with a growing jauntiness.

Will Hutton's voice sounded again: "Who comes? And why?"

"Military apprentice Susanna Clarke!"

Kenneth Larsson had always kept a workshop here at Larsdalen, ever since he was twelve and reading *Tom Swift and His Atomic Earth Blaster* and *Citizen of the Galaxy*, back in 1960. There was more room at the family's summer estate than at the house in Portland, and making things on holiday had been just as much fun as woods-rambling and reading. He'd kept it up even in his hippy-dippy student rebel phase—bell-bottoms and blond Fu Manchu and all— when it had been the only thing he and his father agreed on. Then when he inherited Northwest Holdings, puttering around with a little hands-on engineering kept him sane when the managerial side of the family business threatened to drive him bughouse.

The oscilloscopes and electric furnace and other fancy toys were useless now, and there wasn't any room in Larsdalen proper; the big house his grandfather had built back in 1906 was crowded to the gills with four growing families and the staff. But rank still had its privileges. He might not be the bossman anymore, but he *was* the bossman's father-in-law and close advisor—*closest,* in anything to do with technology. In his fifty-second year—the first Change

Year—his childhood hobby had become his life's work. The big technical library still helped, too.

He'd had this building run up at the west end of the back meadow as soon as they had any hands to spare, or sooner; a long frame rectangle with a brick floor and running water, plenty of skylights and windows, forges and machine tools, desks and worktables and drawing boards, storage closets, and kerosene lamps hanging from the rooftree. It all had a smell of solvents and woodsmoke and scorched metal; designs were pinned to corkboards along the walls—for reapers and mowers and threshing machines, for pumps and windmills and Pelton wheel water turbines. And for war engines, trebuchets and catapults and a flywheel-powered machine gun he *knew* he could get working eventually.

My very own Menlo Park, he thought wryly.

"You can go now, Vicki," he said.

His young assistant ducked her head, shed her many-pocketed leather equipment apron and left; she didn't say anything, but then, she rarely did. Whatever she'd gone through while prisoner of that band of Eaters—cannibals—in central Idaho hadn't left her mute, but she was wary of human contact beyond all reason even after the newly formed Bearkiller outfit rescued her.

Larsson smiled grimly. That was back when he'd still thought his family had been *unlucky* to be in a Piper Chieftain over the Selway-Bitterroot National Wilderness when the Change hit. And Ken had the good luck to get Mike Havel as their pilot when he hired a puddle jumper to run them up to the ranch in Montana.

Speak of the devil, he thought.

A teenaged military apprentice from one of the A-lister families knocked and then swung the door in the middle of the workshop's long west wall open, letting in a flood of afternoon light and cool damp spring air.

"The Bear Lord is here, Lord Kenneth," she said formally, her face and voice serious; she would have been about ten at the time of the Change.

Mike Havel stood in the doorway, still in the war harness

that doubled as formal dress for ceremonies. He was eating ice cream out of a cup with a little wooden spoon, which was a rare treat these days—sugar was an expensive luxury again. A glance at the apprentice, and he handed her the bowl. Larsson hid a smile of his own, as she fought to conceal her delight.

"You might as well finish this," Havel said. "And don't let anyone but the names on the list in."

"Yes, Lord Bear!" the apprentice said. When the door swung closed Larsson could see her through the panes, eyes watchful on the open ground as she spooned up the fruit-studded confection.

Havel shrugged at Larsson's look. "Lost my taste for the stuff, anyway," he said a little defensively. "Too sweet."

He was a big man, but without quite the height or burly thickness of his father-in-law—a finger under six feet, broad shoulders and narrow hips showing under mail and gambeson, long in leg and arm. He moved lightly, hugely strong without being bulky, and graceful as a hunting cat, his boots scarcely raising a creak from the boards of the stairs even with the weight of metal and leather he wore. When Larsson first met him he'd been twenty-eight and already had a weathered outdoorsman's tan, with the sort of high-cheeked, strong-boned face that didn't alter much from the late teens into middle age. Apart from new scars and deep lines beside his pale, slanted gray eyes, what had changed was something indefinable . . . *Perhaps it goes with being a king,* Larsson thought, and grinned.

The grin looked more piratical than it had before the Change; the older man had lost his left eye and hand to a bandit's sword in Change Year One, and the patch and hook added something too.

"Hi, *Lord* Ken," Havel went on, smiling a crooked smile, stripping off the metal-backed leather gauntlets. "Got the initiations over with, at least."

In the distance a roaring chorus of voices rose in song, or something close to it, as booted feet clashed in unison to the beat of drums and the squeal of fifes:

"Axes flash, broadswords swing
Shining armor's piercing ring
Horses run with a polished shield
Fight those bastards till they yield!
Midnight mare and bloodred roan,
Fight to keep this land your own—
Sound the horn and call the cry:
How many of them can we make die!"

"I like that song," Havel said, grinning. "It's becoming sort of traditional—another favor Juney Mackenzie did us. What's better, everyone else on the A-list likes it, too." He winced slightly as Ken Larsson raised a brow, and continued: "That is, everyone likes it except Signe. I ducked out when she started glaring at me again—everything associated with our red-haired friend puts her on edge now. Christ Jesus, I don't *need* this. Can't you talk to her? She's your daughter . . ."

Ken Larsson laughed until he wheezed. "Oh, no, son-in-law, I got out of *that* job at the altar. Besides . . . can you blame her?"

"Yeah, as a matter of fact, I can! Yes, Rudi's my kid—but Signe and I weren't married then. She was still back in Idaho when I came west on that scouting mission and ran into Juney. Hell, Signe and I weren't even *involved* then, not really, and she'd made it pretty plain no hanky-panky was in prospect. OK, she said no, I folded up my tent and rode away."

"She'd had a rough time," Larsson said, looking aside. It had been even rougher on him, the night his first wife died.

"And I haven't touched another woman since we *did* get involved," Havel said bitterly. "Christ Jesus, I'm getting the punishment for adultery without having the fun!"

Larsson cleared his throat. "Anyway, Mike, expecting a woman to be *reasonable* about something like that is about as futile as trying to fly to the moon by putting your head between your knees and spitting hard. Have you actually confessed yet?"

"No," the younger man said shortly.

"Well, you should. Grovel and apologize and beat your breast and promise never to do anything wrong again. Keep on doing it while she yells and throws things, and then while she sulks and gives you the cold shoulder beat yourself up some more."

"Shit, I didn't *do* anything wrong!"

"And that is relevant . . . how?" Larsson snorted. "Listen to the voice of experience, son. Besides, there's young Mike. She's probably worried about him."

Havel's lips curled into a smile at the mention of his son's name; then he frowned in puzzlement.

"Worried?"

"About who inherits all this," Larsson said, waving his good hand.

Havel blinked, obviously surprised. "Well . . . well, shit, Ken! Who said the position's hereditary, for Christ Jesus' sake? Even Arminger hasn't gone that far."

"He will," Larsson predicted. "Bit awkward for him that his only child's a girl, but if you read the reports, he's setting things up for Queen Mathilda the First."

Havel shrugged. "Yeah, but I'm not Arminger, by Christ Jesus. Last I heard, the assembled Outfit chooses the boss-man when the old one dies, retires or is impeached; and I should know, seeing as how I *wrote* the damned law code. I've gone along with a lot of Astrid's pseudomedieval horse manure, but enough's enough! No golden crowns for this country boy."

Larsson sighed. "Mike, you might have made the distinction between political and military authority and private property a little more distinct . . . or distinct at all . . . when you were setting things up. Or maybe I should have reminded you, even busy as we were. But done's done; if the Outfit were to select somebody *else* after you were gone, who owns the house? And the lands—the stuff we manage directly from here? The heirs of Mike Havel, guy with a growing family, or the successor to Lord Bear, ruler of all he can see? And if it's the latter, what do your kids get? Parents are *supposed* to be anxious for their children's futures, you know; you can't blame Signe for living up to the job."

"Hmmm," Havel said. "Point. Distinct point."

"Besides which . . . let me ask you a question: How many of those apprentices you just enrolled were relatives of people already on the A-list?"

Havel frowned, thinking. "Four out of seven. Why? Anyone can take the tests."

Larsson sighed again. "Mike, you're a smart guy, but you're kind of . . . focused. This is a low-productivity economy we've got—not as bad as the Dark Ages, more nineteenth-century in a lot of ways, except it's also a pre-money setup most of the time and our population's too small for much specialization. And we've made schooling compulsory, which I approve of. But what do a tenant farmer's kids do in their munificent free time, school holidays being scheduled to coincide with the growing and harvest season?"

"Work their asses off helping their family get the crop in," Havel said promptly. "Same as I did back in the Upper Peninsula, before I graduated high school and joined the Corps. Only a lot more so. We ran that farm part-time; mostly the family lived on what my old man made in the Iron Range mines."

Larsson raised his metal prosthesis and made a check-mark in the air. "Bingo. Now, what does an A-lister's kid do? You know, the people with the big land grants and tenants and full-time household workers."

"Pitches in on the home farm a bit, usually . . . but I see your point."

"You betcha. You insisted on high standards even for getting into the apprentice program, and it's *hard* learning to shoot a bow from the saddle of a galloping horse, or handle a lance. The A-lister's kids have the gear and the space and the trained horses and the leisure to *practice,* not to mention expert coaching from their parents and siblings. Plus one *hell* of an incentive—the land goes with the A-lister rank, and without money, how do you build up alternate investments? Plus the family has to be willing to let the kid go when they're sixteen to *be* a military apprentice, just when they're getting really useful on the farm or in the workshop and starting to pay off the parental investment. A-listers don't need their children's labor so badly."

"It's not all family members," Havel said defensively.

"Not yet. The original A-listers are too young to have many adolescent children; it's mostly their younger siblings so far. But when their offspring are old enough, you're going to find they're a *lot* more than half the apprentice uptake. And watch who marries whom, too, which'll push the process along even faster—the more so since it's a coed setup. I watched the same thing happen in the business world back before the Change in the seventies, eighties. When lawyers and executives were all men, they sometimes married secretaries. When women professionals arrived in numbers, they married other lawyers and executives."

"I hadn't . . . Ouch."

"So it's pretty likely the A-listers will vote in one of *your* kids as successor. Because by then it'll be unnatural to do anything else. So Signe's worrying, maybe unconsciously, if it'll be *her* kid, not just *yours*. Pam tells me that there were a lot of systems like that in the old days—where the throne was elective within a certain family, broadly defined. Like in the sagas—read about what the dozen sons of Harald Fairhair did to Norway sometime. If you acknowledge that Rudi Mackenzie *is* your son, everyone will believe it who's got eyes. He's older than young Mike, too. Old enough to start getting hints of what sort of a man he's going to be; he's smart, and he could charm a snake out of its skin, for starters."

"Well, shit," Havel said, pushing back his helmet by the nasal and rubbing his jaw. "But even if the position goes to one of my kids, I'd want to pick the best when they're old enough—for that matter it could be Mary or Ritva, as easily as Mike Jr. or Rudi."

"That was probably Alexander the Great's plan, watching his kids grow and picking his own successor from the best of them. Unanticipated events sort of took a hand, and nobody's immortal. You ought to be thinking about this *now*, Mike. We don't have a tradition on how to handle succession yet. Note that I have an interest here too—if it's going to be hereditary, I want one of *my* grandkids to get it."

They looked at each other, and Larsson changed the subject. "When did they start that 'Lord Kenneth' business?" he asked. "It fits for you and your shining-armor crowd, but why humble mechanical *me*?"

"You know perfectly well, and it's your own damned fault," Havel replied, smiling. "They started it when your youngest talked them into it. She'll have them forsoothing next. You're not an A-lister, but you're my father-in-law and you're our ... wizard, I suppose. Astrid loves that idea, by the way."

"Astrid's perverted imagination is not *my* fault!"

"She's your daughter, isn't she? You let her slide into the Mistress of Ceremonies position, didn't you? You're also the one who let her wallow in all those doorstopper books with the lurid covers and knights and princes and warrior elf maids and wizards and walls of ice and quests for the Magical Dogtag of Doom and whatever."

"I thought she'd grow out of it," Ken Larsson said weakly.

Havel's boot knocked the sheath of his backsword aside with practiced ease as he sat on the stool before a drill press and went on: "She landed *me* with the Lord Bear nonsense before we'd finished who-eats-whom with Mr. Bruin. I'm surprised it hasn't turned into a *talking* bear conjured up by an evil sorcerer, and gotten slapped down in that goddamned illustrated journal she keeps."

"Illuminated, not illustrated," Larsson said.

They shared a chuckle at the thought of the—profusely illustrated—Red Book of Larsdalen. Sheer dogged persistence had let Astrid Larsson hang names out of her favorite books on a good many things, post-Change. A fanatic for Tolkien and his imitators could do a world of linguistic damage, particularly when things were in flux anyway and she was part of the ruling circle of families; Astrid hadn't shown any signs of growing out of it at the ripe old age of twenty-two, either. The younger generation was alarmingly given to humoring her—or even to taking up her enthusiasms simply because they sounded cool and torqued off their elders.

"I think it's the isolation, too," Larsson said. "If we had

more outside contacts, people would laugh us out of it. As it is, every little bunch of us is free to go off on their weird tangent of choice."

Havel nodded. "Sounds plausible, in a horrible sort of way. So, what's up?" he went on, dropping his bear-topped helm on a table and running his hands over his bowl-cut black hair. "I've got to go read some reports by Signe's intel people about bandit trouble up on the northern border. *Anything* you've got to say will be more interesting than more goddamned reports."

Larsson's single blue eye gleamed. He turned to a desk piled with papers and bearing a mechanical calculator he'd salvaged out of a museum, and pulled out a sheet covered with graphs from beneath his slide rule—the results of months of experiment over the winter.

"I think I've got a handle on the Change!"

Havel snorted. "How many times have we chewed the fat about that? Starting the morning after. I thought you'd gotten the reaper binder working. *That* we can use. Harvest is tricky. Or more penicillin. We could get another outbreak of the Black Death anytime and we're clear out of tetracycline."

"No, not just a hypothesis this time—a theory with experimental confirmation."

"You can *do* something about it?" Havel said, sitting bolt upright.

"Oh, hell, no, Mike. Do I look like an Alien Space Bat from an arbitrarily advanced civilization? Arbitrarily Advanced Alien Space Bats . . . sounds like a lobbying group. But I've gotten some idea of what's happening. Look at this."

Larsson pointed to a piece of apparatus on a bench, one that involved a gasoline lantern burning under a blackened cylinder. He turned up the wick with the tip of the metal multitool strapped in place of his left hand, and tapped the metal casing with it. The flywheel off to one side gave a halfhearted turn and then stopped.

"This is what they called a Stirling-cycle engine—sort of like a steam engine without the water, using a gas as the working fluid in a closed cycle. This one comes from a museum in Eugene; I traded some moonshine to a scavenger who had it in a load of miscellaneous junk. I wanted it because it doesn't depend on fast combustion—explosions—like IC engines. Result: It doesn't work anymore either."

"Why am I not surprised?" Havel said.

He sounded patient, in a heavy sort of way. *But then, he puts up with Astrid, too.*

Larsson went on: "A Stirling engine is like the theory of heat engines made manifest. Put concentrated heat in *here,* raise the temperature of the gas, and you get mechanical work out *there.* OK, mechanical work and diffuse heat. All you need to make it work is a temperature gradient between one end and the other. And like all heat engines since the Change it just doesn't work to any useful degree."

"What about guns?"

"Guns *are* heat engines—first ones to be widely used. But."

He swung the lamp out from under the cylinder, engaged a crank and worked it with his good hand. Crankshaft and piston and flywheel spun up with a subdued hum; after a moment he released it to run down.

"You see, one of the interesting things about a Stirling engine is that if you run it in reverse—if you put mechanical work *in*—it acts as a refrigerator. You get *cold* out the other end. They were used for that in labs and some manufacturing back before the Change. And that still *does* work."

Havel's brows went up. "Well, that could be very useful," he said. "We could really use some refrigerated storage for food, particularly if we could do it in bulk. It just doesn't get cold enough in the Willamette to make icehouses practical—one of the few advantages we had back when I was growing up on the Upper Peninsula, and man, did *we* have ice and to spare. We could run this Stirling thingie in reverse off a waterwheel or a windmill?"

"Yes, or the sort of horse gin we use for threshing machines now. But think about it for a moment. Why would the heat-to-work cycle not function, while the work-to-cold cycle *does*? And when you're cranking it, it works *ex-*

actly the way it did pre-Change. It's like you can only play a film backward."

Havel shrugged again. "Presumably your Alien Space Bats, or Juney's gods, or the Reverend Abbot's Lord Jehovah wanted it that way. I never did think the Change just *happened.*"

"Neither did I. It's too . . . *focused.* A random change in natural law would most likely just collapse everything into quark soup. And everything is too neatly scaled, the effects kick in at the precise level necessary and no earlier; it lets any biological process go on just fine, our nervous systems work, fish can still use their swim bladders, but that"—he pointed at the engine—"is screwed. Somebody *did* this to us."

Havel slapped a hand against the brass bars that made a protective basket around the hilt of his backsword. "Give me a clear run at whoever did it, and I'll carve them a new one."

"Yes, yes," Larsson said, a testy edge to his voice. "But this gives me a handle on *how* the Arbitrarily Advanced ASB's are screwing it up—the heat engine side, at least, that's easier to get a grip on without instruments than the electrical problems. It isn't nanobots with unobtanium force-field generators watching our every move and selectively intervening whenever we try to fire a gun or run a generator. What's happened is a change in the Ideal Gas laws—or more accurately, a forced change in the behavior of near-ideal gasses—"

"Whoa, partner," Mike said, raising a hand. There was a rustling chink as the elbow-length mail sleeve of his hauberk brushed the vambrace on his forearm. "I knew my way around a motorcycle engine, but that's about it, techwise. You're talking to a high school graduate who just squeaked by in math and fudged a lot to get his pilot's license."

"OK, it's a change in the way gas molecules act under certain very specific circumstances, so there's no increase in pressure with heat beyond a low threshold. Like there's some added force that glues molecules together, so instead of producing work, the heat energy or the work put into mechanical compression gets locked into some weird form of *potential* energy."

He pointed to another apparatus, a cylinder with a gauge attached, a piston rod sticking above it, and a framework for dropping weights on that.

"This is the one that's really been driving me nuts. It turns out the pressure limitation is same-same with pumping air mechanically into a reservoir. After a certain point, all you get for more pumping is sweat—same glue-the-molecules effect."

Havel looked at the apparatus and frowned. "You mean if you drop that weight, it doesn't compress the air in the cylinder? OK, we've got infinitely efficient shock absorbers?"

"Oh, yeah, it does compress it—up to a point. Then the *volume* of air keeps getting smaller as you push, same-same as it would have before the Change if you exerted the same force, and it resists a push just as it would have before, but more like a liquid or solid than a compressed gas. The *pressure* doesn't get any higher after that cutoff point. There's a falloff in the extra push-back pressure you get for each input of energy applied; it starts small and then goes up in an asymptotic curve—ever-steeper curve, to you scientifically illiterate types. Pretty soon it reaches something close to infinity—like trying to go faster than light with a rocket."

Havel ran his hands over his hair. "That's *crazy*."

"Well, *duh*, my armor-plated son-in-law. Of *course* it's crazy. It simply fucks parts of the laws of thermodynamics, just for starters. That's what confirmed my mental certainty about the glue-the-molecules effect. Watch."

He walked over to the cylinder and tripped a release.

Whank!

The weight slammed down, and the gauge twitched. Ken jerked a thumb at it.

"OK, as far as I can tell, the piston went down *exactly* as far as it would have before the Change under the same weight. But see the pressure gauge? Barely a fraction of what it would have been with that reduction in volume. As far as I can tell, what happens is the air gets sort of . . . *thicker* . . . as it gets compressed . . . the molecules get closer together and the energy input goes into mashing them tighter and tighter, but they don't leap apart when it's removed. They just expand again, they fill additional volume but they don't *push* at it the way they should. The same thing happens with any other compressible gas, by the way, but *not* with non-compressible liquids like water. Which means you can use hydraulic systems just fine."

Larsson rubbed his good hand on the leather support of his multitool. "You know, if you could get that energy back *quickly,* this would make a hell of a battery, or an explosive."

"You can't get the energy back? It's *gone*? Conservation of energy I have heard of—"

"Oh, you can get it back; thermodynamics isn't *totally* screwed up. You just can't get it back very *fast,* or in any form that's any fucking use at all."

He turned a valve, and there was a long hiss; the piston rod sank down. "When you do this, the exit valve and the air around it heat up more than they should. For that matter, the air in the cylinder gets hotter than it should when you drop the weight; not *much* hotter, just barely enough difference that I can detect without electronic instruments. I *think* the potential energy trapped by the glue-together effect leaks away gradually in the form of diffuse low-level heat as the molecules 'unbind.' The slow burning with explosives is probably part of the same effect; the extra force keeps the molecules of a fuel from spreading fire as fast. There seems to be a relation between pressure and . . . never mind. I think something similar was done to set an upper limit on permitted *voltages,* too, maybe by increasing the degree of electron localization in solids. That would—"

"*Whoa,* Ken. Look, this is all very interesting, and I even think I understand parts of it . . ."

"That's more than I do," Ken said, grinning. "I understand *what,* but I've got no earthly idea *how,* much less the theories behind the effects. I'm like Imhotep the Pyramid Builder confronted with a TV set, trying to understand how the wizard got all the miniature people in the funny box. We're multiple paradigm shifts away from being able to understand it. We just don't have the intellectual vocabularies—hell, the *grammars*. And with our toys taken away, we can't get from here to there."

Havel frowned and continued: "... but I'm trying to keep thousands of people alive around here. And we're running out of *stuff*. Things are wearing out. We've got plenty of food and enough basic shelter now, and a fair start on weapons, but we don't have enough tools or cloth or shoes and we *certainly* don't have enough medicine if the plague breaks out again, and every time we shift people from one thing there's another that goes undone, and Christ Jesus but that bastard Arminger up in Portland *is* going to take another slap at us soon, so I have to keep our military up to snuff, which costs. So could we please concentrate on things that'll actually *help* us?"

"Eventually this could be useful, a heat sink can—oh, all right, Mike. I get your point. It does have some practical implications, though. It means we can get enough concentrated heat to run a foundry, say . . . but a lot of other industrial processes, most high-pressure chemistry for starters, are just . . . forbidden."

"Thanks. That'll save us time and effort." Havel slapped a hand on the older man's shoulder. "We couldn't have done it without you, Ken."

Kenneth Larsson unscrewed the multitool from the hardened-leather cup strapped over the stump of his wrist. As he fastened on the hook-grasper he used for everyday work he shook his head.

"No, Mike, we couldn't have done it without *you*." He held the hook up like an open palm. "Yeah, I've done a lot of useful work for us, and I'm damned proud of it—prouder of it than of anything I did as CEO of Northwest. So have my kids, and so have Will Hutton and Josh Sanders and Pamela. But you're the guy who found us all—"

A knock at the door interrupted them. The apprentice opened it. "My lords, it's A-lister Naysmith. He says you told him to look you up, Lord Bear."

Ken got up and left, giving his son-in-law a slap on the shoulder. He waved his hand at the man entering, who ignored it—but that was probably from the terror that left his face like a mask carved out of lard. With the crowd at

Larsdalen for the holiday, this was about as private a place as could be found without ostentatiously riding out somewhere beyond the defenses. For a moment Larsson paused at the bottom of the veranda steps. Somewhere a rooster crowed; behind the workshop was a broad stretch of pasture where horses grazed, slanting up southwestward to a fringe of forest. The foundations of a citadel showed there at the highest point of the Larsdalen plateau—raw earth and sacks of cement, rebar and quarried rock. Beyond, the steep scarp of this outlier dropped to the flatlands around Rickreall; beyond *that* was the low green line of the Coast Range.

And behind him he could hear Mike Havel's voice. The workshop's walls were thin.

"—there's a reason you got the big farm and the help to work it and the rents and the Justice of the Peace appointment, Naysmith. And it *wasn't* so you could sit on your ass and drink beer and chase girls who didn't want to get caught. You're supposed to keep yourself and your people ready to fight, and administer *justice*. Christ Jesus, you *do* know what the word means, don't you?"

An inarticulate murmur, and then Havel's voice rising to a roar: "—will not abide trash behavior, Naysmith! This is your *last* warning; next inspection, I expect your holding's A-listers *and* the militia to perform by the numbers and on the bounce. And the next complaint about you bullying your people or taking more than the compact allows will be the last; if there's a petition against you I *will* have that hauberk off your back and I *will* strike you off the Brotherhood's rolls. And your assessment is doubled for this harvest—it'll come out of your share too, not the farmers. If you want to work for a squeezing bandit, you can take your sorry ass over the border and try your luck with the Protector."

The apprentice stood stiffly at the foot of the stairs, eyes front, left hand on her sword hilt, right hand carrying her targe—small round shield—tucked across her chest. She was a little pale around the mouth; listening to a chewing-out from Mike was alarming at the best of times.

Another mumble, and Havel's voice was kinder: "Look,

Mark, you've been with me since Idaho. We fought Iron Rod together. I *know* you can do better than this. So what's the problem? Tell me, for God's sake, and I'll help you."

Larsson grinned, taking a deep breath of the cool air. *Think I'll go visit my newborn, or my grandchildren,* he thought, and ambled off. He'd had his bellyful of being CEO back before the Change and had never liked it one little bit. It was *good* to have someone else to handle that stuff.

I'm a pretty good engineer, and I was passable as a businessman, but I really don't think God gave me what it takes to be a warrior king.

CHAPTER THREE

The M1 motorway that ran north from London was still passable beyond the edge of cultivation in the commandery of Whipsnade, in the sense that you didn't need to hack your way along it with a machete or ax; the six lanes and thick deep foundation under the pavement were putting up more resistance to the encroaching armies of revengeful Nature than most of man's works.

Nigel Loring still found it eerie to ride down it with walls of vegetation taller than the tip of his lance on either side, the more so as evening fell and his borrowed remount's hooves dragged beneath him. The sun was a red ball on the horizon, filtered through canes and branches. Runners and growth from the median strip and the verges were most of the way across the pavement; many of the autos and trucks were mere mounds of foliage. A fox sat on the roof of a pantechnicon and watched him until he was close enough to see the sun gilding its rufous fur and its tongue lolling through its sharp white teeth, then dropped to the ground and disappeared into the tangle of tree and shrub and bramble west of the roadway. There was a brief whiff of the dog-fox's musky scent as they passed, rankly feral beneath the warm green sweetness.

"Four men riding by and it's scarcely bothered," Alleyne Loring said. "You can tell there's not many riding to hounds in this county just of late. I hope those antifoxhunting fanatics were pleased, in the short interval before their hideous deaths."

The joke was sour, but Nigel Loring smiled; his son had been brooding alarmingly, and most of the remaining youth had left his handsome features, though he was still two years short of thirty.

"Watch out, Reynard," John Hordle called after the departing animal, as they rode under two overpasses. "You'll get scragged for sure if you 'ead that way—it's Milton sodding Keynes."

Nigel Loring chuckled. *Odd. I'd have thought his cheerfulness would be irritating, under the circumstances, but it isn't. Maude always liked him, of course. She'd have given one of those gurgling laughs of hers if she were here now. I remember that was the first thing I noticed at that do of the vicar's—she was talking to him across the garden and I heard her laugh. She was wearing one of those absurd floppy hats . . . it was seventy-three . . . enough!*

"I think we cleaned it out fairly thoroughly, back in CY3," he said. "There weren't many of the poor devils left by then, anyway."

"It's like cockroaches," Archie MacDonald said. "Ye'll no get the last of 'em, not with a whole kettle o' boiling water to the floorboards."

The farmworker was sweating a little, and he kept his bow across the saddle despite its awkward length for a mounted man. He started when three red deer rose up from the shade of an Aston Martin that must have cost three hundred thousand pounds once; the big russet animals poised for a moment, then turned and trotted swiftly away with their muzzles up and their horns laid on their backs, bounding over a three-car pileup of wrecks and running northward until they vanished from sight. Hordle looked at them and thoughtfully twanged the string of his bow.

"Not worth the trouble," Sir Nigel said. "We've got enough food to reach the Wash."

"Wasn't thinking of that, sir—though that yearling hind looked fair tasty. I was thinking they looked like they'd been hunted before. You do much deer hunting around here, Jock?"

MacDonald squinted after the vanished animals. "We've no seen any, near the farm—not Bob's, nor the ones Gunnar and I have filed for, we've done a bit of work on both, keeping the access roads clear and the buildings tight, ye ken. Hunting around here's mostly birds, rabbits, wild pig, fallow deer, and those little muntjacs—the ones that bark like dogs—they do love a bramble thicket. And you see some gey strange beasties from the Safari Park—there's rhino about yet—but no the red deer."

"The nearest herds of red deer were in Cornwall," Alleyne said thoughtfully. "Fairly remote areas, mostly. The Lake District."

"Aye, an' Scotland, the Highlands. And they'll no ha' gotten a lift south on the *Cutty Sark,* the way we crofters did from Skye."

"I would expect them to spread south, though," Alleyne said. "Or it could be red deer from the Woburn herd, if any made it through. They'd be likely to move north for the grazing, and to get away from the settlers, this last little while."

He rubbed his chin, fingers rustling on soft blond stubble; there hadn't been much time for shaving. Like his father he was riding one of the farmer's horses, an undistinguished cob of about fourteen hands, and like the elder Loring he'd removed all his armor save for breast- and backplates and the helmet dangling at his saddlebow. Their own mounts followed behind, carrying the gear in sacks slung over the war saddles.

"But if they haven't spread to the edge of the farming country, why should they be wary of men?" he went on. "That bally fox wasn't. *Ergo,* they *have* been hunted."

Hordle and Nigel exchanged glances. That was a good point . . .

"We should be getting near the turn," Nigel said aloud, consulting the map in his head.

It was disconcertingly easy to lose your sense of place and distance, when the landscape looked so different from the way memory painted it. He'd driven through here countless times . . .

"Isn't there a Welcome Break sign about here? Has a flying goose or something of that sort painted on it."

"Nae, ye've gone too far if ye see that," Archie said. "It's three miles north o' here. Junction Fourteen—yes, that's it."

He pointed to a sign that rose thirty feet in the air with the upper part of its rusted, pitted surface above the vegetation; it was blue with a white band ending in a pointed tip at the top, and another line pointing leftward. A mile went by, steady riding at a fast walk—the stalled vehicles made it difficult to go faster. They were on the right side of the motorway, the southbound lane before the Change; Junction Fourteen was on their own right, curving up from the main thoroughfare. Another sign loomed.

" 'Milton Keynes, Newport Pagnell, A509,' " Hordle read. "And 'The North,' at the top—that's original, innit? Specific, too. Better be careful, sir," he went on, as they turned their horses up the eastward-leading access road. "This is the slip road for oncoming traffic. We'll cop a ticket if we're seen going down it the wrong way."

"You are incorrigible, Sergeant," Nigel snorted.

There was no need for him to ask why he got so much encouragement; and they *were* careful as they passed a blue-and-white sign with an arrow directing drivers to the M1 for Luton, London and points south. The lesser road that led to the town itself was far more densely overgrown save for the narrow path Buttesthorn's men had hacked, and a good deal of it had been ripped at by heavy floods, starting with the wet spring in the year of the Change. There were sections where only a scalloped edge of pavement remained above overgrown mud and there they had to dismount and lead the horses. Nobody was maintaining levees anymore; even in late summer he could see patches of reed and livid green marsh grass to his left as they rode. The arched 1920s roof of the Aston Martin plant had slid quietly into the silt . . .

Stay alert, he told himself. The bubble of misery sitting below his breastbone threatened that; it would be so easy to plunge into gray apathy—or worse, tormenting memories of Maude. *Work is the best remedy for care. You have other lives depending on you now, including Maude's son.*

The graceful arch of Tickford Bridge was still clear of vegetation, save for vines crawling along the railings and up the cast-iron lampposts; the bridge itself was iron, built in 1810 when that was still a novelty. The tiny Lovat ran below, thick with reed and sedge, flanked by tall willows and oaks that had spread upslope in both directions in waves of saplings. Over their tops ahead and to the right he could just see a slip of the tower that crowned St. Peter and St. Paul Church, looming above Newport Pagnell town as it had since the Wars of the Roses. But when he looked directly ahead, up St. John Street . . .

"Not much left," he said.

Fire had passed through the little market town, fire and flood. The buildings to his left were nothing but mounds under second growth; the forest was reclaiming them faster than it was the open fields, and tall saplings reared among the rampant bramble and thorn. To the right, on the higher triangle of ground between the meeting point of the rivers where the original settlement had stood, occasional snags of wall or even roofs remained—though many of the newer frame buildings had simply been ripped apart by Russian vine pressing on their joists. Under the scent of vegetable decay and silt was a fainter one of wet ash and crumbling, moldy brick—the taint of corruption was probably his imagination.

Insects and rats had picked the bones clean long ago.

"Major Buttesthorn's men said it was clear to that pub where they hid the canoes, sir," Hordle rumbled. "But tricky in the dark."

It was eight thirty, and the long twilight of an English August was drawing to a close. Nigel felt the drain of exhaustion, sand in his eyes and the feel of it in his joints.

John Hordle gave a low whistle as they walked their mounts forward, cautious on the bad footing. "This is a good place to hide something, and no mistake. It looks like it's been abandoned for a hundred years, not less than ten."

"Why's it called a *port*?" MacDonald said suddenly.

"Odd name for a town sae far inland. Na'er seen it before, mind you."

"It wasn't named a port, originally," Nigel said. "It was *porta*, that's Latin for a trading post. This was the border with the Danes, in those days."

"Danes?" the Scot said, turning in the saddle to look at him.

Nigel smiled and inclined his head towards his son; perhaps a friendly voice would keep the farmworker steady.

The younger Loring said, "Founded in 917, before Edmund Ironside completed the reconquest of the Danelaw. Then given to Sir Fulk Paganell by William the Conqueror for services rendered at Hastings in 1066."

MacDonald grunted. "Ah. Like this Commandery business of the king's."

He spat aside to show what he thought of *that*. Sir Nigel winced a bit behind his impassive face; the bones of the idea had been his as much as the monarch's—a quick and simple way of organizing and defending the resettlement of the mainland, with the existing guards and SAS units as a framework. He hadn't meant to take it quite so *far* towards outright neofeudalism, of course . . .

Alleyne smiled. "The labor levies, you mean?"

"Aye, that in particular," MacDonald said. "It's a nuisance that drives you fair mad, when there's so much wants doing to haime."

The younger Loring pointed over his shoulder at the path Buttesthorn's men had hacked through the vegetation on Tickford Street. "Of course, without the levy, all the roads south of here would look like *that*."

"Weeeel . . ." MacDonald said reluctantly. "Perhaps ye've a point."

They rode up the curving High Street; many of the two-story Georgian storefronts had collapsed into the streets, from fire and subsidence and sheer decay, but there was enough brick and pavement to keep the trees and brush from growing too thick yet, though saplings and shoots showed where its infinite vegetable patience was at work. The horses snorted and rolled their eyes as their hooves clattered and crunched through the uneven footing; there were scuttlings and scurryings through the piles of rubble and wreck, behind the blind windows like sockets in skulls where a piece of wall survived.

"Where'll we put the horses?" Archie MacDonald said. "This is no' good for their hooves."

Sir Nigel nodded; the three beasts they'd borrowed to supplement their own were a substantial share of Jamaica Farm's capital assets, and the man was entitled to be worried. In fact, he felt a sudden liking for the wiry redhead. Archie MacDonald had no particular reason to feel any loyalty to the Lorings. He could simply have gone to his local Commandery and turned them in, and gotten a good farm ready-stocked out of it, rather than breaking his back for years to earn one. Instead he was risking his life in this tangled, sodden wilderness to help a man he'd never met before, for his friends and because he thought it was right. And if he seemed a bit nervous, well, he wasn't a professional soldier as were the Lorings and Hordle.

"The churchyard," Nigel said. "If the fencing's still intact—it should be, it was iron palings. Hmmm . . . one watch here with the horses, the other up the street with the canoes. We'll want to get an early start."

Despite his exhaustion, he would have preferred to start now, if the sky weren't already turning purple-blue in the east, and the first stars appearing. They'd be following the river, north and then eastward to the Wash and King's Lynn where the ship was supposed to meet them. But . . .

God knows I've done water work before, and mostly at night. Not to mention Borneo and Belize. But the Ouse will be difficult. Full of obstacles and winding about, breaking its banks and retaking the old floodplain, and it's a long journey. I wouldn't care to try it in the dark, not when losing a canoe would be a disaster. We can afford the time: the king won't send pursuit overland. It's too late to do any good, and he'd have to arrest Knolles, and he certainly can't afford that, politically—it would touch off revolt for certain if he turned on one of his most loyal officers. A night's delay will give him more time to set something up at sea, but that's less of a risk than blundering about exhausted in the dark.

They turned in past the great silvery gray bulk of the

church; the moon was up now, and it seemed to make the ancient limestone glow. Hordle lit a lantern from their baggage, adjusting the wick and then lifting it on the tip of his bowstave as the two Lorings pushed the tall doors open. Inside the hundred-foot length of the nave things were less orderly than the nearly untouched exterior suggested. The pointed arches and pillars along each side still stood, but in spots the white plaster had been discolored by smoke, probably from the missing pews. There were ashes and fragments of bone near the altar, where the rood screen had been, and blasphemous, incoherent graffiti scrawled over the walls. Hordle reached up to hook the wire loop of the lantern over one of the dead electric candles around a pillar, then knelt, taking a pinch of the ash between thumb and forefinger and bringing it to his nose.

"This isn't eight years old, sir," he said. "Nor one, neither, I'd say. Early this spring?"

The two Lorings joined him. Alleyne leaned over the discolored stone where the fire had been, his blue eyes bright with a hunter's keenness. "You're right, Hordle. Hmmm. That knucklebone there, it's pig. And these . . . that's a red deer's leg bone, by God. Someone's been using this place since the Change, not very recently, but several times at long intervals."

His father wrinkled his nose slightly. "Someone with a very elementary sense of hygiene," he added. The smell wasn't all that obtrusive after months, but it was still detectable in this damp climate.

Archie MacDonald called from the entrance: "What's there?"

"Someone's been using this as a campsite," Nigel said. "Brushwood Men," he went on. "But not just lately, I'd say."

That was the standard euphemism for those who'd made it through the Change on the mainland—usually by devouring the less successful—the handful who'd merely hid in remote places and been very, very lucky had come in and joined the resettlement in Change Year Two. There weren't very many of the Brushwood Men, but they lingered in the unsettled zones—and even a few in the vast, tumbled, half-flooded ruin of London, by rumor, surviving now on rats and rabbits and what they could scavenge from park and riverbank.

"Filthy buggers," MacDonald said, with a shiver.

"Right," Alleyne Loring said, returning from a brief tour outside. "The fencing around the churchyard's intact, and there's plenty of grass down towards the river. We'll hobble the horses, and you can start back with them tomorrow morning, MacDonald. A little luck, and nobody will be any the wiser."

The two warhorses were Irish Hunters, seventeen hands and towards the heavier end of that mixed breed; they'd do well enough as draft animals, especially on an isolated frontier holding. Hordle's cob was an unremarkable beast and would fit in with Jamaica Farm's trio very nicely. Three good horses were as many as most farms could afford; six would enable them to get a good deal more done, with less human exhaustion.

"What about the harness, sir?" Hordle asked.

Nigel nodded at the heavy war saddles, specialist gear of no use to anyone who didn't intend to ride to war armored cap-a-pie and carrying a lance.

"We'll take those along to a deep place in the river and sink them. No sense in dragging a hundred pounds of tack around the world. Your saddle's standard issue, Hordle, so your farmer friend can have it with the horses." He looked at MacDonald. "Which watch do you want to take, and where?"

They were standing near the church doors; the Scot looked up the ruined length of Newport Pagnell's High Street. The slumped front of the Cannon pub was only fifty yards east; the canoes and traveling gear were hidden in the function room at the back. From there it was easy carrying distance down to the stone bridge over the Great Ouse.

"If it's all the same, I'll take first watch here," he said, looking at the stout stones of the church. "Forbye, could I keep the lantern?" The three ex-SAS men looked at him blankly.

"Whatever for?" Nigel asked, curiously.

Hordle snorted. "It might not do any harm 'ere. But Jock . . . if there was anyone lurking about . . . well, you might as well hang up a sign, 'Sneak Up and Kill Me,' mate. All a light does at night is blind you and mark you out." More kindly: "I'll be back to relieve you in three hours, and we'll save you dinner."

Nigel reached for a canvas duffel bag; it held the rest of his armor. But Hordle was before him.

"I'll take that, sir," the giant said, and took them both, besides the war saddles, hefting the two-hundred-pound total without visible effort, despite his own gear.

Nigel and Alleyne followed, eyes wary in the dark and hands on their sword hilts. The front of the Cannon had collapsed into the street; they had to climb a long sloping surface of rubble before wiggling through between a section of half-collapsed ceiling and the top of the mound into the function room.

The door to that had survived; Buttesthorn and his men had been hard at work there, as they saw when they let the section of blackout curtain fall to hide their entrance and turned up the lantern. The rubble had been pushed back from a section of stone-flagged floor, and any cracks in the mostly intact rear and side walls had been roughly patched with mud and planks, from the inside. Three aluminum canoes waited, with bundles of gear neatly packed and trussed beside them. Trail food, extra arrows, two more longbows—Nigel and his son were both excellent shots, but neither could bend Hordle's monster stave—sleeping bags, clothing, fishhooks, lines . . .

There was also a little spirit stove. Hordle grunted appreciation and lit it as he rummaged through the sack of supplies they'd brought from Jamaica Farm.

"Right, I knew that Gudrun was a kind-'earted girl. Pity we couldn't stay a little longer, but needs must. Sausages . . . bacon . . . bread . . . butter . . . onions . . . tomatoes . . . spuds . . . mushrooms, even! We can do a proper fry-up. Fair scrammed, I am. It'll be salt horse and Old Weevil's wedding cake on the *Pride of St. Helens,* I'll wager. Ah! She put in four bottles of Scarecrow Best Bitter, all the way from Arreton; it must be love. Bob'll be livid."

"I'll take first watch outside, then," Alleyne said. "Give me a shout when it's ready, Hordle."

Sir Nigel sat, unlacing the bag with the rest of his suit, going over the pieces—pauldron and vambrace, spaulder and sabaton and greave—checking for nicks in the enamel, flexing the leather backing and straps and buckles. The armor didn't need nearly as much maintenance as the medieval originals. They'd used some of those in the first year or two, taken from museums and country houses; after that the armorers had rigged water-powered hydraulic presses to stamp copies out of sheet metal salvaged from warehouses and factories. The Lorings' suits were of the best, and the nickel-chrome-vanadium alloy was much, much stronger than the rather soft medieval steel; besides that it didn't corrode easily, if at all. Still, it was best to take no chances, and it was as important as ever to keep the leather supple.

And the homely, familiar task let his mind wander while he kept it on impersonal things.

He looked around the ruined pub; how long would it be until this was a town again? At least it *would* happen; there had been times in the first Change Year when he feared it would all collapse, that England would be totally wrecked as most of Europe and the Middle East had been, beyond hope of recovery. There *was* an England again, however tiny and impoverished; and at least he could comfort himself that he'd played some part in building it. Perhaps in laying the foundations of a new age of greatness. The Irish might have had the starring role this time if they hadn't indulged their taste for bashing in each other's heads so wholeheartedly, but as things were old England had the field to herself . . .

And how will they think of these years, in that age to come?

When this was a pub again, or housed a weaver or a merchant or a blacksmith, how would the chronicles fit this age into the long, long vista of the island story? Beside the Black Death, he supposed, or the Viking invasions; a great catastrophe, long ago, which ushered in a new age. But there would be none of his blood in it, for the first time in many centuries. There had been Lorings at Tilford before the first stones of Woburn Abbey were laid, although for a time the land had passed through a female line before the name returned through marriage to a distant cousin.

Lorings had carried their blazon of five roses to Crecy and Agincourt; one had gone ashore at Cadiz in the first Elizabeth's time, beating a drum in the surf as his men put King Philip's Armada stores to the torch—and drank up an amazing cargo of sherry found on the beach. A scion of the house had died under Rupert's banner at Marston Moor, and the mother of his infant son had stood siege as commander at Tilford against Cromwell's Ironsides— Charles the Second had made the Lorings baronets shortly after the Restoration, as a cash-free way of paying off the debt. Others of his ancestors had left their bones from Delhi's gates to the Crimea. Nigel's own father met his end leading a jungle patrol in Malaya against communist guerillas in the 1950s, and his mother died of a fall while pursuing Charlie James Fox over a hedge not long after. Nigel himself been raised mainly by his grandmother, whose young husband Lieutenant Eustace Loring had vanished under a storm of German shells in the retreat from Mons in 1914. She'd lived long enough to see him married . . .

Maude . . .

The wound was still raw, but it didn't scrape at his whole mind quite as much, now. The first pain had subsided just enough to let him feel lesser hurts.

The fact of the matter is that we were very happy, these last few years, politics aside—if Alleyne had settled down and produced some grandchildren, it would have been perfect.

He wouldn't have chosen the Change—no sane man would—but . . .

To be completely honest, I'm more at home in an England of farmers and squires and parsons than one of cities and motorways and the Internet, he acknowledged ruefully. *If it weren't for the . . . eccentricities . . . of the king . . . a dozen hitch of Shires couldn't have dragged me out of the country again.*

Maybe I should *have taken the offer of Gibraltar,* he thought, accepting a plate from Hordle with a word of thanks, and beginning to stoke himself methodically.

Gibraltar wasn't quite an island, but the only connection to the mainland was a narrow peninsula. The town and garrison there had managed to barricade themselves against the hordes and live off the huge stores cached in the tunnels of the Rock, plus a providential bulk carrier full of Argentine wheat that drifted by just close enough. Expansion into the empty spaces of southern Spain and northern Morocco had required help from the mother country, though—men and tools and leadership. An intriguing challenge; a job worth doing.

I might have accepted if I were a bit younger—and then I wouldn't have been involved in politics here and Maude would be alive. There was a hint of a title, too . . . I'd have retired quietly in another decade—and all that was Queen Hallgerda being cunning.

Alleyne returned from his watch at Hordle's soft-voiced imitation of a barn owl. The archer loaded another plate with eggs, sausage, fried potatoes and buttered bread.

"I'll take this over to Jock and send him back when he's finished," he said.

Alleyne smiled—a charming expression that reminded Nigel forcefully of his wife for a moment. "Excellent fry-up, Sergeant."

"I take a good bit of feeding, sir," Hordle said. "So it pays to do it right. Maybe a bite to eat will cheer up that mournful Jock git. I think the ruins put him off, like."

"You were always the best field cook I knew. Something Sam Aylward *didn't* teach us, eh?"

"Christ, no, sir. Samkin could burn water. I swear a can of bully beef tasted worse if he opened it."

"I'll relieve you in four hours, then."

The two Lorings settled down in comforting silence for a moment as Nigel prepared to take his own turn; the younger man had a thick hardcover book out. It was his copy of the *Fellowship of the Ring,* of course, a signed edition salvaged from Oxford in CY2. He'd brought along all three volumes.

Nigel was reaching for his sword belt when they heard Hordle's owl hoot, repeated twice.

"When I saw the fire, I thought that Jock had done it," Hordle said grimly. "He was nervous of the dark here—with reason, as it turns out."

The Lorings helped each other into their war harness as they listened to the report and watched the archer draw in the thin film of dirt that overlay the flagstones with one long thick finger. It took them only five minutes to don the plate that way; the redesign had been thoroughly ergonomic—not something that the original medieval smiths had emphasized.

"So I came up quiet-like, to show him why it's a bad idea to light a fire in hostile country," he said. "Which was fortunate, or I'd have run right onto their sentry—as it was, I smelled him first. He was hiding a treat, he was, though, and probably he could smell the soap on *me* if I got too close. Once I'd located him I went around the rectory side of the church and scouted that way. Six women, five kids and eight or nine grown men. The men all have bows of a sort and good long knives, and there's a fair number of spears and such, couple of axes—woodchoppers. Two sentries out—here and here. The rest all in the nave of the church. They must make a regular circuit of it with this as a stop, and we got unlucky on the timing."

"You're sure MacDonald is alive?" Nigel said.

"Had him tied to a pillar, sir. Stripped for his clothes and banged about, but not hurt bad yet. They had a couple of deer hanging up, probably the ones we saw earlier today. I don't think they'll eat him if they kill him . . . but they want him to talk, and from what I overheard, they're thinking of keeping him to show them how to look after the horses. Those've got them excited, but they're dead nervous too. And I think they came up from the river, sir."

"Hmmmm." Sir Nigel thought, then shook his head regretfully. "We don't have time to do this with any subtlety," he said. "We'll just have to go in and win, and hope we can get MacDonald alive out the other end of it."

* * *

Hordle had been right; you *could* smell the Brushwood Men's sentry a dozen paces away, if you were downwind of him—the heavy, sour, metallic-fecal scent of an unwashed body and unchanged clothes in a wet climate. Otherwise there wasn't much to quarrel with in his choice of a sentry box, squatting inside a window ledge that a sign proclaimed had once been Odell's Bistro; that was on the south side of High Street, just beside the bend that held the church. It gave him a clear view both ways along the street, and kept his eyes away from the firelight that flickered red and sullen through the stained-glass windows. His ragged clothing broke up his outline, save for an occasional gleam of eyeballs or teeth, and he was admirably motionless.

Well, the clumsy ones got eaten long before this, Nigel thought, as he counted his heartbeats. *Four hundred forty four . . . five . . . now!*

He stirred in his hiding place, deliberately letting his armor clank against a loose brick. Moonlight shone on eyes again as the sentry's head twisted—no showy leaping up, just the minimum movement of head and vision, and another as his bow came to the ready. He scanned the street; then his eyes went wider still, and he began to turn as he realized someone was creeping up behind him.

Nigel winced very slightly as two great hands came out of the darkness and clamped on either side of the man's head, gripping the matted hair and beard and then twisting sharply. The sound was like a green stick breaking; the body gave a single twitch and went limp. More smells added themselves to the unlovely aroma. Closer, he saw that the ragged appearance was partly deliberate: swatches of cloth had been sewn to the dead man's trousers and the jacket he wore over bare skin, breaking up his outline and making better than passable camouflage. The bow slid down and Nigel picked it up for an instant to examine; it was yew from some churchyard, crudely made but serviceable, and cut by someone who knew enough to use the sapwood for the back and heartwood for the belly.

They're learning, he thought with a slight chill. *Well, of course. Process of elimination, what?*

Nigel and Alleyne moved forward cautiously; it *was* possible to move silently in plate armor, if the interior surfaces and edges of the plates had linings of soft thin leather glued on, and you had the knack. Light flickered through the stained glass of the church; they came in low, and he knelt and raised his visor to peer through a gap in the stained glass into the nave of the church. The savages had built a fire on the same spot near where the rood screen had once been; smoke drifted high under the hammer-beam roof, and flickering ruddy light cast shadows in the great rectangular space of the nave. A deer hung gutted and headless from a rope around one pillar; another was being butchered by two tangle-haired women, knives flashing not unskillfully . . . and that made you think how they'd probably learned their way around a carcass, which was unpleasant. An aluminum cauldron bubbled over the fire. As the women cut gobbets free they tossed them into the boiling water. Another stirred it, and added handfuls of chopped wild greens and feral vegetables. For a moment that surprised him, but they'd all have died of scurvy if they hadn't learned *that* much.

Archie MacDonald was trussed up to one of the pillars, much like the deer; he was naked save for a set of bruises already turning purple, and one eye was swollen nearly shut. One of his captors had appropriated his plain homespun jacket and trousers, his shoes, his bow—far better than theirs—and his belt and sword, which was the only longblade in the group. The clothes were far too big for the man, who was short and had a ratlike face thrust forward from slightly stooped shoulders and three rings that looked like wedding bands through the septum of his nose. He was also a bit older than the rest; unkempt hair and rotten teeth and scabby skin made it difficult to tell, but the leader looked to be about thirty-five and the rest of the men mostly a decade or so younger. They'd have been in their midteens when the Change came. The women were about the same, or a little less; the six children who lay on heaped blankets in the corner ranged from toddlers to six or so. Two of the women were visibly pregnant.

The men were crouched around the fire, roasting bits of

organ meat from the deer on sticks as appetizers, the fire-light winking on crude tattoos and gold rings and plugs in body piercings. One got up and walked over to the prisoner, juice running down his chin from the kidney he'd been eating. The smell of them all in the nave and their leavings mingled with the odor of roasting and boiling meat in a particularly nauseating mixture.

"He looks plump," the man said, showing snags of tooth when he grinned. "In the old days, he'd have been right tasty! If you want him to talk, Viggers, why don't we 'ave one of his legs off? He don't need *them*. We could offer him some, done just pink in the center."

The rat-faced leader moved with astonishing speed; there was a meaty *thump* as his shoe slammed into the other man's crotch.

"Shut up!" he screamed. "We don't talk about that! Ever! We did what we 'ad to do but we don't talk about it! *Ever!* The Netherfield Avengers are real men who look out for their own, not fuckin' animals like them Brummie cunts!"

He punctuated the words with a few more hearty kicks. The man threw up helplessly, then crawled away, leaving a smear of half-digested venison behind him. Some of the others dropped their eyes when the little man glared around; others laughed when he unbuttoned and pissed on the writhing form.

"We've got them horses," the leader said, hands fumbling with the unfamiliar fastenings. "We can do a lot with horses! When the others come in we'll be able to carry all we'll need, and then we'll go far north, take some land . . ."

Nigel drew back and nodded at the others. A few signs conveyed his meaning silently: *Hordle, you keep MacDonald safe. Alleyne, with me.*

Then he gently lowered his visor; when it clicked home it covered his face to the lower lip, overlapping the bevoir to make a ridged mask of steel from chin to brow with only the long eye slit to break it. The bad part about a close helm was that it restricted your vision, particularly around the edges. The good part about full plate was that you were near-as-no-matter invulnerable to ordinary cutting weapons and very, very hard to stab. And that you didn't need to worry about glass ...

He took four steps back and then sprang forward, curling his limbs together in midair, with one arm around his knees and the other holding the shield over his face. Impact with the stained-glass window was peculiar—half crisp pops and crunching, half the soft, heavy resistance of the thin lead strips between the glass panels. Nigel landed and rolled, coming up on one knee with the shield under his eyes and the sword flicking out into his hand.

Reality broke into fragments, images glimpsed through the visor slit as he turned, moving like a living statue of green steel. A woman scuttled towards MacDonald, raising a knife in a hand where fragments of deerflesh clung. Hordle's bowstring slapped against a bracer, and an arrow went through her swollen belly without slowing in a double flash of red; she went down shrieking endlessly and clutching at herself. A savage drew his own bow, aiming at Hordle in the window; Nigel's backhand slash caught him behind the knee and he went over on his back, thrashing like a beetle. The shaft went wickering up into the arched darkness of the nave to slap into plaster.

"King's Men!" one of the savages screamed. Nigel had rarely heard such raw hate. "Kill 'em! Kill! *Kill!*"

"A Loring!" Alleyne's voice rang out, given a peculiar muffled quality by the close helm.

"A Loring!" Nigel replied, shouting from the bottom of his lungs. "*A Loring!* St. George for England!"

Hordle leapt into the room, out of the vulnerable spot framed by the window. His bastard sword was in his hands now, held in the double-handed grip as he moved across the floor towards MacDonald in a pounding rush, astonishingly fast and light on his feet for a man his size. A savage started a thrust at him with a spear, then turned the movement into a frantic attempt at a block. The great blade came looping up, then down through the tough wood with a sharp *crack,* through the man's right arm above the elbow, and then the tip went through three-quarters of his neck. The corpse spun away as the sword swept through the rest of its arc. Hordle danced in a circle of his own with the follow-through, turning it into a thrust that went through a belly . . .

The leader of the savages—or Netherfield Avengers, if there was a difference—leapt around behind his people, urging them forward. They didn't need much encouragement. A few seconds and they boiled towards the two Lorings in a wave of screeches and stinks. Alleyne and Nigel stood shoulder-to-shoulder, then back-to-back. Nigel punched his shield into a face and felt bone crumble and break, then laid open a neck with a short overarm cut. Blood sprayed through his visor, blinding him for an instant; a body landed on him, sending him staggering sideways. An arm closed around his neck, legs around his middle, and a knife sawed and stabbed around his throat, probing for a gap between bevoir and sallet helm. And there *were* gaps, if you had long enough to look . . .

He reversed the blade and stabbed backward blindly. There was a screech and puff of rotten breath next to his ear, but the knife continued to probe; something cold and hard ticked at the leather collar beneath the steel.

Nothing for it, went through his mind.

Nigel kicked out with both legs, throwing himself backward; the weight on him helped him fall in a controlled topple. The savage on his back screeched again as they came down on the stone floor, with the baronet on top— and though he wasn't a large man, the sixty pounds of armor brought his total to a little over two hundred. Something cracked beneath him, and the scream turned into a gurgling wail. Another savage loomed over him, swinging up a weapon—a sledgehammer, and that *could* kill him in his harness. It was too late to try to rise or roll aside; instead he kicked out with one spurred foot, felt the blunt metal point catch in flesh, and ripped it down. He was three-quarters back to his feet when another savage came at him, swinging an ax. It struck into the middle of his breastplate with a loud unmusical *bonnngk* of metal on metal, with a tooth-grating harmonic beneath it as the curved plate shed the blow—and the impetus helped him make the last few inches onto his feet. Nigel slid forward, using his shield to bind the man's arms against his own body, stabbed downward deep into a thigh and twisted the point—

And the room was plunged into near-darkness, as someone upset the stewpot onto the fire with a long *shhhhsssss* of steam.

Nigel snapped his visor up. Some scattered coals still glowed redly, enough to show him shadowy figures clawing at each other in the doorway, and others diving through the broken window. Hordle roared and flung his sword with a sweeping two-handed motion like a hammer toss; it turned in the air and drove point-forward into the back of the last savage, sending him forward on his face with the blade and hilt sticking up like the mast of a ship.

"After them!" Nigel wheezed, suddenly aware of how his breastplate seemed to squeeze at his chest as he heaved for air. "Get them running fast—"

Alleyne went by him, blade raised high, shouting something that sounded like *Wait for me, Grishnàkh.*

Hordle followed, snatching his longsword free as he passed the man it had killed; more shrieks and screams sounded outside. Nigel leaned against a pillar with his sword hand, then let his shield fall free with a clatter and raised his canteen to his lips, swilling a mouthful and spitting it out to clear his mouth of gummy saliva, then drinking. Light flared up again; Archie MacDonald had collected some of the coals and dropped them in the piled brushwood the savages had collected.

Then he limped over to Sir Nigel, peering anxiously with the one eye not swollen shut. "Are y' injured, sair?" he said.

"Not—" Nigel coughed, took a deep breath and held out his canteen. "Not as much as you, my friend. Just rattled about a bit inside my shell. I'm getting a little long in the tooth for this sort of thing, I fear."

MacDonald took the canvas-covered metal in a hand that suddenly started shaking. "I've no bones broken," he said, steadying it with both hands and putting it cautiously to his mouth, where the lips had been bruised and torn against his own teeth. "And I'm better than I was before I heard ye're voice, sair."

The crackling light threw their shadows high on the walls. MacDonald huddled closer to the fire, seeking the warmth his naked skin and the fringes of shock needed. Nigel went around the bodies lying about, counting and making sure that the dead savages were undoubtedly and permanently so with quick, merciful, sword stabs; distasteful work, but necessary—he'd be responsible if they crawled off and recovered enough to be dangerous again. By the time he was finished his son and the archer were back.

"Got another one, but they scattered fast in the dark," Alleyne said. "Most of them ran for the riverbank. I think they had boats there, from the marks in the mud."

"We got about half of them, or a little better," Hordle said. "But—"

A whimper interrupted him. The children of the Netherfield Avengers were huddled together in their filthy nest of tattered blankets. Nigel looked at them and sighed.

"This is going to be complicated," he said. And then to the children: "Don't worry, little ones, we're not going to hurt you."

Alleyne snorted: "They're not going to believe *that,* Father, any more than a fox cub would."

MacDonald muttered something under his breath, on the order of *Nits breed lice.*

Nigel gave him a quelling glance, but the man was right in the literal sense—the youngsters *would* be lousy. At least they were young enough to forget the horrors of their upbringing in a couple of years. The new England needed all the hands and backs it could get.

Hordle grunted as he cleaned his sword on a rag, then rubbed it down with a swatch of raw wool. "This is like the one about the fox, the cabbage and the sheep," he said.

Nigel yawned convulsively, politely covering his mouth—although that was a bit risky, considering what clotted his gauntlets. "I think the best thing would be to put them on the horses and get them back to Jamaica Farm tonight," he said. "Then of course we'll have to come back here ourselves . . . and someone will have to come with us to take the horses back . . . the gear here will have to be guarded too . . . I'll give Mr. Bramble some names of people around Tilford who'll take them in. Thank goodness there's no more of that bumf with identity documents."

"No rest for the wicked," Hordle said. "There goes a night's sleep. Of course, it's just a merry cruise down the Ouse afterward. With one big bastard of a problem."

"Yes?" Nigel said. There seemed to be sand in the cogs of his brain.

"The kiddies' dads have boats too."

CHAPTER FOUR

Juniper Mackenzie scowled slightly as she looked down at the pilings of the bridge that ran over the Willamette and into Salem's Center Street—the ruins where Salem had been, rather. The piles and the spaces between them were thick with rubbish: logs, brush, general trash, wrecked cars and trucks and campers. Now the spring water was foaming high over that barricade, water blue-green and then surging white in the bright noon sun, throwing waves half the distance up to the deck of the bridge, and spray high enough to strike her lips with the chill wet smell of it. The roaring power of the spring freshets made the pavement tremble beneath her feet and the ponded-back water spread, flooding streets on both banks and covering the low islands just upstream where the waste ponds had been.

It also brought more rubbish tumbling down to join the growing dam every day, and the vehicles made the assemblage too strong for the water to just push downstream. One of the few sensible things the state government had done in the brief months between the Change and its own total collapse had been to get the stalled cars off the main roads in and around the state capital. Otherwise the number and nature of its manifold idiocies had surprised even a former unwed teenaged mother who'd kept and homeschooled her profoundly deaf daughter in the teeth of welfare officers, bureaucrats and Uncle Tom Cobleigh and all;

they'd disregarded how much in the way of useful metal and springs and formed parts an automobile had in it, and also the cargoes in the trucks.

Except the food, she thought. *Even they weren't that stupid.*

So those on the bridge had just been shoved over the side, including one eighteen-wheeler full of perfectly good blue jeans. Perhaps not a great fault, when their other mistakes had denied so many who might have survived any chance of life, but . . .

Rudi looked down through the railings and then solemnly up at her. "The river spirit's angry, Mom," he said. "*Really* angry, 'cause She's all tied up with stuff. We oughta quiet Her."

She put a hand on her son's small hard head. "That She is, *mo chroi.* We should also get that wreckage out of the way, come summer, and free the waters."

"That's what I *said,* Mom," he replied, looking as if he'd like to stamp a foot but too well mannered for tantrums.

And sometimes I get a bit of a chill at the things you *say, my heart,* she thought, beneath her chuckle.

She remembered presenting him to the altar in the *nemed,* at his Wiccanning near nine years ago. And the words Someone had spoken through her:

> *Sad Winter's child, in this leafless shaw—*
> *Yet be Son, and Lover, and Horned Lord!*
> *Guardian of My sacred Wood, and Law—*
> *His people's strength—and the Lady's sword!*

Perhaps it was her imagination that he was . . . *sensitive* to things. But perhaps it wasn't, too. The Gods knew, but they hadn't told Juniper Mackenzie, High Priestess or no. Not yet.

"Nothing I can do about that, sure," she muttered to herself, looking down again. "The bridge, now . . . if we don't clear the piles the next time a dam breaks"—and several of the upstream ones had already, as locked spillways and lack of maintenance took their toll—"this bridge is going to go bye-bye, taking the other and the rail bridge with it. And that will be a royal pain in the arse."

Then they would have to go *miles* out of their way south to cross the river, and back north again on the other side to get to Bearkiller territory, which meant an extra day's travel on bicycle or horseback and four to six with wagons. Or hiring people from Corvallis to do it, at vast trouble and expense. So they *should* fix the problem before the utterly irreplaceable bridges went down. The problem with *that* was that it would take hundreds of workers a month of hard graft and considerable danger to life and limb, plus scarce equipment like winches, and there were a dozen other things more *immediately* important to be done between now and the harvest, and why should her clansfolk bear all the burden of doing something that would benefit everyone in the Valley?

That's what they'd say—or yell loudly—at the clan assembly, and she hadn't let the system become an autocracy. More of a town-meeting anarchy, tempered by the fact that most survivors of the Change years tended to outbreaks of hard common sense now and then . . .

Deal with that later, she thought, and raised her head to look east.

You could see the snow peaks of the High Cascades from here, floating on the eastern horizon with a tattered veil of cloud streaming from their tops, blue and white and disturbingly lovely over the corpse of the city. Fire-scorched, the forlorn pride of the capitol stood off to the right, with its bearded, ax-bearing pioneer atop the drum-shaped dome. Little else that was human remained in the old state capital except bare-picked bones. Whatever could burn had gone up in the great fires, and the quick-growing lowland brush and vines crawled over the blackened rubble, spreading out from park and lawn, roots prying at concrete and stone with the long slow strength of centuries. For the rest, roaches and rats had multiplied beyond belief, then eaten each other and died in a ghastly parody of the human dwellers' fate.

Or the fate of not quite all *the dwellers.*

The Mackenzies had halted here because on the bridge nobody could sneak up on them; it would be otherwise in the narrower streets. The city wasn't altogether dead; nor were the only folk to be met those using the bridges or scavenging for useful goods. She grimaced at memories of her own—clutching hands and mad screaming-grinning faces and breath stinking of shreds of human flesh caught between rotting teeth.

Eaters aren't the problem, not anymore, thanks be to the Lord and Lady. Perhaps a last few skulking solitary mad-men remained, but the shambling terror of the cannibal bands was mostly a memory of the Dying Time now, passing into folklore.

No, the real risk around Salem this ninth year of the Change is from plain old-fashioned bandits, who are a lot smarter and better-armed.

As travel and trade revived a bit and farms grew worth raiding there were always those who thought stealing easier than working; and there was little law in the Valley now save what communities like hers enforced within their own bounds. That the bandits would leave your stripped carcass for the Goddess' ravens instead of eating it themselves wasn't much of a consolation to the victims. Nor was the prospect of being sold for a slave in some of the less civilized areas if captured; ironically enough, places that had fought to turn away refugee hordes in the months after the Change were now nearly as desperate in their desire for more hands to do all the things machines had once accomplished.

She also strongly suspected that the Protector slipped the reiver bands help to distract the southern valley while he prepared for war; it was just the sort of thing Arminger and the Portland Protective Association would do. Some of the outlaw gangs used the taller buildings in Salem as bases for bicycle-borne raids, with their binocular-equipped lookouts lurking about the top-floor windows like maggots hiding behind the empty eye sockets of a skull. It was a lot harder for pursuers to run them to earth here in this stone-and-steel wilderness, too, so that noose and blade could put an end to them.

And to think I was once strong against capital punishment . . . to be sure, I'd never seen people killed by bandits, then. Plus Salem plain gives me the willies.

The physical stink of death was long gone, but surely Earth herself bore the memory of despair and terror, in the place where so many had passed untimely to the Other-world. She thought Eilir felt it too, and Rudi more strongly than either—though he simply set his lips and endured it, with composure beyond his years.

"So, Sam," she called to the First Armsman of the Mackenzies, and nodded towards the ruins. He'd picked her escort, and ridden with it. "Fast and loud or slow and cautious?"

"About equal risk, Lady Juniper," he said.

Sam Aylward's voice had a slow south-country accent from deepest rural Hampshire, a yokel burr as thick and English as clotted cream. An adventurous life in the SAS and sheer chance had landed him in Oregon when the Change came, hiking the mountain paths. She'd stumbled across him while she was hunting for meat for the pot, lying trapped and injured after a tumble into a ravine in the Cascades above her cabin.

Cernunnos sent luck to him and us both that day, she thought, watching him nod thoughtfully, his gray eyes narrowing as he scanned the ruined city. *Praise and thanks, Lord of the Forest!*

"I'd say go for loud and fast," he concluded, running thick fingers through short, curly brown hair now showing a few streaks of gray; he'd been just turned forty the year of the Change, and newly retired from the British army, traveling on an unexpected inheritance. "There's no bandits in the middle valley that'll tangle with this many of us, if they know the odds."

The square Saxon face was calm as he waited for her answer, the thick-armed, barrel-chested body utterly at ease. He looked slow, to someone who hadn't seen him move when speed was called for.

"Fast and loud, then," she said. "We'll go down Center, turn south out of town on Twenty-fourth, go past Turner and Marion . . . We can make Lebanon before nightfall, if the horses all hold up. But lunch first."

A packhorse carried food in two large baskets strapped to its cargo saddle; round loaves of good brown bread still slightly warm from Larsdalen's kitchens, butter, hard cheese and sausage salted and dried and smoked until eating it was like chewing rather tasty steel-belted radial tires. Plain food, but riding long hours was hungry work, and most of them remembered times when this would have been better than a feast.

She drew the little *sgian dubh* knife from its sheath in her right boot top—eating with a ten-inch fighting dirk like the one at her belt was not advisable, unless you *really* disliked the shape of your nose—and sketched a figure on the surface of a loaf, chanting:

> *"Harvest Lord who dies for the ripened grain—*
> *Corn Mother who births the fertile field—*
> *Blessed be those who share this bounty;*
> *And blessed the mortals who toiled with You*
> *Their hands helping Earth to bring forth life."*

Everyone present was a Dedicant at least; many echoed her, and they all joined in the final "Blessed be" before pitching in.

Mom? Eilir signed, with her mouth full. *Remember when you used to busk at the state fair in Salem before the Change, and we'd go to that Jaliscan place on Silverton Road? Lord and Lady, but those shrimp in garlic butter!*

Ah, that was fine indeed, mo chroi! Juniper replied.

Carefully, she did *not* wonder what had happened to Jose and Carlita. If you didn't know someone's fate by Change Year Nine, the probabilities ranged from a quick death to something *really* bad.

Eilir's face fell a little, probably at a similar thought. She got up to join the other youngsters but stopped for a second to say: *Mostly that all seems like a dream—the old days—as if it was just a story someone told me. Other times just for a moment, it's* this *that doesn't seem real.*

Juniper smiled and ate in friendly silence, listening to the water's roar and the wind's whisper, watching Eilir and Astrid and their friends chaffing at each other; watching a young man take the time to groom his horse, and a girl pick wildflowers growing in cracked pavement, weav-

ing some into the mane of her horse and tucking one behind her ear.

Aylward munched stolidly, his eyes never leaving the
road they'd take, scanning methodically. The horses bent
their heads to piles of cracked oats and alfalfa pellets, and
drank from buckets hauled up from the river.

At last he dusted crumbs off his hands and raised a brow
at her. She nodded at his unspoken query.

"Right, you lot." He turned to the rest of their party,
who'd repacked the panniers and stood by their horses.
"Gear up and string bows, if you haven't already."

Gearing up meant stuffing the flat beret-like bonnets in
a saddlebag and putting on helmets—round steel bowls
with hinged cheekpieces that clipped together under the
chin. They were already wearing their brigandines—rows
of small metal plates riveted between the layers of a
double-ply jerkin, the outer layer green and carrying the
clan's sigil, the crescent moon between branching antlers.
Many wore padded arming doublets underneath them,
with short mail sleeves and collars attached. All the adult
Mackenzies also bore short broad-bladed swords in the
Roman style on their left hips and long fighting dirks at
their right; hooked over the scabbards of the swords were
round steel bucklers the size and shape of soup plates,
ready to be snatched up by their single handgrips.

But you didn't string a yew longbow until you had some
prospect of using it. Wooden bows tended to "follow"—to
develop a permanent weakening bend—if left strung too
long. Even the reflex-deflex models Sam had taught them
to make, with their subtle, shallow double curve heat-
treated into the staves. Archery and hunting had been his
hobbies for decades before the Change.

Juniper watched with fond pride as Eilir pulled her
longbow from the carrying loops beside the quiver slung
over her back. Then she put the lower tip's nock-piece of
polished antler against the outside of her left boot and
stepped through between string and stave. That let her
brace the riser handle against her right buttock; she pulled
down sharply with both hands as she flexed her body
against the heavy resistance of the seasoned wood, using

one hand to slide the cord's loop up into the grooves of the polished elkhorn tip. The movements had the easy, practiced grace of an otter sliding down a riverbank.

That left her with a smooth shallow curve just under six feet long, D-section limbs of oiled and polished yellow yew on either side of a black-walnut riser grip; forty-five arrows jutted over her right shoulder, fletched with gray goose feathers and armed with a mixture of delta-shaped broadheads and narrow six-sided bodkins designed to punch through armor. Juniper bent her own bow as well; it had a fifty-pound draw, which was the lightest in the group. Aylward's was more than twice that; she'd seen him put a shaft right through a bull elk's ribs and have it come out the other still going fast—and once knock an armored man off a galloping horse at two hundred paces.

Lord and Lady, it doesn't even disturb me to think about that anymore, she thought with a slight mental shudder. *Not that I was ever really a pacifist, but ...*

She cut a last section of sausage so that Rudi would have something to worry at, cleaned and sheathed the knife and swung into the saddle with a creak of leather, tucking up her kilt into a comfortable position—she wore good woolen boxer-style underwear anyway—and signaled to the bannerman.

He put the horn to his lips again and blew, a dunting howl of jaunty defiance.

"Ill-doers flee! Friends take heart! The Mackenzies are riding!" she called, a great high shout in her trained singer's voice, and the horses clattered down towards Center Street.

Eilir Mackenzie rubbed the fingers of her right hand on the tooled leather scabbard of her dirk as she rode; tracing the intricate interwoven patterns was her equivalent of whistling idly. It was pleasant to ride out on a bright spring day after being pinned so long in the Hall at Dun Juniper by the wet gray gloom of a Willamette winter. Not that the Black Months were all bad: there were the great festivals of the Year's Wheel; and making things, sports and storytelling, visits and books and games to pass the time; raw chilly days hunting in dripping woods, and long drowsy evenings to follow, lying on sheepskins before the hearth, roasting nuts and sipping hot cider; and of course chores.

So winter has its points, but spring's like throwing open a window when a room's gone fusty and stale.

She looked over her shoulder at Salem for a moment as the dead city faded in the living horsemen's wake, then turned back with a slight shudder. It was good to get out of *there,* too. Her mare Celebroch kept to the same walk-trot-canter-walk cycle as the rest of the group, but she did it with a high-tailed, arch-necked Arab grace that only Astrid's Asfaloth could match; the horses were twins, silky-maned and dapple gray. The feel of the great muscles between her thighs was like coils of living steel, longing to run . . .

They'd needed less than an hour to clear the built-up section and reach open country southeast of the last outskirts, only the occasional vine and creeper-grown mound showing where a burnt-out farmhouse had stood, its flowers and rosebushes lost among weeds. The hearing members of the Mackenzie party—everyone except her—were probably having their ears numbed and attention distracted by the rumbling, clattering, clopping beat of hooves on the asphalt.

She wasn't, and noticed something odd out of the corner of her eye—movements in the roadside thickets. They were level with a peach orchard gone wild; thin spindly volunteers sprung from fallen fruit, and a tangle of whiplike unpruned branches starred with a first few pink blossoms. A streak of red fire blurred out of it . . .

That fox broke cover and went across the road before *the rabbits did. And none of them paid any attention to* us. *Game's gotten less wary, but not* that *much less wary. They were both running from something. Or somebody.*

Nobody honest lived around here; too close to foragers and Eaters in the early years and too solitary now; the only towns still living on the river itself were Corvallis and Portland. Her eyes probed the fields as she emptied her mind and let the patterns show themselves.

The lush fruit of the Valley's rich soil and reliable rains gave the land a disheveled dryad beauty. The stretch east past the old orchard was bushy and overgrown: weeds and grass that rose stirrup-high or better, a new growth of yarrow rank and tall through last year's dead brown stalks, shrubby Oregon grape with spiny hollylike leaves and clusters of yellow flowers. The field had been cultivated for flower bulbs before the Change; amidst the strangling invaders early tulips and iris pushed up forlorn in crimson and blue; darting swarms of rufous hummingbirds hovered around their blossoms. Patches of waving reeds showed livid green amid a buzz of gnats and swift predatory dragonflies; that was wetland returning as ditches were blocked and field drains silted up and the untended levees along the Willamette and its tributaries broke down.

An abandoned tractor near the road was already a mound of blackberry vines and golden pea starred with pale gold blooms, with only the regular curve of the rear wheels and the shape of the square cab showing the hand of man. Patches of wood left along creeks and field boundaries before the Change now sprouted thick fringes of saplings, young trees as tall as her own five-eight or higher. There were red alder and black cottonwood, fir and pine and oak spreading out as the skirmishers of the triumphant forest's march. The fresh spring leaves fluttered like the banners of a conquering army; maroon trillium bloomed in the shade beneath their feet, bright orilachrium coins scattered beneath the victor's feet.

More small animals ran across the road. Birds went by overhead. They'd bred back fast, but there were still a few too many to be chance; she spotted tree swallows flying in swooping curves, grebes, scruffy-looking jays . . . And everything going north to south.

Eilir made a sharp clicking sound with her tongue. Astrid Larsson turned in the saddle. Her pale brows went up as Eilir's hands moved. Then her eyes narrowed, startling blue rimmed and veined with silver.

Can you hear anything unusual that way? Eilir signed. *North?*

Astrid's long, narrow head turned, flicking the rope of braided white-blond hair across her back. *Nope,* she signed. *Too noisy right here. Come on!*

The two young women reined their horses aside, down through the roadside ditch and into the field north of the road. A skull hidden by rampant goldenrod crunched under an iron-shod hoof. Elessar and Undomiel were agile as cats and just as smart, and they could tell something a little unusual was up, their nostrils flaring and ears swiveling radarlike. Eilir kept her eyes busy. Her friend ostentatiously closed hers as she took off her helmet to rest on her saddlebow, frowning in a pose of concentration.

Even under her gathering anxiety that made Eilir smile a little. Astrid was her oath-sworn *anamchara*—soul sister and best friend—and had been since they met when the Bearkillers came west over the Cascades late in the first Change Year. She was her own age to the month—fourteen then, twenty-three in a few days. And they'd put together the Rangers, who even the Bearkiller and Mackenzie elders had conceded were useful over the last year or two. She was just plain totally cool to hang with, too. But there was no denying . . .

Astrid's a bit of a flaming goof at times. "Self-dramatizing" was the way her mother put it. *Like that vest.*

It was good, supple, black leather, sleeveless and thigh-length, and lined with tough nylon, with a layer of fine chain mail between; so far, so practical, if she didn't want to wear the whole elaborate panoply of an A-list Bearkiller on a ride through—mostly—safe country, and the color went well with her dark brown pants and boots. But what she'd put on it wasn't the stylized, snarling bear's head of Mike's outfit or the moon-and-antlers of the Mackenzies; it was a white tree topped by a crown and seven white stars.

Not to mention the helmet.

It had a good steel pot underneath, but it was also covered with a raven built up from individual feathers of black-lacquered aluminum, the wings covering the cheekpieces down to her chin, and the eyes were genuine rubies salvaged from a jeweler's shop. Yes, it looked even cooler than the white tree and stars and crown; she was a *stylish* goof even at her worst. And yes, Astrid had chosen the Raven sept when she was adopted into the Clan; Eilir and her mother were Ravens themselves. But Raven wasn't just the sept's totem and tutelary spirit. It was the bird of the Threefold Warrior Goddess Badb-Macha-Neman, the Morrigu Herself. Seriously big mojo, not to be invoked lightly; and the Gods had a tendency to show up in the aspect you called. As within, so without.

Astrid had been the one who insisted on calling their gang the *Dunedain* Rangers, too.

She really *ought to find a boyfriend and get her nose out of the Tolkien. Yeah, it's a* great *story, none better, I love it too, but she needs to relate to the* real world *more. Plus she's still a* virgin, *sweet Lady Arianrhod witness and pity her.*

After a moment Astrid spoke and signed: "Yes. I *do* hear something, I think. Dogs—a lot of 'em."

Feral pack? Eilir asked, following both—she read lips well. Then, since Astrid preferred the term: *Wargs?*

There were a lot of dogs who'd managed to avoid going into the pot in the Dying Time, outliving their masters, or been turned loose before people got really hungry, and by now they'd had several generations of descendants, mingled with coyotes. There weren't any actual wolves this far south and west—yet—but the dog packs still in business were *real* survivor types, big and fierce, and they'd gotten used to eating manflesh in the bad times. That made them a lot more dangerous than real wolves, though more to children or individuals caught alone than an armed group.

"No," Astrid said and signed, her hands moving fluidly above the saddlebow. "No, they sound more . . . *organized* than a warg pack, sort of. And they're not just barking. It's more of a baying sound, like hounds. Like the ones Mike keeps for hunting."

The rest of the Mackenzies had passed on another few hundred yards, long bowshot; heads were turning back to look at them. The two put their horses up to a hand gallop—Arabs had jackrabbit acceleration, too—then jumped them over a section of wire fence still standing, overgrown until it was like a shaggy hedge, landed in a spurt of gravel, and reined in beside Juniper. The Mackenzie chieftain smiled for a second at the casual display of horsemanship; then the smile died as she saw their faces.

She frowned when Eilir explained, and flung up a hand. The loose column came to a halt, riders facing alternate directions, looking hard and listening as they fingered bowstrings. First one and then another waved and called that they'd heard the dogs too.

"Should we push on southeast?" Juniper said thoughtfully, looking down at Rudi's excitement. Then: "No. The university and Mike and Mt. Angel all agreed this is Mackenzie land, even if we're not using it much at the moment."

The extremely theoretical western border of the Clan's territories ran along the river and Highway 99W, I-5, south from Salem to Eugene, and east to the crest of the Cascades—eastern Linn and Lane Counties, and a chunk of southern Marion. Most of it had been too close to the cities, and now it was empty and reverting to wilderness; the Clan's cultivated land and people were in the southeastern part tucked up against the foothills, ending at an outpost in the ruins of Lebanon.

Grimly, the Chief of the Mackenzies went on: "That's someone's hunting pack. Let's see who's on our land without our leave, and what it is they're hunting. I suspect it isn't deer."

We Rangers should scout it out, Eilir signed; Astrid nodded vigorously.

Another hesitation, and then: "Be careful, *mo chroi,* and you too, Astrid dear. Don't be long, and come right back when you've learned something."

I'm always *careful, Mom,* Eilir signed, and the Chief of the Mackenzies winced.

"Rally the Dunedain!" Astrid called. "Lacho calad! Drego morn!"

Four others fell out to join them—three young Mackenzies and Reuben Hutton. Astrid pulled her own bow from its saddle sheath and laid an arrow in the riser's cutout shelf; her weapon was in the Bearkiller style, shorter than the Mackenzie longbow—a recurve horse-archer's model built up of sinew and wood and horn, glossy with the lacquer that waterproofed it. You could carry one of those ready-strung and they were a lot easier to use from the saddle. She let the reins fall on Asfaloth's neck, turning the horse with knees and balance.

"Check your gear," she said. None of the other Rangers was over twenty, and their faces were gravely attentive or excited or both. "Everyone check your *anamchara*'s, too."

Besides her bow, Astrid wore a Bearkiller-style sword—single-edged, as long as her leg, and basket-hilted—and had a round shield about two feet across slung at her saddlebow over the bow case, with the bear's-head sigil on its elk-hide surface. Marcie and Donnal and Kevin were kitted out much as Eilir was. Reuben Hutton was a Bearkiller himself from an A-list family, with the blue mark between his brows and the full panoply on his back, armored from throat to ankle. In a minute or two they were ready.

Astrid led the way; the others spread out behind her in a blunt wedge. The road vanished quickly behind them; field and meadow followed for half a swiftly cautious mile, with nothing more startling than the odd pheasant breaking out of the grass at their feet. Then they splashed through a flooded field with black muck and sparkling droplets flying up from the horses' hooves amid a yeasty smell of vegetable decay, over a deep creek by a small decrepit bridge with water flowing over its sagging middle, and into a ten-acre woodlot. Luckily it was mature timber, the lowest branches mostly higher than a rider's head if you ducked and wove a little; then they were up to the edge of a broader clear stretch, more than long bowshot across—four hundred yards or better.

Eilir let her binoculars drop for a second. *Careful,* she signed. *Let's take a look first.*

The Rangers all knew Sign; like Sindarin it was a requirement for initiation into the Dunedain, and many younger Mackenzies learned it anyway, useful as it was for war and the hunt. They stopped a horse's length inside the wood's edge; that way undergrowth hid you from anyone out in the light, but you could see out from the shadows. First Eilir scanned the tangled growth of the field for fence-posts and gaps—the chest-high growth could hide tangles of barbed wire or abandoned farm equipment, both mortal risks to a horse's legs. Then she did a broader sweep . . .

A sounder of feral pigs headed towards them, making the tall grass and weeds sway against the westerly breeze. Luckily they split around the silent party of riders as soon as they scented them; swine had come back fast because they were clever as well as tough and prolific. Something else came bounding behind them, half glimpsed, also mainly a waving in the tall grass and reeds—

Watch out, Astrid signed. *That may be the boar.*

It wasn't. Eilir had only time enough to recognize the rushing black-striped golden deadliness before it was past, vanishing in the wood's depths. Bows were half drawn, and Reuben managed to get his ten-foot lance leveled with a strangled yell. Horses crow-hopped in belated panic . . .

Before the Change, private American enthusiasts had owned more than half the tigers in all the world. *After* the Change a lot of the obsessed owners—and you had to be an obsessive in the first place to keep a cat that weighed three hundred pounds and up—freed the beloved pets they couldn't feed. It turned out that tigers were opportunists when feeding themselves—which in plain English meant they turned man-eater with ease and joy, almost unnoticed at first amid the Great Dying. The Willamette's burgeoning mix of swamp and prairie and forest was ideal country for tiger, too. Without firearms they were a standing menace to flocks, herds, isolated farms and anyone who traveled alone.

Worse every year, too, Eilir thought disgustedly. *They breed like . . . well, like cats.*

"If those guys with the hound pack are after Sher Khan there, more power to them," Reuben said. There was disgust in *his* expression too as he swung his lance back upright and checked his bow case. "Those things are fucking *dangerous.*"

Quiet! Sign only, and wait, Astrid signed. *One tiger wouldn't have caused all the disturbance Eilir saw.*

They didn't have to wait long. Eilir stiffened as she scanned the opposite woodline.

People coming, she signed, then made a broader pulling gesture that meant "bows ready" in their own code.

The two Bearkillers stayed in the saddle, but edged their mounts a little farther back into the shade; they were equipped to shoot from the saddle, of course. The others slipped down and dropped their knotted reins—another requirement for the Rangers was the ability to train a horse to stand stock-still without being tethered. Eilir reached over her shoulder for an arrow and stepped behind a tree, checking to see that everyone else had too. Their gear was all green and brown save for their kilts and plaids, and the Mackenzie tartan was the same colors with dark blue and a very little orange added; it made excellent camouflage.

Eilir bared her teeth as the newcomers darted out into the sunlight, running and stumbling and looking over their shoulders. There were four adults—two couples. Both women were carrying infants, and the men had older children piggyback; a teenaged girl ran with a burlap sack clutched to her chest. The youngsters limited their speed severely, and so did their staggering exhaustion, sweat runneling down the dust and dirt on their faces despite the cool fair day, chests heaving. The children were crying, but their mouths kept shut. They and the adults were ragged, their patched, pre-Change clothing torn anew by the brush they'd forced their way through, bleeding scratches adding to old scars.

All four of the adults had steel collars riveted around their scrawny necks, hastily wrapped in bits of cloth with rough raw spots and calluses beneath. Both couples looked enough alike to be peas in a pod, save that one pair and their children looked Anglo-fair and the other mixed, the man Hispanic of a darker kind, Guatemalan or Mexican.

Eilir's eyes met Astrid's.

Well, this is the sort of thing we made that oath about, she signed.

"Yup. 'Protect the helpless' and I've never seen a clearer case," Astrid replied.

Her dreamy eyes looked thoroughly alert now. "OK, I can hear the hunting horn too and it's not a Bearkiller or Mackenzie one. Those people are out of the Protectorate, or I'm an orc. So are the ones chasing them—who *are* orcs."

Eilir turned to Marcie. *Get back to the Mackenzie and tell her we've got trouble. No estimate on their numbers, but we're going to have to cover these people one way or another.*

The younger girl nodded, sprang into the saddle and flicked her mount into motion, galloping with her head bent low over its neck.

The refugees looked up; they'd probably heard the sound of the hooves that Eilir could feel as a fading vibration under the leaves and fir needles of the forest floor. They cried out in mindless despair and halted as Astrid rode out into the sunlight. The three clansfolk walked beside her horse, Eilir on her right, Donnal and Kevin on her left.

"Look, it's OK!" Astrid called; she gestured broadly, calling them forward. "This is Clan Mackenzie land—keep going south, we Dunedain will hold them off!"

The teenager looked more alert than the others. At the clear female voice she darted forward again, breasting the tall grass and weeds with difficulty. The others followed like water through a broken dam; Eilir could smell them when they came closer, a rank feral odor. The children were barefoot, the older girl wore some sort of light shoe and the others had only sneakers—cracked and worn and held together with thongs and rawhide patches—or bundled rags. The darker man had a woodchopping ax in his right hand; he kept it ready as he sidled around them, and his companion likewise gripped a hoe with the head bent forward and sharpened to make a crude spear. The children watched the armed and armored strangers with huge frightened eyes.

Trying to question them would be useless—even if they knew how many were on their tracks, they'd been beaten into mindlessness by fear and exhaustion. It would take hours to get anything coherent. Eilir fought down another surge of anger; one of the children was the same age as her brother Rudi, and they were being hunted with dogs. They cowered at the sight of a sword or bow.

She needed control now. *Breathe in.* Suck it down into the diaphragm, then let it slowly out to carry away rage and fear and worry. *Breathe out. Ground and center, ground and center.* The metallic taste in her mouth lessened, and the fluttering under her diaphragm. The buckskin that covered the grip of her longbow drank sweat and stayed steady under her palm.

"Go! Run!" Astrid snapped, and the refugees did, faster than they had, a little hope lending strength to their legs.

"Here come the dogs," she went on, with a tightening of her lips.

The animals were almost as invisible as the pigs had been, and more so than the tiger; just a massive waving in the grass, a glimpse of whiplike tails lashing in the pleasure of the hunt, and tan-and-white patched hides. Occasionally a floppy-eared head came up . . .

But not all were hounds. Five were huge mastiffs, shaggy gray-furred creatures heavy as men, with long legs and great square heads like barrels—barrels that split open to show wet, yellow teeth like knives. Mastiffs were sight hunters, and these had been trained to follow human prey—to follow and to kill. Now they charged, like hairy orcas rising out of the chest-high sea of grass at every bound.

"*Shoot!*" Astrid snarled.

She loosed first, having a better vantage point from the saddle. A mastiff's leap turned from a thing of grace to a broken cartwheel, and the young woman reached back over her shoulder for another shaft.

But the dogs were fast. Eilir waited until hers was close, then drew as Sam Aylward had taught her—throwing the left arm forward and matching it with a twist of gut and torso that put all the muscle of her body into the effort as well. She needed that; the stave had been made with Sam's own hands, a birthday present a year ago. It was tillered for her full growth—a war bow and not a hunting tool—with a draw just under eighty pounds. She'd punched shafts through chain mail with it on the practice field.

A smooth breath out as she drew, until the triangular broadhead she'd filed from a stainless-steel spoon touched the riser's arrow shelf, and the kiss ring on the string brushed her upper lip at *precisely* the right spot.

Hold the draw, until the unseen line met the next leap . . .

The bow surged a bit as the string snapped against her bracer, but Aylward's bows had little hand shock. The arrow was a flash, a blurred sweet streak that *had* to meet the white triangle at the base of the mastiff's throat fifty yards away . . .

Got him! she thought with cold glee, as the big animal somersaulted backward and disappeared. *You're not going to tear open any more kids, you son of a bitch.*

She was already wheeling and setting another shaft. Kevin had brought his beast down too, a clean hit slantwise from the left shoulder and out at the right hindquarter, the arrow speeding off into the grass after razoring a path through heart and lungs and guts. The mastiff twitched and fell, an almost comical look of surprise in its eyes. Donnal had taken the fourth but didn't have time for another shot. Instead he went diving forward under the fifth big mastiff's leap, as it spread its paws to knock him down and open his throat to the killing grip. It landed ten feet behind him and had barely started to spin in place when three more arrows struck it—Reuben's first, through the neck, Astrid's into the body behind the shoulder and Eilir's smashing home in the spine above its hind legs. That dropped the animal limp as a sack of flour.

Eilir blinked, suddenly conscious of the sweat running down from the foam-rubber padding of her helmet and into her eyes, and the dryness of her mouth.

"Here they come," Astrid said. "I can see riders, and hear them—there goes that stupid trumpet again."

Down! Eilir signed.

"Good idea," Astrid replied. "Look, everyone, we've got to give those people all the time possible—and hope the Mackenzie gets here quick, too. I'm going to try talking. Reuben, you *stay* back there unless I call you. You may have to cover our retreat."

The three Mackenzies dropped to one knee. That put their heads well below the feral growth in the open field; it also nerve-rackingly cut off Eilir's vision of what was happening. Astrid let her right hand fall down by her side, and signed in an abbreviated warrior version of the visual language that they'd worked out for situations like this.

Three riders. Servants make dogs quiet . . . More. Boss-man. Two men-at-arms. Four mounted crossbowmen.

Uh-oh, Eilir thought. *Two-to-one is long odds if it comes to a fight!* Then, brief and heartfelt along with the Invoking gesture: *Dread Lord, Master of the shining blade; Dark Lady, raven-winged and strong, Chooser of the Slain, be with Your people now. Grant us luck and victory. So mote it be!*

Astrid waited, her face calm under the raven-crested helm. Eilir could see her cock her head slightly, listening, then stand in the stirrups to shout back:

"Only the two of you, if you want to parlay! You're on Mackenzie land!"

Her hand went on: *They come. Bossman, one man-at-arms. Wait . . .*

The old field was four hundred yards wide; it would be a while before riders could see the crouching archers. Eilir used the opportunity to switch off the broadhead shaft for one with an armor-piercing bodkin point, an arrowhead made like a miniature metalworker's punch. Those had a pip on the nock, so you could tell the type by feel.

Up.

They rose smoothly, shafts nocked and fingers on the strings, but with the arrowheads pointed down. That didn't matter much, except as a symbol—they could all draw, aim and shoot in under three seconds.

Eilir noted that the two riders only checked for an instant, not long enough to make their horses do anything but miss a half stride; her eyes went first to the tiny figures of the crossbowmen. None of them had snuck off to work his way around the flank, and none had dismounted so that they could use their weapons better. Possibly they were being honest; more probably, they hadn't been told what to do if the situation altered, and weren't going to chance acting on their own. That was the Protectorate for you.

The two riding forward . . .

One was *huge.* Not far short of seven feet and broad enough to look squat, the bulk heightened by a long hauberk of stainless-steel washers riveted onto leather backing, with steel-splint protection on his forearms and shins and metal-backed gloves. His helmet was bullet-shaped, only a T-slit in front to show glimpses of crude thick features, and it had a tall plume of black-dyed ostrich feathers waving from its point. A greatsword was slung over his back, the genuine article with a two-foot hilt, a big ball pommel and a four-foot blade as broad as Eilir's palm; a war hammer was thonged to his right wrist and rested across his saddlehorn, a forged steel shaft a yard long with a serrated head. His horse was in proportion, a German warmblood that must weigh in near a ton, eighteen hands high if it was an inch but long-legged and probably fairly agile, of a type used for dressage before the Change. It was an entire stallion with a savage barbed bit in its mouth.

Uh-oh, she thought. *I think I remember him. In jeans and a T-shirt, that time. The night the Change happened, when we were in Corvallis and the 747 crashed. Which means the little guy has to be . . .*

The bossman was different, a slender man of average height in civilian garb: a jacket of embroidered yellow silk, black trousers and boots and a broad-brimmed hat with a curling feather at the side. He had the Protector's sigil on his shoulder—a red cat-pupiled eye on a black background—and another device over his chest, in a circle like a Japanese *mon,* but the symbol was a Chinese ideograph. The sword at his side was a Chinese type as well, a curved *dao,* heavier towards the tip of the broad blade. He halted his mount—an excellent quarter-horse gelding—and leaned his hands on the horn of his saddle. His features were thin, and might have been handsome except for the crooked teeth that his slight smile showed. There was a scattering of acne scars across his nose and high cheekbones, and his slanted eyes were an incongruous blue as bright as Astrid's.

Yup, that's Eddie Liu. Gangbanger, thief, murderer, rapist and general scumbag, she thought. *What a pity we can't just kill him now, except that it'd start the war early and Mom wouldn't like that* at all.

He'd come up in the world, since that evening in Corvallis. Now everyone knew him as *Marchwarden* Liu, overseer of all the Protectorate's southern flank, and Baron

Gervais—lord of that town and the surrounding countryside. The Protector's hatchetman on this border, and a close confidant, which said all you had to know. A rat to Protector Arminger's hyena; and it was a little surprising he was here himself—unless he just thought chasing people with killer dogs was great sport, something entirely possible.

"Parlay," he said.

He raised an empty hand and then waved over his shoulder. The crossbowmen raised their weapons, showing them unspanned, and slung them over their shoulders on the carrying straps. Scowling, Astrid made a gesture and dropped her shaft back into the quiver. Eilir and the other Mackenzies did too; that added a full second to their response time, but you had to abide by the formalities.

"There, now we can talk like civilized people. Hey, it's Astrid 'the Elf' Larsson, ain't it?" he said genially, with a nasal, east coast, big-city accent. "Or is it a hobbit these days?"

"Numenorean, actually . . . this week," Astrid answered calmly.

You go, girl! Eilir thought.

Astrid continued: "Could I ask you what you're doing on Mackenzie land, Baron Liu?"

"My charter from the Portland Protective Association says this is part of the Southmark," he said. "Part of the Barony of Gervais, at that. So I can do what I damn well like on it."

"We say differently."

"Yeah, I sorta thought so," Liu said. "We can talk about exactly where the border is later. Maybe with your brother-in-law, or the dummy's old lady. Right now I'm looking for some people who owe me. They skipped out on the vig. Bad for business."

"You're not going to find them," Astrid said. "I suggest you turn around and ride away. We Bearkillers have sort of severe penalties for enslavement and the Mackenzies are even more hung up about it."

"Hey, who's talking that slavery shit? They can split as soon as they work off the debt to me—or whoever I sell the debt to, sort of like a mortgage, right? Society would fall apart if people didn't pay their debts."

Astrid spat into the long grass.

Liu chuckled. "Hey, what's with the attitude? Here I am, doing my—as the Lord Protector says—'civic duty,' peaceable as anything, and you come on my land, hang with escaping criminals, steal my property, and then you go and kill my *dogs.* I *liked* those dogs."

"And I bet Mago there raised that snake from an egg," Astrid said dryly.

Eilir gave a silent chuckle; she'd watched that tape with her mother before the Change. To her surprise, Liu smiled in recognition as well; it was a disconcerting, and very unwelcome, momentary link. She flushed, and let her fingers move, suggesting in Sign what the baron could go do with his pet troll or vice versa.

Another surprise. Liu raised an eyebrow and chuckled, obviously understanding what she'd signed.

"Nah," he said. "Mack and I are just good friends." Eilir scowled, conscious of having lost points. "I've heard about you and blondie here. You found the Ring of Power in her Crack of Doom yet, or are you still having fun looking?"

The giant's shoulders shook; he boomed out a laugh as Astrid bridled and Eilir scowled harder. Liu went on: "We met before, didn't we? Back around the Change, you and your momma."

Yes, Eilir thought. *You were robbing a jewelry store and attacking a cop under cover of the big fire where the 747 crashed.*

She signed: *We beat you and your friends up and chased you all off, as I recall. I always wondered how a nice town like Corvallis had festering boils like you and Big and Stupid there on its butt.*

"We were just passing through, sort of doing some business with a few of the students there. I do remember Chico, though. He was a friend of mine."

Eilir winced—inwardly, this time—at the memory of her mother standing incredulous in the flame-shot darkness, the hickory ax handle in her hand and the dead ganger at her feet.

Liu's mocking eyes slid back to Astrid. He looked her up and down and his gaze settled on her helmet. "Did you notice you've got your head up a crow's ass?"

"Better that than up my own, like you, Baron Liu," Astrid said sweetly, and the Protectorate noble's composure showed a crack or two, letting the banked hatred and bloodlust show just a little.

"Yeah, it's been fun chatting, but I've got a debt to collect, so take your girlie-toy soldiers in their miniskirts and get the fuck *out of my way*. Please. Wouldn't want some of you cuties to get hurt."

Eilir looked at the crossbowmen again; *they* couldn't get into any fight in time. Her gaze went back to the hulking armored figure sitting his horse in stolid silence. Mack—he'd been named for the truck before the Change, she heard—was another matter. He was only fifteen feet away, and if he managed to get among them at arm's length before they shot him down it would be like trying to fight a tiger with your fists. He wasn't just three-hundred-odd pounds of armored muscle; unless rumor lied he was fast with it, and skilled. Liu used him like an elephant-sized Doberman on a choke chain, ready to be loosed at any target, as well as personal insurance. That hauberk was a problem as well, the washers were nearly a quarter inch thick and as likely as not to shed even a bodkin point. Getting a shaft through the T-slit of the barbut helm was . . .

You'd have to be dead lucky, as Sam would say. And how I wish he was here!

The giant moved in anticipation, his armored fingers clenching on the grip of the war hammer. Liu smiled a nasty smile. *He* wasn't wearing armor, unless there was light mail in the lining of his jacket, but Eilir had learned even before the Change that, myth to the contrary, bullies were *not* necessarily cowards. Arminger's protégés most certainly weren't; he tested them thoroughly first. The tales of those testings were gruesome. Of course, they also tended to have a lively sense of self-interest . . .

"That isn't a parlay, Liu. That's a threat." Astrid smiled again. "Check," she said, and pursed her lips in a way that told Eilir she was whistling.

Hooves thudded on the soft ground of the woodlot, like muffled taps on the soles of her feet. In the instant that Liu and his bodyguard were distracted by Reuben's exit from the woods all four of the other Rangers whipped their hands to their quivers and set arrows to string. The distant crossbowmen had orders for *that;* she could hear their shouts as they spanned their weapons, dropping the hooks over the strings and winding the cranks.

Reuben changed the odds considerably; he wasn't nearly a match for Mack, but he *was* a big young man, a trained A-list fighter of the Bearkiller outfit, fully armored and with a ten-foot lance in his fist. And while Mack's washers might turn *one* hastily aimed shaft, four wasn't nearly as good a bet.

Uh-oh, Eilir thought. *Liu isn't looking as defeated as he should. And it isn't just his crossbowmen coming up—*

"Check and mate," he said.

His eyes went to the woods behind them and then went wide—nearly bulged—in surprise. Whatever he'd expected there, it wasn't what he saw. Eilir took a step back and to the side, so she could keep her aim clear and dart a glance behind. There were a *lot* of figures moving there, all of them in kilts. One carried a bundle of Protectorate-model crossbows, raising them mutely into view and then dropping them. Another prodded four men forward; they were stripped to their ragged underwear, and all were wounded; one was on an improvised travois of poles and had a seeping bandage across his belly. The Mackenzies waited with their bows up, a shaft to the cord and ready to draw, except for Juniper Mackenzie.

She came mounted, the crescent moon on the brow of her helmet, and a white compressed look about her mouth that her daughter recognized—the look she had when duty drove her to something distasteful.

Such as ambushing ambushers in the woods, Eilir thought, and fought down a silent giggle of relief. Out of the corner of her eye she saw Astrid blow out her cheeks for a moment in a gesture that made her look younger and less stern-warrior-elvish.

Liu's narrow blue eyes swept back and forth, obviously

calculating odds, which weren't good. Four archers were a serious risk. Twenty-four longbows shooting every five seconds weren't just a risk; they were an arrowstorm in the making. Sam Aylward stepped up beside Juniper's stirrup, his war bow in his hands and his face mild and calm.

"Baron Liu," he said courteously, inclining his head slightly. "My lord, I hear your man there is very strong. Is he strong enough to live with a dozen arrows through his chest, do you think?"

He politely didn't mention what the same shafts would do to the man in the cloth coat. Juniper rode out, stopping to Eilir's right—careful not to mask her shot. Behind Liu the other man-at-arms and the crossbowmen were coming up, close enough to see faces. They'd been busy, loading short heavy bolts into the arrow grooves when they'd bent the thick spring-steel bows back and hung the spanning cranks at their waists. Now they slowed and faltered, as they saw who awaited them.

"Go," Juniper said. "Take your men, leave our land, and go."

Her eyes were fixed on Liu, and Eilir gulped slightly at the look in them. The Lord and Lady had ten thousand thousand aspects, and meeting some of them was . . . stressful. Liu felt it too, but he snarled with the courage of a cornered rat, and Mack raised his iron club. It was the crossbowmen behind who looked most rattled; some of them were clutching crucifixes or muttering prayers as they realized who it was they faced.

Juniper Mackenzie.

The Witch Queen.

"Go," Juniper said, and stood slightly in the stirrups, her eyes unmoving, hands raised upright and palms out, arms making a V, face pale as milk.

"*Go,* or I will call on the Dread Lord, and curse you in the name of the Devouring Shadow. You and all with you. And that curse will follow you to all the ends of Earth, run you never so fast. So mote it be!"

Uh-oh, Eilir thought. *Mom's in Maximum-spooky mode. She really means it.* Juniper Mackenzie didn't even swear at people, normally; she took the Threefold Law and the perils of ill-wishing far too seriously for that. *On the other hand, there's the self-defense exception . . . and on the arrows-and-swords level, the fact that we now outnumber them four to one won't hurt . . .*

Liu backed his horse, wrenching at the bit with a savagery that made the beast squeal, stabbing a glance at his men to judge their mettle as the prisoners stumbled forward. Several of the mounted crossbowmen were zealously helping their friends to mount behind them or hitching the poles of the travois to a saddle, thus making it impossible to fight.

"I'll get you for this, bitch," he spat.

Eilir grounded her bow and leaned it against her shoulder; the motion caught Liu's attention, and her hands moved: *You keep* saying *you'll make us pay,* she signed, grinning. *But you never* do *it.*

CHAPTER FIVE

"Why is it called *adventure*," the elder Loring asked. "Instead of—"

"Discomfort? Fear? Unending toil?" his son called back over his shoulder.

"Being stuck in the middle of a complete balls-up?" John Hordle grunted in agreement and took a hand off his paddle long enough to swat a mosquito. "I'd rather be sitting in a good pub with a girl, sir," he said. "Say that Gudrun from Bob's place. *Talking* about me adventures."

The three men paddled in silence for a moment; the three canoes were traveling roughly abreast, usually close enough for easy conversation as the winding banks of the Great Ouse passed by slowly on either side—except that those banks were far less firm and definite than they had been a decade earlier. Most of a millenium of banking and diking and drainage had been undone in eight years, as the waters broke the bonds men laid on them and sought their own level.

Then Hordle chuckled. "What a bunch of bloody liars we are," he said. "If we wanted it all that much, we'd be *in* the bloody pub right now. Nice enough now and then, but right boring if you do too much of it."

"Speak for yourself, Sergeant," Nigel Loring said. "I'm at the memoir-writing phase of life's progress. Good God, man, I *was* writing my memoirs just last month. Maude said—"

He halted abruptly, but there had been a hint of returning life under the mock severity of his tone.

Glad to hear that, Hordle thought. *I can understand it and all, but I don't half like the way he's acted so . . .* not quite there *when nobody's trying to kill us.* A smile: *Of course, someone's been trying to kill us far too bloody often just lately.*

"You and Alleyne are still young enough to be accumulating interesting incidents," Nigel went on, visibly pushing memories away.

"Interesting like this bloody swamp, sir?" Hordle asked. "Reminds me of some book my mum read me when I was small—well, when I was young—what was it called? *Swans and Amazons?*"

"That'd be 'the Coot Club' in *Swallows and Amazons,* Sergeant," Sir Nigel said.

"About a bunch of kiddies mucking about in boats around here, any rate," Hordle said. "Certainly has changed a bit, eh?"

They all smiled. Even in the dry months of late summer, the stream's course was often not where twentieth-century convenience had put it, and the land on either side showed the glint of shallow open water and patches of green reed bed—patches that had grown larger as they passed ruined Bedford and came closer to the Wash. The standing water and warm weather also bred mosquitoes in stinging swarms, not to mention gnats, and a pervading smell of rotting vegetation filled the hazy air.

"I blame you, Father," Alleyne Loring said. "Watch out, there's a dead tree trunk just under the surface ahead."

They all slowed and carefully swerved to the right; the tree was a large oak that had tumbled downstream in one of the floods that had ripped uncontrolled through the Ouse basin in the years since the Change, and planted itself with the root-ball upstream. That held a dozen sharpened spikes waiting just below the surface.

"You blame it on my bad example, eh?" Nigel said.

"No, it was all those copies of the *Boy's Own Paper* you

kept in the attic for me to discover when I was eight," Alleyne said. "Not to mention the stack of Henty, and the Haggard and Kipling. Other boys of my generation learned to be sensitive and socially conscious, and I was marching to Kabul with Roberts or finding the caves of Kôr and She-Who-Must-Be-Obeyed."

If you'd met my grandmother, you wouldn't have needed Haggard for the latter, Nigel muttered, but under his breath.

"That's right, sir, and he loaned the books to me too," Hordle said. "Fair turned our heads, they did. I'd have been a Labor MP, else."

"Oh, rubbish," Nigel replied. "It's your own dam' fault, my boy; I inherited all that from *my* father. *I* didn't make you take up all those books with the wizards and elves, at least—you came to that entirely on your own."

"Oh, I'd say *those* were rather useful. Certainly the hobbies they encouraged were."

It would be a bit intimidating having Sir Nigel as your dad, Hordle thought, not for the first time. *Maybe that's why young Mr. Loring would hang out with those reenactor burkes.*

He'd gone along with that himself, rather than being very enthusiastic. At least until he'd learned the events were good places to pursue his *real* hobby.

Some of the girls looked good in those low-cut blouse things, even if the boys were a right bunch of pillocks, and the beer was better than passable. Even the mucking about with swords was good for a laugh, before it turned serious after the Change.

He dug his paddle in to turn his canoe aside from a sunken cabin cruiser whose crumbling prow reared above the slow-moving brown water, trailing long streams of algae.

Thank God my dad just owned a pub. Talk about pop-u-larity!

"At least it's an open swamp around here," he said aloud. "Less stressful-like, when you can see what's coming."

Dead trees stood in the fields about, their roots killed

out by winter's spreading water, and the floods had kept brambles at bay as well; the more so as this had been corn-growing land, much of it in great hedgeless fields. Most of the lowland was tall open grass; taller brush and trees survived and thrived rankly on bits of higher ground—ground that often showed the snags of ancient buildings, built in an earlier era where experience showed floodwaters were less likely to reach. Birds swarmed overhead and on the water—mallards the most numerous, but also tall gray herons and snowy swans, grebe and the Canada geese that seemed to flourish like bindweed everywhere on the island. Their gobbling and honking was occasionally loud enough to drown the sound of the water and wind; overhead a hawk floated with the noon sun on its wings, feathered fingers grasping the air. Native otter and alien mink slid down the banks with a plop and flash of sleek fur as the canoes ghosted by.

There weren't any of the feral cattle and Père David's deer in sight that they'd noticed off and on the past few days, but *something* was cropping great stretches of the tall grass.

"Watch out!" Alleyne Loring called again, but there was excitement in his voice this time.

A snorting sound followed, like a great bellows being pumped—or pumped slightly underwater, because there were splashes with it.

"Ahead, to the right, about two hundred yards," the younger Loring said.

Hordle gaped, then shut his mouth with a snap and a deliberate effort of will. Ahead was a section of bank still standing, the left a cluster of buildings and the right now a curving island in the midst of marsh. In the deeper water just below the middle of the curve structures topped by gray knobs and pits floated, like some uncouth driftwood sculpture; for a long moment his mind rejected the sight, despite having seen it before.

Seen it in Kenya, he thought, feeling his inner voice gibber slightly. *But ... hippo in Cambridgeshire!*

"I'm surprised they can endure the winters," Nigel Loring said, curiosity in his voice.

"Anything that lives in the water most of the time must have good insulation," Alleyne pointed out; as you drew closer you could see the massive tubby bodies below the surface. "I don't know how well they'll do in the long term, but these seem to be flourishing as of now. We'd best be careful—that female has a couple of . . . what do you call them? Calves? Cubs?"

"Call them bloody dangerous, sir," Hordle said fervently.

He'd visited Kenya before the Change at the Crown's expense—the British army had long-standing arrangements there to secure open space for training unavailable in the then-crowded homeland. He'd mixed enough with the locals to learn that the comical-looking animals were in fact as belligerent as wild boar, and when you scaled one of *those* up to five tons and gave it four giant teeth like ivory pickaxes a foot long . . . the fact that it ate grass by choice and would spit you out after it bit you in half was no consolation at all.

Just then another sound rolled across the open ground to their left, one he recognized from the same memories as the hippo. A hoarse grunting moan, *oouuughh . . . oouuugh . . .* , building up to a shattering roar.

"Lion. *Just* what the country bloody needs," Hordle said disgustedly. "Not to mention all the lovely sweet wolves and cuddly little bears noshing on our ruddy cows."

"God damn all safari parks," Sir Nigel said crisply. "And double damnation to their curators for living long enough to set all the beasts loose."

"They make good hunting," Alleyne said judiciously. "On the whole, I can't disagree, though."

Hordle nodded. *That's the Lorings for you,* he thought. *None of this* "Let's hunt it, and damn the farmers" *for them.*

"Watch out below," he added. "They can walk on the bottom and come up right beneath you, hippo can."

Now that people were thin on the ground again and most worked the land for their livelihood, nearly everyone had adopted the farmer's fiercely protective attitude towards his crops and stock. Not to mention that the carnivores had all turned man-eater during the first Change

year when the wandering masses of starving refugees were
the main food supply available, and many hadn't lost the
habit yet. A big animal with teeth and claws was no joke,
when all you had was a spear or a knife.

Hordle drove his paddle into the water, angling over
northward, towards the left bank of the river. One of the
hippos raised its head and forequarters out of the water as
they came closer, opening its barrel-shaped head in a raw
bellow of warning, the four giant yellow teeth framing the
huge red gullet. The others rotated their heads like sub-
marines swiveling a periscope, their twitching ears showing
the focus of their attention. Hordle grinned and ducked
down to get a better look at the infants—at that stage, even
a hippo could be cute.

Fwwwwtp.

The arrow went through the space he'd occupied an instant earlier. Reflex kept him crouched as he dug the
paddle into the muddy water of the Ouse with all his
strength. The tough wood bent and the canoe surged forward as the skin crawled up his spine and his gut twisted.
Being shot at by people he couldn't see was among the
many familiar experiences he had no desire to repeat.

Fwwwtp. Fwwwtp. Fwwwwtp.

"Shit!"

The last hiss of cloven air ended in a *ptank!* as an arrow
arched down and slammed down into the bottom of the
canoe not far from his right foot, standing in the thin aluminum. Water began to rill in around the edges, and along
the slit the broad triangular arrowhead had cut. Hordle
dug harder at the water, switching the paddle back and
forth from right hand to left to keep the canoe on a steady
path, and looked behind him. A boat had come out from
around the stretch of island bank, a crude flat-bottomed
thing of planks and plywood and plastic sheeting. It was
large enough for a dozen men—just—half of them poling
it along with long wooden rods, and the rest with bows,
shooting as fast as they could draw.

*Maybe they'll ram a hippo ... no such sodding luck, John-
nie. Not quite that stupid.*

Luckily between the crowding and the uncertain foot-

ing, they couldn't shoot very well—the range was respectable, over a hundred yards. Another flight rose from
the punt as he watched, twinkling in the sun, then fell all
around the three canoes. The hissing of the shafts ended in
a series of sharp, wet, slapping sounds, like hailstones in a
pond. He thought about reaching for his own bow; he'd
have to draw awkwardly, underarm, and the canoe's rocking would throw his aim off. Still . . .

"I can plink a few, sir!" he called.

"Not here!" Nigel Loring snapped. "We'll draw them to
the buildings. You flank them on the right. Go!"

Nigel Loring drove his paddle into the water, gasping
slightly with the effort, feeling the burning strain in his
back and shoulders, the thudding of his heart at the literally life-and-death effort, the hissing *wheep* of passing arrows. The teeth beneath his graying blond mustache were
bared in a snarl of effort; you might not think you cared
much what happened to you anymore, but the body had its
own logic and its own priorities.

Behind him Alleyne paddled with smooth, quick competence, his face set with strain, and the building grew ahead
of them—an old brick lockhouse, the roof collapsed but
the walls still standing, with scorch marks above the empty
windows. There had been other buildings round about, but
none of them were more than brushy mounds; there had
also been a couple of big trees near the lockhouse, but the
fire that brought down the roof had killed them all, except
for a few branches on the far side of one oak. The wooden
doors of the mitre-built locks were slightly open, and water
poured through them in a sluggish current, pooling below
where the lower ones were still mostly shut, though sagging.

Curse it, Nigel thought, as another flight of arrows came
up—and fell short; the canoes were faster than the punt.
They picked their spot well.

The canoes might be faster, but not so much faster that
they wouldn't be caught if they stopped to heave them past
this lock. Then the pursuers would catch up and riddle
them with arrows at point-blank range. They couldn't turn

about, either, with the savages behind them, and it wouldn't do much good to try to don their armor—the enemy could ring them in ...

... and in any case, wading around in this liquid muck with sixty pounds of steel on your back ...

Past here they would be into the fens proper, first a narrow cone of them and then opening out into nearly a thousand square miles of reed and pool and mere. It had been farmland before the Change, some of the richest in the world—but kept that way only by pumps and drainage, a good deal of it below sea level because of the shrinkage of the peat soil.

The prows of the canoes slid into the soft mud of the bank. Alleyne and Nigel each leapt out of his craft, gave a swift wrench to slide it higher so that it wouldn't float away when relieved of their weight, then snatched up their personal weapons and extra bundles of arrows and ran for the lockhouse. The mud sucked at their feet, slowing Nigel's more than his son's, which were young and on the end of longer legs. Arrows whickered down behind them, hitting the bundled supplies in the canoes with dull *thud-shunk* sounds, and the thin aluminum of the hulls with unpleasant metallic pops. Alleyne drew ahead. Even then, with his heart pounding and lungs heaving Nigel knew an instant's pride that the younger man didn't slow—instead he did the tactically sensible thing, and sprinted up the last stretch of tall grass and brush to dive headfirst through the window.

A second later he popped up behind it, drawing his bow—from firm footing, protected to the waist, and with room to work. The arrow that he sent whickering past Nigel brought a yell from behind, faint with distance but sharp with pain. Nigel vaulted through another window himself an instant later, stumbling on the broken boards and rubble within as two arrows followed him in and vanished with snapping and cracking sounds in the tumbled wreckage of the interior, and another slapped into the window frame and stood humming with an evil descending note. Then he forced himself erect and wheeled. It was the work of a moment to string his own bow; you had to be careful with that, though, and the mental effort helped him slow his breathing. The interior of the lockhouse smelled of ancient wet ash and mold and rotting wood; he put his feet carefully on the floor, lest a foot go through the boards and trap his leg. He slung the quiver over his back, drew a shaft and shot—the bow wasn't his primary weapon, but he'd practiced a good deal since the Change and some before it.

There were two of the flat-bottomed boats now, but they were both moving backward rapidly to get out of arrow range. One halted, and a white cloth went up on top of a pole, waving back and forth. When no more arrows snapped out from the lockhouse the clumsy craft edged forward a little and halted within speaking distance.

Nigel blinked in surprise, as his breathing slowed. Sweat soaked his uniform in the muggy heat, and he ran a sleeve over his face, then looked cautiously around the edge of the window. Generally the Brushwood Men simply killed anyone from the settled zone—what they called "King's Men"—they came across. The antipathy was entirely mutual, fueled by disgust on one side and frenzied hatred on the other, born of the days when the island refuges had closed their borders to the starving masses of refugees and enforced it with pike and club and museum swords.

"Keep an eye on the other one, and around us," he said, and Alleyne nodded silently. Then the elder Loring went on, shouting out the window: "What do you men want?"

He recognized the pack leader they'd seen in Newport Pagnell, thin-faced and slight and with his nose bristling with rings; someone had cut Archie MacDonald's stolen clothing short in arm and leg but it still hung on him like a tent. He stood and cupped his hands around his mouth, while the rest of the savages in his craft crouched behind crude shields.

"We wants our kids back! Give them to us and we'll let you King's Men go!"

Nigel's eyebrows went up further. *Wouldn't have believed family affections were that strong among the Brushwood Men,* he thought. *After all, these are the people who ate children to survive.*

"This is a bit awkward," Alleyne said as he peered out the west-facing windows to make sure a party weren't sneaking around to take them from that direction. "Yes, our friend Grishnàkh from Milton Mordor Keynes . . . very awkward, seeing that we don't have their children and can't go back for them."

"Let's hope they don't realize that the government probably *would* trade them for us," Nigel said, thinking hard. Then: "It's fairly obvious we're fugitives ourselves. Nothing for it but the truth, or at least part of it." He shouted again: "We don't have them with us. You can see that—there isn't room in these canoes."

"Where the 'ell are they then, you bastards?"

"We sent them into the settled zone for fostering. They're south of Winchester and they'll be split among a dozen farms by the end of the week, where they'll have plenty to eat and wear, and a good education. And be better off than they were with you! Now get out of our way, or you'll get more of what we handed out in Newport Pagnell Church."

The leader of the Netherfield Avengers screamed with rage and snatched a bow from one of his men. The arrow rapped off the stone wall of the building, and the two Lorings shot in return. Nigel's arrow stood quivering in a shield; Alleyne's flicked between two and set up a shouting and thrashing as the flat-bottomed craft was poled back to join its companion.

"You give me back my boy! Give me back my 'arry, or I'll eat your fuckin' liver and lights while you watch it!"

"So much for the repentance of the Netherfield Avengers," Sir Nigel muttered, and shot back; the arrow thunked into the side of the crude barge, and the men with poles frantically redoubled their efforts.

He still felt a little uneasy at the raw grief and rage in the voice of the savage. *That is not a man who intends to give up,* he thought.

Faint and far, Nigel heard the leader shout as his boat halted again out of range: "Take 'em alive. Anyone scrags 'em, I'll scrag him myself!"

"Diplomacy never was my great strength," Nigel said.

"And I'm afraid they're not as stupid as we hoped, eh?" Alleyne replied calmly. "They'll wait for night, then, and come in under cover of darkness. I count twenty of them, all fighting men."

Nigel nodded; they were a blur to him, but Alleyne's eyesight was considerably better than normal. "We could probably eel our way out past them once night falls," he said. "But we'd have to abandon the canoes—which would leave us stranded. Our ship isn't going to wait forever."

"Let's see what Hordle comes up with," Alleyne said, climbing a sloping section of collapsed roof for a vantage point above the level of the windows. "He's quite a resourceful chap."

"Good man," Nigel agreed. "Good as any I've ever served with, poor old Aylward excepted."

"Hunh!"

With a last savage dig of the paddle, Hordle forced the prow of the canoe into the reed-grown mud at the stream's edge. Then he leapt over the side, instantly sinking calf-deep, grabbed the thwarts and wrestled the little craft forward by main strength, over a ridge of dirt and into a shallow water-and-mud patch the consistency of thin porridge. The sucking sounds his feet made as he struggled towards the higher ground of what had once been the stream's bank were like porridge cooking as well.

Blighty doesn't want to let me go, he thought whimsically.

The thick glutinous mass tried to suck the boots off his feet as he waded forward with his sword and bow lying across the crooks of his arms; the sewer smell of marsh was thick around him. Reeds swayed on either side; his head would have been above them if he hadn't bent over, which made his progress slower yet. When the ground grew firmer he went down on his belly and eeled forward, over the low ridge and into what had been the field beyond. The edge of that was a ditch, and water and silt coated the front of his body like thick paint. The whole field was more like swamp than dry land, but not as bad as the river side of the bank. He stopped as the coarse grass waved over his head, ignoring the hum of mosquitoes stabbing into the soft skin behind his ears, and listened as he forced his breath to slow.

Wind in the tall stems. Voices shouting, muffled by several hundred yards' distance and the slight ridge of the former riverbank with its willows and alders. That let his mind paint a picture; the water came in behind the shallow C-shaped section of riverbank, making an embayment behind it where the savages had hidden their boats. The water there must be very shallow, less than a foot deep, but that would be enough for something flat-bottomed and broad.

Have to be ruddy careful with this, he thought, and raised his head for an instant's scan before pulling it down again fast but smooth; jerky motions attracted the eye.

They'd left no sentries on dry land he could see, save for one in the limbs of a tree on the former riverbank who must have been their lookout. The tree was thirty yards away, and he was standing on a bough twenty feet up, hugging the tree trunk with one hand and peering out around it to keep track of the action. Hordle checked his bow, but the string was a precious pre-Change one, absolutely waterproof—not that well-waxed linen took much harm from anything but a thorough soaking. He leopard-crawled a little farther forward, trading distance for angle, then brought his feet carefully beneath him and took a deep breath. He'd have surprise on his side, for thirty seconds or a minute . . .

But twenty-to-one odds is a little steep, even for Little John Hordle.

Stand, feet already planted in the T he'd learned before the Change when it was just a hobby he shared with the heir to Tilford Manor, Sam Aylward instructing them both on visits. Draw . . .

Snap. The first arrow took the sentry in the back of the head, slanted up through the brain and broke through his forehead from the inside; he was using the bodkins designed to punch through steel plate, and the impact was an unpleasant triple crack—bone, bone, tree trunk—less than a second after the shaft left the string.

Snap. Snap. Two more, one in the upper torso and one through the lower back, balancing the noise of the bowstring and the sound of arrows thudding home against the attention that would be drawn when the sentry fell out of the tree. Pinned thrice to the living wood he slumped instead, twisting very slowly. The body would fall, but only when the arrowheads pulled free of the trunk, or the shafts broke, or the body's weight pulled them entirely through.

Go!

He sprang erect and raced for the low ridge, teeth showing in a mask of dark brown mud that coated him to eye level. *Though what I'm supposed to do when I get there ... maybe I can take half a dozen with me ...*

His rush broke through a screen of young willows, the flexible stems beating at him like whips; he held his bow at arm's-length over his head, which put it nine feet up, to keep the string safe. There were the two boats full of savages, not fifty yards away ...

Ah. Yes. Bloody hell, that would be ruddy entertaining, wouldn't it, then?

The hippos were between him and the Netherfield Avengers, their backs out of the water where they'd backed up, but their attention firmly on the dangerous, noisy, annoying humans in boats; pretty soon one of them would get the idea that discretion was the better part of valor and they'd all come out of the water and walk away into the fields behind him.

Unless something hurt one of their precious calves. "I hate to do this to the little kiddie, I really do, Mabel. But it's him or me."

Snap.

The arrow flashed out in a long shallow curve and plunged into the right buttock of the nearest hippo calf with a wet smacking sound, like a soaked towel flicked onto a man's back. The little animal opened its broad mouth and screamed as only a three-hundred-pound baby could do when it called to its mother in distress.

Mother weighed four tons. Taken with her sisters she had about the same mass as a medium tank.

The hippos had been resting quietly, their big rounded feet touching lightly on the mud of the river bottom. The sound of the infant's pain, seconds later the scent and taste of its blood through air and water, sent them bellowing and shaking their heads, roaring out their challenge to the world. The savages probably hadn't much noticed the big beasts, with their mind on human prey. Now the shallow-draft boats rocked as they looked around, eyes going wide at the sight of the animals lashing the water into silt-choked foam less than half a bowshot away.

They responded as undisciplined men always would: keyed up for a fight and with weapons in their hands, presented with a fresh danger. At least half a dozen of them drew their bows and shot at the massive weight of enraged aquatic mammal.

"That's right, you dim Herbert, let Mum know who hurt her darling little babykins," Hordle chortled.

The hippos lunged forward, mouths gaping as they headed towards the threat in a torrent of spray and hoarse squealing. The screams of the savages added to the tumult; half of them tried to pole their craft away, while the quicker-witted jumped•overboard and swam for it, and a few simply stood and shrieked out their terror.

Behind him the sentry's body pulled loose from the tree and dropped. Nobody noticed, or saw Hordle's tall troll-broad shape as he spun and ran crouching through the trees and brush to his canoe. A heave and two lunging steps brought him into it, paddle driving him towards the locks. He gave a whoop and waved as two smaller shapes darted out of the lockkeeper's house and launched their own. There was no need for words in the quick, hard, coordinated work of getting the canoes over the locks and into the broadening stream below. Half an hour later only an endlessness of reeds surrounded them, waving well above their heads.

"That was inspired, Hordle," Sir Nigel said as they paused in a broader open stretch, and leaned over to shake his hand.

"Just making use of opportunity, sir," Hordle said, grinning broadly. "The hippo's great fat arse was there, me bow was to hand . . ."

Alleyne chuckled. "Got us out of a very sticky spot," he said. "Speaking of which, I think my canoe is sinking. Those arrows, don't you see."

His father gave it a quick look. "We can patch the other two, but this isn't worth salvaging," he said. "I doubt we've seen the last of our friends from Netherfield, either; they seemed far too full of civic spirit to me. Alleyne, you take the bow position in my canoe. We'll redistribute the loads and discard most of the food—weapons and armor are the first priority."

Hordle gave a mock whimper, but joined in tossing the rations overside. Even working hard, fit men could go several days without eating before they lost much strength, and at a pinch they could forage. When the damaged canoe had been stripped, he took a moment to smash a hatchet through the bottom in several places; there was no sense in giving the Brushwood Men a free gift of it.

Sir Nigel looked ahead, to where the tall gray tower of Ely's cathedral rose above the marshes. "We'll stop there to repair the canoes and take a look about," he said. "I'd like to keep to the levels beyond, but . . ."

"But probably the river's changed course." Alleyne nodded. "The canals are all above general ground level. Pity Hereward the Wake isn't about when you need him."

Fwwwpt.

The paddles flashed as the first arrow went by, throwing drops of spray in arcs to the sky as the two canoes drove desperately northward through King's Lynn. The Lorings were propelling their canoe Canadian voyageur–style, kneeling in the bow and stern; Hordle sat in the rear of his, alternating strokes to either side and making about the same speed by raw power. All three men were gaunt and filthy and haggard, dark circles of exhaustion under their eyes, their uniforms caked with dried mud and stained white with rimes of sweat; fresh patches showed damp under arms and around their necks.

"They're gaining on us!" Hordle said, as the snap of bowstrings came from behind them.

Fwwwpt. Fwwwpt. Fwwwpt. Fwwwpt. Fwwwpt. Fwwwpt.

Nigel bit back a desire to shout: *Well, that's ruddy obvious, isn't it, man?*

The flight of arrows hit the water of the Great Ouse only a few feet behind them, stuttering in like hail. About twenty of the savages were still on their track, but they had switched to another boat some time ago, one they'd had hidden somewhere. It was a pre-Change hull of some sort, cut down and rerigged for oars, and it was *fast.* Six long sweeps worked on either side, which let the Netherfield Avengers' chief steer and six of his band shoot. Which they were doing with dismaying frequency and accuracy; their only problem was range, and the rowers were about to solve that.

Nigel's head whipped back and forth as he looked for a spot they could land and make a stand, even as arms and shoulders and breath worked on automatically. Leftward was only flooded rubble with an occasional snag of wall standing, densely overgrown where it wasn't standing water covered in ten-foot reeds. Eastward the old medieval core of the little city still stood, as was often the case—most of it was on a natural levee, above the usual flood line. He could see the bulk of the old Hanseatic warehouse, and beyond it the barley-sugar columns and waterfront tower of Clifton House, which had been used as a lookout for ships in the old days, and the Purfleet Quay jutting out into the river beyond it. Ships sunken or canted at their moorings hid much of the shoreline, and others stood awash in the stream, their upperworks making obstacles the canoes had to dodge with loss of precious time.

Fwwwpt. Fwwwpt. Fwwwpt. Fwwwpt. Fwwwpt. Fwwwpt.

One of the shafts went into the bag of armor ahead of Nigel, a dull *chunk* sound as it hit a piece of his harness. It would be suitably ironic if one hit him—went through and then stopped against the protection he couldn't wear. The rest fell all about them, plunking into the turgid water of the river and floating away head-down with their draggled flight-feathers bobbing uppermost.

"There!" he called. "Head in for the quay. We'll make a stand in the customshouse tower."

In fact, we'll be shot down like dogs well short of there, but one has to try, he thought, as he bent to the paddling. *What an end for the Lorings! Killed by swamp cannibals not forty miles from Cambridge . . .*

It was Hordle's happy shout that alerted him, so total was the focus of his concentration. Two longboats were pulling out from behind the quay, a towrope lifting from the water as they did. At the end of it was a ship, a three-masted schooner with her poles bare. A banner broke out from the mizzenmast, a blue background with the stars of the Southern Cross on it in silver and a Union Jack in the top corner. The Australian flag, and nowadays that of the Tasmanian Commonwealth.

Her name was the *Pride of St. Helens* after her home port, and he'd last seen her tied up at Southampton when King Charles went aboard as part of the diplomatic formalities.

"We're not there yet!" he called, feeling an absurd impulse to laugh welling up under his breastbone, suppressing it lest it break the rhythm of breath and effort. Then, more quietly to his son: "Just like something out of Haggard, eh?"

"Not . . . if . . . we're . . . killed . . . at . . . the . . . last . . . minute!" Alleyne panted, timing the words to the stroke of his paddle. "That . . . would . . . be . . . entirely . . . too . . . ironic . . . and . . . postmodern . . . for . . . my . . . taste!"

Fwwwpt. Fwwwpt. Fwwwpt. Fwwwpt. Fwwwpt. Fwwwpt.

Something scored across his shoulder, white-hot chill, then pain and a trickle of blood. Alleyne almost looked around at the involuntary hiss of pain.

"Flesh wound," Nigel bit out. "Ignore it."

It hurt like fire, with the salt of his sweat running into it and the coarse cloth of his jacket rubbing the wound with each stroke of the paddle. The edge of the arrowhead had sliced the taut flesh of the shoulder muscle like a razor, and working it hard wasn't doing it any good at all.

"Keep paddling!"

The next volley would have them bracketed. Men were

clustered at the rail of the big schooner ahead of them; then they stood back from around some piece of equipment that crouched there.

TUNNNG!

It was a deep metallic sound, like a huge saw blade being wobbled between the hands of a giant. Something went by overhead, moving in a blurred streak faster than an arrow. His head swiveled involuntarily to follow it. The line of its flight bisected one of the rowers on the savages' boat, and his head went tumbling overboard while his body thrashed and spouted.

TUNNNG-WHACK!

The sound was different this time, and the missile. A globe flew wobbling through the air, trailing smoke from a ring of tarred hemp. It went overhead as their eyes swiveled to track it, and then struck the surface and burst not far from the savages' prow. With a loud *whoosh!* the contents spread out on the water and roared into orange flame, trailing twists of black smoke into the bright summer air.

The improvised galley was a little over a hundred yards from the three fugitives, two hundred from the schooner. Both weapons looked as if they could shoot considerably farther than that, and the savages seemed to realize it. There was a brief squabble, and one of them pushed the chief aside from the tiller; the dead oarsman's body was tumbled overside, and an archer flung himself into the vacant position. One side of oars backed water, the other plunged theirs deep and heaved, and the new steersman threw his weight into the effort as well. The boat turned in its own length and began to flee south, the blades of the oars beating froth from the water.

And the chief stayed on his knees, staring at his escaping enemies, both fists clenched and shaking as he screamed a curse; the voice was thin with distance, but Nigel could hear sobs in it as well.

Beside him, Hordle had turned his canoe and come up precariously on one knee. His great yellow bow bent into a perfect arc as he aimed . . .

"No!" Nigel called.

The archer looked at him incredulously. "Sir, I swear I could put one—"

"No, Sergeant. Let him go." At the wide-eyed question in the other's eyes, he answered, "We took his son."

CHAPTER SIX

"Hakkaa paalle!"

Mike Havel screamed the ancient war cry of his ancestors as he pounced—or the war cry of about half of them, if you subtracted the Norwegians, Swedes and Anishinabe-Ojibwa from the Finns. The backsword blurred in a glittering arc, a running cut that started with the point forward, made a wide looping flourish around the head and slammed down with the advancing foot. It was a very powerful attack, but a bit slow.

Unless you had the strength and reflexes to do it very, very fast . . .

Crack-tinnng!

The surface of his opponent's targe was there, precisely sloped to shed the steel with minimum transfer of force—which didn't mean *no* transfer; the armored figure went back a quick sliding step to avoid being rocked off balance. A weapon just like his licked out in a economical under-arm stab; he beat the blade aside with his own, flicking the parry from the wrist and then a double cut to both sides of the neck. Backswords were about a yard long, single-edged with a basket hilt to guard the hand, suited alike to a swift thrust or a solid smashing cut.

"Hakkaa paalle!" he shouted again, driving his opponent back ten feet in three seconds, the point darting at knee and sword arm and neck.

"Hakkaa paalle!"

That barking shriek meant "Hack them down!" and the Outfit had copied it from him. Four centuries ago the same war cry had rung out behind the banners of Gustav Adolf, the Lion of the North, on battlefields from the Baltic to the Danube, from Russia to France. So had the Church's special prayer: *From the terrible Finns, good Lord deliver us!* Now the Bearkillers had made it as dreaded in post-Change Oregon as it had been when the Suomi swarmed out of their forests to lay half of Europe in ashes.

The two fighters were toe-to-toe, moving in a complex dance of movement too blurring fast for an observer to follow unless they were already expert themselves—a crashing skirling *tingggg* of steel on steel and *thwack* of sword on shield and the occasional duller sound of a blade making contact with armor.

At last he locked the other's sword with his, hilt-to-hilt. For a moment they strove, legs churning like stags; then he got room for a buffeting slam with his shield. The other armored figure went down with a crash, and he slid forward catlike to present the tip of his sword before her face.

"OK, you're still getting better," Pamela Larsson—nee Arnstein—gasped. "I admit it."

"Nowhere to go but up," Havel replied. "You're the one who did this shit *before* the Change, step-mom-in-law."

She shoulder-rolled back to her feet. He was panting too, in a controlled fashion, lungs working like bellows. He'd been drilling hard for hours before he started a round of practice bouts; the Bearkillers usually did, on the assumption that you weren't going to be lily-fresh when the manure hit the winnowing fan. And actually fighting in this Renaissance cut-and-thrust style with fifty pounds of gear on you was brutal physical labor, worse than cracking rocks with a sledgehammer, plus with an opponent at Pam's level you had to go to ten-tenths of capacity every second. The slightest holding back meant defeat.

"Besides which, I'm starting to slow down a bit," Pamela said. "Hell, I'm *forty-one* now, Mike, and it was a *real* struggle getting back into shape after the last baby. I don't think I've got much left to teach you."

Signe Larsson looked over from where she'd been practicing lunges at a leather target hanging from a timber frame, with an apprentice pulling on a rope to make it swing unpredictably. The point went home with a hard *crack* every time, aimed at a spot six inches behind the man-shaped rawhide cutout.

"You still beat me most matches, Pam. Mind you, I've had *three* babies to your pair since the Change," she said. "Granted, the twins were a twofer time-wise, but the principle's the same."

"*You're* twenty-seven," Pamela said. "You recover faster. I'll keep sparring with you—unlike your maniac of a husband, you're not a third again heavier than me and strong enough to bend horseshoes with your hands. Whacking great bruises distract you from the finer points of swordplay. Also childbirth's easier on you because you've got better hips for it than I do."

"You calling me wide-assed, Oh Wicked Stepmother?"

"Compared to my skinny backside and snake hips, you've got the Great Butt of China," Pamela said, grinning as she pulled off her practice helmet. "Or Sweden."

"There's Astrid, though . . ." Signe said, with a sly smile. "*She* doesn't mind sparring with Mike."

"Your younger sister is a goddamned *mutant*," Pam grumbled. "Some rogue virus infected her with nonhuman DNA."

The helm had a mask of thin steel rods across the face, rather than the simple nasal bar of combat gear. The face beneath it was slender like the woman's long whipcord body, olive-skinned, with a beak of a nose and large hazel eyes; sweat plastered a lock of dark brown hair with russet highlights to her forehead.

Mike Havel let one of the apprentices help him out of his armor—he could do it himself, but it was slow and awkward; putting it on was much easier, since gravity helped there. Then he stripped off the sopping gambeson and leaned back on a bench with his back against a rough board wall, a towel around his neck and a mug of cold water in one hand, feeling the heat come off him in the cool damp air like a horse steaming after a hard ride. He'd

built what Pam called the Salle d'Armes in the same style
as a timber-frame barn, to give the maximum open space;
the high roof of the giant building was watertight, but the
plank walls let in a lot of light and weather, and the floor
was packed dirt—this was where the garrison and apprentices did a lot of their advanced-skill training in winter.

Bitchin' cold sometimes, too, he thought with satisfaction, fondling the ears of a hound that came over and laid
her head in his lap.

"Good dog, Louhi," he added, as she slapped the ground
with her tail.

There was very little point in learning to fight unless you
made the training conditions as realistic as possible, and
the enemy—the dirty dog—often refused to meet you at a
convenient time and place. Right now the weather was
good, and so most of the action was in the broad fields
around the building, lit by a high, hazy blue sky; only the
foot-fencing and unarmed-combat classes were inside. On
the bright green grass beyond riders galloped by targets,
loosing arrows from their stiff recurved bows, or using
sword or lance; sometimes at rings suspended on ropes, or
trying to pick wooden pegs out of the ground, or at straw
figures—that served to train the horses out of their fear of
charging home, too. Mock mounted combat was done
under careful supervision, riders hammering at each other
as the mounts circled and snapped; the training was as
much for the horse as the rider.

Not far away a section of newly mustered military apprentices were starting to sweat their way towards the coveted A-list status; stretching, tumbling and running courses
in weighted armor, working out with free weights or practicing stances before some tall mirrors. A dozen more staggered in from the ever-loathed cross-country run in armor
and pack; that included a trip up and down the steep scarp
behind Larsdalen, popularly known as "Satan's Staircase."

Havel grinned nostalgically as he listened to the
distance-muffled scream of the training-cadre instructors:
". . . stop puking, Apprentice Latterby! You can puke on
your *own* time! You make *me* want to puke, the way you'll
bring disgrace on my beloved Outfit! You idle little mag-

gots aren't home on Daddy's manor anymore! Bearkillers can fight on horseback, on foot, or while we fucking *swim*, and we don't get tired. The enemy gets tired and then we *kill* their sorry ass. *Move! Move!*"

It took him back—back to Parris Island, in fact; he'd managed to acquire several other graduates or Camp Pendleton alumni as part of his training staff.

It'll be interesting to see how performance goes when everyone's the product of the apprentice program. They've already lots of motivation; getting on the A-list means climbing into the top drawer. You can throw anything *at these kids and they'll still kill themselves trying.*

There was a damp earthy smell; pine-wood sweating tar, old sweat, horses, leather and metal; the noise was booted feet on dirt, hoof-fall from outside, the clash of metal and wood, grunts of effort—it all reminded him of a very martial health center, the sort they'd improvised in the Iraqi desert back in ninety-one, waiting for the dance to start. By now it had become homey, almost comforting.

A little stir went through the watchers as two men came in. Havel looked up, dipping another mug of water from the plastic barrel fastened to one of the Salle's posts.

"Hi, Ken," he said, nodding to his father-in-law. "Eric," to Signe's brother.

Father and son made their greetings. Eric Larsson straddled a bench, elbows on knees. He was Signe Larsson's twin and as tall as their father, several inches over six feet; broad-shouldered and long-limbed, but rangier in build than his male parent. Much like Havel, in fact, but scaled up—a tiger to the Bearkiller bossman's leopard, and with a similar smooth ease of movement. Scars showed as white lines in his short blond beard, or as seams against the tanned skin of hands and neck. When they'd met just before the Change, the younger Larsson had been a sullen jock teenager—but even then, he hadn't known the meaning of "quit."

I thought *he'd turn out to be a dangerous man,* Havel thought, reading the calm blue eyes. *We could have used him in the Corps. A natural for Force Recon. Well, he's had a lot of pounding on the anvil to test the metal since the*

Change. All that does not kill us, makes us stronger, as Conan said ... that was *Conan, wasn't it?*

"We scouted up north around McMinnville, as per plan," Eric said. "While Will took a troop into the Amity Hills, visiting and distracting any attention headed our way—"

Havel grinned. "Good news there, if you haven't heard. The Brigittine monks have decided to tell Arminger's pet pope in Portland to go to hell, and get square with Abbot Dmowski. Your father-in-law sort of persuaded them."

Proving Will Hutton is twice the diplomat I'll ever be, he added to himself.

"They've got a good little fighting force and some useful farms and craftworkers and they're right between us and the enemy," he went on aloud.

"That *is* good news," Eric said, but his face stayed grim. "The word from McMinnville itself is worse than we thought, though."

"It *is* a new castle? Not just an earthwork fort?"

"It's a fucking nightmare—bad as the one at Gervais, and bigger. South of town."

"Just north of the Yamhill River, on the road by the old gauging station, I'll bet?"

Eric looked mildly startled. "Yeah, Mike. How'd you guess?"

"It's where I'd put it," he replied absently, his eyes hooded in thought as he called up terrain and distance. "Kills two birds with one stone: plugs the gap between the Coast Range and the Amity Hills, and gives them a base that's perfectly placed to launch raids on our farming country down south at Amityville and Rickreall; it'll be staring right down our throats. On the good side, it probably scares the bejayzus out of those idiots in Whiteson. Neutrality, my ass ... they'll *have* to make up their minds now, or at least as soon as the walls start to rise."

Signe cleared her throat. "Careful how you go at the neutrals, Mike. Honey and vinegar and all that."

Havel shrugged and grinned. "Yup. I can control my natural disgust with their yellow-bellied wavering, you bet." He turned his head back to her brother. "Details?"

"They're working on the foundations now, but you can

see the outlines. It's concrete again; no more of those telephone-pole motte-and-bailey specials that burned so nice. Ferroconcrete. Accent on the *ferro*. We got close enough to see that they're stacking I-beam as well as rebar; they must have a couple of hundred workers on twenty-four-hour shifts. Josh"—that was Josh Sanders, an ex-lumberjack and ex-Seabee and their expert on field fortifications—"got detailed sketches and extrapolated what the finished product will look like, based on the way they're digging and standard Protectorate practice. Says he'll debrief tomorrow, he's working up his notes."

Ken Larsson nodded and held up a sheaf of papers covered with pencil drawings. "I think Arminger's working from historical models."

"Hand 'em over, hubbie dear," Pamela said. She flicked through the pages. "Oh, yeah. Kerak des Chevaliers, I'd say, maybe Shobak." At their blank looks she sighed and went on: "Late Crusader types, from the Middle East. Add in a bit from Harlech and Edward the First's other Welsh castles, and modern touches like barbed wire. As good as you're going to get for pre-gunpowder fortifications. Or *post*-gunpowder, in our case."

"Nice to have an expert," Havel said, smiling crookedly.

"Hey, bossman, remember I was a *veterinarian*."

"At a zoo," Ken Larsson put in. "And still are, in a manner of speaking."

Pamela thumped him on the shoulder and went on: "The historical stuff was my *hobby*, like prancing around with swords. The Protector's the guy who was a real gen-u-wine history professor."

"The Demon Professor . . . from *hell*," her husband said. "We *would* get one who specialized in medieval history, too. It gives him entirely too many clever things in his bag of tricks."

"Where's he getting all the *materials*?" Eric asked, giving his father and stepmother a quelling look. "The concrete alone—"

His sister spoke up; she handled the intel files. "There were at least two big bulk freighters in Portland loaded with cement, according to what we've got from travelers and debriefing refugees," she said. "And another in the Columbia, and God knows what in Seattle, which he's been scavenging lately—incidentally, he controls everything from the Columbia to Tacoma now, too, which means quite a few cement *factories* with their stockpiles of finished product—like the one down here where we get ours. Not hard to haul the building materials on the railways, now that he's got them cleared of dead locomotives. There's a Southern Pacific branch line in through McMinnville and he's done better at keeping up the bridges than we have."

Eric rubbed at his beard. "Now that you mention it, we saw a couple of big trains—horse-drawn, and oxen. Didn't get close enough to see the loads under the tarpaulins, that could have been anything. I just thought it would be grain and such. And little handcarts on the rails too—you know, the ones with a couple of guys pumping at levers, like you used to see in old movies. Zipping along real fast, too, faster than a horse—faster than anything I've seen since the Change."

"Clever," his father said, and tapped his hook absently on the sketches. "And Portland's a big asset. You know, back before the Change, the United States produced about a hundred million tons of steel a year, and imported more. And *lots* of it went into buildings, or other uses where it'll last a long time; Portland was a fast-growing town, plenty of skyscrapers—millions and millions of tons, just in those alone. Considering that we've mostly gone back to using a few pounds of metal per head every year rather than thousands, it'll last a *long* time. We're so fixated on the Change that all we associate with cities is death and chaos. But if you can get at it, today a big city's a *mine*. Steel mine, glass mine, copper mine, asphalt mine—you name it, high-quality metals and alloys already smelted, plus gears and shaped stuff. And that gravity-flow water system in Portland gives Arminger a lot of hydraulic power; he's rigged up machine tools to run off it. It gives him manufacturing capacity."

"So Arminger isn't short of materials," Eric said. "He's still doing a *lot* of this building. It must cost something fierce in terms of other things he *can't* do."

Well, my brother-in-law has *absorbed basic logistics,* Havel thought.

"Notice what he and his barons've been buying, during this latest so-called truce?" he said aloud. "Food, mostly. That lets him pull workers out of the fields and build up a reserve." He called up a mental map. "With McMinnville, that gives him a string of castles east to Dayton, St. Paul, then down to Woodburn-Gervais, then over to Yoder. Plus all the smaller works, and what he's been doing in his HQ. A bit south of the old Yamhill-Marion county line. Defense in depth and he can screen the full width of the Valley; it counterbalances our advantage with the way the Eola and Waldo hills pinch in towards the river around the ruins of Salem."

Pamela nodded. "When a country's fully castellated"—she paused—"I mean, when it's got lots of castles, war turns into a series of sieges; even without camp fever, that'd be no fun at all. Unfortunately, we don't have anything comparable, apart from Larsdalen and Dun Juniper and a few other spots. And that city wall the university put up at Corvallis. Our A-lister steadings and most of the Mackenzie duns, they're a lot smaller, about like his second string. And we *know* he's got a good siege train now."

"There's Mt. Angel," Kenneth Larsson said. "I'd hate to have to try and storm that."

"Yeah, although that's geography as much as fortification," Havel said. "The abbey's on a nice, steep, three-hundred-foot-high hill to *begin* with, besides what they've put in in the way of walls."

Ken Larsson looked at his eldest daughter. "What news out of Portland?"

"Nothing unusual that my people can detect. There's a rumor he's going to announce that his daughter Mathilda is his heir, some big church ceremony with his pope laying on a blessing; she's over with Baron Molalla right now, has been for six months—some fosterage thing."

Eric snorted. "And I can see *that* bunch obeying a nine-year-old girl," he said.

"I can see anyone obeying Sandra Arminger as Regent, if our dear Lord Protector kicked off early," Signe said.

"She's got a following there, particularly among the old Society for Creative Anachronism types who think the gangers need to be scraped off their shoes, and she scares a lot more. Scares *me* sometimes! Besides, I doubt he plans on dying anytime soon, which is a pity, and there's a matter of Mathilda's marriage when she's of age—that is going to be one highly courted debutante."

"Given up on having a son, has he?" Havel said meditatively.

"Pretty well. It isn't like he hasn't tried—he's the 'If it moves, screw it, and if it doesn't move, shake it' type but none of them's ever caught. Maybe he had the clap sometime."

"Hmmm," her father said. "Is it certain young Mathilda—he must have named her after Mathilda of Flanders, what a thing to do to a kid—actually *is* his?"

"Certainly from her looks," Signe said. "I've seen portrait pictures taken at her birthday last October and it's unmistakable. Pity, we might be able to do something with it if it weren't."

Havel shrugged. "Hopefully he won't have a successor anyway. Is he mobilizing?"

"Nope, not beyond the usual," Signe said. "Mostly he's been spending a lot of time with those Australians—Tasmanians, actually—who showed up in Portland before Gunpowder Day. I haven't been able to get any of my people close to them, though. Odd . . . it'd be nice to hear what's going on in the rest of the world, but why is he putting so much effort into them, with a big war brewing?"

"Maybe he's decided to just defend what he has?" the elder Larsson said hopefully. "After all, he's got most of western Washington, and the Columbia Valley nearly to the Dalles. Going on for a couple of hundred thousand people, too. That's the biggest, well, *country* anyone's put together on the whole west coast between Acapulco and Alaska, as far as we know. Biggest single political unit this side of New Deseret, probably."

Havel shook his head; everyone else except the elder Larsson echoed him.

"Nah, Ken. Wishing don't make it so. That string of castles are meant as a base for attack—they're a lot more than he needs for defense, or even holding down the countryside, and like Eric said, it's costing him a lot. It's the shield to his sword, it lets him use small garrisons for cover and put the maximum numbers into a field army. He's got more full-time troopers than anyone else but he doesn't have a big militia he can call out when the balloon goes up."

Signe nodded. "Plus he's just not the type to stop; and besides, the Willamette's the best farmland around and he hasn't got more than a third of it. Plus we're the only real opposition this side of Pendleton and the Yakima; the rest, it's just odds and ends, little villages and a few towns that made it through, and the ranchers over in the Bend country. If it weren't for us at his back, he could snap it all up as far as Idaho and south to California—that's empty, but a lot of it would be worth resettling eventually. He's gobbled up everything he can without taking us on directly, so now he's going to do that."

"And he's bigger but we're growing faster these last few years, which is likely to make him sort of impatient," Ken acknowledged. "Not least because we keep getting escapers from his territories."

"I'd want to run away too, the way he squeezes his people." Eric scowled. "I saw more of that than I like to remember, up McMinnville way."

"Which is how he *can* do all that building," Havel said. "You can build big without machinery; that's how the pyramids got made. But it costs." He contemplated the map in his mind's eye for a moment longer and went on: "Not to mention keeping all those soldiers drilling year-round. Hmm . . . There's still a gap in that chain of forts. Just east of the river—the French Prairie."

"Foundations," Ken said. "The subsoil there's like jelly, and getting worse. I wouldn't want to put in anything with a forty-foot curtain wall and towers. Chancy."

In a fake-British accent he went on: "*But the fourth time, it* stood!*"

Pamela snickered, but the younger Bearkillers gave him blank looks.

He threw up his hands: "Christ, didn't any of you people

watch Monty . . . oh, never mind. Anyway, that area was half swamp in the old days and it's going back that way."

"Damn it, if he put as much effort into keeping up the levees and drains as he does into soldiers and forts, he wouldn't *need* to try and take away our land!" Eric Larsson snapped.

"To be fair, I don't think there are enough people left in the Valley to keep the old drainage system up with no power tools, and even without it there's more land than we can cultivate anyway," Signe said. "Not that I want to be fair to Arminger. I doubt any of the people on our side do."

Havel growled with exasperation. "That's the problem. We don't have a 'side.' *Arminger* has a side. What *we've* got is an alliance of four major and *twelve* smaller . . . university-run city-states, theocracies, clans, village republics, whatever-we-ares . . . trying to fight a single dictatorship. A damned *loose* alliance, at that. The only way we can do anything collectively is for all sixteen of us to sit and argue until it's unanimous. You know the definition of a committee? The only life-form with more than four legs and no brain."

"Makes you miss the good old US of A," Kenneth Larsson said. "Gridlock and all."

"I always did," Havel replied seriously.

"How come you never pushed to start it up again, then?" Eric Larsson said curiously. "I mean, you never let us use the Stars and Stripes or anything when anyone suggested it."

"Because that country's *dead,*" Havel said, an edge in his voice. "It died the night of the Change. I met a guy in Europe once who said the basic thing about Americans was that we'd never had a Dark Ages, just the Enlightenment. I've got news for you: the Dark Ages arrived, in spades, March seventeenth, nine years ago. Flying Old Glory would be . . . disrespectful. Like someone digging up their mother and using the old girl's skin for shoe leather. I may have lost my country but I'm not going to desecrate its grave."

Eric winced. His mother, Mary, had been injured when their Piper Chieftain crashed in Idaho the day of the

Change, and then was killed by bandits in a rather grue-some fashion not long after. The other Larssons glared at Havel.

"Sorry. Tact not my strong suit." He sighed and rose. "OK, we'll get the reports circulated and have a staff coun-cil meeting day after tomorrow. Christ Jesus, but I hate an-notating reports and holding meetings!"

Ken Larsson relaxed and chuckled. He'd been a busi-nessman, and the son and grandson of wealthy magnates, while the Havels had all been miners since they arrived from Finland in the 1890s—and got their unpronounceable *Myllyharju* changed to something the Czech pay clerk found easier to write. When they weren't feeding the steel mills they enlisted in the marines, or went logging, or worked a hardscrabble farm they'd bought around 1900. All very worthy and salt-of-the-earth, but . . .

"Welcome to the executive suite, my proletarian son-in-law," he said. "Ain't it grand?"

Havel snorted. "C'mon, Signe. I need a bath."

And now I need a shower, he thought several hours later, lazing with his hands behind his head and feeling the same vague longing for a cigarette he'd had at times like this since he quit in 1992.

The master bedroom of Larsdalen still showed the influ-ence of poor Mary Larsson, Ken's Boston-Brahmin first wife; the pale wood of the window frames and the furniture, the light graceful lines and perhaps a lingering odor of patchouli. They'd made changes: Signe's collection of stuffed animals and horse prints, a few of her own paintings, book-shelves, and the stands holding their armor and weapons. He didn't like sleeping with the hilt more than arm's-reach away.

He watched as Signe went through into the nursery to check on Mike Jr., who was napping, then watched appre-ciatively as she walked back in, honey-pale curves dappled by the evening light through the west-facing windows, sleek as a leopardess. The big house was comfortable enough for walking around in the buff; Ken Larsson had rerigged the central heating system to work on wood fuel.

"So, how's the big fellah?" he asked.

"Sleeping like a baby, which is sort of appropriate."

Havel chuckled. She went on: "Got to get his rest, if he's going to be Lord Bear Two. Or even just help one of his sisters be *Lady* Bear ... that sort of sounds funny, you know? Like Goldilocks."

It wasn't anything he said in the silence that followed ...

"One of them *is* going to be Lord Bear Two, right, Mike?"

He stretched. "A little early to be thinking about that, isn't it, *alskling*?" he said casually. "I'm not planning on retiring anytime soon. And the Outfit will have some input too, hey?"

"And what about your *bastard*?" she suddenly hissed.

I would really have preferred this subject not come up when I was naked, Havel thought. *It's sort of a psychological disadvantage.*

With the thought, he swung out of the rumpled bed, belted on a bathrobe and went over to the sideboard—another innovation—to pour himself a stiff bourbon. Then he turned, leaning back with his arms crossed.

"OK, Signe, you want the lowdown on it, yeah, he *is* my kid. At least, it's possible—I can't swear who Juney was seeing about then, but his looks do make it highly *probable,* you bet. I'm not denying it. I was willing to let it pass, but I'm not denying it. Not here in private, not to you. I won't make it public unless you insist."

Two spots of red had appeared on Signe's cheeks; the flush spread downward in a way he found distracting even now, as her chest heaved.

"Is that all you've got to say?"

"No. In the whole time since the Change, I've been with exactly two women, you and her—and with her, it was exactly once. Run the timing, *alskling*. That was in goddamned *April* of Year Zero. We weren't married. We weren't *involved*."

"That was because—"

"Yeah, I know. I was there when we came back and killed the Three Stooges from hell, right? But the fact remains that we *weren't* involved. Yes, if I'd been screwing around, you'd have a right to want to carve my liver out.

But I haven't been; not by any reasonable definition. You're the woman I want to spend the rest of my life with."

"But little Rudi makes it a bit awkward, doesn't he?"

"Yes. Kids have a habit of doing that."

He tossed off the drink, considered getting another, and decided not to—he'd had relatives who tried to solve problems that way.

"But I can't exactly have him killed, now can I?"

Signe opened her mouth, closed it, then stalked to her clothes, pulled them on and walked to the hall doorway.

"Fixing things is *your* problem," she snapped, then slammed the door behind her.

Well, shit, Havel thought, looking after her. *Guess I didn't grovel* hard *enough.*

She'd be all right in a while.

I hope, he thought, with an unfamiliar hollow feeling under his breastbone.

CHAPTER SEVEN

Carefully now, Dennis Martin Mackenzie told himself.

Even these days, it wasn't often he got a chance to carve a whole twenty-foot section of black walnut log in a mixture of low and high relief; he grinned, feeling himself drooling metaphorically as he prepared to take out another chip, savoring the strong, slightly oily-bitter scent of the cut wood.

This sucker would have been worth thousands *before the Change, but I'm doing something better with it than turning it into veneer.*

The trees weren't even native to Oregon, although they did well in the Willamette, like nearly everything else except tropical stuff. Juniper Mackenzie's great-uncle the banker had planted thousands of them in the cut-over Cascade foothills around his hunting cabin starting back around 1920, fancying himself a practitioner of scientific forestry and having the period's innocent calm about introducing alien species into an ecosystem. This one had been harvested a year before the Change, along with a lot of other mature timber, something Juniper had done as the only alternative to losing the land she'd inherited from him for back taxes. Then the timber company had gone belly-up and left the logs stacked to season while the lawyers sharpened their knives . . .

Dennis's stepson Terry stopped working on a prentice-piece clamped in a vise on a nearby bench and came to look. It was getting dark, and Dennis's workpiece was surrounded by lamps; the wall of the dun to the west meant that sunset came a few minutes early. The shadowless light was pretty good, but you had to be careful about judging depth. He took the gouge and laid the sharp V against a section, tapped with the wooden hammer . . .

Tock. A large chip flipped away to join those littering the gravel beneath the X-shaped wooden rests that held the great baulk of hardwood.

"And that's it for today," he said in satisfaction, caressing the dark wood with its dense hard grain, feeling the strength of it through his fingertips, the gloss it would take when it was oiled and polished and varnished just right, and set up with its twin . . .

"It's gonna look *great,* Dad," the twelve-year-old said. "Maybe even better than the gateposts here."

"As good, at least, if I do say so myself, Terry," Dennis said happily.

Even after nine years he was a little self-conscious about calling the boy *son,* although "blended" families like his were more common than not these days, given the accidents of survival in the Dying Time, and Terry hardly remembered his birth father. Certainly he had the love of the wood in him, and he wasn't half bad at leatherworking, either, which was Dennis's other trade, and had been his second hobby before the Change.

Terry was half Vietnamese, slender and fine-featured, and he made Dennis Martin Mackenzie feel almost as much of a hairy troll as his mother Sally's slight-boned prettiness did. She seldom talked about her first husband, who'd been working late at Hewlett-Packard in Portland that March seventeenth, and had simply never made it home.

She had the guts and sense to take Terry and get out of Dodge before things went absolutely to hell. She is one fine lady.

He smiled as he caressed the wood with a broad hand, callused from his work and scarred by the accidents inevitable when you used chisel and gouge, knife and awl and waxed thread. The dividing channels for the knotwork were finished, running in sinuous interlocking curves and angles up three-quarters of the log's smooth surface; that left rounding the serpents and the delicate work of putting in the scales. The interlacing patterns and gripping stylized beasts' mouths had their inspiration from the Book of Kells, but he'd made changes of his own—elongating the pattern, and changing the animals to coyotes and black bear . . .

With wood this beautiful, I'm almost sorry to do any inlay work. Just a little to pick out the mouths and eyes of the dragons and wolves. More up top, of course.

He touched the rougher wood at the log's end. That was where the face of the Goddess would go—and that was the real challenge for this piece of work. He'd spent nights and days thinking of it, while he worked on other things or just stood looking. Sutterdown wasn't using the Celtic pantheon to represent some aspect of the twin divinities of the Old Religion, the way most Mackenzies did. They wanted to be different . . .

Hmmmm. Yeah, the outer form is Aphrodite. But I want elements of all three Aspects here. Sally for the Mother-of-All this time. Eilir for the Maiden? Maybe Astrid, if I can get her to sit for it. Or Luanne Larsson, if I could get her over here for a couple of days. I like the way the bones of her face go—that Spanish-Indio-African-Anglo blend would be just right for the Goddess in this aspect—

"How much is Sutterdown paying you for this?"

He started out of his trance, suppressing a flash of irritation. "Hey, Chuck. Is it that time already?"

Chuck Barstow was in his brigandine and sword belt, with twin sprays of raven feathers on either side of his round bowl helmet for ceremonial swank; privately Dennis thought he was given to wearing headgear all the time because his sandy hair was getting real thin on top, and he wore his beard trimmed to a rakish point. He was also taller and younger than the woodworker—forty to his fifty-odd, lean whipcord and gristle to the other man's broad muscular hairiness.

He *wasn't fat before the Change,* Dennis thought, with a trace of satisfaction at his own waistline—not exactly narrow, but without the rolls of surplus tissue he'd worn there from his late twenties until the aftermath of the Change. *But then, he was a gardener by trade, not a pub manager like me, and he did all that knightly SCA shit in his spare time, too.*

"Yup. The Dun Fairfax people sent a horn-call up when the party went past and the road sentry relayed it. Sam's stopped off home there, by the way."

"Damn," Dennis said mildly. "I wanted to talk to him about the latest batch of cedar for the arrow-making shop before he got all caught up in farmwork. Oh, well, it ain't a long walk and Melissa's a hell of a good cook; I'll drop by tomorrow . . . no, that's Ostara, everyone'll be busy. Day or two after."

He brushed chips out of his beard and off his carpenter's apron, laying down his tools. Terry hurried to help put them away in the workshop that huddled against the inside of Dun Juniper's wall beside the family cabin. Dennis grinned: Terry was a good kid, if a little serious. He grinned wider as he put on a clean white shirt with biblike ruffle, tucked it into his kilt, wrapped his plaid and belted and pinned it, and arranged the flat Scots bonnet on his head with the tuft of coyote fur at the clasp.

He'd teased Juney for years before the Change about the way she put on the Celtic thing, however much it went with her style of music, and about how her coveners were always pulling some sort of myth out of the Irish twilight— of course he'd been a cowan then, an unbeliever, and hadn't understood the symbolism. Juniper Mackenzie might have been the one who told the band gathered at her cabin that to survive they would have to live like a clan, as it was in the old days—but he didn't think she had meant to be taken quite so literally. It had been Dennis who christened it the Clan Mackenzie, and started the kilt-wearing fashion when they salvaged that warehouse-full of tartan blankets. He'd come up with a good deal else that caught on too, in the years since, and mostly she'd had to go along with it.

It drives her bananas, Dennis thought with a smug grin, and only a slight pang at the metaphor—he hadn't tasted a banana in nine years.

Chuck raised an eyebrow, obviously following the thought: "Dennis Martin Mackenzie, the Clan's very own Astrid Larsson."

"Oh, now you're getting *nasty*," he protested. "Astrid's a compulsive fantasist. I just have a well-informed sense of humor."

The other man grinned. "It may be a joke to you, Dennie, but have you noticed how the younger generation takes it? Like they really *mean* it?"

Urk, he thought. *You've got a point there.* He glared at the Armsman.

Chuck spread his free hand and replied, "No offense. It's done us good, I think—*looking* different helped people believe things *were* different." A sly smile. "And speaking of Celtic motifs, how much *is* the covenstead at Sutterdown paying you to carve this tree? And in what?"

"Pain in the ass not having money anymore, isn't it?" Dennis said with a wink. "I mean there's only so much wheat or bacon you can use and keeping fifty bushels and a sow around until you can swap for something you really want is clumsy. They offered gold, originally, but I took it in wine, instead. Lot of our people still leery about gold."

Chuck raised a brow: "Not payment in Brannigan's special ale? Juney made a song about it, after all."

Dennis mimed taking an arrow in the ribs. "Traitor! I think that blowhard Brannigan spikes his with magic mushrooms, and mine's all natural ingredients—barley malt, hops and mountain spring water. But I will admit Sutterdown's got the best vineyards in our territory, even if they're not as good as the Bearkillers'. They agreed to store it for me."

Chuck's grin was honestly admiring. "Lost none of your innkeeper's instincts, I see," he said, laughing and leaning on his spear. "The longer *they* keep it, at their expense, the better it gets."

"Since it's a red blend that's mostly pinot noir and less

than a year in the wood, yeah, pretty much. And running the Hopping Toad was fun, sorta, but it was just my eating job. Wood and leather, that was where I got my kicks. Well, I like brewing, too. Anyway, it ain't strictly Celtic like the ones here; some of the knotwork, yeah, but the faces are classical as much as anything. Everything's an aspect of the God and Goddess, right?"

He looked down at the wood, smiling, and touched it lightly with his fingertips again. "It's all gonna look damn good, if I say so myself."

"Sutterdown *ought* to be concentrating on getting their damn town wall finished," Chuck grumbled.

He wore two hats in the clan: Lord of the Harvest, which translated as Minister of Agriculture, and Second Armsman, which in peacetime meant going around chivvying people to keep their training and defensive works up to scratch.

"No rest for the Wiccan," he went on with a sigh, settling his helmet and heading for the gates.

And he puns, too, Dennis thought with a wince, and set about closing up shop.

Dun Juniper was bustling with preparations for the Chief's homecoming and the big pre-Ostara dance by the time he and Terry had swept up the chips for the kindling box and dragged a tarpaulin up to cover the workpiece. Terry's mother Sally was over in the Hall, helping with the decorations and cooking—her usual jobs were principal of the Dun Juniper high school and Lore-Mistress for the Clan as a whole, overseeing the schools and Moon Schools, but the kids were off for the day.

Dennis decided that the best contribution *he* could make was to go up and lean on the battlements and watch the sun set and Juniper and her party arrive; if he didn't someone would find him real work to do. There were ladders at intervals between the cabins built up against the wall. He went up one with the ease of long practice and emerged puffing on the fighting platform, surprised as always at how *high* things looked from there.

Higher outside than inside, of course; Juney's cabin—the core of the Hall—had stood on a little oblong plateau jutting southward into a larger hillside bench. The steep slope around its edge gave the walls fifteen feet more height on their outer surface.

In the summer of Change Year One the growing clan of the Mackenzies had put up a log palisade around Dun Juniper. Then they'd had a couple of practical examples of how well that style of fort could burn, and nobody had grudged the work of renovations next year—much. They'd used the *Murus Gallicus* as a model—the Gallic Wall of the old continental Celts. It was a crib-cage of horizontal squared logs, each layer at right-angles to the one below; the gaps between the logs were filled with fitted rock and rubble before the next layer of timbers was spiked down, until the wall was as high as you wanted—thirty feet, here—and an outer layer of mortared fieldstone concealed the ends of the horizontal logs. There were U-shaped towers half again as tall at the corners, plus a pair facing each way to bracket the gate, and they'd improved on the Celtic original by working cement and rebar into the rubble as the wall went up.

Add a solid coating of waterproof stucco from an abandoned building-supply warehouse over the outside, give the fighting platform a pavement of remelted road asphalt six inches thick and it was weathertight and low-maintenance, too.

Hell of a lot faster and easier than building a real stone wall, he thought, putting an elbow on one of the waist-high embrasures that alternated with the seven-foot merlons along the platform; the merlons each had an arrow slit in the middle. *And remembering how much sweat it cost us, that's saying something. Stronger than stone alone if someone comes calling with a battering ram, too.*

"Which the Lord and Lady forbid," he murmured, and made a gesture as Sally and Terry came up the ladder he'd climbed; she had infant Maeve on her back in a carrier, and eight-year-old Jill scampered up behind her, confident as a squirrel on ground she'd climbed over all her life.

The girl pointed upward with a cry of delight. A flight of swans went by overhead, their V headed westward towards the distant river.

* * *

Juniper Mackenzie looked up at the swans as they went overhead, flying down from the mountains to the river; here at the top of the road she was near level with them for an instant, close enough to see their snowy feathers turned ruddy by the light of sunset. Their voices floated down, majestic as the slow beating of their great white wings, sad as the sunset. Then they were past, shadows against the greater shadows in the west, where crimson and gold castles towered above the trees and slowly faded towards blue-black as the first stars shone.

She felt a song moving, a stirring behind the breastbone, the music weaving with the words; not the fiddle or guitar for this, but the harp Dennie had made for her over the winter with its sounding board of seasoned, polished Engelmann spruce; she could forgive a great deal of his foolishness for that. Her lips moved, singing in a half whisper, with a hum to carry the tune:

> *"Where does the wild swan wander?*
> *On lonely shores where salt foam tumbles*
> *No roof but leaves, above a bed of moss*
> *By silver streams that shun the homes of men.*
> *So flies my heart over mountain rock:*
> *My brother the deer, my sister the wolf;*
> *To run alone in the cold gray wet of autumn*
> *With the harsh tapping of twigs*
> *And the flutter of wind-stripped leaves . . ."*

She stopped, confident that she had the beginning of it at least. To work the rest she needed solitude and quiet—which in her position were unfortunately hard to get.

Damn! I never wanted it! All I wanted was to help my loves survive. I could see what must be done, and one thing led to another . . .

"Sorry, friends," she said, noticing that the column had halted; and feeling once more the chill, chafing discomfort of soaked clothing. "Didn't mean to keep you here cold and wet!"

"Sorry?" a woman said, laughing, tossing back long yellow hair darkened with the rain despite her slicker—Cynthia Carson Mackenzie, commanding the escort now that Sam had dropped off at his home at Dun Fairfax down in the little valley below. *"Sorry?"*

"We're sorry we won't hear the rest of it, Lady Juniper!" Astrid said.

I like the words, Mom, Eilir signed; she read lips well. *A lot.*

"Then you'll all hear the rest, though not today. And now let's go see if there's a hot bath and a dry robe, and what's on the hob for dinner!"

Mom . . . it's Ostara eve. You can bet *there's something special!*

They pressed their tired horses up to a trot, out westward onto the broad bench in the side of the mountain that held Dun Juniper, away from the creekside path up from the head of the valley. The level land beyond ran east-west, an oval nearly a mile long and half a mile wide at its broadest point, making an interval of rolling meadow between steep tall forests upslope and down. The graveled road wound through the spring flush of green meadow dotted with huge Oregon oaks; some from the days when her father's line settled here fresh out from East Tennessee a century and a half ago; more planted since—along with maple and walnut—by her great-uncle Earl, who'd prospered in town and bought back the family homestead as a hunting lodge and played at forestry.

She thought of the strange, solitary, childless old man and smiled fondly; he'd loved her in his way—probably— although she'd seen little of him, even when the family visited in the summertime. Willing the property to a teenager with an illegitimate deaf daughter had astonished the family nearly as much as it surprised *her,* but by then a whole generation of potential heirs had predeceased old Earl. Maybe he'd laughed from the Summerlands as she buckled down to make a modest success of her music, as much to hold on to the land as to keep a roof over her and Eilir's heads. And she had—just, if you counted selling some of the timber occasionally to make up shortfalls. They'd been doing well enough right before the Change . . .

And if only he could see it now! she thought.

The first blue camas flowers starred the meadows; they'd turn to sheets of color by April or May, and twinberry glowed dull gold, henbit reddish-purple. Cattle black and red, horses squat and powerful or tall and long-limbed drowsed behind plank fences or young hedges of white-flowered hawthorn, some raising their heads to watch as the riders went by. The Mackenzies kept their best breeding stock here for safety, the precious Suffolk punch roans, Arab and quarter horse saddle-breeds, fleecy square-set Corriedale rams and Jersey and Angus bulls. There were fewer fields than in the first desperate years; most of the grain came in now from more fertile parts of the Clan's lands westward in the Valley proper. But some brown plowland showed the green shoots of potatoes or the blue-green of oats, and a stretch of old gnarled apple trees painstakingly brought back into bearing with more new-planted, all showing the first creamy froth of flowers.

The little waterfall off to her right leapt down the steep mountainside into a pond fringed with reed and willows, larger now that they'd put up a turf-covered check dam. The waterwheel below it was still just now, without the querning sound of grain being ground or the *ruhhh . . . ruhhh* of the saw; the wood of the millhouse walls silvery with age—they'd rescued it from a tourist trap. A furrow from the pond watered acres of truck garden and berry bushes.

And westward Dun Juniper itself, still like a dream that might vanish and leave only Uncle Earl's lodge. The white walls grew solid enough as they neared, silver and then stained reddish with the dying sunlight behind it; spear-heads glinted on the battlements, and the banners flew, and a few first gleams of lamplight showed through arrow slits in the towers. The heavy *boom . . . boom . . .* of Lambeg drums came from above the gates, and the squeal of bag-pipes, and the little figures of people growing until she could identify one or another—probably the whole four hundred or so who dwelt within.

"*Is é do bhaile do chaisleán,*" Juniper murmured.

"What's that, Lady Juniper?" Astrid asked.

"Very freely translated: *A woman's home is her castle!*"

Everyone in hearing chuckled. "And never were words more true!"

The road kept going westerly, through the flower beds just outside the Dun—her secret guilty indulgence in the fruits of power, although they were useful for ceremonies, too—and then one branch climbed along the side of the rise to the gates, exposing any attackers' defenseless spear-arm side to missiles from above. The people there *were* throwing things: flowers, in fact, or little braided grass figures of the Green Man, for luck. She waved and grinned; being Chief might be a pain in the fundament some of the time—much of the time—but Juniper Mackenzie knew how to work a crowd, by Ogma the Honey-Tongued!

She halted at the top of the laneway, amid an iron clatter of horseshoes on the small flat area paved in flagstone that spread before the entry. The gate was closed—had *been* closed so it could be symbolically opened again. Its frame was heavy timbers close-fitted into a solid baulk a yard thick, but the surface on both sides was quarter-inch sheet steel, painted bark brown. This last winter they'd had the leisure to get a little playful with it, and Dennis had directed a project that laid on designs in copper; Astrid and Eilir had done the drawings. At first glance it was just more of the swirling abstract knotwork, the bronze bolts which held the facing on part of it, but when you looked closer the patterns running down the middle sprang out at you.

The Triple Moon above, waxing and full and waning, like a circle flanked by crescents; below that a man's face, wildly bearded and surrounded by a halo of curls, with horns springing from his forehead.

Juniper halted her horse and swung down from the saddle, not without a groan—riding for hours in cold rain did middle-aged joints no good—and thumped the side of her fist against the gate. It felt like striking a cliff of living rock, and she called up: "It's Juniper Mackenzie, Chief of the Clan Mackenzie by the Clan's own choice, asking for the gate to open!"

Dennie and a few others had tried to get her to refer to herself as *the* Mackenzie, the way a lot of other people did. She'd drawn the line there, successfully for once.

Inside someone shouted, and there was a long rumbling quiver as the great horizontal beams were drawn back into slots in the tower walls on either side; there were vertical ones as well, but they weren't used except in emergencies. Then came a rhythmic shouting, as teams pulled back on the gates. Each had heavy truck wheels built into its middle and the end where the leaves joined, and they rolled back easily enough.

Chuck and Judy Barstow walked out through the gateway, between the shaped and painted pillars—the God as Lugh of the Sun on the left, with his spear and solar disk and head wreathed in carved holly; the Goddess as Brigid on the right, with the flames of wisdom and the sheaf of abundance, crowned with rowan. Judy—once Maiden of Juniper's Singing Moon Coven and now High Priestess of her own Wolf-Star—poured wine from the pitcher into the long silver-mouthed horn Chuck held; that had started out as one of a pair over the bar of a Western-themed place in Sisters. Then he handed it to her.

"Welcome home, Lady Juniper," he said, smiling warmly. "A hundred thousand welcomes to the Mackenzie!"

Juniper nodded to him, and took the horn; she'd rather have had hot chocolate with a marshmallow—lost paradise!—or mulled mead, but wine would do well enough. She raised it overhead in her right hand, then poured a few drops before the image of Lugh, holding it expertly with the curling tip over her forearm:

"Shining Sun, God of the skillful hand and piercing mind, strong Defender, Wise in Council, gentle Father, we thank You for guidance on this journey in the works of hand and word and heart. May this place be rich with Your gifts of knowledge and of craft."

"Blessed be," came a hundred other voices, murmuring on the heels of her own.

She drank. The wine was strong and mellow; when you gave to the Gods, you gave your best. Then the libation to the Mother-of-All—and here Dennie had been guided, for while the God's image was beautiful, the carven eyes of the Goddess rendered here always seemed to lift her beyond herself:

"Goddess of the ripened corn, Lady whose flames are the warmth of wisdom, You who inspire the poet's tongue, Mother gentle and strong, whose womb is source of all things, we thank You for the protection of Your arms while far from hearth and loves. May this place be a sanctuary of Your compassion, to nourish all who enter in perfect love and perfect trust."

"Blessed be."

Another long sip, like the spirit of berries and fruit and the autumn earth, and she passed the horn on to the others, for each of them to make the thanks-offering and take a swig. A four-footed figure burst through the legs of the crowd inside the gate—her old mutt Cuchulain, limping and dim-eyed, but still determined to claim his mother/pack-leader/comrade. She bent to thump his ribs and push aside his usual attempt to sniff under the kilt, and then straightened.

"And the Lord and Lady witness, if we're going to have that dance tonight I need a *bath*. We old ladies get cranky and creaky without a good hot soak."

> *What of the bow?*
> *The bow was made in England:*
> *Of the true wood, of yew-wood*
> *The wood of English bows*
> *So men who are free*
> *Love the old yew-tree*
> *And the land where the yew-tree grows!"*

Sam Aylward sang the old ditty softly; his bass voice was still rough as a rasp, and he warbled out of tune now and then—music had never been his strong point. The sheep never seemed to mind, though, here or back on his father's farm, and it did seem to make them a little less flighty. It was hard to tell for sure with woolies; they were near as brainless as a new-minted lieutenant fresh from the drill fields of Sandhurst.

"Come on, Dolly, let's get the little bugger born and you comfortable," he said, interrupting himself, then went back to the work and the song. "You should have done this a month ago like the rest of your woolly mates. Breeding out of season, shame on you."

His broad hands moved with surprising gentleness, as the ewe bleated and struggled in the straw of the sheep shed he'd built at the highest point in the big plank-fenced field. Fingers traced the leg; the joint went the right way this time, which meant it was the *front* legs, the ones which should be facing this way, at last. He reached in to make sure that it wasn't twins, and the ewe gave an indignant wiggle.

Most of the breeders could drop theirs out in the pasture, in this gentle climate, but he preferred to have them dry and out of the wind on a raw afternoon like this. The rain had barely stopped when he arrived, beneath a sky colored like old iron and darkening towards the early spring nightfall. He'd come home soaked, and then it was out to check on the last of the flock to deliver with no more than a quick word to the wife. The weather had turned nasty the last half of their trip back from Larsdalen, though now the clouds were breaking open to show belated blue sky in the west.

As well I did check.

No single family here at Dun Fairfax had very many woolies, so they managed them as one flock to save time and work—and Larry Smith, the shepherd, had been off after a couple of strays. Dolly and the lamb both would have died if Aylward hadn't been there and pitched in.

It was turning dark; the cries of a flight of swans went by overhead, and outside his eldest son Edain was romping with the dogs. His stepdaughter Tamar was waiting not far away, crouching in the straw with her arms around her knees and singing along with him as he worked, and doing a much better job of carrying the tune:

> "... *so we'll all drink together*
> *Drink to the gray goose feather*
> *And the land where the gray goose flew!*"

"All right, girl, keep her steady," he said. "Firm but gentle, now."

Tamar knelt and held the ewe's head and forelegs while he grasped the lamb's feet and began a steady pull; his grating bass and the girl's clear contralto sounded together over the frantic bleats as the nose came free.

> *"What of the men?*
> *The men were bred in England:*
> *The bowmen—the yeomen—*
> *The lads of dale and fell.*
> *Here's to you—and to you—*
> *To the hearts that are true*
> *And the land where the true hearts dwell!"*

"There we go, Dolly old girl!"

The newborn came clear of the birth canal in a final slippery rush; not much blood, he'd gotten the legs turned in time, though only just. The ewe lay panting for a moment, tongue out.

"I knew you could do it," he said encouragingly, stripping off the birth sack to make sure the lamb didn't suffocate and toweling it down with an old burlap sack.

Edain came in as he finished—all over mud as might be expected of a healthy six-year-old; luckily he wasn't wearing much but a singlet and his kilt which left a lot of easily washable skin exposed—and he crouched to watch with his damp, sun-streaked fair hair plastered to his forehead.

Dolly was exhausted—this was her first lamb and a hard delivery—but she had plenty of strength to turn and sniff her offspring before licking it clean; it got to shaky legs and butted at her udder, feeding naturally and not needing a helping hand as they sometimes did. Which was as well; hand-rearing a lamb its mother rejected was a royal pain in the arse. He put down a little grain and hay for Dolly, who had the lamb tucked in against her now.

Tamar brought over the big tin bucket of water and the towel and washcloth and a chunk of strong-smelling homemade lye soap.

"There you go, Dad," she said, and wrinkled her nose slightly.

"It's a messy business, girl," he said. "And that's a fact."

She nodded undisturbed. A farmgirl didn't grow up squeamish, and she'd lived two-thirds of her lifetime in the Changed world. She was thirteen this year, a gangling girl just tipping over the edge of adolescence, all legs and knees and elbows, with a shock of yellow hair and blue eyes and a round cheerful face. She might have been his own as far as looks went; there was even a trace of Hampshire to her talk now, for all that her blood kin had been farming around Boone's Lick and thinking about the Oregon Trail while Aylward's great-great-grandfather froze his toes off in the Crimea. He supposed that in a few more years he'd be beating off the boys with a stick and grumbling that none of them seemed worthy of her.

He stripped off the canvas apron, stained with the blood and fluids that gave the air a tang of iron and copper under the smells of wet turned earth and straw and manure. Beneath it he wore only kilt and boots, showing a matt of grizzled brown hair on his chest and the ugly white scar-tracery left by bullets, blades, arrows and grenade fragments on his muscular stocky body.

Plus Arabic letters on his stomach, where someone had started to spell out the name "Abdullah" with a red-hot knife. The last letter trailed off, fruit of a terminal interruption.

I wonder what happened to Colonel Loring? he thought, not for the first time; it had been his old commander who provided the interruption—hand over the mouth, Fairburn knife through the kidney. *Well, if anyone survived, it would be Sir Nigel Loring—not that it's likely anyone much in Britain did survive.*

He grew conscious of his children's gaze, shook himself free of the brown study that had gripped him for a moment and bent over the bucket with busy hands. Their mother Melissa was finicky about what she let in the door too. Tamar and Edain sat on a stall partition and swung their feet as he washed, filling him in on what had gone on around home and at school and Moon School while he was away with the mission to the conference at Larsdalen. Tamar was beginning algebra, which she didn't like, archery practice, which she did—

At that point Edain sprang up and took an ax handle, holding it out vertically in his left hand with the arm parallel to the ground, the strengthening exercise for the bow arm.

"We do that at school for a whole *hour* every day now!" he boasted, beaming, a gap showing where two of his milk teeth had gone recently.

Tamar rolled her eyes. "Just the same way *you* showed *me,* Dad," she said with the heavy patience of thirteen for six.

"That's the way to raise children," Aylward said with grave approval in his tone. "Good lad."

He'd been the one who got Lady Juniper to put that in the curriculum for all the Clan's schools, back in the second Change Year. Edain dropped the ashwood and went to examine the lamb, poking it with a finger and earning a suspicious look and bleat from Dolly.

"And what else?" Aylward asked.

What else for Tamar turned out to be herb lore, and the use of the spinning wheel, which she could take or leave, plus the usual chores. And making colored eggs to be buried around the hamlet for the sake of the crops, and practicing the Ostara dances.

Aylward nodded tolerantly at her enthusiasm; he gave the predominant local religion the same grave formal courtesy he'd always extended the Church of England, but neither moved him much. Melissa was the High Priestess of the Dun Fairfax coven now, though, and strong for the whole business—also slightly irritated her husband had never become more than a Dedicant. She'd have preferred him as an Initiate at least, and preferably her High Priest.

Can't see meself prancing around under the moon with antlers on me head, he thought with a grin, then spat as the expression let some of the harsh soap into his mouth. Larry Smith had that job here at Dun Fairfax, and looked, in Aylward's considered opinion, a complete prat in the role. *I must admit, it's a good religion for farmers. The festivals all make sense that way.*

He'd seen Juniper's faith spread through the Mackenzie territories and beyond over the years like fast-growing ivy over a wall. Starting with the core group of coveners and friends who'd gathered at her cabin days after the Change, and out from there as they took in refugees—*One recently retired English soldier caught out on a hunting trip, for instance*—and then became the seed crystal of order and survival in this corner of the Valley. Now Tamar's generation was growing up, and to them the whole thing was as natural as water to a fish. *Their* children would probably forget that their pre-Change ancestors had mostly been Christians.

Lady Juniper's charisma hurts not a bit, too. She's come close enough to convincing me more than once, just by being what she is, not by preaching.

"I wish I could have come with you to Larsdalen, Dad," Tamar went on. "It must have been *so cool* with all the Dun Juniper people. You know, back when I was just a little girl, right after the Change, Lady Juniper gave me a candy bar? I can remember it clear as anything, when I went out in the road and asked her if she was a Witch? And now we're *all* Witches. That was right before the battle, when those people chased us out of Sutterdown and she called the Dark Lady to help us."

"I remember that, poppet," he said.

It had lost nothing in the retelling since; watching fact grow into legend and legend become myth in a few short years had been eerie, and the original skirmish had been weird enough. He splashed his face repeatedly to get the lye soap out of his eyelids, and then stuck his whole head in the bucket, coming up blowing before he scrubbed vigorously at his curly brown hair with the towel.

"I was at the battle meself, remember. And you haven't reminded me about the candy more than a thousand times."

His smile took any sting out of the words. Inwardly: *And that put the plums in the pudding, beating back that probe the Protector sent. Herself going wild like that, running at them screaming like a bloody banshee and everyone following just as stark raving bonkers . . . And the Reverend Dixon dropping dead after the battle, too, he was her only rival in the faith-will-save-us brigade around here. If she'd been a Buddhist, we'd all be spinning ruddy prayer wheels by now.*

He shook off memory: a chalk pale blood-spattered face, eyes showing white all around the rims, red hair bristling like a fox's crest, and a voice that had echoed down from his head into his gut . . .

Edain took up the ax handle again, this time wielding it like a sword—or a six-year-old boy's conception of how you used a sword, tempered by watching adults practice the real thing fairly often.

"When Lady Juniper called the Lord 'n Lady 'n they *smote* the wicked!" he said with bloodthirsty enthusiasm. "She's *great*. She sings real nice, too."

Baraka and to spare, she has.

"And Dad was a *hero*. I'm gonna be a hero too!"

"I'll teach you better than that," Aylward snorted. "Heroes run themselves onto spearpoints. I *won*, is what I did. Now come here, young'un."

He held the squirming boy by the neck while he did a quick daub-and-wipe with the towel. "There, that's got the worst of it off."

When he'd pulled on his shirt and jacket Tamar hopped down and proudly took up her light bow; he picked up a spear leaning against one of the poles that held up the lean-to roof of the open-fronted structure. It was six feet of smooth ashwood, with another foot of steel on top, ground down from a leaf spring to a knife shape that tapered to a vicious point along two razor edges, and he politely declined Edain's offer to carry it for him. One thing he'd gotten into the boy's head good and proper—via a few smart smacks on the backside—was that he didn't touch a weapon without permission. Of course, Edain craved the day when he'd be able to walk abroad with dirk and bow like his elder sibling, rather than just shooting at the mark under close supervision.

He balanced the spear over one shoulder as they all left the long shed, and whistled up his dogs—a big Alsatian and an even larger shaggy mutt, both rescued as pups. They'd been lying outside the shed, eyeing the sheep wistfully but far too well trained to do any bothering. The herd looked apprehensive; sheep didn't really like either men or dogs, and these had the comically naked look woolies always had right after shearing. At least there weren't many nicks or cuts this year; everyone had finally learned how to use hand shears on a wiggling sheep held clamped between the knees.

"Garm, Grip," he called, and they fell in behind him with eyes alert and tails wagging, accepting an ear-ruffling from Tamar and an arm around each neck from Edain. "We're off home, mind. No chasing rabbits. Heel."

They followed the humans down the gentle slope and towards the gate—he cocked a satisfied eye on the hawthorn seedlings he'd planted along the fences here and elsewere; they were growing fast, already chest-high, glowing with their early-set white flowers, scent a faint cool sweetness. By the time the planks had rotted out, they would be good cow-tight barriers that needed no sawn timber to repair; he'd learned how to lay, stake, pleach and ether a hawthorn hedge when he was about Tamar's age. His hands remembered, and others were learning.

Me dad didn't get a tractor until I was Tamar's age, either. The house never did have running water, just a hand pump. Until that sodding burke of a stockbroker bought it for a weekend place.

That made him smile again; the same mix of stubborn conservatism and sheer poverty that doomed his father as a farmer had given the younger Aylward a set of archaic skills that were coming in very handy indeed, post-Change.

The laughingstocks of Crooksbury, we were . . . but this *Aylward's laughing last.*

A collie wagged its tail as they opened the gate, but stood alertly until they'd hitched the wire to close it again. A little further along the fence a man leaned against a post with resigned patience, his bow in his crossed arms and a spear propped beside him.

"G'night, Larry," Aylward called, while the dogs exchanged sniffs.

"A good night as long as it doesn't rain, Sam," the shepherd said with a brief wave, then turned back to his charges.

He had his supper in a cloth-tied bundle at his feet, and a good thick coat and rain slicker, but Aylward didn't envy him—the more so as a kilt was a bit drafty at times, even with drawers beneath. The fashion had taken strong hold, though. Everyone teased you if you didn't wear one most of the time, and teasing was no joke living close with the same faces every day.

"I'm shrammed already," Smith grumbled.

Got that word from me, Aylward thought, with a wave and a nod. *At least he got it right.* It *was* a cold and shivery night, at least by Willamette standards. *And* I'm *headed back to a hot dinner and a nice warm kitchen.*

Dun Fairfax had been built around a century-old farmhouse left vacant by the Change—the owners been elderly Latter-Day Saints, and very, very diabetic—to be a base for those who worked this stretch of the clan's land. The graves of the Fairfaxes stood on a slight rise not far from the gate, well-fenced and with a stone marker. Juniper Mackenzie had gone to some trouble to get Mormon rites said for them; several of the residents also made small offerings now and then, from courtesy and because the supplies in the old couple's barn and basement had helped to keep the proto-clan going for crucial months. He didn't know what they'd think of becoming the tutelary spirits of a Wiccan farming hamlet . . .

The Mackenzies had added twelve more homes, ranging from log cabins to frame buildings built from salvaged materials to what the Yanks called a double-wide, that last hauled in by a four-hitch of Suffolk punch draft horses. Then they'd enclosed it with a ditch, bank and log stockade, plus a square-set blockhouse over the gate. The circuit included the old Fairfax barn, a meetinghall-cum-covenstead, more sheds, storage and workshops, and room enough to drive all the livestock in come an emergency. The whole was in a west-tending valley with Dun Juniper perched up the slope to the north.

The high peaks to the northeast were touched with pink by the setting sun, and tall ranks of Douglas fir stood north and east and south where the rolling bottomland crinkled upward into high hills or low mountains. From here he could see down a swale in pasture, over a fence and a trickle of creek, up through an apple orchard with the buds just burst, and past the truck gardens that surrounded the dun to the pointed logs of the palisade itself.

The original farmhouse was his—he held sixty-four acres from the Clan, a good little bit of a farm, the biggest in this settlement—and it had been built on a rise; that and its own two-story-and-attic height left the top of it visible from here over the wall.

As he watched a lantern came on behind a window, showing soft yellow flame through glass and curtains, and then another and another. No other lights flickered within eyesight, though Dun Juniper was just up the slope to northward. The chuckle of Artemis Creek a little to his south was loud tonight, full with the spring rains and the beginning of snowmelt on the heights; underneath it he could hear the low humming moan of a spinning wheel, rising and falling and then abruptly cutting off as someone laid it by for the night. An owl dropped out of the woods to the north and soared over his head to the pasture beyond, on the lookout for field mice and rabbits.

He laughed softly as he took a deep breath of the fir-scented air down from the mountains; it mixed with the damp grass, a whiff from the pigpens, woodsmoke and cooking from the dun. Edain's patience broke, and he ran on ahead; the dogs looked for permission before dashing off in pursuit.

"What's funny, Dad?" Tamar asked, putting her free hand in his.

"Well, girl, I was just thinking that it's an ill wind that blows nobody good."

Or even an ill disaster-beyond-all-reckoning that didn't leave *someone* better off.

No fault of mine the Change happened—it came as near as bugger-all to killing me too, slow and nasty. But all I've ever liked doing is soldiering, hunting and farming; and here I get to do all three as much as suits me—with chick and child thrown in, which I never expected. None of that frabbling with the bank and the prices and regulations that broke Dad, either; we eat what we raise, or trade it straight-

*up for what else we need. And when I fight, I do it for my
own family and friends and the land that feeds us.*

He'd taken the queen's shilling before he was old
enough to vote, gone where she sent him and fought whoever the officers told him to fight, and given it all he had.
The whys and wherefores weren't rightly any of his business; he was a soldier, and it was his trade.

Defending his own was . . . *Sort of . . . direct-feeling—
more personal, like.*

"Where does that song about the yew tree and the bows
come from, Da?" Tamar asked as they walked along; she
was getting old enough to be curious about the family history. "I mean, not just from England?"

"God"—he caught himself and added—"and the Goddess know, girl. I learned it from my grandfather. Tough old
bugger—must've been eighty as I first remember him and
still strong as an oak root; I was the youngest of four, the
rest all girls, you see, and *my* dad married late. We Aylward
men do. Granddad fought in World War One, he did. Came
back limping."

She nodded understanding, walking along beside him in
the gathering dusk. "Yes, I know, Dad. But the song?"

"Well, *he* said he'd got it from *his* grandfather, who got it
from his—who fought bloody Napoleon if you can believe
it—who got it from *his,* and I don't know how many more
generations. Tell you the truth, it's what first got me interested in bows as a nipper. I liked to play at Hundred Years
War."

She gave him a puzzled look: "You were a soldier over
in England, Dad. Didn't you always shoot a bow?"

"That was before the Change, remember. We used guns."

"Oh," she said with a shrug, obviously dismissing a time
that distant.

*Never heard a firearm set off, probably, and doesn't re-
member cars or the telly much,* he thought, shaking his
head a little. *And to Edain, they're fairy tales, like Robin
Hood to me, or Jack and the Beanstalk.*

"But that's cool about the song, though," she went on
generously. Aylward hid a grin.

They walked up the graveled way to the blockhouse.

The gateway through the man-thick palisade logs was open; it was just wide enough for a two-horse wagon, built up of heavy timbers covered in bolted-on steel strapwork. The forging was crude—Aylward had turned his hand to smithing a little, but was no expert—yet immensely strong. The villager on gate-guard duty for the night was just lighting a lantern and hauling it up a flagpole before climbing the steep plank stairs to the platform under the parapet.

"Cheryl," Aylward said, nodding. "Seen a young boy go by, well-plastered?"

"Hi, Sam, Tamar. Edain went up the street in a rooster-tail of mud a couple of seconds ago," she replied, settling her steel cap with a sigh and going up with a lunchbox in one hand and her bow and quiver in the other. "Followed by two mud statues shaped roughly like dogs," she added over her shoulder.

That was one more reason you couldn't live alone on your land; there had to be enough to trade off chores like guard duty that needed doing the clock round.

The laneway between the cottages within was graveled too; chickens pecked about in it until a couple of children shooed them off towards their coop for the night, and ducks and geese came up from the pond for their evening feed—they had a good strong perennial spring here. Dun Fairfax was a well-to-do settlement, with much of its draft-work done by horses rather than oxen; one nickered off in the stable sheds built up against the inside of the palisade; there were eight of the beasts, including two mounts of his that doubled for riding and light farmwork. Keeping riding horses was a bit of a luxury, but necessary for his other job as Armsman; the rest of the families all had at least one bicycle, and it was going to be yet another pain in the arse when those started to unfixably break down.

He passed various neighbors with a smile and a nod; Katherine Doors came by from the big pre-Change barn where all the households kept their milch cows along with the communal straining tub, and barrel churn and cream separator; two big plastic buckets of milk rode at either end of a yoke over her shoulders. Several interested cats followed her, noses and tails up as they traced the swaying of the pails and hoped for a spill.

"This is working a treat, Sam, just like you said it would," she called, tapping the fingers of her steadying hand on the smooth garry-oak stave he'd carved for her. "Saves a lot of work."

"You're welcome, Kate," he said.

Everything's relative, he thought silently. *Those buckets must weigh eighty pounds, together.* But it *was* saving a good many trips back and forth. At least Dun Fairfax had piped water to everyone's kitchen.

He circled the old two-car garage of the Fairfax house, now a bowyer's workshop and spinning-and-weaving room with the sliding door replaced by salvaged windows for light. What had been the backyard of the house was his wife's herb garden, with roses trained up against trellises on the walls, and a bordering edge of dahlias and peonies; Edain waited with the dogs, suddenly a little apprehensive as he looked down at the state of his shoes and kilt.

"Can't have that," Aylward said, and gave the dogs a bucket of water each and a brush with an old burlap sack; they laid back ears but submitted to the rough cleaning.

"Dad? What about me?"

"Talk to your mother about that."

Man and girl walked down the brick pathway to the kitchen door, savoring the good cooking odors that came out the opened window, and stamping to get the mud off their soles. The leather went *splat* on the wet brick and Tamar suddenly started kangaroo-hopping down the path, giggling as she landed, her bow held over her head in both hands, and her brother joined her.

"Boots! Boots, all of you!" his wife Melissa cried, sticking her head out a window; she was a comfortable-looking woman in her late thirties, with a halo of yellow-brown curls just touched with the first gray strands. "I cleaned the floors for Ostara while you were gone and I'm not doing it again!"

Aylward snorted. *Wipe yer web feet, ninny!* he heard, remembering his mother's voice when he came in from the fields with *his* father.

"And watch out for the hob's milk!"

His mother had put out a bowl too, come to think of it—ostensibly for the barn cats, though, rather than the house hob, but the moggies around here wouldn't mind who got the credit for emptying it.

"*Edain! That kilt was clean this morning! You were supposed to be with your father, not rolling with the pigs! Get to the bathroom and clean up* this instant. *And don't you* 'aw, Mom' *me, you little hooligan!*"

Melissa's own mother was speaking in the background; Aylward groaned a little inwardly at that. Eleanor was . . .

Not quite stark raving bonkers, but not quite normal, either, since the Change.

"Why potatoes with the meat again, dear?" she asked Aylward's wife. "Wouldn't some nice steamed rice be pleasant for a change?"

Melissa *growled,* and he heard something heavy slammed down on a counter.

"Mother! Yes, I'd like to use rice. And *coffee* and *chocolate.* But we don't have any! We don't *grow* any. We don't know anyone who grows any!"

Eleanor's voice went on as if she hadn't spoken: "And all this butter with the vegetables, and cooking with all this cream, it's a little *heavy,* isn't it? You've got to watch your figure, with the baby coming. It's so difficult to lose weight again afterward."

Tamar glanced at him and rolled her eyes as he waited for a second with his hand on the latch, mouthing silently: *Grandma's nutsoid today and it's making* Mom *nutsoid.*

Melissa's voice rose and something slammed on a counter, even harder this time. "I got up at five o'clock this morning to milk the *cows,* including Kathy's cows because she carried the milk for me. Then I helped make breakfast for eleven people. Then I spent the morning working in a five-acre *garden.* And collecting eggs and feeding our chickens. Then because I'm pregnant, I got to sit down all afternoon in the garage, *weaving* so we'd have clothes next winter, and in the intervals I can look after Richie and help get *dinner* for twelve ready, and if I weren't pregnant I'd have been out planting *potatoes*! And this is the *easy* part of the year! I need every calorie I eat! And if you can't help, get out of the way!"

He heard the sound of feet rushing off, and Melissa's half-guilty sigh. Tamar and Aylward obediently used the scrapers and brush kept beside the door, then went in and let the spring bang it closed, blinking a little at the bright lamplight and buffing their soles one last time on the interior rug mat. His wife waved from the direction of the stove where she was stirring the soup, and he turned to put his spear in brackets above head-height. His bows hung there too, and the belt with his sword and dirk and buckler, and the rest of the household's weapons—you had to be careful with your killing tools when there were toddlers about.

"Sorry," Melissa said to him over her shoulder from the huge cast-iron woodstove with its attached bread oven and water heater.

It was the envy of Dun Fairfax. Compared to an electric range, it was primitive. Compared to cooking over an open hearth . . .

"Not your fault she's barmy, luv. She forget the Change 'appened again?" Aylward said.

"She remembers, when she wants to," Melissa said, then made herself relax, with a visible effort. "Sorry if I was sniveling about things. But if *I* can adjust to this, why can't she? And when she gets like this, it makes *me* remember, and I don't *want* to."

"It's all what you're used to. Easier for me, considering the way I was raised."

Melissa laughed. "I should count my blessings, then. Dinner's nearly ready. Everyone should be down in a moment."

He'd knocked down some partitions to make the kitchen larger; it had plenty of room for a table that seated twelve, with benches on either side, a seat at each end for him and his wife and a lantern slung from the roof above. Right now a braided equal-armed straw cross hung not far from it, for the Ostara blessing—the images of the Lord and

Lady over the hearth were year-round. A high chair stood beside one of the seats; Richard Aylward came stumping across the floor, chubby arms outstretched.

"*Daaaada!*" he caroled. His father swept him up; he wiggled delightedly, then stretched his arms out to his half sister. "Tama-tamaaar!" Then to the dogs, who stood looking up at him, giving tongue-lolling grins full of the mild benevolence of canines faced with puppies or infants, wagging their tails: "Gri-gri-gri!" which might do for either of their names.

"Well, I can see who *you* prefer, Dickie," Aywlard said, setting the boy down. "Romp away, then." The two-year-old said his favorite word—*No!*—and then fell to with a will.

"How did the last lambing go?" Melissa asked.

Tamar played with her brother and the dogs on the floor. Edain came back in, his light hair sticking up in three or four directions, despite last-minute attempts to slick it down with his fingers, then joined them.

"The delivery went well enough, love," he said, wandering over. "After I turned the lamb. Fair bollixed up to start with, it was, and no mistake."

A small wooden keg rested in an X-trestle of boards on the counter, with mugs on shelves above; he took one down and tapped himself some beer. He'd paid Dennis up at Dun Juniper for it with hops and barley, since the man had the true brewer's knack and Aylward didn't.

"Want one, love?"

"Later, thanks, when I can sit still and enjoy it. The ewe's OK?"

"Dolly's fine, and the lamb should live. Larry shouldn't have had to deal with the whole flock, not this time of year, not the way it's grown. He's well enough with a birthing ewe, but Tamar will learn the way of it better, I think. We might put her and, mmm, young Hickock to work helping him when school's out for summer."

She grinned over her shoulder and whispered. "Not matchmaking, are you?"

"Lord and Lady forbid!" he answered, equally quiet. "Though she and Billy Hickock get on well enough. Give it six or seven years, though."

The rest of the household came in, from the other rooms or from work outside, and busied themselves setting out the cutlery and butter and bread and beer amid a cheerful crackle of conversation about the day's work and gossip and the Ostara dance that would be held in the big threshing-barn after supper. There was Eleanor, over her temper now, Aunt Joan—a nice enough old bird, and unlike her older sister, fully functional, thank God—and the aunt's two children, a boy named Harry about eighteen and a girl called Jeanette a little younger; also two unrelated young men from Sutterdown and their wives. Both couples were working for him to get experience while they saved up to start and stock their own crofts; one of the wives had a new baby and the other was expecting, but not as far along as Melissa.

Not a bad crew, he thought. *And very helpful around the farm.*

As the First Armsman he could call on the other households to fill in for him when he was called off on duty by the Chief, and they could deduct it from their dues to the Clan in turn. It wouldn't even cause much resentment, given how the rest of them had leaned on him for teach-and-show in the early years, when they were learning the farmer's trade and mistakes could mean empty bellies. Still, he preferred to manage from his own resources as much as he could—nobody liked having to neglect their own land. The last of the spring plowing was still to do, barley and potatoes to plant . . .

Though all the youthful energy makes me feel me own age now and then, right enough.

He snaffled off a roll from a pan Melissa had just taken out, tossing it in one callused hand until it was cool enough to eat; it had been a long time since bread and cheese in the saddle at noon, and the steaming-fresh wholemeal was good enough to eat without butter. She smiled sideways at him while she held the oven door open and prodded the meat, then stood and gave him a kiss; a little awkwardly, since she was six months along.

"That's ready . . . make yourself useful then, Sam," she said. "We're supposed to eat it at the table, you know."

The main dish was a roast of pork; the Smiths had slaughtered recently, and everyone swapped around to even out the fresh meat. He lifted the pan out and set it aside to stand for a few minutes before he carved, while Melissa made the gravy; the side dishes were potatoes roasted in the juices, and winter vegetables—boiled parsnips and carrots in a butter sauce, sauerkraut from the crocks in the cellar, and a dried-apple pie with whipped cream for dessert, which latter they'd been having more often since he managed to track down a hand-cranked beater whose owner felt like swapping for a bow.

He brought the great pot of soup to the table first, nose twitching, and ladled it into the bowls handed up. It was potato-and-cream, with bits of onion and densely flavored chunks of bacon that had been cured over applewood in an old Aylward family recipe.

Melissa seated herself at the other end of the table, and said the blessing—another advantage of Wicca, he'd found, was that you could shove off things like that on the lady of the household. He put his spoon to the soup, and lifted it—

"Sam! Sam!"

"Oh, *bugger,*" Aylward said, at the shout and the sound of a fist pounding at the door; then he blew on the soup and swallowed hastily.

Larry Smith stuck his head in, the fog beads in his chin beard glistening. "Sorry, but something took one of the sheep, one of yours—a wether. I didn't hear anything, but Lurp"—the collie—"started barking. There's blood-sign but I couldn't pick up any tracks. It's down in the corner of the field, by the road."

"Bloody hell," Aylward sighed. Then: "You did the right thing."

Larry had been a bookseller before, but he was a fair tracker; he'd actually hunted deer a fair bit even then, and more since. Surprising to an English way of thinking, but the Yanks had had a lot more woodland than old Blighty even before the Change. If he hadn't seen anything, that meant there probably weren't any really obvious tracks.

"It could be anything, dogs or a big cat or some human dinlo," Aylward said.

Men were least likely; it would be bold bandits who went this deep into Mackenzie territory, and such wouldn't settle for one sheep. They'd go for horses and cattle—more valuable and easier to drive off—and for bicycles, tools, cloth, stored food.

Or it might be a trap meant to draw us off and then *raid the dun.*

"Get—" He thought, mentally crossing off the stumble-footed, feeble and incompetent, women pregnant or nursing, and a few steady types to keep an eye on things here. "—yourself, Bob, Alice, Steve, Jerry, and Carl. Full kit, but spears, not bows. It's going to be too dark to shoot worth shite and I wouldn't want to tangle with a cat in the dark without a nice big cat-sticker. Double guard on the wall and everyone else can kit up too, just in case. Meet me at the gate."

Larry nodded, turned and dashed back out. Aylward turned. "Wally, you come with me. Shane, Deirdre, Allison, Nancy, you kit up but head for the walls with the others—it might be a trick. Lively!

"Probably just a hungry dog gone wild," he said to the rest at the table. "But we have to check."

A few of the youngsters on the verge of adulthood looked mutinous about being left out of the search party, but they knew better than to complain openly—this was something that came under his authority as an Armsman, and he didn't tolerate indiscipline.

Someone did mutter plaintively, "Does this mean the dance is off?"

He pulled on his arming doublet with its short sleeves and stiff leather-backed collar of chain mail, the fabric still wet and smelly, and swung his brigandine down from its hook on the wall; the accordion pleat in the leather along the left side let you put it on over your head like a jersey, and then tighten it and strap the catches. Then his sword belt, a bow—he took down and strung his hunting weapon, an eighty-pound popper, better suited to this work than the great war bow—plus quiver and spear; he left the cheek-pieces of the helmet pushed back for a moment.

Melissa and a few of the others had been busy cutting and buttering bread and slicing meat while those he'd named armed themselves. She wrapped the bundle in a cloth and put it into the haversack, then clipped that to the rings on the back of his brigandine and handed him a piece of the pork—the outer cut of the roast with some of the crackling, his favorite.

"You be careful, Sam," she said.

Wally and he knelt and bent their heads briefly as she made a sign over them and went on:

> "Through darkened wood and shadowed path
>   Hunter of the Forest, by your side
>   Lady of the Stars, fold you in her wings
>   So mote it be!"

Then: "I'll put the soup back on to keep hot."

"Thanks, luv," he said.

He gave her another kiss, longer this time, nodded to his children, then stuffed the meat into his mouth as he turned to the door, dogs eager at his heels.

There were tendrils of mist outside, thickening even as he watched. Which would combine with the darkness to make tracking through the woods a total joy . . .

Could be worse, he thought, chewing on the savory slice. *Could be raining.*

Juniper perched on her carved oak and walnut chair cross-legged and made the fiddle sing, swinging into the quick jaunty beat of "Mi ni Nollage," with the bodhran and the flute accompanying her, and a guitar backing up her flourishes, and the sweet wild tones of the uilleann pipes behind it all.

Lanterns and candles lit the ground floor of what had been her great-uncle's lodge and her home, before they rebuilt it and added the upper story and loft; now it was one great high-ceilinged chamber a hundred and twenty-five feet by thirty, surrounded by verandas on three sides and with doors to the new kitchens flanking the hearth in the middle of the north face. The walls were packed with people in their festival best, and more hung through the windows, leaving an oval clear in the middle of the room; all the adults and adolescents who lived in Dun Juniper were making merry tonight, plus many guests from other parts of the Clan's holdings, and a few from outside it. Cedarwood logs crackled in the big stone fireplace, scenting the air.

The last set had been youngsters doing a lively jig—Chuck and Judy Barstow's adoptees, Aoife and Daniel and Sanjay, plus their friends, all in their late teens and enthusiastic. This beat was faster and more complex, though; she looked around the room as she fiddled, to see who'd attempt it.

It's changed a good deal and no mistake.

The logs of the walls had been smoothed and carved in colored running knotwork and faces over the years since the Change—the Green Man peering out through a riot of branches, stag-antlered Cernunnos, goat-horned Pan; Brigid and Cerwidden and Arianrhod and more. In the wood around the upper band and over the hearth were set the symbols of the Quarters; comfrey and ivy and sheaves of grain for North and the Earth; vervain and yarrow for Air and the East; red poppies and nettles for the South and Fire; ferns and rushes and water lilies for West and the Waters.

Eyes shone in the light of pastel candles and lamps set in wrought-iron brackets, hung tonight with ribbons in the same colors, plus baskets of colored eggs. Wreaths of flowers were on many heads, and woven-straw crosses hung from the ceiling—equal-armed, Brigid's crosses, for the Wheel of the Sun. A shout of laughter rose as the Jack-in-the-Green came prancing through. That was young Dave Trent, although you weren't supposed to remember his name tonight; he wore a tight green body stocking sewn all over with vines and leaves, a snub-nosed grinning wooden mask with gilded carved leaves for hair, and flourished a vine-stock wand. The way he handled it made *phallic symbol* entirely plain to the slowest perceptions, and so did his

early-Elvis pelvic gyrations. Then a mob of girls and young
women tried to grab him—or touch the wand, which was
lucky, especially if you wanted to conceive—and he
bounded out with comically exaggerated terror and a goat-
bleat that Juniper matched with a long note on her fiddle
before swinging back into the tune.

The tables had been taken out with the last of supper,
but the doors to the kitchens were still pulled back, and
trays came out laden with pastries shaped like rabbits with
raisins for eyes, dried-fruit confection and slices of cake,
along with mugs of herb-flavored mead and Dennie's
foaming beer and glasses of wine. Hands sought hands . . .

*I'd be guessing we're going to have a fine crop of new
Mackenzies come Yule . . . Well, it* is *a fertility festival, is it
not?* she thought with a wide grin. *The young God rises
ready and randy to wed the Maiden!*

"Well, come on, you cowards!" she called to them all.
"The music's for dancing to, isn't it? We're tapping our feet
on the earth to waken Her from sleep!"

Happy shouts came through the wide-open front doors
as someone leapt over one of the fires for luck; the night
was cool, but the body heat and the blaze on the hearth
and the lanterns kept it warm enough in the hall that the
breeze from outdoors was welcome. She heard the stepping of feet in time to the music, scuffing on the ground
and tapping up the stairs and over the floorboards of the
veranda, and cried greeting with the rest as Astrid and Eilir
burst through the door and out into the open space, making someone taking a shortcut to the jakes dodge aside.

They were both in kilts and singlets and light dancing
shoes with jeweled buckles, their hair done up in braids
under the feathered Scots bonnets, and long staffs in their
hands. Eilir loved dancing, taking her cues from the movements of the musicians and her partners and from vibration felt through the soles of her feet; and Whoever had
presided over Astrid's cradle had filled with extra physical
grace the portion of her that should have contained common sense.

Ah, the Dance of the Spears, Juniper thought as they
went across the floor in file, their feet flashing in unison,

twirling the long poles like batons in blurring arcs, left hand on hip . . .

Sweet Goddess! she realized, almost but not quite startled enough to lose the beat; then she didn't dare alter a note.

Those weren't props; they were real battle spears, seven feet of stout ashwood and sharp-edged steel, as deadly in reality as the legendary Gae Bulg of the Sedanta was in story. One slip—or even one bad stroke of her own fiddle bow throwing the dancers off their stride—

The tune went faster and faster, and they switched to a face-to-face posture; mock-combat, synched to the rhythm, and a *ting!* as steel met steel and *crack!* as wood met wood, leaping, whirling, feet blurring as fast as the silver arcs of the spearheads. Across the room her eyes met the wide, appalled and unbelieving gaze of Chuck Barstow, who'd practiced with edged weapons for years before the Change and every day after it. The crowd gasped; now the two were whirling the spears wrist-over-wrist like quarterstaves as they danced, moving them in huge figure eights and then leaping into the air and letting the momentum pirouette them completely around one last time, kilts flying up to show the strong slender thighs. The spears slowed as they each went down on one knee facing Juniper, the polished heads out and nearly touching the floor as the music crashed to its finish.

The two young faces grinned up at her, sweat-slick and happy, and the crowd was up and cheering and stamping. Astrid and Eilir handed the spears off to their friends—

Accomplices! Juniper thought, torn between pride and fury.

—and stood, arms around each other's shoulders, free arms waving as they turned to take the applause. Rudi dashed out to hug his sister, and the two of them grabbed him and tossed him up between them, throwing him nearly to the ceiling.

A sudden pang took her heart as she looked at them; could life offer them better than this moment? Eilir her heart, and Astrid who she loved nearly as well.

Certainly there's more and better; they're at the springtide of their lives, she thought. *Loves and children of their own, and the wisdom of age, and then the Summerlands . . .*

Though there were likely to be problems there. They weren't lovers, as many assumed—in fact, they found the thought inexpressibly funny, and Eilir had been dragging the odd boy into the bushes these four years past.

It would be easier if they were, Juniper thought. *They're everything but that to each other, which leaves little enough room for a man—or at least a man you'd want.*

For a moment a thought moved in her, formless as roiling cloud, and she closed her eyes—then her will gave it words and purpose. She murmured beneath her breath, moving her hands in certain symbols:

"Sweet foam-born Cyprian, send them each the love that will be best for them. As the Young God rises to wed You in this season, to each send him, send him on the wings of Your wind, send him on the tides of Your sea." Then, surprising herself: "And for me also. By Your Cauldron, by the spear of the Horned Lord, by the joining of the two that brings all creation, *so mote it be!*"

She could feel the spell prayer leave her like a dart cast into a tempest; feel it borne up by winds that smelled of apple blossom and fresh-cut hay and somehow also of musk and heat. Laughter sounded in her ears, proud and fond.

The thought barely had time to bring unease when there was a buzz of comment from outside, and the sound of the gate horn. Seconds later a youngster ran into the Hall, panting and disheveled and slightly damp; she stopped to take a deep breath and smooth down her kilt and plaid before she came to Juniper in the high seat and shyly dipped knee and head, pulling off her bonnet.

Why, it's Melissa's Tamar! Juniper thought. *Must have run all the way up from Dun Fairfax.*

It wasn't that far, even counting the way the hidden direct path wound back and forth up the hillside, but it was steep and awkward in the dark.

"Lady Juniper," she said. "My Dad, he's sent me with a message. Private message."

The girl was fairly bursting with the importance of her mission, and Juniper smiled indulgently.

"*Is i an eorna nua tú a fheiciáil,* Tamar. You're as welcome as the first shoots of barley, and every Mackenzie has a right to speak to the Chief."

She signaled the other musicians to keep going, laid down her fiddle and bent a little to let the girl whisper in her ear. More dancers moved out onto the floor, and the bustle built back.

"He says you should come. Come with Chuck, he said, and no more others than you must. He's found something you need to see."

CHAPTER EIGHT

North Sea/Grand Canaria
August 21st–30th, 2006 AD—Change Year Eight

The captain's cabin of the *Pride of St. Helens* held a bunk, a desk, several chairs, and a curved couch running under a set of large portholes in the stern; drawers and cabinets were built into the walls and under the seats. It was an efficient use of space, giving an impression of room without actually being very large. Three shelves held books; a cutlass, crossbow, helmet and leather tunic with metal inserts were clipped to the bulkhead by the door. On the desk was a photograph—post-Change from the slightly blurry black-and-white look of it—of a handsome middle-aged woman with an eight-year-old boy and a girl a few years younger standing beside her, and an infant in her arms. The other picture on the wall was an oil painting, a landscape with sheep and rolling green hills and a long masonry bridge with a village of stone-built Georgian houses in the background, all looking English but somehow not quite.

"Thank you very much," Sir Nigel said to Captain Nobbes, fighting down a slight pang of envy at the family portrait. *Alleyne's alive; that's what really matters.*

The Tasmanian was a slim man only a few inches over Loring's five-foot-five, snub-nosed, with graying brown hair and close-cropped beard and dark blue eyes, his face tanned dark and lined from years spent at sea. He poured brandy into two glasses, then handed Nigel one before seating himself behind the desk.

"To your escape, Sir Nigel," he said.

Nigel lifted his glass, sniffed and sipped; the brandy was excellent, with a complex fruity aftertaste beneath the bite.

"A Tasmanian brand?" he asked.

"Kiwi. Nelson, South Island," Nobbes said. "I've Bundaberg rum, if you'd rather, six months old and fit to grow hair on yer chest."

He laughed at the flitting expression of distaste on Nigel's face, and went on: "The Kiwis helped finance this expedition—New Zealand's a sort of federation centered on Christchurch, nowadays. I'm afraid the North Island got knackered, with Auckland at one end and Wellington at the other, but the South Island took surprisingly little damage—about like Tasmania, in fact."

"Tasmania sounds rather paradisical."

Nobbes chuckled. "Maybe, compared to the rest of the world. It was tight, but we brought ourselves through with no famine or plague or warlords. Though you should hear how the folk from Hobart and Launceston complained at having to move out to the country and do some real hard graft."

Sixty million dead here would have been thankful for the opportunity, Nigel mused grimly, hiding his thoughts with a sip of the brandy.

He remembered driving refugees back into the waters of the Solent at pike point, and improvised galleys ramming boats where gaunt women held up their children just before the steel-plated bows struck.

And towing rafts of bodies out to sea, with the fish and gulls at them. You fellows had an easy time of it with the Bass Strait and distance between you and the worst.

The ship heeled a little more as a gust of wind struck her sails; Nobbes cocked his head at a volley of orders and rush of feet, and nodded absently in approval at the "Heave-ho!" of a deck team hauling on a rope.

"Taking you in wasn't pure good nature," Nobbes admitted. A smile: "And not just that King Charles gets my royal Aussie hackles up. You've got knowledge and skills that'll be useful on the other part of my mission."

Nigel nodded. "What do you actually *do* with the nuclear weapons?"

"Put them in big steel boxes, fill the boxes with molten. lead—the *Pride*'s ballast is lead ingots in stainless-steel boxes—then dump them in subduction zones off the edges of the continental shelves," Nobbes said.

"Hardly seems worth the trouble," Nigel said. *It will work—thank God for plate tectonics—but . . .* He went on aloud: "Seeing that even if the explosive triggers would function, which they will not, chain reactions are inhibited somehow. Certainly the power reactors just sit and glow, even without the cooling systems. The boffins in Winchester think they'll keep doing that until the isotopes decay."

Nobbes shrugged. "Prime Minister Brown is a raving Green with a bee in his bonnet, and he's popular enough that even those who disagree humor him. Certainly the plutonium is still just as toxic as it was before the Change, and radiation will still kill you just as dead. We *did* have problems with oil tankers, bulk carriers loaded with toxic chemicals, and so forth."

"British ships have orders to scuttle them too," Nigel said. *And how nice it must be to have the chance to worry about environmental issues, rather than starving or having cannibal savages climb down the chimney.* "We've more or less cleared the Atlantic as far south as Gibraltar, come to that."

Nobbes finished his brandy. "Another? No? And then there are the war gasses. We certainly don't want *those* to fall in to the wrong hands. We can't do anything about the ones stored in places like Kazakhstan, but those nearer the coastlines—"

Nigel smiled. "My dear fellow, you don't have to convince *me*. You've saved my life, and my son's, and Hordle's—and Hordle left everything behind and risked his life to save ours, which is a debt I can only repay through your generosity. You're offering us asylum in what appears to be the last outpost of civilization. I'm perfectly willing to work my passage, and I'm well used to implementing plans I consider total codswallop, simply because I'm told to do it. Dealing with the war gasses isn't even that dangerous, if you're careful. The organophosphate nerve agents can be neutralized with running water in quantity—it takes out the chlorine atom, and you can burn the others—though granted, you'd best be a good bit upwind when you do it. And you'd best be *very* careful about containers that have become leaky, what?"

"Beaut!" Nobbes said decisively. "I can't tell you how comforting it is to have a bloke who really *understands* this garbage."

Nigel went on: "And more concretely, Alleyne and I have both had experience at sea. Small-boat training before the Change, and on sail since; we can both shoot the sun and lay a course. Sergeant Hordle . . . well, he can hand, reef and steer, and if you're in the habit of sending shore parties into danger, then you could travel about the globe twice before finding as good a man of his hands as Little John Hordle. Crack shot, too; he's been rated Archer Instructor for the Guard these three years now."

Nobbes's eyes lit. "Now, all that will be *immediately* useful. I lost my second and third lieutenants in a job-up with pirates off Diego Garcia this spring, and it's been a bloody nightmare with only myself and the XO as watchkeepers. Let's do a tour, shall we?"

The deck of the *Pride* was a long clear sweep, fore and aft, one hundred eighty feet of decking with only a slight raised coaming before the wheel, and another forward of the mainmast that led down to the forecastle. Two launches lay keel-up on either side of the mainmast, and another hung in its davits over the stern. Under tarpaulins five catapults crouched with shrouded menace, two on either side and one abaft the wheel. Nigel strolled forward to the mainmast, returning cheerful smiles and nods—the crew had evidently taken to them after that little brush at the Wash.

"That went rather well," Nigel said, after the captain had left, as his son and John Hordle joined him.

Hordle still had a chunk of bread in one hand and a chicken leg in the other, not being afflicted with seasickness, and his hazel eyes shone with contentment. They leaned on the railing and watched the dark blue-green waters of the North Sea rushing past in a long foam-tipped curve down the gray steel hull of the schooner; the wind was out of the west where the low coast of East Anglia showed in the distance, and the deck's smooth yellow huon pine planking was canted like a low-pitched roof as the ship leaned away with her sails swelling in taut beige curves. Bursts of spray sped back along the deck as the bowsprit pitched up at the top of every swell, tasting cold and salt on the lips.

"Positions on the *Pride,* and asylum and probably land if we want it at the other end," Nigel went on. "Tasmania's well beyond the king's reach—or the queen's, more to the point."

Just then a voice rang out from the masthead a hundred and twenty feet above their heads: "Sail ho!"

The three Englishmen tensed. Beside the wheel the vessel's executive officer turned her head up and raised the speaking-trumpet in her hand; long strands of black hair flew out from under her billed officer's cap as she called, "Where away? What rig?"

"Nor' nor'east, ma'am! Barque-rigged, three-master."

"What colors?"

"I can't see . . . wait a bit! Well, fuck me! It's a jumbuck *holding* a flag, on their flag!"

The three relaxed. Nigel frowned as well; the Australian concept of discipline had never appealed to him, and this troop of merry-andrews made the pre-Change Australian military look like the Grenadier Guards. Still, they got things done . . . And he knew who used a sheep holding a banner as their blazon.

"Lieutenant Flandry!" Nigel called. "That's the Visby arms. She'll be a Norlander, a Swede out of the island of Gotland, probably heading for Dover with paper salvaged from their mills."

Dominique Flandry nodded. "Thank you, Sir Nigel. I remember that briefing paper you had done up for us when we made Southampton."

That had been back before his arrest; he'd done up an appreciation from the survey reports—some of them from survey parties he'd led in person. The Tasmanians had naturally wanted to know the state of Europe. That was extremely simple for most areas west of the Vistula:

Everyone died. There were exceptions, of course. Born-holm and some of the other Baltic islands like Gotland and Oland and the Alands were among them, analogous to the Isle of Wight as opposed to mainland Britain. And a fair-sized clump of towns in northern Norway had made it through the Change, courtesy of isolation and a huge NATO ration dump they'd discovered, along with villages in the more remote parts of Sweden. That came to a quarter million in total, and lately they'd cobbled together a loose federation called Norland under a scion of the Norwegian royal house, to resettle the empty death zones of southern Scandinavia. They claimed adjacent Germany as well, and there wasn't anyone to say them no, except for a few thousand neo-savages.

"Nothing to worry about this time," Alleyne said. "But."

Hordle tossed the fleshless chicken bone over the side and wiped the dark red furze on the back of one of his hands across his mouth.

"Right you are, sir. *But.* Twenty people knew what we were planning to get you out; there wasn't time to set it up bit by bit. What're the odds on a secret staying secret when that many know it?"

"Somewhere between twenty to one against and zero, Sergeant," Nigel said crisply. "For that matter, the *Pride*'s course will look dashed odd, given that she was supposed to be heading for the Americas."

They looked at each other. "It depends on what the king decides to do," Hordle said. "He *could* just decide to forget about us, I suppose. Even though we've made him look a right burke."

"And the queen. You'd be closer to the truth if you said it depends on what she talks him around to doing," Alleyne replied. "Having met the woman, I'd say that's pretty well anything, given time. And she's spiteful."

"Perhaps I shouldn't have lost my temper with her in public," Nigel admitted, remembering eyes gray as a glacier. "And I should have remembered her namesake, and that her people's literature is entirely concerned with blood feuds and revenge."

They all looked at each other again, and then out to the

English coast. "Not time to relax just yet," Hordle said with a sigh.

"I think we'd best acquaint ourselves with our duties on this ship," Nigel said. "And leave the matter of pursuit to the evil day."

Because there's damn all we can do about it, he thought.

John Hordle sucked at a barked knuckle as they slid down the ropes to the waiting longboats. Above them the side of the *Kobayashi Maru* reared in a rust-streaked iron wall. The big tanker had been listing hard to port when the *Pride*'s lookout spotted it, with an oil slick behind it a hundred miles long. Even as the boarding party left you could see how she'd begun to settle as water flooded into her spaces from the open scuttlin-cocks. For a moment he wondered idly where the crew had ended up. According to the log they'd rigged the ship's lifeboats with improvised masts and sails ten days after the Change, meaning to try for the coast of Argentina and then come back with help.

Must 'ave been a bit of a shocker if they made land, and found out the truth, he thought. Then he shrugged—if they'd survived at all, they'd done better than most of the human race.

It was a hot late-August day on the Atlantic; they were standing off the Portuguese coast, with land out of sight on the eastern horizon. The water stretched like hammered blue-green metal around them, riffled by a mild breeze and a long low swell out of the west. Like many of the crew, he had a bandana tied about his head; like all of them he wore loose blue trousers and bloused shirt, belt with a sailor's knife, and bare feet. Most of them were Tasmanians, with Kiwis second and Aussies from the mainland third; a few were wildly varied, picked up all over the world on the *Pride*'s great survey voyage.

Sir Nigel and his son wore the same outfit as Hordle, but with shoes and peaked caps—officer's garb. That had caused a few minor problems—the elder Loring was no martinet, but the Ozlander conception of rank was still a little too casual for someone who'd started in the Blues and Royals. Also, he didn't regard *"She'll be right, mate"* as an appropriate attitude to problems.

"That was a proper job of work," Hordle said; the supertanker's manual scuttling-cocks had been awkwardly placed in dark narrow spaces and rusted solid to boot. "Why bother? It was going to sink soon anyway. Hull must be like a lace tea cozy beneath the waterline."

"British ships have the same regulation, Sergeant," Sir Nigel said, taking the tiller with an expert's hand. "Hulks are a navigation hazard. Besides that, tankers do less damage if they sink in deep water rather than break up on a coast, and we're over the Iberian Abyssal Plain here."

"Ah," Hordle said; that made sense. Eventually the black goo decayed naturally, but it could foul a shoreline for years, and there had been a *lot* of tankers at sea eight years ago. *The only thing crude oil's good for now is killing fish.* "Funny how everyone wanted the stuff before the Change, and now we want to get rid of it."

There was a murmur of agreement as the longboat's crew ran out their oars and sculled for the *Pride* where she lay hove-to half a mile away. Some ships had cargoes that were still valuable even after all this time—medicines and luxury goods mainly, though even intact toilet paper was worth a fair bit. He knew men who worked full time at salvage, although merchantmen still afloat were growing rarer and rarer as time and tide and storms had their way with them.

Hordle stood in the bow of the longboat, ready with the boathook. The Lorings and he had fitted easily enough into the *Pride*'s crew, since their small-boat skills were readily transferable; they'd all gone together on expeditions up the Seine and Loire, and once overland to the Rhône, down it and out through the Med in a ship that met them there. The Tasmanians also struck him as being a little less belligerently Aussie than most Ozlanders he'd met before the Change, which was pleasant; he'd worked with the Down Under SAS on his single deployment east of Suez.

Good-enough blokes, good fighting men, but always putting on the Digger and trying to show up the whingeing

Poms, he thought. *You'd think they'd all landed at Gallipoli last week, with a jolly jumbuck under each arm, straight up.*

The ship grew from a bobbing toy to its respectable two-hundred-foot length. Hordle looked down the length of the longboat, to where his opposite number was ready to hook on at the stern; she was named Sheila Winston, a pleasantly shaped brunette of twenty-two with snapping eyes whose usual job was in the galley. He'd had his eye on her, and he suspected vice versa. Being on a ship with a mixed crew did make things a little less dull, although he'd have liked it better if the mix had been more even, instead of three men per woman, or the regulations less strict. Still, he had the advantage of not being in the *Pride*'s chain of command—formally, that was.

"Oars . . . *up!*" Sir Nigel called.

The long wood shafts went up in bristling unison; where it counted, the Tasmanians were perfectly capable of doing what they were told, quick and neat. Hordle reached out deftly and caught the boathook in the rope that ran along the scuppers. A petty officer on deck made a polite request that the boat not scuff the ship's paint, and added more obscene embellishments as the boat crew went up the Jacob's ladder and the smaller craft rocked and swayed; two stayed for an instant to hook on the hosting tackle. Then the cry of "Haul away" came, and a dozen deckhands tallied on to the gear. The boat rose dripping from the water, with Hordle and Sheila Winston fending off still as it was swung inboard and hung from the davits.

Think I'll go bother the cook, Hordle thought as he stepped down to the deck, the worn huon pine smooth under the skin of his feet.

The *Pride*'s chief of galley was a genial Fijian who'd been in Nelson on the South Island at the time of the Change, and who outweighed Hordle though he was six inches shorter. It smelled like the midday meal was under way, and the fresh provisions loaded in Britain hadn't quite run out yet, plus overside fishing had yielded fairly well. They weren't quite down to salt pork and ship's biscuit yet.

You know, there's a good deal to be said for not *having anyone on your trail,* he thought happily.

Alleyne Loring turned at a nod from Captain Nobbes: "Set all plain sail," he barked.

The crew sprang to the ropes at a cascade of orders from the bosun and mast-captains; Hordle tallied on to the nearest. The *Pride*'s sails unfolded as the gaffs rose up the masts, the free outer edges shaking and thuttering as they swung, then cracking taut. The schooner's nose turned south as she fell off the wind and the staysails up forward bit, and the movement grew swifter as steerage way came on her and the wheel turned. Water began to chuckle down the sides, and the bowsprit tracked a long slow corkscrew, a rise-swoop-and-fall motion instead of the short hard pitching she'd made with her nose into the swell.

A voice rang out from the topmast: "On deck there! Sail ho!"

"Where away?" Captain Nobbes called upward through his megaphone.

Good-enough sailor, Hordle thought. *Not that I'm any great judge. Thinks he's Horatio sodding Hornblower, that's the problem. Or that other one, in the books Sir Nigel likes, written by the Irishman.*

"A bit north of leeward, Skipper. Nor' nor'east."

"What rig? What colors?"

"Ship rig; three masts; all sail set. Flying the White Ensign. A bloody big drongo of a ship, Skipper! Coming on fast."

Well, stone the crows. I shouldn't have tempted fate like that, not even on the quiet. He ducked into the forecastle. The crew racked their personal weapons under their bunks.

Nigel Loring adjusted easily as the *Pride* heeled, and watched the crew at work. They totaled forty-five, more than were necessary to work the schooner—this rig was economical of labor—but on an exploratory voyage these days you could expect to fight, and to lose some before you returned. Right now the booms of the big fore-and-aft sails were swung out over the water to port, and the schooner's sharp bow cut across the swell directly southward, at ninety degrees to the wind. Then that died down, stuttered back, shifted and backed, coming more from the north. The sky was cloudless save in that direction, an arch of perfect blue turning paler where shadows fell towards the west. In the north clouds piled like thick beaten cream, shading to gold and black where they towered high.

"Set gaff topsails!" the captain called. Then: "Lay aloft and loose main and fore t'gallants and square topsails!"

A topsail schooner carried square sails as well as fore-and-aft; in the *Pride*'s case, two each on the upper main-mast and foremast. They helped considerably when you weren't working into the teeth of the wind, but they re-quired more work: someone had to climb out the yards and let them loose, whereas the fore-and-aft sails on their booms could be worked from the deck. Crew rushed up the ratlines and out along the slender-seeming spars, their feet on the manropes, bending to wrench at the hard knots that held the sails bundled. Canvas thuttered and cracked a hundred and twenty feet up, like distant gunfire, and taut beige shapes of New Zealand flax bellied out in the wind. The ship heeled further as the wind caught in the four square sails and levered down through the masts and keel. Nobbes kept a careful eye aloft, wincing at loud creaks.

"That's the disadvantage with wooden topmasts," he said. "They're just not as strong as steel."

"But more replaceable," Nigel pointed out. *It's all very well to love your ship,* he thought. *But Nobbes takes it to an extreme.*

Of course, it was Nobbes's ship in a very special sense; before the Change he'd owned it, and run it around the South Pacific on excursions for people who wanted a taste of life in the old days. He'd been in St. Helens on the east coast of Tasmania when the Change struck, and ended up in the Tasmanian navy fairly quickly, albeit mostly running cargo and passengers. Some of his old attitude remained.

"Well, there is that," he said. "They're building a new class much like this back in Tassie, but wooden-hulled with steel diagonal bracing on the ribs. I'm supposed to get one—compensation for the government taking the *Pride,* and all the years I sailed her for 'em. I've some cobbers who'll help me find cargoes, then it's up to Malaysia for rubber, and over to Burma for teak and rice, Ceylon for tea and coffee and cinnamon and back again. I could use a good man or two to help with that—it gets bloody lively, what with the pirates and all. Couple of years and I'd go partners on a new ship."

"I'd rather thought I'd take up land," Sir Nigel said. "I understand there's a good deal available, and it's what I know, allowing for differences in the climate."

"Plenty of room on the mainland, sport, right enough, or on North Island," Nobbes said absently; his eyes were still on the rigging. "But the land's cheap for a reason; things can get pretty rough there. Tassie and South Island are full up, what with all the people out of the towns and on the farms and stations—there's agitation to break up the bigger ones. Fancy themselves as bunyip barons, some of the stationholders do; and over on the mainland, a lot of them *are* bloody barons. Accent on the bloody, too."

Nigel nodded. From what he'd heard, the big cities of mainland Australia and New Zealand's more densely populated North Island had collapsed as thoroughly as any in Europe or Asia or America, and they'd taken circles of countryside two hundred miles across with them. Of course, that left a lot of Australia untouched—the circles hadn't overlapped as they had in more densely peopled lands.

Still, Alleyne and Hordle and I could handle any roughness *where we wanted to set up, I suppose . . .*

The sound of the water slapping its way along the *Pride*'s hull changed, becoming a little louder, a little faster, like palms beating out a choppy rhythm on a drum. The motion altered as well, turning longer and smoother, a rocking-horse surge that spoke of sea miles gone away.

"With the wind on our beam like this, that'll give us an extra knot, setting the t'gallants," Nobbes said with satisfaction. He turned to the binnacle just forward of the wheel. "Eleven . . . eleven and a half knots."

Then he looked back over the fan-shaped rail at his ship's stern, over the tarpaulin-clad shape of the catapult crouching on its turntable.

"Odd running into another ship here," he said meditatively.

"Not so odd as all that. Southampton-Gibraltar is the busiest shipping route we have now—that Britain has now. Which isn't saying much, I grant you."

Nobbes grunted. "*Bloody* odd Gibraltar made it," he said.

"A combination of luck and geography," Sir Nigel said. "Though it took considerable ability to organize it all."

Nobbes brought up the heavy binoculars that hung around his neck.

"She's just hull-up now," he said. "Sailing with the wind abeam is the best point for a square-rigger, but even so she's very fast . . . she'll pass us in a day or two on this heading. There's not many ships could come up from behind on the *Pride,* if I do say so myself. They're cracking on, though. I wonder what their hurry is?"

A suspicion coiled in Nigel's stomach. "Hordle, step up here if you please," he said. The big man did. Nigel went on: "You were stationed in Southampton for a while, weren't you? At the dockyard, while I was off on that diplomatic mission to the Principality."

"That I was. Didn't envy you a trip to Ian's Rump, either, sir."

Nigel frowned slightly; in fact, he shared the opinion. The Principality of Ulster might loudly proclaim its loyalty to the king, and to his brother Prince Andrew—chance had stranded the latter there when the Change came—but he didn't particularly like the bloody-minded military–Orange Order-cum-Free Presbyterian junta that had ended up ruling the northeastern quarter of Britain's sister island—or what was left of it, between starvation and mutual pogrom.

"Take a look," he said, handing over his own binoculars. "Tell me if you recognize that ship."

Hordle looked for a moment, and pursed his lips. "No doubt about it, sir. *Cutty Sark.* I saw her in for repairs, after she shuttled in her last load of Icelanders, back in CY3."

Nigel whistled silently, and Nobbes went slightly pale. Partly, Nigel thought, because that might mean the king had decided to give chase regardless, and to hell with offending far-off Tasmania; the *Cutty Sark* was a Royal Navy vessel now. And partly because the ship was legendary, the last and greatest of the China tea clippers, brought back to sit in glory in drydock on the Thames after a career that had included record-breaking runs on every route she sailed.

"But sir?" Hordle went on. "They had us doing fetch-and-carry work there, and from what I heard of the dockyard maties talking, she wasn't what you'd call sound even then. Even for something a hundred and thirty years old."

Alleyne's regular-featured face was thoughtful as he nodded. "I read the report, Father. Her keel—the wooden keel—is waterlogged, and the corrosion on her frame . . ." He turned to Nobbes. "Captain, you know she's iron-framed, with plank sheathing?"

Nobbes snorted. "Yes," he said, in a tone that also meant *And the sun comes up in the east too, my gracious Pommie-lad.*

"Sorry, sir. Well, the frame's been corroding—not just weakening it, they could cure that with riveted patches, but the rust is pushing the stringers away. She needed to be stripped bare in drydock, chipped down to solid metal, and rebuilt from the keel up. Instead they just did what they could from the outside, pounded in more caulking, and kept putting the basic work off. Perhaps they thought it would be easier simply eventually to scrap her and build new."

"She's still almighty fast," Nobbes said thoughtfully.

"Not as fast as she was once," Alleyne said. "They also cut down her sail plan, to lessen the strain on the hull and the working of the planks. Not so many studding sails and such."

"What have they been doing with her?"

"Refugees at first, starting in March of 'ninety-nine. Then cargo on the Gibraltar run," Alleyne said. "Manufactured goods and settlers out, food and fiber back—sugar, cotton, wine, citrus, olive oil."

Nobbes grinned in a lopsided way. "England has an empire again, eh?"

"In a way," Nigel said; the irony of it had struck him too. "Interesting to see how that turns out ..."

"It'll be interesting to see if the *Sark*'s loaded with troops and out to see us knackered," Hordle said bluntly, jerking his head northward. "Sir."

Nigel winced slightly, but there was no point in delaying further. "Perhaps it's rude of me to ask, but what will you do, Captain, if it is?"

Nobbes looked embarrassed, and spoke reluctantly: "I'll run like buggery, Sir Nigel. If they catch us up and it's just a matter of dodging, or trading catapult bolts at long range, I'll do that. But if it means saving my ship and crew, I'll have to hand you over, and that's the dinkie die."

"I appreciate your honesty, Captain Nobbes," Nigel said courteously.

And Hordle looks like he's thinking of ripping your head off in that event, and I think you're beginning to notice. Best defuse matters and change the subject.

He relaxed and smiled. "Let's hope we can avoid such a choice, eh? And that ship *could* just be running down to the Rock. We're ... they're ... resettling the choice bits of southern Spain and northern Morocco—the Gibraltarians and immigrants get farms, the realm gets trade, everyone's happy. Though the ghosts must be raining curses on us in Spanish and Arabic."

"Thought of moving there meself, sir, and taking up land," Hordle said, glad of a chance to break the momentary chill. "Nice climate and the brambles aren't as thick about the edges as back in old Blighty."

"Maybe God *is* an Englishman," Nobbes said. "The world drops dead, and the Poms get the whole of Western Europe out of it."

"Only if we breed very enthusiastically," Alleyne said. "Killing off all but one in every two hundred of us seems an odd way for the Supreme Being to show family-feeling, even if it does make many corners of foreign fields forever England in times to come. Though I think it's definite that He isn't French, what?"

Nigel nodded. "On the evidence, my boy, He seems to be Tasmanian."

"I thought Australia was bad, until I saw Europe," Nobbes said, with a gesture of half agreement. "And America's worse if anything . . ."

"Most of the parts we can reach are bones," Nigel said judiciously. "Some islands did well and we don't know anything about the interior or the western portion."

Alleyne put in: "There's quite a few Italians left, though— ten thousand in the Alps, fifty thousand in that clump in Umbria, two hundred thousand on Sicily. A fair number of Greeks farther east on Crete and Cyprus, and of course as you get east of central Poland . . . It *will* be interesting to see how things shape in the next couple of generations."

Nobbes nodded. "Right now we'll see if *Cutty Sark* really is chasing us. Clear for action!" he called. "Helm, come about—right ten degrees. Let's see how high that beaut can point."

"Damn my eyes, but she's fast," Nobbes said, standing by the wheel of his ship and watching the *Cutty Sark* in the double circles of his binoculars as she tacked, beating up into the wind.

For the *Pride,* that was easy—just put the helm over, let the fore-and-aft booms swing across the deck above head-height, and the ship was making another leg of its zigzag course upwind. A square-rigger couldn't point nearly as close to the wind, and it was much easier for her to be "caught in irons," left bobbing helplessly with her sails pressed back against the masts and yards. The *Sark* was crossing her bowsprit over the eye of the wind nearly as nimbly as the schooner.

"And . . . mainsail *haul*," Nobbes murmured, the command that would set the crew to pulling the big square sails round on the clipper.

I think our good skipper is envious, Nigel thought, amused despite the tension of the moment. *But then, what sailing-ship captain wouldn't be?*

As they watched, the tall sail pyramid of the pursuer passed through the vertical and lay over; the sails that had been clewed up to the yards dropped down again and her bow-wave grew taller, until white water raced from her knife-sharp prow down the long sleek sides and her mizzen chains were nearly buried in the foam.

"My oath, but she's *fast*," Nobbes said again. "If she weren't sailing four miles to our three, she'd have caught us by now. *And* she's got three times my displacement and a crew to match."

"Do you think there's much hope?" Alleyne Loring said.

At Woburn Abbey, Sir Nigel and his wife had been under administrative detention on vague allegations of sedition. If the Lorings and Hordle were recaptured, they would face court-martial on very specific charges: desertion, murder and levying war against the forces of the Crown for all three of them—a noose for Sergeant Hordle, and the gentleman's ax for the officers. Swords and armor weren't the only ancient things that had turned up resurgent in the aftermath of the Change, and the Emergency Powers regulations were still very much in force. That had been one of the matters Sir Nigel had objected to.

"Well," Nobbes said, then unexpectedly grinned. "Not much hope on a straight chase like this. What's more, a few hundred more miles and we hit the westerlies—and running before a wind, we wouldn't have a chance in hell of keeping ahead. But the glass is falling, and those clouds look dangerous."

"Ah," Nigel said. "And in a blow—"

"Right, sport. I've a solid welded steel hull under me arse, and steel lower masts and steel-cable running rigging. That beaut old lady has fragile bones. The worse the blow, the better for us. Let's see what the weather has in mind."

Be careful what you pray for, Sir Nigel thought six days later. *You may get it.*

The bowsprit of the *Pride* rose and rose, until the on-rushing wave seemed to tower above them like a mountain of steel-gray water, sliding down towards them with a ponderous inevitability. The top began to curl, collapsing under its own weight and the fury of the northerly gale. Long streamers of spray and foam flew out from its top, ghostly in the half-light through the dense cloud overhead. More surged down the slope ahead of the breaking wave . . .

. . . and struck.

White water leapt ahead of the surge as the bows went under, and the wave raced the length of the *Pride*'s deck towards him. He braced himself, involuntarily flinging up an arm before his eyes, and then the water struck—first a foam like the head on a giant's glass of beer, then a solid smashing blow of cold sea. The cord that linked his belt to the safety line stretching fore and aft kept him from going over the taffrail as he was tumbled and pounded in the darkness, but when the wave passed he was on his knees, coughing the wrack out of his lungs as he blinked his eyes and checked that the two helmsmen were still on either side of the wheel.

They were; one of them was John Hordle, and he grinned under his dripping sou'wester. His mouth moved—he was probably shouting, but the keening wail of the wind through the rigging and the white roar of the water made it impossible to hear at all, much less to understand. One moment's error by either of them, and the *Pride* would broach to, tumble as the waves took her sidewise and sink like a rock with all hands in thirty seconds of terror.

Nigel scrambled up; the schooner was cresting the wave like a chip of wood washing onto a beach, and as she cleared the crest the force of the wind snatched the breath from his mouth and made the skin of his face burn. For an instant he could see for miles, across a seascape of waves three-quarters hidden by the white froth that tore from their tops, as if the ship was sailing through the storm clouds themselves rather than the ocean. Then the two scraps of staysail set forward to keep her nose into the wind caught the full force of the gale and jerked her forward with an acceleration that made his teeth snap together. She skidded down the steep north face of the wave like a skier down a mountainside, faster and faster, the high whine of the rigging turning to a deeper note as the walls of water gave a momentary protection from the storm. Another burst of seawater came over the bows and raced along the deck as they slid into the trough of the wave and dug in for an instant; this time the wave was only waist-high when it struck the quarterdeck, and he kept his feet easily enough.

As the *Pride* began the long slow climb up the next wave rain slashed down. At first Nigel didn't notice it—everything was thoroughly wet as it was—but soon it cut visibility noticeably. The cold chill that made his bones ache in the spots where they'd been broken and put knives in his joints was no worse, but it *felt* so. It took him a moment to realize that the two dim figures in their gray rain slickers were newly on deck.

"You are a good relief," he said semiformally to Alleyne—or as formally as you could when you had to shout to be heard—and then smiled. "And a very welcome one! Is the galley fire lit?"

"It is, Father. And plenty of *actual tea.* I'm getting quite used to it again."

The other was Captain Nobbes. He shouted something, then repeated it as he came closer, snapping his safety cord onto the lifeline with practiced ease.

". . . you taste it?" he was asking. "The rain!"

Well, it's rain, Nigel thought, then concentrated; he knew better than to dismiss something an expert said about his own field. He took a mouthful of the downpour and ran it over his tongue—it was pleasant to get the salt taste out of his mouth anyway.

"*Grit!*" he shouted back. "*There's grit in the rain!*"

Nobbes grinned back under his sou'wester and came close enough to bellow into the Englishman's ear. "We're off the coast of northwest Africa, then—I thought so, from the way the wind was turning, and that clinches it. Read about the grit in an old book they dug out of a museum for us. It's Saharan sand. Means the storm will blow out soon."

"I hope God's listening—or Poseidon, Captain!" Nigel shouted back cheerfully.

And I actually feel *cheerful,* he thought in mild amazement, as he and Hordle went down the companionway. *I rather thought that wouldn't happen again.*

The bigger, younger man held the door open for him— no easy feat, with the wind this strong. The howl of it gave way to a low toaning moan as the rubber-edged steel shut behind them, and they hung their oilskins and sou'westers on a rack over a trough to catch the drips; a dim lantern behind thick glass lit the narrow corridor. Hordle hurried forward then, and while Loring was still struggling with his boots he came back with a great covered mug of tea and a small basket of the scone-like soda bread the Australians were fond of, buttered and spread with marmalade—Royal Cornish Reserve, probably a gift from someone at court to the Tasmanian emissaries.

"Thank you, Sergeant," he said, yawning. "You should go get some rest."

Hordle's face was still running with seawater. "Going to go chat up that cook's apprentice some more, sir," he said. "Sheila, her name is. I can see she fancies a well-set-up lad, and I can sleep when I'm dead."

Or when you're fifty-two, Nigel thought, as he toweled himself down in the tiny cabin.

Weariness struck despite the strong hot tea, despite the pitching and rolling. He barely had time to finish the last scone before his head hit the pillow.

"Sound as a bell," Captain Nobbes said happily. "Didn't even lose a sail."

The *Pride*'s nose was west of south now, and the wind was behind them, on their starboard quarter. The sun was hot despite the fresh wind, and the ocean was a deep purple-blue frothed with lines of whitecaps; the schooner bucked almost playfully as they cut the swell. The deep iodine scent of the sea and the tarred rope of the running rigging went together well; Nigel found himself looking forward to lunch, which was to feature tunny steaks in cheese—the lines trolled overside had been productive this morning.

"That's La Palma?" he asked. The mountain was rising gradually from the sea ahead.

"Unless we're all worse navigators than we're likely to be, or the chronometer's gone for a Burton," Nobbes said. "We stood farther out to sea on our way up from the Cape, but we'll see about wood and water here this time. It's uninhabited now, eh?"

"Nearly," Alleyne said grimly. "Unless you count Moorish corsairs stopping in now and then."

"I thought you said . . . never mind. Later. We'll keep a sharp—"

"Ship ho!" called the masthead lookout, sitting braced where the t'gallant yard crossed the main topmast. "Over that spit ahead."

"What rig?" Nobbes called sharply.

"No bloody rig at all, Skipper!" the lookout called. "And she's not alone, either. Looks like boats putting in and out from the shore, or something like that."

Nobbes looked at his XO without needing to speak.

"Helm, fifteen degrees west—thus, very well, thus," she said.

The schooner turned smoothly, falling off the steady westerly breeze. The island ahead was an irregular cone, greener higher up the slopes, arid-barren below where the irrigation systems had collapsed. Before the Change it had lived mainly off tourism with a minor sideline in exporting specialty crops; neither had proved much help afterward. But there were still sheltered coves, and springs where you could get good water, and wood in the ravines if you didn't mind the scattered bones. There were even feral goats and pigs whose ancestors had hid very, very well, and a few villages of survivors further south.

"That's the *Sark!*" Alleyne said as they rounded the spit of land.

The bay beyond was a perfect semicircle, with white ruined houses on the shore above the rugged cliffs, and a fringe of palms at the top. The ship was afloat half a mile away from the northern point the schooner rounded, and anchored an equal distance from the shore.

"Poor bitch," Nobbes muttered.

It took Nigel a moment to realize that the seaman meant the ship; he leveled his binoculars for a closer look. The *Cutty Sark* certainly seemed deserving of pity; down by the head and listing to port, with all three masts off at the tops and the rigging a crazy tangle of broken wire and knotted rope amid a few jury-rigged scraps. Water spurted out from her decks as the pumps worked in what was obviously a losing race with the inrushing sea; her gunwales were far closer to the surface than they should be. At a guess sections of planking had come loose in the storm, and she'd limped in here hoping to make repairs—or at least find a spot where the crew could wait for rescue when she went under. Ropes over the side held sails fothered over patches of the bottom. Two longboats put off from the shore as he watched, pulling hard for the ship and abandoning a fire that sent a slim pillar of smoke up into the azure sky.

The other boats coming around the southern point of the bay were worthy of attention as well, and certainly why the shore party was hurrying back. The pumps also stopped as he watched, the jets of water pulsing and then dying to trickles as the crews went scrambling for harness and weapons.

"Moors," he said grimly to the Tasmanian captain. "And far too many of them for comfort."

The boats that spider-walked into the bay were long and low and narrow, with sharp knifelike prows and sterns that looked identical; they were giant versions of the Senegalese sea-fishing pirogue, and those ocean-going canoes had often been up to sixty feet long even before the Change. These averaged a hundred feet, fitted with twenty oars a side rather than paddles, and each had a single mast and lanteen sail. Their hulls were caravel-built, made from overlapping planks adzed to fit and painted a blue-green color that made them surprisingly hard to see even at close range; and they were dark with men. He suspected the interior bracing was salvaged metal, though that was much rarer in Senegal than Europe—still, there were the ruins of Dakar and St. Louis to mine.

"And there are a round dozen of them," Nobbes said. "How many men?"

"Alleyne?" Nigel asked, handing him the glasses.

"Rough counting, sixty to eighty a hull," the sharp-eyed younger Loring said after a moment. "Call it between seven and nine hundred in all."

Nobbes grunted; half thoughtful, half sounding as if he'd been belly-punched. The *Pride*'s total crew was less than a tenth of even the lowest estimate. The whole British army wasn't much larger these days. Africa below the Sahara had suffered gruesomely in the Change and its aftermath, but not as badly as the lands farther north.

"Well, we know we're not being chased any bloody more," he said. "Those poor bastards on the *Sark* aren't going anywhere."

"The Moors don't take prisoners," Nigel said. "Except as slaves. And they, ah, surgically modify those."

Nobbes winced and licked his lips, glancing around, obviously conscious of eyes on him from all along the deck. He looked at the calm surface of the bay. "Not much wind in there," he said meditatively. "If we go in, we'll have to break them before we can get out—wouldn't be able to run if it went against us. The land shelters the bay from the westerlies . . . think they could hold out on the *Sark* until we arrived?"

Unexpectedly, it was Hordle who answered; the two Lorings stood silent, respecting the Tasmanian's authority as Captain.

"Yes, sir," Hordle said. "They might not be able to drive them all off, bunged about as they are, but they'll put up a stiff fight." Pridefully: "They'll know they've had English archers to deal with! Best thing Charlie ever did was make practice with the bow compulsory, and those'll be professionals, regulars."

Nigel waited, willing himself not to tense. At last Nobbes shook himself and shrugged. "Blood's thicker than water," he said, and went on with a laugh: "especially among the First Families of Tasmania—who were transported pickpockets married to whores, like my great-great-great-great-granddad. Sound to quarters, Number Two. I want us two hundred yards off her stern, and we'll anchor with the bow to shore, make it a T. And get the toaster ready."

Nobbes glanced at Nigel as the hoarse beat of a drum and a volley of orders broke the immobility of the crew, turning them from spectators to a purposeful mass, breaking open the weapons locker and pulling the tarpaulin covers from the catapults. Others bustled about pulling bolts and raising what looked like sections of the deck. Those turned out to be heavy wooden screens, secured to the rail with quick-release metal clamps to make a continuous chest-high barricade around the bulwarks save where the catapults needed a clear field of fire.

"They'll come in on either side of the *Sark*?" Nobbes asked.

"Two deep," Nigel agreed. "They're a vicious lot and they hate us like poison, but they're not stupid in my experience. That'll let them maximize their numbers, and they'll try and finish the *Sark* before we can intervene. Alleyne, let's get into our harness."

"Those Ned Kelly suits?" Nobbes said. "You'll go down like Ayers Rock if you go overboard in those!"

Nigel grinned; he felt a good deal more comfortable coming to the rescue of his countrymen than he did running away from them.

"Well, Captain, we'll just have to make sure that the enemy are the ones who fall in, eh, what?"

"There they go," Hordle said, his voice taut.

The *Pride* was ghosting into the bay, with all sails set. That did less good than they had hoped, with only the faintest breeze from over the ridge to the west to help; the sails were hanging nearly slack, rippling at their edges with each puff. She moved with a dreamlike slowness, while the Moorish galleys darted like water bugs. That made him feel like a spectator, and he didn't like *that* at all. The hot late-summer sun made him sweat like a horse, too; he could feel it soaking into the gambeson under his mail shirt, and smell it along with the hot pine of the deck. The leather-wrapped grip of the bow made patterns in the skin of his left palm until he forced himself to relax.

The Moors were closing in on the British ship; the *Sark* lay silent. The schooner was close enough for them to hear the yelping, screeching war cries of the corsairs, as they swung up on either side of the crippled sailing ship. He could see a black giant, naked save for a twisted rag loincloth, in the bows of the lead pirogue swinging a grapnel on the end of a long rope, then tossing it with a shouted *Wau-wau*-ho!

A dozen more flew out from the pirate vessels, trailing

their cords like a malignant spider's web. The rowers snatched their oars in, moving in trained unison, and then tallied on to the lines and drew them hand over hand.

"Are those useless Poms going to do *anything*?" Sheila asked, fingering the cutlass at her side. The crew waited, armed and tense.

"They will," Hordle said. *Though I don't know how many are fit for duty, after the battering the ship took in that effing storm.* "Just about . . ."

Scores of strong arms drew the corsair vessels in alongside the British ship, two on either side and one under the stern. More crowded in to grapple with those, making a bridge of boats for boarding. Men crawled over the long slender craft like flies on dead meat; each of the corsair craft had twenty oars a side, and most carried as many men again as the forty needed to row. Many of the pirates were olive-skinned Moors in long robes and turbans, some with an end of it drawn across their faces, or darker Peul dressed likewise; others were tall, muscular, ebony-black Serer and Wolof tribesmen in anything from scars and nakedness to long white nightshirtlike garments now kirted up around their knees. Some wore crude armor of leather with bits of metal sewn on and a few had helmets under their turbans; their weapons were broad-bladed spears, machetes, axes and some crude, curved, slashing swords hammered out of scrap steel. Edge and point sparkled and swirled in the bright sunlight as they crowded forward screaming their war cries, and a flurry of javelins went before them.

"And . . . about . . . *now!*" Hordle said, feeling his teeth skin back from his lips.

The sides of the *Cutty Sark* seemed to ripple for a moment in a wave of greenish brown, as the men who'd been lying flat on their decks came erect, standing in three staggered rows on each side—forty to port and as many to starboard, drawing their bows to the ear.

The savage screaming of the corsairs cut off with a horrified suddenness, and the command came over the water, thin with distance but distinct: "Wholly together—*loose!*"

Then a hundred bowstrings snapped as one, a massed

cracking sound like bamboo breaking. The archers were shooting at point-blank range, and that close even the best suit of plate could not stop a shaft. The broadheads went through the simple hide-and-wicker shields and improvised armor of the corsairs as if it were the cloth and naked skin that was all the protection most of them had. Many of the shafts went through two men each in a quadruple splash of red, or through one man and through the planks of the pirogues' bottoms.

"Rapid fire!"

The archers drew and shot, drew and shot; the pirogues along each side of the ship were suddenly wallowing funeral barges full of the dead, and of a heaving, moaning carpet of the wounded and maimed. The delta-shaped arrowheads slashed wounds the width of a man's paired thumbs through limbs and bodies, and almost instantly the water around the locked vessels turned from blue-green to pink. A few questing triangular fins were there already, as the first men staggered overboard and screaming into the water with arrows through limbs and torsos and faces.

If they break . . . Hordle thought.

That was probably what the *Sark*'s commander had counted on and why he'd held fire until the last minute, the sudden massed shock at close range sending the rest fleeing. But they did not. Instead more men poured forward as the arrows slashed into them, leaping across the piled dead and screeching out the name of their god. The islanders answered them with a crashing threefold bark—a deep-chested *Hurrah!*—and a hissing sleet of arrows. The honed edges of the arrowheads twinkled briefly as they flew, like the sun sparkling on bits of glass.

Hordle answered it with a shout of his own, half encouragement and half aching frustration: "Eat that, you sodding pirate bastards!"

At the stern, the Moors had no arrow storm to face. Instead the full-armored men who commanded the company of bowmen stood along the rail, rising from their crouch with their shields up and their visors down. Most carried longswords, held up overhead with the blade parallel to the deck; a few had poleaxes, or war hammers with serrated heads. He saw one of those come down on a pirate climbing up with a curved knife between his teeth, smashing the man's head like a melon dropped on concrete; the ugly, thick, wet pop-*crack* sound was clear to his mind's ear. The swords flashed, bright silver for a few moments, then throwing red arcs as they chopped and stabbed; the knights stood like a wall of steel along the rail, but a dozen spearpoints probed for each.

A pain in his jaw from the force with which he clenched his teeth brought him back to full awareness of his surroundings, and he made himself breathe. Not far away Sir Nigel and Alleyne stood; the younger Loring was literally quivering with eagerness, the plates of his steel suit rattling. His father stood in earnest quiet talk with Nobbes. The Tasmanian kept shaking his head, and then reluctantly nodded.

"Volunteers!" Sir Nigel shouted; he wasn't a large man, but the call went from one end of the *Pride*'s deck to the other effortlessly. "Volunteers for a longboat sortie. No members of the catapult crews or the first deck watch—half with Lieutenant Loring, half with me. Quickly now, and we have them!"

There was a stampede; Hordle helped sort it out, and draw the two launches alongside. Alleyne took one, sliding down the boarding rope with nerveless aplomb, as if he didn't have sixty pounds of steel strapped to him—and it was a long muddy walk across the bottom of the cove to shore. Hordle went into the other boat along with eleven of the *Pride*'s crew and Nigel Loring. The little baronet was peering out from under his raised visor—and probably seeing things a bit blurred, but that never held him back . . .

"Stretch out," Nigel said. "We'll hit that clump of corsair boats tied up by the *Sark*'s stern—take them in the rear. No shouts until we reach them."

The crew tumbled into their places, shoving off from the schooner's side with the long ash oars and then pulling in unison, quiet save for grunts of effort. Sir Nigel was at the tiller, his shield with the five Loring roses propped up against his knee, his face shining with sweat under the steel sallet. Hordle gave him a quick nod and went to the bows, holding his bow high to keep spray off it, then went down on one knee, with his right foot braced solidly behind him against the foremost rower's bench.

Two weeks since I drew bow, he thought, nocking a shaft. *But you don't lose the knack that quickly.* It had been old Sam Aylward who'd started him and Alleyne Loring, when the old soldier visited Crooksbury and the two of them were hero-worshipping youngsters. *Gave me a headstart, you did, Samkin. Well, if thanks can do you any good where you are now, you've got them.*

The ruined ship and the circle of corsair galleys grew swiftly as the clear green water hissed by beneath the long-boat; he could see the bottom thirty feet down: clear white shell-sand and patches of waving green, and silver-blue fish flitted through it. The backs of the pirates came clearer as well; a great mob of them on four or five of their long narrow hulls, crowding forward towards the stern of the *Cutty Sark*. The rail was hidden, a broil of men and robes and swinging weapons; now and then a figure catapulted backward with flailing limbs, trailing red as a sword took him, but there were scores of them crowding in. And more boosting them up to the rail, pushing forward despite their gruesome losses. Others thrust with long spears or poles over the heads of those in the front line, several men on each shaft, beating the knights back from the ship's edge by sheer main force.

One man chanced to look back, doubtless glancing to check that the other infidel vessel was still safely distant. His eyes bulged as he saw the longboats driving forward, and he opened his mouth to shout a warning.

Snap.

It was near two hundred yards, and from a moving platform. Hordle gave a snarl of satisfaction as the arrow drove in between the gleaming white teeth and smashed out through the pirate's neckbone; he dropped as limp as a sack of grain, and none of his comrades noticed. The Englishman's hand flashed back to his quiver, and he set another shaft on the arrow rest.

"Another conscientious cunt," he snarled quietly as a Moor in dingy white noticed him.

He shot, but the arrow flew over the enemy's shoulder—close enough for the flight feathers to brush his cheek and make him throw himself down in the bilge of his pirogue with a yell; then he was up, dripping and shouting, grabbing at shoulders and kicking backsides and pointing at the longboats, jabbing his finger to drive home his point.

"Faster!" Hordle shouted.

He emptied his quiver in a ripple of archery that sent forty shafts downrange in the time it took the longboat to reach its target. *His* target was densely massed, and even shooting into the brown every shaft would find a target.

The last went through a shield and twelve inches into a spearman's chest at point-blank range. Sir Nigel threw the tiller over, and the crew raised their oars and brought them down like wooden threshing-flails on the Moors crowding to contest the edge of the first pirate vessel. The heavy varnished wood cracked down on heads and shoulders and arms with the meaty sound of mallets hitting a chicken carcass. Alleyne Loring leapt from the prow of his longboat, Sir Nigel from the stern of his, and the crews followed with a shout and a flashing of cutlasses, making a blunt wedge behind the two full-armored men. Hordle followed, leaving his buckler by his side and taking the bastard sword in the two-handed grip, filling his lungs for a shout as he jumped and landed in ankle-deep water in the swaying fragile pirogue.

A spearhead slammed towards his face. He crouched and spun and cut diagonally, and it flicked away, leaving the pirate staring at the cut shaft until Hordle stabbed through his body on the return. Another step forward, another—

Sheila Winston stooped beside him and cut a man's ankle out from under him. A palm-broad spearhead took her in the face as she straightened, punching through nose and jaw with sharp crackling sound. She dropped with a bubbling shriek, cut off when another stabbed through her throat and into the wood of the pirogue's bottom. Hordle roared and swung the greatsword in a looping cut that took both the man's arms off at the elbow; he turned, and tried to run backward, spraying blood into the faces of his comrades. Something struck the Englishman in the gut, a short-gripped spear whose point didn't strike hard enough to cut the links of the chain mail. He snarled and struck downward with the brass ball on the pommel of his sword, driving it like a hammer onto a skull protected only by a mat of woolly hair ...

Suddenly they were on the last of the pirate craft, under the overhang of the *Cutty Sark*'s stern; the bulk of the corsairs had never realized they were under attack from the rear until the swords struck. Now they bolted for either end of their long slender craft, or leapt around the curve to those lashed on either side of the clipper. Visored sallet helms showed above the rail, and then red sweat-streaming faces as the steel protection was pushed back. Rope ladders followed; Hordle stuck his sword point-down in the planks beneath his feet and paused to help the two Lorings up the swaying thing of wood and rope, then snatched it free and followed himself.

The deck of the *Sark* was chaos come again; bodies lying in heaps, on the poop deck and down in the waist, all amid the tangle of fallen spars and sails and cordage from the storm. Archers held the sides and forward edge of the poop, but most of the center of the ship was a mass of men—guards archers and corsairs and Royal Navy crew-folk—all locked together in a swarming brawl, naked extreme violence breast-to-breast, with superior numbers balanced against better weapons and training.

Nigel Loring paused only for an instant, surveying the situation. Then he clashed his visor down and shouted, pointing his sword forward: "St. George for England! *Follow me!*"

A roar went up, short and harsh and savage. The knights formed beside him, and the *Pride*'s crewfolk and the surviving archers in a wedge behind. The armored men smashed their way down the companionways, stabbing with shortened swords, battering their way with sheer mass and even with blows of their steel-sheathed fists and head-butts into vulnerable faces. The mass conflict on the main deck altered with the suddenness of a saturated solution when a drop of catalyst is added. All at once the corsairs clustered forward, the islanders below the break of the poop deck, both in compact masses facing each other across a space empty save for the wounded and the dead. A moment of panting silence broken only by the screams or whimpering of the hurt, and then from three hundred throats a call went up:

"Aaaallllahhuuuu-Akbar!"

The crashing *Hurrah!* answered it—and Hordle felt something change. He risked glancing over the side and saw a massive bolt from one of the *Pride*'s catapults skewer four men still in the vessels lashed to the side of the *Sark*; its companion smashed into the bottom of the pirogue and cracked a plank clear across in a spray of pink-tinged water. Seconds later a glass globe struck, shattered, spread clinging inextinguishable fire. The schooner herself slid into sight, still moving with that stately grace. A figure showed in a gap in the protective shields, dressed in a pre-Change airport fireman's getup—complete to clear face shield and silvery overrobe. Cradled in the figure's hands was what looked like a thick clumsy gun, with a tube running back to an apparatus of pipes and tanks; two more pumped frantically at that, swinging the levers up and down.

The silvery figure raised the weapon, and a long thin stream of amber liquid poured out of it, down onto one of the corsair galleys. With a *pop* the stream caught fire, then went up with a rush of orange flame and black smoke, playing back and forward along the hundred-foot length of the pirate craft. Wood and canvas and human flesh burned; men turned into torches that danced and leapt into the water shrieking, but the sticky, clinging flame floated there too. Beyond, the sea was thick with high triangular black fins . . .

Hordle's fighting snarl turned to a broad grin as his great red-running blade went up in a sweeping gesture of invitation, sending a spray of blood across the planks of the deck as it did. He laughed as he shouted: "After *you*, Abdul!"

Half the pirates bolted for their pirogues, dropping their weapons and running screaming to the bulwarks, leaping down and hacking at the ropes that bound them to the *Sark* and to each other, pushing with oars and throwing their own casualties overboard in their haste.

The other half knew themselves dead men and charged, shrieking. Hordle shifted to a one-handed grip on the long hilt of his sword and drew his dagger with his left hand . . .

Nigel Loring coughed to clear his throat; it was hoarse with shouting, and he labored to draw air into lungs gone dry as mummy dust, air wet and hot and foul with the stink of blood and less-pleasant bodily fluids. He pushed up his visor with the back of his sword hand, heedless of the smear that left on his face, and peered at the blurred images.

The clash of metal had stopped for an instant, one of those odd pauses that happened spontaneously in hand-to-hand warfare as men stopped to breathe and shake the sweat out of their eyes. The last of the pirates grouped around a kneeling figure on the foredeck, a thin white-bearded man with a green-dyed turban. He bent in prayer, a small book done in delicate Arabic calligraphy open before him, a string of beads in his left hand, a small carpet unrolled beneath him. When he rose again, his eyes met Nigel Loring's, calm and unafraid.

Curse it, what's the word for "surrender"? the Englishman thought. *My Arabic's completely gone . . . "rendez," that's the French, would he understand that?*

Then the moment of calm shattered as a crossbow bolt struck one of the men around the marabout. There was a last rush, surging past Nigel to be in at the kill; he saw Hordle's great blade swinging in a blurred horizontal arc, and the old man's head went bouncing to the rail and over; the body knelt upright for a moment, blood fountaining from the neck, then collapsed in an ungraceful tangle. The last corsairs died around it a second later, hacked into gobbets of flesh and organ and raw pink bone by dozens of blades swung with hysterical strength.

Nigel grimaced and slammed his sword point-down into the deck. An armored hand came into his field of view, holding a British-issue military canteen; he took it with a croak of thanks and splashed some onto his face before taking a deep draft. When he turned to return it, he saw that the man he'd taken it from was armored as he was, also with the visor raised. A young face, fair, blue-eyed and handsome—much like his own son, and nearly as familiar.

"Prince William!" he said, shocked. "What on earth are *you* doing here, Your Highness?"

The younger man smiled. "Getting my life saved by you, Colonel Loring—again, it seems."

Their eyes met, in a flash of perfect mutual understanding. *So the queen has already started putting the heirs in harm's way.* And the prince was unafraid—not young man's bravado, but coldly so. Sent south on this deathtrap of a ship . . .

Loring smiled. "I see I trained you well, Your Highness."

"You have, Sir Nigel. I suppose that technically I should arrest you—"

They both looked about. The deck of the *Cutty Sark* was far closer to the water now; barrels bobbed and floated against the underside of the gratings that covered the hatchways, a bonging, rubbing sound like water-filled drums beating in the halls of sunken Ys. Alleyne had organized working parties, dragging the British and Tasmanian wounded from the piles, carrying them over to where the ships' medics and their helpers were bandaging and sewing at the long ghastly wounds made by scimitar and shovel-headed spear. The *Pride of St. Helens* edged closer, and so did her longboats.

"—except that I have no choice but to beg your assistance, if we're not all to drown."

"It's my pleasure to serve, Your Highness. There's a village not far up the coast that will accommodate you all, and your wounded, until a cutter can reach Rabat and send a navy ship down to fetch you."

"You realize this is going to make . . . certain parties at court look complete fools," the prince said.

"All the better, Your Highness."

"Sir Nigel . . ." The younger man stepped forward and grasped his forearm. "Sir Nigel, if you could come back—"

"That would mean open rebellion," Nigel said softly.

"Are you willing to go that far? Do you want me to set you on the throne with the sword's point?"

"Well . . . no," the prince replied.

"I didn't think you would, somehow," the baronet said, smiling grimly. "And I don't think you need to, if you keep your wits about you. Build on this. Tony Knolles will help, and Oliver Buttesthorn. They're both good men."

"I'll remember that, Sir Nigel," the prince said. "But where will you go?"

Nigel shrugged, and looked westward, blinking a little as he saw the sun was already setting. It made a path of blood and fire across the water, stretching clouds like hot gold and molten copper along the horizon.

"There, Your Highness. This part of the Lorings' story is over, and we've pulled up our roots. Somewhere there's new earth waiting for them."

He looked down at the sword that stood quivering in the wood, and his steel glove fell on its pommel. *Good-bye, Maude, old girl,* he thought. *I wish you were here.* Aloud he went on as he tapped the sword hilt: "Tilled with this, I fear."

Behind him, his son also looked out over the long slow swell of the sea. "*Dawns like thunder,*" he murmured.

John Hordle ran the swatch of raw fleece down his sword, swearing mildly as that revealed where the steel had taken a knick cutting through bone.

"Sort of traditional," he said. The younger Loring looked at him, and Hordle hefted his blade meaningfully. "Well, it's how we got England in the first place, innit?"

CHAPTER NINE

Dun Fairfax, Willamette Valley, Oregon
March 21st, 2007 AD—Change Year Nine

"Where's it to, Larry?" Aylward said.

"Over this way, by the road."

The Dun Fairfax party rose out of the mist like waders from water as they went up the low rise in the center of the pasture, then sank again as they walked down towards the fenceline, the vapor rising up shin and thigh and torso like an impalpable gray sea. Aylward waited for an instant before he descended into it, straining his eyes against the gathering dark, but there was nothing to see. The spear-points of those ahead of him were last to disappear, right after the spray of raven feathers at the clasp of a man's Scots Bonnet. The air was cool and clammy-wet against his skin, perfect for carrying smells. Garm and Grip were getting excited at the scents, quivering eager but too well mannered to bark out of turn.

"Around here," the shepherd said as they slowed and the fence loomed out of the fog like a darker shadow in the gray-black.

"Just a bit of light, then," Aylward said.

Then as the shutter of the bull's-eye stayed open too wide and too long, glowing through the mist: "I said just a *bit,* Larry!"

"Sorry, Sam."

"You can close the shutter now."

Aylward went to one knee, leaning on his ashwood

spear, and touched the bloodstain. The tacky, slightly lumpy feel was unmistakable when he put his fingertips to the wet ground and rubbed thumb over forefingers; so was the smell when he brought them to his nose. When the moon broke free of a cloud the ground had the black glistening look that blood-crimson took on in low light.

And I know that look, now don't I just? I know it bloody *well.* His smile was grim.

This edge of the pasture was down near the southwest corner; just over that was the road out into the Valley proper, with Artemis Creek running along its southern side. There was a dense belt of trees along the running water, a narrow strip of grassy field, and then the steep forested hillside, covered in Douglas fir and ponderosa pine. Night and the damp air brought out the scents; turned earth from the field of spring-planted barley just west, and stock and woodsmoke from behind them, an intense sap-laden forest breath from the south, chilly and wet and green.

It also made his left thigh ache a bit, where the Argentine bullet had broken the big bone back in '82, and his right shoulder as well—he'd spent days with it dislocated, lying at the bottom of a ravine, before Juniper Mackenzie stumbled over him back just after the Change. He'd recovered full function, but it still hurt in damp, cold weather.

Well, you were forty then and forty-eight now, he told himself. *Not a lad anymore; old flesh doesn't heal like young. Learn to like it; when you're hurting, you're not dead.* Aloud he went on, pointing south towards the road:

"That's where they've gone. Over the lane, over the water, and up."

"You think it's people?" Larry Smith asked.

"Stands to reason, doesn't it? There's blood, lots of it, but no bits of wool or skin like an animal would have left. Someone cut that wether's throat, let it bleed out, and then ran off with it. They'll not go straight down the road westward, because that leads into open country—my oath, that's probably the direction they came from. And Dun Juniper's up on the slope to the north. So they'll go south, up the hill, before they work back towards the lowlands. That's if they've any bloody idea where they are at all."

He looked around. Even the men close to him were simply darker patches in the misty night. Once over the river and among the trees, it would be like standing inside a closet—except that in a closet you didn't have to chance a branch taking your eye out, and you generally weren't in the company of men carrying razor-edged blades on the ends of awkward poles.

"Everyone, be careful with the stickers, all right?"

He was glad he'd told everyone to kit up. The brigandines were twenty-five pounds of inconvenience each, but they didn't make any noise and they'd be extremely helpful if someone *did* accidentally run his spearhead into a neighbor. Plus they'd be *very* helpful if it came to a tussle. Any mixup would be at arm's length; even Sam Aylward couldn't shoot well in pitch-dark.

"Spread out so you're just in touch, and *please,* don't any bloody fool get lost, right? And keep it quiet."

"Aye, sor," someone said, in an excruciating Mummerset growl. "As ye wish."

Aylward snorted quietly to himself as he wiped his hand on a clean patch of grass and dried it on his kilt. One thing the post-Change, Oregon-version Clan Mackenzie had in spades was bad put-on British accents, most of them sounding like they were out of old pirate movies by way of *Monty Python,* and the closer you got to Dun Juniper the more of them you heard.

Although I'll grant that Lady Juniper herself can do a perfectly authentic County Mayo brogue when she wants to. And of course I'm an 'ampshire 'og of the purest breed— seven hundred years of Crooksbury farmers.

The imitators, though . . . He supposed the others had caught it from the reenactors and Renaissance Faire types who'd made up much of her original circle. What they'd all end up sounding like a few generations down the road when the soup had had some chance to simmer didn't bear thinking about . . .

He turned to the dogs, whistling softly. "Garm! Grip! Take the scent. Seek, boys. Seek!"

The dogs were mere dark shapes weaving in and out of the

mist, but he could hear their interested snuffles. Then they stopped, muzzles to the ground; he moved up between them, watching their black nostrils quiver over the grasses that bent down under the beads of moisture that condensed on them. Gram growled low in his broad chest, and they began to move purposefully to the south.

"Slow, boys. Slow!"

He'd hunted the dogs long enough and trained them well enough that they knew not to leave the humans behind. The boards of the fence loomed up out of the dark, and there was a clatter and someone's mild curse as they climbed it, cut off by a sharp *shush!* A little more light glimmered on the graveled road; the white dust and rock seemed to glow, and the drifts of fog moved with a breeze from the west. The group halted at his *sssst!*—they weren't SAS troopers by any manner of means, but he'd been training the clan in general and this lot in particular for nine years now, and the most of them hunted for the pot on their own quite frequently. The dogs cast about again, zigzagging across the road with concentrated attention, then moving off eastward; after a moment they doubled back and halted where a trail took off from the road and plunged through the creekside trees.

Now isn't that interesting? he thought. *Whoever it was missed the trail down to the water, then turned back and got it. Right . . . straight down to the river, eh, boys?*

They all moved down through the brush, breath and feet loud in his ears. "Larry, let's have the light again for a second—the rest of you keep your sodding boots back, will you?"

There *were* tracks this time, amid the mud and trampled ferns of the creekside. Aylward grounded his spear and crouched, his hand pointing to direct the light.

"Well, cor' stone the crows," the Englishman said mildly. "It's a tribal migration, it is."

He turned to the others. "They stopped here."

"More than one?"

"Six at least, mate," Aylward said, indicating tracks with the point of his spear. "Eight, more likely. What's more, a couple of them were youngsters—see the bare footprint there? Six-year-old or thereabouts. There's four different sets of shoes, only one without holes in 'em."

There was a murmur from the others. A thought struck him. Aylward cast his mind back; yes, there was just enough time, given that Lady Juniper and party had stopped overnight at several duns and for a whole day in Sutter-down despite Ostara being so close. Herself had stayed with the local Baptist minister, Reverend Jennings, at that. Pointedly driving home a point about toleration of the suddenly minority faith.

Separation of Covenstead and State, was the way she'd put it.

Coming cross-country from the spot east of Salem, there was just enough time . . .

"I think I may know who this is," he said slowly. "But I could be wrong. On the one hand, they have kids with them. On t' other, they could be bandits or even Eaters. So let's be careful, shall we?"

The water was nearly to the waist and snarling-cold as they crossed the ford, snowmelt from the high mountains to the east, enough to numb his thighs and feet and set at least one set of teeth chattering. There was nothing to be done about that; the dogs didn't seem to mind at least, por-poising up on the other bank and shaking themselves vig-orously in the murk. One advantage of kilts was that you could hold them up out of the wet, and the merely damp wool cloth felt good when he let it go again on the other side and it swung down to his knees.

"That settles it," he said, when the dogs picked up the scent again. "If they were regulars at sheeplifting, they'd have waded upstream to break their trail. They just went across and scarpered."

"Wade upstream? In *this?*" stuttered the one whose teeth had chattered; he was rail-thin, an ex-architecture student who'd wandered in years ago.

"Better to be cold than caught, Carl-me-lad," he said. "And they won't be far. Not carrying that weight of mut-ton, and hungry with it. And with children. It's getting cold, too. They'll figure nobody'll be after them, and stop to cook it and eat. Now quiet."

They moved on through the woods and up the steep slope at an angle, a dense forest of tall candle-straight trunks, Douglas fir and western hemlock interspersed with brush and yew, the weed tree of the understory. There was a method to it; you didn't try to hurry, or be absolutely silent—that was impossible. Instead you stopped after you'd made a noise, waited for a second or two, then went on again. A forest at night was full of noises, creak and crackle and vegetable groaning, the drip of moisture from that afternoon's rain, the clicks and whirrs of dark's creatures, the *whoo-whit!* of an owl, the far-off yipping of a coyote. Footfalls and the occasional crackling of a branch could fit right in, especially if the ones listening weren't woods-wise.

The dogs whuffled, coursing back and forth—faintly contemptuous of how slow humans were, he sometimes thought. The slope grew steeper, and he carefully used the metal spike on the butt of the spear to anchor himself.

Soon.

Garm and Grip froze, a little ahead of him and to either side, their noses pointing like the sides of a triangle. All he had to do was draw the lines out into the night; he even recognized where he was, a bit where the angle of the slope went from forty-five degrees to a more comfortable twenty or so for a brief space. For getting to know the lay of the land even the best scouting didn't equal living on it for years and hunting over it regularly.

His *sssssst!* froze everyone in place. He left the spear and eeled forward on his belly for a dozen feet, and his dark-accustomed eyes caught light—low, reddish, more reflected off overhead branches than seen directly. He took a long deep breath through his nose, and caught the unmistakable scent of roasting meat. When he went backward Larry Smith and Alice Dennison were waiting close enough to see his hand signals, and to pass them on. He waited while the clock in his head ticked, and wiped his hands on his kilt to make sure they wouldn't be slippery when he grasped the ashwood of the spear.

"Now," he said, in his ordinary conversational voice— whispers carried further.

He stood and walked forward, the spear grasped like a rifle-and-bayonet combination. His teeth skinned back a little; he'd *used* the bayonet, in the Falklands—that had been his first taste of action.

The figures seated around the low fire were intent on the meat grilling across the coals; the little spurts of fire when a drop of fat fell and hit them illuminated faces. Two men, shaggy-bearded; a trio of women—no, one was a girl, sixteen, seventeen at most. Two older kids huddled together under a scrap of canvas, holding it over their heads to make an improvised tent with the open end towards the fire, while two infants lay wrapped like papooses between them.

Proper lot of gallybaggers, he thought, looking at their scarecrow rags and gaunt faces.

The yearling sheep had been butchered with some skill, and a rack of ribs rested above a net of green branches; the kidneys and liver were on sticks, and almost ready. Everyone in the little party watched the food with a dreadful single-minded intensity, the youngsters whimpering now and then.

Until they heard the footsteps, and saw light breaking off the honed edges of the spears. The children shrieked, but the adults and teenager sprang up—an improvised spear, an ax, branch-clubs, stones, the girl with a good knife.

"Hold it!" Aylward barked. "Nobody do anything bloody stupid, and nobody needs to get hurt. Drop the stickers. Throw down! *Now!*"

He watched the adults count the spearheads, and turn to see that they were ringed around. The man with the hoe-spear slumped in despair as he let it fall; there were thuds and thumps as the others followed suit. The girl, he noted carefully, sheathed her knife rather than following the letter of his instructions.

"Look, mister," the fair-bearded man said. "Look, please . . ." Then anger burst into his voice: "What harm have we ever done you?"

"You're eating our sheep," Aylward observed.

"Our kids are hungry, goddammit!"

"Ours aren't," Aylward said. "One of the reasons they're

not hungry is that we don't let people steal our sheep . . . Wait a bit, though. Were you lot up north a couple of days ago? Running away from a right nasty little sod who calls himself Baron Liu? Keeps company with a big bugger called Mack?"

The man gaped at him, and the others clutched each other. "How'd you know?"

One of the others grabbed at a crucifix and whimpered. Aylward grinned at that. There were enough rumors about Lady Juniper's people in the free sections of the Valley; he supposed it was natural the Protector should be spreading even more ridiculous propaganda about them in his baili-wick, and using his puppet church to spread the message. Enough of his subjects ran off as it was. Telling them tales about the Wicked Witches would be a cheap way of keep-ing them home and working.

"Because I was *there,* you dozy burke!" he said genially. "If you'd just stopped after that, we'd have seen you right. We're the Mackenzies. If you'd *asked* for help, you'd have gotten it."

That seemed to frighten them more, and the women clutched at their children.

"You shouldn't believe all you hear," Alice Dennison said. Then: "By Cernunnos and the sweet Lady, Sam, these folks aren't a threat to anyone but that sheep, and it's dead already."

The teenager spoke. "Jeff, Miguel, we shouldn't believe *anything* the Protector or the Baron or their tame priests told us."

That seemed to get home, but these people had been afraid so long that it had become a habit, and one proba-bly hard to break.

"Right," he sighed, and grounded his spear.

Then he reached back into his haversack and pulled out the bundle Melissa had made up for him. "This is ready to eat. Have your cruncheon on me."

He tossed it, and the cloth-wrapped food fell at the teenager's feet with a thump. She didn't waste any time, and when the others saw the bread and meat, and the roast potatoes and twist of salt his wife had packed, their resistance crumbled. The other members of the Dun Fairfax party followed his example. The adult fugitives looked as if they felt like crying as they crammed roast pork and cheese and hard-boiled eggs into their mouths; the children *stopped* crying as they were fed.

"Careful there," Aylward said. "Don't do yourself an injury."

One of the women nodded, and made the children slow down—by force, mainly. The teenager had been pacing herself from the start. She had striking light eyes, and they met his levelly.

"Do you know the Queen of Witches?" she asked.

"Yes, love, but she wouldn't be overjoyed to hear you call her that," he said. "Lady Juniper's good enough. Sam Aylward's my name."

"Aylward the *Archer?*" one of the men asked, sounding incredulous.

"I shoot a bit now and then, yes. And you're not four miles from Dun Juniper right now, and herself's in residence."

That got attention, even through the food. The two men looked at each other, but the girl didn't hesitate; instead she stood up and approached him, holding out a squarish bundle wrapped in coarse cloth.

"I took this from the castle," she said. "Baron Gervais's castle. From the office. I was part of the cleaning staff."

Ah, Aylward thought, taking it and stripping off the container. *Probably his bar bills. On the other hand, it might explain why he was out after this lot personal-like.*

Larry Smith stepped up and shone the bull's-eye on the pages. His eyes opened wider, and Aylward gave a long whistle. The text was in some sort of code, but the maps were plain enough.

"Alice," he said, rewrapping it. "You know your way back?"

"Hell, yes, Sam."

"Get back to the dun, then. Send someone to Lady Juniper and tell her to come—to bring Chuck, and no more else than she must, and come quickly. Send Tamar, and tell her to hurry. We'll get these people back to my place," he concluded. "And everyone, don't chatter on about what you've seen. Alice, you hop to it!"

Alice nodded, tossed her spear to her husband and went downslope in a controlled fall. Aylward looked at the quasiprisoners and sighed as he stuffed the documents into his haversack. Garm and Grip had discovered the guts and head of the sheep, and looked up at him questioningly, waiting for permission. Aylward used the blade of his spear to crack open the skull for them, and they dove in noisily as he stabbed the steel into the earth to rough-clean it.

"All right, you two go first," he said to the male refugees. "And we'll carry the kids, ladies. Someone pack up the meat from that wether. No sense in letting it go to waste."

The direct way down the steep scarp to Dun Fairfax was rough, twisting back and forth through the darkened forest; it had been a logging road, long ago. That was why most traffic took the longer U-shaped route westward along Artemis Creek, then north with it and so onto the bench that held Dun Juniper, even though it tripled the distance. But the horse knew this trail, and Juniper Mackenzie did as well from long years before the Change. She still took it slowly, as mist curled between the great trees, flattening the sound of hooves; the moist air beaded on her hooded cloak, and more dripped from branches over the trail. Tamar clung, perched behind her with her arms around Juniper's waist, and three more horses followed; she'd pulled the tail of the cloak around the girl to give her a little extra protection. It was made of unfulled wool—with the natural grease left in the fiber and then the thread hard-woven— and it shed water nearly as well as a pre-Change rain slicker. Those were getting worn and brittle and hard to find, and weren't nearly as good at keeping you warm. It *did* smell rather strongly of lanolin, though, particularly when it was wet.

Wet wool, wet horse, wet me, Juniper thought, as the fog drank the dull sound of hooves on soft dirt, and moisture dripped on them as steadily as rain. *Just when I'd gotten comfortable again. This had better be good, Sam!*

Under that went a chill. She knew it would be. Sam

wasn't the sort to start at shadows . . . unless something important was doing the shadow-casting.

They came out of the woods, and Tamar hopped down lithely to open the gate in the plank fence that edged the Dun Fairfax farmlands. Then she trotted along beside Juniper's horse, one hand gripping the stirrup leather to ease her pace, tireless as a yearling deer. The gates of the dun were abustle, with people standing about and dogs barking and lanterns burning bright; the hum of conversation rose as the riders from Dun Juniper drew near.

Juniper stood in the stirrups and held up a hand: "Merry met," she said, and then waved down the greetings. When silence fell, she went on: "I know you're all fair ruptured with curiosity, Mackenzies . . . but as a favor to me, could you keep it quiet for a wee bit?"

"That means keep your sodding mouths *shut*," Sam said as he came out of the gate, genially enough, but with an edge to it.

There were murmurs at that; the folk of her clan tended to be talkative, and to love argument and assembly and debate—it had become as much a mark of a Mackenzie as shooting skillfully with the bow. Probably they'd caught it from her original core group of coveners and re-creationists, who could talk black into white and up into down, and loved to do it—plus it was entertainment to replace TV.

On the other hand, they also tended to take what she said seriously, sometimes excessively so. The little crowd broke up as people went back to their homes—doubtless to hash over the events of the evening, but at least they weren't getting in the way. Most of them would delight in keeping the news within their own dun, too, and hug a secret close until they couldn't bear it anymore.

Sam whistled sharply, and several of his household people came up to collect the horses as the visitors swung down.

"Started with a missing sheep," he said quietly to her as they walked towards his house. "And from there . . ."

"Hmmm," she replied when he was done. "Let's go see."

"*And* they're frightened at the name of you, Lady Juniper. But most anxious to see you, as well."

"Not the first time it's been like that."

"Not a bad bunch. They made it out with Baron Liu chasing them, after all."

"Thanks to Eilir and Astrid," she said quietly, looking over her shoulder at the pair in question. *As well try to keep water from flowing downhill as keep those two out of it.* "But I see your point."

"Plus some little things . . . they've been eating short for years and running hard on next to nothing for days now, but we didn't have to stop them from rupturing themselves. Thanked us polite-like when we used the bolt cutters on those dog collars around their necks."

Juniper nodded, and took off her cloak to shake free the moisture before she walked into the warm, well-lit space of Aylward's hearth room and hung the garment on a peg; there was a mat underneath to catch drips. Then she made a gesture with one hand and bowed her head towards the family altar over the fireplace.

Melissa Aylward smiled as her kin cleaned away plates and bowls. "Merry met and welcome to our home, Lady of the Clan," she said, and extended a plate and cup.

"Merry met and thanks, Lady of the Hearth," Juniper replied, taking a cookie and popping it into her mouth—she wasn't hungry, but symbolism was important. The hot mead was soothing, though.

Melissa grinned then, and said less formally, "Sam's always bringing home something that needs cleaning up and feeding, Juney."

"A big softie, under that gruff shell," Juniper agreed.

The children Sam had mentioned were being borne off by members of the household, to be bathed—and deloused—and tucked into beds; several of the younger were already lolling limp into sleep by then, between the warmth and full bellies. Others of those who lived here had suppressed their natural curiosity and scattered off to the rest of the big farmhouse. That left only Sam, her, Chuck, Eilir and Astrid apart from the two refugee couples and the teenager. She looked at them . . .

Something. Something important. The worm biting its tail, things yet to be casting their shadow through the circles of time . . .

The power points of her body flaring in an electric tingle, a cool wind blowing through her mind, a hint of a starshot darkness that glowed with an inner light . . . She damped down frustration at the uncertainty of it.

Even to her most beloved child, a mother doesn't reveal all her mind—she can't, because the child can't grasp it yet. How then does the Divine speak to us? In song and myth, dream and vision, like a serpent in a bed of reeds, coil upon counter-coil.

The dark Hispanic-looking man gulped at her green-eyed stare. *"Ojos garzos"*—*The eyes of wizardry*—he said softly, and crossed himself.

Juniper shook herself back to the waking world, and remembered discussions she'd had with Jose and Carlita over platters of *camarones al mojo de ajo.*

"Si," she whispered in his tongue. *"Si, garzos, pero para el bien, no el mal. Bruja, si, bruja de los buenos—Sacerdotiza."*

He inclined his head. *"Queen* of Witches."

Her smile grew wry as she swept aside the tail of her plaid and sat, tossed her bonnet on the table and ran her hands through unruly red curls where the first gray threads had made their way this winter past.

"Yes, but that doesn't mean what you think it means. Look, let's be practical, shall we? First, you don't have to worry about the Protector or Baron Liu anymore. You're free of them now. We'll find you food and decent homes. And work, but work for yourselves—rely on it—and land of your own eventually. We don't turn anyone away who's running from those . . . I won't call them swine because it would be an insult to that noble beast the pig, sure."

One of the women buried her face in her hands and began to weep. Juniper suppressed an impulse to give her a hug—more likely to scare than not—and signaled Melissa to lead her away; she'd probably feel better close to the children anyway. The others seemed to slump where they sat.

"We made it," the dark man murmured. "Before God, we actually made it." He crossed himself again. "Even at peril of our souls, it's worth it."

Juniper sighed. "First, Mr. . . . Lopez, isn't it?" He nodded. "We've got freedom of religion here; and we'll help you pass on to the university people, or the Bearkillers, or the good monks at Mount Angel, if you prefer. Frankly I've been sort of embarrassed at how many people here have taken up the Craft, but there are still Christians among us . . . Why *didn't* you head for Mount Angel, by the way? It's closer."

"I think of that first, but too many damn soldiers in the way," he said frankly. "Those *hijos,* they kill us all slow, they catch us, even the *niños.*"

Sam grunted agreement. "The Protectorate's got continuous cavalry patrols along there—and the border's well marked."

Miguel nodded; he was a stocky brown-skinned man with shaggy hair so dark that it had blue-black highlights. "*Si.* So Jeff"—he indicated his lanky Anglo companion—"say we should go west first, then turn south before the river, around Salem. Nobody go near there much, too scared. *Territorio bandido.* Some of the bandidos, they do things for the Baron, too, but we figure we hide better than from soldiers."

"That was wise of you," Juniper said.

She flicked a hand, and Astrid and Eilir sat down on the benches across from the fugitives. Chuck went and poured mugs of beer for everyone, then resumed his stance a little behind Juniper, watchful without being tense—this *might* be a trick. With four of the most formidable warriors in the Willamette Valley at hand to protect her, Juniper didn't feel particularly threatened. She didn't want the fugitives to feel pressured either, and wasn't sure whether having Chuck behind her in full fig was a good idea, but *he* certainly thought so and she didn't want to argue about it.

Instead she teased the story out of the three of them. Miguel Lopez had actually been a resident of the town of Gervais before the Change and had managed to survive hiding near it, which was a rarity; his family had arrived a few years before from Jalisco in Mexico, migrant farmworkers like many in that town. He'd moved around hiding from Eaters and refugees and the plagues—living mainly on a pickup load of cracked oats, livestock feed his family had hidden in a woodlot—come out late in the first year, and started a small place of his own, before the Protector's men arrived.

"We didn' fight much," he said bleakly. "Too many of them. And they promise to protect us against Eaters and bandits, get us seed and tools, at first it sound pretty good. Then—" He touched his neck where the collar had left raw patches and calluses.

His friend Jeff Dawson had been a high school student in a Portland suburb—and as he confessed, lucky to end up in one of the Protector's labor gangs rather than driven out to die with so many others. He'd come to Gervais as part of a group sent to help construct the castle, and stayed as a general worker around the place.

"But I wasn't going to take it forever," he said. "And then there was Crystal."

That, evidently, was his sister, who was sixteen or so and strikingly pretty, with wide blue eyes and long tawny-colored hair; she looked a little younger than her age, and she was shorter than Juniper would have expected from her brother's six feet.

She'd have been about seven or eight when the Change came, Juniper reminded herself. *Probably undernourished since, which would limit her growth. And she can't be as much of an innocent as she looks, or she wouldn't be alive, no matter how much her brother tried to help her.*

"She was working in the castle," Jeff said. "That bastard Mack, he started sniffing around her."

He flushed and his hands clenched into fists on the table. Juniper raised an eyebrow, though she'd heard rumor and reports. Jeff couldn't speak; it was Miguel who went on:

"*Malo,* that one. *Bastardo.* He don't just bother girls, he hurt them. The Baron, he don't give a damn."

Why am I not surprised? Juniper thought.

So far it wasn't an unfamiliar story; they'd had hundreds of similar refugees. But . . .

"But Crystal brought us something," she said softly. "Something important. Important enough for Baron Liu to come after it in person, with such a small escort, as if keeping it all quiet was important to him. Very important."

Sam handed her the papers. They were bound, making a bundle about the size of a hardcover book, but the spine was held with steel post-and-clamp fasteners, allowing leaves to be removed or added. She riffled quickly through it; mostly columns of numbers, written in a small neat hand—someone from Arminger's own chancery, at a guess, and they might be able to identify who from the fist.

"Sam?" she said.

"I'd wager it's an Altendorf substitution code," he said. "The numbers'd refer to the pages, to lines, and then letters within the lines. They're a right nightmare to decode if you don't have the book, because if they're careful they don't even give things away with word frequencies—*the* and *and* and bumf like that. I'm no code breaker, but I do know enough to recognize that."

He leaned over and turned the book to the back pages. Her lips shaped a silent whistle; those were maps. Maps of the central and southern Willamette, and the coastline—one of Newport was very detailed, with all the post-Change corrections, and that was the coastal town closest to Corvallis. It had a good pass over the mountains, too. A final foldout map covered the whole of western and central Oregon as far as Umatilla, with copious notes in the same frustrating columns of numbers.

No convenient arrows and dates. Pity the buggers aren't that stupid. All this tells us is that they're up to no good.

And there was a printed sheet of numbered paragraphs in the back cover of the booklet. There always was, in the Protector's publications intended for his overlord cadre.

Number One read: *If I capture my worst enemies, I will not stand over them gloating and boasting and telling them all the details of my secret plans and then keep them alive for torture in an escape-proof dungeon. Instead I will just kill them instantly.*

For the first time the girl spoke, in a soft shy voice. "I was in the Baron's office, hiding in a closet—I knew we were going to run that night, and I wanted to steal some of the new silver money." A flash of anger: "He owed us all of it and more!"

Then she licked her lips. "And then the Baron and . . . and Mack came in, and they talked, and he put this in the desk, and locked it. When they left, I came out and took it."

Juniper's eyebrows went up. "I thought he locked it?" she said.

Crystal smiled, and reached into her blouse. She was wearing something like a housedress cinched over culottes, ragged with her trip through the brush but looking as if it had started out much better than what the others of her party wore. When her hand came out, it held a small sack of soft leather, held closed by a thong threaded into eyelets around the top. That chinked with a musical and—literally—silvery sound as she dropped it on the table.

"I had a copy of the key. He put it down where I could reach it, weeks ago, and I had Jeff copy it."

Jeff grinned sheepishly; it made him look more his real midtwenties age. "I sort of learned how in shop class," he said.

Juniper sipped her mead and thought. Then Crystal cleared her throat. "When the Baron was talking . . . he said something very strange." Juniper nodded, and the girl went on: "He said it all depended on the Tayz Maniacs."

"Tayz Maniacs?" Juniper said, puzzled.

"And the Brits."

Brits I understand, but what are . . . wait a bit. Take out his accent and his sense of humor—so-called. She'd always had a good ear for regional patterns of speech, and Eddie Liu's was purest New Yawk, without even a trace of Cantonese; his mother had been American born of remote Polish ancestry. *What would it sound like if Liu said it?*

"Tasmanians?" she said. "But that . . . what would he mean by that?"

Chapter Ten

Near Amity, Willamette Valley, Oregon
May 12th, 2007—Change Year Nine

Michael Havel reined in and aside, dead weeds and new grass crackling under Charger's hooves. The big gelding halted in the lee of a house that was deserted but still standing, a large frame bungalow with a small red-painted barn whose walls showed gaps; someone's dream place in the country, its shattered windows gaping like eyes weeping for broken dreams. Young saplings from the ornamental trees had overrun lawn and garden, providing welcome cover. Beside him Will Hutton flung up his right hand, clenched into a fist inside its mail-backed leather gauntlet, and the little column of mounted Bearkillers came to a halt with a sway and a surge, the heads of their long lances safely hidden from anything beyond the crest line ahead as well. This was about as far north as the Outfit patrolled regularly and well beyond the settled zone, but nobody would take too much notice of the horse soldiers—except to keep well-hidden, in some instances.

Lancers have a lot of punch, but they're not what you'd call inconspicuous.

Hiding still had its uses—this operation was one—but visibility wasn't equivalent to death, the way it was when he'd learned the pre-Change art of war.

Though hiding armies *is still a good idea, and easier than it was, no radar or sensors beyond Eyeball Mark One. But when the actual killing starts, you have to run right up to the other guy to noogie on him and he can just stand there giving you the finger until you do. It* still *feels weird.*

Havel and Hutton and Signe dismounted along with Eric Larsson and his wife Luanne, handing off their reins. The patrol got their mounts into the shelter of the building. A very good eye might see the trail they'd left cross-country from some distance, but the rolling land made that unlikely. So did the combination of shaggy second growth and forest that covered a lot of it.

Havel nodded to the patrol commander and went walking forward with the others, then stooping; finally they went to their bellies as they came to the ridge ahead. That was no knife-edge crest, just a long low swelling that rose perhaps fifty feet above the level of the countryside and well below the Amity Hills to their west. A sagging board fence grown up in brush and vines marked it, and a few tall firs; they crawled into the undergrowth carefully, pushing forward with helmeted heads and armored shoulders against the thick spiky growth. An occasional muttered curse sounded as a thorn or twig slipped between the rings of chain mail and through the quilted padding beneath.

Then they all uncased their binoculars and pushed back their bowl helmets—the nasal bar made using field glasses impossible unless you did that—and looked through the last screen of tall grass and brush towards the north. There was a burned-out farmhouse not far down the slope, snags of wall reaching up through rampant vine and brush. The ruin stood in a clump of trees; those that lived at all were half dead from the heat of years past, their bare limbs stretching towards the overgrown mound with their other sides in leaf, quivering in the mild breeze from the north. A broken-down barn stood beyond, and after that neglected fields running down to a creek lined with trees; beyond *that* was another stretch of burgeoning wilderness; the edge of the Protectorate's plow-land and pasture was out of sight at the north end of this stretch, what used to be called the Dayton Prairie.

Two roads ran north-south down the lowland to his right, the easternmost crossing the river on a bridge still intact; someone had gone to the trouble of clearing off the vehicles from that one.

"And that's where the Crossing Tavern is," he said. "Just this side of where Webfoot Road crosses the creek."

"Where the innkeeper's feeding travelers to Crusher Bailey's gang for a cut of the take. The ones who won't be missed too bad," Will Hutton replied grimly.

"Let's not jump to conclusions, Unc' Will," Signe said. "Crusher's gang *is* working this area, but we don't know their MO and we're not sure the innkeeper's in it with them. My people haven't been able to find out anything one way or another."

Havel pulled a grass stem and stuck it meditatively between his teeth, enjoying the fresh sweetness and inhaling the welcome smell of new spring growth crushed under the rings of his hauberk.

My darling wife has *come a long way,* he thought, grinning inwardly. *She was a vegetarian before the Change, and now she's head of the CIA, as well as a mean hand with a backsword. Well, we probably suit a lot better than I would with Juney Mackenzie—that woman's conscience can make you feel* real *uncomfortable.*

"You been able to find out what the hell the Protector is doing up the Columbia?" he said.

"He's back, but not with most of the troops," she said. "Haven't been able to find out what he was doing. He just ordered a task force together and sailed out of Portland, leaving the Seal with his wife. Then he got back two days ago, headed straight out of Portland west with an escort, and while he was on the road there *Sandra* called out a hundred crossbowmen and fifty knights and their banners and sent them east over the Willamette—towards Molalla, remember? Arminger went after them hot-foot. Must be something important going on over there. Those visitors of his were involved."

"Can you guess at anything?"

"Well, his daughter's staying with Molalla. The guy was a Blood before the Change, name of Jabar, but he's more sensible than a lot of Arminger's baronage. Firm supporter of the Protector, worse luck."

"Well, whatever's going on over there, it *does* make it the perfect time to take care of Crusher Bailey," he mused.

He looked carefully at the roadhouse that stood just south of the creek and the bridge, nearly hidden by the trees. He'd never been up here himself, not this far eastward at least; no sense in giving the Protector a free chance at a coup de main. There was a fair amount of traffic on the road; the Protectorate and the other Valley communities were formally at peace despite the occasional skirmish, and everyone benefited from trade in the meantime. He could see individuals on foot, mounted on bicycles or on horseback, carts of wildly varied construction ranging from wooden replicas of nineteenth-century models to cutdown pickups, small herds of sheep or cattle . . .

The ridge they were using for cover was the last easternmost outlier of the Amity Hills, themselves the northern fringe of the Eolas; none of the heights were over a few hundred feet, but in sharp contrast to the flat open land ahead and to his right. For a while he examined the territory, and the wisp of smoke rising from the sheet-steel chimneys of the way-stop.

"It's on the south bank of . . . Holdridge Creek, right?" he said.

Hutton nodded. "That runs east into Palmer Creek, an' that goes north to meet the West Fork and join the Yamhill at Dayton, then that hits the Willamette past the big east-trending bend."

The Texan pointed slightly north of east: "That bit there, though, the sloughs over a couple-two miles thataway, they're a lot worse than they were before the Change, comparin' the maps to the firsthand look I had last week. Swamp and nothin' but. Braided channels and islands, all shifted around. What roads an' bridges there were are damn near all gone and we couldn't tell which wasn't yet, not without being pretty noticeable."

Eric whistled agreement; he'd been on that downriver scouting mission too, drifting along disguised as a barge-load of grain.

"No shit!" he said. "Part of that area was a state park, wetland preserve. Lordy"—a trick of tongue he'd picked up from his Texas-born father-in-law—"but it's wet now! A duck could drown in there if he didn't know the pathways."

"Yeah, and the bad guys can hide out in it," Havel said. "They *do* know 'em."

Signe chuckled. "It's like the Debatable Land," she said. "*Que?*" Havel said.

"Something my esteemed stepmother mentioned. Pam says a long time ago there used to be this stretch of ground between England and Scotland; they both claimed it, and neither one would let the other put in its laws and sheriffs. So there *wasn't* any law—not even as much as the rest of the border had—and outlaws made their home there."

"Sort of like the Hole in the Wall gang," Hutton said meditatively.

Will Hutton had been a noted wrangler and horse tamer before the Change, with a small ranch in Texas and customers for his horses all over the Western states; a delivery had caught him in Idaho that March nine years ago. He'd never graduated high school, but he was widely read in Western history and anything to do with horses.

"Yeah," Havel said. "Only this Crusher Bailey bastard's a lot nastier than Butch and Sundance, and too many of his hits are around here. His gang's not going to go on raiding our people and stealing our cattle and horses. Now that I've eyeballed the terrain, I say we go with the plan. The Protector's barons are having some sort of kerfuffle over on the east side of the river, a problem with raiders or something like that—less chance they'll try to interfere right now. There won't be a better time."

Signe sighed. "Yeah, and Arminger still has some of his cadre at Bonneville, after the whatever-it-was he was doing up the Columbia. Let's get moving, then."

"You sure you want to do this, sis?" Luanne Larsson— nee Hutton—said. "I thought you were . . ."

"Lost it," Signe replied shortly. "It was only a month along, anyway."

Eric grumbled in turn as they turned and slid down towards the Bearkillers waiting in the swale. "I still say you should let us do it, bossman."

Havel snorted. "It's not so easy to get known by sight without pictures or TV, but there still aren't many six-foot-two blond guys with wives who look like Luanne wandering around the Valley. You two are both pretty well known by name and general description this close to Larsdalen. People would be a lot more likely to twig if they saw you side-by-side."

Oregon had been a pretty white-bread state before the Change, particularly outside the cities, and the survivors had tended to be rural folk. You saw the odd Asian around, some blacks and rather more Hispanics, but all were few enough that they stood out. Some contrasts would just attract the eye and prompt the memory; Luanne's chocolate-colored features were a compromise between Hutton's blunt face and the strong-boned Tejano-Mexican comeliness of her mother, Angelica, all the more striking next to her husband's Viking looks. It was a pity; they wanted a woman along on this because it tended to disarm observers a little, and Luanne's skill set would have been perfect. Signe would do nearly as well, though, with a little cosmetic work.

"You just want all the fun," Eric said.

He grinned as he spoke, but his eyes flickered to his sister in momentary unease; this would be dangerous in ways that a straight-up fight wasn't.

Havel shrugged. "It beats reading and annotating reports on sugar-beet production and having meetings about management of the mint, but then so does getting nibbled to death by giant cockroaches."

He *did* feel a bit guilty about taking over this mission—it was really a job for an NCO—but ... *Time I got away from home for a little. Maybe I'll be appreciated more that way when I get back! And anyway, the Pentagon's ruins and bones. We're back to kings leading from the front.*

"And we have to do it smart," he said. "Riding in with our lances all shiny and bright, they'll just run away again—plus the Protector's men might object; like Eric says, they claim this area too. We don't want to start that war just yet. So ... let's waddle and quack like decoy ducks. Might be fun, at that."

"So you admit it's an abuse of rank for personal gratification," Eric said.

"Shut *up!*" Luanne said, then snorted and rolled her

eyes. "Signe's got her an actual reason to do this, since her fellah's going, but *will* you please stop volunteerin' to get me kilt, husband? Men! It's like you're fighting over the right to muck out the stables!"

"It's a dirty job, but—" Havel and Eric began in unison, then grinned at each other. Luanne turned to her father and threw up her hands in exasperation:

"Idiots, every one, starting with Dumb Blondie here. I make an exception for you, Daddy."

Hutton shook his head. "You're too easy on me, honey pie. When I was Eric's age, I was still ridin' roughstock at rodeos and it don't come no more stupid than that; the brains kick in when you get past forty and slow down a bit. You should be gettin' to your years of discretion soon, Mike, if you live that long."

Ouch.

They'd hidden the decoy material several miles back, in an overgrown orchard just south of the Amityville–Hopewell road, with an observer in a tree up on Walnut Hill to make sure nobody was snooping. A group of senior apprentices waited there, and they helped Havel and Signe out of their war harnesses—you had to be a bit of a contortionist to shed a hauberk by yourself. The slow fall of white blossom in the mild wind made it more pleasant than usual.

Signe looked at herself in the mirror; her naturally wheat-gold hair was now a dark glossy brown; and she brushed off a few pink petals clinging to the damp locks and sighed: "Well, Miss Clairol still works. Long dark hair and short blond roots after this."

"You look a lot more convincing as a brunette than I would as a blonde, sis." Luanne smiled; then she turned to Havel and snapped open a makeup kit. "Let's get to work on the bossman."

When she'd finished he took the mirror and looked at himself. His bowl-cut black hair was now cropped until it looked like a homemade crewcut just growing out; she'd stained the distinctive white scar that ran from the corner of his left eye up across his forehead, which made it much less noticeable, and covered the little brand mark between his brows. Luckily he had a naturally dark complexion and took the sun well—probably a legacy of his Anishinabe grandmother, given that the rest of him was a mix of Finn, Swede and Norse—so the stain went well with his usual weathered tan. Contact lenses salvaged from an optometrist's in Salem turned his pale gray eyes brown-black.

The clothes were what a pair of well-to-do stock farmers from east of the Cascade mountains might wear; tough pre-Change hiking pants with cargo pockets and a couple of neatly repaired rips, check cotton shirts, boots, broad-brimmed hats, duster-style leather jackets that fastened with toggles across the left side of the torso, sewn with links of chain on either shoulder to offer a little protection from a downward blow. Their plain round shields were unexceptional, and so were the Bearkiller-style backswords and powerful recurve bows in saddle-scabbards; that type of equipment was made over much of Oregon these days, not just in the Outfit's territory, and anyway smiths in Larsdalen and Rickreall had a nice sideline in selling blades and fighting gear.

All was not quite as it looked. The leather coats were of much thinner material than they appeared, and were lined with light chain mail made from fine steel wire, with an under-layer of nylon; the hats held what Pam called "secrets"—steel skullcaps concealed by the crown of the Stetsons.

Havel's flat Upper Midwestern vowels were at least a bit different from the way a native of the Valley spoke, and Signe could sound like someone from the Bend country at need. The fifteen loose horses actually *were* from over the mountains, ranch-bred of good working-quarter horse stock; the type was a steady export of the eastern slope. The last element of their ensemble was a light but sturdy two-wheeled cart, also genuine—it came from a shop in Bend owned by someone who'd made equipment for rodeos before the Change—drawn by a single horse between shafts, and bearing bundles and bales covered by a tightly roped tarpaulin, as well as a little surprise cooked up in the elder Larsson's workshop laboratory. The driver was a tow-haired teenager, a military apprentice named Kendricks picked for his wits and ability to keep his mouth shut, with his bow slung on the frame beside him, along with a spear in a holder and a hatchet and long knife at his waist. Everything was in good repair, but appropriately dusty and battered, the way you would be after weeks on the road.

Signe exchanged a brief embrace with Eric, then hugged Luanne and Will Hutton too. "Don't worry, sis, Unc' Will. I'll keep Mike out of trouble."

"You do that, honey-pie," he said gruffly. Then to Havel: "Take us about an hour and a half to get into position."

"I don't expect they'll try and jump us at the inn or on the road there, there's too much traffic. More likely to try something tomorrow, north of the crossing," Havel said. "Crusher's too smart to crap where he eats, or we'd have strung him up by now. He's been working this stretch for more than a year."

"Got me a rope ready and a tree all picked out," the Bearkillers' second-in-command said grimly. "That big one back to the tavern would do right nice."

Hutton hated bandits with a cold passion; three Idaho amateurs had jumped him just after the Change, and they'd figured out what had happened to firearms before he did; plus they'd been survivalists of a particularly nasty breed, the Aryan Brotherhood. They would have killed him and raped his wife and daughter and then probably killed *them* if it hadn't been for Michael Havel and Eric Larsson stumbling onto the scene, fresh out of the wilderness where their plane had crashed.

A mirror flicked a signal from atop Walnut Hill: the *All clear*. Havel swung into the saddle—a plain cowboy-Western type, not the more specialized military models the Bearkillers had been making the last few years. Signe got the herd moving; she'd grown up around horses, at Larsdalen and the family ranch in Idaho, and she was still better than he was at handling the beasts *en masse*.

He leaned over to speak a last word to Hutton. "Just get in place on the north side of Holdridge Creek and keep a sharp eye out for the signal," he said. "We'll take it slow to let you have time to do it without drawing attention to yourselves, and there's plenty of cover. We'll come on in the afternoon, or next morning, depending on what we find at the Crossing Tavern. If they jump us anywhere, it'll be between there and the Protector's border, so they can hide the horses in the marshland. The reports are pretty conclusive that nobody gets snagged at the tavern itself."

Of course, if they blow our cover, they might make an exception.

Hutton nodded and gripped his hand for a moment; Havel waved to the others and followed. As he went he turned and looked over his left shoulder at the Amity Hills—at Walnut Hill, in particular.

Would it be worth keeping a permanent lookout there? he thought.

The hilltop posts were useful for keeping an eye on things—he'd scavenged telescopes and binoculars everywhere they could be found—and lights and mirrors let them flash a message quickly. But building them high enough to be useful was expensive in labor and materials, and each required a crew who could be doing something else . . .

Like plowing this land, he thought.

They were down from the low rolling heights, cutting eastward across open fields. There had been farms in the hills—undulating country you could call hills only by contrast to the flat alluvial Valley floor—and even more orchards and vineyards, but more forest than anything else. The lowland was all cleared except for the banks of the odd stream and small woodlots, or had been before the Change; and this close to the high ground it was all naturally well drained, unlike the bottomland farther east. Right now it was tall green grassland getting shaggy with brush, spots half blue with May's camas flowers. Ready for the plow, but the trees were starting to encroach and the orchards to degenerate into pathless thickets. In a few decades it'd be twenty-foot trees and heavy brush laced together with feral grapevines as thick as your thigh; in fifty, dense mixed woods. He'd grown up working-class of a deeply rural sort in the Upper Peninsula of Michigan, and he knew what it was like to take down a big tree with ax or a crosscut saw, and to get the roots out without dynamite or a powered winch.

The problem is that there just aren't enough people around—to do that, or anything else. So my grandchildren will have to bust their asses . . . or . . .

"Signe?" he said. She glanced over and he went on: "Didn't you tell me once most of the Willamette was grass-land when the pioneers arrived? Looks like it's growing up in forest pretty quick now."

She nodded. "That was the Indians. They used to set fires in the autumn to kill off brush and saplings, so there was a lot of prairie and oak meadow. Grazing for deer and elk, and plenty of camas root in the prairies. This would all be solid forest otherwise."

"We might do some burning," Havel said. "Be sort of dangerous, though . . . have to do it after wheat harvest and be real careful the fires didn't get out of control . . ."

He made an exasperated sound between his teeth. Running a country, even a little one, turned out to be a lot like being a juggler, only you couldn't help dropping an egg now and then—if you were lucky, you got to pick which one went ker-splat.

And eggs don't scream when you fumble them. And to think I wanted this job . . . OK, let's be honest in here where it's private: I still want this job. I like making things happen instead of having them happen to me, and I'm pretty good at it, which is good for everyone. And I will purely and surely do whatever it takes to win a fight, which is just what we need with Arminger around. I just don't like some parts of it much.

Signe loped her mount back a little west and waved her coiled lariat at a horse visibly thinking of straying, helping to keep the herd bunched until they crossed an overgrown ditch and swung onto Webfoot Road, turning north. The beasts saw no particular reason not to stop and take a drink from a pond or eat a little of the succulent new grass now and then, but they were reasonably used to doing un-reasonable things because humans told them to, and the lead mare was well trained.

Still, I get daydreams about just being a rancher or a farmer myself, he thought. *Just honest work to put food on the table and lay something by for the kids. But someone has to run things, or Momma-threw-away-the-baby-and-raised-the-afterbirth types like Arminger and Crusher Bailey will do it.*

He glanced eastward; about half a mile thataway you could see why the little county two-lane called Webfoot had gotten its name, but big parts of the swamp looked new, too. There were dead trees in it, their roots killed out by standing water.

"That must have happened when the Keene Reservoir broke," he said. "Damn, but I hate to see things get run down that way."

"Hey, Mike, remember you're not Lord Bear today, and staggering along carrying the Outfit on your shoulders," Signe said, reading his mind with disconcerting ease; that happened more and more often as their marriage accumulated years. "You're Mr. Brown from Cottonwood Ranch, and it's a fine spring day with the sun shining and no cares in this world—except getting our skulls crushed by Crusher Bailey, or our bodies shot full of arrows, but Mr. Brown wouldn't know about that."

"Yeah, life is good for Mr. Brown," he said, grinning back.

There really *was* a John Brown of Cottonwood Ranch, and they'd met fairly often at conferences. He was one of CORA's movers and shakers, and the Central Oregon Ranchers' Association was as close as the country east of the Cascades had to a government nowadays, not that that was saying much.

"Not that the poor man would appreciate it," Signe replied, and they both laughed.

The rancher was also a serious chill-dill-pickle-up-the-butt worrier, which made Signe's comment sly as well as to the point. He'd always liked her sense of humor.

We get along pretty good most of the time, he thought. *Which makes it more of a contrast when we don't.*

He relaxed a little and took a deep breath; it was only slightly seasoned with the dust and smell of the horses.

Under the rumble of their hooves was a deep quiet; the sough of wind though the grass and an occasional roadside tree, a rookery of pigeons sitting on a section of telephone wire still standing, small animals flashing across the road; once he glimpsed the flicker of something bigger along a field boundary. He guessed at a buck from the brief glimpse of a black-tipped tail, but possibly a feral cow. Wild game was coming back nicely the last few years with all this rich edge-habitat land to feed off. In a way the ghastly outbreak of plague in the refugee camps back in Change Year One had been fortunate—there hadn't been time to strip *every* living thing from the Valley lands before the Black Death finished what starvation began, with assists from cholera and typhus.

And keep focused. This isn't like riding out to find some deer or wild pigs. We might get attacked before we reach the tavern.

The land went by slowly; you didn't push horses past walking pace when you were taking them to sell and wanted them in prime condition at the end of the trip. Distances that had been a quick run to the mall before the Change meant hours of walking, now.

I wonder when we'll stop comparing things to how they were before the Change? he thought idly.

Then, with wry honesty: *Never. I was a man grown by then and I'm always going to be a stranger in this world. Signe and Luanne do it less than I do—they were teenagers—and Ken does it more—he was past fifty. Astrid less than any of them, but then, she was just fourteen and never really touched down much on Planet Consensus Reality anyhow. Our kids will probably think we're lying through our teeth about the old world and get bored as hell with our stories.*

The sun crept by overhead, getting on towards afternoon. Two big carts went by them southbound drawn by eight yoke of oxen each—car-wheeled, but with new-made frames of timber and metal, both loaded with tall pyramids of PCB pipe lashed down with rope; no doubt the tubing was ripped out of a derelict town or Portland itself and was headed out to repair someone's plumbing system. The oxen were red-and-white Herefords, not the best for the work but passable, plodding along with splay-footed patience along the cracked and potholed asphalt. The drivers walked beside the wagons, spears in their hands, and not looking too badly off—even a sadistic son of a bitch like Arminger couldn't afford to make *everyone* in his territory miserable. The wagoneers weren't looking too worried, either; but then nobody was likely to pick a fight over half a ton of plastic pipe.

Only governments stole on that scale, and Crusher Bailey hadn't quite gotten up to the robber-baron level.

Two lighter carts came by, each drawn by a pair of mules; Signe called a question, which was in character, and the driver told them what they carried: shelled filberts, nut oil and smoked salmon—the runs were improving on the Columbia since the dams at Bonneville and The Dalles broke, but not very far up the Willamette as yet. The rest of the cargo was salvaged goods from the dead cities, fine fabric and cutlery and edge tools, plus aspirin, antiseptic ointment and Tums, things you rarely saw anymore. Not surprisingly, that wagon had more guards, mounted ones. They looked more alert than the spearmen guarding the load of pipe, and also looked like they were Protectorate men-at-arms; gleaming oiled chain or scale hauberks covering them neck to knees, big kite-shaped shields slung over their backs, conical nose-guarded helmets over mail coifs on their heads and long double-edged swords at their belts, lances in their hands with the butts resting in rings riveted to their right stirrups. The morning sun shone liquidly on the metal of their armor, and their eyes were hard and wary, constantly moving.

Back right after the Change, Arminger had mistaken dressing men up in military gear for the much more difficult process of turning them into real fighters, but experience had taught him and his new-made lords better since.

Maybe they're moonlighting, Havel thought, eyeing the men-at-arms narrowly. *Or possibly someone, Baron Emiliano for instance, has an interest in the shipment and lent them to whoever organized it.*

Northbound traffic was mostly beef cattle and some

sheep, together with oxcarts loaded with sacks of grain or potatoes, butter and cheese in tubs. Their horse-herd swung wide around the slow-moving obstructions, and once nearly came to grief with a herd of yearling shoats that used the distraction to evade their minders and make a break for the river swamps; from childhood experience, he suspected pigs were smart enough to know why people kept them around and act accordingly. A horse-drawn wagon passed them northbound; the dozen guards walking beside it looked like university people—the pikes half bore were the more complex sixteen-foot takedown model the Corvallis militia favored, and the other six carried long-bows or crossbows. That many guards meant a valuable cargo; from a quick look he thought it was beeswax in blocks, expensive and valuable for half a dozen purposes, starting with candles that didn't stink and drip as much as tallow dips, and small kegs of honey.

He and Signe took their horses around the ox wagons, and well off the road for a while when the horse-drawn wagon came up behind them; perfectly sensible, if you didn't want animals inconveniently bolting. He dismounted and faced away from the road, taking up one of Charger's hooves and holding it between his knees as if he was getting a stone out.

If anyone can recognize my ass, I deserve to get caught, he thought, smiling down at the perfectly sound hoof; luckily, Charger was a good-natured horse.

When they got moving again, Signe unslung a small guitar and began strumming and singing:

> *"Run softly, Blue River, my darlin's asleep*
> *Run softly, Blue River, run cool and deep—"*

Havel joined in, his bass more tuneful than it had been before the Change; if you wanted music these days, it had to be live, and practice helped even if you had little natural talent. He liked country, but his tastes ran more to Kevin Welch or Bob Schneider tunes, and he'd developed a taste for the Cajun sound, zydeco, while he was in the Corps. On the other hand, he could take Johnny Cash. The

Huttons' tastes had been influential, and they tended to really *old-fashioned* country—some of their stuff was so old that it sounded a lot like Juney Mackenzie's songs.

At least it beats that sixties boomer crap Ken loves. I shouldn't have let him build those wind-up phonographs; if I have to listen to a scratchy Sympathy for the Devil *or* We Are Stardust *one more time . . . oh, well, the records will wear out eventually and he hasn't figured out how to make more.*

Singing on the road was perfectly normal these days, too; it wasn't as if you could plug a Walkman into your ear anymore. It had been surprisingly difficult for townie types to realize that life didn't come with a soundtrack.

Up ahead to the right was a fair-sized vineyard along Palmer Creek; some of it had died off near the water, but the rest of it had been painstakingly restored, pruned and cultivated, leaves bright against the old gnarled brown-black trunks. Then there was a patch of woodlot, green shade flickering above them; the Crossing Tavern had a sign there, nailed to an old telephone pole. It claimed, fairly implausibly, that the owner had certificates of protection from the Brigitine monks, from Mt. Angel twenty miles away across the Valley, from the Protector, from the Bearkillers, and from the independent town of Whiteson all together—he knew the one about the Outfit was a bare-faced lie. Below that were the services offered, and the terms of barter. The series of boards ended with one that read: *Mastercard and Visa accepted. No, just kidding.*

Havel barked laughter. "I do hope the owner's not in on it," he said. "I'd hate to hang a man with a sense of humor like that, bandit or not."

"I wouldn't," Signe said grimly.

Deadlier than the male, Havel thought silently.

He pulled his recurve bow out of the case and set an arrow on the string before he entered the woodlot, his eyes wary amid the firs and cottonwoods and big-leaf maples. Havel had been a crack shot with a rifle—particularly a scope-sighted Remington 700—but it had taken years of dogged practice to make him more than passable with a horn-and-sinew composite bow shot from horse-back. Signe was better than he was, Luanne could beat her, and Astrid Larsson could beat anyone in the family; she'd been an archery enthusiast before the Change. Some of the Outfit's younger generation looked to be downright uncanny.

Just beyond was what had once been a large building of some sort, probably a gas-station-cum-convenience store; there was no way to tell for sure, with signs down and the way it had been modified. The building had originally been shaped like a long T lying on its side with the narrow end pointing at the road. New construction had turned it into a narrow E with the three arms facing westward towards him, using the former parking lot as a floor. Some parts one-story and some two; the walls were a double layer of cinder block with rubble and concrete between, and the windows had heavy steel shutters pierced by arrow slits. It looked untidy, but immensely strong; there was a small greenhouse of plastic sheeting on metal arches, and a mature orchard—cherries, by the froth of pink blossoms, and apples in the next field just showing white—off behind it were paddocks and a big truck garden covering several acres, with more orchard on the other side of Holdfast Creek.

The Bearkillers' intel said the place had started out in the first full Change Year, someone who'd managed to survive God-knew-where-and-how settling and claiming the area together with his extended family. He'd made a living the first little while off the truck he grew and for-aging, but mainly by rigging a hand pump and selling the fuel from the gas station's underground tank, essential for lighting and half a dozen other uses. Then he'd branched out into a rest stop, as people began moving around once more.

A suspicious number of whom don't make it through these parts . . .

There were horses and cattle in the paddock nearest the building, unhitched wagons, saddles resting on a rack by the door, and a few folk walking about. A makeshift tower three stories tall held a watcher, who began beating on a piece of sheet metal as Havel came out of the trees, louder than the *clang-ting!* of a smithy somewhere in the background.

Several more people came out at that, one of them holding a pre-Change compound hunting bow, immensely valuable while it worked and impossible to repair or replace when it didn't anymore. A woman flanked him, with a polearm—a long curved cutting blade on a four-foot shaft, a *naginata*. The younger man on the other side had a spear and a bowie knife, and a double thong with an egg-shaped lead ball in its soft leather pouch, held deftly in his right hand—a sling, David-and-Goliath type. There was a family resemblance to all three, stocky and big-boned—the sort who'd have been overweight before the Change—with strong black hair and beak noses and bony faces.

Havel carefully returned arrow to quiver, slid his bow into the saddle-scabbard and held up his hands in sign of peace. "I'm traveling in horses," he said, jerking one thumb towards the herd behind him. "Name's John Brown; got my wife Anne with me, and a boy who works for us."

The man in his thirties stroked his bushy black beard and nodded, looking them over and considering their gear. Several more people, probably customers or employees, came out of the heavy metal door—it looked as if it had been salvaged from a warehouse—and stood watching.

"Welcome," the proprietor said. "I'm Arvand Sarian, and I keep the Crossing Tavern."

There was a slight guttural accent to indicate his fluent English wasn't his native language, but he didn't look Mexican and the accent wasn't Spanish, or anything Havel had met when posted to the Gulf. He also looked past Havel as Signe bunched the horses up; one of them made a half-hearted bolt and she turned her mount in pursuit with a sharp whistle, the lariat whirling over her head. Then the noose shot out and settled neatly about the fleeing mare's head; it submitted meekly as she led it back to the others. Sarian's shaggy eyebrows rose slightly; the eyes beneath were small and so black you couldn't see the line between pupil and iris.

"You're not Bearkillers," he said. "Not from Mt. Angel, or Corvallis either. And certainly not Mackenzies!"

Havel shook his head. "We're CORA folks," he said. "Cottonwood Ranch, south of Sisters. Came over 20 as soon as the pass opened, with a horse herd and them carrying packs; hides, tallow, wool. Sold most of it in the Mackenzie country and Corvallis. I had this lot left, and heard the Protector's man north of here was buying, so I sent the rest of my hands back and brought 'em up. The Bearkillers didn't object but they weren't what you'd call friendly."

"Baron Emiliano is buying horses, yes," Arvand said, his voice neutral.

"Well, we'd like to stop a spell. See to our horses' shoes, if you've a farrier, rest up, groom 'em, have a meal better than trail rations . . . maybe stay the night."

Arvand nodded. "What have you to barter?" he went on briskly. "Or I'll take gold or silver—coined, if you have them. Corvallan or Bearkiller dollars, or Protectorate marks or rose nobles. Or I'll take it by weight, or any of the usual trade goods." He looked aside to the younger man, probably a son or brother. "Aram, help the lady with her herd—the paddock by the north wall."

"I've got some precious metals, a little," Havel said, nodding thanks. "Or I can trade"—he nodded to the cart—"from what I picked swapping up for the horses. I've got windup alarm clocks, Swiss army knives, needles and pins, sewing thread, combination padlocks, fishhooks and synthetic fishing line, eggbeaters, sausage grinders and such like. And some Fruit of the Loom underwear and good hiking socks, still in the plastic."

Arvand beamed at him; those were light high-value goods.

And I wouldn't have told you about it all, *if this were on the square. Just the thing a bandit would love to steal, to go along with the horses. But go ahead, think I'm stupid.*

They began to dicker. That went briskly, and Havel had an obscure sense that he'd been skinned afterward, even though the price wasn't unreasonable. He and Signe turned over their horses to Arvand's workers—half of them had that same family resemblance—and went in through the tavern's front doors, their saddlebags over their shoulders after politely declining an offer to lock them up in a strongbox; he bustled in ahead of them.

Havel blinked as he strode into the main room. Places like this had been springing up at natural stopping points over the past couple of years, as the simple scramble to survive lifted a little and men began to learn or relearn, a little, how to live in the Changed world. A few things were ordinary: a big common room with a fireplace and a bar, tables and booths, stairs to rooms above, a kitchen that served as a barrier between the inn proper and the quarters of the owner and his family and retainers. This one was bigger and tidier than most, although neither people nor clothes nor boots could be as clean now as in the lost days of washing machines and cheap abundant soap and no manure-producing animals close to the house. It didn't stink here, though; it smelled of cooking and woodsmoke, and the food looked to be more than the usual bread with stew from a pot kept eternally bubbling on the hearth. Not that he didn't like a good savory stew, but it wore if you were traveling a lot—especially when "savory" translated as "thick and brown."

Better lit than most, too. Christ Jesus, they've even gotten a blackboard menu up! The shish kebab look tempting, but . . .

"Double bacon cheeseburger with fries," he said, when the innkeeper had led them to a booth and a waitress poised. There was even catsup—doubtless homemade under the lying Heinz label, but he suspected it would be good.

"Me too," Signe said eagerly.

The other surprise was the rugs—not on the floor, which was clean-swept asphalt still bearing faint yellow and white stripes, but hanging from the walls, the only ornaments except for some not-quite-Russian-looking religious images. The colors of the rugs were deep and rich, wine reds and blues and purples, in patterns that combined geometry with stylized flowers and animals; they reminded him of some the Larssons had had in the big house from before the Change. A couple of them had unusual combinations of colors, paler and more delicate. He recognized the ones weavers in the Bearkiller territory and its neighbors had produced from wild indigo, safflower, berries, and some new to him as well.

"Those for sale?" he asked Sarian.

"My friend," the man said, smiling whitely and stroking his curly black beard; it fell halfway down his chest. "My friend, the only things not for sale here are our land, our weapons and our women. I sell food, I sell lodging, I buy and sell horses and tack and doctor horses and have them shod, I trade bulk grain and foodstuffs, and I sell the goods people trade to me for these things . . . and I sell rugs, yes."

Havel pointed at the carpets with the colors of home-made dyes. "Looks like you *make* them, too."

"My aunt, rather, and my wife, and some girls they've taught. Just this little while, but it is a tradition in my family, in the old country." He grimaced. "I came to America from my homeland not long before the Change—we lost everything in the war there, when we had to flee Baku. I fought with our army until we won, but then there was no making a living. So, we build up a little business here, brought over some of my relatives, and then—*poof!*—the whole world goes crazy. At once I saw that Portland was doomed."

"You got out with the rugs?" Havel said.

The majority hadn't realized what was happening until far too late, and had then fled the fires and fighting in panic with nothing but what they had on their backs; most hadn't gotten twenty miles before they just laid down and died, of hunger and thirst and sheer heartbreak, although you found bones along every road even now. The others . . . well, a lot of them had been eating each other by then, and not long after that the plagues started.

"We had bicycles and we made a cart of them, to pull, you understand, with all the supplies we could gather. I had a restaurant . . . The rugs we hid after a day or two on the road. We lived in the woods for many months—from hunting, the supplies we had, and a few cows and pigs and chickens we . . . found. Then I come here when the worst was over, see it is a good place when things get better, and . . ." He glanced around, pride in his eyes.

"What's your price on the rugs?" Signe said, sounding genuinely curious. "New and old?"

"More for the old than the new. The new are good, very good, but we are still . . . what's the word, experimenting with dyes. And we need more alum, to fix the colors."

Sarian glanced aside at Havel. He shrugged in turn: "Anne knows cloth better than I do. Bargains good, too."

Which is true enough. She's got a better natural head for logistics than I do.

The food came, and glass steins of beer; the latter was as cold as you could get by keeping the barrels in a cellar. The waitress also had a little scale, and looked at the scraps of silver with a practiced eye as she weighed them. He ate the hamburger with appreciation; the food at Larsdalen was excellent, of course, but he spent a lot of time in the field. The fresh tomatoes must be among the first of the season, started under glass and then planted out, and they were delicious, the onions pungent and strong, the lean ground beef a meaty delight set off by the rich tang of the cheese and the smoky-salt bacon.

Food often tasted better since the Change—when it was fresh, particularly. Out of season you got things dried, pickled, canned, smoked or salted, if at all, and hoped like hell nothing went dangerously and undetectably bad. At that, the Willamette growing season was longer than most places; diets got a lot more monotonous east of the mountains, or further north.

Sarian nursed one stein of beer as he had carpet after carpet brought over. At last they settled on a price for a dozen, six of the new and six of the old.

"There'll be a good market for these back home," Signe said.

Which was true for their assumed characters and their real ones both. There were plenty of A-listers prospering enough to want to spruce up their fortified farmhouses, not to mention some Bearkiller traders and craftsmen doing very well. And no doubt the rugs would be popular with wealthy ranchers in the Bend country too; not only were they pretty, but hung on a wall they'd do wonders with cold drafts in the high-country winters now that central heating was mostly a nostalgic snow-season memory.

Signe got a deal that would leave us a profit if we were who we're pretending to be, and I still feel obscurely certain we've been took. Again. I'd hate to buy a used car from this guy!

"Good," Havel said, as the three of them shook on the deal. "We'll pick 'em up on my way back."

"Chicory?" the waitress said—she'd been the one with the *naginata*. "Or more beer? There's wine and brandy and whiskey available too."

"One more beer," Havel said. "Chicory's just enough like real coffee to make you miss it more."

"Bring it along, John," Signe said as she put down her napkin and rose. "I'm not going to let anyone put their hands on our horses without I look 'em over first."

"You said it, honey."

The farrier's forge was in what had been the repair bays of the gas station, which was a clever use of space; one bay had a frame and winch-worked hoist for shoeing working oxen, ending in a big canvas bellyband—unlike horses, cattle couldn't stand on three legs, so you had to hoist their weight off their feet before you could get at the hooves. The smith himself didn't look like one of Sarian's relatives; he was pale, with brown hair and beard and a thick pelt likewise on his broad chest, freckles on his muscular arms; he was in jeans and steel-toed boots and a new-made leather apron and arm-guards, otherwise bare above the waist. His wife had the innkeeper's stamp, though, and he dropped a word or two of the guttural-throaty language the Sarians talked among themselves into his conversation with her as she pumped the bellows.

Signe watched him work and nodded to Havel, satisfied. He wasn't surprised. The big brick hearth with its metal smoke-hood, the double-punch cylinder bellows, the workbenches and rows of tools and four specialized anvils, all argued for competence. So did the abundant store of blank horseshoes on pegs. The way the farrier handled the job he was on confirmed it, and the customer led his mule away with a satisfied smile.

"Like you to have a look at my drove stock," Havel said to the smith; Sarian observed with his arms crossed on his chest. "Our riding mounts are fine, and the cart beast, we had them done in Corvallis, but the others've come a long ways on asphalt. We'd like the ones who need it trimmed and new-shod before we sell 'em."

"Be glad to—" the smith began, then stiffened.

Havel had heard the hollow booming *clock-clop* of hooves on the pavement of the bridge over Holdfast Creek just north, and the more solid crunching sound as they reached earth once more. Two men had ridden into the E-shaped front yard of the Crossing Tavern, on horses that looked shaggy-ungroomed but healthy and fast. Both wore bicycle helmets covered with straps of bent steel; one had a short sleeveless scale-mail shirt that looked a little small for him, the other a vest of braided rawhide picked out here and there with metal—cheap gear, but much better than nothing. The bigger of the two had bib overalls on under the armor, and he carried an odd weapon with the head resting on his right hip. The business end looked as if it had started life as a rock-breaking sledgehammer, but someone had sawn a couple of inches off each side of the head to bring the weight down to something reasonable, and then filed the metal striking surface crisscross until it was a series of small pyramids, like a giant meat-tenderizer.

Which is exactly what it is, Havel thought; the head was mounted on an ashwood shaft a yard long, with a hide-wound grip. *Have to be a strong man to use that, though.*

The two dismounted and led their horses over to the smithy. The man with the hammer *was* strong, Havel's height but broader, his torso a rectangular block the same width from wide shoulders to hips with arms as thick as the blacksmith's. He also had a bit of a kettle belly, and spare flesh elsewhere; not something you saw all that often these days, and his hair was as red as Juniper Mackenzie's, though it had started to fade back from a high forehead. The face below was broad and cheerful-looking, with small blue eyes and tufty eyebrows and a squashed-potato of a nose, a few broken veins there and on the cheeks. The face of someone ready with a joke and to knock back a few with friends, a smiler; there was a broad one on his face now as he listened to something his companion said.

That man was smaller and wiry, despite a certain family resemblance, and a bit older than his companion. He wore jeans and a checked shirt that were solid and untattered, which meant he was reasonably affluent; so did the good hiking boots. He had a hide bucket slung over his back like a quiver, but it held short spears instead of arrows, each about a yard long and tipped with narrow metal points. One of them was in his hand, and he rolled it over his knuckles and then twirled it with fingers alone, tossing it up and catching it, all without looking at it—his eyes were fixed on the travelers, particularly on Signe. He smiled too when she glanced around at him, revealing several missing front teeth; his mouth had a long parallel scar across the upper lip, as if someone had tried to grab it and slash it off and nearly succeeded. Two big knives completed his ensemble, not on his belt but strapped to his thighs.

"We need our horses done," the man with the javelin said. He looked at Havel. "Out of the way, you. We're regular customers."

The bigger man with the hammer made a soothing gesture at his companion. "The lady's first in line, little brother," he said. "We've got time. Those your horses in the paddock, ma'am?"

"My husband's and mine," Signe said distantly, nodding towards Havel.

"Those are some fine animals," he said. "They'd fetch a good price a bit north—Baron Emiliano wants some remounts for his crossbowmen."

Havel hitched his thumbs into his sword belt. "You interested in buying?"

The big man shook his head. "Carl Grettir isn't that rich, nor are his friends. Good luck with the Baron; he's a hard man and he'll drive a hard bargain."

There's always something strange about people who refer to themselves in the third person, Havel mused thoughtfully, watching as the two men handed off their horses and went inside. Signe blinked and seemed to be mentally searching for something, then shrugged and shook her head.

"You know," the Bearkiller leader said to Sarian, "if you put in a small water-race from that dam there"—he pointed northwest to where a pre-Change earthwork dam made a pond about a thousand yards away—"you could have a mill too, with an overshot wheel. That would be mighty useful, and not just for grinding grain. We've got one like that on the ranch, but we had to build quite an earth dam for it. It's drier, where we live."

The innkeeper shook himself a little, as if casting off some bitter thought. "Yes, Mr. Brown, it would be useful," he said. "And if there were a mill as well as a tavern, more settlers might come, a wainwright's shop, livery stable—a town, and farms around it. But I could not protect that many; I keep the peace within bowshot of my house and my bridge, and no more. Also I haven't enough hands to build such. And most of all, it would attract attention. I will not build up just for some warlord to take."

If this guy were in the Outfit's territory, I'd see he got loaned what he needed to expand, Havel thought, as he dipped his head to acknowledge the point and Sarian walked off. *I may be a warlord, but by Christ Jesus I'm not a stupid warlord, and I heard the fable of the goose and the golden eggs a long time ago.*

The tavern's smith was honest as well as competent; the seven horses he picked for reshoeing were the ones that actually needed it. Havel and Signe hung around, and weren't the only ones. He'd expected that; in any small community with a blacksmith, the forge tended to be a center of gossip as well as work, particularly before summer got really hot. Most of it was the usual dead-boring crops and weather—and weather in western Oregon was just too consistent to get very excited about, nothing like the Midwest where he'd been raised. People were curious about happenings east of the mountains, but not to the extent of being troublesome, since it was too distant to really affect their lives. There was more speculation about the Protector's intentions; everyone dreaded the prospect of another war. Havel suppressed a grin to hear himself described as a *brass-assed son of a bitch, but honest.* There weren't any Mackenzies present; when the discussion turned that way there was a mixture of superstition, dread, bewilderment and liking—the Clan had helped a lot of people pull through the second and third Change Years, mostly by loaning them seed corn and arranging deals for stock with the ranching country to the east.

Nobody mentioned Crusher Bailey until the two disguised Bearkillers brought up bandits in general, which was natural for their *persona* of outsiders traveling through strange territory. Probably the locals had been subconsciously afraid that talking about the man would make him more likely to appear.

"Yeah, *muy malo,* that one," a traveler from Gervais said. "Likes to break your knees and legs and leave you to die, I hear."

"*I* hear he *sells* people . . . up north," a woman declared.

Travelers from the Protectorate looked uneasy, or shrugged. "He certainly sells stock and stuff there," one of them said, spitting into the hearth; it made a sharp *fissst* sound. "Or his fence does, he doesn't show his face there. Baron Emiliano ought to get off his ass and do something about him, or the Bearkillers ought to. There'd be more trade on this road, and less wasted on guards, if he were gone."

"The Protectorate and the Bearkillers probably won't *let* each other take care of it," another commented. "Dog-in-the-manger stuff."

The spitter spat again. "Useless bastards, for all their armor and swords," he said, which was sufficiently ambiguous about who precisely he meant that he wouldn't get in trouble for it back home in the Protector's territory. "Goddamn it, what is this, America or Guatemala?"

"After the *Change,* you doorknob?" the woman said, and got a wry chuckle. "It's fucking *Braveheart* country now."

"Always preferred *Rob Roy,* myself," someone else said. "More realistic—and don't we know it, nowadays?"

The people who'd been adult at the time of the Change

settled in to the ever-popular rhythm of a 'remember that scene' conversation, and the younger ones tried to change the subject.

Havel took a cup of the chicory the next morning as he sat yawning in his booth; the effect might be psychosomatic, but it did help pop the eyelids open. Signe looked disgustingly fresh; she'd slept like a baby. Apprentice Kendricks had too, but *he* was sixteen and sleeping on the floor hadn't bothered him.

Everyone's gotten less finicky about privacy, Havel thought. *But there are still limits.*

Sarian came over to them after the waitress had dropped off their plates—bacon, scrambled eggs, toast, sausage and home fries. Havel cocked an eye up at him as he ate; the stocky, bearded man seemed to be hesitating, torn, as his guest mopped his plate with a piece of toast.

Which on short acquaintance I'd say is not his usual MO. I'd peg him for a can-do sort, Havel thought.

Decision firmed behind the heavy bearded face. He looked around, and bent over to speak quietly:

"I would go right now, friend, if I were you. Or wait until more are leaving, so you can go together."

Havel opened his mouth to ask a question, but Sarian shook his head and turned away.

"Aha," Signe said, lifting a spoonful of fried pickled green tomatoes onto her plate. "Now *that* was interesting, bossman."

Havel nodded. "And I think we should do precisely the opposite of what he advised. Take your time with breakfast, and we'll head out alone. If people are bunching up that way, the road'll be temptingly empty."

"And we'll be trailing a broken wing." Signe grinned back, but there was a tightness around her mouth.

Sarian didn't come to say good-bye as they left; a serious breach of good business sense with a newly won and valuable customer. Havel whistled silently as they left the Crossing Tavern's northernmost perimeter, marked by another set of signs nailed to a telephone pole. It was comforting to know that Will and the patrol would be hanging on their left, just out of sight to the west.

It was six miles to the edge of cultivation around Dayton, at the north end of the Dayton Prairie; two hours travel at the gentle walking pace they were using, much less if you pushed your mount. The grass and quick-growing bush were tall on either side of the road, turning most of the abandoned cars and trucks into mounds of vegetation; now and then bits of a burnt-out building showed above a similar hillock.

He frowned at the cars as the herd rumbled and clattered along; Charger's hooves clopped slowly, insects buzzed, and small fleecy clouds drifted through deep blue sky. In Bearkiller territory the dead vehicles hadn't just been pushed aside; they'd all been dragged off and systematically stripped of everything useful—particularly the leaf springs, invaluable for swords and knives and edge-tools of all sorts; they'd stored the surplus in old buildings, greased for protection, supplies sufficient for generations of smiths.

Then they were in a section where the fields had burned last fall, and the new grass was only knee-high, shot through with blue camas flowers. What had been a small store of some sort stood by the side of the road not far ahead to the left, and a line of willow and alder and oak on the right showed where Palmer Creek swung close. The two Bearkillers pretending to be ranchers cantered about, using shouts and waving lariats and occasionally the whirled end of a rope to remind the horses that spreading out through the rich meadow wasn't on the agenda for today.

"Heads up," he said softly, as seeming chance took them closer together.

Adrenaline dumped into his bloodstream like a jolt of electricity in the old days, and he seized control of his breathing. Movement . . .

Two mounted figures . . . and three more behind them, and a dozen on foot. He looked right; sure enough, half a dozen more coming out of the fields there, angling in towards the road behind them. He reached into a saddlebag for his field glasses—carrying a pair of binoculars around was a rather too obvious way for someone of his pretended identity to invite robbery—and leveled them, turning the focusing ring with his thumb.

Aha.

"It's the guy from Crossing Tavern, the one with the cut-down sledgehammer," he said. "Three guesses . . . Why waste time? It's Crusher Bailey, all right."

Grinning now as he waved and whooped his men on, and the grin looked less friendly and less fake than his expression back at the wayside inn. The horse herd was nervous, tossing their heads and turning back and forth as shouting humans closed in from three sides.

"Why am I not surprised?" Signe said. "Wait a minute . . . Crusher . . . didn't he call himself *Grettir?*"

"Yeah?"

She slapped the heel of her palm on her forehead. "*That's* what I was trying to remember! Dad told me about it ages ago, when we were kids and he was reading us those old squarehead stories." At his glance she went on: "It's what Grettir means in Old Norse. *Crusher.* You know how those Viking guys all had nicknames, Iron Fist or Blood Wolf or Skullsplitter or whatnot? There was a saga hero named Crusher—Starkad, Starkad Grettir."

"Big chuckle, ha, ha, a bandit with some education," Havel said. "He's probably going to try to get us to surrender, which gives us an opportunity. Kendricks! Ready!"

The apprentice threw back the tarpaulin that covered the back of the two-wheeled cart; below was a complicated piece of machinery, most of which consisted of coil springs from the suspensions of heavy trucks, all screwed down tight. In the middle of it all sat a rocket-shaped projectile. Kendricks flicked open the top of his lighter, an old-style model with a wick, alcohol reservoir and little steel wheel that ground against a flint. A quick motion of his thumb, and a pale blue flame topped it.

"Wait for it," Havel said without looking around. "Wait for it . . ."

His right hand went over his shoulder for an arrow.

Crusher's men were behind them, spread across the road, and getting closer to the right; Bailey himself was only fifty yards away ahead and northward, rising in the stirrups to cup his hands around his mouth and shout across the milling horses.

"Now!"

Kendricks touched his lighter to the stub of fuse on the side of the finned dart and then jerked a lever. There was a huge metallic *crunnng—WHUNNNG!* as the springs uncoiled, and the dart vanished skyward in a streak too fast for the eye to follow. At the top of its trajectory two seconds later there was a muffled *fump* as the little parachute deployed, and orange smoke billowed out a thousand feet above the surface of the Willamette.

Explosives didn't explode anymore. Lower-speed combustion, for example the type in a smoke flare, still worked like a treat.

Crusher Bailey had no leisure to watch. Even as the apprentice worked the machinery Ken Larsson had made, Larsson's daughter and Mike Havel drew their recurve bows to the ear. Horn and sinew and the thin sandwich of yew wood between them creaked as the curved staves bent into smooth C-shapes, and the long shafts slid backward through the arrow rests. Havel's bow drew at a hundred and ten pounds, and he'd worked with its like most days since the Change; Signe's was lighter, but she was an even better shot.

Whap-whap, as the strings slapped the inside of their left forearms; the chain mail and leather absorbed most of the force, but not as well as the metal bracers he was accustomed to; they'd have bruises, if they survived the day. The broadheads twinkled as they blurred downrange, the curve of the fletching twirling them like rifle bullets. They covered the fifty yards to the bandit chief in less than a second.

Bailey had excellent reflexes, and he was moving even as the two Bearkillers raised their bows. He threw himself flat on his horse's mane as Signe's shaft went through the space his chest had occupied an instant before. Then he screamed, as Havel's sliced across the outside of his left thigh; screamed and threw himself out of the saddle and onto the ground. The man behind him jerked as Signe's arrow went through the space where Crusher had been and thumped into the center of his chest, smashed through the shirt of braided rawhide, through his breastbone and into his spine. Then he slid boneless out of the saddle—a shaft thrown by these heavy recurves would cut the best chain mail like cloth at close range, and it ignored anything less.

Plenty of people carried saddle bows these days, but not many had that sort of eye-punching accuracy from horseback, or could drive a shaft so hard. *That* required constant practice.

Shit. I wanted Crusher.

The highbinder was lying in the long grass, hidden from Havel by the same horse herd that prevented his men from charging right in, and he was screaming orders.

As the two adults shot, Hendricks had been busy too: he snatched up his bow with one hand, and flicked the carriage whip across the cart horse's back with the other.

"Make for the ruins!" Havel shouted.

The boy did just that, yelling and whacking the beast across the rump; the cart drove off the road, one wheel bouncing high and nearly throwing it over, then heaving and jouncing through the meadow. Havel turned his horse with thighs and balance and shot again, at the bandits who'd swung onto the road south of the ruins. A man screamed and began hopping around, waving an arm with an arrow through it, but things came back at the two Bear-killers as well—the unpleasant *whhht* of a crossbow bolt, and the whickering *whissst-whissst* of arrows. Most of the bandits carried blades or polearms, but at least half a dozen had missile weapons as well.

"Go!" Havel shouted, and leaned forward as he clamped his legs to Charger's sides.

Signe followed suit. The superbly trained warhorses broke into a gallop from a standing start, leaping the roadside ditch and breasting the tall grass in the field beyond. Havel turned in the saddle and shot three more times in the thirty seconds it took to reach the ruined building; two misses, and one hit a horse in the shoulder. The beast screamed, a huge hurt sound of bewildered, uncomprehending pain; that was one of the manifold evils the Change had brought back into the world—Humvees didn't shriek in agony when they got shot up.

They pulled up their mounts and got out of the saddles in a hurry. Signe slid to the ground like a seal down a wet rock, or like someone who'd been riding for fun since she was six. An instant later she had the two horses inside the gutted building; their eyes rolled and they snorted at the slippery linoleum under the layer of debris and dirt and sprouting weeds beneath their hooves, but they obeyed. Hendricks snatched things out of the cart and dove after her. Havel turned, saw the bandits trying to push their way through the crowd of horses from three directions, deliberately set himself in the archer's T.

The arrows punched out in a steady rhythm, whickering away in smooth shallow arcs blurred with motion; the bright midmorning sun glinted on their sharp-edged heads.

Snap.

A mounted man took one in the shoulder and started to shriek; he slid out of the saddle, then clutched at it as his feet touched the ground—if he went down here, a large herd of horses would walk all over him.

Snap.

The next shaft sank up to its fletchings in that horse's neck. The beast bugled in a gurgle that sprayed blood out of its mouth and nostrils, glittering drops flying into the air, and half bucked, half staggered away. The wounded man dropped flat as his support was torn away, and then screamed again as the dancing hooves of the panicked horses came down on him—each with a thousand pounds behind it.

The scream was brief, and Havel bared his teeth in a snarl of satisfaction.

I don't enjoy *killing people,* he thought. *Really, I don't. Correction. I* do *enjoy killing bandits.* People had done what they had to do to get through the Dying Time, but nowadays there was plenty of honest work to hand. Crusher's men were jackals who attacked the weak and robbed, raped and killed because they liked it. *Hanging's too good for these scum.*

None of the bandits he could see were more than a hundred and fifty yards away, and at that range the hornbow was about as effective as his old Remington 700.

Snap.

A bandit staggered into view; he'd been bumped by one of the horses he pushed aside to get to the west side of the road. That put him less than fifty yards away. The arrow struck just above the bridge of his nose, and he pitched backward.

The mounted outlaws had all *dis*mounted in a hurry. That gave them a little cover behind the horse herd, but the horses protected the disguised Bearkillers for a little while too. A glimpse of movement to the south, and he pivoted smoothly on his heel, drew and shot.

Snap.

This time he was close enough to hear the wet thick *smack* as the point struck; the bandit was bent over as he ran for cover, and the steel lashed into him just below the floating rib on his right side. It hammered down and through, burying itself in his pelvis. He dropped sprattling to the pavement, screaming for his mother and letting his longbow skid into the ditch.

"Die slow, you son of a bitch!" Havel said, scanning for another target.

Whuppt.

The crossbow bolt went past too fast to see, but he could feel the ugly wind of it between face and bowstring as his hand went back for a new shaft.

"Get the fuck in here, you maniac!" Signe shouted.

Havel started out of the killing haze and obeyed, rolling through the empty window nearest him; the light mail in the lining of his long leather coat protected him from the jabbing spikes of glass still in the frame. The inside of the cinder-block building was bad footing, dirt and weeds and rubbish over linoleum, with fallen shelves and racks of videocassettes ready to tangle your feet. Signe was fumbling with the lock of the door, which was metal with a hollow core; Havel reached out and turned the dead bolt himself, twisting with all the strength of his hand and wrist. It shot home with a grating squeal of rusted steel.

A quick look around showed that there were only two windows, and both had shutters that were made up of squares of steel strapwork; the fragments of glass had paper glued to their backs. As Havel grabbed one of the toppled racks he saw why—the garish cover of the video-tape showed something highly unlikely involving two women, a dog and a piece of electrical apparatus. He saw a few more covers as others fell from the steel shelving; some made the first look rather tame.

"Didn't think I'd make my last stand in a prono-video store," he grunted.

He and Signe grabbed one of the heavy metal racks and slammed it up behind the door, then added a half dozen more, shoving at them until they were a tangled mass.

"Last stands aren't my inclination anyhow," Signe replied, as they put another in a corner where the sky was visible between the bare stringers of the roof, to serve as a ladder. "But I wouldn't mind killing Crusher Bailey from one."

Havel nodded. "Kendricks, get up there and tell us what you can see," he said.

He considered the interior of the video store as the youngster scampered up the framework, squirrel-agile. Havel sneezed once as dust flew up, smelling of old rusty metal and rat droppings and weeds and very faintly of rotten meat. There was a counter and cash register close to the door—the drawer of the register lay smashed open, mute inglorious testimony to someone being stupid enough to steal *money* right after the Change, of all useless things. The two small windows looking out on the parking lot and the road were the only openings here, but a door gave out on the other side of the open space; probably to a storage room and office. Signe was thinking on the same lines; she stuck her head through and looked around.

"Windowless," she said. "Just one door, and it's solid with a bar across the inside—it'd be easier to smash through the wall. Nothing here but some bones." A moment later, as her eyes adjusted to the dim light: "Burned bones, human ones. And split for the marrow."

"Let's block this too," he said, and they heaved another set of frames over the connecting door. "Cinder block doesn't have much strength."

Then they took station next to the windows. The bandits were driving off the horses, heading for the trees along the creek two long bowshots to the east; through his binoculars he could see hints that there was a camp there. Havel took a mirror on a collapsible rod from his belt and snapped it open, using the glass to check angles he could not see from the window without sticking his head out.

Well, here's a distraction from our domestic problems, and no mistake, he thought. *OK, two behind the pickup, another two behind the planter, and a third pair behind the bed of the overturned SUV. They'll all have something to shoot with, they're there to keep us pinned down while the rest get ready to storm the place.*

"Anything?" he called up to Kendricks.

"No sign of Lord Hutton," the teenager said. "But I think I see bandits moving in the field behind the store—there's a big old propane tank about twenty yards out, and some trees. Lot of bush, too."

"Oh, hallelujah," Signe said quietly. "Lordy, but I'll be glad to see Unc' Will and Eric and the rest. Weren't they supposed to be here by now?"

"Yeah, but . . ." Havel grinned at her. *"I still live,"* he quoted.

"Wasn't that Tarzan's saying?" she asked, flashing a smile back at him. "The ape-man'll save my rosy-pink ass?"

He'd been a Burroughs fan in his youth, and he'd gotten a set to read to their daughters, something Signe and he did together as often as not. It was a partial antidote to Astrid's fixations, at least, to which the young seemed appallingly vulnerable.

"John Carter, *alskling,*" he replied, wondering if she was as nervous as he was. Hutton should have been here by now. "It was the finest swordsman on two worlds who said that."

"Ah, the guy from Virginia who made it with the big Martian bug and produced an *egg?* You'd be more likely to have a fertile mating with a cabbage!"

"Well, granted, Dejah Thoris was . . . what did Ken call it? Oviparous? But that doesn't really make her a *bug*. Or at least I hope not."

"It lays eggs, it's a bird, a bug or a gator—careful! That one's got a crossbow!"

Kendricks ducked and yelled. A bolt slammed into the rusty metal roofing near his head and stood quivering in a stringer. Havel and Signe stepped up to the windows and shot. The crossbowman dove back behind a flat-wheeled trailer cart that bore a powered water-ski and had for nine years. He gave a yelp of fear and they could see bits of him moving behind his cover, enough to know that he was spanning his crossbow.

"Uh-oh," Kendricks said. "Lord Bear, they're bringing stuff back across the fields."

Havel used his mirror-periscope once more. They were carrying planks, boards and a set of bicycles; the whole party disappeared from his view as they angled behind a truck that blocked the way. They kept coming until they were right up against it, too; he *could* see their feet below the body, far too close for comfort.

That was close enough to hear snatches of conversation, as well as hammering and knocking.

". . . pile stuff out back and burn them out," someone yelled. "That's quicker. I don't like that flare thing they sent up for shit."

"This meat's more tender raw than roast," said the booming genial tones of Crusher Bailey. "We don't have all day, and we don't want to send up a big signal fire of our own. There's only one man, and a boy and the girl."

"Christ, Crusher, look what they did to Sumter! That's a *world* of pain. We got their horses. Let's split! If I wanted to be a fucking soldier, I'd have joined the monks or gone to Portland."

A jeering note from the bandit chief: "Didn't know you were a girl too, Willie. Goddamnit, didn't you hear what they had in that cart? That's the price of three *hundred* horses! With that much, we could buy our way into half a dozen places and live easy."

"How do we know they've really got all that stuff?"

" 'Cause the innkeeper told me, and as long as we can squeeze him, he'll come across right. Now shut up and get to work, or you'll find a world of hurt a lot closer than that door."

There was a thud and a yelp, and Bailey's voice went on: "If this many of us can't take three fucking farmers, we're in the wrong business. We'd have the whole Valley laughing at us once it got around. Move it!"

Interesting, Havel thought. Suddenly conscious of his thirst he uncorked a canteen and drank, leaning over to pass it to Signe. *The innkeeper* is *feeding Bailey information but he's* not *doing it voluntarily.*

"Sorry I got you into it this deep," he said.

"Didn't hear myself saying no," she replied. "Things should have worked smoother than this." Then she took a quick look out the window and set the canvas-covered plastic bottle down. "Uh-oh."

I know what Uh-oh *means,* Havel thought. *It means we're screwed, usually.*

"Siege cat," Signe went on.

"Well, shit," Havel sighed, and used his mirror. "No, make that *two* siege cats."

The siege cat was a big square of double-thick plywood, mounted on a timber frame with wheels, a trail for pushing and steering, and slots to shoot through; it looked as if the bandits had had it ready, needing only to be put together. Another just like it followed out behind.

"Pretty fancy, for bandits," Signe said. "I *really* hope Unc' Will shows up soon. He was supposed to shadow us *close*."

Havel studied the mantlets-on-wheels. "They're not sturdy enough for real siege work against a fort. But they'd do fine for storming a farmhouse, say. Plenty thick enough to stop an arrow. They probably cart them round whenever they're away from their base."

This is starting to look rather bad. There were twenty or so of the outlaws, not counting their dead and wounded.

Individually none of them were much of a much, but ten to one were very unpleasant odds. *Maybe I should have stayed home. Signe sulking is better than Crusher Bailey crushing. Where the* hell *is Will? He was supposed to keep us under continuous observation!*

"You six, keep their heads down!" the bandit chief yelled. "Let's go!"

Arrows and crossbow bolts whined and zipped through the open windows; more slammed and tinged off the rafters where Kendricks sat—until he fell, with a grunt and a sharp cry of pain, a bolt through his clavicle. A roar of triumph went up from the bandits; then a scream of pain, as Havel popped up from below the window and shot. A man hopped out from behind one of the siege cats, shrieking and shaking one foot with an arrow through the boot. One of Signe's punched into his chest and he fell.

Havel ducked back again as an arrow sliced the leather over his shoulder and exposed the wire mail beneath; the sensation was like being whacked—hard—by a wooden rod. There was just too much flying through the slatted bars of the shutter to stand up and draw; he duckwalked over to Kendricks and checked the wound instead. The bleeding didn't look too serious, internally or externally, and the boy had thumped his head on something coming down and was half conscious. All he could do was arrange him on his back and shove something under the back of his head.

Probably for the good he's knocked out. That'll dull the pain and he couldn't do anything anyway, with that. He'll be months in bed, if we live.

"Mike!" Signe said. "They're getting close!"

He moved back; the shooter behind the cat was uncomfortably accurate, and they would have a view of the interior when it was shoved right to the window, so the only safe spot would be plastered against the wall between the window and the door. Then both cats were up against the windows, blocking them and leaving the interior of the porn store lit only by the triangular patch of light from the broken corner of ceiling. He dropped his bow, swept out his backsword, tugged at the leather strap that held his targe over his back and slipped his forearm through the loop and grip as it swung down. Signe was doing the same; they waited on either side of the door. Behind them the horses moved, shifting and rolling their eyes at the noise and stink.

"Well, it's been a lot of fun," Havel said, making himself grin at her in the dimness.

"We still live!" she shot back; from the sound, it was only half a joke.

"Axes! Axes!" Crusher Bailey's voice called. "Shooters ready for when the door comes down! Let's have the lobster out of the shell!"

Metal beat on metal, and the door sagged. "First after you with the woman, Crusher!" someone shouted.

The door fell, half-in and half-out of the opening. Someone used the hook on the back of a guisarme to haul it back; it fell flat on the steps with an echoing crash, and Havel squinted against the flood of brightness. A blast of arrows and bolts came through, smacking into the plaster of the interior wall and standing like bristles, or punching through into the corridor beyond, but they would be shooting blind. The room would be very dark from the outside.

The shafts were intended to drive the defenders back from the opening; a first bandit ran in, shield up—and ran straight into the metal racks propped up over the space where the door had been, screaming a curse as his arms tangled in them. Havel danced in and thrust through an opening, a motion as precise and swift as the flicking of a frog's tongue. The point ran into the man's throat with a series of crisp popping and rending sounds, felt up the hilt as much as heard. Signe's sword flashed past that one's shoulder at the next, an overarm highline thrust that slammed the spring-steel point under the brim of a helmet hammered out of sheet metal. It grated and crunched against facial bones, and she freed it with a jerk.

Then they both stepped aside as more arrows came through—many bounced off the frame of the racks. Hands used that cover to drag the bodies out, and the rocking door that made the footing uncertain. There was plenty of blood to keep it slippery.

"Guard my left!" Havel said.

The bristling heads of a dozen polearms came next, spearpoints and heavy glaives and crude guisarmes with hooks, probing for the frames to push the obstruction back, but that meant the bandits were packed shoulder-to-shoulder and blocked their own bowmen. Havel and Signe stepped neatly in from the sides of the doorway; he broke one spearpoint off with a smashing blow of his shield's metal-rimmed edge, and thrust at the hands gripping another in the doorway, making one bandit drop his polearm with a clatter and a cry of alarm. Signe chopped at others, and wood splintered under her edge. Havel pressed in closer to strike at the men rather than the weapons, but that meant the bandits could see him too. Points probed for him from the second rank; they drove him out of sword range amid a volley of scatological curses and vicious threats, and the others heaved to move the piled racks.

Havel snarled and skipped free as they tilted and rocked back into the room with a jangling crunch and screech. A bold thief came through under the spearpoints, stooping and holding his shield over his head, sword ready.

"Hakkaa paalle!" The war shriek filled the dusty room, and Signe echoed it.

"Shit, *Bearkillers!*" someone shouted, panic in his tones.

The bandit ignored it and thrust underarm with his double-edged weapon; Havel caught it on his blade, let the swords slide together until the hilts locked, and then twisted it with all the strength of wrist and shoulder. The thief's eyes were blue in a stubble-cheeked face. They flared wide, with pain and shock at the raw strength of the arm opposing his. The outlaw sword flew free, and Havel whipped his hilt up and across like a set of huge brass knuckles. Bone cracked and the man wailed, dropping as he pawed at his face. Havel knocked a spearpoint aside with his targe and another with his sword, stamping down with a spurred heel; the moaning cut off abruptly. A thrust struck him in the stomach, not hard enough to penetrate the mail beneath the leather, but winding him. He snarled, chopped sideways with the edge of the targe and cut backhanded with his sword into a neck. Blood sprayed into his face, salt and iron, but there were just too *many* of them—

Then there came a thunder of hooves from outside, and a huge ringing battle cry: "St. George for England! *A Loring! A Loring!*"

"What the *hell?*" Havel shouted.

CHAPTER ELEVEN

Whap-tunnng!

The string slapped at Juniper Mackenzie's bracer, and the longbow surged and hummed. The arrow snapped out, rising in a smooth sweet arch, seeming to hesitate at the peak as the bright afternoon sun struck the honed edges of its point, and then plunged faster and faster down towards the mark. That was a circle drawn on the grass of the meadow with an eight-foot set upright timber at its center; a two-inch-broad white stripe was painted down the middle of the post. She could *feel* the connection between them, arrow and target, bow and archer, all one in a perfect harmony, like the wind and the blue camas flowers themselves.

Thunk!

The sound echoed back, faint with distance as the arrow slammed into the massive fir-wood baulk two hundred and fifty yards away. Juniper's hand was already swinging back over her shoulder. It paused at the empty quiver; she stopped, blinked, looked around, jarred out of a centered focus that made her one with the world and her task.

"Forty-five shafts, two minutes forty-six seconds," Sam Aylward said loudly.

A couple of people clapped. Juniper held her bow in her left hand and worked her right arm to get the strain out of muscle and tendon, then switched off to do the other. Shooting this far and fast and hard was strictly for battle drill. When you went into the woods after venison the range was usually less than fifty yards, plus the target ran away if you missed—not towards you with shield up and a sword ready to spill your guts.

The thought was melancholy, but she sternly forbade herself much nostalgia about the peacefulness she'd known before the Change. That had been sheer personal luck. War had happened then too, just not around *here,* not on her doorstep. But wherever it happened was *somebody's* home, and the consequences weren't all that different whether it was AK-47s in Somalia or halberds in post-Change Oregon.

I knew I lived in a lucky country in those days, but not quite how *lucky,* she thought wryly. *And this is a day for practice, not real fighting, sure. Lighten up, girl!*

Most of the folk of Dun Juniper were out this Sunday morning with their bows, and more up from Dun Fairfax, in clumps from the big truck gardens near the millpond at the east end of the benchland meadows to the beehives and tanner's yard at the west. There was a sweet smell of crushed grasses in the air, and underneath it the cool resinous scent of the great mountain forests stretching eastwards, together with smells she'd stopped noticing—woodsmoke both fresh and soaked into people's hair and clothing, manure, lye and tallow boiling to make soap, tanned leather, horse sweat, a whiff of charcoal and hot metal from a smithy inside the dun's walls.

Aylward handed her the gold watch he'd been using to time her; an old-fashioned oval type with a chain and a cover that snapped open to show a tiny portrait picture. The heirloom held a black-and-white photograph sixty years old and considerably younger than the instrument itself: a faded portrait of her grandmother, a sad-looking, care-worn woman in a long dress, with a shawl over her head and an infant girl in her arms—that being Juniper's mother, fresh from her baptism. Achill Island had been a hard bitter place to make a living in those days, and Juniper's own mother had left it early as most youngsters did. She'd been waiting tables in a London pub when she met

Juniper's father, serving there as a sergeant in the USAF in the sixties.

No surprise that Gran looks twice her age. The wonder is that an Achill fisherman could hang on to a gold watch, and still eat!

Juniper took it back and tucked it into a special padded hard-leather pouch on her belt; the considerable sentimental value aside, it was too useful to risk, literally irreplaceable—and it couldn't be repaired if anything serious happened to it, either.

The less advanced pupils were shooting at circles on tripods or deer-shaped outlines propped up against fence posts; many of *those* archers were as young as six or seven. They included Rudi Mackenzie, just now getting grabbed and rolled in the grass by a gang of friends, most of them a year or two older, after he sank another bull's-eye with his light child's bow.

It's proud I am of him . . . but . . . It was a little disturbing just *how* good he was at such things. *And him so young!*

It was Clan law that everyone between six and sixty had to practice at arms unless they were medically unfit, but a budding custom already stronger than law meant archery had become the Mackenzies' favorite leisure-time sport as well. There were practical advantages, but shooting skillfully with the longbow had also become part of being a Mackenzie—a badge of identity like the kilt back in the first Change Year. And group identity had a fearsome power, in this new-old world where you worked and lived with the same faces every day and a mile was a long way.

I understand what "clan" actually meant *in those times a lot better than I used to,* she thought. *I understand the old songs with my bones now, don't I just?*

"Score of forty-five, forty, twenty-eight, eight," a boy said, trotting up breathlessly with Juniper's arrows; he'd had to clamber over a board fence on the way.

All her arrows had landed within the twelve-foot circle around the post, forty within the six-foot, twenty-eight had hit the post, and eight had been in the vertical white strip—"splitting the wand," to use the ancient term.

"Seventy-eight out of a possible one hundred," Aylward said. "Congratulations, Lady Juniper."

She grinned and waved at the clapping, and held the bow she'd named after the Greek archer-goddess overhead. Then she stepped back a few paces to check the heads and fletching on her shafts, wipe the broadheads and bodkins clean of dirt and slide them back into her quiver. A seventy-eight score wasn't bad at all, well above average. There were plenty of things she liked better than archery; from meditation to weaving . . . but archery could be a form of meditation itself, and with her mind and soul still full of the singing peace from last night's Sabbat circle in the sacred wood, she wasn't surprised that mind and hand had knit together so well.

Astrid Larsson was up next in this group, the only one on the field not using a longbow. Another thought struck Juniper. "Just how many archers do we have, exactly, now?" she said.

She leaned on her bowstave to watch Astrid, with the lower antler-horn tip resting on the toe of her boot. "A little over two thousand, isn't it?"

"In a full levy?" Sam Aylward said. "Twenty-two hundred and seventy-three as of the muster this last Imbolc. That's everyone who passed the minimum standards test for field service, of course. I'd rather the qualification test was tougher, but quantity has a certain quality too. You don't need to split the wand when you're shooting at men packed in shoulder to shoulder and sixteen deep, or cavalry moving boot-to-boot."

She shook her head. "And we had, what, forty-five for that first brush with the Protector's men? How we've grown!"

Though the big rush of accessions was over now; most survivors in western Oregon had gravitated to one of the larger groups or another, depending on where they'd ridden out the early years and what they thought of its leadership and customs. To be sure, people were also breeding about twice the pre-Change rate, but it would be a long time before the children stepped into their parents' shoes . . . or took up their bows.

"Start!"

That was Chuck Barstow's voice; he was using a wind-up kitchen timer. Astrid had a slight smile on her face as she emptied her quiver. She did it with a smooth efficiency that raised eyebrows even among those who'd seen her feed the bow before, regular as a machine but infinitely more graceful. The *snap* of the hornbow's string on the young woman's bracer and the *thunk* of arrows punching into wood sounded crisply as she walked a line of shafts down the length of the "wand." A few arrows were pushed aside by unpredictable gusts of wind, but they plunged down point-first not far away—at better than six hundred feet you had to drop the shaft onto the target, not shoot level.

She'd been an archery enthusiast *before* the Change, of course.

Astrid bowed and waved to the applause with studied graciousness, unconsciously assuming what Juniper thought of as a Tolkien-cover pose; the noise covered Eilir as she approached from the rear with an evil grin on her face and prodded her friend with the tip of her longbow.

Astrid squealed and leapt and whirled.

Show-off! Eilir signed, and grinned as she stepped forward to the mark herself. The crowd began counting the score as she drew and loosed . . .

Juniper lowered her voice. There was enough background noise to let her speak privately with the stocky brown-haired man next to her.

"Any progress?" she said.

"Judy's pretty sure I was right about it being a Altendorf code," Aylward said. "But for what, we don't know. My guess . . ."

She raised a brow, and he went on: "My guess would be it's an updated operational plan—a contingency order, so he only has to give a codeword and set things in motion. But that's just a bloody guess. Maybe they could work it out over to Corvallis. Judy's a bright lass, but . . ."

Juniper frowned. Judy Barstow Mackenzie—nee Lefkowitz—*was* bright. She was head of the Clan's healers, and had been a registered nurse and midwife before the

Change, with three languages under her belt to boot, not counting English.

Not to mention a good grasp of Yiddish and Russian profanity. She'd gotten that from her grandfather, who'd fought from Moscow to Berlin with Zhukov and then taken off his uniform and kept right on westward until he reached New Jersey. *But she isn't a cryptographer, either.*

The university people would be far more likely to have someone with relevant skills. An Altendorf code was based on correlations with a book or other document, and it was infernally hard to break—you had to have not only the book it referred to, but the right edition so the page and line numbers corresponded. Or you could break it by sheer number-crunching, but *that* really required computers.

On the other hand . . .

"We have *some* chance of keeping a secret. Corvallis does everything by 'committees of the whole' and leaks like a sieve," she said. "The Bearkillers can keep their mouths shut, but I don't want to get Mike in more trouble at home . . . And I really don't want the Protector knowing that we've got a hold of a copy of his little scheme."

"You think his faithful marchwarden the good Baron Gervais hasn't told him?" Aylward said with a grin.

"Is a bear Buddhist? Does the Dalai Lama defecate in the shrubbery?" Juniper said.

"Tsk! Why-ever-for shouldn't he tell his old gaffer that he had a folder of plans stolen?"

Aylward spoke with a wolf's grim amusement; he was enjoying Marchwarden Liu's possible discomfiture a lot more than she was. Not that she could blame him, but . . .

"Arminger . . . Goddess, I don't like imagining what he'd do to the man if he found out—even Eddie Liu wouldn't deserve *that*."

"I'd say it's poetic justice, Lady Juniper. Hmmm. I don't suppose we could blackmail Liu by *threatening* to grass him up?"

"Now isn't *that* the interesting thought, now!" Juniper said. "I always did prefer being sneaky to straightforward bashing . . . tricky, though. Perhaps we could blackmail him into giving us *more* information about the Protector's schemes? By the Threefold Shadow, I don't think he'd hesitate out of loyalty."

"And speaking of the Threefold Hecate . . ." Aylward said, jerking his thumb over his shoulder.

Which means Judy's back from her mission of mercy.

Juniper gave him a reproving thump on the shoulder—her friend wasn't *that* terrifying—and turned to look. A buckboard wagon drawn by two horses was bumping along the gravel road westward from the watermill, with six Mackenzie archers on bicycles following along behind as escort. They peeled off for the gates of Dun Juniper as the wagon turned towards the Chief's party, whooping and increasing their speed as they pumped the pedals towards home and baths and beer. Judy Barstow was driving the buckboard—she and Juniper had been classmates in high school in Albany back when the other's name was Judy Lefkowitz, and they had discovered the Craft together in their seventeenth year.

Right now Judy looked a bit travel-worn; it wasn't an easy journey past the ruins of Eugene, especially if you were taking the overgrown back roads and dodging bandit gangs often dozens strong.

"Juney!" she called, waving.

"Judy!" Juniper replied, reading the other's pursed-lip expression with the ease of long experience as meaning roughly:

For this *piece of limp celery I missed the Sabbat?*

She had a passenger, a woman Juniper knew only by correspondence since the Change, though they'd run into each other a few times at RenFaires and Pagan gatherings before that. Laurel Wilson wasn't any older than Juniper's late-thirties, but from her looks could have given her a decade or more; those were the lines of privation and strain, and there were streaks of gray in her long dark hair. Bright sunlight brought out the wrinkles and weathering. She was looking around at the bustling scene with open awe, and even more so as the real size of Dun Juniper's walls became apparent—the shining white of the stucco coating and the painted roundels of flower and vine under the battlements gave an appearance of grace that belied the sheer massiveness of it.

"Merry met, the both of you!" Juniper said, as Judy pulled on the reins and the horses halted, bending their heads to graze. "We'll be through in just a second."

Judy's children—Tamsin, a girl of twelve, Chuck Junior, still toddling, and the three adoptees, who were nineteen or twenty now—abandoned their father's scorekeeping station and came trotting over; or the teenagers did, with Tamsin running at their heels and Chuck the Small toddling in their wake and setting up a howl as he tripped and fell on the close-cropped turf. Judy tied off the reins, jumped down and comforted the two-year-old with brisk efficiency.

"This is worth watching," she said over her shoulder to the visitor; Laurel stood, and shielded her eyes with a hand.

Westward down the meadow men and women were following loaded carts, taking out scores of target outlines shaped like a man with a shield, made of a double layer of thick planks. The targets were propped up against successive fence lines at fifty-yard intervals out to three hundred yards, with each figure a few feet from its neighbors to left and right—the same formation as armored footmen would have in battle. This was a harder test than battle in some respects, because the real thing would involve shooting at a formation many yards deep; a little over or under usually didn't matter much.

Of course, nobody's shooting back *at you,* Juniper thought, settling the baldric that carried her quiver with a shrug of her shoulders. Not far away, a signaler raised a silver-mounted horn to his mouth and blew *Assemble in line,* a long modulated dunting howl.

Those of her clan with pre-Change battle experience had told her the hardest thing to unlearn had been the instinct to spread out and take cover. You couldn't do that in a big battle these days. Longbows were deadly, but they weren't machine guns. To stop a mass of armored men charging with bladed weapons you had to pack your archers together, which meant you had to stand upright and just take whatever came back at you.

The shooters drifted over from the other clout rings and the butts, chatting as they did. She heard Aylward sigh, and hid a smile; he'd taught them all a great deal, but they weren't the Guards, or the SAS.

"Line up by squads, you horrible lot!" he barked, and scowled harder at the genial remarks he got back. "Sod this for a game of soldiers, you idle, useless maggots—move it!"

The nonshooting spectators had a high proportion of nursing mothers and the visibly pregnant, including Melissa Aylward.

"Watch your tongue, Samkin!" she called, and laughed at his scowl along with more than a few of her friends and fellow onlookers. "I know where you sleep!"

The squads each had nine bows, with subgroups of three—mystically appropriate and solidly practical as well; there were three squads here from Dun Fairfax and eleven from Dun Juniper's larger population. A hundred and twenty-six archers in all, not counting the juveniles, overage and hopelessly shortsighted who helped hustle more arrows up to the shooters. The arrangement had the added advantage of keeping everything friends-and-neighbors, which put heart into ordinary folk if they had to fight.

Juniper stepped into her place beside Chuck and the Dun Juniper banner, looking to either side with fond pride. They might not have quite the guards snap that Sam remembered nostalgically, or the Bearkiller habit of doing everything at a run, but they got where they were going— a staggered triple line formed, with a yard between each of the Mackenzie warriors.

"Nock shafts!" Aylward barked.

There was no chatter or nonsense now. A hundred and twenty-six hands brought a nock to the cord and a shaft to the cutout arrow shelf that ran through the middle of their bows. The first target was the line of shields three hundred yards distant. Each was about man-sized—or thumb-sized, at this distance.

"Let the gray geese fly!" Sam shouted, his own bow ready: "Wholly together—"

The yellow-limbed yew bows came up, pointing at the same angle—they would begin with dropping shots at extreme range. Juniper drew until the kiss-ring on the cord touched her lip.

"—shoot!"

The slap of strings on bracers sounded so close together that it was like a lightning crack. Beneath that came the deep whining *humm* of the cords, and the whickering massed *sssssst* of the shafts as they rose in a dense cloud, louder than sleet in a bad storm. She emptied her mind and became one with the rhythm of it: breath out as you drew, open the chest, close the back, throw the left arm forward and twist with hip and gut until you reached full draw, sense the right angle for release, let the string fall off the three draw fingers of the right hand, follow through, reach back for another, and another . . .

"Second target!"

They adjusted their aim; now the arrows flew on a shallower arc.

"Third! Fourth!"

"Point-blank, maximum speed!"

The muscles of her shoulders and arms were burning in truth now, but that was a distant background to the dance, her hand darting down now where the helper had stuck the next bundle of shafts point-down in the turf and ready to grasp. Arrows blurred out from the Mackenzie line, scores every second for one last long burst, slashing across the meadow in a ripple of sleek destruction. The heads struck the plank shields with a hard *tock* repeated so fast it sounded like a whole flock of mad woodpeckers; they were using broadheads, not greased bodkins, but many were hammering through the double layer of tough wood anyway, and the rest bristled out thicker than a porcupine's spines.

"Halt!"

They did, suddenly aware that they were puffing and blowing. Juniper blinked a little as she looked at the long oval where the arrows stood in ground and shield—thousands upon thousands of them, fired in the time it would take armored foemen to cross the killing ground. She couldn't help but think what it would be like, trying to keep your shield up and march through *that*. Much less ride a horse into it; the poor beasts didn't wear much armor, and had even less reason to let themselves be hurt and killed in the quarrels of men.

Well, shit, *as Mike likes to say. I'm proud we can do it, but Goddess gentle and strong, I wish we didn't have to!*

The line broke up; people started helping each other out of their brigandines for shoulder-rubs—you had to be careful about repetitive motion injuries—or went off to practice sword-and-buckler or battle-spear work for a change of pace, or just to socialize, gossip, dicker and swap.

"So, what do you think, Sam First Armsman Aylward Mackenzie?"

"I'm . . . not quite satisfied, but not unhappy either," Aylward said. "Or rather, we'd have nothing to be un'appy about if every dun in our territory were up to this standard. They're still not real soldiers . . ."

"But they aren't any kind of soldiers at all," Juniper said gently. "They're farmers, and blacksmiths and carpenters and schoolteachers and weavers, who fight when they have to."

The Englishman nodded. "I grant you that, Lady Juniper. And for that, they're bloody good."

Tamar ran up, with a smile at Juniper, and her stepfather put an arm around her shoulders. "And I'm a farmer who fights when he has to meself, these days."

Juniper ruffled the girl's hair, unstrung her own bow—something you had to be careful with; it could take your nose off if you slipped, or poke out an eye—and walked over to the wagon.

"Long time no see, Laurel," she said, extending a hand.

You look terrible, she didn't add. The other woman was wearing patched jeans—patched with a piece of badly cured hide across the seat, for starters. She didn't quite look like a homeless gangrel, but she wasn't all that far from it either.

"I'm glad to see you, Lady Juniper," Laurel said humbly.

Juniper sighed inwardly at that, and at the tone more than the words. She'd gotten used to people calling her that, or Chief, or *the* Mackenzie—from some of them, like Aylward or Dennis or her old covener friends, it was just a half-teasing gesture of affection. Hearing it *this* way from someone she'd known back in the old days drove home how irrevocably lost those days were, and the weight of the responsibility on her shoulders. She didn't challenge Laurel's choice of words, either. People wouldn't understand.

Ah, here I am the great Chief, Herself Herself, and I can't so much as tell someone to knock it off and call me Juney.

"Come on, let's get you settled, and then we'll talk."

"So, you were a self-initiated solitary back before the Change?" Juniper said gently.

The four Mackenzies and Laurel Wilson were in the attic loft of the Hall, Juniper's bedchamber when she unrolled the futon now neatly stored beside Rudi's on a shelf, and also her office and workroom, and the place she kept her fiddles and guitars and the big harp. There was a desk, typewriter and adding machine, racks of ring-binders and filing cabinets; being head of even a very decentralized state turned out to involve a lot of paperwork, something she loathed with every fiber of her being. It was also the place where she kept her Craft tools and books, and the site of her private altar, over on the middle of the north wall beneath one of the dormer windows and beside the lectern that had her Book of Shadows under a black cloth. The smell of incense still clung, although the tiny brazier between the figures of the Lord and Lady was empty and clean; around it stood the black-handled athame, a white-handled knife with a curved blade, vials of oils, candles . . .

The woman sitting across the table from her made a reverent gesture towards it. "I hadn't actually got that far," she said. "We'd just started our Circle but . . . well, I'd read a *lot* of the books, though."

"Which books, if I might ask?"

"*The Woman's Encyclopedia of Myths and Secrets.* And Silver Ravenwolf . . ."

Behind her back Judy Barstow grimaced with clenched teeth and pummeled her temples with the heels of her hands.

"I tried Starhawk, but it was sort of hard to get into."

Judy went pale and made gagging motions, then mimed tearing out hanks of her hair.

Judy! Juniper thought, hard. *Be nice!*

The Tradition that the Singing Moon belonged to had always insisted on a year-and-a-day of intense instruction before Initiation, and an unbroken line of descent from Initiate to Initiate; in fact, for Wiccans they were traditionalists. They'd bent their rules—they'd had to, after the Change and the huge influx of new believers—but no more than they must. Particularly for those who went on from simple Dedicant status to full Initiation. Still, this wasn't the time to get all sniffy.

The Lord and Lady don't check your ID at the door, if you come with love and trust in your heart.

She managed a flicker of a quelling glare at her former Maiden; Sally Martin did rather better, and covertly nudged her with an elbow. Chuck Barstow kept his face carefully blank.

Be kind, Judy, Juniper thought, projecting a soothing calm. *They've managed to survive this long.*

"Well, let's stick to the immediate practicalities, Laurel," she said. "You've got . . . what, eighty people in your group these days?"

The long room had three dormers on either side, and more windows at either end; down at the east end was her big eight-harness loom with its treadles and shuttles, an old friend from before the Change, surrounded by baskets full of skeins of dyed wool yarn. Duplicates of it were working in half the Clan's households, used by her own pupils and the ones *they* had instructed. A bolt of finished tartan cloth four feet across stood nearby, ready to be taken for fulling. Laurel's clothes weren't all that ragged, and they were clean, but the leather on the seat of her jeans was the only thing she wore that hadn't been made before the Change.

"About," Laurel said. "We're over the scurvy now—thank you for telling us about the rose hips!—but . . . it's one thing after another. All our stored fruit going bad was just the last of it; and we spend so much time hiding, and we lost six people the last time the gangs raided us . . ."

"We'll help," Juniper said soothingly. She looked down at her notes. "I think that your problem is basically a skills shortage and sheer lack of enough numbers to defend yourselves, rather than resources or effort. You've certainly been working hard enough, and you're producing enough food, just, but it's keeping it that's the problem, between bandits and wastage."

Silence stretched. "Well," Juniper said at last, "we're certainly willing to welcome you to our clan, if you'd rather join us than the McClintocks . . ."

"Oh, thank the Goddess," Laurel said, and her eyes brimmed over. "You've been helping us for years, and I feel so—"

Judy bent to put an arm around her shoulders. Juniper made soothing noises while she smiled to herself; the High Priestess of Wolf-Star wasn't nearly as much of a tartar as you'd think from the way she talked sometimes. Sally handed her a handkerchief and filled her a cup of chamomile tea.

When Laurel could go on, Juniper did as well: "This is going to be a major effort, relocating your people. You do understand you have to move? We can't possibly have an outlier south of Eugene, it's just too far away—and too dangerous."

Not to mention how Corvallis and half a dozen others would howl at our annexing more territory. Can't have more quarrels . . . especially not with the Protector watching.

Laurel nodded. "It's . . . well, it's hard to abandon so much work, but it just wasn't *working* anymore. I thought we'd pull through, after the first year—those seeds you gave us saved us—but now . . . I think the only reason the bandits haven't killed us all is because they want us to be there to steal from next year."

"Eugene's a problem," Chuck said, speaking for the first time since the meeting started. "We, all the honest valley communities, are going to have to do something about it. If the scum working out of there ever get a leader, we could be in real trouble . . . The MacGregors would help, and the McClintocks, and some of the towns and neighborhoods down Ashland way. When the Protectorate isn't distracting us, we'll have to see about an expedition."

Which may not be for years, or in our lifetimes . . . if the Protectorate doesn't destroy us in the interim, Juniper thought grimly, then brought her mind back to the business at hand.

"This is about the best time of year, the next two months," she said. "We've enough to spare from essential work now to give you a guard to get you safe up here."

Chuck nodded. "We might get Astrid's Rangers in on it." A grin: "Pardon me, the Dunedain Rangers."

Laurel looked impressed. "The . . . Astrid *Larsson?* And the *Dunedain?*"

Juniper nodded solemnly. "And Eilir."

"Can we get the tartan we'll need?" Laurel said, looking over at the loom. "For the kilts . . ."

Juniper winced slightly. "That's not a . . . ummm, maximum priority, really," she said.

Dennis, go n'ithe an cat thu is! she thought. *And may that moggy eat you raw, with mustard!* launching her exasperation like a mental spear at the one who'd come up with the fashion. *Although . . . be what you want to seem, the sage said. It will probably make them feel better to look like the rest of us.*

"We'll see what we can arrange," she said, and tapped a point on the map. "I think there, on Courtney Creek, would the best place for your folk to settle. It's only ten miles from Sutterdown and about thirty from here; I'll have you shown around it. There's plenty of good land vacant there, isn't there?"

Chuck closed his eyes for a moment, calling up information, before he answered:

"Yes, any amount, and first quality light loam with good natural drainage; if you planted shoelaces there, they'd sprout. There's even some orchard—it won't bear much this year, too neglected, but it could be reconditioned, pruned and cleaned out this winter. Apart from that, there's the vineyard Brannigan in Sutterdown claimed, he's done some real work on that so it's his, of course, but I imagine he'll be happy to have people closer he can get to help bring in his grapes. There's a convenient old farmstead with good wells we can use as a core for a new dun, still mostly intact, even the windows. We'll have to put up a windmill and water tank for starters."

"How's Alex fixed for time?" Juniper asked. "They'll need palisades, too, and then there'll be houses and barns, worksheds . . ."

Chuck's younger brother Alex had been a house-builder before the Change. Now he was the Clan's inspector of fortifications, and *still* built houses. There were a lot of vacant ones, but they were usually in the wrong places and useful mainly as a source of materials and fittings—Sutterdown was the only town in the Mackenzie territories that was still occupied, and the pre-Change farmsteads were all too scattered. They'd have to requisition draft horses and ox teams . . .

But everyone will be glad to have someone plugging that gap, she thought. The new dun would cover the approaches nicely. *Plus the extra hands. Always more work around than we can do with the people we've got.*

"Alex is busy like you wouldn't believe with getting the Sutterdown town wall finished, but I'll tell him to draw up some plans." Chuck looked at the map. "That's close to the Ward Butte sentry station anyway. Not too hard to keep an eye on."

Juniper looked back at Laurel. "Now, we're going to have to *loan* you a good deal of equipment, stock and tools," she said. "You understand, Laurel, I can't just give it to your people; mine have worked too hard to make and grow what we're talking about. It'll be some years before you can pay it all off, pay it with work and a share of your harvest . . ."

Laurel nodded wryly. "I understand, Lady Juniper. You do think the vote will go through your assembly?"

"Oh, yes," Juniper said. "I'm quite certain. Everyone—everyone suitable—who joins us is like another baby born, another candle in the night. Now, we'll also have to think about training and apprenticeships . . . some of your people apprenticing to our craftsfolk . . . although you've got some excellent carpenters, I must say, and that'll help immensely, but you also need someone about the dun who knows basic smithing, to repair tools without losing too much time."

Those two young couples from Sutterdown working for Sam could settle with you, for starters, she thought. *They'll do nicely, plus Sam says they've three really decent archers among 'em, and there are a few others who're ready to start their own crofts or take up full-time trades.*

"And you'll all have to think about which sept you'd prefer to join—that'll take meditation, you'll want to hold a Circle . . . in fact, perhaps my Maiden, Sally, could give you some pointers."

Judy opened her mouth and then shut it again; she might be a purist, but she could see this wasn't the time for another of her who-gets-into-what-sept talks. There were times when Juniper thought she'd be happier in a hypothetical First Congregational Church of Wicca, Calvinist, sitting around with the church elders discussing whether an applicant was truly of the elect.

"Could . . . could we use your *nemed* here?" Laurel said eagerly.

The Singing Moon's sacred wood had been famous among Oregon's pagans long before the Change. Now the name trailed numinous clouds.

"Surely," Juniper said, smiling. *The wood deserves its fame, even if I don't.* "And another near where you'll be settling, to find the right place for your covenstead. Beltane would be perfect for that; new beginnings and fruitfulness, after all. There'll be a festival of dedication at Sutterdown this Beltane anyway."

The discussion went on for some time; when it was over and Laurel went glowing on her way, Judy blew out her lips with a sound like a skeptical horse.

"Oh, great. The septs of the Clan Mackenzie: Wolf, Bear, Coyote, Elk, Raven . . . and now the Fluffy Bunnies. Robin Wood? No Starhawk? What about Matthews . . . even Zee Budapest?"

"They'll do very well, once they've settled in," Juniper said stoutly. "Nobody who's survived this long can *really* be an F-B. Lord and Lady witness, looking back on it *we* seem like F-B's."

The others of her advisors trickled in; she hadn't wanted them all there during the discussion with Laurel. That would have been too intimidating.

And what's to come intimidates me, she thought.

She sighed and closed her eyes, controlling her breathing, let calm if not peacefulness flow through her. Then she opened them again and looked around the table.

"*Cogadh*," she said. "War. Whether we will or no. Not *very* soon, not this month, but not more than a year's grace, either, I'm thinking."

"August at the earliest," Andy Trethar said. "When the harvest is in."

His wife Diana nodded. They were alike as long-married couples sometimes became, both slim and dark, with a little salt in the pepper of Andy's beard. They'd run an organic foods store and restaurant in Eugene, then done the cooking for the clan when all they had was the Eternal Soup, and now they looked after food supplies in general besides running the kitchens of the Chief's Hall here at Dun Juniper.

"We've got plenty stored, and so do the Bearkillers and Corvallis and Mt. Angel. But the Protectorate isn't nearly so well off—they'll be short, until *their* harvest comes in. That's why they're buying grain now."

Sam Aylward nodded. "Right you are. He'll want to conquer our storehouses, not burn our crops. And he's got projects under way that will take time, things that would improve his position when the balloon goes up. Those ruddy great castles, for starters. More likely after next year's harvest, but possibly this autumn. He's not the sort to attack before he's ready, worse luck."

Chuck made a gesture of agreement, and then one of Invocation. "It's too early to say for sure, but the Lord and Lady willing the harvest this year looks excellent, we ought to average fifty to sixty bushels an acre on the wheat and better on the barley and oats, potatoes look good, and our herds are doing well."

"Plenty of spare weapons," Sam said. "And a reserve of five hundred made arrows for every archer, besides what they keep at home. Chuck?"

"We've got bicycles or horses for the whole levy, and enough draft animals for the supply train; full equipment for everyone, and enough gear to replace losses." He looked at his wife.

"I wouldn't call all the medicos *doctors*, exactly," Judy said. "Any more than I am. But they know what they need to know, and we've got enough medical supplies . . . such as they are and such as we can make."

Juniper nodded decisively. "We're agreed he probably won't attack until after the grain harvest, at the earliest?" After a chorus of nods, she went on: "That's what Mike Havel and Luther Finney and Captain Jones think, and the abbot for that matter. But there's the matter of those refugees . . . what about them, by the way, Sam?"

"If Wally and Leigh are leaving me to set up with this new lot, I'll have room for them, and work in plenty. The girl—"

"She's following Eilir and Astrid around like a lost puppy," Juniper said with a chuckle. "But I had in mind her little gift."

Her chuckle raised eyebrows. "It's Laurel," she said. "Or rather her husband, Collin. It occurred to me while we were considering what to do about them that *he'll* be useful."

"How so?" Judy said. "Frankly, he seemed dreamier than the lot of them, and that's saying something!"

"He's a stereotype of a professional mathematician," Juniper said, grinning as the others sat up straight. "And he *is* a genuine PhD. Which would be rather helpful to us, now wouldn't it? It would mean, with luck, we could figure out just *what* the Protector has planned, as well as *when*."

A chorus of agreement. Juniper's smile was not at all her usual amiable expression. "And in any case we should do something to him, first, shouldn't we?"

She laughed at the surprised expressions. "We can't loosen his hold until we break his spell of fear. That requires . . . practical demonstrations. We've been stinging him like mosquitoes. Time to become hornets. Also to demonstrate to him the folly of ruling a hostile countryside, to be sure. You can't be too careful in which enemies you make, and how many, and where."

CHAPTER TWELVE

Near Amity, Willamette Valley, Oregon
May 13th, 2007 AD—Change Year Nine

"St. George for England!"

The bandit in front of Havel started to turn, jolted by the unfamiliar cry from behind him. He jerked his head back with a scream of panic as he realized what he'd done by dropping his guard, then looked down incredulously at the yard of steel through his stomach.

Havel wrenched the sword back. Muscles tried to clamp on it, but the knife-sharp blade severed them as they did; the sensation was hideously like carving a pork roast. The man doubled over with an *oooff*, like someone who'd been punched in the gut—except that he wouldn't be getting up. Havel turned the motion of withdrawal into a loop, ending in a short economical overarm chop at the man behind the one who collapsed hugging his gut. The sword smacked into bone, and when the bandit clutched at his left arm with his other hand the limb came off in it. He stared at it for an instant and then turned, shrieking like a machine grinding through rock, spraying blood into the faces of his fellows.

"Hakkaa paalle!" Havel shrieked, sword and shield working together in a blur of speed.

A spray of red drops flew through the air as he cut backhand; the frame of a shield cracked like a gunshot, and the arm bone beneath it. He smashed the edge of his own shield into the man's face as he dropped his guard, then thrust over the falling body; the point went home in the meat of an upper arm, and he twisted it like a coring knife . . .

"Oh, shit, *Bearkillers!*" one of the outlaws screamed.

"Hakkaa paalle!"

Signe screeched the war cry and killed the man in front of her with a stepping thrust to the neck that snapped out and back in a blurred glitter of steel. Then the bandits broke, backing up fast, crowding each other in the doorway and then turning and running. Havel followed. The sunlight outside made him blink for an instant, shield and blade up. Nobody struck at him; they were too busy running away.

And dying. Another horse stood nearby; the rider had dismounted, a big man plying a longbow with wicked skill.

It was the two mounted men close by who were *really* startling. As he watched, one pulled his lance out of the back of a fleeing bandit—running away from a lancer on foot was an exercise in futility—and swung the long shaft into an upright position. His companion sloped his red-running sword over one shoulder; both used their bridle hands to push up their visors as their horses turned back towards the ruined video store and away from the dozen or so outlaws flogging their horses east across the tall grass of the fallow field.

Visors, Havel thought, mentally gibbering. *Yikes!*

The two horsemen were in full plate armor, cap-a-pie, head to foot, the sort of thing people before the Change would have thought of as a King Arthur knight-in-armor outfit. It was enameled in green, and he blinked and squinted to see the details.

Sallet helms. Milanese style, he thought. *Fifteenth century. Agincourt armor, Henry V, Wars of the Roses, once more unto the breach, St. Crispin's Day, Joan of Arc and all that good shit.*

The Larsdale library had a book on it, part of a series on the history of arms and armor with illustrations and diagrams. He'd gone through it when they'd considered making some like it; the plate harness was good equipment, not much heavier than a mail hauberk, nearly as flexible, and better protection against arrows or crushing weapons. In the end they'd decided it wasn't worth the trouble. Plate had to be shaped to the individual the way a tailor hand-cut a good formal suit, and the level of time and trouble required was a whole order of magnitude greater than with the mostly chain armor they were using.

"Good day," the first armored horseman said; both bore a blazon of five red roses on their shields. "Saw you were in a spot of trouble with these bandit chappies and mixed it in. Hope that's all right, eh? Had to clear the way, in any event."

The accent was English, in a rather old-fashioned plummy Eton-Oxford-Guards way Havel had heard only in movies before the Change. Mild eyes regarded him from beneath the raised visor, blue and a little watery; a fair mustache shot with silver confirmed his estimate for the man's age, a bit north of fifty. He rode a big yellow horse as if he'd been born there; the saddle was a high-cantled war model, and the stirrup leathers were long, leaving his legs nearly straight. The man beside him was bigger and younger, a lock of yellow hair plastered to his forehead with sweat, eyes blue-and-worried.

"Many thanks," Havel said, containing a burst of questions; he hadn't seen anyone from farther away than Montana for years, and now . . .

"Quite welcome. We'll be moving along then, we're actually in a bit of a hurry, you see—"

"Mike, Unc' Will's arrived!" Signe called.

Do not succumb to information overload, Havel thought, his head swiveling west. A trumpet sounded from there. *About time,* he thought, and threw up a hand as Will Hutton reined in with a spurt of gravel, his lancers dusty and foam on the necks of their horses. He pointed northward with one gauntlet and spoke. "Bossman, Arminger's men are comin' down the road. Troop strength at least. More off to westward, that's why we were late—had to get around 'em. Looks like they're beatin' the bushes for someone, and they want him *bad.*"

Havel bared his teeth as he looked around once more; there wasn't much time, but going off half-cocked wasn't the answer.

"I presume you're no friend of the Protector's?" he asked the older man in the plate armor.

"Rather! The rotter's after our heads, I'm afraid." A calm smile. "Name's Loring. Sir Nigel Loring. Late of the Blues and Royals, and the Special Air Service regiment. My son, Alleyne, and the big fellow there is Little John Hordle."

Havel blinked in shock. *All right, information overload has arrived.* Then he nodded coolly—it didn't really *matter*. There wasn't time to gibber and rave and run around waving his arms.

"Believe it or not, I've met a friend of yours, Sir Nigel, and he's told me about you . . . later, later! Will, get Kendricks patched up and out of here."

"Ambulance wagon's about a quarter-mile back," Hutton said, and made a motion to his signaler. The young man put the trumpet to his lips and blew a complex pattern.

Havel went on: "Then throw out a screen and tell Arminger's men to get the hell out. If they come at you, skirmish and fall back. Eric, Luanne, you come with us. *Move.*"

He turned to Nigel Loring. "My name's Mike Havel. Aka *Lord Bear* around here. Also no friend of the Protector, as you've probably heard. I knew there were some Australians or Englishmen in Portland, but . . . later! I was doing some bandit-ambushing when you showed up—"

. . . and nearly got me killed by delaying Will . . .

"—but I'd rather not restart my war with the Protectorate just now. I do offer sanctuary; we don't extradite fugitives from that bunch. My men'll keep Arminger's busy, and sure you're still running directly south. You come with me; we'll finish up my chore, and then head home. Where I'll be *very* interested to hear your story."

Loring looked at him steadily for an instant, then nodded with a brisk decisive gesture.

"Sanctuary . . . will be very welcome. Lead on, Lord Bear."

He was evidently making a snap judgment on Havel's character as well. His followers had all been waiting for that small gesture; the big longbowman grabbed the bridle of a horse whose bandit owner would never need it again and swung into the saddle. The knight and his son fell in behind Havel, and the Bearkiller leader waved.

"They went thataway," he said, pointing to the clump of woods a bowshot distant to the northeast. "Follow me!"

Will Hutton stood in his stirrups and chopped a hand forward. The Bearkiller troop rode northward, swinging out to make a single line across the road and the fields on either side. That kept their pace down to a canter, which was just as well; the Protectorate force ahead was coming on at a round trot, in column of fours, a massive rumble of hooves and rustling clatter of equipment and bristle of lances, with a few mounted crossbowmen out in front. Those turned back when they saw the Bearkiller, and the column of men-at-arms writhed for a moment and began to shake out into a two-deep line about two-thirds the width of his. There were more than thirty of them, all well mounted; he stood in the stirrups and used his binoculars. The big kite-shaped shields were matte-black with the Lidless Eye, not quartered with a baron's blazon—the Protector's household troops, then. Beyond them the ground dipped a little, but he could see sunlight breaking on edged metal there, too; probably infantry coming up at the double, but quite a bit behind.

"Halt!" Hutton said, swinging his fist up. Then: "Wings forward! Extend to the west!"

The formation shifted, each end thrown north, the one to his left stretching further and a pair of the riders from the right trotting over to join it. The shorter wing to his right was anchored on Palmer Creek; a steep bare bank running down to a broad marshy channel—the Protector's men could get around there, but they'd have to take quite a while at it. One thing Hutton had learned long ago was that hooves didn't go well with soft footing, particularly when they were carrying two hundred pounds plus of armored rider and gear, so he didn't have to worry about *that* flank.

The Protector's horsemen were coming towards him in a line centered on the road, but it was a line that rode deeper into an unequal-armed V every moment.

They're getting uneasy about it, too, he thought, grinning whitely. *Good. I do purely hate that man and all his crew.*

The enemy formation slowed an instant or two before their commander signaled a halt about two hundred and fifty yards away, the limit of practical archery. He rode forward a little with his trumpeter at his side; Hutton tightened his thighs to move his mount out from his own formation. At that signal of mutual intent to talk they both trotted forward to meet midway between the two war bands.

The Protector's man halted his mount without needing to use the reins; Hutton nodded slightly in acknowledgment, and glanced approvingly at the big glossy black animal. They both removed their helmets and propped them on their saddlebows, another bit of the etiquette that had grown up over such matters in the last few years. Arminger's commander was in his late twenties, around six feet tall and broad-shouldered, with the hard muscular look anyone got if they trained every day in armor. His face was harder still, high-cheeked and snub-nosed; his corn-colored hair was cropped closer than a crew cut over the area behind his ears, and a few inches longer forward of that. That was the fashion among the Protectorate's military elite; it looked deeply silly as far as Hutton was concerned, but it helped prompt his memory.

Alexi Stavarov's boy, he thought silently. Then: "Lord Piotr."

Alexi had been one of Arminger's original backers in Portland just after the Change, according to Signe's research; if he wasn't second-in-command it was because the Protector was careful to keep the power structure of his realm at the level just below himself full of bickering rivals competing for his favor, without any clear chain of command. What the arrangement lacked in efficiency, it more than made up for in security. At least from the Protector's point of view, and Hutton thoroughly approved from his own.

The odds are long enough, without them gettin' their shit together, he thought, waiting with raised brows. *Take your time, Russkie-boy, take your time. Time is my friend.*

"Lord William," Stavarov replied, equally polite. "Might I ask why you're blocking the road?"

"Might be I could ask what you're *doing* on this road, Piotr Alexandrovitch?" Hutton said. "Wouldn't be thinkin' of crossing our border, would you?"

Piotr Stavarov flushed; he was fair enough that it showed despite an outdoorsman's weathered tan. "This is Protectorate territory," he snapped. "It's a long walk to your border. We're patrolling. You are trespassing."

"Don't see any of your people on the ground hereabouts," Hutton pointed out. "And we're here because we're hunting bandits. So you *don't* patrol it, or not enough to keep road agents down. Seems to me your claim is sort of mostly talk."

"We're pursuing dangerous criminals ourselves," Stavarov replied. "Are you assisting them deliberately? Because standing in our way makes it more likely that they will escape."

Which was brass, if you liked, since his father had been a smuggler, drug runner, extortionist and loan shark before the Change and a mass murderer after it. For that matter, he'd been a KGB agent back before the Berlin Wall fell. Back when what happened on other continents mattered . . .

Hutton spread his gauntleted hands. "You folks and us, we've got different ideas of what a *dangerous criminal* amounts to," he pointed out. "That's why we don't have no extradition treaty with y'all."

Stavarov opened his mouth, then visibly realized that argument would be playing into Hutton's hands; with every second the fugitives he sought were that much farther away.

"Get out of our way or we'll kick you out of it," he snarled, and reined his horse around, spurring back to his own men at a gallop.

Hutton grinned to himself, looking up at the sun to estimate the time; it wasn't a good idea to try wearing a wristwatch under armor, particularly since nobody was making any replacements for wind-up watches that got smashed.

Around two o'clock; say they think the people they're chasing are moving at ten miles an hour . . .

"Bows out and ready," he said to his own trumpeter. "One shaft, then Parthian retreat. And pass the word, aim at the horses when you can—but hit the men if you have to."

That took only a few seconds; Hutton grinned harder as he thought of young Stavarov's dilemma. Unlike the Outfit's A-listers, Protectorate men-at-arms didn't carry saddle bows as well as lances; they relied on their infantry for missile fire, and had to get within ten feet of you to do any harm. They could wait for their crossbowmen to come up . . . but that would take time, which was the whole point of the matter, and Hutton could just pull back out of range and make them deploy all over again. They weren't trying to *beat* him, they just wanted him to go away so they could barrel on south and catch those weird refugees, whoever they were.

He could read a snapping of temper in Stavarov's savage gesture. The long curled trumpet Arminger's forces favored rang out, and the lances came down in a glittering wave. The horses went forward . . . walk . . . trot . . . canter . . . Then they settled into a steady hand gallop, and the earth shook under the pounding of a hundred and twenty hooves. In the fields on either side of the road divots of earth flew up as the horseshoes churned at the turf; he could see Stavarov himself coming straight at him, his kite-shaped shield sloped up under his eyes and covering his whole left side, the double-edged blade of his lance head aimed at the Bearkiller's midriff.

"Now!"

Hutton raised his bow, drew, loosed. A volley slashed out from the Bearkiller ranks; carefully aimed, and at no more than a hundred yards' distance. The arrows twinkled once in the sun as they reached the top of their shallow arcs, then snapped down towards the Protectorate's men-at-arms. Hutton's horse turned in place under the pressure of his thighs and rocked into motion. He'd been directing the Bearkillers' breeding program for most of a decade now, and he'd folded a good deal of old-style quarter horse into the mix, for the jackrabbit acceleration that their powerful haunches produced. The Protectorate men-at-arms were well mounted, and a long race would be a toss-up, but the Bearkillers had a definite edge in acceleration.

Hutton could see that, as he drew another arrow and turned in the saddle to fire over his mount's rump. That let him see the results of the first arrowfall. Some of the shafts stood quivering in shields, or had glanced off the mail of hauberks despite the bodkin points, or simply missed. Others had penetrated, and riders were down, one being dragged by a foot caught in the stirrups, some simply falling out and clutching at the steel and wood in their bodies.

What really disrupted the charge was the arrows hitting the *horses*. Wounded, they bolted, or turned bucking and plunging, or fell under their neighbors in a chain-reaction of tumbling and tripping thousand-pound animals. They were much larger than their riders, unarmored, and they had far less ability to face pain and injury for the sake of obeying orders.

Which makes you wonder who's smart and who's dumb, he thought, wincing slightly at the piteous screams the wounded animals made, full of an uncomprehending agony. He'd always liked horses . . .

The rest of the men-at-arms bored in, grimly intent. Hutton shot again, aiming low, and a charger reared with an arrow through the fleshy part of its left forelimb. The distance between the two forces narrowed until he could see the flared nostrils of the horses, then opened out again.

"Trumpeter," Hutton called. "Sound *fall in, column to the enemy's right*."

That would let the Bearkillers shoot, and if the Protectorate force turned to chase them . . . why, then, they could *still* shoot at their pursuers, and the enemy would be heading away from the fugitives.

Gonna be one frustratin' day for that Russkie-boy, Hutton thought as he angled his horse westward; hooves rattled on asphalt, crunched on gravel, and then the animal bunched and gathered itself and leapt the roadside ditch.

The bandits' tracks were clear enough to Havel in the field to the east of the road. They ran straight eastward towards the Willamette, went past an overgrown drainage ditch and became clearer still where they'd ridden down the wooded stream bank beyond, straight into Palmer Creek. That was where they'd hidden and waited for the tempting ranchers and their horse-herd to come north from the Crossing Tavern. They'd abandoned their plunder and those eastern-bred horses ran free through the roadside meadows, but all the gang members who'd managed to run away had done it on horseback. Havel leaned over in the saddle as they passed the mess of blankets and cooking pots and buzzing flies that told of the outlaws' wait, and kept to the front as they moved down the low slope to Palmer Creek.

His mount breasted the stream and the others put their horses to it as well, the beasts tossing their heads as they felt for footing; cold water poured into his boots and lapped at the—waterproof—lower edge of his bow case. His eyes scanned up through the trees and brush on the other side, and the edge of the water. The hoofprints there were fresh, still filling where they'd stamped down through the leafmold, bits of dirt fallen where the horses had taken the bank ahead. His own surged beneath him as it climbed out of the water in their wake.

"I make it eleven," he said.

Luanne Larsson kicked one boot free of the stirrup and leaned far over in the saddle, holding to the horn. "Twelve," she said, pushing her round bowl helm back by the nasal to examine the soft black soil. "Blood trail, there, though—don't know if it's the man or the horse," she went on, swinging back erect.

"Halt for a bit, then. I want to get back into my gear."

Signe and Havel dropped to the ground; their regular battle mounts were along on leading reins, and their own war harness was bundled across the saddles.

On the one hand, we're going someplace marshy, Havel thought, as they helped each other into the hauberks. *On the other, it's someplace people might try to kill us. On the balance, I'll wear the armor. And we can handle a dozen raggedy-assed bandits, but there may be more of them—* probably are *more of them . . .*

"I like a man who knows his mind," Nigel Loring said;

which was both a compliment and a hint. He looked Havel up and down. "Good gear, by the way."

Havel nodded. "Easier to make in quantity than what you're wearing," he replied. "Not that it isn't a pretty suit."

"We took the design from museum pieces, actually," the Englishman replied, pronouncing the word as *ekshually*. "Now, as to what we're doing . . ."

Havel settled his palm-broad sword belt, bloused the hauberk above it slightly—that shifted some of the weight to your hips—and pulled a map out of Trooper's saddle-bag. The well-trained horse stayed steady as he spread it against the saddle.

"I originally planned to trap Crusher Bailey wherever he jumped me," he said. "But the troops I had planned for that are now screening against the Protector's men who are chasing *you*. I . . . *really* don't want to let Crusher get away and rebuild his gang, either."

He looked at his party; Signe and him, Eric and Luanne, and the three Englishmen; he knew his kinsfolk's quality, and from the look of it the foreigners were good men of their hands too. That wasn't surprising, from what he'd been told . . .

"So we're it. Let's push them hard enough they don't get any fancy ideas, like setting ambushes."

Sir Nigel leaned over and looked at the map, then up at the country ahead. "Seems to be something that requires action," he agreed. "And we certainly owe you a debt for your hospitality, Lord Bear. Alleyne, John?"

The other two nodded, Loring's son gravely, the bow-man grinning from ear to ear. "Whatever you say, sir," John Hordle said. "Never a dull moment!"

He had an accent that reminded Havel of Sam Ayl-ward's, though not so thick. He was younger, perhaps in his late twenties, with a face like a ham, hands the size and shape of spades, little russet-brown eyes above a nose something had squashed years ago, and a shock of dark auburn hair and orange-hued close-cropped beard that did little to hide a thick scattering of freckles. He wore a green-enameled chain-mail shirt, and carried a longbow in the old medieval style, a simple tapered stave of yew, a full quiver of gaudily fletched arrows across his back; a long double-edged hand-and-a-half sword and a dagger hung at his waist. Eric blinked at him, obviously not much enjoying someone looming over him the way he did over most others; the Englishman would be six foot seven in his stocking feet, and Havel thought his shoulders were as broad as a Bearkiller sword was long, scabbard and all. The battle-gear made him look like a cross between a young Santa Claus and some ancient heathen god of war.

"Let's go, then," the Bearkiller lord said, putting his foot in the stirrup.

They broke back into the sunshine, instinctively spreading out in the bright sunlight; past an abandoned sheet-metal building that bore the faded logo of a fruit-packing company, past derelict farmhouses and collapsing barns, through meadows blue with camas flowers and iris, red columbine and pale pink twinflower growing more common as they headed southeast; bird and butterfly started up as the horses breasted the tall grass and weeds. The fleeing outlaws were not in sight, but their path was obvious enough. Then Luanne cried out:

"Horse! And man too, I think."

The horse was standing with its head down and hidden in the rank growth nearly as tall as it was. The head came up as the Bearkillers and their guests approached, and it whinnied at them—or more probably, at their horses. A man struggled up too, clinging to a stirrup, falling back with a cry of despair as the horse shied, then scrambling awkwardly back into the saddle as it steadied. Luanne gave a whoop and unlimbered her lariat, whirling the loop of braided rawhide over her head as she charged. The fresher horse closed quickly. Luanne had been ranch-raised in Texas and an up-and-coming junior-rodeo star before the Change; the circle of leather rope landed neatly about the man's shoulders and jerked him screaming from the saddle as she snubbed the lariat to the horn of hers.

The others reined in; the man was lying half-stunned, weeping and cursing and trying to staunch a stab wound in one shoulder which he couldn't reach with the lariat on him. Luanne kept the tension on the braided rawhide ex-

pertly tight, backing her mount whenever the outlaw tried
to get any slack on it.

Havel smiled grimly and swung out of the saddle, drawing his sword. The outlaw howled as the Bearkiller's boot
caught him on the wound; he could do no more than paw
feebly as he was disarmed. The cries of pain and panic died
away to a frantic gurgle as he felt the prick of a sword point
under his jaw. The fallen man bared yellow snaggled teeth
in a doglike grin of submission, their look fruit of malnu-
trition and neglect since the Change; Havel judged he'd
been about twelve back then.

"Look at me, you worthless sack of shit," Havel said,
pushing the helmet back so that his face was clear; he'd dis-
carded the irritating contacts some time ago. "Who am I?"

The sweating face went even paler beneath its fuzz of
mouse-colored beard. "Oh, Christ, *Lord Bear.*"

"Bingo first time, asshole; the guy you just tried to rob
and kill. You listening?" A fractional nod and a wince as it
moved against the shaving-sharp point of the sword. "So
you know my word's good. Here's the deal. Lead us in to
your hideout—we know pretty much where it is, so don't
get any bright ideas about stranding us in the swamp—plus
telling us everything we want to know, and you get to live.
Yes or no?"

"Shit—Crusher, he'll—"

Havel put a little pressure on the sword point, and a
bead of blood appeared; the outlaw jerked fractionally,
turning it into a trickle. The Bear Lord transferred the
point of the long blade to the tip of the bandit's nose; it
followed his movements with mechanical precision, and
he stared at it with cross-eyed fascination.

"What exactly is Crusher Bailey going to do to you that
I can't?" Havel asked reasonably. "And I'm right here. He
isn't."

The bandit's eyes shifted to the ring of figures around
him, then desperately to the bright world beyond. It would
be hard to die on a spring day . . .

"OK, you promise?"

"Yeah, I promise."

You get to live, Havel thought. *The only convincing ar-*

gument I've ever heard against capital punishment is that being dead doesn't hurt much. You'll haul rock and break rebar out of concrete twelve hours a day seven days a week, but you won't be dead. If you're real unlucky, you'll still be alive and doing it twenty years from now.

The prisoner swallowed at Havel's expression and stuttered: "OK, man, OK!"

"Signe, patch him," he said, stepping back, sword still poised.

"Do I *have* to?" Signe asked.

"Unfortunately, yes. Hard to get information out of his corpse. Luanne, get his horse."

The Lady of the Bearkillers ripped open the outlaw's dirty shirt and even filthier denim jacket and applied the field-dressing without any unnecessary gentleness. When he yelped, she backhanded him across the face and snarled, "You the one who yelled '*First after you with the woman, Crusher*'?"

"No, ma'am, it wasn't me I swear . . ." He gabbled, then took another look at her and became more panic-stricken than before, if that were possible. "You ain't, you can't be—"

Signe shook her brown locks: "Hair by Ms. Clairol, asshole. And *I* didn't make any promise to let you live. Did you notice that, lover boy? *Did* you?"

"OK, I'll shut up!"

Havel grinned. *How we think alike, my gentle spouse and I!* The prisoner flicked his eyes away from Signe to him, but did not seem to find the expression on his captor's face reassuring. In fact, he seemed to think of it much the way a coyote would about the smile on the muzzle of the very last wolf it ever saw.

"Where's Crusher's camp in there?" he asked, flicking the sword through the air from the wrist. It made an unpleasant *vwweep!* sound.

"Ah . . . look, we, uh, *they,* camp a couple of different places. Mostly near the old gravel pits, you know, on the west bank downstream from Woods Landing about maybe half a mile, a bit more? There's a jetty on the east bank, Crusher keeps boats hidden both sides, sorta flat-bottomed things, so he can get stuff back and forth, you know?"

Havel nodded. That explained a good deal about how Bailey's gang had ranged so far, and been so hard to find or track, but he wondered where Crusher Bailey had gotten the boats. He didn't think they were the types who'd run them up themselves. And if they simply ran for their boats and took them all with them, there wasn't much he could do but go home and try again another day. Bailey could go look for a new hangout, in another of the burgeoning swamps along the Willamette, or in the ruins of Salem, or even farther south in Eugene, or in the mountains near one of the roads that crossed the Cascades.

"Put him on his horse. Tie his hands together and then to the reins, and lash his feet to the stirrups."

The outlaw gave a moo of panic at that—it meant almost certain battering death if the horse fell or bolted—but went quiet again after a look at the faces around him. They put him at the head of the little column, and the Bearkillers all pulled out their recurves and set a shaft to the string. So did John Hordle; Havel looked over at him curiously. It wasn't impossible to use a longbow from horseback, just immensely awkward and difficult; he'd seen Sam Aylward and Eilir Mackenzie do it, and read about samurai using seven-foot bamboo bows from the saddle.

"Can you shoot that thing mounted?"

"No, sor, I can't, not to speak of," Hordle said cheerfully. "But I can get off a horse right quick, I can."

Havel nodded; the big Englishman's feet were near the ground anyway, on an ordinary-sized mount. Then he cocked an eye at the sun—it was behind them, about three hours past noon—and waved them forward, his eyes busy. They crossed an old railway embankment, a line of weeds and saplings now, with the two streaks of rusted iron mostly hidden, then down into another neglected orchard, the sweet-sour smell of years of fallen fruit strong and the spindly saplings crushed by the passage of the fugitives they were chasing.

"Halt," he called softly in the insect-buzzing gloom. "There's a steep slope ahead of us, wooded, and then open country that was swampy even before the Change. It runs into a loop of the Willamette, the Lambert Bend, and the bar upstream broke in the floods three years ago. Easy to bog down. Eric, you did the scout, you ride right after our guide here. First time it even looks like he's leading us into a swale, put one through his gut. Asshole, your *only* chance of getting out of this alive is for us to win, understand? Rest of you, we go in fast and hard, get stuck into them and kill 'em all—I'd have preferred to take Crusher alive to hang, but there aren't enough of us. Any questions? Then *go*."

They came out of the orchard into a stretch of woods that sloped eastward; flickers of light came through the canopy above, and the hooves pounded and then began to squelch as the land leveled out. Suddenly the trees about them were dead, bleached white ghosts, and reeds waved about them higher than a mounted man's head.

"Here!" the outlaw at the head of their column said. "Left here!"

They turned on to an old dirt road; it was muddy, and gobbets of the soft black soil flew high as the horses loped forward, but it was passable—just. Havel kept his reins knotted on his saddlebow, guiding Trooper with thighs and balance; the outlaw wasn't up to that standard of horsemanship, but the other Bearkillers were. He noted with interest that the Englishmen were too, at least the two in plate armor.

The directions kept coming, and they were making good progress. Suddenly the reeds were past; the ground was still soft and boggy in spots, but the trail led among trees, big black cottonwoods and willows and red alders, with blue ponds—probably the old gravel pits—on either side. The ground sloped down very slightly from the levee to dense woodland and brush along the river; amid the trees were tents and crude huts, and hearths smoking. Men and women boiled among them, gathering bundles with frantic haste and scurrying down towards the river's edge and the boats hidden there.

Raw screams of panic came as the Bearkillers rode into sight; then a great booming voice: "There's only seven of them, you pussies! There's better than thirty of us—do you want to lose all you've got? Take 'em!"

Uh-oh, Havel thought, and shot. *Total mindless panic would have been nice.*

Arrows and crossbow bolts came whining back at them; some distant part of his mind grinned in amusement as the first of them struck the bandit they'd captured and made their guide, leaving him flopping limp in the saddle to which he was lashed. The outlaws were shaking themselves out into a rough line or elongated clump, but there were an almighty lot of them; it wouldn't have mattered if he'd had Will's troop at his back, but he *didn't.* It wouldn't have mattered in open country, either; horse archers could peck footmen to death easily if they had room to run. This wasn't open country; he couldn't go a hundred yards in any direction without needing webbed feet, and on the muddy tracks they'd used to get here the outlaws would probably be quicker than horses.

"OK, work to be done," he said. "Let's give them a charge."

Get ironclad fighters in among the lightly equipped outlaws, and they could still turn it around. He cased his bow, whipped out his backsword and slid his targe onto his left arm; out of the corner of his eye he saw John Hordle slip from his mount and raise his longbow. Eric and Luanne pulled their lances free of the saddle scabbards and leveled them.

The bandits waited, grounding spears or jeering and shaking bows and crossbows. Then—

The brush can't be moving, he knew.

That was exactly what it looked like, brush and tangled shoots standing and shaking itself along a hundred-yard line. Then he saw the kilts and plaids below the ghillie cloaks—war cloaks, the Mackenzies called them—and heard a familiar deep voice cry out: *"Let the gray geese fly!"*

Forty longbows snapped, and the broadhead shafts twinkled in the mix of shadow and sun, flashing as they came out of the shade of tree and grass. The range was close, less than a hundred yards. Half of the armed bandits fell in the first volley.

The rest charged the Bearkillers, but it was less of an attack than a desperate attempt to get by them and into the swamps. John Hordle's bow snapped three times, and three men went down—two with arrows in the leg, one shot through the gut; the armored riders chased targets that dodged and squealed in panic. Havel stabbed one with a slamming thrust down by his own left leg, freed the blade and rode another down, Trooper's shoulder sending him spinning into the downward stroke of the backsword. It jarred on bone with a butcher's-cleaver sound, then came free in a great fan of blood that sparkled bright red on the rank wet grass. That put him in position to strike for Crusher Bailey, but the outlaw chief's companion threw a javelin that made Havel duck. Bailey gave a cackle of relief as he dodged past, trademark hammer held high.

It turned into a yell of alarm as John Hordle stepped into his way. The hammer beat down, but the Englishman stepped in and caught the wooden shaft just above Bailey's hand. His great red paw closed on the hickory, ripped it from Crusher's hand and threw it casually behind him. Then his bear grip closed around Bailey's torso, trapping him with his arms pinned to his side; the bandit weighed well over two hundred pounds, but Hordle raised him high and squeezed, squeezed . . .

Crusher screamed and thrashed, and went limply unconscious. Luanne's lariat fell around the body of his javelin-throwing companion, and she signaled her horse into a short trot, dragging any fight out of him. Mackenzie archers sent a flight over the heads of the last fleeing outlaws, the long arrows burying themselves in the soft turf with only their fletchings showing, bringing the crowd to an arm-waving stop.

Another voice called, a soprano, high clear: "Throw down! Now, every one of you! Hands high! Anyone whose hands aren't high will be shot!"

Silence stretched, and then the outlaws began to shed their weapons. Havel legged his horse forward, the others following in his wake. A red-haired figure waited for him, standing beside a broad-shouldered man leaning on his bow as Mackenzies rounded up and bound the surviving members of Crusher Bailey's gang—and protected them from a group of women clad in rags and bruises heading their way with weapons snatched up from the ground, or in a couple of cases with kitchen knives and roasting spits. A few men likewise ragged and hot-eyed came with them; those were mostly limping heavily, from smashed kneecaps or broken legs left to heal crookedly and make escape impossible. Other nonfighters, women and some children, stood uncertain or looked daggers at the warriors who'd destroyed the outlaw band.

Well, even bandits probably have families who love them, Havel thought. Then: *This ought to be interesting,* as he reined in by the Mackenzie leaders.

"Juney, Sam, good to see you," he said. "Lucky you happened to be in the neighborhood. *That's* why we got reports the Protector's men out east were all running around like headless chickens!"

"You always were a bit too headlong, mate," Aylward said.

Juniper Mackenzie made a *tsk* sound. "Mike, how often do I have to tell you there's no such thing as coincidence?" she asked, grinning slyly, then nodded to Signe. "Merry met!"

"Hi," Signe said flatly. "I'll get this organized. Looks like the gang had a fair number of prisoners here."

She turned her horse aside, towards a series of wood-and-wire cages that gave off a stench even more noisome than the rest of the bandit camp. Eric and Luanne slid from their saddles; the young man whooped as he threw his arms around the Chief of the Mackenzies and swung her around. His wife was almost as enthusiastic; Havel snorted and turned his eyes away.

He watched Sam Aylward instead. For once, the air of hard cheerful competence deserted the ex-SAS archer. He looked at his compatriots with his eyes bulging and his jaw dropped; he stuttered for a moment before he managed: "Sir Nigel? Young Mr. Loring? *Little Johnnie?*"

The big bowman grinned at him. "It's not King Arthur and the Round Table, nor yet Robin Hood neither." Then his eyes dropped to Aylward's kilt. "Oh, sod all, Samkin! Don't tell me you've gone Jock?"

Havel gave a snort of laughter. "Lot of explanations coming," he said. "But this isn't the time." He slapped a mosquito. "Or the place."

The land around the Crossing Tavern was crowded; with Will Hutton's troop, twenty-one Mackenzies, a dozen freed captives from Crusher Bailey's camp babbling their thankfulness—and, beneath a great garry oak, a row of men who sat bareback on horses. The rope nooses about their necks ran up to where the ropes were fastened to the outspreading branch above; most were silent, and a few who'd babbled or begged were gagged. From where Michael Havel watched, the tall round shape of the tree was silhouetted against the sun going down behind the hills to the west; birds twittered in it, rising in a cloud when the humans disturbed them too badly—once when a bicycle-borne Mackenzie came up from the south and started calling for Juniper; the clansfolk hustled him off. Havel noted the action out of the corner of his eye and then ignored it; he had more pressing business.

Crusher Bailey was the last of the row, glaring, his lips moving silently as he mouthed curses. A sign hung around each bandit's neck, written in charcoal on a board: ROBBER. MURDERER. Crusher Bailey had that, with additions: RAPIST—HORSE THIEF—HOUSE BURNER—CHILD STEALER.

The folk of the tavern watched silently. Will Hutton walked down the row, holding a coiled lariat in his left hand, the end loose in his right. Each time he flicked a beast's rump with the knotted end, the startled animal lurched forward and another figure hung swinging and kicking below.

Mike Havel looked up at Crusher Bailey when there were only three left. "Got anything to say, Crusher?" he said calmly. "I'd really like to know about your connections."

"Yeah, I've got something to say," Bailey said, and spat at his captor. The gobbet went *splat* on the ground between them. "I say you aren't any better than me, just got a bigger gang. And you ain't worth a pitcher of red piss, either! None of you are!"

Bailey clapped his heels into his horse's flanks, and the

animal bounded forward. His body twitched and kicked briefly, then hung limp as it swayed gently back and forth; the outlaw's heavy frame had given him a quicker death than that of most of his followers.

A murmur of surprise came from the onlookers, and Will Hutton stopped in his progress down the line of nooses. Havel smiled a crooked smile and shrugged as he looked at the older man: "Business aside, some men it's just a pleasure to hang, Will."

"Yep, purely a joy," the Texan said.

The last outlaw looked down at them from where he sat his horse, between Crusher's body and the rest of the swinging gallows-fruit; it was Bailey's brother, the slight ferret-faced man.

"I should have gone first," he said. "I'm the eldest of the Bailey brothers. It was me got Crusher through the Dying Time, and we didn't eat nobody neither."

Hutton nodded gravely. "Sorry about that. Your brother sort of broke the flow. You ready?"

The outlaw looked up at the setting sun. "Figure so."

Will slapped the rope across the horse's haunches, then looked down the row of dangling bodies. "Dirty job, but someone's got to do it," he said.

"Bingo," Havel said. "Now people around here can sleep a little easier at night—and use this road more."

A long sigh went through the crowd as the last of the outlaws died; a cool wind from the west went through the leaves of the tree above, making a sound louder but not much different. The limb was nearly as thick through as Signe's waist, but it creaked under the burden it bore. Havel glanced around—nobody was within immediate earshot, if he spoke.

"Sorry about Reuben, Will. He was a good kid."

The older man's face grew harder still; he glanced up at the bough. "He was a good kid, once he was away from that trash father of his—even before, I reckon. And he was growin' into quite a man, too. Reminded me of my boy Luke . . ."

Havel nodded, hiding his surprise. He hadn't heard Hutton mention his eldest child in years; Luke Hutton had been in Italy the day of the Change, doing a hitch as a paratrooper.

"Just one more score in the bill Arminger's runnin' up," the Texan went on. "I expect Angel will want to hear Astrid tell the story ... sort of hoped ... Well, never-no-mind." He sighed and set his shoulders. "There's always work, thank the good Lord."

Havel nodded. "Speaking of which." Then he turned and called: "Arvand Sarian! Front and center!"

The black-bearded innkeeper came forward uncompelled, and he looked Havel in the eye, his arms folded across his chest, standing silent and proud. The Bearkiller lord nodded somber approval, and called over his shoulder.

"Signe! Get that boy out here, would you?"

His wife came forward, leading a boy of about five by the hand; he was dark-haired, and despite gauntness and haunted eyes had the strong family resemblance Havel had noticed among Sarian's kin; Signe patted his head as he looked up at her with a tentative smile.

"There's your dad, little guy," she said, turning him towards the innkeeper and giving him a gentle swat on the bottom of his ragged cutoff jeans.

The boy's eyes went wide. He ran shouting to the tavern keeper, to be swept up in a huge embrace. Havel waited until Sarian had handed the boy off to the child's mother—the decencies had to be observed. When the tavern keeper turned back, the eyes that had been coldly defiant were wet with tears. When he spoke it was in his own language; it took a moment for him to shift back into English, and the accent was stronger when he did:

"For this ... this gift of my son ..." He sank to his knees. "I give myself to your judgment, Lord Bear. Let me be punished, not the rest here; they only did as I told them."

Havel nodded again in approval; it was well said, although the man didn't have much choice in the matter, considering how many troops were on hand. He took off his mail-backed gauntlets and tucked them into his belt before standing with his feet planted apart and his left hand on the hilt of his backsword.

"We found your son in a cage and a good deal else in Crusher's camp, Sarian," he said. "So, you weren't feeding strangers to them because you wanted to. You still did it, and they're still dead, or worse."

Inwardly: *If I'd been in Crusher's boots, I'd have made you take a share of the loot to get you in deeper. But I'm not Crusher, thank God.* Aloud he went on: "You admit I've the right to hang you? It's certainly what the families of the dead would want." Sarian nodded silently, bowing his head.

"Then hear my sentence," Havel said coldly. "You settled and built this place, Arvand Sarian, but now it's mine. You'll hold it from me, and be my man in all things. You and all yours; and your heirs will do the same for mine. This is now the northern border of Bearkiller territory and you're subject to the Outfit. Understood?"

The heavy swarthy face blinked at him in astonishment, then nodded with a quick decisive movement, fighting down a grin. "Yes, Lord Bear. I hear, and I will obey."

He held out his hands, palms pressed together; that showed he had some knowledge of Bearkiller custom. Havel held up his right, palm out, for a moment.

"Just a minute, Sarian. Up until now, you haven't owed me a thing. Once you swear, you *will*. They say every dog gets one bite; you've already had yours. Now you'll be running with *my* pack, and you don't get a second chance. Stand by me, and I'll stand by you; turn on me, and you die. Understood?"

This time Sarian smiled. "I've heard you're a bad man to cross, but also a man of your word," he said. "That seems to be true."

Havel took the other's hands between his. Sarian knew the Outfit's pledge; few who kept their ears open wouldn't, in this part of the Valley. The form for an ordinary dweller in the Outfit's territory was different from an A-lister's, although anyone who knew Astrid Larsson would have seen her fingerprints on both:

"I, Arvand Sarian, pledge obedience and loyalty to the Bear Lord. I will pay his tax and keep his peace, heed his laws and his appointed officers, follow him in war and in peace with arms and council, I and my blood after me. So I swear. So witness earth. So witness sky."

"I, Michael Havel, pledge in the name of the Bearkiller Outfit and my own honor that from me Arvand Sarian shall have fair justice and good lordship, protection and aid at need; and so long as he keeps faith with me, he shall keep holding of all that is his, no man compelling him, he and his heirs after him. So I swear. So witness earth. So witness sky."

The Bearkillers watching gave a cheer. Sarian rose, and chuckled: "So, my lord, I suspect your first command is that I feed all these," he said, waving a hand around at the gathering. "I can. We baked today, and there are the hams, we butchered a beef yesterday and I can slaughter a couple of shoats for ribs and chops, chickens . . ."

Havel grinned. "That *was* going to be my first command," he said. "The next . . . remember that mill we discussed, while the horses were being shod?"

Sarian did, but seemed a little surprised that Havel had. "Yes?"

"You're going to build it, and I'll see you get a loan if you need it. I may be a warlord, Sarian, but I'm not a *stupid* one."

"Hard man, your Havel," John Hordle said.

He leaned back in the booth with the glass beer stein looking like a teacup in his massive fist. Aylward took a swallow of his own while casting a discreet eye around; nobody was near enough to overhear them, as the Crossing Tavern bustled with the effort of feeding so many—most of them outside around their campfires. There was laughter from the booths around them, and snatches of song from the camp; the strange fruit dangling from the old oak hadn't dampened spirits for long. People had gotten tougher-grained since the Change, and nobody was going to miss Bailey's crew much. Some of those passing by paused to spit on the bodies.

"Not exactly mine," Aylward said. He held up a hand. "I'm Lady Juniper's Armsman now . . . run her militia, pretty well; not to mention she saved me life right back after the Change. *And* her territory is where I've settled for good and all, Johnnie—I've a wife and children over there in the Mackenzie country, and a bit of a farm. It's my 'ome now." Unspoken: *So don't tell me anything Lady Juniper's Armsman shouldn't know, because I'll use it if you do.*

Hordle nodded in his turn. Aylward's quirked smile said: *Looks like we still understand each other, mate.*

There was little left of the hulking awkward youth who'd listened to Aylward's stories in the taproom of the Pied Merlin. Hordle had still been young when they last met nearly a decade ago; very young to leave ordinary regimental service and pass the almost insanely rigorous SAS tests, but he'd shown promise. Now he was a man grown; not yet thirty, but with a matter-of-fact confidence. He also had an interesting collection of scars on face and hands and arms, when you had time to look—none from bullets, but a fair number of the thin white puckered lines you got from blades.

"As to our Lord Bear," Aylward went on, "he's a bad enemy but a good man to have at your back if he's your friend, and that's a fact. Now do some ruddy talking, John. Any news on my sisters?"

He'd had two still living when he left England ten years ago. He blew out his cheeks in relief when Hordle smiled and nodded: "We got 'em both out, and their families," he said. "Even with the Change, Sir Nigel wasn't going to forget, eh?"

"Bless 'im," Aylward said, raising his mug.

And I'll wager he got Hordle's kin out too, and the families of any other troops he had under his command. One reason Sir Nigel had been an effective commander had been a thorough understanding that loyalty had to run both ways.

"I've 'ad nine years of wondering what went on back in the old country. What happened to Lady Maude, for starters?"

"Killed when we broke Sir Nigel out of Woburn Abbey," he said.

"What the ruddy *hell* . . . no, I'll let you get on with it."

Hordle finished his stein and filled it again from the jug

on the table; then he took a small loaf out of the basket beside it, tore it apart and began to eat it.

"Get on with the rest, then," Aylward said after a moment.

"Ten years in a word, Samkin?" Hordle said, cheeks bulging as he chewed meditatively.

"Ten thousand for a day, unless *you've* changed."

"Right, then: the Change happened—I was dead asleep in barracks when it did, first thing *I* knew besides the light and headache was gettin' rousted out at four o' bleedin' clock to stand on a street corner with an SA80 even more useless than it was when bullets worked. Well, it had a bayonet. Day Two they gave us halberds and pikes from the Tower and turned the Tin Bellies up in their fancy kit."

"Must've been bad, in London."

"Bad? Mate, you've no idea—we scarpered early, morning of Day Three, and there was fire and smoke from one horizon to another already, and crowds in the streets, and when the water went off, and then . . . The politicians had *no* bloody idea what to do."

"Now isn't *that* a super sodding surprise."

Hordle nodded. "But Sir Nigel and the Household Cavalry got the queen out to the Isle of Wight; she died that winter, poor lady, of grief and overwork—wouldn't take a crumb extra. And when we left London Sir Nigel had notice sent to officers he trusted, to use the islands as rally points—Wight, Man, Anglesey, Arran . . . he could see what would happen if things didn't go back the way they'd been, and that the rally points would need defending."

Aylward nodded. *And smart enough to figure things wouldn't change back,* he thought. *And hard enough to see what had to be done. If they hadn't defended those islands, they'd have been overrun and eaten out, which is what I thought had happened.*

"Blair was supposed to follow along when the civilians finally started taking it serious-like, by the last message we got out of London, but he never did— the riots were bad by then, and the food had run out."

"Bet it had. Small loss with Blair, is what I think. I never did like the bugger's greasy great smile—you could wring the man out and do a proper fry-up with the oil."

"No argument then or now, Samkin. And that's probably exactly what happened to 'im."

They laughed grimly, and Aylward went on: "What about the prince?"

"Sir Nigel took an SAS team to Sandringham to fetch him; we used the back roads and rejoined at the coast— quite a gypsy caravan by then, the prince'd been thinking, like, and he had us sweep up all the horses and livestock we could; seed grain from Highgrove too, and tools, and some farmers he knew. And we *towed* a bloody great grain ship out of Southampton on the tide, with sodding rowboats . . . Christ, talk about hard graft!"

He shuddered at the memory and tilted his mug back.

"Isle o' Wight, eh? Might have guessed that. How many lived?" Aylward said.

"Of our folk? Three hundred fifty thousand; Jocks, Taffies an' all. Two-thirds of that on Wight."

"I'm not surprised," Aylward said, wincing a little despite himself; that was one in two hundred of the British population. Better than he'd expected, in fact. Still . . .

"Six hundred thousand by now, though."

"That's fast work with the dollies even for you, John!"

Hordle snorted laughter and shook his head: "We brought in a lot of foreigners from Iceland and the Faeroes, you see. They lasted out the first year at home on sheep and fish, but they were up against it by then, and proper glad of a place to go, and we needed the hands something fierce by then to get the crop in . . ."

"Sir Nigel said something about the prince getting eccentric."

Hordle grinned, without much mirth. "He did good work at first, mind you, but then . . . eccentric? I think *went bloody barking mad* was more what he had in mind. Sir Nigel and some others were going to do something about it, only Charlie decided to do something about them first— or rather Queen Hallgerda did. Those Tasmanians had a ship in, they agreed to give asylum—Charlie had put their backs up something frightful—so young Mr. Loring and

Major Buttesthorn and a few of the lads and I broke Sir Nigel out of Woburn, and got him down to the ship—just like Robin Hood and Bad King John, it was—and here we are."

"Gotten short-spoken in your dotage," Aylward said. "What happened once you got here, then?"

"Ah, well, Sir Nigel would be the one to tell about that."

"Now," Havel said an hour later, "we have time to talk, by Christ Jesus."

The Englishmen were around the table, Juniper Mackenzie with them; the Bearkiller leaders flanked Havel; everyone was slightly damp from the baths. The room was private—Arvand Sarian's people had laid it, lit the lanterns and brought the food: lentil soup, fresh bread, butter, spring salads, kebabs of chicken and lamb and garlic-rich yogurt on the side, platters of smoking pork ribs with a hot red sauce, French fries, roast vegetables. They'd also set out jugs of wine and water, cider and beer.

Will Hutton spoke as he reached for a rib: "I don't think Arminger's men were pushin' hard, Mike, not once they realized these English folks was past 'em for good. We may have killed a couple; had about half a dozen wounded ourselves. Susanna Clarke got a lance point on her shield and went over the crupper: broken thighbone and half a dozen ribs stove and a nasty cut on her face, but she'll pull through."

Nigel Loring stirred. Michael Havel held up a hand: "Everything in its place, Sir Nigel. Let's hear Lady Juniper first."

Juniper took a pull at her beer. "*Is túisce deoch ná scéal.* A story begins with a drink."

To her surprise, Sir Nigel answered in the same tongue: "But *Nuair a bhionn an fion istigh, bionn an ciall amuigh.* When the wine is in, the sense is out!"

Juniper chuckled and inclined her head. "Ah, but beer, now . . . Well, it all started a little before Beltane—May Eve to you cowans," she went on, her storyteller's voice clear without loudness, the words smoothly knit. "We'd gotten word that the Protector and most of his household troops were out away past the Columbia Gorge."

Signe nodded; so did Sir Nigel.

"We were with him, worse luck," the Englishman said. "Pretty country, but deplorable company."

Juniper chuckled. "And it struck us that since Witches are *not* obliged to turn the other cheek, a good ringing slap across his was due for the breaking of our border. I was killing half a flock of birds with one stone. . . ."

CHAPTER THIRTEEN

Juniper yawned as she set the big basket of eggs down on the wooden counter, then went to one of the smaller sinks to wash her hands—getting their potential offspring out from under sitting free-range hens wasn't the most sanitary procedure in the world. Besides which, the birds pecked even when you thanked them politely and explained your need, which was understandable but annoying. A cook grabbed the basket and bore the hundred or so eggs off to be washed, cracked into bowls, mixed with cream and chopped scallions and cooked into fluffy scrambled form.

"Thanks, Juney," Diana Trethar said absently, sitting at a table and making notes. "I'm trying to come up with something *different* for this Beltane feast coming."

"Diana, it's going to be a potluck anyway! Do a pig or two, roast venison if Cernunnos sends us a deer, Bacchus pudding and wreath cake, and leave the rest to people's imagination!"

The slim dark woman returned to her lists, obviously not having heard a word. Unlike most people, her current job wasn't all that different from what she'd done before the Change—in her case, running MoonDance restaurant, where she'd been in charge of the kitchens and researching recipes.

"I just want something *new,*" she said after a moment of pure focus, eyes blank as she tapped the feather of her quill pen against her lips.

Juniper gave a peal of laughter. "Remember when the problem was making food for twenty feed thirty-five?"

Diana flashed her a quick grin. "That's what the Eternal Soup was for," she said. "Most efficient way of feeding a big group ever invented."

"Most boring, you mean."

"That too. But we were usually too hungry and too scared to be bored back then, if I remember it right." Her eyes went back to the paper. "Hmmm . . . custards for dessert, maybe . . ."

The rest of the long kitchen set against the rear of the Hall was bustling; ancient Mackenzie tradition, hallowed by all the years since their very first harvest, was that the Chief kept open house and a free table—for clansfolk, visitors, and even for gangrels and tramps. Bakers reached into the arched brick ovens with long wooden paddles, bringing out rolls and fruit tarts and round arched loaves of bread with an eight-spoked Wheel cut into their brown crusts; the ovens and the bank of woodstoves made it warm even early in the morning with doors and windows all open, and pleasantly full of a medley of good scents that made the saliva rush into her mouth: the sharp odor of brewing herbal tea, bread and biscuits baking, pancakes in butter-greased skillets bubbling and developing lacy crusts around their edges, porridge giving off smooth thick *pooofh . . . pooofh* sounds, and then there were bacon and ham and sausages sizzling and popping . . .

Dishes were already coming back on trolleys. At one of the large sinks salvaged from the kitchens of a hotel, a team of "corks"—individuals who could be stuffed into any empty chore that needed doing—were scrubbing briskly and setting the plates and saucers and mugs to drain. One of them had a braid of white-blond hair down her back and a slightly mutinous look on her long sculpted face.

Juniper grinned inwardly. *Sorry, Astrid dear,* she thought. *Chores are for everyone, and this isn't Larsdalen. You're an adopted Mackenzie in Dun Juniper, not a princess!*

She let the washing continue until the current stack was done, then called her name, jerking her chin towards the main Hall. Astrid tapped Eilir on the shoulder, and they took off their bib-aprons and dodged out into the great room, tossing them at two others who were on the duty roster and looking reasonably finished. There were more folk at the long tables than was usual, making a cheerful clatter of cutlery and of voices as they called back and forth; most of those who were going to Sutterdown for the ceremonies had chosen to eat here rather than in their own homes. Juniper went to the sideboard where food and crockery waited, filled a big bowl with oatmeal porridge— it was studded with dried fruit, cherries and chunks of apple and pear and crumbled hazelnuts—poured on thick yellow cream, put a mug of the tea on her tray, and made her way to the head table. That was raised on a low dais, and her chair was a thronelike affair carved from oak and maple and walnut by Dennis himself, the pillars behind ending in stylized raven's-heads for Thought and Memory and arching to support a Triple Moon.

That and a view over the room were privileges of rank. The sun was just up, and the verandas outside made it a little dim here without artificial light; god-faces and colored symbols loomed out of the tall dimness above. Racked spears and swords glittered near the big side doors; men, women, children and dogs wandered in and out, along with a damp, chilly spring morning air.

She threw *hellos* and *good mornings* left and right as she walked up to the head table; eating there had come to seem normal, albeit a little like living forever in a hotel. Sometimes it was a relief to sneak down to the kitchens late at night and have a muffin with just Eilir, or make something herself with a few old friends.

"At least when I was a singer, I wasn't on display *all* the time," she muttered, after she'd set her tray down and made the blessing and Invocation over the food and began to ply her spoon.

"Getting nostalgic again?" Chuck Barstow said.

He set down a tray heaped with eggs and fried ham and potatoes and biscuits beside her and started stoking his leanly muscular frame; Second Armsman and Lord of the Harvest were both jobs that kept you sweating. In the seat beyond him Judy yawned and blinked over a bowl like Juniper's. It was just six o'clock and she'd never been a morning person, one of the few serious incompatibilities she and Juniper had; it was also one reason she and Chuck lived in the Hall, where you didn't have to get your own breakfast. Her black cat clambered painfully onto her lap, curled up and went to sleep, not even waking up for the cream-pouring, but then Pywackett was fourteen and a bit decrepit, which made it natural. Cuchulain thumped his tail on the floorboards behind her chair and then went back to sleep himself, despite determined attempts at dog-bothering by a couple of young Hall cats just out of kittenhood.

"Noooo," Juniper said uncertainly. "Not nostalgic in general, if you know what I mean. Just nostalgic for, well, being just *myself*. I'd undo the Change if I could, of course, but otherwise . . . I like this better. It's more the way human beings were meant to live."

"It's gotten so I feel that way most of the time, when I forget what we had to go through to get this far," Chuck said. He used his point-trimmed beard to indicate the table at the other end of the great room. "But I doubt those poor bastards do."

That was where the gangrels and beggars sat; they had to be washed first, of course, since lice and fleas carried disease, but they still looked shaggy-ragged and unkempt, their faces weathered and often scarred or gnarled. Some twitched or spoke to nothing; others cowered on their benches; more hunched over their food, snarling at anyone who came too near. Juniper looked at them with pity, even though most of them chose a wandering life, depending on casual work now and then, eked out with charity and petty theft. Certainly anyone willing to *really* work was welcome to stay past the hour-and-a-day granted mendicants, here or at one or another of the clan's duns. Food was abundant now, but producing that or anything else just took so much sweating-hard effort!

I think most of them are mad, poor souls, probably since the Dying Time. Just functional enough to survive . . . for a while. Or too haunted by what they did to survive to settle among ordinary folk again.

Chuck sighed and shrugged: "Well, they're not much worse off than homeless people before the Change."

"There are a lot more of them, relatively speaking," Juniper said.

"And I suspect some of them are spies, you know. It'd be a perfect way for Arminger to slip his men through here."

"You're probably right," Juniper said soberly; it was part of Chuck's job to worry about that.

Then she flashed him a grin: "But some may be the Lord or Lady in disguise, or some other spirit you wouldn't want to offend. Remember why we leave an empty place at Samhain!"

He nodded—joking aside, they both knew that was entirely possible—and changed the subject. "Judy and I should be coming with you," he said.

"No, you shouldn't," Juniper said, firmly but with a smile. "I have to be at Sutterdown for Beltane"—the reasons were essentially political; the Clan Mackenzie's only town thought *it* should be the Chief's residence—"but Dun Juniper's folk need a High Priest and High Priestess for the rites too, don't they?"

Unspoken, her eyes added: *And if you* and *Sam Aylward* and *myself disappeared afterward, there wouldn't be much doubt as to what we were up to, would there? Plus an Armsman's needed here, in case quick decisions have to be made.*

Judy was coming back to consciousness halfway through her breakfast. She stretched, yawned, poured on more cream and returned to her latest hobbyhorse: "This sept thing isn't working out the way we planned."

"No, it isn't," Juniper said cheerfully, enjoying the intense flavor the dried Bing cherries cooked into it gave the porridge under the smooth richness of the cream; the clan's milking herds leaned heavily to the Jersey breed. "So they're spread between the settlements, instead of each being concentrated at one. So what? Sure, and it'd be dull if things always went as planned. It's actually better that way. You can always look up another Wolf or Raven if you're away from home; it ties all the Duns together."

"Well, yes, but how do we know people are picking the *right* totem?"

Juniper looked at her, blinking. "Well, how do we know they're *not?* Meditation and dreams seems a pretty good way to me. I suppose we could . . ."

She paused to think of methods, the loopier the better. *Flip coins? Throw dice? Do the I Ching? No, that would work. Blindfold people and spin them around until they point at a totem sign?*

"I've got it! We'll make a *magic hat,* and put a really powerful spell on it so it can *talk,* and let that sort people when we put it on their heads!"

Judy snorted, then laughed; she didn't do it all that often, but the deep rich chuckling was worth waiting for. "Time you were off, then," she said, as Juniper scraped her bowl. "Merry met, and merry part . . ."

". . . and merry meet again!"

The party from Dun Juniper relaxed when they reached the base of the streamside road that sloped southward down from their hillside bench; they had the Sutterdown god-posts with them, and together the two carved black-walnut trunks weighed enough to make anyone cautious with a horse-drawn wagon and its elementary brakes.

Everyone halted and gave a cheer, where the road and Artemis Creek reached the head of the valley and both turned westward. From here you could look down the long swale, where the rolling patchwork of field and wood opened out towards the valley proper. Behind them the sun was just up over the low green mountains and the higher Cascade peaks behind, throwing their shadows before them. Dennis started a song—his deep voice could carry one a lot better than it once had, with nine years' practice:

> *"The weasel whistles and the herons hum*
> *And the pixie pirouettes upon my thumb*
> *So I know the day has finally come—*
> *It's . . . time . . . to . . . roam!"*

Juniper laughed at the familiar tune and reached for her guitar, joining in:

> *"Pack our bags and harness the horses*
> *For the dog just danced, the cat just grinned*
> *I've now heard from reliable sources*
> *That we're bound out on the festival wind!"*

Four great brown-coated Suffolks drew the wagon, which was a much-repaired Conestoga that Chuck Barstow had ... liberated ... from a living history exhibit the night of the Change, along with the mares who'd borne the present team. On level ground and smooth roads the massive ton-weight beasts moved it along easily enough, with a thudding clop of plate-sized hooves and a crunching pop of ironshod wheels on gravel, though the personal baggage of twenty-five people was piled over the tarpaulin-covered pillars. A few rode horses or bicycles, but most were on foot; the wagon wasn't moving very fast, nor were the smaller children riding on it part-time, and the whole party had to go at the pace of the slowest. The only other wheels in their group were on a replica carriage that had carried tourists through Salem before the Change and was along to give a lift to those who couldn't walk the distance and needed the comfort of springs and cushioned seats. Swords rested at belts, bow and quiver over shoulders, here and there a spear or ax or bill, but that was only because nobody went far from their doors without, these days.

More and more voices joined in:

> *"A kilt, a brooch and a plaid of wool*
> *And a tin cup, spoon and a wooden bowl*
> *And some sweet potcheen in a cruiscin full*
> *Is what—we'll—need!"*

Dennis Martin Mackenzie laid a proprietary hand on the tarpaulin-clad wood while he sang and strode along beside the fruit of his labors; his wife and daughter rested atop it, and the eight-year-old kicked her heels in time to the tune. He carried a four-foot Danish bearded war ax over his shoulder, one his brother John had made for the collector trade before the Change, along with the Roman-style short sword that now swung at Juniper's hip. Both had been widely copied since, but not by John Martin; he'd been on Nantucket when the Change hit. Rumor born of the last radio broadcasts had it that the Change had *started* there.

The song ran on to its conclusion:

> *"When we arrive at the village faire*
> *Banners and ribbons bright fill the air*
> *Crofter, blacksmith and tinker are there*
> *Magic and music extraordinaire!"*

Dennis flourished the massive weapon in sheer exuberance. "I swear, this place gets even more drizzle over the winter than Corvallis does," he said. "Isn't it grand to have some bright sunny weather for a change?"

"Speak for yourself," Juniper said, touching a finger to her cheek and the fair freckled redhead's skin that made her vulnerable to even the mild sun of western Oregon. "Come summer, I roast, even here. I *like* rainy days, I'll have you know, you . . . you . . . *Californian*."

"Now you're getting *nasty*," Dennis chuckled. "And I like a rainy day too. Or even three, maybe. But not thirty in a row, with just a stray sunbeam to separate it from the next month-long set of rains."

"Better damp than frying."

Though it *was* a splendid day for a long walk, with Artemis Creek bawling and leaping in spray over rocks to their left, and the low forested mountains rearing green on either side, scenting the air with fir sap. Ahead the long reaches of the Willamette faded into blue-green haze, the Coast Range barely visible as a line at the western edge of sight.

The sky was clear save for a few fleecy white clouds drifting through blue heaven, and it was just cool enough to make walking pleasant, with recent rain ensuring they raised only a little dust even from this graveled road. The young peach and cherry orchards on the hillsides to her right were past the peak of blossom, but the apples and pears were sending drifts of white petals over the road and the wayfarers, cuffed free by the wind that bore their scent.

The spring wildflowers of the lowlands were at their best these last days of April. The thick grass along the roadside verges was bright with blue violet, the deeper blue of camas, yellow iris and Engelman aster; along the stream pink-and-white flowers waved over the big round leaves of umbrella plant, and red monkeyflower gave nourishment to hummingbirds and sphinx moths. More flowers were scattered through the pastures and orchards on either side, along with the red clover blossoms, and some spotted the fields of grain and roots as well. You couldn't weed them all out by hand, and chemical herbicides were a memory fading into legend. Juniper was profoundly grateful for both despite the calluses on her fingers and palms from hoe handles and weed-pulling.

And now that we know what we're doing and have enough tools and stock, this isn't a land where you really need to squeeze an acre until it squeaks, she thought. *If you have to farm, the Willamette is about the best place in the world to do it. We've got the gifts of the Lord and Lady in abundance. Blessed be!*

Dennis cast an interested eye at the bees buzzing amongst the flowers and smacked his lips absently; he ran Dun Juniper's honey-wine operation as well as its brewery, and his mead was sought after throughout the clan's territory and beyond. They halted briefly at the turnoff for Dun Fairfax; the Aylwards were there, and a few others. Sam Aylward nodded gravely to her, touching his bowstaff to his flat bonnet, as if a pleasant trip to Sutterdown was all he had to think of in the world.

Which is precisely what you should be thinking, woman! Juniper scolded herself. *Keep it out of your mind, if you want it secret!*

Young Rudi Mackenzie and Terry Martin yelled to the Aylwards' Tamar—Rudi's friends were usually a few years older than he was. Grip and Garm dashed out to meet them; each boy hooked a hand in one dog's collar as they ran to meet her.

"Ice cream!" Terry shouted. "Sutterdown says they've got their ice machine working, and we're all going to have *ice cream!* Lots of it!"

Tamar whooped and tossed her light bow in the air and caught it, then did an impromptu jig. Juniper grinned to see it; one of the things she liked about the ninth Change Year was that kids could spend their childhoods unselfconsciously being children. The Aylward toddler, young Richard, wasn't with the rest of the family, and Juniper looked a question at Melissa when the greetings were over.

"We left Dickie with Kate," she said, and mimed fainting with exhaustion. "This is supposed to be a *holiday*. Tamar and Edain and the little stranger"—she patted her stomach—"are enough."

"Oh, I know *exactly* what you mean," Juniper said.

She and Aylward handed the heavily pregnant woman up into the carriage; then the man went to throw their dunnage on the Conestoga. Melissa was wearing a loose linsey-woolsey shift with an *airsaid* over it. That was a heel-length tartan cloak, pinned at the breast with a brooch like a plaid, and wrapped and fastened lightly around the waist with a belt; they were increasingly popular with Mackenzie women as a maternity dress, being less awkward than the "little kilt" when you were huge. It was also a way to show off your weaving skills, something of which Sam Aylward's wife was rightly proud.

Juniper went on: "To be sure, though, having raised one child before the Change and one after, I'd say it's easier now if you're lucky with the illnesses, which Brigid grant."

"Certainly it's easier to get someone reliable to fill in for you when you need it," Melissa said out the window of the carriage, settling herself and taking her knitting out of the basket she carried. "And vice versa, of course."

Sally Martin had dropped off the Conestoga, and walked up with Jilly's small hand in hers; Dennis took the child up piggyback, after checking that the leather blade guard was tight on his ax. Her round face and slanted blue eyes looked over his shoulder, and then she went to sleep with limp finality and her cheek resting on the shoulder pad of his brigandine.

"Right," Sally said. "And Jennie didn't mind wet-nursing Maeve while I was gone. Try finding someone to do *that* before the Change."

Melissa nodded. "Though oh, do I miss formula and disposables! Sometimes it seems like it takes a whole dun to raise a child nowadays."

"That it does," Juniper said. "Better for the mother, better for the child, and better for the dun, come to that."

They walked on as the valley of Artemis Creek opened out into the broader Willamette: hilly fields gradually turned to rolling plain laid out in squares of cropland and pasture and small woods as the road gradually curved north of west, with the heights always on their right hand. They stopped at Dun Carson and Dun McFarlane and others along the way, each yielding its party bound for Sutterdown and the festival until there were scores and then hundreds straggling along. They could see dust plumes from other parties converging on the same destination.

Juniper cast a satisfied Chief's eye on the tight strong log walls of the duns, and a countrywoman's on the well-kept fences and hedges of the crofts and small farms into which the land was divided, and the well-managed woodlots. On the grainfields as well, spring-planted oats and barley just showing against the dark brown-black plow land, winter wheat already calf-high, flax up to her middle and blooming blue; and on the neatly pruned orchards of apple and cherry, peach and plum, wine grapes and filberts and walnuts, with the wild mustard blooming yellow beneath. Sheep grazed, looking as if they were wearing longjohns as they recovered from shearing, and red-coated cattle stood up to their hocks in thick grass and clover, while horses drowsed beneath trees or trotted along field verges, whickering to their kin on the road. Folk busy with hoe and spade and animal-drawn cultivator paused and waved and called as they went past; this wasn't the busiest season of the year, but farmwork never entirely went away.

Déanann sparán trom croi éadrom, she thought. *Possession makes for satisfaction!*

Particularly when it's the things you and your kin need for your very lives. I never see a well-tilled field now without a nice little glow, mostly in my stomach.

This was the heartland of the Clan Mackenzie, the territory she and her friends and the ones who'd joined them put together in the first Change Year, working against time to get a crop in and salvage what they could from farms round about. Bellies empty save for the thin nourishment of the Eternal Soup; the terror of the plagues spreading from the refugee camps, fighting off Eaters and bandits and the collapsing remnants of the state government, the Protector's first probes this way . . .

And finding out how to live in this new-old world. Odd how we elder folk can't stop thinking about the times before no matter how hard we try to forget, she thought. *Maybe that's why so many have taken up the old ways or what they think were such; we Mackenzies, the Bearkillers, the monks at Mt. Angel—even Arminger, in his twisted dreams of a dark past.*

She shook off the thought, taking deep breaths and calming her mind. *Ground and center,* she told herself. *Live in the moment, for only the moment is real.*

Someone had lent Laurel a kilt, though it was entirely too short—the hem was supposed to brush the upper edge of your kneecap when you were standing. Sally Martin was walking near and talking theology with her—which was a charitable way to describe it; Judy would have called it "Starting with the basics of Wicca 101."

"—so it's just as much a matter of *becoming* the God or Goddess as worshipping them; or both and neither; remember, they're not sitting outside the universe on a mountain looking at us in a magic mirror. They *are* the universe, that tree, that horse, me, you—"

She'd trained to be a schoolteacher before the Change, and was one these days; Mistress of Schools for the Clan now and Lore-Mistress of the Moon Schools as well, and she made as good a Maiden as Judy had, or better. Her knowledge was as broad, now; she loved the Craft as much; and she had endless kindly patience, which was a thing Judy's best friend—

Which I am, Juniper thought.

—wouldn't claim for her. Judy had been born to be a High Priestess. Melissa Aylward leaned out the window of the carriage, listening and offering her own observations now and then; some of her advice was more relevant, since Laurel was going to be living in a little farming dun like hers.

Someone in the straggling collection of Mackenzies began singing again, and everyone took it up. "Sweet Betsy from Pike" to start with, then "Lucy in the Sky with Diamonds," then—in honor of their destination—Juniper's own "Brannigan's Special Ale"; under the racket she could hear Dennis adding his own obscenely scurrilous verses to the tune, and gave him a glare. His rivalry with Brannigan was a joke, most of the time, but the festival to dedicate the town *wasn't* the right time. Sutterdown took a good deal of soothing, particularly when the Mackenzies' biggest settlement remembered how much it would like to be the Mackenzies' capital too.

Many of the teenagers and younger adults walked with arrows on their bowstrings, and shouts of *Dropping shaft over the oak and into the stump!* or *The patch of poppies!* told of impromptu games of rovers, punctuated by mothers calling shrilly for children to stick to the road and not wander into someone's field of fire. Astrid and Eilir and their Rangers played games of their own; mounted catch-me-who-can across the countryside, and hair-raising wrestling in the saddle at a gallop.

Which shows the strength of their arms and the strength of my character, Juniper thought. *That I don't scream* Stop before you break your necks *to the young idiots!*

Lunch was a huge chaotic picnic prolonged by an intersept softball game, and they made camp for the night in an open field near a tree-lined creek an hour before sunset. The distance from Dun Juniper to Sutterdown was about an hour in her old rattle-trap pickup; these days, three hours by bicycle, four on horseback pushing hard, one long serious day's walk, or one and a bit at the leisurely holiday pace. The nearest dun had contributed fresh milk and greens and an oxcart full of firewood to the camp; families and groups of friends or totem-brothers swapped things back and forth from their campfires; folk set up tents or just put their bedrolls in a likely looking spot, since it didn't seem likely to rain; everyone pitched in to dig slit trenches well away from the water, deal with the working stock and set the night watch.

After dinner was past and the first stars appearing over the hills to the east Juniper found herself sitting on the tail of a wagon, looking over a small low fire at a circle of children's faces, huddled with their plaids or sleeping bags across their shoulders—night could still be chill, towards the end of April. They nibbled at cookies or pastries, with a little prodding and whispering and giggling towards the back; the moon shone silvery through a whisp of cloud, turning it into a glowing mist, and the stars were scattered thickly across the sky. Noise died away as she asked: "Well, which shall it be, then?"

While the little ones clamored, she checked that her mug was easy to her hand on the boards of the wagon bed, and nicely full of Dennie's home-brewed ale, a large crock of which had been standing in the cold creek waters since they camped. Talking was thirsty work, and she'd be at it until the parents carted off the last protesting tot. She blew foam off the top and took a swallow as they cried out:

"Toad and the gypsies!"

"Bilbo and the trolls!"

"Treasure Island!"

"Rob Roy and the Duke!"

"Pinocchio!"

"Robin Hood and the Sheriff!" her own son cried; Rudi had a weakness for hero-tales of derring-do.

That last one had special relevance. Motor cars and talking toads were equally the stuff of misty legend now, but oppressive kings and wicked sheriffs were unfortunately all too real—the word "sheriff" had already become a synonym for "lord" or "ruler" in many places. Especially so east of the Cascades, where deliberate archaisms of the sort favored by most of the Willamette communities weren't so common. Not all of them were that much of an improvement on Arminger or his new-made barons; you could be just as thorough a weasel-souled bastard of a man as John Lackland or the Sheriff of Nottingham without picking a fancy title out of a book.

"None of those!" Juniper said, dropping into her storyteller's voice—it had a bit more of the brogue in it—and laughed at the groans. Children wanting a favorite story over and over hadn't changed, either.

"No, it's a tale of Toad I'll be telling you, but a new one; how Toad and his friends fought off the wicked weasels who tried to seize Toad Hall. Now, you know Toad had a good heart, but he could be a foolish fellow when the mood took him—perhaps Robin Goodfellow had been about his cradle, eh? Like a little person I could name but won't, the one with the sunset-colored hair there."

Rudi grinned and ducked his head. Juniper put her guitar across her lap, and strummed a cord; she'd be speaking mostly, but an occasional tune didn't hurt, nor a little background music to help out the magic of the words.

"Difficult Mr. Toad found it to remember that *is minic a bhris beál duine a shrón,* it is often that a person's mouth broke their nose."

She could see lips moving as they memorized that. A few didn't get it, and their friends filled them in, miming a punch in the face.

"So long ago, when Toad and Mole and Ratty and Badger lived along the river in a land much like ours, and the people of feather and fur and stream spoke everyday with our heavy-footed kind . . ."

There was a mass sigh from the children, and they leaned forward, their eyes bright in the firelight.

Beneath the happiness, a small cold voice spoke at the back of Juniper's mind: *Enjoy yourself while you can, Chief of the Mackenzies. Storm clouds fly, and ravens gather.*

"Heave-*ho!*"

The cry rang out again, and a dozen hands hauled at the rope. The Lady's pillar swung erect, the base thumping down into its bedding, and more Sutterdowners with padded poles held it erect while the braces were fixed that would keep it so until the concrete dried. The tackle and pulleys were taken down from the arch above, and the ceremonial gate at the northeast quadrant of the circle was complete.

Juniper had to admit the folk of Sutterdown had spared nothing to make their covenstead splendid; in fact, seeing

such a thing openly put the town's heart left her a little uneasy, after long years of discretion before the Change. She
knew consciously that in the Mackenzie territories the
Craft was the faith of the majority these days, had been for
years in fact, and of a *large* and ever-growing majority at
that. Unconsciously . . .

Two hills anchored the western edge of Sutterdown,
each a hundred and forty feet above the general level of
the town. The covenstead was on the summit of the
southern hill, with a magnificent view of the curling Sutter River glinting in the noonday sun—town and stream
had been named after the same pioneer who'd built a
ferry here in 1846—and the farmlands beyond to west,
south and north, the low shaggy hills rising towards the
mountains to the northeast. Downslope were the crenellations of the new town wall and its low towers with their
witches'-hat roofs; beyond that was a great green park in
the U-shaped bend of the river, an expanse of trees and
flower-starred spring meadow speckled now with the
tents of visitors come for the festival. The new-planted
Sutterdown *nemed*—Sacred Wood—was in the park too,
a broad circle of oaks and beeches that would be majestic in a generation or two.

The top of the hill was so already. It had been planed
flat, then replanted with grass, flower banks red and blue
and white and purple, bright bushes and young trees. The
center held the big open-sided circular building itself; great
pillarlike Douglas fir trunks supporting a truss roof covered in wooden strakes, the ends of the rafters carved into
the animal-head shapes of the Mackenzie totems. Inside
was a brick pavement with the symbols of the Quarters at
their stations and swirling patterns elsewhere; the altar at
the north was a block of blue-green nephrite acid-etched
in curling knotwork. Today the four Quarters held gifts;
images of the God and Goddess as Apollo and Aphrodite
in the north, done in some hard white stone; a ritual
sword in the south; great straw-wound glass firkins of
wine in the west—that had been Astrid—and Dun Juniper's contribution, covered with a cloth marked with
the pentagram in the east.

The bowl-shaped hearth in the very center of the pavement was full of split oak, stacked ready to light. That would be the Sutterdown *teine eigin,* the needfire; all the community's hearths and the Beltane bonfires would be kindled from it.

Warm spring wind cuffed at Juniper's robe; the hood was back, and a garland of lilies and verbena covered the headband that held the silver crescent moon on her brows, with green ribbons fluttering. The air held a scent of incense and flowers; and of damp coolness from the river, of fresh timber and mortar and brick. Most of the other robed participants about her wore garlands as well, and many carried thyrsi, long willow wands decorated with bells and ribbons and cowslips; their slight silvery music made a pleasant undertone to the murmur of voices from the crowd on the slope below. Then a great cheer came from the eastern gate, and roars from the others; the winners of the race about the town's outer boundaries were coming.

Soon Juniper could see the first of them running up the steep way from the town square and city hall to the hilltop, the leader with the yellow banner of the East and of Air waving it aloft. Grinning and panting the others followed, spreading out around the pillar circle to place their banners at the Quarters.

Dennis Martin Mackenzie, High Priest of the Singing Moon, was beside her as she moved forward then; he had a solid dignity to him in the robe and antlered headdress, a gravity that his smile did nothing to dispel. The High Priest and Priestess of Sutterdown—Tom Brannigan and his wife Mora—followed, as Juniper took up the bowl of May wine and poured a libation to the new-set pillars.

"Aphrodite, Foam-born Goddess, Bringer of joy, Lady of our hearts' delight! Apollo of the Sun, Lord of Light, God who loves justice and due proportion in men and cities! Sutterdown today dedicates itself to the God and Goddess in Your shapes. Bring Your gifts within its walls, and within our hearts!"

She sipped from the bowl; strawberries and cool wine, flowers and ground woodruff. Another cheer rose from below, and a sudden thudding of drums; drums and chanting to drive the power outward, out to the markers beyond the walls where the banners had been. She looked up to meet the carven eyes, and blinked a little; Dennie had been at her all winter to advise him on the work, but she'd told him to go meditate and ask the deities how *they* wanted to be shown. Evidently, he'd done just that, but you could only see the full fruit of it when the pillars were in their appointed place.

At first glance the face of Apollo was purely the Olympian, balanced and clear, the ever-victorious Light that dispels darkness. But if you looked a little longer the eyes seemed dark themselves, fathomless with incommunicable wisdom . . .

Apollo Loxias, the voice from the fissure in the navel of Earth. Pythian Apollo. The words of the ancient poet rang in her heart: *He came down the mountain like the shadow of falling night . . .* and the words became a vision in her heart, of a tall striding darkness edged with fire.

The delicate beauty of the Cyprian was more than it seemed as well; one minute a woman in the full flush of beauty whose parted lips promised, next a shy girl, then someone older, stern and wise . . .

Dennie, you are wiser than you know or will admit. These will remind anyone who sees them that the forms the God and Goddess take are true—but that They are also more than any form can contain.

Juniper took up the sword and made the first ritual cut in the space between the carved pillars, closing the Circle to create the sacred space; then paced around it sunwise:

"I conjure you, O Circle of Power, that you may be a meeting place of love and joy and truth; a shield against all wickedness and evil; a boundary between the world of human kind and the realms of the Mighty Ones . . ."

Sutterdown Dedicants tossed and twirled the banners as she called the Quarters. The Sutterdown High Priest and Priestess knelt to receive the gifts on the Eastern table; wands, crowns of silver leaves and moon opal, of antlers and gold; and the trifold woven cords that Juniper and Dennis bent to tie around their waists, white and black and red.

"Priest and Priestess are you, as are we," Juniper said, raising them and exchanging the ritual kiss. "Free are you, and your folk, as are we."

She'd known Tom Brannigan for a decade and a half now, since she first drove herself through Sutterdown to visit the land she'd inherited from her great-uncle and stopped for a beer and to try to set up a gig playing her brand of music. Most of that time he'd seemed a slightly stolid sort like his wife, Mora, people whose imagination came out in his brewing and a mutual gift for making others feel at home in their tavern. She had no doubt he'd taken up the Craft because everyone else in Sutterdown seemed to be converting after the Reverend Dixon dropped dead, which made it a likely looking thing to do, and had risen in it because he was shrewd and popular, ambitious for his town and himself as well.

Together, Juniper and Dennis chanted; and now there was a look on Brannigan's face that she had never seen there before, but recognized without a moment's hesitation—recognized from the inside. A wild torrent that was joy and terror and neither, a communion with something utterly Other and yet as familiar as a parent's touch in the night; vast beyond knowing and woven into every atom of your being.

When he rose the Dun Juniper pair stepped back and bowed low and listened as he called the Goddess into his High Priestess, and tears of happiness poured down her cheeks.

For Juniper the feeling was different this time; more like warm hands pressed on her shoulder, and the shadow of an infinite smile: *Well done, daughter of our hearts.*

Speeches, Juniper thought. *Do I* never *get away from them?*

Brannigan and Mora were still shaken; joyful, but not all that coherent. And it took a *lot* to leave Tom Brannigan speechless. . . .

There were about a thousand people living in Sutterdown, and double that here for the festival; more than one in eight Mackenzies, and a rather higher proportion of the teenagers and adults. All of them seemed to be looking up at her, grouped in a big semicircle on the eastern slopes of the hill that held Sutterdown's great covenstead. Behind her the needfire crackled in the new covenstead's hearth, and torchbearers stood ready to race out with the *teine eigin* blaze to kindle festival bonfires and household stoves.

"Mackenzies!" she said. "Ostara is the promise of spring, and Beltane is the promise fulfilled as summer comes back to us. We've pruned and we've planted, plowed and sown, sheared and doctored our stock and seen to the lambing, swept winter out of our houses and our hearts. I think we've earned a little celebration on this night when the veil between the worlds is thin, don't you?"

A roaring cheer spread up the hillside; the bagpipers were at it again, and the massed drums at the foot of the hill thundered, until she raised her hands once more.

"Now, we've dedicated this town to the God and the Goddess, and that's something else to celebrate. There's one thing I want each and every one of you to remember, though: That does *not* mean that it's any less the hometown of our friends and kinfolk who still follow other ways. There are many pathways; what matters is that they head for the same place, and rightly walked, they all do. Remember that!"

And don't be unkind to poor Reverend Jennings and his flock, she thought, nodding to where they stood among the crowd. Dwindling and aging though they were; not more than one in five here in Sutterdown, less elsewhere in the Clan's territories. And few of them under thirty these days; she suspected their children would be the last Christians among the Mackenzies. *Poor wee, well-meaning, bewildered man.*

She raised her arms and her voice, casting it to reach them all. *"And listen to the words of the Great Mother, Who of old was called Artemis, Astarte, Dione, Melusine, Aphrodite, Ceridwen, Diana, Arianrhod, Brigid . . . Sing, feast, dance, make music and make love, all in My presence, for My law is love unto all beings . . . all acts of love and pleasure are My rituals."*

She paused, put her hands on her hips, and tossed her

head. "Well then, what would you be waiting for the now? Didn't you hear what the Goddess just said? Get out there and have fun, by Divine command! Go! Scat!"

The drums roared, and a long chain of dancers began to weave its way through the flower-decked streets.

It was the third night of the Beltane festival, and Juniper Mackenzie and her First Armsman were down in the parkland outside Sutterdown's western gate. Juniper's mask was that of a raven; it overshadowed her mouth without covering it, which was convenient as she watched the dancers and nibbled on a skewer of chicken grilled with an intriguing honey-mustard-garlic glaze. By unspoken convention, festival masks meant you weren't really you, and so nobody could approach her on business.

She felt a little hoarse from the singing she'd done over the past days, and the talking; her legs were slightly sore with all the dancing. She'd been around a dozen maypoles, and presided at games and contests, in archery and swordplay, running and wrestling and jumping, music and dancing, judged pie-baking and embroidery and cabbages of unusual size and children's cherished hand-reared prize sheep. The festival *had* been fun; also useful, taking the pulse of her folk, chatting with leaders from this dun and that, quite a few quiet sessions with the Brannigans and others prominent here in Sutterdown; they'd agreed to repay help they'd had with the town wall by assisting several smaller settlements to improve their defenses, and take a lead in the building of Dun Laurel.

The likelihood of another serious clash with the Protector had been glumly accepted.

Other needful things had gotten hammered out: the new high school, a preliminary consensus to clear the pilings of the bridges in Salem at low water, after Lughnassadh, if they could get the Bearkillers to help, which she was fairly confident of. The look and range of goods brought to sell or swap also told her much about how farms and workshops and trade were going, as much as Andy Trethar's record books. Things were going well, or would be if war wasn't looming over them; in some ways her people were better off than the Bearkillers. They seemed to have a broader range of handicraft skills, if perhaps less machinery, and they didn't have to support a group of full-time fighters either, or Corvallis's heroic but slightly crazed determination to keep their university in being.

To top it all off, Rudi had led the Juniper Ravens—his Junior Little League team—to triumph in the inter-sept competition just that afternoon, and was now sleeping off a well-earned ice-cream gorge back at the hostel Sutterdown's Ravens had set up in an old building for the use of visiting members of their sept. Most of the town's residents were of the Elk totem, and many had been Elks even before the Change, but there were a fair scattering of others.

Juniper gave a reminiscent smile that verged on a purr. *Speaking of topping . . .* On the second day of the festival she'd also managed a *very* pleasant time of her own in a Beltane bower with a friendly Sutterdown shoemaker of her acquaintance, a handsome man who had extremely educated hands.

And Sam and I got something still more private yet put together, too, she thought with a mixture of grim resignation and wistfulness. *I've plenty of good friends, but love, that hasn't come my way. Someday, Goddess willing . . .*

The pair near the bonfire were doing a sword dance in modern Mackenzie style, only distantly related to the old Scottish version. Here the swords were Clan-style short swords rather than claymores, and they were laid in turf with one edge down and the other up, points inward to make a circle divided into four Quarters. The dance was done with a partner, though still with one hand on the waist and the other high, and it involved a good deal of stepping and leaping; the tune was "Ghillie Chalium," which began slow and then went more and more swiftly as fifes and pipes squealed, bodhrans rattled, and the fiddle rang.

She'd managed to insist that the sword blades be dulled first, and that had become the rule—she hoped. She'd never been one to think that life could be made smooth and safe altogether, but . . .

It's appalling, the younger generation's attitude towards risk!

"I'm keeping an eye on that young man," she said aloud.

"Me too," Aylward replied; his wolf mask was pushed back so that he could tip up the mug he held, full of Brannigan's Special, a dark Guinnesslike malt brew of extraordinary potency. "Moves like a big cat, doesn't he?"

The dancer in question was Rowan Carson Mackenzie, one of the leading lights of Dun Carson, whose heart had been his father's farmstead before the Change; he'd changed his name from Raymond when he became a Dedicant. He was in his midtwenties, a broad-shouldered long-limbed man two inches over six feet, arms heavy-muscled from his trade of blacksmith and bladesmith, with a jut-jawed face. Like most male Mackenzies his age he shaved his beard save for a mustache and wore his hair at shoulder length, spilling from under his flat bonnet in a flaxen torrent and whirling with the effort of the dance. His sister Cynthia was dancing with him, and their feet flashed and blurred as the pace of the music picked up and they sprang from one Quarter to another.

"He's big, which rarely hurts," Aylward went on. "Strong as a bloody ox, which *never* hurts, and he's very quick, which is even more important. Works hard at it too; you've seen him with that ax he's made."

Juniper nodded, finishing the kebab and tossing the stick into a trash barrel. She had seen it; the weapon was much like Dennie's, built to the ancient Viking pattern, and Rowan handled it like a willow switch at practice or in competitions. He'd fought with it, too—against bandits, and in a few border skirmishes with raiders from the Protectorate—and won a fearful name. She had her doubts about that ax ... And before that, he'd been just barely old enough to be in that initial battle with Arminger's men, back in the harvest summer of the first Change Year.

"Good shot, too, if not quite as good as Cynthia," Aylward enthused. "Bends a heavier bow than hers, of course—heavier than me. And he's clever, and he's got motivation."

"That's why I've got my eye on him," Juniper said. "Perhaps a little too much motivation, Sam?"

"Natural enough, Lady," he said. "After all, Arminger's men did kill 'is father, back in the first Change Year."

Juniper shook her head. "Cynthia hates Arminger because he killed their father," she said. "Rowan's . . . obsessive about it. I meant that I was keeping an eye on him to see if I could help ease his soul, somehow. Black hatred like that damages you more than the one it's aimed at."

Aylward shrugged and spread his hands, and Juniper sighed in turn. They were close friends, but that didn't mean they saw everything the same way—or that they should, of course.

"Perfect for this job we have in mind, though," he said. "Both of them are good at rough-country work."

Juniper nodded. "At least they're well past twenty-one," she said. "I don't want to second-guess you on your job, Sam, but aren't most of the rest a bit . . . young? I doubt the average is much above voting age. Sanjay and Dan Barstow don't shave much more than their sister Aoife."

He nodded towards the Carsons. "They're older than those two were, the first fight we had," he pointed out.

"We were desperate and fighting at our doorsteps."

"Thing is, Lady, it's the younger ones who've had the most training now, and at the most impressionable ages, especially the ones we've picked for this job. The best archers start with the bow as a kiddie. They've grown up rough, too, rougher than anyone our age. On this trip they'll need all the youthful endurance they can get. And they're . . . more adjusted to the circumstances, if you take my meaning. Also they're less likely to have young children of their own."

"What about you and me?" she said, with a quirking smile.

He shrugged again. "I've got enough age and treachery to make up for youth and strength," he said. "And you're needful for the political side."

The dance ended with a long-drawn roll from the bodhrans and squeal from the pipes, and a chorus of hoots and claps. Flushed and happy, the brother and sister came over to where they stood—which was near a table that bore beer kegs and mugs, and trays of eatables.

She smiled at their greetings as they tapped the barrel. "Rowan, Cynthia, merry met. All's well at home? Are

Joanne and Jack along? I should have asked before, but the Sutterdowners have been running me from one thing to the next."

"Joanne's fine and sends regards, Lady Juniper, but she didn't fancy the trip seven months along," Rowan said. "Besides which, little Morianna has just learned how to say *no*."

Juniper winced and laughed, and raised her mug. "All my sympathies. And you, sir, are a black traitor to run out on Joanne at such a time. And yours?" she went on to his sister.

"Sean's well over that fever, and little Niamh's fine too—I keep telling this hulking lout, all you have to do is say *Want to take a nap?* and then right afterward *Want a cookie?* Do that a couple of times, and they learn *no* isn't the answer to every single thing. Jack wanted to keep a close eye on the new vineyard, though, and we're just putting in the foundations for the crusher."

"Brannigan's vineyard needs some competition," Juniper agreed.

Cynthia's brother smiled a wolfish smile. "And neither of our spouses are around to try to talk us out of . . . something."

"Ah, and here's two more," Juniper said, giving him a quelling glance.

A chant went up in the middle distance:

> *"Fire, burn this Beltane night*
> *Fire to greet the Sun—"*

Then it turned into a cheer as a pair took a run and leapt over a bonfire flaring in a trench. The group broke up in laughter and shouts, streaming away to the high-school amphitheater where *Robin Hood and Guy of Gisborne* was being put on. All but the pair who'd leapt for luck and love; they walked over to Juniper, and turned out to be Astrid and Eilir. They joined the two from Dun Carson at the barrels, and then in a circle around the Chief.

I finally got her out of the covenstead, Eilir signed. *Meditation and prayer, prayer and meditation! It would be too much for Samhain, and this is* Beltane, *for Her sweet sake!*

Astrid flushed a little and opened her mouth, but Juniper held up a hand. "Dear, Eilir's right. For us, this world isn't a preparation for another. The God and Goddess *are* the world, and it's our rightful dwelling-place; to know Them, you have to live *in* it. It's the Summerlands that are a preparation for coming right back *here*—another life is a gift, not the loss of nirvana. Remember the Charge of the Goddess!"

The tall girl with the silver-streaked eyes pouted slightly, but nodded. Cynthia nodded as well, and Rowan raised his mug: "Well, we'll need Working for what we have in mind, too, Archer," he said, and winked as Aylward scowled. "The Lord of the Spears and the Lady of the Crows . . ."

Eilir and Astrid both looked as if they were suppressing a grave excitement. The pair from Dun Carson were openly eager. Juniper sighed. This too was the work of a leader in the Changed world.

Or perhaps any other.

Chapter Fourteen

"I thought you had some direct action in mind, back on Gunpowder Day," Mike Havel said. "Good for you. If Arminger's barons think they can violate the truce on the quiet whenever they like, I'll be damned if we can't do likewise."

He grinned. "And each of us can blame it on the others."

Juniper nodded. "It's a cunning fellow you are, Mike. We left Chuck and Judy in charge at Dun Juniper, and the fair at Sutterdown this Beltane was a good cover for what we had to do. No better time to gather the right people secretly, and to leave unnoticed."

What a wealth of living that packs into a couple of sentences, Juniper thought, looking around the Crossing Tavern's private room at them. Mike's eyes, friendly and shrewd and as ruthless as a wolf in winter as his strong white teeth ripped the meat off a pork rib; his Signe's blue gaze, intelligent and not in the least friendly; the calm strength of Will Hutton that always reminded her of Sam, and the polite curiosity of the English group.

"Arminger has been nipping at us for years, and we've been nipping right back," she said, taking a sip of her ale. "It was time to sink some real fangs right in his arse. And while there may or may not have been an underground of Witches in Europe in the old days, there most certainly is in the Protectorate this ninth year of the Change, and other folk who're friendly to us and not him—secretly, of course. Relatives of those who've made it out and settled among us, for starters. First our people gathered by twos and threes, slipping away and eastward, up into the mountains on the old tracks."

"Safer than trying to sneak over the border around Salem, say?" Mike asked.

"Less conspicuous, certainly," Juniper said. "Except for the odd hunter not many go up into the high country these days, and most of those stick to the lower levels; the game's thicker there, and it's safer. We've never been able to scour the mountains completely clean of bandits and Eaters, not north of Route 20 at least. Too big, and too far from our duns. We can't spare the people for constant patrols. Plus there are too many ways to slip over the mountains."

"Yeah," Will Hutton growled. "Them CORA folks, they don't watch any of their side as close as they should, 'cept maybe the main passes. Lots of wanderin' folk and broken men east of the mountains, always a few coming on to the west. Worse these last two years, with the war in the Pendleton country."

Juniper nodded. "But nothing that's a threat to a big well-armed party, so we drew together at Elk Lake, and worked our way north to Table Rock in three separate groups, not too far apart. Forest country, still a bit chilly and wet in May, but tolerable if you know how. The Protector doesn't entirely ignore that area, though. It's where runaway serfs head for, to begin with . . ."

Table Rock Wilderness, Willamette Valley, Oregon
May 6th, 2007 AD—Change Year Nine

Not enough birds, Juniper thought suddenly.

This land near Table Rock was home to many; she'd been listening to a golden-crowned kinglet until just a second ago. All at once they were silent, on both steep slopes above and below the trail . . .

"Whoa!" someone exclaimed, up near the head of the column.

The Mackenzies halted; it was eight, just two hours after sunrise, and May was still chilly enough in the mountains for the horse's breath to show as white plumes of steam in air crystal-clear and scented with fir sap and pine. Juniper could see over the heads of the dozen or so on foot ahead of her. She went mounted as a concession to age and rank; there wasn't enough grass on these upland trails for more to ride, unless you wanted to get into a circular-argument trap where more horses carried fodder so you could have more horses carrying fodder. She still didn't see what was ahead for a moment, because her mount was forgetting its training, snorting and trying to rear on the narrow forest track. From the sound of it, so were the four packhorses behind her. Where they thought they could go was a mystery, since the land was forty-five degrees from vertical in all directions and densely covered in big trees and underbrush.

Bear was her first thought, when she saw what blocked the trail, along with minor irritation; they were common here in the western Cascades and most likely it would trundle off soon enough. Then she got a better look; brown, higher at the shoulders than the rump, dished face, and big—very, very big.

Grizzly! What did the man say? "I expected this, but not so soon!"

There had been rumors of grizzly sightings in the last couple of years, but nothing confirmed—like wolves and buffalo, they'd been half wishful tale rather than fact. This was Old Eph right enough, an adult male with the beginnings of the whitening on his hump hairs. Probably he'd been born right after the Change, and wandered in westward from the Montana-Wyoming mountains, or down from British Columbia, looking to stake out his own feeding ground. Grizzlies needed big territories to support their bulk, and with guns gone and humans scarce again they were spreading fast throughout their historic range. In Oregon that meant everywhere except some of the southeastern deserts, but she hadn't thought they'd make it this far in only nine years. A jolt of excitement went through her as she watched the majestic beast move its long neck back and forth enquiringly.

At least Earth is healing Herself. Thanks and praise, Lord Cernunnos of the Forests, Lady Artemis of the Beasts!

Then she decided it was perhaps more pleasant to contemplate the bear's majesty at a distance; say, viewed through binoculars across a valley and a nice swift creek. And that up close like this it was perhaps more exciting than she wished; grizzlies were a *lot* more temperamental than ordinary black bears. This one looked to be still slightly gaunt from winter, and hungry. It also seemed to be sniffing the air with mounting interest, which was unfortunate—it could smell the horses. And even more, the blood-and-meat scent of the butchered mule deer carcass slung over one of them.

They'd split the Mackenzie war band into three to work their way through these mountains, with the Rangers scouting on ahead and carrying messages between the columns. Sam was with one group, Cynthia led another, and Juniper presided over this, with Rowan handling most of the actual leading. He was near the head of the column, and flung up a hand to freeze everyone in place. Two in the lead leveled battle spears; the rest put arrow to string and made ready to draw; the movements were quick, fluid. The razor edges of the broadheads glinted in the olive-green gloom of the morning forest as light flickered through the needles of the Douglas firs and hemlocks.

"Shall I shoot?" someone said.

The archers sidled out to get a clear field of fire; that wasn't easy given the footing, but the path did curve a little towards the west. Between them they could probably put a dozen shafts into the beast inside a second, but . . .

"Don't be a fool," Rowan said, his voice steady but pitched low. "There aren't enough of us to use the meat and we can't pack the hide out, and he might get through to us anyway. Shoot if he charges or I say so. And get those horses under control!"

Juniper did; she was riding Eilir's Celelroch, and the well-trained beast quickly subsided into tense quiet. Between her daughter's knees the Arab mare probably wouldn't have started acting up at all; Juniper was a good rider, Eilir a superb one. The people tending the pack animals took a little longer, and the bear was getting more curious about the smells of blood and meat.

Rowan stepped up between the spearmen—although one of them was a spearwoman, if you wanted to get picky. His shaggy hooded war cloak made the big blond man look even larger—it was loose-meshed cloth mottled in shades of green-brown, and sewn thickly with narrow dangling loops. This last day, they'd all taken the time to stick twigs and vegetation in the loops, which made you look bulkier except when you were keeping very still, in which case it made you near-as-no-matter invisible. Rowan faced the bear and slid his bow into the crook of his arm. His right hand reached out, and effortlessly snapped off a thumb-thick, arm-long branch from a hemlock that rose from lower down the slope to stand beside the trail.

"Peace between us today, brother bear," he said. "You go your way, and we'll go ours. Everyone get ready!"

Juniper echoed the thought in her head, her hand making a sign, concentrating her will like a dart. *So mote it be!*

Rowan took the branch in his left hand; now his right moved to his belt, slowly and carefully, and brought out a lighter. The alcohol-soaked wick caught immediately as his thumb spun flint against steel in a shower of sparks, and the hemlock needles went up with a *woosh* as he touched the flame to them. Then he waved it overhead, yelling; to the bear's senses a twelve-foot figure tipped with the terror of fire. The rest of the party raised their arms and waved them as well, shouting nonsense—or in a couple of cases, prayers. The bear half reared, nostrils wrinkling, and let out a deep moaning grunt of protest that showed its long yellow teeth.

Juniper had noticed years ago that predators were less afraid of humans since the Change; even before that they'd known the difference between a man with a gun and one without quite well, and they'd quickly realized that the dangerous noisemakers were gone. They were still wary of fire, though, and by now the bear's weak eyes and keen ears must have noticed that there were a good many of the irritating, noisy bipeds as well as the tempting smell of food. Hunger and aggravation warred with caution, and

then the great beast turned and crashed off into the rhododendron thickets. The noise of its passage gradually
dwindled, and the normal forest sounds replaced it.

Phew! she thought, shaken. *That could have been unfortunate!*

The clansfolk waited until the bear was obviously gone;
a member of the sept named for him gathered tufts of cinnamon fur from the bushes, chuckling with delight as he
wrapped them in a rag and tucked them into a pouch—
they would make much-admired marks for his bonnet
clasp, and fine gifts for friends who were of his totem. The
rest kept their eyes busy, then calmly resumed their steady
ground-eating pace; a few discussed the meeting in low
tones for a while, then went quiet again. She knew that was
mostly simple prudence; they weren't very near enemy-
controlled territory yet, but they were well north of any
area the Mackenzies controlled or made safe. Yet most of
it was that they simply didn't care much, beyond having an
interesting story to tell when they got home.

I do not understand the younger generation of our Clan,
she thought, shaking her head a little. *I love them, but I do
not understand them, even my own dear son. And even Eilir
is stranger to me than she would have been, in the old world.*

Most of those here were younger than her daughter,
who'd been fourteen nine years ago; Rowan was the eldest at twenty-six. Only blurred childhood memories of the
time before the Change remained to the youngsters, and
that had left its mark. It was more obvious on this venture, days alone with her juniors.

What is it exactly? she thought. *It's not just that they're
hardy and tough. So are Sam or Chuck . . . or myself myself,
to be sure. Or that they're devout Witches; so am I, and a le-
gion of our converts are wildly so, like drowning folk clutching at a sturdy log. I think it's that they just . . . take it all for
granted. They're not haunted by the Change, this is their
world. And it's not that they believe in the Craft; it's the way
they do. It's not an affirmation with them; they believe the
way we believed in atoms.*

Plus they didn't hold themselves quite like late-
twentieth-century Americans, or walk like them, or sit like

them . . . and there was an indefinable something in their speech, too. *And in the way they treat me.* It wasn't the sometimes embarrassing reverence of those who'd joined the Clan in the Dying Time and lived because of it, although there was a deep respect. They were ready enough to banter with her, or argue for that matter, but underlying it . . .

The fact of the matter is they really do *think of me as the Goddess-on-Earth, and they're easy with that, too—a lot easier than I! They've grown up foreign to me and their parents, and that's the long and short of it. Their children will be more alien still.* Juniper shook her head. *Later,* she decided. *Time to think of such things later.*

The season was less advanced than down in the warmer lowlands to the west, earth wet underfoot, a damp chill in the air whenever they were out of the sun, but the effort kept them all warm. The path wound through forest still as the long day wore on into midafternoon; they were pushing to reach their destination well before nightfall, and merely gnawed biscuit or other trail food as they walked, and swigged from canteens. This had been private land, mostly regularly harvested for timber and replanted. Nine years hadn't changed it all that much, although fires had left patches of open ground where bushy thin-leaf huckleberry grew thickly in a profusion of small yellow flowers, mixed with manzanita pink. Wildlife and birds were thicker too, in this rich edge habitat without many human hunters; the paths and trails more overgrown, kept open more by paw and hoof than boot or wheel.

The peaks about weren't tall, even their destination was a bit under five thousand feet, but they made a tangle of sharp ridges and deep V-shaped valleys, mostly densely covered in trees right to their summits, woven with a net of creeks and small lakes. Now and then a view opened up to the east and showed the white cone of Mt. Jefferson, and sometimes the Three Sisters farther southward, less often Mt. Hood far to the northeast. Mostly the land reared in close about them. Then they passed an old fallen park sign, deep in a swale, and angled east behind a tall butte.

A sound not quite like a chickadee greeted them. Using

the signal was wise; when the war-cloaked figure rose from the side of the trail nobody sank an arrow through the body beneath. A hand in an archer's glove threw the hood back above a Mackenzie helmet covered in the same fabric, and an implausibly young face grinned at them. Black eyes snapped in a brown face beneath a shock of raven hair that showed around the edge of his bowl helmet—it was Sanjay Barstow Mackenzie, one of the adoptees Chuck and Judy had rescued from a stalled schoolbus just after the Change, while they were on their own journey from Eugene to Juniper's cabin.

"The Archer sends greeting, and you're where you were supposed to be," the young man said; he was just turned nineteen. His voice held a slight sardonic edge, as if he was surprised to find them there. "He says Nohorn Butte there will hide you from Table Rock if you're careful with your fires."

"Tell Sam to teach his grannie how to suck eggs," Rowan growled. "What sort of idiot does he take me for?"

Sanjay's grin grew wider: "Well, he didn't specify what *sort* exactly, but if you want me to *guess* I could come up with a few—" He cut off at Rowan's snort, and went back to business: "The Dunedain say it's just as our secret Witch-kin in Molalla said: a launcher, and a lookout station there. They'll lead us into position before dawn, and you're to be ready for the frontal attack on the signal—three fire arrows, out over the gate."

Juniper nodded. "We'll be ready," she said.

Sanjay took in the disassembled mule deer slung across one packsaddle; they'd done a rough job of draining and butchering, then packed the meat and edible organs back into the hide in a shapeless blood-wet bundle.

"Ah, you were lucky, by Cernunnos!" he said.

"Ah, you mean we were *quiet*," Rowan boasted. "He crossed the path not a hundred feet ahead of me. One shaft—the heart—ten paces and he dropped."

To be sure, he's still a young man, Juniper thought, smiling to herself.

"Lucky I said; lucky I meant," Sanjay jibed.

"Ah, you mean we can *shoot*," another of the party chuckled. "And Cernunnos rewarded us for it."

"Well, the Horned Lord may have taken *pity* on you," Sanjay returned.

Even as they joked, two of the Mackenzies were lifting the hundred-odd pounds of meat to the ground; they opened the hide, cut some of the raw leather loose and rewrapped a thigh and half the ribs in it. Others helped Sanjay load it into his oiled-leather backpack. The slender fine-boned young man's step didn't falter when another forty pounds went on his back, along with the weight of his brigandine and weapons and gear. He touched the stave of his longbow to his helmet brow in salute to Juniper and disappeared into the woods upslope, climbing the hillside in a series of springy elastic bounds without touching his hands to ground or trunk, kilt swirling around his thighs, the dandy-gaudy peacock fletchings of his arrows bobbing.

"This is a good place," Rowan said, looking around. "Aidan, Donnal, Susie, get water. Tom, Ed, Silvermoon, you're first watch. The rest of you, set up camp here. I'll make the fire."

Juniper rubbed her jaw to hide a smile; evidently he'd taken Sam's warning to heart. She went to help those setting up a picket line to hold the horses; that was a rope stretched between two trees, and a pile of oats and alfalfa pellets from the sacks for each beast. They were out of the logged-over section here, into what had been National Wilderness territory; the trees were tall, a hundred feet or better in mixed stands of hemlocks and firs—Douglas, silver and grand—mostly grown up since the last wildfire went through here over a century ago. By the side of the stream a little southeast were some Douglas firs that looked to be four or five times that age, towering living columns near two hundred feet high and twelve through at the base.

All these mountains will look like this, when Eilir's grandchildren walk them, Juniper thought, looking up into that majesty.

Undergrowth was sparser under the shade of the canopy, save where the steep rock just north kept out the roots of the big firs; the crest was five hundred feet above them, and Aylward was right—it would hide anything but a pillar of smoke nicely.

"Sunset's in about five hours," she said.

Rowan put the lower tip of his bowstave to the earth, looked at the length of the shadow it cast and nodded; then he glanced up at the three-quarter moon—up since two hours past noon, and it wouldn't set until about the same before dawn.

"Hmmm," he said. "Rendezvous on the way with Cynthia at two hours past midnight. Call it four and half miles to Table Rock as the raven flies, another three on foot . . . three hours' travel, and the pace to leave us fresh at the end. Plenty of time if we leave at sunset, and we'll all be the better for a meal and some rest."

She opened herself to the weather, looked at the sky, sniffed deeply. "More cloud later, though not soon. Perhaps a little rain. Damp and heavy dew, certainly. That'll lay scent and muffle sound."

Rowan nodded again; he broke the deadwood for the fire himself, feeling to make sure it was bone-dry all the way through, to burn without smoke. Then he set up a screen of woven branches before he kindled it with his lighter, making a fire that quickly turned to embers low and hot. The meat of the deer was cut into chunks and strung on sticks, with no seasoning but salt as it sizzled at the edges of the fire. Soon he was saying over and over again:

"Keep that back there, the Dagda club you dead, don't drip more grease on the coals, keep it off to the side, it makes less smoke that way!"

To go with it two thin griddle plates were set over the coals; onto them went a batter made from stream water and the coarse meal everyone carried in their haversacks. It had baking powder and salt already mixed with the stone-ground flour, and it quickly rose and bubbled and browned into a thick biscuitlike wheat cake that went well with the last of the strong-tasting sour-cream butter in its Tupperware container. Despite the packhorses, they had only the most basic foodstuffs along; the bulk of the loads were weapons and tools to make them—bowstaves, strings, arrowheads, bowyer's draw knives and little printed booklets on the art of turning Pacific yew into longbows.

Gifts, so to speak, Juniper thought a little grimly. *To the Protectorate's common folk.*

She juggled a hot gobbet of deer's liver from hand to hand until she could bite into it and lick the delicious juices from her fingers. Someone made an inarticulate sound of pleasure, then said:

"Venison always tastes better like this."

"When you're famished?" Juniper said. "Of course! *Is maith an t-anlann an t-ocras.* Hunger is a good sauce."

A small cauldron boiled water for herb tea—they had some water-purification powder along, but it tasted bad and the folk in Corvallis charged the earth for it. Bringing creek water to a hard rolling boil for fifteen minutes killed the giardia parasites just as dead, and a few handfuls of herbs were easy enough to carry. Cold, the excess would go into their canteens.

One of the watch came in to report, and to take food back to his companions. "Silvermoon's up on the crest," he said, jerking a thumb in that direction. "And yes, I reminded her not to let the binoculars flash when she had them pointing west. Nothing between here and there that she can see."

He made a wide circling gesture. "No man-sign on any side, either; not recent enough to see, at least. I don't think they patrol this far."

Juniper nodded. "That post is there to watch for people trying to get *out* of the Protector's territory," she said. "There's nothing east of here for a hundred miles except the Cascades, and he holds Highway 25 and 26. And Hood River northeast, but he has that too."

When Tom had gone off with two bark plates loaded with food for his friends there was nothing much to do but smother the fire with shovelfuls of dirt—and only then with a bucket of water. They all made a murmured apology for disturbing the earth here, laid out their crumbs as an offering for the birds and the spirit of the crag, and settled in to wait. Some went over their gear again, checking the fletching on their arrows, flexing their brigandines to make sure all the rivets that held the metal plates between the layers of canvas or leather were sound, scanning every inch of their longbows for cracks and the horn tips to make sure they were still tightly glued.

The *veeep . . . veeep . . .* of steel on hone sounded quietly, as the blades of swords and spears and dirks, the edges of arrowheads, were ground a little sharper. It was the sort of obsessive detail-work you did on tools that might mean the difference between life and death; then everyone went over the maps one last time. When that was done, many of the young warriors sat in facing pairs, painting each other's faces and hands with triskeles, spirals, abstract patterns, or the forms of their totems. Sam disapproved of the fashion for painting up before a fight—he claimed it reminded him too much of football hooligans in the old days back in England—but even the First Armsman hadn't been able to forbid it. When it was finished Rowan's face was overlain with a dragon's in gold and black and scarlet, with the tail curving around his neck.

And to think I once thought I was joking when I told Dennie that he'd have them all painting their faces blue if he kept up with the Celticity, she thought. *Little did I imagine! Here I'm to blame, though. The patterns are all from my library. Who knew just loaning books would . . . well, there's not much else to do in wintertime, at that.*

Those who'd finished set gear by and rested quietly; a few lovers went aside—they might be dead this time tomorrow—and others played cards, tossed dice, or told stories. She heard a snatch of that: ". . . and then he said as the outlaw turned at bay: 'This is the most powerful war bow in the clan, and even I can't hold the draw forever. So tell me, punk, do you feel *lucky?*'"

Rowan took extra care with his great war ax, rubbing a swatch of raw wool up and down the smooth ashwood shaft, checking the rawhide binding at the lower end, taking out a pocket hone to touch up the broad curved cutting surface. That had a blade of hard spring steel, welded with forge fire and hammer into the mass of a head made out of twisted bundles of softer low-carbon rebar; that let the rear face serve as a smashing hammer on targets that would shatter the cutting edge. When he was finally satisfied he rubbed the wool over the metal—the lanolin kept rust from starting—and slipped on a leather cover fastened with a snap.

It was a trifle cruder than Dennie's weapon, but skillfully made, and graven with runes and symbols that had made her blink a little the first time she'd seen it bare and close enough to read them.

And made me wonder where he dug those up. They weren't in any book I lent to Dun Carson! Bane and blight and ruin were worked into that metal with every hammer stroke. I'd as soon go into battle with a rattlesnake in my naked hand! Yes, it's a terrible weapon, but it will betray him in the end; doesn't he realize that?

Quiet fell. Juniper Mackenzie set herself cross-legged, controlled breathing, brought up the image of a still pond reflecting the crescent moon and sank inward. More and more of the others followed her, unless they had immediate tasks to do. When she stirred it was just short of the time for leaving; the westering sun touched the distant Coast Range, and eastward the high Cascade snows burned crimson along the horizon of encroaching night. Overhead the moon shone through patches of clear sky and glowed when streamers of white haze covered it; the air smelled moist.

"Come," she said, and they knelt in a Circle around symbols scratched into the dirt with a dirk for an athame—but the best symbol for a sharp knife was still a sharp knife.

Here could be no elaborate rite; nor was this one she would have chosen to lead, except from hard necessity. The quiet words still rang in her mouth and in the cold wind that blew along her spine and into mind and heart. And at last:

". . . so come to us, Lugh of the Shining Spear, Dread Lord, mighty Warrior, All-Conquering Sun; come to us, Badb-Macha-Neman called the Morrigan, Great Queen of Battles, raven-winged and strong, Chooser of the Slain! Your own faithful people call upon You, and to You we dedicate the acorn harvest of the red field. Arise and come with storm and terror, in blood and in wrath! So mote it be!"

Then they clasped hands, chanting:

*"I am the wind that breathes on the sea
I am the wave, wave on the ocean
I am the ray, the eye of the Sun
I am the tomb, cold in the darkness
I am a star, the tear of the Sun
I am a wonder, a wonder in flower*

*Who but I can sing the meeting of the mountains?
Who but I will cry aloud the changes in the moon?
Who but I can find a place that hides away the sun?*

*Through a word of great power,
I am the depths of a frozen pool
I am the song of the Raven black*
I am the spear that cries out for blood!"

They rose with the last words and set out, all but the pair
watching the horses, filing into the shadows of the trees.

A figure came ghosting up the pathway behind the
Rangers, where it wound below Table Rock. Eilir stepped
into the shadows of the trees with the rest, but Astrid made
the *Safe* gesture; it must be Kevin, their rear guard, the one
who wielded brushwood to wipe out their tracks. He was
panting a little, and jerked a thumb over his shoulder.

We're being followed. The hands moved in starlight and
moonlight; that washed his freckled face pale, or perhaps
tension did. *They're a half mile behind me. Six of them.*

And there were six Rangers in the nighted woods below
the mountain. The Protector's men evidently did patrol
this close to home. She watched Astrid bite her lip, then
sign swiftly: *Upslope, then back along our tracks. Linear
ambush. Quick and quiet, Dúnedain!*

They'd been moving north along an overgrown old dirt
road, upslope from a creek brawling with snowmelt and
about a mile east of Table Rock. The water would cover
most noise. A lifetime among the hearing had taught her
how to calculate such things; the vibration was perceptible
beneath her feet, and it was only a few hundred feet to the
water—the pitch was at least a foot of descent for every

three or four laterally. The woods upslope were thicker than those towards the creek, but neither was thin, and it was a mile or better to the enemy lookout; as long as they stayed under the branches, at night they might have been ten miles away, or a hundred. Tattered wisps of mist trailed from the treetops above, drifting down the slope towards the water and half covering it as they thickened.

They eeled through the woods east of the road, racing back along the direction of their own travel and trying not to break the brushwood in their paths; it grew darker, and she drank in her surroundings through her fingertips and the movement of air on her face and arms. It was cold and damp now, dew beading on grasses and ferns and moss, dropping down her neck and wetting her kilt and legs. The scent of needles and leaves decaying under her feet was strong, though the fog gave a muffled feel to everything, as if her nose was stuffed with soft cloth.

Here, Astrid signed. *We can't stop and swap arrows with them. Too much chance one might get away and warn the lookout station—it's only a mile upslope from here. Eilir and I will shoot at the leader, and so on down the line; everyone shoot twice at the same first target as your anamchara, move down one, then out blades and at them. No prisoners, no battle cries, and do it fast. We can't let any get away.*

She disposed them along twenty yards of the road, each in a position with a clear sight of the trackway. Each stood where they would shoot, drew four arrows from their quivers and stuck them lightly in the ground at their feet, then stepped back behind the chosen tree. It wasn't hard to find ones that offered complete concealment; they folded their shaggy twig-woven war cloaks around them and drew up the hoods, looking through the wide mesh of the gauze masks. From the moonlit road, the space beneath the trees would be caverns of blackness.

Eilir turned her eyes to Astrid, got a grin, and gave one in reply. It wasn't a fake, but not as easy as her soul sister's either. *That's the thing about playing a role all the time,* she thought, with tender exasperation. *After a while, you* are *what you* pretend. *And Astrid's been pretending to be utterly fearless so long she really* is.

Then they settled in with their backs to each other, ready to step around the tree in opposite directions. Calm was a little harder for Juniper Mackenzie's daughter. She controlled her breathing, drawing the chill wetness slowly in through her nose down into the bottom of her lungs, and sought through open eyes the image of a single star appearing on the horizon of morning. After a moment thought died down, and with it flashes of memory, of sights and smells and horrors. Instead the awareness of the night flowed into her, drops trickling on her skin, the bite of an insect. Time seemed to slow and lose the herky-jerky quality of tension. A moth went by heedless of her, less than hand's-breadth from her face. Then there was a flash of pointed leathery eight-inch wings behind a yellowish brown furry head, and the moth was gone save for head and wings tumbling towards the forest floor in the departing killer's wake.

Hoary bat, she thought with mild detachment. Then: *Here they come.*

Five men, walking in a long staggered line down the brush-grown dirt road below, with the gathering fog reaching to their knees in patches where it lay thick. Two had floppy-eared hounds on chain leads, and the animals pulled forward eagerly, noses to the ground. They wore uniforms of a sort—much like pre-Change camouflage hunting garb—and carried crossbows; they didn't seem to be wearing armor, though they might have light mail under the loose jackets. Besides that they wore small backpacks, with knives at their waists and machetes in place of swords—what the Protector insisted be called "falchions" in his domain.

In a way Arminger is Astrid's evil twin, she thought with a distant corner of her mind.

The rest of her was focused on the ... *targets. Just targets.*

They walked fast, their eyes raking the sides of the road upslope and down. The man in the lead drew closer, clearer in the bright moonlight that washed the road at intervals. He walked gracefully, though he looked to be older than his followers; he had a pointed beard that was gray-streaked brown, and a silver badge pinned to the turned-up brow of his floppy hat. That was in the shape of a rampant lion holding a broad-bladed spear.

Lord Molalla's sigil. They must be his foresters. And that one, he was a soldier before the Change, or a hunter, or both. Probably both.

Foresters were huntsmen—of runaway peons and serfs not least—and border guardians; the town of Molalla was down in the center of the barony, although the river it stood on had its source in these mountains. Their leader was scanning the ground, not entirely trusting to his dogs but following the Rangers' tracks; that was no easy feat, at night and after a skillful attempt to disguise them, and through the rampant brush and grass that had hidden most of the bare ground. Occasionally he would stop and toe aside some vegetation to get a better look at the damp earth.

At last he came level with them. Eilir felt a nudge from Astrid behind her, and each hit the quick-release toggle on their war cloaks, letting them fall as they took a stride forward, pivoting and bringing up their bows in the same motion.

Loose. A sharp quick rap as the bowstring slapped against her bracer, and the hum of recoil in her bow hand.

The arrow had only a hundred feet to go, but it was downhill, and the man with the pointed beard was already diving forward towards the Rangers' side of the road, going under the trajectory of the shafts. The dogs went down, and several of the huntsmen; a spatter of crossbow bolts came back from the rest. Eilir's hand went down for one of the arrows she'd stuck in a moss-grown root and the lead huntsman popped back up again; *he* hadn't wasted the one quarrel of his slow-loading weapon on a reflexive shot at an invisible target. He aimed with careful speed and then fired, dodging back behind the roadside growth at once. The bolt didn't come anywhere near the two young women; instead another figure toppled down the slope towards the track, clawing at stems and branches.

No time to think which of her friends it had been. The bearded huntsman was out of sight even as the two return arrows hissed down and thumped into the place he'd been.

Another was fleeing down the road but he dropped with limp sack-of-grain finality and two long arrows in his back.

Astrid dropped her bow and swept out the long Bear-killer sword she wore slung with the hilt jutting beyond her left shoulder. Eilir drew her short sword; in the same motion her left hand snatched the buckler from its hook on the weapon's sheath. Then they leapt down the steep rocky mountainside, their boots kicking up black basalt gravel and clods of dark wet earth. Steel glimmered under the moon, almost matching the sheen of the fog . . .

And Astrid's probably busting a gut not shouting A Elbereth Gilthoniel! *as loud as she can,* Eilir knew.

Since Juniper's daughter couldn't talk without using her hands she contented herself with a wide carnivore smile; opponents often found her silence disconcerting.

Come on, soul sister, you may be a goof but you're a swordswoman *goof!*

They both jinked and dodged as they came down the slope, the rest of the Rangers on their heels; not too difficult, when you were running at speed down an unfamiliar steep slope in darkness, caroming off trees and trying as hard as you could not to trip on the things that snatched at your feet and wanted to throw you helpless at the feet of men with hungry swords. By unspoken agreement they were both headed for the leader with the pointed beard; he was far too deadly skilled to be granted even a few seconds to draw his band together or take thought, and there were no points for fighting fair.

Both thought he might be waiting as they burst through the brush with a quarrel in the groove. Instead he'd done something even smarter, realizing that this fight was lost; they caught the sway of weeds and saplings on the other side of the road, as he headed quick-foot for the stream below. There he could break his trail, get around them and warn the lookout station on Table Rock.

A buckler was useful for running through a forest at night. You could hold it up to protect your eyes from things that would otherwise poke them out. Their legs were long and they were young; the man was only halfway across the brawling snow-swollen creek when they crashed onto the gravel on its bank. Fog came to his waist over the water, ripped aside now and then for an instant as the current pulled eddies through the air.

Mustn't let him out of sight. He'd disappear too well.

None of the three had a distance weapon. Or at least, none had a bow—the man stooped instantly, came up with a fist-sized rock and threw with a motion that said he'd played baseball once, whatever his other lifeways. Astrid ducked in her headlong charge, but not quite quickly enough; the rock slammed into the front of her helmet instead of her face, and ricocheted up into the darkness. The young woman's head slapped backward and her heels shot out from under her as she pitched flat on her back, disappearing in the ground mist.

Uh-oh, Eilir thought. *Wild Huntress, help!*

She didn't pause, even though she knew exactly what the man wanted—to get her into the water where the knee-deep flow and bad footing would soak away her agility. If she waited until he got to the other bank chances were he'd escape altogether. The stream was sickeningly cold as she jumped in, and the smooth rounded rocks shifted under the soles of her boots. She knew an instant's fleeting gladness she was in a kilt rather than trousers—that much less sodden cloth to cling to her legs.

His mouth moved, but between moonlight and intentness of purpose she couldn't read the words. They didn't matter, compared to the way his hands went crossways down to his waist and came up with two blades, the heavy machete chopper and long bowie. They moved in small precise circles as he crouched and grinned at her, backing away slightly towards the eastern bank . . .

He's not frightened. He just wants to get away before anyone else gets here, so he can report us. I have to kill him fast.

Closer. Blue eyes that turned pale in the cold light, and a golden earring. Three inches taller than her five-eight, and long arms—enough lines around his eyes that he was probably over forty, but strong as well and likely still quick enough. Scars on his hands and under the beard showed fights survived and opponents who'd died.

It's not my first time either.

The bowie knife stabbed for her belly, swift enough to blur in the moonlight and very hard. She knocked it aside with the buckler; the collision sent pain shooting through her left hand and wrist, but she drove the point of her short sword towards his face at the same time. He got the machete-falchion in between, and the guards locked. He braced shoulders and feet and she let the strength of it throw her backward; no point in getting into a wrestling match. But the water turned what would have been a cat-quick bound into almost a stumble; if it hadn't slowed him a little too the backhand cut would have taken off half her face. As it was, she felt a featherlight sting along the line of her jaw, and a hot trickle on her water-cold skin.

His eyes went a little wide as he dodged her counterchop; the edge touched cloth, and grated on mesh mail beneath. That *almost* let her shin-strike to the crotch succeed, but the water slowed her again. His bowie lanced towards her thigh; time slowed as she poised, let the point go past and then struck with the edge of the buckler at the exposed wrist.

The impact sent a grisly thud up her arm, and the knife flew free as bone crumpled. *One hand down.* She snarled and struck again, a stooping chop to the outside of the knee. He blocked again with his machete in a shower of sparks, ducked aside to turn her gut-punch with the buckler into a glancing blow ...

And hit her—hit her impossibly in the face with his broken left hand. The cheekpiece of her helmet took some of it, but her head snapped back and she staggered off-balance, tasting salt in her mouth and feeling her knees buckle. He launched himself forward, striking lizard-swift with the machete; one stroke she blocked, but the other landed on her stomach. The brigandine's small plates held, but the blow still had a strong man's shoulders behind it and she went down winded, a great splash throwing water chest-high as arrows sprayed from her quiver and she pancaked on her back. Again the river clutched at her, leaving her roll half-completed when he landed on her, water flowing into nose and open mouth as heaviness crushed her into the stones of the creek bed. Alone in utter darkness, the fog and water together like the inside of a closet.

He felt like boulders atop her, weight half again hers, his elbows on her shoulders and his good hand closing around her throat. The universe vanished in wet blurred blackness, and the blood pulsed in her throat as she tucked her chin down to try to stop the terrible crushing power in his callused fingers. Red shot across her eyes as she fumbled for the hilt of her dirk and got it out; the mail beneath his coat turned a stroke gone feeble as her starved lungs robbed her arms of strength.

Relief, then agony—reflex sucked ice water into her lungs as the iron grip on her throat vanished. She lunged up, and found herself nearly face-to-face with the man who'd been killing her, his distorted countenance looming at her out of the fog. A foot of steel poked out of the front of his jacket, and blood flooded out of his slack mouth into her face as she coughed and retched out river water, the blood black as the water in the moonlight, tasting of copper and salt and iron. Then the body swung aside as Astrid wrenched her backsword free with a ruthless boot on the man's body.

You all right? she signed, wiping the blade and sheathing it over her shoulder.

Ffffffff- Eilir stuttered as cold and shock froze her fingers for an instant, sitting in the river. *Fine.*

A hand clasped her forearm and helped her up; she stooped to cough once more, felt carefully for her sword and dirk in the dark water, and waded to the western bank. There she went to one knee for an instant, panting and hacking to clear her lungs and suck in air. The weight of her sodden armor-padding and plaid dragged at her already, and there was a mortal chill in it. Astrid handed her a flask; she took a brief nip of the Larsdalen brandy to let the sweet fire warm her belly, then poured a little more into her palm and rubbed it over her face—an old trick against cold Sam had taught them years ago. Then she signed:

How are you, *anamchara? I thought you were knocked out at least.*

To herself: *And I thought I was dead. Not ready for the Summerlands, not just yet. Things to do and be first.*

Just a bruise, and woozy for a few seconds, Astrid said,

though the aluminum-feather raven on her helmet was slightly the worse for wear—the rock had bent its neck and beak, and knocked out one of the ruby eyes.

Eilir nodded; it couldn't have been a real concussion. You didn't get up from one of those and prance around as if you'd woken up from a nap, as she knew from painful experience.

Then I didn't know where on earth I was or which way was up, lying in that ground mist. Come on, you've got to keep moving or you'll stiffen up.

Thanks, by the way, Eilir signed, as they puffed up the slope to the road.

You're still one ahead in the save-your-oath-sister's-life league, Astrid replied.

Eilir felt a little better as she moved, despite the cold water dripping from every portion of her. A thought made her smile.

You know how stretch fabric gets unstretchy when it's been washed too many times?

Yeah?

That was why pre-Change underwear still in the package were worth their weight in gold and more. Most people were back to rag loincloths or less. Drawstrings just didn't work very well at keeping boxers up, either.

Well, getting soaked like this made me think. What are we going to do when the last sports bra dies?

Astrid grimaced, then shook her head: *The same thing we did when the tampons ran out. Improvise. Use very thin well-tanned kidskin, maybe. Or if we could tan your sense of humor, it would stretch!*

Then it was Eilir's turn to twist her mouth. That turned from mock horror to the real thing as they came onto the road. The rest of the Rangers had dragged the bodies under the slope on the west side, where they couldn't be seen from the heights above. There were four, two with wounds where arrow shafts had been pulled free for reuse, the other pair spilling all their blood from sword wounds; it glistened black in the moonlight. The wet cold kept the smell down a little, but nothing could hide the undignified sprawling look of sudden violent death.

It wasn't the enemy dead who left her stricken, though—they'd chosen to carry blades for one of Arminger's barons, and it was up to them to make accounting to the Guardians—Reuben Hutton was lying bleeding as well.

Kevin looked up as they came to Reuben's side; he was the Dunedain's best medico, and he shook his head slightly at their questioning glance. Eilir felt a chill that had nothing to do with the cold water; Reuben had played and trained and then fought with them for a long while now.

The young man probably knew what the crossbow bolt angled up under his floating rib meant, and he'd had just time for the first shock to wear off; his pleasantly homely face was milk pale and contorted as he tried not to scream. Drowning as a slashed artery drained into your lungs wasn't a very slow way to go, but it *hurt*. Astrid reached down and pulled a silver cross on a chain out from under the Mackenzie-style brigandine he was wearing; Reuben clutched it convulsively and brought it to his lips. He was Christian—Catholic, specifically, like his adopted family. Eilir didn't know precisely how he'd ended up with the Huttons; there was something about his birth father and mother dying heroically in a fight where Will's wife, Angelica, was nearly killed, back when the first Bearkillers were making their way westward from Idaho. Nobody seemed to want to go into the details, and she'd never wanted to push it.

Kevin brought out one of the hypodermics they all carried in a padded boiled-leather pouch; poppies grew well in the Willamette, and homemade morphine was available, though scarce. Eilir signed *Two,* which was a fatal dose and didn't matter anymore, and then went on to Astrid: *Hold him.* When she looked surprised, Eilir went on: *Just do it! Now!*

Astrid put an arm under his broad shoulders as Kevin stabbed one hypodermic and then another into the angle of neck and shoulder. Reuben's face relaxed quickly as the drug took effect. He kept the cross before his lips; Astrid bent down and pressed hers to his brow for a moment. He tried to smile, tried to speak, stiffened and jerked as blood ran out of the corners of his mouth. Then his chest moved in a sigh, and he went slack. More blood ran down his lips and onto Astrid's black jerkin with its sigil of white tree and stars.

The five remaining Rangers put his body beside a massive fallen log and covered it quickly with brush. Eilir took advantage of an instant of privacy as she and Astrid recovered their bows. *I told you to do that because he'd been in love with you for years,* she signed. As the silver-blue eyes went wide in shocked surprise: *Don't ask. I'll tell you about it later, my dearest doink. We've got work to do.*

Kevin went ghosting down the trail; when he came back he had part of the work with him, in the person of Sam Aylward's stocky form, striding along cradling his bow in his arms just as he had his rifle when he yomped his way to Port Stanley a generation before. The shrewd eyes took in the scene as he and the Ranger eased into the woods beside the roadway, and Eilir felt a rush of relief. She thought Astrid did too, from the way she shifted slightly in the darkness.

Nice quiet job, he signed. *Nobody got away? Anyone cut out for the river?*

More reasons than Eilir's status had made knowledge of Sign widespread among the Clan Mackenzie, although that had probably started the fashion—that and children's love of secrets and codes. It was useful in a surprising range of tasks, especially talking while you were hunting or fighting.

One, the leader, Astrid signed, and reported the facts with stark simplicity.

Too bad about Reuben, he was a likely lad and always gave his best, the stocky bowman replied. Then, with a veteran's stoicism: *Good work otherwise. Of course, there were six of them originally. They sent one back to the trail up Table Rock when they ran into your tracks, before they chased after you. Downy bird, whoever was in charge of them. Glad you scragged him. Speaking of which, the one they sent back ran straight into me and my lot.*

He reached behind himself with his hand and patted the arrows that jutted over his right shoulder.

Urrk! Eilir thought, and saw him wink. Astrid went on:

We've got a way up the slope to the cliffs—the turnoff's about two thousand yards north. Then around a mile and a half through the woods to the base of the cliff. Our contact dropped the codeword, so we know that's OK.

Aylward grinned, not unkindly. *Or we know that evil bugger's Inquisitors tortured it out of our contact, and we're walking into a trap,* he signed. *But I don't think so, and you've got to take risks in this business.* He looked up. *Two hours to moonset. Just right, with a little margin for taking it slow. This fog's thickening—that'll help.*

"Mist," Juniper Mackenzie whispered. "Blessed be!"

"Straight from the Cauldron of the Goddess," Rowan agreed.

His sister Cynthia nodded; her band had rejoined at the base of Rooster Rock and made the climb with them. Several of the others made Invoking signs, and glanced aside at the Lady of the Mackenzies. Juniper bit back an impulse to snap *I'm not your good-luck charm, you adolescent idiots!* Or *the Wiccan pope-ess!*

Though she *had* been wishing hard for something like this, and what was magic if not the trained mind and will directing the forces of the universe? Useless to feel guilty at the impulse to bark, either, as long as she didn't actually do it; nerves were natural enough. She'd never pretended to be a fighter by trade, even when she embodied that Aspect of the Powers. And the Mighty Ones were at work here.

How not? There's nowhere they aren't *at work.*

Table Rock stood before them to the north, looming out of the rising tide of silvery fog as the moon sank towards the horizon, growing larger to the eye as it did. Rooster Rock stood behind; it was several hundred feet lower, but straight up and down in its central parts and harder to climb. The Mackenzie war band had crept up the slopes of the long ridge that connected them, something made possible by the dense forest that grew to the top, and easier by the fog. That was rising even as she watched, and it turned the flat-topped height ahead into a black island amid the vapors, muffling every sound in the nighted wilderness. She unshipped her binoculars for a last look.

The outline of the low mountain hadn't changed since she came through here, backpacking through the wilderness with some friends . . . *Lord and Lady, going on twenty years ago!* She pushed aside a wistfulness; as far as she knew, every one of that little group was dead save Judy Barstow—Judy Lefkowitz, she'd been then. A long finger of land sloped gently up to just under five thousand feet; the last half mile was surrounded by cliffs on three sides, leaving only this approach. When she saw it as a young woman there had been only a trail, and the summit had been like a rock garden of wild rose, parrotbeak and kinnikinnick. There was a wall across the top of the trail now, less than a fortress and more than a fence, three feet of dry-laid stone and a six-foot-high stretch of thick boards nailed to posts on top of it; the roofs of several buildings rose over the wall, and a tall timber-frame tower reared skyward. It was like seeing an old friend whose face had been slashed. A little lantern light showed behind it, even at near two in the morning. She looked up at the moon; another hour and a half until it set, and then—God and Goddess willing—they could get on with it.

Eilir goes into danger first, Juniper thought. *And Astrid and Sam and all the others with them.* Silently, beneath her breath, lips barely moving, she chanted:

> *"Through darkened wood and shadowed path*
> *Hunter of the Forest, be with my loves:*
> *Lady of the Stars, fold them in Your wings*
> *So mote it be!"*

Then she settled down under her war cloak to wait. Behind her, three-score and ten Mackenzies did likewise, relaxed as tigers, bows waiting by their hands.

Here, Eilir signed, no farther from the recipient's eyes than his nose. Eilir followed him, the last of the party, as the five Rangers and Aylward's picked band of six slipped under the lee of a black basalt cliff that made them utterly invisible to anyone above. A great semicircular chunk had fallen from the base of it here long ago, and made a broad shallow cave; likely the fog would have hid them anyway, and it made moving through the darkness like walking in a giant broom closet. They waited in the blackness, waited to see if anyone had heard the noise from their crossing of the boulder field and scree that lay a little north. She worried about that less than the hearing; the everlasting silence she moved in allowed her to concentrate more. She'd long since learned how to move silently, starting with long summer days in the woods with her mother before the Change observing beast and bird. When one could sneak up unheard on a ground squirrel or get close enough to a deer to touch it, it wasn't hard to avoid human notice . . .

Nothing; the moon hung huge above, blurred through the mist, then dipped below the edge of tree-clad ridges. Darkness became more absolute, and silence stretched as they waited. She reviewed the layout above mentally: the fence and gate across the neck of the rising finger of land, then frame buildings on either side of the old trail with a narrow lane between, then a long timber-and-metal ramp out to the summit, with the signal tower beside it. She'd memorized the maps thoroughly before they left Sutterdown, though.

That left an uncomfortable amount of time to think. This would be a famous deed, if it went well. She enjoyed thinking of that; there was nothing wrong with being proud of doing right, and getting recognized for it; and if fighting the Protector's men wasn't right, nothing was. But watching Reuben drown inside, with all his life unlived . . .

Is this sort of thing what I want for all the rest of my life? she thought. *I love the travel and outsmarting the bad guys and sneaking under their eyes and making them look like idiots, and hanging with Astrid is great—someone has to keep my darling sister-soul from flapping her arms and flying off with the wild geese—and the Dunedain are my best friends, and yes, I get a rush from the danger, but watching friends die . . . well, we all have to risk that.*

When the Mackenzies went to war, everyone strong enough marched and fought; if you didn't like that, you were welcome to go live somewhere else.

I really don't know . . . this is something I do well, and it helps everyone. I do know I want children. And a man who's more than short-term fun, I'm getting too old to be satisfied with that. And I think Mom wants me to take over her job someday, but Rudi . . . of course, while I'm with the Dunedain, everyone knows Sign, which is really a help.

There just weren't many deaf people around these days—partly because there just weren't as many people, period, and partly because a smaller share of the deaf had survived the Dying Time. Not more than a score or so in the whole of the Clan's territories, certainly, including kids born since.

She sighed silently. How did that old saying go?

> *The lame can go horseback*
> *The handless tend herds;*
> *The deaf are undaunted in war;*
> *Better to be blind than burnt on your pyre*
> *No deeds can a dead man do.*

Of course, that was Odin talking, and He was a notorious fink . . . Just then one of the others tapped her on the shoulder, and she moved forward with eagerness blazing up again. *Yup, I'm* undaunted, *all right!*

Three ropes had fallen from the top of the cliff, good strong hemp. There was no need to talk; everyone knew what they were supposed to do.

Her bow went over her shoulder into the loops beside her quiver; that was new-filled with a full load of forty-five shafts. All the rest of her equipment was padded against noise. Sam Aylward spat on his palms and took the middle rope, climbing rapidly hand-over-hand. Eilir and Astrid flanked him, going up inchworm-style—locking the rope between crossed feet, holding on with their hands while they slid the feet up, locking them again and pushing with their legs. Halfway up they came out of the fog, and faint starlight showed on the surface of the mist like reflections on a dully phosphorescent sea, doubly so by contrast with the black basalt cliff. Then the ropes grew close to the rough, pitted surface of the rock as the overhang grew less, and she had to switch her feet to the cliff surface, boots scrabbling at it as she pulled herself up with arms and shoulders burning. They all reached the top at the same time, sweating and breathing deeply after the hundred-foot climb, but not winded. A figure darted forward and Eilir's hand went to her dirk for a moment, then upward as the stranger bent to offer a hand to help her. There was more light here from lanterns and fires, just enough to see that it was a woman in a housedress and shawl, but not enough to read lips well.

Eilir took the hand for the last scramble, then smiled and touched her own lips and an ear with two fingers and shook her head: *I can't hear you or speak.*

The woman blinked surprise but then seemed to grasp what she meant, and went over to Sam Aylward, bending and listening; then she ran quickly back towards the long low frame building that faced the cliff edge only ten feet or so away. It was blank on this side save for small windows, darkened now—barracks and stables, according to the briefing. The three of them made a triangle in front of the ropes, waiting with their bows ready as the nine others below climbed up behind them.

Five minutes, Aylward reminded the six in the gate party, pointing southward.

They nodded and ghosted away. The others waited until they saw them reach the building and two make stirrups of their hands, throwing the others up to the roof one by one in vaulting leaps, then hauling their comrades up. They crawled along below the ridgeline, planting their feet carefully on the wooden shingles of the roofing until they were in position to sweep the rear of the fence and the gate in it. One turned and used the broad gestures that communicated over distance: *Six men by the fence. Quiet. End of their shift. We're ready to support main attack on gate.*

Aylward nodded. "Let's go," he whispered, easy enough to read in the darkness.

It was just past four in the morning, the hour when a sleeper's life and mind flicker lowest. Even so Aylward's party had the hardest task, silencing the signal tower before the men there could light their beacon. *That* would alert posts north and south of here and be relayed deep into Baron Molalla's section of the Protectorate, reaching Portland itself not long after sunrise. The tire-tread soles of their boots went swiftly over the stony surface as they ran stooping. Even the dogs were mostly asleep; one raised a questioning head as the Mackenzies ran into the open space between the two rows of shacks, then sprang to all fours in alarm.

Eilir pivoted on one heel, drew, shot at the flash of teeth and collar, turned back and ran on. The arrow flickered through darkness and the hound flopped back down, transfixed from the left side of its neck to its right hip, dead before its body struck the ground.

Sorry, brother dog, she thought. This one wasn't a killer, just a loyal beast, helping to guard its pack territory and puppies. *Enjoy chasing the rabbits in the Summerlands and think kindly of me. Now let's get going. The others will smell the blood soon, or us.*

The building was along one side of the old trail to the summit; there was another on the other side, and then only the signal tower—and a long ramp of two-by-fours and rails curling gently upward at its end, with a shape at its beginning covered by a tarpaulin. Eilir's eyes were on the tower, and those with her too. It was a mere unenclosed framework with a ladder running up the center, but the platform at the top had a signal fire waiting in an iron bowl, and mirrors for flashing messages.

Aylward held out a hand and they halted. Then he chopped it forward. Sanjay dashed past her, and his two sibs; they hit the ladder running and went up it with their feet and hands moving at sprint speed, scampering like squirrels. The rest of the scaling party stood back, arrows on their strings. Eilir risked a quick glimpse over her shoulder. That was just in time to see three more shafts arching upward, southward towards the fence that enclosed this outpost; the five minutes were up. She could see them clearly, for each had a gasoline-soaked rag tied around it behind the head, and lit before they were fired. They traced arcs of fire across the night, southward over the outpost's fence and gate.

OK, most excellently sorcerous Mom, she thought, switching her gaze back towards the platform above. *Over to you, and the Lady!*

* * *

"Now!" Juniper Mackenzie shouted, as the three fire arrows arched skyward above the dimness ahead—headed safely out of the outpost, which must *not* burn. *"Up and at them, Mackenzies!"*

Around her there was a mass rustling as seventy clansfolk shed their war cloaks and sprang to their feet; then a frenzied shout, a howling like wolves, hawk screeches, the bellowing of bull elk, all uniting into a long ululating wail like catamounts at war, with more than bit of rebel yell in it. Now they *wanted* to be heard. They dashed forward, packed into a blunt wedge on the narrowing finger of stone, rising up out of the fog as the rock rose beneath their feet and the outpost stood stark before them, a solid darkness against the black sky. Shouts of alarm rose behind the wall, and lanterns flared in the predawn blackness. At a hundred yards, Rowan flung his arm up.

"Halt! Four shafts! *Shoot!*"

The Mackenzie onrush looked disorderly, but that was illusion; each knew what to expect, by long practice. They halted as one, raised their bows for a dropping shot behind the wall. The massed crack of bowstrings on bracers sounded in the darkness, and then the whickering hum of the arrowstorm, the dim flicker of the arrowheads at the height of their arc, and the hissing plunge of steel-tipped cedarwood as it fell out of the sky like sleet, the second and third shafts in the air before the first struck. Plunging fire was doubly terrible in the dark, invisible until the last second, impossible to dodge or guard against. Screams of pain followed the shouts of alarm.

"Forward—"

The mass loped on.

"Halt! Four shafts! *Shoot!*"

Juniper fitted another nock to the cord of her bow. *For Eilir!* she called to herself, and drew the cord to the ear.

Eilir knew when the terrible baying screech of the Clan's war cry struck the Protector's outpost. Light flared behind her among the buildings, as panicked hands turned the knobs and raised the wicks of lanterns, or set lighters to candle. Feet pounded, many and hard enough to let her feel the vibrations on the soles of her feet. And a hundred feet above her, three men ran to the edge of the tower's platform, peering southward towards the gate.

Aylward, Eilir and Astrid drew their bows to the ear and loosed within a half second of each other. A man spun back with a shaft in his shoulder; another pitched forward, turning and turning with his mouth open in a great O until he struck not far away and bounced—once. The third threw himself flat and rolled away from the edge, probably to light the alarm fire near the center.

But also towards the hole where the ladder comes up, Eilir thought grimly.

She knew pretty much what he'd be seeing there; Sanjay's face coming through the trapdoor, grinning in the dark around the dirk clenched in his teeth. After climbing all that way expecting to see a crossbow aimed down at him, he wasn't going to be in any mood for half measures, either. Seconds after the thought two more men in the Protector's gear soared out from the edge of the platform, one limp, one falling windmilling and head-down until he landed not far from his comrade; the skull broke open on the rock and spattered.

Ouch, Eilir thought. An instant later Sanjay and Aoife and Daniel waved from the spot he'd fallen and then faded backward.

The three on the ground turned at once, going to the earth and crawling away. More and more figures were spilling into the trail between the buildings. Time to sow a little confusion.

Eilir rose, crouching, and ghosted forward to the corner of the building, waited until a door opened on the other side, drew and shot . . .

Juniper ran panting towards the gate, but the mass of the Clan's war band surged past her on either side—all but her standard-bearer and the three told off to accompany her. The kilted mass struck the arrow-studded wood of the heavy fence and scarcely paused. One with a raven painted on his face in black and gold hit the low stone wall running

and leapt clear over the points of the uprights with a banshee howl, chopping with his sword even as he landed on
the other side. Others were less flamboyant but nearly as
quick; one in each three would brace his back against the
wood with knees bent and fingers linked into a stirrup, and
toss the other two up as they jumped and planted a boot in
his hands. Then hands would come down and haul them up
to drop down on the other side of the fence.

Getting too old for that! she told herself, following in
Rowan's wake with the banner bearer at her side. The
green-and-silver flag flapped in the wind of their passage,
the crescent moon cradled between antlers.

The gate was of iron bars, welded into a diagonal lattice
with openings palm-broad; the bars themselves were
twisted from lengths of rebar heated and hammered together. A crossbow bolt flashed out and a clan warrior fell
with a shriek of pain, but an instant later a Mackenzie
arrow fired from behind him struck the crossbowman in
the small of the back. He dropped; boots trampled across
him in the darkness, and bones broke. Then the foremost
Mackenzie rank was up to the iron, a murderous scrimmage with swords and short-gripped spears and dirks used
at close range through the openings. The gate heaved and
rattled against the bar that held it against the weight of
many strong bodies, but it held.

"Room! Give me room!" bellowed the man who was a
blacksmith in peacetime.

They did, and the hammer side of his ax struck once,
twice, and again. Sparks blasted out where it hit on the outside of the rightward edge, over the hinges. One blow and
it sagged; another, and the upper corner came free. A
dozen Mackenzies launched themselves at it then, some
recklessly feetfirst. The iron grille fell inward, taking men
down with it and beneath it.

Screaming, the warriors of the clan surged across it and
into the narrow lantern-lit space beyond. There had been
two dozen of Baron Molalla's foresters here, and as many
ordinary soldiers. She had watched her folk do well against
odds; with surprise and numbers on their sides, they were
terrifying. The Protector's men tried again and again to

form in ordered lines as they'd been taught, but the Mackenzies were all around them, fighting three on two or two on one, each a leaping, dodging blur of stabs and chops and smashing blows with the buckler. Everyone was too close-packed for distance weapons, and the sound was like a dozen loads of scrap metal falling on a stone smithy floor, with the white-noise surf of human voices thrown in.

Then the men-at-arms came out of the commandant's house; it took time to put on that gear. There were only four of them, but they were armored from neck to ankle, their kite-shaped shields broad and heavy and strapped with metal, held up face-high until nothing showed but the glaring eyes on either side of the helmet's nasal bar. They formed up in a blunt wedge and trotted forward in a jingle of steel and pounding of boots. An eddy of combat erupted around them and the Mackenzies drew back, one clutching a slashed arm, two dragging another more seriously wounded. Protectorate survivors elsewhere fought their way towards them, and a knot of civilians followed, including babes in arms. It would be difficult to shoot them down without injuring the noncombatants, but they couldn't let them escape either—and swarming them under would cost gruesomely.

And behind them, a glimmer of flames through the windows of the house; they must have set a blaze before they left. *We've got to get that fire out!* she thought.

She opened her mouth to make a call for their surrender. Rowan forestalled her, loping forward with his teeth showing in a fixed rictus of bloodlust amid the gorgon menace of his painted face, helmet gone and flaxen hair blowing wildly, a beacon in the dimness that drew clansfolk after him. And fighting, he shrieked, an ululating wail like fingernails on slate.

"Haro!" the knight shouted, sloped his shield and cut downward with the Norman longsword.

Rowan's headlong rush had been a trick. His ax met the other's blade in midair and steel crashed on steel, sparks and clamor; sheer battering and mass swept the lighter weapon aside and nearly out of his opponent's hand, and the armored man staggered. His wrist and arm must have been numb with the impact, robbed of strength for a moment. The ax looped up overhead in a deceptively graceful motion, held at end and middle, and then Rowan's hands slid together at the end of the shaft as it slammed down again with all his better than two hundred pounds of muscle and bone behind it. The edge bit through the good riveted mail, through flesh and bone, and the knight dropped to the ground with a metallic crash, thrashing and bleeding from an arm half-severed at the shoulder.

Cynthia had been holding the man on her brother's unshielded left in play with her battle spear, using it like a bladed quarterstaff, the head and butt cap like streaks of light in the darkness, booming on the shield, sweeping towards his face, stabbing down at a foot. The baron's trooper was so fixed on it he never noticed the hammer side of Rowan's ax until it crashed into his neck below the flare of his helmet. Bone snapped, and the others were falling . . .

"Scathach!" Rowan shrieked in terrible exultation, whirling the weapon up again.

Then Juniper was moving, faster than she thought was in her, leaping before him. She spread her arms wide and met his eyes; there was an almost palpable shock as green met blue—although the pupils of his had expanded to almost swallow the iris, like windows into night.

"No!" she said, driving her will forward like a spearpoint of her own. "These aren't fighters, Rowan!"

For a moment she thought that dreadful ax would come down on her, and then humanity flooded back into the younger Mackenzie. He staggered, mouth loose and slack; well she knew that weakness which flooded in when you returned from beyond the world of common day.

"Get the fire out," she snapped. *An order will help him come to himself.* "Quickly, before it shows at a distance."

The fight was over—nothing left but pursuit and killing amid the shadows, and the long scream of a man who'd chosen the cliff over the red blades and painted grinning faces running behind him. Juniper grimaced as she slid her own unmarked sword back into its sheath.

Then, very softly, she murmured to herself: "What is it

we've brought back, to run wild once more on the ridge of the world?"

Sixteen hours later and twenty miles to the west, the Mackenzies turned to watch stars appearing over the Cascades as night came towards them like a moving wall of shadows. They were encamped on an island of firm ground in a new swamp; the smells of evening were abroad, woodsmoke, cooking, horses and cut grass over by the picket line. Other stars appeared against the mountains now—great fire beacons burning in the gloaming, distance-shrunk to trembling candle flames dancing against encroaching night; first one north of Table Rock, then more to either side, and racing past them to the northward, heading west.

Juniper shivered as she looked at them. *Like the old days,* she thought. Very old days, along the frontier between England and Scotland; half her ballads came from there, from the ancient tales of her father's people—the folk who'd given the words *blood feud* and *unhallowed hand* and *black mail* to the English language.

There had been nights like this there, when the balefires burned from hilltop to hilltop, from the North Sea to the Irish Channel. Warning laird and crofter that the great reiver clans were out, swarming from Liddersdale and Teviotdale and a dozen other nests, riding a thousand lances strong to break the Border.

And now the Mackenzies are out, she thought mordantly. *Granted we're on foot and carrying longbows, but the principle of the thing . . .*

"They've twigged," Sam Aylward said, coming to stand beside her with a piece of sausage in his hand, his prosaic matter-of-fact tone doubly welcome. "Probably those prisoners got loose—well, we knew they'd not stay tied up forever. Everything gets harder now."

Juniper nodded. "But *they're* reacting to what *we* do," she pointed out. "Now we have to move faster, and always be doing something new before they can deal with what we've done. It's only thirty miles to cross the Valley; a day's travel, maybe two."

Sam smiled. "This will draw their troops away from the southern border, too, pull them north and east," he said. "That'll make it a lot easier for our folk and the refugees."

"And we're appropriately dressed," Juniper said, touching kilt and plaid. At his look she grinned and went on, quoting a poem from wars older and more savage than any this land had yet known:

> *"On foot should be all Scottish war*
> *Let hill and marsh their foes disbar*
> *And woods as walls prove such an arm*
> *That enemies do them no harm.*
> *In hidden spots keep every store*
> *And burn the plainlands them before*
> *So, when they find the land lie waste*
> *Needs must they pass away in haste*
> *Harried by cunning raids at night*
> *And threatening sounds from every height*
> *Then, as they leave, with great array*
> *Smite with the sword and chase away.*
> *This is the counsel and intent*
> *Of Good King Robert's Testament."*

CHAPTER FIFTEEN

"So that's why they are all stirred up, Juney," Mike Havel chuckled. "Tweaking him, as you said back at our conference. We thought it would be the perfect time to clean out Crusher Bailey, with the Protector himself doing something up the Columbia, and his reserve cavalry all east over the river. Either they've got a lot more cavalry than we thought, or our English friends here are more important than we thought. Perhaps we'd better hear from them before you fill us in on the details of how you got from Table Rock to the Willamette."

Juniper nodded. It had taken only half an hour, spaced out between bites; the good food was welcome after a week of riding, fighting, and snatching meals catch-as-catch-can.

"I'm curious too, to be sure," she said. "And poor Sam's fair bursting."

Sam Aylward grinned his thanks at her—he'd been smiling a good deal since he saw Sir Nigel and the others. He'd spoken of the Lorings, but not often, probably because memories of home were too painful when he thought everyone he knew dead.

"I might as well make the introductions," he said. "Sir Nigel was my CO in the SAS for quite some time, and we were neighbors before that. Tilford Manor's not far from Crooksbury and my father's farm—where it was before he sold up, that is."

"Two of the least successful agricultural enterprises in Hampshire," Nigel Loring said, with a slight self-deprecating smile. "Aylward's father and I were in a sort of race to see who could drag out the agonizing process of bankruptcy longest. I won, but then I had my munificent officer's wages to offset the yearly losses, and I had more assets to borrow against. No, I lie—we did make a clear profit, twice. 1974 and 1987."

I think I like this little Englishman, Juniper thought, smiling back. *And if he had a hand in the making of Sam Aylward, he must be some considerable sort of a man.*

"And this great lump of a gallybagger here, his father ran the Pied Merlin," Aylward went on. "*And* he's a second cousin of sorts. Bad blood coming out there, inbreeding ..."

"Led me astray with tales of soldiering on his visits home, Sam did," John Hordle said, beaming. "Lies, lies, nothing but lies!"

"The more fool you to believe them, then," Alyward said. He turned to the younger Loring: "And you must have been just down from Sandhurst when things Changed, sir."

"I was, and it was luckier than I thought at the time. But Father was more at the center of things."

The elder Loring took up the story, eventually summing up: ". . . quite an efficiently managed coup and purge, and we'd been very reluctant to openly confront His Majesty. If it hadn't been for the Tasmanian ship being in port and willing to take us into exile . . . well, the king *might* have allowed me and mine to retire to Tilford Manor eventually. On the other hand, he might not have, after the queen had been at him for a while. I'm afraid we'd all become deplorably case-hardened by then. We took Captain Nobbes's offer and sailed from King's Lynn—"

"Ah," Mike Havel said. "And you pulled into Portland in . . . what, early March? Sorry if I'm cutting you short, it's very interesting and I'd appreciate the whole story when there's time, but we *do* have immediate local problems with your former host there." A crooked smile. "As did you, I understand."

"Their ship got in the first week of March," Signe said. "But the Protector kept it under very tight security."

"Yes; the *Pride of St. Helens* was on a world survey voyage, you see."

Juniper leaned forward as well. Aylward felt his ears prick; this wasn't just a matter of far-off things long ago. It affected his new home, and his family and people.

Loring went on: "Well, at first everything went quite well. I can't say that I liked this Arminger chappie even on first acquaintance, but I didn't take against him at once the way poor Captain Nobbes did, we'd seen plenty of worse rulers thrown up by the Change ... and when I did realize there was no dealing with him, I flatter myself I didn't show it. Then it became obvious that he was delaying our departure for some reason ...."

Portland Protectorate, Willamette Valley, Oregon
April 6th, 2007 AD—Change Year Nine

It was a fine bright spring day as the Protector and his guests rode out from Portland, westward to a manor that he'd suggested as quarters for their visit. The burnt-out suburbs were almost behind them now, although for most of the trip you'd scarcely suspect humans had ever lived there anyway, save for the road itself.

Tall trees left standing before the Change reared among saplings already twice man-height, above a tangled mat of vegetation, vines and brambles and hedges gone wild into shaggy walls; forest had gone even further towards reclaiming the abundant pre-Change parks and natural corridors. It was all washed by recent rain, intensely green, starred with flowers, swarming with insects and loud with songbirds. There was game trace of everything from rabbit to elk and boar, and even emu—plus one astonishing set of pugmarks that were unmistakably tiger, although nothing beyond butterflies and birds showed itself with so many carriages and riders on the pavement. The sound of their hooves rumbled and echoed as the road wound between hills crowned with tall firs.

Reminds me of parts of England, Nigel Loring thought— of the thorn jungles and spreading woodland that had taken over where resettlement hadn't reached, right down to the descendants of game-farm escapees haunting the new wilderness. *Like those hippo in, of all things, the Fens.* Only an occasional snag of wall or stretch of concrete or asphalt showed the hand of man, or a creeper-grown lamppost.

"Portland's virtually the only large city we've seen that isn't completely deserted," Captain Nobbes said, turning in the saddle to look behind them at the skyscrapers, and at the unearthly white cone of Mt. Hood floating against the eastern horizon. "*Partial* destruction is very rare."

"I'm not surprised," the overlord of the Protectorate said. "From my scouts' reports, it's certainly the only one in western North America of any size that isn't empty of anything but bones—usually gnawed bones."

Nobbes nodded. "We've been around the world, and anything that had a population of over a quarter million is dead, and has a dead zone around it. The bigger the city, the bigger the dead zone—and in places where they overlap, there's nothing left. Most of Europe west of the Vistula, both sides of the Mediterranean, pretty well all the Middle East, Turkey, Japan, Korea, eastern China . . . Well, there's Singapore, but that was a special case—they all moved out in an organized mass."

Lord Protector Arminger—Nigel Loring assumed that was a bit of a joke—nodded graciously.

"The circumstances here were rather exceptional," he said. "I saw that the population had to be reduced, and quickly, or everyone would die. So I and my associates— the Portland Protective Association—seized whatever bulk foodstuffs we could before they were wasted or lost. Forty percent of American wheat exports to Asia went through Portland. The amount in the pipeline was considerable, and we took over elevators, trains stalled on the tracks into the city, ships in port and in the Columbia. And then we, mmm . . . encouraged the surplus population to leave and shift for themselves; with that, there was enough to keep more than thirty thousand people alive for a year.

After about six months we began to expand into the countryside round about, most of which was as you say a dead zone—dead from Seattle in the north as far south as Eugene, except for some enclaves of . . . troublesome bandits and cultists on the fringes. You can imagine the difficulties—lack of tools, lack of skills . . ."

"Remarkable that you've accomplished this much," Nobbes said, his voice neutral.

Well, you Tasmanians had a good deal of luck, with the Bass Strait to protect you, Loring observed to himself, slightly irritated by the unspoken distaste.

The thought made him feel a little more sympathetic to Arminger than his first impression had left him, and he had to admit that the man had been scrupulously polite. Portland's ruler was a tall man in his middle forties with a square chin and knob-strong cheekbones, light-brown hair falling to his shoulders, dressed casually in loose black trousers tucked into high boots, crimson jacket, a dagged hood with long liripipe, and a broad-brimmed hat with a peacock feather tucked into the band. A dagger and double-edged longsword swung from his belt, the hilt a surprisingly plain affair of steel crossguard and worn, sweat-stained leather-cord grip. He looked fully capable of using it effectively, too. For now he held the reins in his left hand, and a peregrine falcon in hood and jesses on his gauntleted right wrist.

Nobbes evidently felt the silence as they came out into settled country; Arminger was the sort of man who could use quiet as a weapon, and Nobbes one of the more numerous variety made nervous by it.

"This reminds me of parts of Tasmania," he said, speaking rather loudly to carry over the rumbling thunder of hooves. "Near Launceston, and up the Tamar. Even to all the people in the fields, and my, didn't all those yobbos from the towns complain!"

"You seem to have made a remarkable recovery, though," Arminger said. "We lost nine in ten or more of our population, and you?"

"We were hungry, but lucky with it—no famine at all, ah, my lord Protector," Nobbes said. "But we've found a number of islands that did as well as Tasmania—the South Island in New Zealand, they've got nearly a million survivors, and Prince Edward Island in Canada with over a hundred thousand; Bornholm and Gotland in the Baltic; no famine there either. And many more that did worse than that but well compared to nearby mainlands—Fyn, Sicily, Crete, Cyprus. And Iceland held out for a year, before the British evacuated them."

"Logical," Arminger replied. "Most of the farming countryside in the advanced countries produced huge surpluses of food for people far away. Even with the massive drop in productivity after the Change there was enough for the few residents and they could readjust in time—unless they were overrun by starving refugees. Islands that weren't too built up would be safe from that, just as the far interior was here—Idaho, for instance. Or at least an island could defend its borders."

He went on, like a genial host: "I've been told the landscape here is like England, too, Sir Nigel," he said to Loring.

"More like parts of France," Loring said. "The Loire Valley, Anjou or Touraine . . . near Bourgueil, for example. Except that you can't see mountains from there, of course. Perhaps more like the Dordogne country, as far as the view of the middle distance . . . larger scale, of course."

Arminger looked pleased. "Yes, now that you mention it, this does look a little like parts of France. I visited Tours as a student, long ago . . . how is France doing?"

"It's empty, save for the dead," the Englishman said flatly. "The king sent a mission through a few years ago to salvage works of art and take a survey, and I was in command of the escort. We've planted a few outposts on the Norman coast, and at the mouths of the Loire and Gironde. Everything else is scrub thicket reverting to forest, with the odd pocket of neosavages, no more than ten or twenty thousand in all."

"Pity," Arminger said. "It was a beautiful country, don't you agree, my sweet?"

His wife looked up from her accounts in the open carriage; Sandra Arminger was a woman in her thirties, brunette but with something fox-faced about her, and clever dark eyes.

"It was overpriced and they never did learn about changing their underwear regularly," she said. "The food was good—as long as you didn't think too much about the kitchen or what was under the chef's fingernails."

"Think of the art, and the chateaux, and the scenery," said Arminger.

"Think of the bad-mannered waiters, and the drivers all intent on killing you."

"Philistine."

"Romantic."

The lord of Portland turned to his guests again: "We're past Beaverton, out of what used to be called the Silicon Forest. Now it's the New Forest. I'm keeping it and the big parks west of town as a hunting preserve . . ."

Loring gave an involuntary snort of laughter. "A hunting preserve called the New Forest? I say, you're following Norman precedent rather closely, what?"

Arminger's grin was charming. "Touché!"

His wife spoke: "Your family is of Norman origin, isn't it, Sir Nigel?"

"Remotely," he said. "But yes, there was a Loring in the Conqueror's train—a *miles,* or household knight. He was rewarded with land in Hampshire, which stayed in the family . . . until last year, in fact."

"Remarkable," Arminger said; his enthusiasm seemed genuine. "Unique, perhaps?"

"Rare, but not quite unique. There were the Berkeleys—descendants of Eadnoth the Staller, a Saxon nobleman who went over to the Conqueror and was killed in 1068. His descendants held land in the West Country right down to the Change, which I'm sorry to say they didn't survive."

"I'm sure you could tell us a great deal of interest about the Old World," Sandra Arminger said.

"I'm merely a soldier, my lady," Sir Nigel demurred. "A straightforward type, I'm afraid. You probably know a good deal more of history and matters of state than I."

"Not all that straightforward," she said thoughtfully. "Despite the charmingly boyish smile—your son has it too."

"The smile?" he said, feeling a prickle of apprehension as Arminger raised an eyebrow and looked between his wife and his guest.

"The charm, and the hidden depths, I think," she said, and returned to her account books.

Arminger nodded, the considering look still in his eyes as he went on: "We're entering the farming part of Washington County now. Thank God the Change didn't wait a few more years, or this would have been built-up too."

Arminger *was* genial enough; until you remembered that at a word his men would cut you down, or drag you off for worse. Or you thought of the sick, brutalized eyes of the labor gangs in Portland, and the weeping sores under the iron neck rings.

Nigel Loring cast an appraising eye on the escort. A dozen were mounted crossbowmen, with mail vests, simple conical helmets, knife and short sword at their waists, small round shields over their backs. Another dozen were what Arminger called his men-at-arms: equipped Norman-style in knee-length hauberks, big kite-shaped shields and nose-guarded helms, but with plate vambraces and greaves on their forearms and shins added, equipped with longsword and eleven-foot lance. All of them seemed tough, fit, probably good with their weapons, and well-mounted—they were certainly expert horsemen, as was their master, and good at riding in formation to boot. The escort's commander had the plume on his helm and little gilded spurs on his boots that he'd been told marked knightly status.

It seems Charles isn't the only one given to romantic terminology, Loring thought, stroking his mustache to hide a smile; he was a baronet himself, after all. *Still, I've seen stranger things since the Change. And Arminger here was one of those Society chappies.* The medieval reenactment group had offshoots and equivalents in Britain, and a fair number of those had ended up on the Isle of Wight; his own son had been involved with them since his teens. *Very useful they were, as instructors. I do wish they hadn't given Charles so many ideas.*

Sandra Arminger rode along in an open carriage, reading through some files. Servants jogged along behind on nags, but the mounts of the armed men and the guests were superb, spirited but beautifully trained—the tall yellow hunter he'd been given was a joy to ride, and he hadn't been able to resist naming it *Pommers* after his favorite horse back home . . .

No. Back in England, he told himself sternly. *England will never be your home again. You'll have to carve yourself a new home somewhere—land for the Lorings to hold, and I suspect by the sword.*

Nigel took a deep breath. The air was fresh, a little warmer than Hampshire would be in April, with an intense green scent. Now that they were out of the overgrown ruins the landscape was gently rolling; steeper ridges in forest of oaks and firs, the hillsides and valleys between a patchwork of greens—pasture with clover and trefoil blooming red among the grass, young grain, a pink froth of cherry blossom scenting the air, hillside vineyards putting out shoots and leaves. There were blue-flowered flax, and hemp and beets as well; cattle and sheep grazed in substantial herds, overseen by herdsmen on foot with slings and simple spears.

But no scattered farmsteads except ruins. Odd, that.

From what he remembered, villages weren't common in the United States, not in the European sense of farmers and farmworkers living clustered together, but that was what he saw here. Homes were tightly grouped at crossroads or near a stream, several dozen in every clump, ranging from modest comfort to mere shacks. The villages were slung along laneways with an open square at the middle, each house surrounded by kitchen gardens and sheds. Every cluster was bounded by a fence of palings with a gate and watchman's house, and each had a church, a larger-than-usual home functioning as a tavern, a smithy and sometimes a water mill. There was usually a larger building some distance from the hamlet, surrounding by a ditch, earthwork bank, concrete or fieldstone-and-concrete wall, and tower; from the look of it each of those was the center of a separate farm, and a large one at that.

It did look rather like some rural parts of England, save that it was more systematic, more consistent, and the village homes were less varied—whether substantial or squalid, most of them looked as if they'd been knocked together since the Change out of salvaged materials. Children and a few women were busy around the hamlets, caring for small stock and weeding in the gardens, or looking after toddlers and infants; he recognized the moan of spinning wheels and the rhythmic clattering thump of looms as well, and several times the distinctive sound of wooden hammers in water-powered mills fulling woolen cloth. Most adults were in the fields, largely weeding at this season when the spring planting was complete. There were a few horse-drawn machines helping, particularly around the fortified manors, but mostly it was hoes, and workers kneeling or stooping to use trowels or their bare hands.

Hmmm, he thought, judging the density and the spacing. *One or two square miles per village, on average; call it a hundred people per square mile. Most of the territory this Lord Protector claims to control must be empty, or he'd have a million subjects, not the hundred and fifty thousand he boasts about. Islands of cultivation in a sea of wilderness, probably.*

The field workers looked up at the sound of hooves; some in rags with iron collars about their necks, some drably but warmly dressed. Loring could see expressions ranging from naked fear to cultivated blankness when they saw the long black banner flapping from its cross-staff. Frenzied cheers burst out, and smiles more artificial than anything he'd seen in Madame Tussaud's as a boy down from Winchester College. As it came closer they dropped to their knees, still cheering, then bent their necks in silence until the standard had gone past; the whole procedure was repeated in reverse as Arminger's party drew away.

I wonder if anyone dares spit or curse when he's out of sight? Loring thought.

Nobody who'd experienced the frightened court at Osborne House in the days of the madness of King Charles could miss the smell of tyranny when it sweated out of the very earth beneath his feet.

No, probably they don't *dare. Charles was never as bad as this.*

Still . . .

And the field layouts are interesting, too. Big fields, but I'd say they're worked in strips, from the markings in the crops. Like the old open-field system, except with clover-lays instead of fallow. Demesne home farm around those fortified manor houses. It's not like England; it's like a dream of medieval Europe in general . . . like something out of a book, in fact.

And twice that morning they passed genuine forts, like some demented modernist version of a medieval castle, done in frowning gray ferroconcrete with gangs of plasterers working to cover them in stucco, and complete to the pointed circular roofs over the towers and the wet moats grown up in waterlilies.

Just then one of the servants, a lean, dark-bearded man in a leather jerkin, rode up and pointed.

"Heron, my lord!"

Arminger looked up, and he grinned as he reined in and unhooded the falcon; the column halted as he did. The bird saw the prey and mantled, feathers splayed and wings spread as it crouched, then launched itself into the air with a sweet chime of bells and a fierce *skreeek!* Loring strained his eyes. The heron was high already, traveling from north to south; it broke even further skyward when it saw the peregrine's upward rush. He'd never practiced falconry himself; foxhunting was his sport, and since the Change he'd taken up pursuing boar. This did have a certain excitement.

"She rings, my lord Protector!" the servant—who must be the falconer—cried. The falcon was circling, rising in an upward gyre. "She's going to get above him! I told you that was the finest peregrine in the mews."

"No, she's way below. Ten rose crowns she's not going to get altitude on him, Herb," Arminger said with a grin.

The falconer paled, beneath a short-trimmed black beard. "My lord, I'm a poor man. I couldn't pay that."

"Well, then, let's bet a kick in the ass against the kitchen girl you've been sniffing around," the lord of Portland said. "She's yours if—"

"She stoops!" someone cried. "The falcon stoops!"

The tiny dots merged. "She binds!" the falconer said. "She's bound, all right!"

The dot grew, until it showed as two birds tumbling around their common center of gravity, the peregrine's talons locked in the heron's body. Then the falcon released its giant white prey and ringed again, climbing for a second strike. It climbed almost to the edge of visibility as the heron flapped heavily for a forested ridge, then stooped again—falling like a guided missile; they could all see a burst of white feathers as it struck, and then killer and victim tumbled together to the ground. The falconer ran out into the pasture to the north of the road, twirling his lure, and returned with the falcon on his wrist, tearing at gobbets of meat he fed it and then submitting meekly to the hood. The big white bird dangled from his free hand by the feet, its wing tips brushing the ground despite his attempts to hold it high.

"Annie's yours," Arminger said. "That's her name, isn't it?"

"Yes, Lord Protector," the falconer said.

"You want to marry her? She's a bondservant, isn't she? Peon?"

"Yes both times, Lord Protector." A flush this time. "And I do want to marry her. She's willing, too."

"Well, I'll pay her debt," Arminger said. "Can't have the household staff marrying beneath themselves. And you get the ten rose crowns, too—call it a wedding gift. Take the heron over to that village; give it to the priest with my compliments."

He waved away the thanks. The rest of the day passed in inconsequential chat—or seemingly so; Loring noted how skillfully Arminger drew out bits of information.

But not as cunning as he thinks he is, he thought. *Or perhaps he was once, but having nobody to tell him no for the last nine years has blunted his edge. His wife's even better; she does it without letting you know what she's about.*

Towards evening they passed through a pleasant small town, tree-shaded streets full of Victorian-era homes; the more pleasant because it lacked most of the usual fringe of ruined strip malls and abandoned, burnt-out subdivisions.

The hills around were dense with tall fir, and the trees within the town included—

"Those are sequoias, are they not?" Alleyne Loring asked, looking up at the thick columns that towered one hundred fifty feet over their heads. "I didn't think they were native to this area. I saw some in California, long ago, in Yosemite." A quirking smile. "I was more interested in Disneyland, at the time."

"They're not native," Sandra Arminger said. "Planted from seed a little over a hundred and twenty years ago."

"There seem to be a good many people about here," Sir Nigel's son observed, his blue eyes alert. The streets didn't exactly bustle, but more than half the homes seemed to be occupied.

"We're resurrecting the Pacific University here," Sandra said. "The library survived, and even some of the staff. Structured on a new basis, of course, with a charter from the Protector. We can't live on pre-Change training forever. We need a supply of younger professionals; engineers, accountants, priests. And to put some cultural polish on the scions of our baronage; you may have noticed that many of them are rather rough diamonds. I do wish you'd consider staying, Sir Nigel—it would raise the whole tone. Ah, here's the turnoff."

Arminger dropped back from Captain Nobbes to ride beside Nigel Loring. "It's an interesting place," he said. "Built by a Montana mining king back in the nineteenth century. Redone as the center of a vineyard estate in the 1980s."

"Pinot noir, I expect?" Sir Nigel said.

His tastes in wine had always been conservative. *Like most other things about me,* he thought ruefully. *But I have heard of Oregon's pinot noirs.* There weren't all that many places which did really well with the great Burgundian red-wine grape.

"Yes, and a pinot gris that went very well with seafood. Also a very nice crisp gewürztraminer, an off-dry Riesling and a *very* nice Müller-Thurgau. I always rather coveted the place, in a daydreaming sort of way, and had it taken in hand when we resettled this area in the fall of the first

Change Year; there are three knight's-fees' worth of land attached to it, plus the woodlot and forest; two large villages and two gristmills, and I built a small castle nearby as a stronghold for the fief—you'll see why I didn't put a wall around the house itself. It's convenient to our new university town, near a working rail line to Portland, and the hunting's spectacular—everything from rabbit to tiger, with the Coast Range close. But it's too far west to be really handy, held by me directly, so I've never been able to spend as much time here as I'd like. A pity; my daughter loves the place."

I doubt that it's all that awkward for you, Loring thought. *It's a day's travel on horseback, and railroads aren't any faster than the horses pulling them these days, but with a handcart you can do forty or fifty miles an hour.* They'd used them in England, in regions with enough people to keep the tracks clear; they were the fastest form of land travel in the Changed world. *You're just making the bribe more credible, my lord Protector. And a succulent one it is; land enough for me, my son, and a good farm for Hordle as well.*

If they were trying to buy him, at least they weren't trying to do it on the cheap. They turned in past ivy-grown stone gateposts, under tall century-old oaks; the evening sun dazzled him for an instant as he looked down a long allée of the great trees, sinking into the heights of the Coast Range. Vineyards lay on left, and a squarish building that was probably the winery; horses grazed to the right; beyond them was plowland and pasture where the sunset cast long shadows. Closer he could see that the center of the estate was a great white-painted house, with two tall pillars supporting the portico.

Not excessively grand by British country-house standards, even with the more recent wings added and the post-Change dependencies and stables. To begin with it was wooden, not stone or brick; but the gardens were very lovely; wildflowers thick in the lawns, and roses as good as any he'd seen back home—back in England.

Oh, he's a clever one, is our lord Protector, Loring thought. *Even on short acquaintance knows what sort of bribe to offer* me. *I wonder if Nobbes has noticed? He's a well-meaning man but not very acute, unless I've wasted six months' observation at close quarters.*

"Very nice," Captain Nobbes said.

"The chef here is marvelous," Sandra Arminger said as servants ran out to take their horses, and the captain of the guard led his men away. "And the wines are very good as well."

As long as there's nothing in the glass but wine, Loring thought. *It would be a fine place to live, Lord Protector, if it weren't in your kingdom.*

Crossing Tavern, Willamette Valley, Oregon
May 13th, 2007 AD—Change Year Nine

"Yeah, he's smart enough to know that you catch more flies with honey than vinegar," Havel said judiciously. "He just can't resist pulling the wings off, though. Two questions, Sir Nigel: Why did you turn him down, and what did he really want?"

Loring stroked his mustache. "My dear young fellow, credit me with some brains at least. 'Out of the frying pan, into the fire' didn't appeal to me! I'd seen entirely too much of how the Lord Protector ran his little kingdom to accept his offer, however tempting. Compared to him, even His Majesty's worst . . . eccentricities . . . were rather mild. And bore hardest on the commanderies and their officers, not ordinary people. He never tried to clap ballygreat iron dog collars on the commons."

John Hordle looked to where his longbow rested in a corner. "Charlie may live to regret making everyone keep a bow and practice with it, sir," he said. "If he ever did incline that way, that is." Aylward smiled grimly and nodded.

Loring went on, catching the ex-SAS man's eye: "As to why, I think it was snobbery. His barons and knights are, as his wife said, something of a bunch of rough diamonds—the reenactors being the best of the bunch, and a minority. He probably wanted a genuine English baronet, however reduced in circumstances, as a . . . trophy, as it were."

I know that look, Aylward thought. *It means,* more, later, *and* privately. Aloud, he said, "That's him to the inch, sir."

Something in his voice made several others look at him sharply—Lady Juniper first, then Signe Havel, then her husband. Imperceptible nods went around the table as the leaders agreed.

Juniper Mackenzie's smile was genuine enough when she spoke: "Then perhaps we'd better fill you in on what we did once we were inside the Protector's border."

But her foot kicked Aylward in the ankle, ever so lightly.

CHAPTER SIXTEEN

"This way," the farmer hissed to Juniper.

He was sweating with fear as he led the Mackenzie party down the old private road with woods and scrub close on either hand, and vines twining across the cracked surface. It was an early May dawn, and there was an intense stillness—as if life waited while the gray gloaming faded into light that trickled down through the leaves overhead. The mosquitoes were unfortunately all too active, little itching needles stabbing at the backs of her knees and face and hands as bodies brushed through dew-wet grass and bushes.

They passed the rusting hulk of a car still resting where it had swerved off the road and struck a tree nine years ago, mostly covered in vine and weed; through the dirt-encrusted window Juniper could see there were still some wisps of hair on the skull that rested against the steering wheel within. Then they left the roadway and went more slowly along a faint game trail, through older established woods. In a clearing where sun speared down through the broken canopy a ruffled grouse cock stood on a stump and went *boom*-hoot! as the yellow pouches on either side of his neck swelled and shrank amid the white downy feathers.

The grouse took alarm at the farmer's passage. She hissed impatiently at him; he was hurrying along a familiar way, and even so made more noise in his bib overalls than her clansfolk did with all their gear and weapons. Not that it should matter right now, but there was the principle of the thing. The gray look to his skin as he slowed down made her feel briefly ashamed; he was risking his family and home, not just his life.

"Should be around here I left 'em . . ." he whispered, as they came near the eastern edge of this patch of woods.

A bit of branch struck him on the head, and he started violently, leveling the spear he carried and glaring all around him. Juniper smiled reassuringly and pointed up.

The tree overhead was a hundred-foot Douglas fir. The farmer stared into the branches, and still started again when a rope uncoiled from one of them; the figures in their war cloaks hugging the trunk above were hard enough to notice even if you knew where to look. Astrid and Eilir and Sam Aylward came sliding down it; the young women jumped free at head-height and landed lightly as cats, grinning silently. Her First Armsman waited until his boot soles were a foot from the ground before dropping, dusting his palms and walking over to her.

"Just as this gentleman said, Lady," he reported quietly. "The railroad's in use—wear keeping the steel bright, ox- and horse-droppings. Handcar patrol along at the intervals he mentioned, too."

"And the local coven vouches for him and his friends," Astrid pointed out.

She was eager to the point of quivering slightly; this was exactly the sort of trip around Robin Hood's barn that she gloried in. Eilir leaned on her bow and shrugged slightly with a smile. Her expression spoke louder than words, or Sign: *Your call, Splendiferously Supreme Clan Chieftainly Mom-person.*

Juniper looked at the farmer again. He was in his late thirties, probably, or possibly half a decade older; people's looks often aged faster when they got into that range nowadays. He *didn't* look particularly starved or harried— nothing like the refugee couples they'd rescued back around Ostara. Shaggy with brown beard and hair long except for the bald patch on top, and weathered and worn like any outdoor worker, but well fed and shod. He had the spear, too, and a long hunting knife.

"You're a free tenant, and better off than most here in the Protector's lands," she said softly, catching his eye with hers and holding it. "Is it worth the risk to you and your kin, and the loss of all you own? Do you have a particular grudge against Lord Molalla?"

"Yeah," he said, squaring his shoulders and licking his lips. "Sitting in that goddamned concrete castle and telling me what to do and taking a quarter of what I grow! Making me take off my goddamned hat and bow when he rides by! So I'm treated like a better grade of dirt than the poor bastards who ended up as bond tenants or peons. Great! I remember what things were like before the Change; I was born a free man and an American citizen, by God. We're not starving anymore. Nobody would be going hungry, if those bloodsuckers would leave us alone. It's just—"

He lifted the short spear. It was a good enough weapon to frighten off wild dogs; against mail-clad men-at-arms on armored horses it might as well have been a breadstick. The rest of his weaponry was a knife and a pre-Change camper's hatchet.

Juniper smiled sadly. *And it's not surprising that you're the leader in this. It's the man who has a little who wants more, not the starveling with nothing but an empty belly. Also things haven't quite had time to settle down and set hard yet. A generation or two, and our friend's grandchildren here might be fighting for the baron, not against him.*

Aloud she went on: "Well, most places to the south do better than Arminger, sure. And we'll help you; I just wanted to be certain you all knew what you were getting into."

"We do," he said. "And we've heard about what you folks did to the east last week. We're willing to take a chance."

"Go then," she said. "Have your people ready to join in. But be quick. Joanne, Liam, Ibar, go along. You know the signals. And *chomh glic ie sionnach.*"

The young Mackenzies grinned silently at the play on words; they all had wisps of red fur attached to the brooches that pinned their plaids at the shoulder: *Clever as a fox* was the motto of their sept, and she knew they didn't need anything more explicit to make them alert for betrayal. They nodded, touched their bows to their helmet brims and trotted along with the local farmer to make sure he got back to his gathered friends; they would also ensure he didn't survive any treachery. The locals knew where the Mackenzies were, but only in the most general sense. She didn't doubt their hearts were in the right place, but she also didn't doubt that they'd hold back until the Clan's warriors had shown what they could do, and there might be an informer . . .

Juniper turned back to the brushy edge of the woodlot, going the last ten yards on her belly through the rank new spring growth. The crushed stems smelled musky-green as she carefully parted a path for sight with the horn tip of her bow—looking through cover rather than over it was always a good idea, whether you were sneaking up on an enemy or out to watch a mother fox and her cubs at play. The low swale ahead was as the locals had described it: open and uncultivated, shrubby and shabby but not too badly overgrown. The ground was common pasture, for the Baron's stock and those of his town of Molalla a little to the south. The railway ran through it from southeast to northwest, crossing Milk Creek just a hundred yards to her right, on the south; usually a trickle, but now better than waist-deep with spring. At their back floodplain woods ran far to the northwest, with the Molalla River a third of a mile away threading through them, deeper and broader than the creek. On the other side of the open ground and the old Canby-Mulino road were forested hills, two hundred feet or better above the plain.

Six pair of field glasses studied the ground, and threescore sets of keen eyes. Sam nodded to her, and she sighed silently and gave the order. Aylward took the party to the bridge himself; there was nobody else in the clan he trusted to handle the thermite properly. Juniper led six to the rail line several hundred yards farther north. As they jogged across grass rough-cropped by sheep and cattle her eyes went north and east; pillars of smoke stood there, threadthin in the distance. Smoke by day, fire by night . . .

And good Mackenzies should stay out of sight, she told herself with mordant humor. *They know we're out, but they've no idea where, not yet. When they learn, it will be very unpleasant.*

Rowan did the honors when they reached the track; he was a smith, after all. "Lucky this isn't continuous welded rail," he said, fitting a long wrench to the bolts where one rail joined the next. "That would be a real problem . . . hey, a little of that WD-40, would you?"

Old-fashioned rail like this was in forty-yard lengths, joined by butting up the sections against each other and fastening them with a fishplate bolted home on each; that was what made the *clackety-clack* as a train went over them— or had made it, when there were locomotives. There was still a bright strip atop these rails, but rust elsewhere, and a thick scatter of dung showed what the motive power was nowadays. Rowan strained at the five-foot handle of the wrench he'd forged and fitted and tested on rail closer to home, long muscles bulging in his bare arms below the short chain-mail sleeves of his arming doublet.

"Goibniu, Lord of *Iron!*" he wheezed when the first came free. Then he looked at the others: "All right, get those spikes pulled and the rail loose in the chairs, while I do this!" he said sharply.

"Channeling the Dread Lord again, Roe?" Sanjay Barstow grumbled, but they obeyed.

All that took muscle and skills she lacked. Juniper occupied herself instead with looking around, making sure nobody else was visible along the edge of the woods to either side—and taking a last sight and smell and taste of the sweet wild world, in case she passed over this day. When the clanking, clattering, cursing work was done—if the rails had had lives to blast, they'd have been in very bad trouble, and so would the ill-wishers—and the bolts and spikes and keys replaced with replicas of wood and wax, she spoke.

"Pick your spot. We're supposed to have another hour, but that's only a guess."

Sam had selected well. Bushes and patches of tall grass attracted them like moth to a flame; quick work with knives and nimble fingers freshened and thickened the twigs and grass in the loops of their war cloaks to match the meadow. Rowan helped her, despite her grumbling that she'd been woods wise before the Change came.

"Before you were *born*, sure," she went on.

"But you weren't wearing a war cloak then, Lady," he said, infuriatingly reasonable.

"Neither were you. Sam taught us, and I met *him* before you did, too, so there," she grumbled.

"Crawl in under here," he went on.

And is it more annoying to be treated like the Goddess, or like a baby? Juniper thought, obeying.

The cloak covered her like a tent, and like a tent it quickly grew stuffy in the bright daylight. Juniper made her breathing slow, not withdrawing from herself but instead concentrating on every sensation, every itch and tickle and buzz of insect, until she was one with everything about her . . . and unconscious of self, the self that worried and fretted and feared for Eilir and her people, and dreaded having to tell parents why their sons or daughters weren't coming home.

Clickity-clack . . . clickity-clack . . .

Slowly, slowly, her head turned within the hood. Her eyes blinked, bringing her back to full awareness; pupils flared and her nostrils spread to take in a sudden deep breath, but the rest of her was motionless. Motion drew her vision southwestward.

The railcar was silent save for the hum of wheels on steel, the louder clatter as it passed the joins in the rails, and the flutter of the two flags on poles at the prow, Arminger's red cat-pupiled eye on black, and the local baron's lion-and-spear. There was no engine, of course, unless you counted the four men who pumped either end of the big pivoted lever in its center. They were ragged but no more than wiry-gaunt, and not chained to the wooden handles they swung up and down with the regularity of machines, driving through gears to power the wheels beneath. That surprised her a little; it was work that by Protectorate standards should be done by peons—slaves for all practical purposes. Before them a waist-high wooden barricade hid the chair of the man-at-arms who commanded the little vehicle; the plume on his conical Norman helmet fluttered in the rapid passage of the railcar, forty miles an hour and swifter than anything else on land these days. He rested casually, one boot up on the railing, and a hand on that knee holding a pair of binoculars. At the rear four crossbowmen stood, facing out on either side with their weapons in their hands.

I bind you, she thought. *I bind your eyes, your ears, your nostrils. See not, hear not, smell not; by Herne the Wild Hunter, so mote it be!*

The massed wills of every Mackenzie must be beating on the railcar's crew. The field craft that the First Armsman had spent the last decade hammering into them didn't hurt either, of course, or the fact that this select band were all good hunters used to silent waiting.

A moment, then another . . . and the knight's eyes went wide, and he yelled and reached for the brake lever.

That was too late for the fast-moving weight of metal and wood, though the brakes locked and squealed with an ear-piercing shriek and sparks poured from them in a red-gold roostertail torrent. The railcar slid onto the section of rail that had been loosened, onto metal held only by stubs of punkwood and wax painted to resemble steel. The long rails slewed sideways and the railcar leapt free, plowing into the roadbed with a shower of gravel and a chorus of screams.

"Now!" she said, rising.

Six Mackenzies sprang to their feet, tossing aside the camouflage cloaks. The railcar hadn't gone over, quite, but it lay steeply canted with the wheels on one side digging deeply into the dirt of the embankment. The knight had been thrown free and had the wind knocked out of him; he crawled and then began to rise, propping himself up with the lower point of his shield and pushing at the helmet that had slewed half around on his head. The crossbowmen all landed together in a heap in their enclosure, a heap that cursed and heaved as they tried to push each other off and regain their feet. One of the laborers on the pump handles of the railcar screamed as he was flung down and landed on some metal fitting with the point of his shoulder, breaking bone from the volume of sound he made. The others gasped and crouched and glared.

"Throw down!" Juniper shouted, drawing her bow. *"Throw down, now, or you die!"* She was close enough to see the knight's eyes narrow as he cast off shock.

Damn, she thought, as he ripped out his sword and charged.

The range was too close for comfort, and the big shield covered the man from nose to knee, held expertly; her arrow punched through the lion-with-spear painted on the sheet-metal surface and into the plywood with a vicious *crack.* The man checked half a step at the solid slamming impact but came on in his crabwise crouching run.

"Haro! Haro for Molalla!" he shouted, the long glitter of his sword going up for a looping cut. *"Haro! Portland!"*

"Your choice," Juniper said, skipping backward as her right hand reached over her shoulder.

Crack!

That was Cynthia Carson's bow; the bodkin punched through the tough plywood and through the vambrace on the knight's forearm beneath. He screamed as steel and cedarwood cracked bone, and threw out his sword as he twisted to keep balance.

Crack! Rowan's hundred-thirty-pound stave slammed a shaft right through the shield and into the knight's shoulder.

That gave Juniper and four others a shot at the gray chain mail covering his torso. The *snapsnapsnapsnapsnap* of their bowstrings striking their bracers sounded within a second of each other, fractionally before the ugly muffled punching thumps of impact and the low musical *thunk!* of the arrowheads' brutal passage through the strong riveted steel links of the ring mail. Two sank to the fletchings— light-gray goose and Sanjay Barstow's gaudy peacock feathers—and another went into his breastbone and stood there quivering until his knees gave way an instant later.

Sweet Mother-of-All, Juniper thought as the man crumpled, going on hands and knees and coughing out blood and bits of lung. You never got used to it . . . *Dread Lord, lead him home to the Summerlands.* Rowan's ax swung up and then down, in what might be mercy, before he cleaned it on the dead man's cloak and slid it back in the loops across his back.

She turned with a question on her lips. It died unasked as she saw Cynthia Carson lean over the railing at the rear of the car and make two careful thrusts with her short sword; that settled what had happened to the crossbow-men.

Or at least I don't get used to it, she thought, and nodded to Rowan.

"Let's get going!" he said.

Kevin Lewis of the Dunedain was already on the railcar, jabbing a hypodermic into the thigh of the man who rolled moaning on its floor. "Broken collarbone and socket," he said shortly, then cursed as Rowan rocked the vehicle. "Brigid leave just when you need Her, Rowan Mackenzie! Careful! I have to get him down!"

Rowan grumbled but helped lift the wounded man down. Kevin swore again at his haste and laid his patient hastily on the ground; the man's companions followed, staring wide-eyed at the kilted warriors and in awestruck fear at Juniper herself.

"Later, unless he's going to die," Rowan said impatiently to the Rangers' medico.

"Can we lift this without tackle?" Daniel Barstow said dubiously, kicking at the railcar. It rocked slightly under his boot, with a clatter and crunch.

"It's no heavier than a compact, from the report and the look of it," Juniper said. That comparison meant nothing to the younger Mackenzies, and she saw the puzzlement in their eyes. She corrected himself: "Than a draft horse, or a twenty-foot wall log."

"We can do it," Rowan said confidently.

The big blacksmith spat on his hands and reached under the prow of the vehicle for the forward frame. Everyone else crouched and put their shoulders to the sides of the railcar and prepared to lift and shove. Juniper did herself; she was strong for her size, and every bit counted when the twelve had to shift a hundred pounds each.

"And one . . . and two . . . and *three.*"

With a unified grunt they stood, and the twelve hundred pounds of wood and metal came with them.

"Ready . . . *step*," Juniper said, feeling her thighs trembling with the strain, grunting each time a foot came down. *Don't let this come down on anyone's instep. Feel for the footing.* "Step . . . step . . . step . . ."

Wheezing, gasping, they paced forward and lowered the railcar onto the next section of track. One snatched his boot free from under a wheel at the last second, and went white, but that and a few splinters and a little torn skin on some palms were the only injuries; it helped that they all had hands toughened by years of hard labor. Juniper bent to tear a clump of grass free and use it to scrub with a grimace of distaste at the left shoulder of her brigandine, where blood leaking through the floorboards had stained it.

"See who can fit into those mail shirts," she said quickly.

One of the ragged laborers came up. "Ma'am—" he began.

"That's Lady Juniper, the Mackenzie," Rowan said sharply.

Juniper made an impatient *not now* gesture; Rowan had always been a lot more protective of her titles and dignity than she was.

"Ah, Lady, ma'am—you need to know the signals the scout car was using? 'Cause me and Jerry and Luke, we know 'em pretty good. We've been doing this for a year now, since the cow died and Dad couldn't . . . well, for a year now."

"Lady Juniper's luck!" someone muttered. Juniper began to smile.

Rowan grinned too. "All right, let's get those rails looking good again," he said. "Hup, hup!"

"Hup yours, Row," Sanjay said, as he bent to help lift the length of steel rail back into its chairs. He was smiling himself.

Crossing Tavern, Willamette Valley, Oregon
May 13th, 2007 AD—Change Year Nine

Well, that's an incomplete report if I ever heard one, Mike Havel thought. *Something important here, though . . .*

He made a small sign with his hand, saw Hutton's nod.

"And they fell into it, neat as neat could be," Juniper finished, to general applause.

Sir Nigel inclined his head. "Very smoothly planned and carried out, Lady Juniper," he said sincerely.

"Oh, Juniper or Juney," she replied, with an urchin grin. "If you only knew how tired I get of titles!"

"Juniper, then, if you'll call me Nigel." His smile was genuine too. "That sort of guerrilla operation is more difficult to bring off, since the Change."

"So Sam tells me," Juniper said, resting a hand for a moment on the stocky bowman's shoulder. "If I know anything about fighting, I learned it from him."

"You couldn't wish for a better teacher," the baronet said, and smiled back. "But it does show considerable native wit to learn so well."

"Figure I'll turn in," Will Hutton said with a yawn. "We can fill in the rest tomorrow."

Good old Will, Havel thought. *Always picks up on what's needed. And Juney can fib with the best of them. Comes from all that storytelling, I suppose. Sir Nigel seems to take a hint well, too.*

The Crossing Tavern's staff bustled in and cleared the plates. When they left, Havel and Signe confronted Juniper and Sam Aylward across the table; the fire burned low, and the candles as well, scenting the room with the smells of fir-sap and beeswax, tinting the rug-hangings on the wall with gleams of color that were all shades of red.

"So, what really happened?" Signe said; her voice wasn't exactly cold, but it was curiously flat.

"Pretty much what I said," Juniper replied. "It's what happened next that needs to be private, for now, until we can all figure out what to do about it."

Barony of Molalla, Willamette Valley, Oregon
May 10th, 2007 AD—Change Year Nine

I feel completely absurd, Juniper thought. *It would be too bad entirely to die looking like someone eight years old dressed up in her parents' clothes.*

The knight's helmet was bad enough; it had to be padded with a pair of spare kneesocks so that it wouldn't fall down to the level of her upper lip. Wrapping up in the cloak and sitting on a haversack to look taller . . .

Three of the original engine-team and a volunteer stood at the levers; four Mackenzies of suitable size had donned the gear of the dead crossbowmen. It all looked fairly convincing, unless you got close enough to see faces . . . or smell the sewer-and-slaughterhouse stinks of violent death.

"Here they come," one of the clansfolk said.

The knight's seat had turned out to be a swivel, a padded luxury from some office. Juniper used it to turn and look past the lever-pump and over the south-facing rear of the railcar, as her clansmen raised two paddles like oversized Ping-Pong rackets and began using them to semaphore a message: *All clear four miles up the road,* in this case. Normal procedure was for the railcar to dart ahead and then back, from what they'd been able to gather.

The train approached, at a plodding walking pace—the Hereford and Angus steers weren't going to hurry for anyone. There were six rail wagons in the train, each about forty feet long and pulled by eight hitch of oxen. The first held a dozen crossbowmen, eight heavy infantry carrying long spears, a man-at-arms and a tall flag with Baron Molalla's standard; the next four were piled high with cargo under lashed tarpaulins. The last was a covered traveling carriage; part of the roof was a flat space with deck chairs and a table with an umbrella in its center. It was pulled by six big black horses, which was pure swank unless they planned on getting ahead of the freight wagons later, or switching the team around and heading back this way.

The locals said five wagons were normal, not six. Some-

thing unexpected, and in a fight, unexpected *usually means* bad.

There were more horsemen than they'd expected too, walking their mounts beside the slow-moving train, and there were other saddled mounts trailing along behind the rail carriage on a leading line, saddled but with their stirrups looped up.

Call it off? she thought. They could. Just give the signal and streak ahead . . . *No. I've promised that farmer and his friends.* You piled up a debt with Fate when you made a promise, and if you refused to pay when it was due, it was invariably collected later—usually at the worst possible time. *We go ahead.*

Juniper raised her hand and waved; the train would think it a friendly gesture, and Sam would know it for the go-ahead. The passenger carriage rumbled over the little bridge that crossed Milk Creek.

Or the Rubicon, she thought, her heart thudding, then slowing as she made herself breathe steadily as the train came on at the immemorial pace of the ox. *Let them come on, let them get well past, your trusty railcar scouts have checked all this ground for you . . .*

A sound came from the bridge then, a giant's hissing roar. Thermite didn't work quite the way it had before the Change, but it still got very, very hot—more than hot enough to turn the wooden trestle of the bridge into an instant inferno of black smoke and licking yellow flame. Even a few of the oxen looked over their shoulders in surprise at the noise and stink; the men reacted like a kicked-in ant's nest. The frantic milling went on for only seconds before a trumpet blatted; the spearmen hopped down from the leading wagon and trotted towards the rear, forming up before a horseman who waved them on ahead.

The man-at-arms in the front wagon was signaling again, and Daniel replied with more soothing lies. Men boiled out of the passenger wagon at the rear of the train, some of them still helping each other on with their war harness, and began mounting the horses on the leading line. One, two, three . . . five lances. Two more accoutered like men-at-arms, though there was something odd about them.

Uh-oh, she said, carefully not aloud. Everyone knew what *uh-oh* meant; it meant *we screwed up.*

"Best we depart," she said.

More shouts from the bridge; the spearmen had gotten to within twenty yards before a dozen Mackenzie archers hiding in the stream bed came to their feet, standing with only their heads and chests exposed and drawing to the ear. One of them was Sam Aylward. The seven spearmen were five when they'd backed out of range despite their full armor, crouching behind shields that bristled like porcupines, and several of them were wounded.

Juniper's party hopped down from the light railcar, set their shoulders to it . . .

"Heave!"

It went over with a crash, and they dashed for the woods three hundred yards westward. She ran silently, concentrating on her breathing and hoping the men who'd been on the levers could keep up—they had arms and shoulders that looked like sets of steel cable, but they hadn't been getting much in the way of work with their feet and legs, nor been overly well fed. The whoops and cries of *Haro!* from the horsemen proved to be a remarkably good incentive, and they went with the kilted clansmen step for step.

"We're not going to make it to the woods!" Rowan called, looking over his shoulder. "They'll be on us a hundred and fifty yards out!"

Juniper made a wordless but heartfelt inward cry for help as she estimated distances. All of them knew that to show your back to a lancer was death—the problem was that with the numbers nearly even, facing them on open grassland was nearly as bad.

"Get ready to turn on them!" she called. "Not you men, you're unarmed—you keep on for the woods. *Now!*"

She stopped and wheeled. The enemy were coming on in a thunder-roll of hooves, traveling many times faster than a human could run—it was like being chased down by dirt bikes. Five of them in front, lances out ahead of hooves that hammered divots of brown dirt into the air, horse heads with spiked steel chamfrons on their faces and steel peytrals on their chests. The two behind were in knights' hauberks and had shields, but they didn't carry lances, and their horses were different—small and showy and slender-limbed, not the big bruiser warmbloods knights rode . . .

The lances came down with a ripple, eleven feet with the twelve-inch heads included, the honed metal of point and edge glinting in the bright spring sunlight. Devices showed on the kite-shaped shields, old Society heraldry mixed with chop-shop Jesuses and shock-rock album-cover art; even then she was a little surprised to see they were all knights with their own blazons, not just men-at-arms. The faces of the men were hidden save for the eyes, shields up and broad splayed nasals covering most of what showed above that.

Get them focused on us, she thought tautly. *Then—* "Spread!"

The Mackenzies kept running, but to either side, spreading out with yards between each of them. A solid mass of spears or bills or pikes could stop mounted knights—as long as it was very solid, shoulder to shoulder and ranked deep, a bristling wall of points. Most of the Clan warriors here didn't have spears, and there weren't enough of them to make a spear wall anyway—or to drown the charge with sky-darkening arrow storm. There were other ways, though, and this was a picked band of the Clan's best . . .

Except for middle-aged me! went through her. *Well, I'm in 'late youth' at least—*

The lancers hesitated slightly, a fractional check in their boot-to-boot charge as the target spread out to either side. Bows snapped, and arrows began to flicker out towards them; they booted their horses back into a full hard gallop to get across the killing ground as fast as possible, spreading out slightly themselves as they picked targets of their own. She could feel the impact of the hooves through the soles of her feet, making the turf quiver, like the shiver of fear traveling up your legs and into your gut.

One had a sword-wielding zombie painted on his shield with skin tunneled by mocking worms; he headed for her. Her first arrow stuck quivering in the zombie's eye. She shot again, but the peytral on the horse's breast shed it with a bang and a spark of steel on steel. Ten seconds for a galloping horse to cross a hundred yards; she tried to draw again as the lance point drove for her chest . . .

Snapsnap.

An arrow from another bow sank to the feathers in the horse's chest through the triangular protective plate—fletched with peacock feathers, Sanjay Barstow's. Another crunched into the horse's fetlock. The beast went over as if its legs had been cut from under it, with a scream piteously loud. The rider tried to curl himself up as he flew out of the high-cantled saddle, but the loose shield strap that went around his neck made it impossible; the point of the shield struck the ground first, the strap broke and sent it bouncing away and then the knight himself hit in an ungainly sprawl. He staggered half erect as he tried to lever himself up not ten paces from her.

The brown glaring face showed plain at that distance, wet with sweat and with blood pouring from his nose above bared white teeth; a young face with only a wisp of black beard, grown from child to man since the Change.

Snap.

This time her arrow had its way with the armor, through the links on the collar that warded his neck and out the other side. He screamed in a spray of blood, falling on his back and arching in dying reflex as his mail-gloved hands scrambled at the cedarwood transfixing his throat.

Juniper wheeled as the arrow released, knowing where it would strike with the certainty a good shot always brought. That let her see Sanjay Barstow dodge a little too slowly, and the lancehead move with cruel precision to compensate. There was a massive dull *thud* as it drove into the young man's chest, and his whole body flexed and snapped like a whip, face fluid with shock. The lance cracked across as it speared through his breastbone, through the mail shirt and out his back in a fan of blood, and the impact drove the Protectorate knight back against the high cantle of the saddle that cradled his hips. His horse checked, almost staggering for two paces as it recovered its balance.

Aoife Barstow was three yards away. She gave an eerie wail as she saw her foster brother die, and *leapt.* Even then Juniper's eyes went a little wide as she landed crouching, grabbed the knight's stirrup leather, and let the savage jerk of the horse's speed add to her next jump. The young woman flowed upward, pivoting as she rose, the kilt falling back from her long slender legs as her booted heels drove into the side of the rider's head. The knight tried to club at her with the stump of the broken lance, but that and the shield and the sudden violent shying of his horse hampered him; all three went over sideways in a tangle of limbs and screams and the endless banshee shrieking of the Mackenzie woman.

Aoife landed uppermost, riding the tangle down as fourteen hundred pounds of horseflesh and gear crashed across the knight's leg and ground it into the dirt. He lost all interest in his assailant as bone and flesh pulped inside his armor and the horse thrashed in convulsions. The short sword flashed as she grabbed the nasal of his helmet and used it to lever his head back for a slash across the throat. Then she drove the blade down with short chopping strokes. As the three surviving knights reined in and around—you couldn't stop nearly a ton of armor and horseflesh quickly—she rose with the dripping head dangling by its hair in one hand and red sword gripped in the other. She waved both aloft, the red-and-white wolf mouth painted on her skin no more grisly than the contorted shrieking face beneath.

That checked even hardy fighting-men for an instant. Long enough to hide what poured out of the woods behind them . . .

"Down!" Juniper shouted, with all the power of her lungs.

Aoife Barstow ignored her, lost in an ecstasy of fury, the embrace of something beyond men and men's concerns. Her brother tackled her behind the knees, rolling away instantly to dodge the reflexive chop of her sword. Juniper saw it out of the corner of her eye. Most of her attention was on the twoscore Mackenzies dashing forward out of their hiding place in the brushwood at the forest's edge, Eilir and Astrid and the Clan's green-and-silver banner at their head. They halted as they saw Juniper and the others take cover, and the bows came up. . . .

Yikes! Juniper thought.

Any haven in a storm; she rolled and grabbed at the shield of the knight she'd killed, pulling it over her and curling herself into as tight a ball as she could. She squeezed her eyes shut as well; there was nobody she had to show brave for right here and now, and at least she wouldn't have to see death coming if someone overshot. Which was more than likely, with forty archers dropping shafts at an area target a hundred and fifty yards away from their position.

A rising whistle split the air, and another, and another. Someone *did* overshoot, and a long arrow fletched with gray-goose feathers went *shhhunk!* into the ground ten feet away. Underneath the hiss of cloven air came screams of men and horses, and a sound like a brief spate of hail on the shakes of a roof. Juniper threw aside the shield and rose; the knights were a kicking mass of flesh that bristled with shafts. The oncoming Mackenzies flowed over them; dirks flashed in mercy-strokes for man and beast.

Another shout brought her head around. The two riders who'd been behind the knights had drawn their swords and were charging themselves, their whoops oddly shrill. They were in man-at-arms' armor, but . . .

Those horses are lovely, but they're thirteen hands at most, hardly more than ponies for size. One's Arab, the other's an Appaloosa, and even so the riders look too small—

"Rowan!" she called, a prickle at the back of her mind prompting her. "Alive, if you can! I don't think those are fighting men at all! They're kids!"

He shrugged and nodded, thrusting his bow through the loops, drawing his battle-ax from the set on the other side of his quiver and flicking the leather guard off the edge with a quick snap of his wrists. The first rider had Baron Molalla's blazon, unquartered; he leaned forward with his sword point presented as his horse galloped. Rowan crouched slightly, then let one knee relax as the horse thundered down on him. That pushed him to the side with a swooping gracefulness; he turned it into a whirl like a hammer thrower at the Beltane games, with his long arms

out and the four-foot shaft of his ax at the end of them. The
slender horse screamed as the broad cutting edge flashed
through its hamstring with no more effort than a kitchen
knife jointing a chicken, and the beast went over and cast
its rider free. The horse thrashed, ululating its pain; Rowan
frowned and approached it carefully, murmuring an apology as he swung the ax twice—once with the hammer side,
to stun, and then with the blade to kill.

The armored rider had managed to shed his shield and
land well, but he had only begun to rise when Rowan
kicked his arms out from under him and planted a boot between his shoulder blades.

"Naughty!" the big blacksmith said, leaning his ax down
to pin the other's sword and watching with mild curiosity
as his sister faced the other horseman.

She knelt, buckler in her left hand, the other holding her
battle spear—but parallel to the ground, the butt braced
under the instep of her right foot, the head only a few
inches from the ground and hidden in the long grass. Even
if the rider was a child, the mount was far too much weight
in rapid motion to take lightly.

Horses were deeply stupid compared to anything except
sheep, but they had a lively sense of self-preservation and
save in a blind panic would not run onto a point. They
swerved at the last moment instead, swerved slightly if
well-trained, and then a mounted swordsman could strike
from above, inside the longer weapon's reach; that was why
it took a whole hedge of polearms to stop cavalry.

But a horse would not shy from a spearpoint it couldn't
see coming. That was where the stupidity came in handy if
you didn't have a few dozen friends on either side.

Cynthia jerked the ashwood spear haft up with savage
precision, presenting the point at breast-height when the
lovely little Appaloosa was only two strides away. The
sharp foot-long blade knifed into its chest, the weight driving the butt deep into the dirt and slewing sideways as it
made a frantic last-second attempt to dodge with the steel
already in it. That left the strong wood braced between the
immovable earth and the nearly irresistible weight that
even a modestly sized horse galloping full-tilt represented.

It was two feet deep in the bone and gristle of the horse's brisket, and the strain was immense. The snap of its cracking was like nothing Juniper had heard since the Change, ear-hurting loud. The four-foot stub of the shaft blurred sideways and struck Cynthia in the side of her brigandine, knocking her half a dozen paces through the air to sprawl groaning. The horse hit the ground limp, its neck cracking as it tumbled head over heels. The slim rider landed rolling as well, lying stunned where his shield twisted horizontally across him and blocked any more movement, but it had been very creditable to get out of the stirrups and avoid the horse's body.

She moved over to him when a glance showed Cynthia conscious, and paused beside the wounded horse. The legs weren't moving but it still breathed, chest going like a bellows; frothy blood poured out of the nostrils and the great wound in its chest, and the big dark eyes swiveled to look at her, pleading with her to make it better.

Juniper drew her dirk. "Forgive me, beautiful sister," she said quietly, going down on one knee. "Forgive humankind for making you party to our quarrels. All I can give you is a swift end to pain. Dread Lord, take her home to the sweet meadows of the Summerlands. Epona, Lady of the Horses, let her run free with the living wind."

As she spoke she pulled a cloth free from her belt pouch and threw it over the mare's eyes so that she couldn't see the sharp steel, then pressed the point home and twisted expertly. The horse gave a long shuddering twitch, kicked and went limp.

Juniper wiped the blade clean on the mane as she stood. The main body of the wagon train was under control too—a swarm of figures moved over it. An unwilling smile tugged at her mouth despite grief and grimness; that one standing on a tarpaulin-load and kicking someone off it with a tremendous swing of his boot was Sam Aylward, up there with his archers, knocking some order into the farmers who'd swarmed down from the hills while everyone's attention was firmly elsewhere.

Thank you, Horned Lord, she thought; she'd always considered Sam to be a personal gift of Cernunnos.

She turned back to the task at hand. The fallen rider's shield was the first thing wrong. She could read Protectorate heraldry well and was familiar with all the major blazons; it was based on the Society's system anyway, and she'd learned that busking at fairs and tournaments before the Change. This was simply the Protector's, the red cat-pupiled eye on black, with a baton of cadency across it. Cynthia staggered up clutching herself while Juniper toed it aside; the neck loop had broken, the strong leather snapped by the torquing action of the fall. The short slim figure beneath rolled onto its back, fumbling a hand at the empty sword sheath. The helmet was one of the newer model, with a nasal bar flared so broadly at the base that it was nearly a mask covering the lower face. And the armor was of the best, links black-enameled and fine enough that the mail flowed like silk; the sword belt had gold and niello plaques.

"What have we . . . got here?" Cynthia croaked. She was holding herself, arms crossed across her gut. "Just a few ribs sprung, Lady."

"I don't know what we've got," Juniper said. *But I do have a horrible suspicion—who even among Arminger's barons could afford to refit a child in costly first-class armor every six months—*

Greenish-brown eyes blinked open, aware enough to glare at her on either side of the nasal bar. Then they went wide and hands scrabbled at the helmet; half a cupful of yellow bile spewed out on the grass near her boot. To be expected after a wacking great thump on the head like that, and lost amid the savage stinks of battle.

"That's a girl!" Cynthia said.

"Indeed it is," Juniper said wonderingly. "And a young one."

There weren't more than a couple of dozen female knights or squires in the Protectorate, although they hadn't been all that uncommon in the Society; Arminger wasn't what you would call an equal-opportunity employer, and neither were the gangers and thugs who'd made up many of his initial followers. This one couldn't be more than ten. The girl scrubbed her gauntlet's leather palm across her mouth and spat, glaring at Juniper again. Greenish eyes, reddish brown hair, a foxy freckled face . . .

Rowan came up, dragging the other youngster; he was about the same age, but thicker-built and with a coffee-and-cream complexion.

"This one's Baron Molalla's son, believe it or not," he said. "Young Chaka. Now isn't that going to be interesting!"

"Not half so much as this," Juniper said. "Mackenzies, meet Princess Mathilda . . . Mathilda Arminger, the Lord Protector's only child."

CHAPTER SEVENTEEN

Crossing Tavern, Willamette Valley, Oregon
May 13th, 2007 AD—Change Year Nine

"Jesus!" Mike Havel said, spraying a few crumbs from the cookie he was nibbling.

Signe thumped him on the back as he coughed. "Drink some water, darling."

"Never touch the stuff," he said, but obeyed. His mind was racing as he stared at Juniper's cat-ate-canary grin and Sam Aylward's raised eyebrow: *That surprised you just a bit, dinnit?*

"Where *is* she? Where did you put them?"

"Well . . ."

Barony of Molalla, Willamette Valley, Oregon
May 10th, 2007 AD—Change Year Nine

Aoifo and Daniel Barstow knelt on either side of their brother Sanjay, their wails rising to keening shrieks and dying away again in a saw-edged rhythm as they rocked back and forth. Juniper winced at the raw grief of it, even faint with distance, and they weren't the only Mackenzies grieving a friend or loved one. She wasn't looking forward to telling Judy about Sanjay's death, either, and she'd liked the young man herself; he'd been bright and sweet-natured and brave, and there was a girl . . . she'd expected to see them handfasted come Lughnassadh.

But on the whole . . .

"Not 'alf bad, if I say so meself," Sam Aylward said, looking down from the rooftop platform of the passenger carriage. "Of course, it's easy to shine when you take the other side by surprise and outnumber them eight to one, but this sort o' ambush and guerrilla work is a lot harder than it was before the Change. Great force multipliers, explosives and automatic weapons were. Cuts down on the advantage of surprise when you have to run up to a bloke to bash 'im, and do it one head at a time."

About a hundred of the local farmers had turned out to help; twice that, with their families. The ones who were staying had already departed. They carried plundered weapons and war harness to hide carefully in hollow trees and bury under convenient rocks, along with the bowstaves and arrowheads the Mackenzies had brought and a good bit of the taxes-in-kind that had gone into the train's cargo. Practice in stolen hours and lonely places wouldn't turn them into expert archers, or men-at-arms either for that matter, but it would be a great deal better than nothing. The rest were packing loads for themselves and the captured horses from the cargo of the wagon train; that was food, mostly, in the form of double-baked hardtack biscuit, smoked sausage, jerked beef, bacon and hams, along with sacks of beans and dried fruit and desiccated vegetables. Rowan still stood near the smashed-in barrels of liquor, wine and brandy, beer and whiskey. That hadn't made him popular, but she wasn't going to add drunkenness to the difficulties of getting the unorganized locals moving in the right direction.

Some locals stacked railway ties crisscross in a long baulk of creosoted timber, ten feet high, that would serve as a funeral pyre for the Mackenzie dead, and serve the double purpose of wrecking the rails beyond repair as they softened and bent in the heat.

"Field rations," Juniper said, watching a ragged bond tenant stuff pieces of tough salty ham into his mouth as he worked; his jaws moved with the mechanical persistence of a water mill. "And headed for the Protector's main stores in Portland, where he can shift them by road or rail or water. Field rations for an army in the field."

"Right enough. Convenient for us, though," Aylward said, resting his arm on a pivot-mounted heavy crossbow the baron's men hadn't had time to use. "But what are we going to do with *those* two?"

He jerked a thumb at Mathilda and Chaka, where they sat with their arms around their knees, sullen amongst the surviving prisoners—a few heavily bandaged men-at-arms, a glowering priest, some clerks and personal servants. Three trios of Mackenzies guarded them, as much to protect them from the revengeful locals as to prevent escape.

"That *is* a question," Juniper said.

On an impulse she climbed down from the car's observation platform and walked over; there was a very convenient little folding ladder along the side. It reminded her of the private railway cars very wealthy men had had, back in the Gilded Age.

Robber barons once again—literally, this time, she thought, and went on aloud: "And what should we do with the lot of you?"

The priest had been on his knees, praying; he stood as Juniper approached. "We shall remain steady in our faith, even if you sacrifice us to Satan," he said, holding up his cross. "The Holy Father has said—"

Juniper giggled and then suppressed the guffaw that followed. Several others didn't, and the lanky man in black clericals and dog collar glared. He was young as well, with the light of fanaticism burning in his eyes.

"Padre, I'm afraid you'll not be granted opportunity for martyrdom the now," she said dryly, hoping someone wouldn't make a stupid crack about wicker men and mistletoe—it encouraged cowan superstitions.

"Ransom, of course," Mathilda said, standing herself and crossing her arms on her narrow chest; her manner was older than her face, in a way that reminded her a little of Rudi.

She was glaring too, and doing a rather better job of it than the priest. Underneath the armor and padding they'd removed—a quilted-silk gambeson of all things—she wore a black T-shirt and jeans, tucked into polished riding boots. She was slim but not skinny, with the coltish all-limbs look of preadolescence, a tomboy air and no trace of fear at all.

Perhaps she doesn't believe the bits about human sacrifices.

"My father will pay whatever you ask," she went on. "Then he'll come and take it back with the sword! And if you dare to hurt me, he'll kill you all!"

"Let me see your hand," Juniper said, extending her own.

The girl glared for a moment more. "I'm not shaking hands with you!"

"Good," Juniper said dryly. "For I wasn't offering to. Show your hand, or I'll have one of my clansfolk march you over, young lady."

The hand confirmed a guess: callus around the rim made by forefinger and thumb. "Swordsmans' hand," they called it these days. It was just starting with the youngster, but there. Which said interesting things about the girl, and possibly even more interesting things about her father and her father's attitudes and plans.

"I'm not interested in the tyrant's gold, girl," Juniper said, releasing her.

She flushed, something Juniper could sympathize with, being a redhead herself and of a more extreme type. You couldn't hide it when the blood moved under your skin.

"My father is not a tyrant!" she said. "He saved everyone from the Change!"

"And mine is a good lord," young Chaka said, glowering in his turn. "He'll pay ransom for me and all his men here."

There was muscle on his arms and shoulders already, fruit of an early start with the sword, and judging by his hands and feet he'd be a tall man himself if he lived.

"It's true that your father's not so bad as some," Juniper said to the boy. "However, think about one thing—could we have done what we've done, without their help?" She indicated the farmers with a jerk of her head. "And think about why they were ready to help *us*. Ask your father about it, too, when you see him next."

The boy sat again, as if someone had cut his strings; that jarred his head, and he put his hands to it. Evidently he'd taken more of a thump on the noggin than his friend.

"Aren't you going to get him a doctor?" Mathilda asked scornfully.

"Indeed we will, when our medicos have finished with the gravely hurt," Juniper said. "But you can rest easy, we don't harm children."

That got under her composure a bit, and she nearly growled. Juniper hid a smile, and waved Eilir and Astrid over.

This one's going to be trouble, she signed—with her back to the girl.

The others moved so that their fingers couldn't be seen either; no sense in taking chances.

We've got sixty civilians to move a day's march to the border and a fight if any of their cavalry patrols catch us, Eilir signed. *What's the priorities, Chieftainly Mom?*

Getting those people home, Juniper said. *But this girl could be very important politically. Arminger has no other child, and he dotes on this one, from what we hear.*

Astrid's mouth opened to reply, and then her head whipped up. "Nazgûl!" she shouted, a huge, clear, bell-like sound, and reached over her shoulder for an arrow.

So did everyone else, as the slender thin-winged shape of the sailplane banked over their heads. It was a standard pre-Change sporting model, whispering silent through the air overhead, although the Protector's eye on the wings was new, as was the shark mouth painted on the teardrop-shaped nose. Counterweight-powered launching ramps on hilltops could get the gliders well into the air, and the mountain-flanked trough of the Willamette was good soaring country.

Juniper's voice tripped on Aylward's as they shouted: *"Careful!"* and *"Ware the drop!"*

Arrows went soaring up if you shot into the sky. They also came down, pointy-end first, and traveling fast.

Nobody bothered the first time the aircraft came down the line of the rail; it was at over a thousand feet, and probably moving more than sixty miles an hour. It came from the southeast and over the bridge, down to where the wreckage of the railcar lay, then banked sharply to the right over the two wooded hills where the Mackenzies' local friends had hidden. The glide turned into a soar as it struck the updraft over the hills, turning, banking, sweeping upward in a gyre like a hawk circling for height . . . exactly like a hawk.

"He'll see you, and report to the citadel, and my father's men-at-arms will hunt you down like rabbits," Chaka said.

"Shut up, boy," Rowan growled, eyes on the sky as he laid his ax aside and pulled his bow from the loops beside his quiver.

"He's coming back!" Aylward called. "Wants a closer look to be sure what's going on. Ready!"

The glider pivoted on a wing tip, pointed its nose on a downward slant, and came on as it traded height for speed; the pilot could do that safely now that he knew there was a source of lift in easy reach. Juniper felt her breath grow quick, and grabbed it with an effort of will. A flight of arrows went up from the Mackenzies grouped around the toppled railcar, and a groan from everyone watching except the two children, who cheered—the heads winked in the sunlight as they turned, well below the glider.

"Ready!" Aylward shouted. "Nice no-deflection shot, now. Wait for it!"

Juniper didn't bother to set an arrow to her bow; she just didn't draw a heavy enough stave to be useful at extreme ranges. Aylward kept his bow on his back, hands working deftly on the big crossbow instead, moving screws and sighting rings. The bow was a complete set of leaf springs from a truck; it needed a complex crank mechanism to pull the string back against two thousand pounds of resistance, and Sam would get only one shot . . .

Tunggg-whack!

The three-foot bolt of forged steel disappeared northward, its curved vanes twirling it like a rifle bullet. It moved far too fast to see more than an elongated blur, but Aylward's shout of satisfaction echoed the heavy flat plinking sound of the missile striking the light fiberglass of the glider. There was a reason he was known throughout the Willamette country as *the* archer.

"*Shoot!*" he bellowed.

The scout glider staggered in the air when the bolt hit,

but it recovered quickly—apparently neither the pilot killed nor anything vital in the controls destroyed. It *did* lose a crucial three hundred feet of altitude.

Forty bowstrings snapped against the leather and metal of bracers. They would have only one shot as well; the aircraft was doing better than ninety miles an hour, skimming less than a hundred feet up. None of them was used to shooting at targets moving that fast, either.

All but two of them missed; Eilir, Astrid and Rowan would argue for the rest of their lives over whose shots hit. The glider nosed up, up and up until its climb passed the stall point, and then it fell like a fluttering leaf as the wings lost lift.

"We'd best move, Lady," Sam was saying before the sound of the rending crash and the shrill cheers of the Mackenzies died. "He won't be reporting back"—they could see the pilot hanging limp in the broken canopy, and that was splashed red on the inside—"but when he doesn't come back on time, someone with his flight plan will have someplace to look."

Juniper nodded, feeling oddly depressed for an instant at the sight of the broken glider, despite all the other fears and griefs of the day. It had been so long since she saw manmade wings in flight, and it was like a glimpse of the lost world.

She turned to the two children. "Is Chaka here your friend?" she said.

Mathilda stood proudly. "Yes!" she said. "I won't let you hurt him—and he's the son of my father's handfast man."

Juniper hid a quirk of her lips. That was another word that the younger generation could use without the feeling of playacting she suspected even Arminger felt.

"He doesn't look well, and a hit on the head is always chancy," she said. "It would be best for him to rest quietly, not be thrown over a saddle hog-tied. Will you give your oath not to escape or try to escape or give away our position, if I let him go? Leave him here for his father's men to find, that is."

The girl's eyes narrowed. Even at her age, a lifetime being brought up at Arminger's court would have bred wariness. "Why don't you let me go too?"

"You're not a fool, my girl. Neither am I. Make up your mind and do it fast."

"Father said you were a tricky one, too," she said, surprising Juniper. Then she turned: "Father Rodriquez! Bring your Bible, quickly."

Eilir, Astrid, she signed, while the swift ceremony was done. *You'll each take ten archers, the wounded, and all the horses we've got, and half these refugees each. Get over the border as fast as you can; they'll be on our trail and we'll be loud and conspicuous. Eilir, you take the girl, and I wouldn't be expecting perfect trust from her just yet, promise or no. Questions? No? Then move!*

Sam Aylward already had the main column forming up. Juniper swung into the saddle, and waved to acknowledge their cheer as a shout ran down their ranks, marked by bows tossed into the air and caught with flourishes. Someone struck up the pipes, which was safe enough just now, and the rest began to sing as they swung out. Sam cocked an ironic eye at her as the old Jacobite song—highly modified—roared out.

Well, people need songs, she thought defensively. *And it's a great tune!*

Their clansfolk were happy with their victory, and some of the locals looked positively uplifted as the chorus sounded:

> *"Wha wouldna fight for Juney?*
> *Wha wouldna draw the sword?*
> *Wha wouldna up and rally—*
> *At the sacred Lady's word!*
> *See the gathered Clan advancin'*
> *Witchblood hearts as true as steel—"*

Crossing Tavern, Willamette Valley, Oregon
May 13th, 2007 AD—Change Year Nine

". . . and the rest of us headed west, dodging when we could and fighting when we couldn't," Juniper finished. "Eilir and Astrid both got their groups over the border to Mt. Angel—the good baron pulled out the usual patrols to look for us, you see. I suspect he wasn't looking forward to telling Arminger why his dear little Chaka was set free, while Princess Mathilda was taken prisoner."

"That messenger, back when we were arranging for Crusher Bailey's last barn dance?" Havel said.

Juniper nodded. "Little Miss Arminger is now safely ensconced in Dun Juniper, with a good many watchful eyes on her. And leading everyone a merry chase, from the report. Now we have to figure out what to *do* with her."

"That was really quite clever," Signe said. "Making her swear an oath like that—not that Daddy would care, mind you."

Juniper nodded respectfully. "A game you grow up playing and play all your days isn't a game. It's your life," she said.

"Will he care we've got his kid?" Havel said. "Much, I mean. He'll know we're not going to pull out her toenails or anything like that."

"He'll *know* that, but I doubt he'll *believe* it, down in his gut," Juniper said shrewdly. "Since he wouldn't be so . . . squeamish . . . himself. And she's his *only* legitimate child. He's invested a very great deal of himself in being the founder of a dynasty and all that foolishness."

Arvand Sarian had *not* given Lord Bear and his lady the same cramped room they'd shared with Kendricks the night before. Havel didn't know or care if this was actually Sarian's own bedroom; it was fairly spacious, looked on an interior courtyard of the ramshackle building, and had a good clean king-sized bed.

Which is sort of ironic, when you think about it, he mused, leaning back against the pillows with his hands behind his head, unconsciously checking that the belt with his dagger and backsword hung just far enough away for an easy draw.

The room also had an armoire with a good tilting mirror. Signe Havel sat at it, brushing out her long hair and looking thoughtful as the lavender-scented candle flickered beside her.

"I wonder if it would be worth the trouble of dyeing it back to my natural color?" she mused, then glanced at him expectantly in the looking glass.

"By the way," Havel said. "I'm *very, very* sorry. I screwed up. I'll never do anything like that again. Our kids are my sole heirs and I'll announce it whenever you want . . . that's eight hundred and seventy-two."

Signe smiled at him over her shoulder. "I'm holding out for one thousand even, but you're only a couple of months short of it," she said. Then, thoughtfully: "I wish we were the ones holding Princess Mathilda."

She used the title with less irony than he could have, but the thought was worth considering. He gave it a full fifteen seconds before he replied: "By Jesus, *I* don't! Worrying about Arminger's special-ops people swinging down the chimney every goddamned night with knives between their teeth isn't my idea of a quiet life. Yeah, it's an advantage having her on the whole, but the Mackenzies did the raid and we didn't, so they earned it. I don't think we could have done it."

Signe smiled again; this time there was a twinkle of mischief in her bright blue eyes, if it wasn't just the candlelight.

"My darling, you are very intelligent, but there are times I doubt how far you look ahead. Let's put it this way. How old is Mathilda Arminger?"

Havel frowned. "Born late in Change Year One, wasn't she? Come to think of it, Sandra Arminger must have been pregnant when I met them that—what was it—April."

Which had been just before he met Juniper Mackenzie and fathered young Rudi. He winced slightly as Signe let him know she remembered with a glance.

"Mathilda's going on nine; it was unplanned and delivery was by C-section, as you'd know if you'd just read those briefing papers I do at such vast expense of time and trouble. Now, who has a nine-year-old *son* that we know?"

He stared at her, then snorted laughter. "Maybe I am an idiot, but I can't see Juney doing anything like . . . well, shit, you know her, *alskling.* The strongest argument in favor of the Old Religion I can think of is that someone that lacking in personal ambition ended up ruling a quarter of the

Willamette—the gods must have been giving her a boost on the QV."

Signe hesitated, and then nodded reluctantly: "Yeah, honey, I admit *she* might not think of it. But a fair number of *other* people might. Arminger or his wife, for example. I suspect that's why his little bitch was over where she was. Molalla is one of his strongest supporters—or was, before this. A get-the-kids-acquainted visit, I'd guess." A moment of thoughtful silence, then: "Why do you think Arminger hasn't come right out and called himself King Norman the First?"

"Ummm . . . because it would sound so fucking stupid?" Havel said, chuckling. "I mean, unless he wanted people making Elvis jokes behind his back. *The Protector is . . . in the building!* Same reason I didn't call myself the Boss and get the Springsteen snickers. Not all his backers were those Society weirdos who like that sort of thing; a lot of them couldn't stomach him. Plenty of others already think all that pseudomedieval crap he goes in for is evidence of his not being the most stable chair at the table as it is."

"*Grimy arse,* cried the kettle to the pot, my sweet *Lord Bear.*"

"Hey, that was Astrid!"

"But Mike, there aren't that many people around who were even adults when the Change hit—and people over forty were a *lot* less likely to make it through alive. If you ask people the same age as my demented little sister, or the ones who're younger, most of them have never heard of Elvis or Springsteen. They *have* heard of the Lord Protector, and sweetie, they don't think *he's* funny at all. Hell, darling, most of them don't even think *Astrid* is funny, which is funny itself and scary too. By the time Mathilda Arminger and Rudi Mackenzie and the twins are our ages . . . much less Mike Junior . . ."

"Ehhhh." Havel tried to follow the thought.

And I think that was a polite way of telling me I'm a middle-aged fuddy-duddy stuck in a pre-Change mental rut. Aloud, he went on: "Look, Arminger would never put up with Rudi Mackenzie as king of Portland after him—or even, what did they call it, prince consort."

"Yes," Signe said patiently. "But let's look at the alternatives here. Let's say we do really, really well in the war we all know is coming—I mean, God, we're fighting it now, more or less, whenever the Protector feels like it, because if we don't win we'll be too dead to care—so, if we win as big as we can possibly do, are we going to flatten the Protectorate?"

"Not unless they break up hopelessly from the inside," Havel said ruefully. "Too many men-at-arms and too many castles. If we could knock off Arminger in the process, though, or make them turn on him—"

"Then they'd need a figurehead," Signe said. "Depends when and how it happens, of course, but . . . so whoever gets the hand of the little princess might well pick up a big chunk of Arminger's power with it. If it were Rudi, that would make better than half the Valley. Not real comfortable for the Outfit, eh?"

Havel nodded. "But, *alskling,* to get to that point we have to *beat* the Lord Protector *first,*" he said reasonably. "And we're a long, long way from there right now. Long-term alternatives are all well and good, but you've gotta prioritize. If you don't make it through the next six months, six years is sort of moot."

She sighed, nodded, and came to join him. A long moment later: "*Ouch!* That's a bruise!"

"Sorry," he said. "That's the problem with making out when we've both been in a sword fight. Too much like rubbing wounds on wounds . . . *ouch!* Hey, you did that on purpose."

"Damn right I did, darling. Now let's think about this. . . ."

"I'm dreaming, aren't I?" Juniper Mackenzie asked.

"Of course you are, darlin' girl," her mother said. "There! Isn't it just ready, now?"

The plain suburban kitchen was just as she remembered it, down to the chipped white enamel of the old Maytag four-burner gas stove and the crayon drawings she'd made in sixth grade clipped onto the refrigerator with magnets, and the mixing bowls soaking in the sink. Her father's galoshes were by the screen door; it was spring, from the look of the lilac bush outside the window, but a gray, rainy, western Oregon day whose raw chill wind swung the seats of the swing in the middle of the little backyard.

She *knew* this house, the white frame Victorian in the Hackleman District on Elsworth and Seventh. A modest two-bedroom, not quite shabby, the water damage in the upper rear corner of the ceiling from the windstorm back in October of '62 neatly repaired by her father's own clever hands—it hadn't been when her parents bought the house in 1968, the year of her birth, which had cut the price to something they could afford. It even smelled the same: waxed linoleum and a sachet of dried lavender and the peculiar smell of the mutton-based shepherd's pie her mother made, overlaid with the good scent of the raisin-studded soda bread she was lifting out with her oven mitts. The same print of a Madonna and Child taken from a Church calender in 1982, the same checked tablecloth . . .

Mary Mackenzie was in her late thirties, as she'd looked a year or two before the accident, wearing an apron over a plain housedress, the first gray strands in her fiery molten-copper hair . . .

Just like mine, Juniper thought, looking down at herself.

The homespun saffron shirt and patterned kilt should have looked out of place; with the curious logic of dreams somehow they didn't, not even the dirk with its carved bone hilt and the *sgian dubh* in her boot top. Neither did Nigel Loring sitting across from her, smiling as he dropped the little perforated silver ball full of tea leaves into the pot on the end of its chain.

"Never could abide those tea-bag things, Mrs. Mackenzie," he said.

"Inventions of the devil," Mary said, shaking the triangles onto a plate. "A nice cuppa to welcome you to America, Sir Nigel—and sweet soda bread with raisins, if you like it."

"I'm very fond of it," he said, breaking one open and applying the butter and homemade strawberry jam. "My wife and I took our honeymoon in a little place in Donegal, and the good lady there made something very like this at teatime. Just the thing after a long walk in the wet."

Juniper took a piece as well and bit into it; the scent and the rich sweet taste were like a flood that stung her eyes with tears and broke down the gates of memory. Helping Mom with the dishes, standing on a little wooden footstool so she could reach the counter. Judy Lefkowitz and she bicycling on the banks of the Willamette and singing Beatles tunes together at the tops of their lungs. Dad coming in from his beat and her running out to meet him, and he put his cap on her head and hoisted her on his shoulders as he walked up the driveway . . .

"You'll be looking for a place here, then?" Mary asked Nigel. When he nodded, she went on: "Then you'd best be remembering *is folamh fuar é teach gan bean.* A house without a woman is empty and cold."

He smiled, a charming expression in his normally impassive face, one that made him look younger despite the laughter lines beside his faded blue eyes; then the smile died. "Well, perhaps if I could find one like you, Mrs. Mackenzie . . . or my Maude."

She touched him on the shoulder. "Grief is the tribute we pay the dead," she said, matter-of-fact sympathy in her voice. "But they don't ask more than we can afford to give. They've never really gone from us, you know, those we love; they're part of our story, and we of theirs."

Just then the door blew open. Eilir was there, and Nigel's son Alleyne, and Astrid, and the great slab-shouldered form of John Hordle. The youngsters' cheeks were flushed with wind and exercise; there was a minute of laughter and jostling and dripping cloaks before they were seated around the table and fresh plates of the soda bread set down, and tea poured.

Juniper gripped her cup in both hands as she sipped, then set it down.

"Mom?" she said, murmuring under the buzz of conversation. The infinitely familiar face leaned down by her. "Are you . . . are you really my mother?" Her eyes flicked to the blue-robed mother and god-child in the print.

Soft lips touched her brow. "To be sure I am, my heart, my treasure! For aren't all mothers one, in the end?" Her eyes went to Eilir, laughing silently as Astrid showed the two men how to shape the sign for *wet.* "And don't we all return what we're given?"

"Oh, Mom, I've missed you! I hated it when you went away!"

She pressed her face into the apron, flung her arms around her mother's body and felt the infinitely familiar soft warmth and scent. A hand stroked her hair. "Shhh, *mo chroi.* It was only for a little while I left you. . . ."

Suddenly she was sitting up in bed, in the comfortable darkness of the Crossing Tavern's room. With Eilir and Astrid and herself they were near to filling even the big king-sized; the place was too crowded for the luxury of a private room. The girls were asleep, dark head and fair on two pillows, with a tavern moggy curled up at the foot of the bed and only a little starlight and moonlight shining in through the cracks around the shuttered windows.

What a dream! she thought, waiting while her quickened heartbeat slowed. *What a dream!*

She was smiling as she laid her head down once more. *When in doubt, ask the Mother.*

"This is getting to be entirely too much like the *Decameron,*" Juniper Mackenzie grumbled as the leaders sat down to breakfast, with the Lorings present as well.

They were eating al fresco, as much for privacy's sake as for the bright spring sunlight. The stretch of courtyard was still pleasant, with a peach orchard beyond—pink blossom above, and sheep cropping amid grass below starred with yellow penstemon. The cold sweet scent of the peach blossom mixed with cooking, horses and woodsmoke.

"Ah, you like Boccaccio too?" Sir Nigel said. "Chaucer as well?"

"Indeed," she replied. She'd requested soda bread for breakfast, and Crossing Tavern's staff included someone who made a very passable batch. "I do that, professionally and personally."

"You were a musician before the Change?"

"Mostly," she said. *And he seems genuinely interested. It's a rare man who's a good listener on first acquaintance.*

"Celtic and folk. Which meant you were a stage performer as much as a singer, and a tale-teller nearly so."

"And now you're a ruler," he said.

"By some yardsticks," she replied, and they both laughed. "Immeasurably so."

Mike Havel cleared his throat, obviously anxious to get down to business. *It's a grim sort you are at times, Mike,* she thought. *And besides that, it's a terrible habit, putting mustard on bacon like that.*

The sausages were very good; a little spicier than the cooks at Dun Juniper made them. She waited as Sir Nigel sipped his semitea and smoothed down his white-streaked yellow mustache.

"Well," he said, clearing his throat. "It didn't take long to learn what it was that the Protector wanted. The problem was that Captain Nobbes was rather more taken in than I'd have liked. . . ."

Portland Protectorate, Willamette Valley, Oregon
April 6th, 2007 AD—Change Year Nine

The dinner ended with apples and a cheese board; both were excellent. But then, so had been the fresh oysters, the lobster bisque, the crusted stuffed pork loin, the fresh baguettes—and the coffee, a gift from Captain Nobbes's dwindling store.

"So you see," Norman Arminger said, leaning back and turning the stem of his wineglass in his long fingers, "I'm sympathetic to your mission. Certainly I've no desire to see nerve agents brought back into common use! A pity the Change couldn't have taken care of those as well."

The crackling fire on the hearth behind him left his face in shadow, despite the candles on the table—only a half dozen of those had been lit. Nigel suspected that was calculated, to let him see his guests' faces clearly without revealing all of his own. His wife was smilingly inscrutable in her wimple and cotte hardi.

"Dear, I suppose even God has to let *some* chemical functions go on unaltered," Sandra Arminger said, taking a precise nibble of sliced apple and then a bite of blue-veined cheese on a rye cracker. "Or at least that's what Pope Leo says, at great length sometimes."

"There's no danger of their being brought into *common* use," Nigel Loring said. "The industrial processes needed to mass-produce the organophosphates are impossible post-Change. You could make tiny amounts on a laboratory scale, I fear, but nothing beyond that . . . and that would be quite hideously dangerous, don't you know. And they can be destroyed; dropping them into a large quantity of water will do nicely. The sea, or a large river."

"That's a relief," Arminger said. "The storage facility at Umatilla is uncomfortably close, and the area's chronically unstable, currently having a civil war. It wouldn't do to have the gas fall into the wrong hands. You're an expert, Sir Nigel?"

Before he could demur, Nobbes cut in: "S'truth! Couldn't have done half what we've done without this bloke."

"I had some experience with them before the Change," Nigel said. "I wasn't a chemical-warfare specialist, though. More from the other side, if anything, poking around the Middle East and Eastern Europe looking for them."

"As close to an expert as anyone's going to get," Nobbes said with annoying enthusiasm.

"Surely most of it wouldn't be operational anyway," Arminger said.

Loring sighed mentally and cut in. Nobbes would blabber if he didn't, and the information wasn't exactly secret anyway: "Well, most of the artillery and rocket-delivered ones wouldn't be usable," he said. "They're generally binary agents that can't be mixed except by firing the shell or warhead—which is scarcely practicable in our time, eh? The mustard gas is corrosive and I'd be surprised if any is left that hasn't eaten its way through the containers, without preventative maintenance."

"And according to my intelligence, the staff at Umatilla poured gasoline into the storage bunkers and set them on fire before leaving," Arminger said.

His hands clenched on the arms of his chair in anger at the thought. *I don't think we were supposed to see that,*

Nigel thought. *And our good host probably didn't think of checking for some time after the Change.*

"Well, then," Nigel began, a sentence that would end with: *Not much point in poking about there, eh?*

"We'd still have to check," Nobbes said. "We've got protective gear on the *Pride,* right enough. The spray dispensers for the nerve gas might still be functional, eh? Isn't that what you said, Sir Nigel?"

Nigel Loring sighed aloud this time. "Yes, I'm afraid that's a distinct possibility," he said.

"Well, then," Arminger said. "We can't have that. I'll give you all the assistance I can."

Half an hour later, the lord of Portland grinned as he sat alone with his wife in the darkened dining room, cracking walnuts in his fist.

"*Just* what we needed," he said, tossing a few of the nutmeats into his mouth. "We may even be able to win without a war, after a few demonstrations. I'll even offer the idiots in the south Valley fairly easy terms. Subject to subsequent modifications, of course."

A maid came in with a fresh pot of tea; she wore a black-and-white uniform of gown, t-tunic and tabard. "Thank you, Isabelle," Sandra Arminger said, and poured for them both as the girl left.

"I'm glad you got over that fetish period and agreed to have the staff properly clothed," she said. "Body hairs in the soup . . . God, how embarrassing. One lump or two?"

Arminger snorted. "Two . . . I know you, my love. You've got something unpleasant to say. You always bring up an over-and-done-with quarrel before starting a new one."

"Only ones I won," she said tranquilly. "And face it, the skimpily clad maiden thing lost its thrill fairly fast, didn't it? Both the looking and the touching."

"To an extent," Arminger admitted.

"That's why I didn't say anything at the time," she said, with a gracious smile that grew wider when he gritted his teeth. "I knew you'd get over it. I must admit it was fun to watch you have your wicked way with them, occasionally, all the screaming and thrashing. Very occasionally."

"Always room for three," Arminger pointed out.

Sandra smiled again, and drew a line through the air with one finger, as if tracing the edge of a draftsman's set-square used to draw straight lines. "Sorry, dear. Raw oysters never did appeal."

"The point, dearest wife? Besides the fact that being Supreme Overlord turns out to be more like being a bureaucraft than I anticipated?"

"That you tend to confuse fantasy and reality sometimes, my lord Protector, and not just the way you pander to those old Society geeks' taste for romantic terminology. You've . . . nobbled Captain Nobbes, the Aussie extrovert. But Sir Nigel is quite another kettle of fish. Much more subtle under that bluff hearty Squire Western exterior. I think he's seen through you—us, for that matter."

An eyebrow went up on the Protector's knob-cheeked face. "You think so?"

"I *know* he knows you're after that nerve gas for your catapults."

"Gliders too," Arminger said absently. "A very little VX apparently goes a very long way. It might make some of our more independent-minded vassals think twice about pulling their drawbridges up on me as well if I could spray them like bugs from the air."

"Raid as opposed to raids," Sandra said with a chuckle.

He grinned at her. "Insecticide for people. I like it."

"Then strike while the iron's hot, my dear. Before he can talk Captain Nobbes into withdrawing his protective gear and trained team . . . I gather it's not practical without them?"

"I have better uses for the limited supply of people who'll walk into a contaminated poison-gas facility just because I tell them to," Arminger said, picking up an apple and peeling it with a small sharp knife, taking the whole skin in a single long circular strip.

Interesting to know you can peel a human being the same way, he thought, and went on aloud: "It's not really something you can get men to do with a threat of docking a week's pay. But there are more ways of killing a cat than choking it with cream."

"You're really a very wicked man," she said with a smile, after he explained. "Dreadful. A monster."

"Part of my charm, darling."

"Why do you think I married you?"

"You mean it *wasn't* the professor's salary and the faculty cocktail parties? I'm shocked, shocked I tell you."

He put his arm around her waist; they laughed together as they walked out the door and into the corridor.

Nigel Loring had seen many rivers, from the homely little streams of England to the Rhine and the Zambezi; before the Change he'd kayaked down the Amazon, and paddled his way up the Sepik in New Guinea—Sam Aylward had been with him, and insisted on calling it the "Septic" River, for good reason. The mile-wide Columbia Gorge was impressive even so. The water was bright blue this April day, with a wind out of the west beating the surface to whitecaps in the morning, dying away to a glassy calm as the day wore on. Black basalt cliffs closed in on either side, broken by the silver threads of waterfalls and bright-green ferns on the southern shore, then gave way to tall hills forested in somber firs and pines, towering thousands of feet above. When the galley's course brought it close to shore he could see sheets of purple lupin and bright yellow flowers he didn't recognize. And there were glimpses of Mt. Hood's perfect white cone to the south.

"Striking," he said. "A land for giants."

Norman Arminger nodded, apparently taking that as a personal compliment; there was pride in his eyes as he watched the landscape inch past. Some of the small settlements on the shore were abandoned; more were shrunken, but there was a lively traffic of fishing boats and sailing barges and the odd oared craft.

They all gave way as the Lord Protector's fleet went by, the galley *Long Serpent* in the lead, with thirty oars to a side, rowing *a scaloccio* with three men to each of the great shafts. Catapults squatted on turntables on the low planked-in forecastle and quarterdeck; the middle of the ship was open save for a catwalk down the center. The long looms rose and fell, rose and fell, every blade striking the water at a precise angle and breaking free in a trail of spray, to the slow *boom . . . boom . . . boom . . .* of the hortator's mallets on the drumset under the forepeak. The rowers were big brawny men, hugely muscled, wearing only short leather pants, their torsos and shaven heads gleaming with sweat, silent save for the explosive *huuuuff!* of breath as they rose and fell, rose and fell with the rhythm of their work. Half a dozen boys went back and forth with canvas water bottles, directing a squirt into open mouths when they were called. The smell of the rowers was rank and somehow surprisingly dry, like oxen who'd been working in the sun. A score squatted on the forecastle, waiting to relieve the next section due for a rest.

"Row well, and live," Loring murmured under his breath.

Classical reference, he thought—though in fact the film had been wrong about that. Greek and Roman rowers were free men; galley slaves were a medieval and Renaissance invention. To his surprise, Norman Arminger caught the quote.

"No slaves," the Protector said dryly, pausing as several attendants armed him. "That isn't really practical for warcraft, I've found."

Nigel nodded; he'd seen the swords and axes and bucklers clipped to the bulwarks between the benches on the trip up from Portland. From the sewer smell, less fancy tow boats pulling barges loaded with troops and horses and supplies *did* have crews chained to their benches. They'd passed other arrangements, one where bicycle pedals drove a propeller, and one where a big windmill whirling amidships did the same. Probably they were too complex and failure-prone to be practical just yet. Or the Lord Protector just thought galleys made a good show.

"And now if you'll excuse me . . . unless you'd care to spar yourself?"

"Not just now, thank you," Sir Nigel said.

Normally he tried to get in at least a little practice every day, usually with his son—who'd taught *him* the sword, after all—but Alleyne wasn't there. Wasn't with the flotilla, at all, although John Hordle was leaning on the railing not far away, left hand tapping idly on the long hilt of his sword. Loring didn't intend to let a potential enemy get a close-up look at his personal style with a blade. Or perhaps not so *potential* an enemy, either.

Nobody called Alleyne a hostage, Nigel thought, with fury that didn't reach his face. *Not quite.*

Arminger pulled the practice helm with its protective face screen over his head and nodded to the commander of his troop, a squat muscular man with cold blue eyes peering out of a face ugly with thick white scar tissue; that and the shaved head made it difficult to tell his age, but Loring estimated it at about forty.

"Salazar! Johnson!" Conrad Renfrew barked. Then to Arminger: "The usual reward, my lord?"

Arminger nodded again, taking up a practice sword—a yard of oak with an iron core, probably rather heavier than the two pounds or so of the real thing. The two young guardsmen did likewise. One was a little below six feet, the other a trifle above, one fair and one dark, but otherwise they were similar; in their early twenties, broad-shouldered, long-limbed, moving with deft ease in their throat-to-ankle armor despite the light pitch and roll of the deck.

"Let's see if either of you can win that horse," the ruler of Portland said. "Salazar first."

The man raised his shield and advanced; Arminger pivoted on his right heel as they circled, sword over his head with the hilt forward and blade back, the rounded top of the big kite-shaped shield up under his eyes. Then the younger man sprang. The thump and clatter of the match made good cover for a private conversation, especially when you added in the chuckle of water and the hoarse mass breathing of the rowers and the dull boom of the drum; and they both knew how to talk softly without obviously whispering. Loring leaned on the rail beside Hordle, his mild eyes blinking at the sun-sparkles off the water.

"Notice we're not on the same boat as Nobbes's folk," Hordle said. "Keeping us separate on shore too, like, as much as he can without being too obvious about it."

"He's no fool," Loring said.

"Thinks highly of himself, though, just a bit," Hordle said.

"I hope we can make something of that," Loring replied.

"Think he'll scrag us, sir? If we get the VX for 'im."

"I wouldn't put it past him," Loring replied. "But I think he'll try to enlist us first."

"But with Mau-Mau conditions."

"Quite."

That terrorist movement in Kenya had made its recruits break their own culture's taboos, acts so obscene and horrible that they felt cut off from everything but their new allegiance. They weren't the only ones who used that trick, either; it had the dual merit of securing loyalty and weeding out those with inconvenient scruples. Cannibal bands had done the same during the terrible period right after the Change.

I'm almost *glad Maude didn't live this long. Things would be very awkward if she were here.*

"Still, there's opportunities," Hordle said.

His eyes took in the countryside. *And we've heard something about Mr. Arminger's enemies,* they both thought. Anyone who disliked the Lord Protector had to have something to be said for them, and it would be strange if men with their skills couldn't make an escape. *Which is why Alleyne is somewhere they can keep an eye on him.*

Hordle sighed. They both knew that, too. His wide froglike slit of a mouth quirked at Sir Nigel. *He and I rescued you—now you and I will have to rescue him!*

They looked up at the mountains to the south. A heliograph blinked from the top of one, a code but not Morse: *blink . . . blinkblink . . . blink-blink-blink . . .*

They looked casually down at the water sweeping by. "That's quick. Six knots."

And the heliographs would be quite quick enough to report our absence and order Alleyne killed. Their eyes met. *We're going to have to be very careful about this.*

"I'm sure the Lord Protector will have *nothing* to complain about for some time."

The white water of the Columbia broke over the snagged ruins of Bonneville Dam with a toning roar that shook the world, the bright noon sun making the froth shine like cataracts of lace fringed with diamonds as it surged between the remaining fangs of ferroconcrete. Nigel Loring shaped a silent whistle; there was no doubt at all that things were simply *bigger* in this part of the world, starting with the mile-wide expanse of river. The dam itself spanned that breadth across an island; the central portion with the sluicegates was the core of the ruined portion. It wasn't hard to see why, either; the rusted wreck of a big river tug rested halfway through, prow high in the air. The huge barges it had been pushing lay tumbled before it at the base of the dam's low wall, except for one tilted against its side and showing the gravel that had been its cargo; the combined weight must have been thousands of tons, and traveling fast on the crest of a flood wave from the looks of it. What the steel-and-stone battering ram of the barges had begun, the wild water of eight years had continued, until the rapids were not much worse than they'd been before the river was tamed.

"Goddamned inconvenient," Norman Arminger said from not far away, using the point of his wooden sword to indicate the broken dam and then lowering it to the deck. "For transport, that is."

The two young men-at-arms he'd been sparring with stepped back as Arminger pulled off the practice helmet with its facial mask. Below it his flushed countenance ran with sweat, and he was breathing hard; he'd just spent a goodish while sparring in relays with two men who were at least twenty years his junior, trained to a hair, and obviously not holding anything back. Nigel Loring was moderately impressed; he wouldn't have lasted quite so long before tiring dangerously himself, but then he was in his fifties rather than the Protector's midforties. The standard of swordsmanship had been high as well, though the style was different from the one the royal forces used in England, rather more edge and less point, and more use of the bigger shield.

He looked at Hordle, and the big man nodded, seconding his impression: *Quite good, but not quite of the very first rank.*

Arminger tossed his gear to an attendant and pointed to their left, towards the south bank and the locks. A swarm of men and animals and cranes labored around it; their shouts and the clatter of gears came faintly through the distance, until the unearthly scream of a water-powered saw grinding rock cut through the blurring thunder.

"Repairing and adapting the locks is taking *years.* It was a domino effect—dams started breaking up on the Snake in the first Change Year, and when one let go the flood would go downstream, picking things up as it went. But I've got the locks at the Cascades back in operation; those were easier, built in the nineteenth century. At least it's improving the salmon catch. That's been noticeable the last couple of years."

I think the Protector is a lonely man, Nigel mused, with cold appraisal. *Doesn't have many people he can talk to. And he probably thinks it's safe to talk to me, the simple straightforward soldier.*

He'd been a soldier, yes. But a soldier of a particular sort; the SAS was *supposed* to operate behind enemy lines, and in contact with foreigners. You had to be a good judge of men, and not just of your own countrymen or the sort you'd invite to the Club.

Big Chinook salmon were thick in the water below the dam, their fins cutting through the smoother water below. Dozens leapt at the white torrents every second, falling back to rest and try once more or making it through the froth and into the solid surge above. Birds hovered and struck, ospreys and bald eagles and types he couldn't identify. A half-dozen substantial fishing boats were dipping nets slung out on booms, hauling up mounds of struggling silver.

They paused as the Protectorate's fleet came into view: sailing barges full of troops, horses, supplies; and more pulled against the current by rowing-tugs with fifteen oars a side. The Lord Protector's *Long Serpent* was something different, a real warship, long and low slung.

He looked around; the northern bank was hilly but fairly low, closer than most places on this enormous river; the south was steeper, rising to low mountains—or what the

Yanks might call big hills, somewhere around two thousand feet or a little less—sparsely forested in pine. One about a quarter of a mile from the water held the turreted concrete-gray bulk of a castle on a shoulder spur. Banners flew from the turrets, and the drawbridge over the dry moat was down. Lances twinkled as toy-tiny figures trotted down towards the small town that lay beside the locks. You could cover the whole area to the other bank from there, with heavy trebuchets, and most of it with dart-throwers.

The town had a wall under construction—timber forms for the concrete, and he could see wheelbarrows of head-sized rock fill going up board ramps.

"Transportation chokepoint," he said to Arminger. "But you must have a threat nearby?" The castle would have been expensive.

"The Free Cities of Yakima," Arminger said. "North of here. They survived the Change annoyingly well, all that irrigated land, and they've been even more annoyingly independent since."

Nigel nodded. *Which leaves the Columbia as a long, thin corridor of your territory between hostile forces to the north and south.*

Crossing Tavern, Willamette Valley, Oregon
May 14th, 2007 AD—Change Year Nine

"Not exactly," Mike Havel said judiciously, methodically demolishing another fried egg and loading more hash-browns on his plate. "He holds the Hood River Valley and the Mount Hood country. It's Renfrew's fief—he's Count of Odell, as well as grand constable of the Association."

Juniper pursed her lips. "Even so, he's not going to send many men much farther east than that, not for long, not while we're at his backs. The Yakima towns are safe as long as we stand—not that they've ever helped *us*, the creatures."

"Don't know how long the Pendleton folks can hold him off, now that they're fightin' amongst themselves," Hutton observed.

"Or he could be relying on those castles," Havel said. "Sorry, Sir Nigel. Old strategic discussion."

Loring nodded. "We saw that—"

Near Boardman, Columbia Valley, Oregon
April 12th, 2007—Change Year Nine

The small earthwork fort had been in a strong position, near the crest of a low hill, with a canal between it and the Columbia, and a stretch of irrigated farmland dark-green against the lighter olive of the higher land southward. The hilltop position hadn't helped it, or the people living in the little town near it. Bodies lay tumbled between the burnt-out snags of frame houses and double-wide trailers, or in the empty corrals. The corpses had been here for several days and that made unsightly tumbled death worse; despite the coolish weather the meat-gone-off stink was fairly bad, sweet and musky and foul at the same time, like having rancid spoiled soup spilled down the back of your throat. Nigel Loring had been fairly case-hardened even before the Change, and he had watched the death of a world after it. He still let his eyes slide slightly out of focus, which was easy for him and one of the few advantages of advancing years and the rock dust in that wadi long ago. From the look of things, by no means all of the people had died fighting, or quickly. Many still bore the broken-off stubs of arrows, or lay near the black fan of blood left when sword or ax struck. Some of them had been clumsily scalped—the whole of the hair removed, rather than the proper coin-sized patch, the work of someone who'd heard about scalping but never seen the real thing done in the old style. Some of the bodies were very small. Flies buzzed in clouds, also not as bad as they would have been in high summer, but bad enough.

The local man cursed at the sight; his horse shifted uneasily under him. They were well outside the Portland Protective Association's territory now, and they'd picked up local auxiliaries from one of the several warring parties ripping up northeastern Oregon. Sheriff Bauer had sixty riders with him, a wild-looking crew and mostly younger than his thirty-odd. Like him they wore crude helmets of hammered sheet metal, small shields—most of them with metal covers cut from old traffic signs—and breastplates of leather boiled in wax or tallow and picked out with riveted straps of metal on the more vulnerable points. Their weapons were horn-and-sinew recurve bows, knives, and heavy-bladed sabers that looked like scaled-up machetes slung from their belts or over their shoulders.

"It's them murdering redskin devils," Bauer said; the remarks from his followers tended more to scatology. Then he looked up sharply as Arminger snorted, and barked: "You think that's *funny,* mister?"

"No, no, not at all, Sheriff Bauer," Arminger said, rather obviously fighting down a smile, and holding up a hand when his guards bristled at the local leader's tone. "It's just . . . that I've never actually heard anyone *say* 'murdering redskin devils' before. Not . . . not in real life, that is."

The leader of the horsemen visibly restrained himself. *Arminger can't resist taunting,* Loring thought. *Bad tactics, Lord Protector. You need this man.*

The sheriff's restraint was hard won, but it was there. The Protector's personal guard probably helped, twenty knights in their black mail, mounted on big glossy-coated horses. The little army of four hundred men marching along the graveled road up the slope behind helped even more, their spears neatly aligned and glittering in the spring sunshine, the ripple of lance points, slung crossbows swaying, the beat of booted feet and ironshod hooves. Light carts followed behind, some carrying supplies; a few bore dart-throwers on two-wheeled carriages. The roadway was gullied in spots where flash floods had struck or culverts blocked, and some of the bridges were down, but it was still passable for wheeled traffic if you weren't in a tearing hurry.

"I suggest you go look for the, ah, *murdering redskins,* Sheriff," Arminger said. "Take some of my scouts with you."

The sheriff did; the scouts were on range-stock quarter horses, lightly armed with horn bow and sword and dagger,

wearing only mesh-mail vests and open-faced helmets beside their wool-and-leather uniforms. They spread out in a
broad web and trotted off; Bauer's riders shook themselves
out into clumps and bands and straggled away after them
over the rolling country eastward, some of them whooping
and showing off with riding tricks, standing in the saddle for
a moment, or running along beside their trotting horses and
leaping back up.

"What are they fighting about?" Loring asked, as the
Protector and his men fell in at the head of the column,
heading eastward and a little south of the river.

"Who's to rule, essentially," the lord of Portland said.
"This is harder country to make a living off than the
Willamette, particularly without powered farming machinery or pumps or hybrid seed or fertilizers. And there were
more survivors here initially, so the rare good bits like this
irrigated land are precious. It's just sinking in that the only
way to avoid a lifetime of very, very hard work is to skim
off somebody else's hard work and nobody wants to volunteer to be skimmed. That's it when you boil it down and
subtract the personal feuds and the slogans." He smiled.
"I've acquired quite a few valuable followers from around
here in the past year or so."

One of the Protectorate scouts rode up: a small, wiry
young man on a light, fast horse; the binoculars at his saddlebow marked him as an officer.

"About three miles that way, my lord, and coming fast
when they don't get in each other's way," he said. "Four
hundred strong, give or take fifty. The locals are mixing it
in with them, but not doing too well."

He pointed eastward and offered a folded map with his
thumb marking a place. The Protector's guard captain
grunted and glanced a question; the Protector gave a slight
jerk of his head, and a volley of orders and trumpet calls
followed. The force from the west shook itself out from
column into a line that straddled the road—blocks of
spearmen alternating with crossbows, with the lancers on
the right where the ground was more open. The men's
faces were mostly blankly impassive under the helms,
sweat cutting runnels through the road dirt; a few grinned

eagerness or the semblance of it, and a few others looked tightly nervous.

Arminger smiled and reached for the helmet slung at his saddlebow. "And I think you might want to suit up, Sir Nigel."

And I don't like the looks he's been giving me, Loring thought. *I think that his lady wife may have been giving him advice before we left.*

He swung down from the saddle while John Hordle acted as squire and helped him into his suit of plate. He'd been wearing only the back-and-breast for the road, which was one advantage it had over the chain hauberks the Portlanders used; you could shed part of it without taking everything off. As the big young man helped strap the bevoir—the chin protector—to the breastplate, he whispered in the older Loring's ear—he had to lean far down to do it, anyway: "I don't feel right about fighting for this git, sir."

Nigel nodded as he lowered the sallet helm over his head, tested that his scalp fitted snugly in the padding, fastened the chinstrap and flicked the visor down and then up again.

"Think of it as fighting *against* the people who did *that,* Hordle," he said, inclining his head back in the direction of the village and the little fort.

"Ah. That's so, sir."

Loring had had a month to get used to the horse, and vice versa, and it had been well-trained for years before. It knew what the clank of armor meant, and even more what Hordle's deft fingers portended when they fitted the peytral to the leather straps on its breast and the chamfron to its face. The big yellow gelding tossed its head and mouthed the bit, lips blowing out over the great square teeth, a puff of dust coming up from the road as it stamped its foot, along with a dry earthy smell under the hard, musky, horse sweat and oiled leather and the sharp scent of metal. Medieval men-at-arms had ridden entire stallions, but that was taking machismo to absurd lengths and Pommers had plenty of aggression. Loring settled himself in the massive war saddle with its high cantle and cradling sad-

dlebow, steel-shod feet braced in the long stirrups. Hordle
handed the reins of his own stout cob to a helper who led
it to the rear and strung his long bow with a wrench and a
twist and a push of his hip.

"The real old-fashioned way," he said, reaching over his
right shoulder to flip the cover off the top of his quiver.
"Always makes me feel me English roots, as King Charlie
says."

"Not really," Loring said, grinning down at the calm,
round red face by the poleyn that covered his right knee.
"Victorian roots, at best. They didn't use back quivers at all
when the longbow was in flower. In flower the first time, I
should say. They used arrow bags, or pushed them through
the belt."

"Sodding fools, then," Hordle grunted. "I mean, where's
your bloody right hand, when you've loosed the string?
Over your right shoulder, in course."

Then he began to whistle to himself, softly and cheerfully. Nigel recognized the tune, a jaunty little ditty with a
chorus that went:

> *We'll run the course*
> *From Stonehenge up to Uffington*
> *On a white chalk horse we'll ride.*

The Protector's force halted just behind the crest of a
low rise; the dust their hobnailed boots had raised drifted
on ahead of them, spreading and falling in a khaki-colored
mist. It was a bit nostalgic for Nigel Loring, given the
amount of time he'd spent in dry dusty places before the
Change. The command group and their guests came forward a few more paces, enough to put their heads over the
ridge and reveal the slopes beyond. Other plumes of dust
covered the expanse of scrubby grass tufts and sagebrush
ahead of them, where knots of men fought, with only an
abandoned farmhouse and trees that had died when the
pumps failed to break the monotony. Men and horses were
insect-small at a thousand yards or better, vanishing into
little hollows and then appearing again, the clatter of
weapons like faint memory, a twinkle of edged metal

throwing sun-bright blinks through the curtain of powdery soil hammered up by the hooves. Arrows arched between galloping clumps and saddles were emptied, or horses went down thrashing and shrieking; then bared steel crashed on steel, thudded on shields or armor, smacked home in flesh.

The chaotic swirling suddenly took form: Sheriff Bauer's force was riding pell-mell for the ridge, dropping the odd wounded man or injured horse behind; the pursuers clumped together more tightly as they followed, their whoops and screeches loud even over the thunder of hooves. Fewer arrows slanted out from either force; their quivers were mostly empty, and neither had the organization for resupply.

Loring leveled his own binoculars. His brows rose behind them. Bauer's men had looked wild enough; those they fought were . . . *Well, painted savages, perhaps,* he thought. Feathers in the braided hair or feather bonnets, fringed beaded leathers, face paint. Weapons and gear looked very similar to those of Bauer's men under the ornamentation, though some were bare to the waist.

Hmm. Not all really Indians, unless that one's bleaching his hair. Including his chest hair.

The sheriff's men managed to put some distance between themselves and pursuers, spurring their horses ruthlessly.

The Indians probably think they're heading for that little fort, Loring mused, as the defeated men dashed by, some clutching wounds, some fleeing mad-eyed and heedless, but most reining in and turning their horses a hundred yards behind the Protector's force. The medics with the baggage train saw to their wounds; servants brought canvas water bags and bundles of arrows. Bauer himself paused only for a drink and to let the water run over his upturned face, then cantered back to Arminger's side.

"I hope this works," he grated; there was a cut on one cheek, dripping blood into the short brown beard that covered his jaw. "I lost better'n a dozen good men."

"Cost of doing business, Sheriff," Arminger said. Then he chuckled: "And now . . . what a disappointment this is going to be for our Native American brethren. Yet another bitter blow of fate; how tragic."

He waved his sword around his head, and then pointed it forward. A bugle sounded. The entire force broke into a trot forward, pouring over the hillcrest in a line six hundred yards long, spears bristling out, giving a long wordless shout as they halted again. The black banner with the lidless eye reared upright beside Norman Arminger, streaming backward from its crossbar.

The whooping of the Indian war band turned to screams, but even their light horses took a moment to halt when the whole hundreds-strong mass was in full gallop. A few arrows flickered out at the Protectorate troops, but an instant later the front rank of crossbowmen knelt to a barked command and their stubby weapons came up to the shoulder.

Tunggggg!

The short, heavy, pile-headed bolts flashed over the hundred yards in a multiple blurred streak. When they hit they hammered home until only their vanes showed, slamming through cloth and light armor alike.

"Reload! Second rank, take aim! Fire!"

Tunnnggg!

The kneeling crossbowmen of the first rank dropped the hooks of their spanners over the strings of their weapons and spun the cranks as the second fired over their heads. The war party ahead was in chaos, some trying to turn their mounts and get through the press to their rear, others charging, more struggling to control their bucking mounts, and then the standing rank of crossbows shot.

Tunnnggg!

"Reload! First rank, take aim!"

Tunnnggg!

Arminger grinned like something that came hungry out of a forest deep in winter, raised his sword again and made a gesture. Over on the right of the line the men-at-arms stirred as a bugle rang, bringing their shields up and around to rest under their eyes. Their horses came forward in a line, walk-trot-canter; then the lances came down with a long falling ripple and the riders booted their mounts up into a hand gallop, keeping their dressing to present a line of points. He could hear their hooves drumming on the hard ground, and their deep uniform shout: *"Haro! Portland! Haro for the Lord Protector!"*

Their long legs made the big horses fast once they got going, despite the weight of man and gear they carried. There was no crash of impact when they struck the war party's milling chaos—you always expected one, but two parties of horsemen weren't baulks of timber or metal. Instead there was a multiple thudding, massive dull sounds as the eleven-foot lances slammed home, lifting men out of the saddle, many of the ashwood shafts breaking under the strain. A few of the armored men went down as horses tripped or staggered. Many more of the Indians fell, spitted on the lance points or thrown as their lighter mounts were bowled over by the destriers. And the warhorses were trained to stamp on fallen men . . .

Then the Protector's lancers were through the loose formation of the war party, turning, dropping lances and pulling out their longswords or swinging maces with serrated-steel heads.

I do *hope the Indians have the sense to run away quickly,* Nigel thought. Lightly equipped, they had no chance at all against full-armored men-at-arms and their tall mounts. *Though if they could get them to chase too far, and scatter, they might give them all the trouble they wanted.*

Hordle grunted agreement to the unspoken thought, then shouted: "Look out!"

Another knot of Indians was there, a dozen men seeming to boil up out of the ground—out of a little hollow that ran southeast towards the river, but startling enough all the same. The man leading them had a classic twin-tail feather bonnet fastened over a steel cap, and red-and-white chevrons painted on his face and leather breastplate. Loring slapped his visor down by reflex, and the bright day turned dark except for the long narrow horizontal line of the vision slit. He began turning his head side-to-side automatically, the only way to keep from being blindsided in a melee.

"Guard the Protector!" the commander of his guard shouted.

Shields snapped up around the lord of Portland. Which was commendable discipline and focus, but it left the rest of the party uncomfortably exposed. Hordle drew and shot in one smooth motion; a warrior went back over the crupper of his saddle with an English clothyard shaft through his chest. Then he threw down the yew bow and swept out his longsword, turning the draw into a two-handed swing that chopped through a foreleg and sent the horse tumbling and the rider falling to die screaming at his feet. Two men in leather and paint came in on either side of Loring. There was no time to feel fear, or do anything but let his body respond with drilled reflex; a hatchet bounced off his shield, and the heavy machete saber of the other was still upraised when the wielder ran onto the point of the baronet's sword. Teeth broke, and then the thin bone of the brainpan; he let the falling man's weight pull the weapon free and then cut to the left over his shield with a savage overarm stroke that laid flesh bare to the bone. Another attacker came at him on foot with a light spear in both hands, but Pommers reared and lashed out with his forefeet. The heavy *click* that he felt between his eyes was the destrier's ironshod hooves smashing bone like matchsticks under a hammer.

Sheriff Bauer and the Indian leader in the feathered bonnet circled, steel beating on steel and cracking on hard leather; then Bauer head-butted his opponent when their swords locked at the guards, and the two men fell to the ground in each other's arms—their horses very sensibly bolted out of the press, away from the sound of pain and the stink of blood. The men rolled beneath the hooves of the melee, each with the other's dagger-wrist locked in his hand; dust hid them, and there was a sound like a dog worrying at a bone, a shriek of pain and Bauer came out on top, snarling in triumph with the lower half of his face wet red with blood. He spat something aside and stamped the heel of his boot down half a dozen times, howling with glee and waving his bowie knife overhead.

The sounds of battle died in midscream; nothing was left of the Indian war party but a few fugitives spurring their horses eastward, pursued by crossbow bolts and Bauer's men, their horses rested and their quivers filled. The Protector's lancers regrouped and cantered back to their place on the right of the line, while stretcher-bearers went forward to pick up the wounded men.

Or at least the Protector's wounded men, Loring amended with distaste as he wiped his sword clean and sheathed it, flicking his visor up.

Spearmen were attending to the wounded Indians.

"That was just dangerous enough to be good sport," Arminger said; his own sword was out, and red. To Loring: "It isn't beating these range-country rabble that's the problem, it's catching them. Damned hard to make them stand and fight if they don't want to—it's big country out here."

That disconcerting grin showed again. "I'm not the first overlord of farmers to have that problem, either. It'll get worse, when we get tribes of real nomads who follow their herds and live in tents—but that'll take a generation or so."

No, it wouldn't do to underestimate this man. I wish I knew more about his enemies, because I suspect we're not going to Tasmania after all. Not via a ship docked in a city the Lord Protector controls, at least.

"Much obliged," Bauer said to Arminger, casually wiping at his mouth with one hand and spitting to clear it of blood, then picking at something stuck in his teeth. "You killed off better'n half of that bastard's 'chete-swingers. We can beat the rest. I owe you one there . . . Lord Protector."

"Think nothing of it," Arminger said, wiping his sword. "And now," he went on, "it's time to go look at some nerve gas."

John Hordle swore with soft, venomous fluency as he looked at the strips of treated paper and watched the reagents change color. The green chemical suit covered him from toe to the pig-snouted, goggled mask; the longsword slung over his back jarred horribly with the high-tech survivals.

"There's enough still here in the soil to kill a regiment of rhinos, slow and nasty," he said after a moment, his voice muffled. "And it's leaking out as vapor all the time. The bastards must have spilled and burnt everything! This land won't be safe for . . . bugger me blind if I know when it *will* be."

"Twenty or thirty years," Nigel Loring said, watching the disposal crew from the *Pride* moving from one bunker to the next, the view dim with the moisture that was fogging the inside of his suit's eyepieces. "Longer if there's a drought and I wouldn't really fancy being a fish close downstream when it does rain at last."

The landscape they moved through must have been bleak enough at the best of times, a stretch of rolling sagebrush prairie. The bunkers were sunk into the dry, gritty, brown-gray soil, with more dirt heaped over the Quonset hut–shaped roofs; most of them had black scorch marks around their doors, where gasoline had been poured inside and set on fire. Those and the tire tracks on unsurfaced roads were the only marks of man, and there wasn't even the odd bird or jackrabbit to enliven the scene. He could see why this area had been picked as a war-gas depository. Sweat rolled down his body in greasy trickles under the stifling cover of the protective suit; it was worse than a full suit of plate armor, which didn't have to be air-tight.

And hauling each breath through the filter added an extra touch of torment, to go with the subliminal fear that the neutralizing chemicals had gone off and you were corroding your lungs out from the inside. Or that the day would suddenly grow dark as a tiny droplet of nerve agent touched your skin. They had syringes of nerve-gas antidote, and it wasn't even a toxin itself like the earlier versions, but . . .

"At least we're not finding much in the way of intact material," Loring said.

Hordle grunted. "We're finding a good deal of bloody nothing, with a scoop of sod-all on the side."

At that moment a series of muffled shouts went up from the squad of crewfolk they'd trained, and green-covered arms waved. Hordle and Loring exchanged glances and then headed over, the sound of their own panting loud in their ears inside the head-covering hoods.

"These look like the spray tanks you told us about, but they're empty," the bosun's mate of the *Pride* said.

"Let me take a look," Loring said.

The sheet-metal dispensers *were* upside down and empty, thank God—but one of the small drums nearby wasn't. Loring rocked it with a foot while he wracked his memory. *Yes, VX, without a doubt.* Not much of it; the container was only about a liter in size.

He froze for a moment, then turned and pointed. "Get a couple of those shells over here, bosun," he said casually. "I recognize the type; it's loaded with VX, sure enough. Use the dollies. We'll decant the nerve agent into these spray tanks; much easier to move it half a mile in these."

The Tasmanian gave him a dubious look, but obeyed; he'd had six months to establish his authority. Hordle bent until their heads were nearly level.

"That's not going to do the Lord Protector much good," he said, nodding towards the shells. "That's a binary mix and you need the shell to—"

"No, it *won't* do him much good," Loring said. The muffling hoods and distance would keep the conversation quiet. "But he won't know that until he tries to use it, will he, now? In fact, even our assistants here don't have a clue."

"And he'll have that one carboy of real VX to test, too," Hordle said. His tone suggested an admiring grin. "You're a cunning old colonel, sir, if you don't mind me saying so. I'll go help move shells."

Crossing Tavern, Willamette Valley, Oregon
May 14th, 2007 AD—Change Year Nine

Mike Havel paused with a forkful of scrambled eggs halfway to his mouth. After a long moment he set it down, and began to laugh. After a moment, the others at the table joined him.

When silence had fallen, Havel looked around at the other leaders; all of them good security risks, but . . .

"We'll have to be careful about this," he said. "That *has* to stay secret."

If true. Hmmm. How to check on it? Aylward vouches for Sir Nigel, which is a powerful argument, but I save perfect trust for God, and He's not eating breakfast with me. The Change . . . changed people, often enough. By Jesus, it changed me!

Juniper nodded. "And Mike . . . we were worried enough about the Protector when all we knew he had was his men-at-arms and castles. *That* hasn't changed."

He nodded. "But he's going to use them differently now that he thinks he has an ace up his sleeve. The way I read him he's the type who thinks of victory as something you get by some smart trick like a secret weapon."

Loring gave him a quick glance at that, and a slow respectful nod.

"Yes. The problem with *that*, of course, was that we couldn't tell anyone whatsoever about what we'd done."

Willamette Valley, Near Portland
May 10th, 2007 AD—Change Year Nine

"No," Captain Nobbes said.

"No, what?" Arminger replied.

"No, you can't keep it," Nobbes said stubbornly. "You promised we'd dispose of it, and sport, that's just what you must do, like it or not."

The Protector flung up one hand. The column halted, the clatter of hooves on asphalt or crunching on gravel slowly dying. The road ran westward, through farmland and then a patch of woods; the mountains of the Coast Range stood blue at the edge of sight, and in the middle distance the towers of a castle squatted on a hilltop. The column had shrunk with every fort and post they passed as they came westward; Loring guessed that Arminger was anxious to have the precious cargo that rested in the two mule carts under lock, key and guard as soon as possible, and in an out-of-the-way place at that.

Probably he'll spend some time biting his fingernails over whether the most trustworthy guards are really all that trust-worthy, Loring thought. *Such a fuss . . .*

Arminger turned in his saddle to stare at the Tasmanian. "You're either a very innocent soul, or very, very foolish," he said, his voice flat and metallic. "To paraphrase Elizabeth. '*Must* is not a word to use to princes.' "

Nobbes went pale. Loring almost winced in sympathy; the man hadn't developed the right reflexes, and it was suddenly coming home to him that the safe, democratic rule-of-law Commonwealth of Tasmania was very much the exception this ninth year of the Change—and that unlike King Charles, the Lord Protector didn't give a tinker's damn about diplomatic immunity.

I wish I could have warned him . . . but that's why we've been kept separated . . .

The moment stretched. Nigel cleared his throat. "I'm sure Captain Nobbes will come to see the necessities of your position as the guarantor against anarchy in this area, Lord Protector," he said heartily. "Certainly the material's yours, and I for one would be happy to show your men how to use the"—*entirely useless*—"weapons properly. They aren't anything for the untrained to get their hands on, eh, what?"

Am I putting it on a trifle thick? Loring asked himself.

Arminger was evidently wondering the same thing; he shot Loring a considering look. Alleyne was smiling broadly too, and Hordle laughed coarsely.

"Looks like the job prospects is better 'ere than Tasmania, Cap'n. Sorry."

Nobbes began to sputter incoherently, going pale and then flushing red; Arminger smiled at the sight. He had just begun to laugh when a shout from the east brought all heads around. Hooves pounded in the gravel by the side of the road, the *tirrup-tirrup-tirrup* of a gallop; the shoulder was a safer place to ride, if you were pushing a horse fast for any distance.

The rider had a sword and dagger at his belt, but he was unarmored otherwise and his horse had a good deal of Thoroughbred in it. Foam streaked its sides, and sweat soaked the khaki jacket the horseman wore, the smell of both rank as he reined in. Loring recognized the uniform of Arminger's court couriers, an elite corps used only for the most urgent messages. Arminger did too, and he kneed his own mount aside, over the roadside ditch and into the field so that the courier and he could talk unheard. The messenger's mount stood with its head down, panting like a bellows. That helped cover the sound of the men's voices.

At least until Arminger stood in the stirrups and shouted: "*Who? They lost who? I'll have that bastard's head, baron or not—*"

Then he sank back, shuddering, and visibly took a moment to master himself. After an instant he turned back and called to the commander of his guard; they spoke for a moment in low tones, and then orders rang out. Three-quarters of the escort turned and brought their horses up to a trot eastward, with Arminger at their head. The commander turned to the troop leader of the remainder before he followed: "There's been a raid out east; those devil-worshipping rebels and bandits, they're over the frontier. Get this stuff and the foreigners to the castle. Fast."

"But, my lord—"

"Shut up and do it! The Englishman knows how to handle the . . . special material." Even now, he used the code name, which was commendable attention to security, as he pointed at the elder Loring. "Get it and them to Castle Tonquin, *now,* and get it all there safe."

"Yessir!"

The guard commander's horse gave a squeal of protest as he wrenched its head around and spurred into a gallop after Arminger. Loring waited until the man was a safe hundred yards distant, then spoke calmly: "Well, Sergeant, it shouldn't be too difficult to get the . . . special materials where they belong. But with the escort whittled down like this, we should show extra care. The Lord Protector would be *very* upset if anything happened to it."

The troop sergeant was a man in his midtwenties, broad-faced and muscular, with a short-cropped yellow beard. He looked tough enough, and from what Loring had observed in the past fortnight, disciplined to a fault—and near to panic at the Protector's sudden rage and even more sudden disappearance. The sound of an authoritative voice from a man who'd been close to the ruler and visibly treated with respect made him give an audible sigh of relief.

That'll teach Arminger to discourage initiative among his noncommissioned officers, Loring thought, as he dismounted. *God knows what I'd do if someone like Sam Aylward were in charge. Die, most likely . . . of course, that could still happen, so put your shoulder to the wheel, old boy.*

Alleyne and he were in their suits of plate within a few minutes. Nobbes was staring at him, blinking, then nodding slowly.

About time, Loring thought, keeping his face relaxed and nodding back. *Don't be so bloody thick, man!*

"Keep your eyes on the woods, Sergeant," Loring said. "I don't like the look of them. It seems like natural ambush country for *rebels or bandits* to me." He used the same phrase as the man's commander with malice aforethought and the noncom jerked slightly, probably thinking precisely what would happen to him if anyone took the cargo in the two mule carts. "In fact . . . why don't you hand out their cutlasses to these men?"

The Tasmanians' arms were in one of the mule wagons, along with the protective suits. Only a half-dozen of the *Pride*'s crew accompanied them, but every little bit helped. Nobbes helped hand out the blades, and had a chance to murmur a few words as he did. Arminger's man was conscientious; he scanned the wooded area ahead carefully, and kept his men spaced correctly along each edge of the road, while the sailors marched closer to the carts. The shade of the trees closed over the narrow two-lane road, and for a moment there was peace, green-tinted, alive with birdsong, white oxeye daisies and blue-sailors blossoming by the roadside. The overhanging branches would make the lances awkward . . .

I almost hate to do this, Loring thought.

"Sergeant," he said.

"Sir?" the man said, turning; then his eyes started to go wide.

The dagger in Nigel's left hand darted upward, taking him under the angle of the jaw; he toppled backward with a thin shriek through clenched teeth, dead before he struck the ground in a clash and clatter of mail. Loring reached across him even as he fell, wrenching the man's lance out of its saddle scabbard as the horse leapt aside in panic and broke into a gallop over the fields. He whirled it overhead in the same movement, stopping the long pole with a wrenching effort and thrusting overarm with desperate speed. It struck between the shoulder blades of another of the escort; he screamed in surprise as the point broke through the mail links and cracked his spine.

Two, he thought.

His right hand swept to his sword hilt and the left twitched the shield down from his back and his forearm went through the loops. He left the visor up for the moment; the visibility was more important than protection in this sort of fight. An arrow from Hordle's longbow went by Pommers's nose with a *whhhfft* of cloven air and struck a man's leg with a hard nasty *crack*. At point-blank range it punched through the hauberk, through the man's thigh and the saddle beneath and went deep into the barrel of the horse beneath. The animal went wild, bucking and bugling as the rider screamed, then slipping on the asphalt and going over with a crash.

Three.

Alleyne's sword flashed, a glittering horizontal blur, first silver and then red as the point slashed beneath the splayed nasal of one Norman helmet. The man-at-arms dropped his sword and screamed, clapping his hands to his face.

Four . . .

And then the Tasmanians poured into the melee, their cutlasses flashing. Nigel held one man-at-arms off with his shield and another with his sword; a blade thumped painfully into the plate coulter over his elbow, but the man's horse went down with a scream an instant later. A moment's chaos, and the Protector's men were down as well—except for one pair who wrenched their mounts around and spurred them westward.

"Hordle!" Loring shouted. "Those two!"

The big man dropped his sword and snatched up his bow again. Both the riders had their long kite-shaped shields over their backs; the first arrow sank into one of them with a sharp *crack*. The man galloped on, then slowly slid left and toppled out of the saddle; one foot turned in the stirrup and the body bounced along behind the horse for a dozen yards before the animal stopped, turning its head to push at the dangling weight. The other man-at-arms bent low over his horse's neck and hammered his spurs home; an arrow stuck at an angle into the shield on his back, and it might have wounded him as well but he seemed none the worse for it. Hordle swore mildly, raising his bow for a dropping shot; it struck a branch and spun off, sparkling as the shaft pinwheeled into a patch of sunlight. An instant later the rider was out of sight around a curve, the drumbeat of hooves fading in the distance.

"That's torn it," Alleyne Loring said. "Get those horses! We'd—"

He stopped, astonished, as the Tasmanians collected their dead and wounded, loaded them on the carts and started off westward at a trot.

He looked at his father. Nigel shrugged, and took a pair of the reins that Hordle handed to him. "For some reason, Captain Nobbes doesn't seem to trust us anymore," he said. "I suggest we head directly south, and quickly!"

Crossing Tavern, Willamette Valley, Oregon
May 14th, 2007 AD—Change Year Nine

"And that's how you ended up outside that porno store just when Crusher Bailey's men were about to overrun us," Mike Havel said.

Then he wiped his lips with a napkin and threw the linen cloth down on the table. "Juney, you'd better sign me up," he said. When she looked a question at him: "You must be right. There *aren't* any coincidences. Or entirely too many. Your Lord and Lady must be running the show. You realize what that message to Arminger must have been, right?"

She looked back at him and began to laugh. One by one, the others around the table joined in; even Signe grinned like a she-wolf.

"Only hearing you'd captured his darling daughter would have made him go apeshit like that," she said, inclining her head in tribute. "We couldn't have coordinated anything like that in a thousand years."

"Jolly good show!" Nigel Loring said, with the slightest tinge of irony in his tone. "You'll forgive me, ladies, gentlemen . . . but at the present, I'm somewhat concerned with my personal future, and my son's, and Sergeant Hordle's."

Mike made an expansive gesture. "After tweaking Arminger's nose like that, you've got a bunk with the Bearkillers as long as you want," he said. "And we can always use a good fighting man; one who's a trained officer can write his own ticket, within reason. Certainly land if you want it."

Sam Aylward cleared his throat. "You might want to come visit us before deciding on what you want, sir," he said. "I'd like you to meet the missus, at least."

"Indeed, Sir Nigel," Juniper said. "There's room at my Hall, sure. And you know . . . I *seriously* don't believe in coincidences." She grinned happily at the three Englishmen. "I don't think you came here by accident . . . and I don't think you've played out the game, yet."

Nigel Loring's mouth quirked a little; he wasn't used to being beamed at in quite that open a way. Then his smile grew, almost involuntarily.

"It's a tempting offer," he said.

Signe Havel tapped her fork on her plate. "Unless you're still thinking of sailing away," she added.

Nigel Loring's smile died. "No, indeed," he said. "I'd have done my best to get him out if they hadn't gone off on their own, but I'm afraid Captain Nobbes isn't in a position to offer asylum to anyone. Not anymore."

Castle Morgul, near Portland, Willamette Valley
May 14th, 2007—Change Year Nine

Nobbes's scream was high and shrill; Norman Arminger would have called it inhuman, if the past decade hadn't taught him the remarkable range of the human voice. The Tasmanian captain was on the vertical rack, limbs stretched out in an X in padded clamps that allowed the maximum tension to be applied without tearing off a wrist or ankle too soon.

The Lord Protector lounged back in the padded chair, his boots up—it was a leather-covered recliner, salvaged from an expensive home in the western suburbs of Portland where some information-company executive had used it to enjoy the movies on his brand-new DVD player.

I wonder if they really would have replaced videotape? Arminger thought.

The recliner did look a little out of place in the dungeon, but then the dungeon itself was a bit of a compromise between his mental image of the Platonic ideal of underground prisons and what was practical, which had its limits even in the Changed world.

A castle required strong foundations, even one made from cast ferroconcrete, and that meant cellars and underground storage were easy to arrange. Small tables on either side of the chair held a bottle of white wine, a glass, and a selection of small pastries made with honey and nuts. He had considered lighting with torches, but they were just too flickery and smoky; the standard alcohol lanterns hanging from the groined archwork of the ceiling cast a suitably low blue glow. The walls were plain gray concrete, but held plenty of racks for tools and instruments; the floor led to a grating-covered drain. There were air ducts at the corners, carefully made just too small for a human being to crawl through. The concrete was slightly damp with condensation, but several glowing charcoal braziers kept it comfortably warm; bits of pine resin covered the scents of sweat and fear and old blood. Filthy straw infested with bugs and rats was lacking even in the corridors of cells about, but then experience had proven typhus was no respecter of persons. Nakedness on cold wet stone was an adequate substitute for keeping his prisoners in the right state of mind.

The attendants were thoroughly traditional, though, besides the two men-at-arms by the door: stocky men bare to the waist, wearing black leather hoods with eyeholes, and pants of the same material. Sandra wasn't here today; she knew his mood was dangerously taut right now with worry.

The scream died away to a mumbling whimper, and then silence.

"Give him another quarter turn," Arminger said, sipping at the wine.

"He's fainted, my lord," one of the technicians said.

"Well, revive him, then!" Arminger snapped.

The technicians slacked the tension slightly, and followed that up with several buckets of cold water. Nobbes came awake enough to try and catch some of that in his mouth, licking up the drops and then screaming again when he sucked a little into his lungs and had to cough and racked himself. Arminger waited until something approaching consciousness returned to the haunted eyes.

"I swear I don't know anything about anyone kidnapping your daughter, oh, God, I don't *know!* Water, please, water."

Arminger nodded reluctantly. "All right, let's move on to my nerve gas. You didn't have time to destroy it, so you must have hidden it somewhere. I'll find it eventually, but I want it *now,* and not just that lousy little bottle I tested. So tell me."

After a moment's silence, the lord of Portland went on: "Look at the wall."

Nobbes did, when one of the technicians knotted his fingers in the Tasmanian sailor's hair and wrenched his head around.

"There are a number of interesting little tools there. Some are sharp. Some are heavy. Some can be made redhot. And some can be heavy and hot *and* sharp. So . . ." He turned his eyes to the technician. "A dose of the hook, I think. Not the barbed one, and just the inner thigh, this time."

When the screams had died down to sobbing, he went on: "Now, tell me where my nerve gas is."

"Buh . . . buh . . ."

Arminger made a gesture with one finger, and a sponge soaked in water and vinegar was held to the prisoner's lips. When he was coherent again he raised his head.

"But if I tell you, you'll just kill me, you bastard!"

Arminger smiled and nodded. "Yes, I will, after checking to be sure you're not fibbing. And when you realize that's the *upside* of the bargain for you, you'll talk. Another quarter turn there."

Several hours later Arminger walked out of the interrogation room and down a corridor with a long row of cells on either side—he'd found that keeping the prisoners within hearing distance of the interrogations was useful for softening-up, and besides, there was a certain aesthetic balance to it. Hands gripped the bars and eyes glared, but he was safely beyond reach, and a brace of guards followed. Captain Nobbes had gone before, on a gurney with a doctor and nurses in attendance. It wouldn't do for him to die prematurely, after all.

"What about us, you bastard?" one of the crewmen of the *Pride of St. Helens* called.

"Shut up, fuckface!" the guard snarled, lashing at his fingers.

"No, no, that's a legitimate question," Arminger said, as the prisoner staggered back from the bars, clutching at his injured hand. "I think . . . yes, I think that when my daughter returns, I'll hold a tournament. We'll have jousts, and a melee, and bear-baiting, and then something new. You're all going to volunteer to fight a pair of tigers, with knives. Knives for you, not the tigers, that is. I think twenty-to-one is fair odds. If any of you survive, I'll even let you live. The salvage and construction gangs can always use new hands. Simple food, an outdoor life, and healthy manual labor."

More curses followed; the prisoners probably thought they had nothing to lose. They were wrong about that, and the ones who wept, or lay curled up and hugging themselves were wiser. What he'd probably do to them all if his daughter *didn't* return soon would make fighting a four-hundred-pound Bengal starved and tortured into madness seem quite desirable.

The one who'd asked first was a brave man. "What if we refuse?" he said.

One of Arminger's brows rose. "Refuse to fight?" he said.

"Of course! Why should we give you a free show, you manky pervo?"

"Well, if you don't fight, the audience will be disappointed." He smiled slowly. "But I don't think the tigers will mind at all."

The local baron had vacated the great hall—he spent most of his time at a nearby pre-Change mansion anyway—and Sandra Arminger waited, pacing nervously back and forth in front of the hearth. Guardsmen stood like iron statues down the wall, their spears glinting dully in the gloom.

"Well?" she said sharply, after waving her attendants out of earshot.

"Nothing about Mathilda," he said. "I didn't expect there'd been any conspiracy there, anyway. It looks like serendipity; she and Molalla's son just happened to be where the Mackenzies were raiding—they'd decided to come home that day on the spur of the moment, no way to anticipate it. And the Mackenzies won't hurt her, you know that."

"They won't hurt her body. I want her *back,* Norman!"

He made a soothing gesture. "So do I, my love. So do I; very badly indeed. But we'll have to be extremely careful. A botched attempt *could* result in her being hurt. At the least, we'll have to wait for them to drop their guard and relax a bit."

She bit her lip, eyes troubled, then nodded sharply; less in agreement than recognition there was nothing immediate they could do. That knowledge made him swallow a bubble of acid-tasting anger, but there *wasn't*. Not yet.

But when the time comes . . . he thought, and saw her perfect agreement.

"What about the VX?" she said, forcing herself to attend to business.

Arminger smiled sourly: "We'll still have to confirm the location he gave us, but I finally managed to persuade him."

She raised an eyebrow and he went on: "You might say I made him an offer he couldn't survive."

CHAPTER EIGHTEEN

Larsdalen, Willamette Valley, Oregon
May 16th, 2007 AD—Change Year Nine

"You haven't built much in the way of forts over in Britain?" Mike Havel said politely, as they rode under the Larsdalen gate.

"More a matter of refurbishing old ones," Nigel Loring said, running a shrewd eye over the stonework. "Mass concrete, really, isn't it?"

"Built like Hoover Dam, but around a framework of I-beams," Havel agreed. "I don't suppose you did need to start from scratch, much, over there."

"If there is one thing England *isn't* short of, it's castles—or Ireland or the Continent either," Loring agreed. "Most of them in nice strategic locations, as well."

Havel shook his head. "Strange to think Britain did so well."

Loring's mouth quirked and he ran his forefinger over his mustache. "More a matter of Britain doing very badly and everyone else in the vicinity doing even worse, actually. Once we restored order, there wasn't much actual fighting. Not in mainland Britain, because there wasn't anyone left *to* fight. We've had to do a bit of sword work on the Continent, and against the Moors. And in Ireland—a bad business, that, and I can't see any end to it."

Havel surprised him by laughing aloud. "Christ Jesus, you Brits *are* getting back to your roots," he said. "What's next, fighting the Spanish Armada?"

"Well . . . in point of fact, old boy, we're colonizing Spain ourselves. From Gibraltar, you see. It was empty, and it was that or let the Moors have it . . ."

Havel's laugh grew. "Another empire 'acquired in a fit of absence of mind'?" he asked, surprising the Englishman.

"To be absolutely honest, that phrase always struck me as a bit silly-clever, if you know what I mean. *Presence* of mind, rather; profit and preaching, philanthropy and plunder, pinching a bit of land for those not welcome at home, and incidentally keeping the bloody Frogs out. Doubtless it'll be the same this time, although now the French aren't a problem, eh? Now, *they* had bad luck . . . I'm a bit surprised you came up with the quotation."

"Got it from my father-in-law; I think you'll like him. Anyway, it hasn't been so straightforward here. Things are less . . . compact. Not as easy for someone to come out on top quickly."

Havel answered the salute of the gate detachment, and then waved to the crowd beyond; it was several hundred strong, and in everything from farmhand's overalls to A-lister armor. Loring cocked an eye at the reaction; not as loud as the cheers Arminger had received, but he judged it to be a good deal more authentic. Havel rose in the stirrups to address the crowd.

"Well, Crusher Bailey isn't going to be troubling the northern marches anymore," he said. "Last time I saw him, he was dancing on air with some crows waiting for lunch after the performance." That raised another cheer, louder and with a savage edge to it. "We had a brush with the Protector's men too, and they came away sorry and sore."

The cheer turned into a snarl; evidently the Protector was unpopular here. The snarl turned into a chant, with fists and swords brandished above it:

"Lord Bear! Lord Bear! Lord Bear! Hakkaa paalle!"

"All right, cut it out! No biggie! Everyone get back to what you were doing, for Christ's sake!"

And he doesn't need to wallow in it, the way Arminger did, either, Loring thought.

With the *Pride of St. Helens* thoroughly lost, it seemed Oregon was where he would stay—and his son, and John

Hordle—unless they felt like an overland trek. Once the adrenaline rush of escape was over, that had been depressingly certain. Finding that some of the Lord Protector's enemies were better company was reassuring. *And, of course . . .* His mouth quirked.

"*Que?*" Havel asked.

"Oh." *Didn't think my musing was that obvious.* "I was just thinking that if I had to land in the middle of a war at my advanced age, at least it's one I could feel enthusiastic about."

Havel smiled, a crooked expression. "I'm glad you ended up in it too, Sir Nigel. There aren't many people whose judgment on a man I'll take at more or less face value, but Sam Aylward is one of them, and he says you're very capable and . . . 'fly' is the way he puts it."

The newcomers dismounted, and grooms led the horses away; Bearkillers and Mackenzies mingled, talking with friends and relations, or being led away to the bunkhouses for visitors. Two girls came running, their blond braids bouncing as they leapt at Mike Havel; he staggered slightly under their combined nine-year-old weights and then turned with one under each arm, the skirts of his hauberk flying. Nigel blinked for a moment; they were identical, and if one hadn't had a scratch on the cheek he couldn't have told which was which from one second to the next as the Bearkiller lord whirled about.

"Mom! Dad!" they squealed; Signe Havel stood with her hands on her hips and laughed.

"Mary, Ritva, if you can leave off trying to murder your old man, there are guests to meet," Mike said.

Loring hid a smile as he gravely shook hands with both; so did Alleyne, and had the effect he usually did on females.

I can't quite understand it, the elder Loring thought, watching them blink and beam at his son. *Granted, he's taller than I was at his age, and a good deal more handsome . . . perhaps it's the smile? He must have gotten it from Maude.*

Then he watched their eyes go wide as they looked up and up and up at John Hordle. The big young man laughed like boulders rumbling as his huge paw engulfed their small hands, then knelt.

"Want a ride, young misses?" he grinned; they hopped on his shoulders, sitting easily with their arms around his sallet helm, and he and Alleyne followed the rest of the party up to the great brick house.

Mike Havel started to follow, when a voice checked him: "Lord Bear!"

The crowd had dispersed, except for a few. One was a determined-looking young woman of about twenty with a man only a little older standing off to one side, obviously trying to look as if he wasn't *with* her. The occasional angry glares they exchanged argued for a close relationship.

"Lord Bear, I've got a petition."

Havel paused. "It can't wait until tomorrow? Dinner's ready . . . oh, all right. You're Yvonne Hawkins, aren't you?" he said to the girl. "Work in the dairy?"

She had an open-air prettiness, work-worn hands, dark hair in braids down past her shoulders, and she wore a sweater and denim skirt and broguelike shoes.

"Yes, Lord Bear," she said, ducking her head. "Milking, and on the separator. My folks farm on Lord and Lady Hutton's land. I've got a complaint."

The Bearkiller chieftain suppressed an impatient snort—Loring thought it unlikely the girl would notice—and set himself, with the air of a man who does something necessary but unpleasant.

"Why didn't you take it to Angelica, or Will?"

"Well . . . it's a complaint against an A-lister, and he's not serving in their household, Lord Bear. And . . ." She twisted in embarrassment.

"And people like to go to the top," Havel said.

True, Loring thought. *More to it than that, I think. At a guess, she thinks you'd be less eager to judge her about something.*

"OK, you're a member of the Outfit, you've got a right to appeal to me, so spit it out," Havel went on. He'd banished his air of impatience, and waited with all his attention on her face.

She flushed and looked around, then steeled herself.

"*He*"— she pointed—"promised to marry me. Now I'm pregnant and he won't. I wouldn't have . . . well, you know, my lord. Not unless I thought we were getting married."

Havel turned on one heel towards the man, stripping off his mail-backed gauntlets. "OK, Morrison, now you. Did you make a promise to Ms. Hawkins here? And you're the father?" The young man hesitated, then nodded twice.

Havel went on, with a chilly glare: "That was smart. Lying to Ms. Hawkins would be bad. Lying to *me* would be *stupid*."

He didn't add *fatally stupid*. From the way young Morrison's tanned face went pale as he nodded again it wasn't necessary, but he kept his eyes level. He was a big blond youngster in his early twenties, with the enlarged wrists and corded forearms of a swordsman, and a small dark scar between his brows.

"OK, there's no law here against being a fink," Havel began, and the girl's face fell. "But there *is* a *regulation* against dishonorable behavior among A-listers, in case you hadn't noticed; we've got more privileges than other people, and more obligations, too. Breaking promises is right up there with things we're *not* supposed to do; and that does *not* mean just promises to other A-listers and their families, in case the regs aren't clear . . . and they are. Any explanation, Morrison?"

"My lord, I . . . I just didn't want to get married *yet*," the younger man said helplessly. "It's not—I don't have a holding of my own yet, I'm still doing household service with my brother Karl, and—"

"Well, you should have thought of that, shouldn't you?" Havel said. "Christ Jesus, son, do I have to tell you where babies come from? Or what to do about it if you're not angling to reproduce yet?"

The girl flushed more deeply; Morrison shuffled his feet. "We did," he said. "I mean, we were careful but . . . it just didn't work, and then Yvonne wouldn't listen to me at all when I said how difficult things were."

Loring stroked his mustache, smiling to himself. Barrier contraceptives still worked, but they were a good deal more cumbersome than the vanished Pill, and a bit less reliable.

"He wanted to get rid of the baby!" she snapped. At Havel's raised brow: "I won't. It's not right. I'm Catholic."

As are the Huttons, I understand, Loring thought.

Havel pointed at Morrison again. "You?" Then: "Speak up, I can't hear you, Morrison!"

"The Old Religion, sir."

There seem to be a good many of them about, here, Loring thought.

He wasn't altogether surprised; accidents of survival in the period right after the Change had left odder imbalances in the lands he'd seen—most of the few people left in Spain spoke Basque, for example. It all depended on who lived; a single charismatic leader or small group could be very influential. Witness His Majesty in England—or for that matter, Colonel Sir Nigel Loring.

Havel's grin was less pleasant to see this time. "And what exactly do you think Juney—I mean, the Mackenzie, would say about the way you've been acting? Something about a threefold rule?"

Morrison winced again, and this time there seemed to be more in the way of genuine fear in his expression. Loring's eyebrows rose. The Mackenzie leader had seemed a mild sort to him, without any of the hard-man menace you could sense under Michael Havel's rough good humor. And her authority here in Bearkiller territory would be religious, not secular, from what he understood.

A lady with unsuspected depths, he thought. *Hmmm. For a woman to emerge as a leader in times like these . . . A lady with* very considerable *depths, I should think. Besides her obvious charm, of course.*

"OK, it's your kid, and you promised to help look after it, so you owe the young lady big-time, one way or another," Havel said briskly. "That's my judgment. You can appeal to the A-list assembled, Brother Morrison, if you think I'm overtreading your rights. I wouldn't advise it, seeing as Brother Hutton would be speaking for Ms. Hawkins, and if I know Will, he and Angelica would be somewhere between furious and ripshit. With you, not her."

Morrison shook his head this time, emphatically. "I'll accept your judgment, Lord Bear."

"Ms. Hawkins, do you still want to marry this man? He's not a bad sort, just young and using his head for a helmet rack and not much else."

She hesitated a moment. "Yes, my lord Bear. He's . . . I'm angry with him, but I still love him."

He grinned again, in more friendly wise than before. "Smart girl. Not everyone can keep the difference between being angry with someone and not liking them straight in their heads. What about you, Brother Morrison?"

"Yes, my lord. Definitely."

Havel's expression softened. He thumped a hand down on the young man's shoulder. "Good." Then he leaned closer, and spoke softly; Loring could make it out, but he didn't think that the girl could. "And just between me and thee, Brother, I was going to assign her a third of your income for the next eighteen years if you said no. Glad you got smart."

He shook his head as the youngsters walked away; as they did, the two figures grew closer. "Christ Jesus, I didn't expect this sort of thing would be part of the job."

"Stranger things have happened," Loring said reminiscently. "There are times an officer has to be a father to his men. And at Tilford—well, you wouldn't be interested in an old man's maunderings."

"You can learn by listening, or by getting whacked between the eyes with a two-by-four. I always found listening easier. Right now, let's go get dinner." He grinned. "You haven't met Mike Jr. yet; he's still in a high chair. But feeding him, thank God, is something I can still unload on Signe and the nanny."

He shrugged again, this time the sort of gesture a man made before settling down to a heavy task. "And tomorrow, it's back to work."

The map room of Larsdalen had been a sun porch before the Change, with half its roof of glass, and tall windows on two sides. The leaders of the Bearkillers and their allies sat at a long table with the glass behind them and the maps before; the military apprentices had set out spirit lamps with pots of herbal tea and platters of oatmeal cookies studded with raisins, then left before the serious talking began. The evening sun gave excellent natural light; the maps looked as if they'd been drawn by hand post-Change, but by experts, and they showed the Pacific Northwest in considerable detail at half a dozen different scales. Nigel Loring appreciated the skill that had gone into them, and their value. Knowing what was where, which roads were passable . . .

"Everyone who hasn't met him, this is Sir Nigel Loring; he's given the Protector's nose a good hard yank; details are sort of classified. Sam Aylward knew him before the Change, and vouches for him. He was an SAS colonel then, and apparently ran the whole British army afterward, until he had a falling-out with the government there. Sir Nigel, this is Major Jones of the Corvallis University Militia," Havel said.

The soldier was a slender, strong man in his thirties, in a green uniform that looked as if it was designed to be worn under armor, and glasses held on with a rubber strap. The map indicated that Corvallis lay south of the Bearkiller territories, and that it ruled a broad swath between the Williamette River and the Pacific.

"And Councilor Edward Finney of the agriculture faculty there."

The councilor was a square-built man of about Loring's age; his hand was square as well, callused and strong. "I'm actually just a farmer," he said. "Air force before the Change—logistics specialist; my dad owned a farm near town, and I got out, got back there. Pete, here, was a teaching assistant in the history department, and in the SCA. The university, or part of it, ended up running things in our area . . . long story."

"Ed's an old friend, too," Juniper said. "I knew his father well before the Change and we worked together afterward."

"I wish we could say we represent Corvallis," Finney said, nodding. "But we're only quasi-official here."

"We represent *some* of Corvallis," the younger man in green said sourly. "The part that takes the Protector seriously."

Havel snorted softly. Loring looked over to Sam Aylward; the stocky noncom nodded slightly. *Right,* Loring thought. *A city-state run by committees . . . which means there'll be plenty who won't acknowledge a problem until it comes and bites them on the arse. Still, they can't be totally shambolic, or they wouldn't be alive now.*

"Sir Nigel's brought us a good deal of information about the Protector's capacities and intentions," Havel said. A grin: "Partly because the Protector didn't intend that he'd ever get loose to tell anyone about it, and indulged his taste for monologuing about the details of his own greatness. Sir Nigel, over to you."

Nigel rose, cleared his throat, and began to recite: numbers, estimates, appraisals of men and weapons that he'd seen. He didn't need to look at the notes he'd made, but Signe Havel occasionally glanced down at her copies. When he finished, the faces of the Corvallans were longer than they'd been.

"Told you, Pete, Eddie," Havel said.

"Yes, you did," the soldier said glumly. "And *we* believed you all along. The problem is, our homegrown idiots are just going to say that means they're right to bend over backward—or forward—to avoid making the Protector angry." He held up a hand. "Yeah, I know, Mike, that means they hope he'll break his teeth on you guys—or at least eat them last. And that's truly, deeply stupid. But it's so."

Havel grunted sourly and looked at Loring. "So, you'd estimate he can put about ten thousand men into the field?"

"Allowing for minimal garrisons in the rest of his territories, yes," Loring said. "If you don't mind me asking, what can you call up to fight him?"

Havel looked at his wife. "The Outfit's got about twenty-three hundred militia," she said. "Infantry—pikes, crossbows, archers. And we've got some field catapults and a siege train."

"Plus the A-listers," Havel said. "Three hundred of them. Lancers and horse archers—you've seen them in operation."

Sam Aylward spoke: "We Mackenzies've got about

twenty-two 'undred; that's everyone who can pull a useful bow. No cavalry, but we can get some help from over the Cascades—the Central Oregon Ranchers' Association."

Havel snorted again, louder this time. "CORA couldn't organize a fuckup in a whorehouse, pardon my French—every rancher over there thinks he's a king. They make Corvallis look like a miracle of discipline. Sorry, Pete, Ed."

Juniper Mackenzie made a gesture. "Still, we can count on *some* help from that direction. The ranchers who've fought with us against the Protector before will turn out, and some others who want to stay on our good side, and if the CORA isn't good at deciding things itself, at least it won't stop them. Say five to eight hundred, depending on the season and what he's doing up along the Mount Hood country, and what they have to guard against on their frontier with Pendleton—that war's a blight on the whole neighborhood.

"Light cavalry," she went on, looking over at Loring. "Bows and swords. Very mobile, and fine scouts."

Aylward looked at his ex-commander as well. "Ranchers and their cowboys," he said. "The ranches are like hamlets these days, they took in a good many of the townsfolk who survived the Change. It's very . . . decentralized over there, so the CORA as a whole doesn't have to vote for war. The ranchers aren't what you'd call well organized, but they can fight well enough by bits and pieces, as it were."

"Which gives us maybe six thousand against his ten thousand," Havel said, breaking a cookie in half. "And apart from my A-list, ours are part-timers, and his are all full-time fighting men, all well equipped. OK, say he has to leave some at home to keep the farmers under control; it's still not good odds, particularly since about two thousand of his are knights and men-at-arms—heavy cavalry and damned hard to stop. And he's got a better battering-train than we do, and we've got a lot less in the way of fortifications. Besides which, standing siege would let him destroy everything we've spent ten years building up."

Everyone looked at the two from Corvallis. Reluctantly, Peter Jones spoke: "We could put seven thousand in the field with a general call-up. But that would require a council resolution and a referendum vote, if our own territory weren't invaded."

"Ah, participatory democracy," Loring said, his tone neutral.

Edward Finney flushed slightly: "When the people who're going to fight do the voting, they really mean it!"

Which was true, but didn't entirely make up for being late to the party.

"He's still not going to attack before the harvest," Signe Havel said. "The logistics are bad otherwise."

"If he's planning on some sieges he'll bring—"

Loring sat back and let the others argue; he was the stranger here, and thought himself lucky to be allowed to listen in, despite the pleasant informality of arrangements. Instead he watched the faces. A man—or a woman—could lie to you with words, but it was harder to deceive a third party—particularly about character.

Yes, our Lord Bear would make a good friend and a very dangerous enemy, he thought. *Just the man for a sudden deadly blow with no warning.*

He recognized the type; Sam Aylward was another, solid noncommissioned officers, perfectly capable of running a company and of seeing that lieutenants didn't mess things up too badly before they learned their trade. Both capable of a good deal more under the right circumstances.

And young Lord Bear has come a long way ... I suspect most dynasties were founded by men much like him. Wit enough, even if he's no genius, but willpower to spare. Not half so dangerous as his wife, though, I would venture. Beautiful to a fault, yet she reminds me a bit too much of Queen Hallgerda. And I rather think she's a good deal more intelligent, not to mention personally formidable. Mr. Havel is welcome to her.

The two from Corvallis had the harassed look of good men doing their best in a situation that they knew was beyond them. Sam Aylward—*he* looked a little different, and not just because he was nearly a decade older. He didn't seem as detached as he would have been at a briefing before the Change; the matter at hand obviously touched him in more than a professional manner.

He's more settled, Loring thought. *He was always a fine soldier, but a bit lost out of uniform. Glad to see he's found a home. And we could have used him back in England after the Change.*

And then there was Juniper Mackenzie. He noticed that she spoke little, but tended to quiet arguments when she did, and help keep people focused. And her voice was interesting in itself, softly musical, the American accent he'd always found rather harsh and flat softened by the trace of a brogue.

West-Irish, at that, I think she said. Fine figure of a woman, too. Pretty in a colleen fashion, but with character too—someone interesting has been living in that face. Friendly, but I suspect there's a volcano of a temper under that red hair as well.

He'd known Witches before; a good few had survived in England by geographical accident or prescient flight to somewhere remote—two dozen had hidden out in the New Forest, evaded the mobs by some cascade of miracles, and greeted the king's men when they came surveying. Juniper seemed to have her feet planted more firmly in the earth than most of the breed that he'd met. At that moment she looked up and met his eyes; there was a slight jolt that left him blinking, and then she winked at him. He hid his smile, smoothing down his mustache with a finger, then bent his attention back to the discussion. When it ended, she cleared her throat.

"That leaves the question of where to keep Mathilda Arminger." At Havel's quick glance she went on: "Come now, Mike, it's not as if it would stay a secret for long, wherever we put her, sure. You can hide people in a city, but those days are gone, and all we have are villages where everyone knows everything about everybody—we could scarcely chain her up in a cabin in the woods. Too many saw her at that fight in Molalla's territory, for what happened to stay secret for long. Too many of my folks *and* his."

Havel exchanged another glance with his wife. "She's got to stay somewhere safe, at least."

Juniper nodded. "That leaves either here or Dun Juniper—unless Corvallis would like to keep her, as neutrals?" The two emissaries of the city-state made quick fending-off gestures, and Loring hid another smile.

"Well, then, Dun Juniper for the present. It's out of the way, and as strong as any of our holds, and farther from Protectorate territory," Juniper said, with a trace of reluctance in her voice. "Though if anyone would care to volunteer to take her off my hands . . ."

Signe Havel nodded slowly and unwillingly. "For now that's the best option, yes," she said.

"Sure, Signe, and we can reconsider later if it seems wise," Juniper agreed. "From what I've heard back, she's not the sweetest-tempered guest ever received in my Hall. But moving her across the valley would be far too risky . . ."

Hmmm, something there, Loring thought. *But there's something about Lady Juniper's voice that makes it hard to stay angry with her, I think.*

"Yeah, it would be an invitation to a raiding party," Signe conceded. "She'd better stay at your place for now."

A little surprised at himself, Loring spoke: "It might be a good idea to give her some additional guards. I and my son and John Hordle have more than a little of experience at clandestine operations between us, before the Change and after it. And we'd like to see a little more of the neighborhood, since we seem likely to settle here at the last."

"Good idea—" Signe and Mike Havel's voices tripped over each other. Havel cleared his throat and continued: "*Very* good idea. Arminger has some sneaking-around-the-woodshed types himself."

CHAPTER NINETEEN

Dun Juniper, Willamette Valley, Oregon
May 31st, 2007 AD—Change Year Nine

So, what's this Sir Nigel like? Eilir asked.

She looked around one last time to check that everything was in place. The sun was setting to her right, westward; the sky there bright towards the Coast Range, while the snow peaks of the High Cascades on her left were touched with a last touch of crimson, and a first few stars bloomed in the purple above. Birds sang towards evening, under the murmur of voices and the eternal sough of the forests above.

From what Mom writes, he's quite a man, she went on. *Sam thinks so too of course. It's enough to turn me against him, almost.*

"I only saw him for a few minutes. He's nice enough, for an old guy, I suppose . . . sort of like Théoden, if you know what I mean," Astrid replied.

Decrepit, senile and playing sub to a bearded top in a dress? Eilir signed, and dodged a revengeful elbow.

Most of Dun Juniper was gathered to greet the Mackenzie and her guests, and to celebrate victory. For some like Judy Barstow grief was uppermost, but since the Change people had learned death wasn't something that happened invisibly to old people in hospitals. Most were happy, and the walls were a blaze of flower wreaths as colorful as the gardens at the foot of the plateau beneath a bright blue sky scattered with white cloud. Even the meadows beyond seemed to celebrate, their green grass lavish with scarlet foxglove, white daisies, purple lupine and trembling sheets of blue camas flower; the year's colts ran up and down the fences and hedges, kicking up their heels at the excitement and noise. Eilir and Astrid stood before the closed gates with Chuck Barstow and a few others; the rest lined the walls, or stood beside the road, or waited inside. Astrid had a wreath of crimson penstemon in her hair; Eilir had her Scots bonnet on, with raven feathers in the clasp, but some of the flowers in the brooch that held her plaid.

How come you didn't stay over at Larsdalen? Eilir went on. *Not that I don't appreciate the company, but you have those horses you were working on.*

The approaching column turned from toy-tiny to human-sized as it rode westward down the winding gravel road through the benchland and towards the Dun. Her mother was there, and Sam Aylward, and three figures who must be the Englishmen, and an escort that included Rowan and Cynthia Carson. They were just close enough to hear Juniper Mackenzie throw back her head and laugh.

Astrid went on: "What, don't you want help keeping an eye on the Little Girl from Udun?"

She's improved, Eilir signed. *Rudi's been showing her around and she's not sulking nearly as much.*

"Yeah . . . but Larsdalen is getting too crowded to stand," Astrid said. "Especially the big house. You know, with Signe's kids and Luanne's kids and Pam's two—euuu, at Dad's age!—and the staff and *their* kids and all. It'll be dull with the visitors gone . . . I've been thinking again we should find a place of our own, you know, a base for the Dunedain. Somewhere strategic, with good hunting and not too many people. Mithrilwood, for preference."

Yeah, I love it here at Dun Juniper, but there are times it drives me crazy the way Larsdalen does for you, Eilir agreed in Sign. *I sort of get nostalgic about the way it was here before the Change, just Mom and me and the dogs, even though I hardly remember it, really. Mithrilwood sort of reminds me of that.*

"Of course, it'll be a bit crowded anywhere, when we're not camping out," Astrid said with a certain resignation.

You had to live behind walls with strong friends at hand, if you wanted to live at all; solitude meant deadly danger. "But not *as* crowded. And not as many kids, running all over the place and yelling and messing things up."

"Wait till you've got some of your own," Dennis Martin said; he was there in peaceful kilt and plaid and flat bonnet, but he carried his great ax, and leaned on the helve.

Astrid shuddered and rolled her eyes at his remark, but stayed silent.

What's with the chopper, Unc' Dennie? Eilir signed.

Chuck's weaponry was part of his role, but Dennis Martin Mackenzie usually didn't carry steel unless he was away from home, and a battle-ax was a lot less handy than a short sword anyway.

"It's to hit Princess Legolamb here with, the minute she starts in with that 'He's just like Barliman Butterbur' stuff again," he said. "To hit her hard. With the sharp side. Many times. Brannigan, OK, you can call him goddamned Tom Benzadril and his wife is Hashberry, but leave me out."

Astrid ignored him, except for a slight elevation of her straight nose and a sniff; Eilir snickered. The cavalcade was closer now. Some of them dismounted at the foot of the rise and came up the rise leading their horses, others riding slowly behind them; a few of the strangers looked up sharply as the Lambeg drums and bagpipes sounded from the gate towers. Eilir waved to her mother, feeling her face blossom in a smile and a load of worry lift. Chuck and Judy Barstow went forward with the welcoming-cup in its long silver-mounted horn; her mother gave each a brief sympathetic hug before she Invoked the God and Goddess and poured their libation. Eilir expected her to turn to them once more after that, but Juniper Mackenzie was laughing again, talking to the older man in the suit of plate-armor. Behind him . . .

Oh, wow, this one's pretty! Eilir signed discreetly.

Alleyne Loring was whipcord elegance in his leather-and-wool riding clothes, a smile lighting his face as he swung down from the tall black horse and looked around with his left hand on the hilt of his longsword, and a peacock-feather curling in the band of his broad-brimmed hat; the animal rested its head on his shoulder, and he stroked its nose absently. Medium tall, broad in the shoulders, narrow-hipped, moving like a cat . . . then he removed the hat and bowed to the images on the Dun Juniper gateway, shoulder-length golden hair swaying as he did, and politely poured out a few drops before he emptied the horn of the last small mouthful of wine.

Eilir glanced sharply aside at Astrid. Her *anamchara* was standing before the gateway, motionless, sighing. The expression on her face . . .

Oh, wait a minute, Eilir thought. *The first time you ever show any interest, and it's one who looks like young Lugh come again? It's not fair!*

Astrid murmured aloud, but from the way her lips moved was probably not really aware of it: ". . . for he was young, and he was king, the lord of a fell people . . ."

Alleyne Loring's eyebrows went up as he took in Astrid Larsson's tall elegant figure. Then he saw the details of white tree and stars on the black leather of her tunic, and his smile widened into a boyish grin.

"*Elen síla lumen' omentielvo,*" he said.

You couldn't be Astrid Larsson's *anamchara* for near ten years and not know that tongue; besides, those were Eilir's favorite books, too, even if she kept a stricter grasp on the boundaries between fantasy and the common everyday world.

He'd said: *A star shines on the hour of our meeting.* But even though she could lip-read Elvish, there was no Sign equivalent. Eilir felt her own lips compress in annoyance.

He went on, upending the empty horn: "*Sí man i yulma nin equantuva?*"

Astrid laughed in delight and clapped her hands together: "That's a special-occasion cup, but there's plenty to eat and drink waiting in the Hall, and I'll be glad to get you a refill."

This is not fair! Eilir thought. *This is my home and you're the one who gets to talk to him about it. This is just not right!*

The young man noticed her and signed—slowly and clumsily: *I'm sorry; I don't know much of this language.*

Eilrir made herself smile and returned a greeting. *Not fair or right* at all*!*

"You've come a long way," Astrid went on, as they all turned and fell into step into the interior of Dun Juniper. "You and your father and your friend."

Behind them the outer gates closed for sunset with a slow soft *boom* that shuddered through the feet, and then the inner leaves. Lantern light blossomed within—from windows, from larger glass-and-metal lamps on the towers and from the ridgepoles of the log homes that lined the inside of the walls, and bright from the windows of the Hall. That turned the carving and color of beam and pillar into a fantasy of shadow and brightness, crimson and gold and green; the timbers of the eaves continued up above the peak of the roof, and the spirals on them curled deasil and widdershins, gilded by the last rays of the sun. The carved totem-heads at the ends of the rafters loomed over their heads—wolf and bear, coyote and raven and more.

Alleyne checked a pace as the great building loomed up; his huge companion shaped a whistle.

"Well, there's a sight, and no mistake," the bigger man said.

"Like the hall of Meduseld," Alleyne said quietly.

"Just so!" Astrid replied.

Hey! My house! My mom's Hall! Eilir thought. *That's where I live!*

"We haven't seen anyone from overseas since the Change, much less from England! You'll have a lot to tell us!" Astrid continued enthusiastically.

"Sí vanwa ná, Rómello vanwa . . . England," he said, laughing again; his teeth were very white. Eilir's nostrils flared; he had a very pleasant masculine scent, clean and hard beneath the usual odors of horse and leather and woodsmoke.

Another figure moved. Eilir started; she'd noticed the man—it was hard not to, since he was six-seven and broad in proportion—but only out of the corner of her eye. He waited until she was looking straight at him before speaking, which was a courtesy she appreciated.

"Nattering on in Elvish again, is he?" he said; it was probably the sort of voice that felt like a bass rumble under your fingertips, if you touched his chest or throat while he spoke. "Bad habit of his . . . John Hordle's my name."

You do Sign? Eilir asked; the lipreading was a bit more of a strain than usual, given his accent.

Little bit. Want more.

Juniper was looking over her shoulder. Eilir started forward with the others, still feeling a slow burn as she stared at Astrid's back.

I'm your anamchara, *not the designated sidekick!*

They led their mounts over to the stables and spent a minute tending to them; she saw without surprise that Alleyne Loring knew his way around horses with an easy competence. In fact he moved so gracefully that—

John Hordle leapt backward, his mouth open in what must have been a shout of alarm. Eilir grounded her pitchfork with a wince and privately thanked the Lady that he'd been wearing a mail shirt; otherwise something rather nasty might have happened.

Astrid looked at her in astonishment: *Where were* you, anamchara? she signed.

Deep thought, Eilir replied, flushing and racking the long two-tined hayfork. *Sorry. Apologize for me, would you?*

Alleyne smiled, and after a moment so did John Hordle.

"That's my mom," Rudi Mackenzie said proudly; the Chief of the Mackenzies winked at him as she rode by and he waved enthusiastically.

"Well, yeah," Mathilda Arminger said, deliberately unimpressed. "I saw her when she attacked my train, you know."

There was the trace of a sulk still in her voice; Rudi ignored it; it was only natural to miss her family, when she couldn't go home. Then she went on: "Who's the guy in the funny armor?"

"That's the real English baron," Rudi said proudly. "He and my mom rescued *Lord Bear*."

"Oh, *him*," Mathilda said, sticking her hands in her pockets; she was wearing a Clan-style kilt, though in a plain gray guest-weave rather than the Mackenzie tartan, and a baggy sweater.

"Don't be a grouch," Rudi said. "Want to go and see if we can get something in the kitchens? I'm starving and it's a while until dinner."

"OK," Mathilda said. "But why can't you just *tell* them to give you something?"

"Did your mom and dad let you eat anything you want between meals?" Rudi said; he knew that was wrong, but it sounded like fun too.

"Well . . . no. I mean, my mom didn't."

Her face crumpled for an instant, then firmed; she shrugged off the sympathetic arm he put around her shoulder.

"She didn't like me hanging around low places and peons, you know."

"Lady bless, hanging around the kitchens is *fun,*" Rudi said. "It's a lot better than arithmetic lessons, that's for sure."

"Yeah, but they make you *do* stuff. Chores. And that's not what lords and ladies are supposed to do."

"My mom's a Lady," Rudi pointed out reasonably. "And she does chores. That's fun sometimes too. Anyway, it's got to be done."

Mathilda considered this and nodded, looking a little uneasy. "I suppose so. I don't think my mom would like it, though."

"Look—" He glanced around. "Want to know a secret?"

"Yeah!"

"My mom got a letter from your dad." He smiled as her face glowed. "He's going to send someone to talk to my mom about you at the Sutterdown Horse Fair, after Lughnassadh. And you can write a letter back. So why don't we go hit the kitchens, like I said?"

After a moment, Mathilda replied, "Maybe they'll have some of those sweet buns with the nuts?"

"And there's some new kittens there," he said.

"I miss my cat Saladin," she said. "But kittens are always fun."

They trotted off through the dispersing crowd. As they

went, Mathilda caught sight of the stars-and-tree sigil on Astrid Larsson's tunic.

"Oh, *that* stuff again," she said. "Doesn't she ever get *tired* of it? She's a grown-up."

"Don't you like the story?" Rudi asked. "I liked *The Hobbit* best, but Astrid says that's 'cause I'm still a kid."

"I think I'll *still* think it's way too long and full of boring stuff when I'm old, even if Dad got the idea for the flag out of it," Mathilda said. She giggled and dropped her voice to a whisper: "Have you heard about the other Ring story?"

"Other story?"

"The one where the hero's called Dildo Bugger?"

Rudi's face twisted in an expression halfway between fascination and disgust. "You've *got* to be kidding, Matti."

"No, really—"

Dun Fairfax, Willamette Valley, Oregon
July 22nd, 2007 AD—Change Year Nine

"It took me two Harvests to really get the trick of this, even though I already knew how to drive a team," Juniper called over her shoulder; then as she came to the end of the row: "Whoa! Dobbin! Maggie!"

There were two horses pulling the reaper, big platter-hoofed draft beasts with dark brown hides, sweating after a long day working in the hot July sun. They stopped as she called and leaned back against the reins; then she rose and rubbed at her backside for a moment; the metal bicycle-seat of the machine was hard, and muscling the big horses around was real work. Her hands and forearms were sore with day after day of doing it from *can* to *can't,* and the long sinews of her legs ached as well.

Eilir waved from the seat of the other reaper, pausing a second. *I'll take the last of it!* she signed, and Juniper bowed from the waist and waved a hand.

"Be my guest, daughter mine! Too much like hard work for us crones!"

They'd been working their way in from the edges of the field since the dew lifted with no more rest than the horse teams required, and only one ten-foot-wide band of standing grain remained, stretching from east to west along the contour of the hillside. It still wasn't nearly as hard as cutting wheat with twenty pounds of cradle-scythe the way they had their first two harvests, though; she didn't have the height or heft to use one of those. And a reaper could harvest many times the amount a cradler did in a single day, which was a blessing. Summer rainstorms were vanishingly rare in the Willamette's reliable climate, but you still had to get the wheat and barley and oats in as fast as you could. Too much delay and the grain would start to shatter, drop out of the head and be lost on the ground.

"It took you a while to learn the trick because of the slope?" Nigel Loring asked, straightening as he bound the last sheaf of a row and rubbing at the small of his back for a moment.

"Yes," she said. "You have to be careful on a thirty-degree slant like this, or you keep heading down and the horses get into the wheat—and you only get to practice two weeks in the year. It's a lot easier out on the flat, say over at Dun Carson west of here. More difficult on a hillside for the team, too, but Dobbin and Maggie are good-hearted and willing for all they're young."

She glanced over at him as he stacked a brace of sheaves, heaving one in each hand—and they weighed sixty pounds each. Loring handled the task with an easy economy of motion, bare to the waist and tanned nut-brown. He was only a few inches taller than she, but broad-shouldered and built like a greyhound; deep chest, flat belly and narrow waist. His tanned skin was scarred here and there, a little loosened with middle age, and his sparse blond chest hair was as grizzled as the thinning yellow thatch on his pate, yet his slender body was nearly as tight and compact as a boy's. Farmwork would keep you fit, but she knew that the hint of dancer's grace in his movements came from martial arts in his youth and sparring with the sword since—one had to be cat-agile for both.

The hillside field they were cutting was one of Sam Aylward's, the last of the Dun Fairfax crop. Eilir's reaper wheeled away as her mother reined in and started to cut the last strip down the center, the long boards of the creel whirling and bending the yellow-gold grain back as the teeth of the cutter-bar snipped it, amid a smell of dust and meal and green juices. Poppies fell as well, like bloodred drops among the gold of the wheat—they were traditional English corn poppies, which seemed to have mysteriously naturalized themselves around here, starting with the Dun Fairfax fields. Juniper suspected Sam's clandestine home-sick hand with a few packets of seed salvaged from a garden-supply store rather than natural spread from garden plots, but either way they were pretty.

Birds and insects and small beasts fled the advancing machine as the straw fell onto the moving canvas belt behind the cutting teeth, and an endless belt of wooden tines raked it into a smooth windrow that fell onto the ground behind. Juniper groaned slightly as she stretched again, then jumped down and bent and put her palms against the ground; the wheat stubble was prickly beneath her hands, but shot through with soft young shoots of the clover sown among it. When the small of her back felt relaxed she straightened and twisted until something went *click!* in her spine, and then bent backward with her hands linked over her head.

And were you watching, good Sir Nigel? she thought with amusement as she opened her eyes. *Hard to tell, with that polite poker face of yours. And of course, would I be pleased or annoyed if you did?*

The reaper left a long row of cut wheat in a snakelike trail over the ground for the workers who bound the grain, a score or better for each machine. Bend and grab a handful, bend and grab a handful, and keep on until you had a bundle as thick as your arms could span. Then take a swatch in each hand, twist it around to hold it, tuck it in, and you had a bound sheaf; eight leaning together in a pyramid made a stook, and they could wait overnight with their heads up out of the dew, ready to be pitched onto a wagon and carted back to Dun Fairfax for threshing. The air was warm and still as they bent to the rhythmic effort, the tips of the trees motionless; it was a relief to have a good excuse simply to watch. She could feel the westering sun beating on her like warm pillows, as the thin homespun linsey-woolsey shirt clung to her body.

Sam's daughter Tamar led up a two-wheeled cart pulled by a pair of little yearling oxen, her own hand-reared pets. It held a big plastic barrel of water and a motley collection of mugs; she filled one for each of them. All Sam's household were here in the field, and most of the able-bodied from the other families who held land in Dun Fairfax. None of the farms were big enough to justify a reaping machine of their own, so the dun kept two owned in common to share around, and everyone worked together getting in the harvest, turn and turn about as fields came ready—the usual arrangement in a Mackenzie settlement. People had come down from Dun Juniper as well, trading working time for future barrels of flour, or simply pitching in for neighborliness' sake since they planted little grain themselves; altogether there were about enough to bind and stook the wheat as fast as the two machines cut it.

"Thank you, sweetling," Juniper said to the girl. "And the horses are thirstier than we, sure. They should have something before they're taken to the pond or they'll overdo."

Juniper took off her straw hat and fanned herself as she drank; most of the scores of people in the field were in kilt and singlet or less, but she wore a long-sleeved shirt against the sun, and kneesocks, and tied a scarf around her coppery hair beneath the hat; even so her freckles had spread and multiplied, as they did every summer. The lukewarm water tasted wonderful in her gummy, dusty mouth, and she wished she could plunge her head into the barrel. Instead she handed back the mug for a refill, with a murmur of thanks; it was plastic too, with the beginning of a crack on the rim. Nigel's was clay and made after the Change, a reddish brown ware plain except for a stylized feather drawn on the side, but skillfully thrown and fired.

"My ninth harvest since the Change," Nigel said meditatively. "And every one seems—"

"Like a reprieve?" Juniper suggested.

He raised the mug of water in salute. "Just so."

"Is this very different from a harvest in England?" Juniper asked; the first year had been hard here, and she suspected much worse in the British Isles, even on the islands.

"The harvest? Surprisingly similar; a bit earlier, and if this weather is typical—"

"It is that."

"—then the climate's more reliable here. In England it can rain any day of the week in any month of the year, and nowadays with no warning at all. It makes getting in the corn a trifle nerve-racking."

He looked north and east towards the towering peaks of the Cascades and the green slopes that were like a wall along the edge of the world.

"We've nothing like *that* in England, of course. I won't say this is the single most beautiful spot I've ever seen, but it's wonderfully varied. I like the contrast, the fields and orchards here—which *are* very much like parts of southern England—and then the tall mountains and wildwood so close, and the changing patterns of sun and shadow . . . beauty on very different scales, but complementary."

Juniper looked at him. "Well, well," she said. "It's hidden depths you have, Nigel."

His slightly watery blue eyes twinkled. "Sandra Arminger said much the same thing. But it was far more alarming, coming from her."

Juniper snorted and threw a twist of straw at him. "I should hope so!"

Her eyes went across the crowded field; Mathilda Arminger was there, running around with the other children, and helping, as they did.

"I'm surprised she's not a total horror, with parents like that," she said quietly. "And she's just a child, when you get to know her. Spoiled more than a little, and with some odd notions, but not spoiled to the point of being really rotten, if you know what I mean."

"Is minic ubh bhán ag cearc dhubh, as the Gaels say," Loring replied, and winked at her.

"A black hen may often have a white egg, yes," she agreed. "But it's what hatches that counts."

"She's young, yet, very young. It takes a good deal to spoil a child that age, and I'd venture that the Armingers would shield her from the worst of the world they've made, for a while at least. Even complete rotters often love their children, in my experience."

He stared a moment, as if lost in memory. Tamar had gone around to fill buckets for the horses; they lowered their massive square heads and drank with slobbering enthusiasm. Down at the other end of the field the second reaper cut the last of the wheat, and there was an explosion of cheers from the folk at work. A half-dozen of them lifted the driver out of the seat and began tossing her in the air amid whoops and screams; she recognized Astrid, and the massive form of Little John Hordle, and the bright head of Alleyne Loring.

And all three of them pitched in to help as if there were no question of it being otherwise, Juniper thought. *Which is a good sign, in my experience.*

Rudi Mackenzie was around the edges there as well; then he and Mathilda Arminger came sprinting up to where Juniper waited.

"Can we take Dobbin and Maggie?" her son said. His eyes sparkled like green-gray gems in his tanned face, and he was still full of energy despite being allowed to work with the binders for the first time this year. "Please?"

"All right," she said. "But remember; get them cooled down a bit before you let them drink."

"I know, Mom," he said, politely not adding an *of course,* though he'd grown up with horses in general and these two in particular—they were half his age.

Juniper and Nigel unharnessed the animals; Rudi and Mathilda sprang onto their massive backs, sitting as proudly as knights on their destriers. The horses accepted it calmly, moving off at an ambling walk towards the pond in the far southwestern corner of the field, where a willow-grown earthen bank held back the creek and made a watering point when this field was in the pasture-lea part of its rotation. Of course, they'd have done that without any guidance at all. Horses were not mental giants, but they usually had enough sense to betake themselves to water when they were thirsty; the problem was keeping them from drinking too much and doing themselves an injury.

"Good-natured beasts," Loring said, as they straightened the harness and draped it over the seat of the reaper. The bells on the great collars jingled one last time. "Mostly Suffolk punch, aren't they?"

"About three-quarters," Juniper agreed. "Chuck, ummm, *found* eight Suffolk mares right after the Change, and I like the breed. Strong as elephants and friendly as dogs, mostly. The stallion we put them to was a Percheron but we've been breeding back."

He cocked an expert's eye. "Your son has a way with horses; I've noticed it before. He reminds me of Alleyne at that age. Maude taught him mostly, of course. She had the better seat, in any case—far better than mine, then."

For a moment a bleak misery of grief settled over his usual mild cheerfulness, and then he shook it off with a scarcely visible effort, turning instead to the scene before them. Melissa Aylward came down from the gate at the top of the field, where a brace of wagons had drawn up half an hour ago. Quiet fell as she halted by Eilir's reaper and took the last grain cut in her hands, plaiting and shaping it into the form of the Queen Sheaf; she was the High Priestess of Dun Fairfax, and it was her right to make the Corn Mother and give Her the first blessing.

Juniper had been a little surprised at how good Nigel Loring was at binding a sheaf—or any other of a countryman's tasks, from handling a plow team to plashing a hedge. When she said so he smiled at her.

"My dear Ms. Mackenzie—"

"Nigel, Nigel! You've been living under the same roof as me all summer! You're being Stiff, Reserved and Proper again, like an old central-casting Englishman! And Dennie accuses *me* of putting it on!"

"Very well, my dear *Lady Juniper*. I grew up in farming country."

"Aristocrats though, I thought? Landed gentry of Hampshire?"

He laughed aloud at that. "Well, we were saddled with an ancient, leaky, slowly subsiding stone barn of a house and a large, very shaggy garden, which we were too stubborn to hand over to the National Trust, yes. Plus a few weedy fields around the mausoleum that raised a regular crop of debt every year."

"I resemble that remark," she said, laughing in turn. "When I inherited my great-uncle's house and land"—she inclined her head northward towards the hills and what was now the Mackenzie clachan—"right up until the Change the real legacy was a continual threat of having it sold from under me for back taxes, with a minor key in unaffordable roof repairs. I had more disposable income when I was living in a trailer and busking for meals than I did with a fortune in real estate."

"And the taxes appertaining thereunto. As the saying goes, Land gives one a station in society and then prevents one from keeping it up."

"*Oh,* yes. Though I'm surprised to hear you going Wilde like that, Nigel."

"In deadly Earnest, I assure you." Loring chuckled. Then he went on with a wealth of experience in his tone: "There are few so poor as the land-poor."

"Although come the Change . . ."

He nodded. "But what with one thing and another, I learned my way around the Home Farm. And Sam's family were neighbors of the Lorings. In fact, until we sold off everything apart from the manor house and one farm in 1921, they rented land from us, and had for generations. My father died when I was an infant, and my mother when I was about three. My grandmother raised me, bless her, and turned me into the Edwardian fossil that I am. Her world stopped changing about the time my grandfather Eustace stood too close to a German howitzer shell near Mons in 1914."

"What was she like?" Juniper asked; her mind conjured up a hawk-faced old dame in a high-collared bombazine dress. *Though that's probably my hyperactive storyteller's imagination at work.*

Nigel shook his head. "She was what is politely called 'formidable'—which meant she terrified everyone, including myself—a memsahib right out of Kipling. Which is one reason I spent a good deal of time over at Crooksbury when I was a lad; Sam and I were always getting into mischief together, and later I used to help out there when I was down from school, until Sam's father gave up the struggle."

"Your grandmother didn't make a fuss? If she was that stiff and old-fashioned—"

"Oh, no, she didn't object at all." He smiled reminiscently. "Grandmamma was of the old breed; it was quite the thing for me to have a friend like Sam while I was young, as long as he didn't, as she would put it, 'presume.' And since Sam would rather have spent a week shoveling muck onto a spreader than one afternoon taking tea with Grandmamma, it all turned out for the best. Though God knows it would have been different if I'd been a girl . . . In any event, I learned a good deal that was extremely useful after the Change; not that anyone could have anticipated it would happen, nor that I would then spend the better part of a decade teaching ex-urbanites how to farm in a very old style."

"I resemble that remark too, except that I was learning with them while I taught," Juniper said. "Although I did have a nice little half-acre vegetable garden before the Change, and an orchard, and Cagney and Lacey—my Percherons—and I took up weaving as a winter hobby in my teens. Thank the God and Goddess we had some *real* farmers around here, and Chuck, and Sam most of all."

Now the rest of the folk were coming towards her. Juniper and Nigel Loring spent a moment unbolting the cutter bar, folding the creel and raising it and the bar to the traveling position.

"This is a good piece of work," he said as they worked with wrench and pliers from the toolbox beneath the seat. "We've . . . they've been making some much like it in England, these last few years. After salvaging the better-preserved working models from exhibits, of course."

"Only the last few?" Juniper said, raising a brow.

"There weren't enough horses left in England before that, or even oxen. We had to breed up our herds from what few we could bring through the first year on the offshore islands, plus a very scanty trickle from Ireland. Mainland Britain was eaten bare, except of animals that could hide well, which mostly turned out to mean noxious vermin of various sorts. It was strictly spades and hoes and sickles for quite some time, and we're . . . they're . . . still shorter than you are here."

Juniper shuddered in sympathy. Farming was sweating-hard work with plenty of oxen and horses to help and the tools and machines for them to pull and power. Doing without that help meant brutal killing toil, and you got a lot less out of it. Unaided humans just couldn't cultivate enough ground to do more than live hand-to-mouth.

"We were lucky—the ranching country over the mountains had stock we could trade for, though getting the working equipment was another story."

She patted the reaper affectionately. "We were certainly glad to buy these and retire the cradle scythes! Change Year Three it was; a stiff price, but worth it."

"They're not local?"

"No, from Corvallis," she said. "We *could* make them"—there was nothing in the simple machine that couldn't be duplicated by any good carpenter and a smith—"but they have machines worked by waterwheels for their little factories, so it's cheaper. Most of the Valley buys from them."

Loring nodded. Just then the others came up in what would have been a procession if it weren't so casual and hadn't included so many children and dogs running around; Miguel Lopez and his family stood a little aside, looking awkward, although his friend Jeff Dawson was an enthusiastic Dedicant now.

Melissa Aylward led, walking before the corn dolly she'd just plaited, impressively solemn. Sam Aylward and Chuck Barstow carried it behind her, held high on crossed spears. This Queen Sheaf would belong to Clan Mackenzie as a whole, as well as Dun Fairfax, which was an honor for the smaller settlement. The wheat-straw figure she'd plaited was four feet from splayed feet past swelling belly to rough-featured head, and crowned with poppies. Melissa herself had shed most of the extra weight she'd put on before the birth of her new daughter, but hadn't gone back to full fieldwork yet and looked solidly matronly and deep-bosomed in her *airsaid,* a fit vessel for the Mother. The more so as she held a handful of wheat as a scepter in her right hand and red-haired little Fand in the crook of her left arm.

Juniper bent her head and Melissa touched it with the stalks; then both High Priestesses fell in behind the Queen Sheaf, leading the harvesters walking two and two to the north end of the field where a great oak stood beside the laneway and the field gate and a young hawthorn hedge. Most of the rest of the settlement's people waited there, the ones who hadn't been in the fields today by reason of age or infirmity or *very* pressing business.

The two men knelt and lowered the plaited figure before Juniper; she made the Invoking pentagram above it. "All hail to Brigid, Goddess of the Ripened Corn, who accepts the given sacrifice!" she called aloud, smiling. "And to the Corn King, Lugh of the Sun, who dies in this season so that the harvest may be reaped!"

Her voice became a little more solemn for a moment as she turned to her people: "With the work of our hands we help the Lord and Lady make this place the fruitful garden that it is—not wilderness nor iron desert paved and bound, but instead our rightful home. For though we here shall die, as die men and trees and beasts and ripened corn each in their appointed season, yet the blood, the house, the field, the woods endure; and every babe and lamb and new-sprouted leaf proves the immortality we share."

Chuck and Sam braced their spears against the gnarled trunk of the oak, so that the Corn Mother could oversee the festivities; the spears stood for the Lord of the Harvest as well. Melissa broke the loaf made from the first sheaf they'd cut and set it before Her, standing for an instant with a fold of her *airsaid* drawn over her head.

"And She says . . . *eat!*" she said, turning and dropping the shawl back on her shoulders.

The harvest workers stood in a circle around her; they gave three cheers, flinging up their joined hands. After that everyone pitched in, helping set the trestle tables and benches and unload the harvest supper, taking turns to run down to the pond in the lower corner of the field and shed their kilts and dive in to slough off the dust and sweat. One of the wagons carried soap and towels, clothes for the Dun Fairfax folk and robes for the guests who'd be walking back to Dun Juniper later. This wasn't the harvest feast proper—that would come on Lughnassadh, next week, when everyone had had a chance to rest a bit, and be a lot more elaborate—but it was the beginning of it. In most duns there was considerable good-natured rivalry between households to outdo each other at a harvest potluck.

Juniper shook out her water-darkened hair, then pinned her plaid with a jeweled brooch done in swirling knotwork of sinuous gripping beasts; she'd brought along a clean set of gear that included silver-buckled shoes and an embroidered shirt with a ruffled front as well as clean kilt and plaid. Someone handed her a wreath of poppies and oxeye daisies, and she set that on her head as well.

Since the Chief must look spiffy where possible, she thought, with a wry inward shrug. *Well, I was used to dressing up in costume like this for a performance before the Change! Now it's different, though. Now these are my* clothes *and the performance is my* life.

Sir Nigel, on the other hand, wore one of the coarse, gray, hooded guest robes with casually regal authority, as if it were his everyday garb, despite the way the hem trailed on the ground. He bowed slightly as she reappeared.

"My word, but you look dramatic," he said. "And quite authentically Celtic, if not quite Scottish."

Juniper turned up her hands. "What can I say? I was just now thinking that I wore stuff like this before the Change to look exotic—and today, it's just what I wear."

"Quite. I felt . . . a proper burke wearing plate armor, as Sam would say, for the longest time after I'd learned to use it well. As if I were trapped in one of Alleyne's tourneys and couldn't get out, or in one of my childhood daydreams. Now it's quite natural, except when I think about it."

He offered her an arm with a courtly gesture, and she tucked a hand through it; the forearm under her hand felt as if it had been molded out of hard living rubber.

"Ahhh!" Sam Aylward said, seating himself and taking a first swallow of beer from a crock kept cool in an old plastic trash barrel full of cold springwater. "Dennis Martin Mackenzie, my thanks!"

The big bearded man doffed his bonnet and showed his bald spot in a bow. "Hell, they're your hops and barley, Samuel Aylward Mackenzie. Plus the mountains contributed the water free of charge."

"But you did the brewing, mate."

"Pity we don't have any ice, to get it really cold," Dennis replied, with a malicious twinkle.

Aylward shuddered dramatically. "Bite your tongue, Yank! If I didn't like to *taste* the beer, I could drink ice water cut with vodka."

Then he looked out at the field of stooked sheaves. "Well, that's done and now we can all relax and lie about eating chockies till next spring."

He was smiling as he said it, and there were groans from most within earshot; the work of the harvest wouldn't really be over until Mabon, still months away—at which time the fall plowing started anyway. Late-planted winter gardens under mulch would yield a bit through most of the cold season. But at least the *main* crop was in, the breadstuff that was the literal staff of life. Plenty of it was on the long plank tables, in the form of biscuits tapped still hot out of thick clay traveling ovens, and of baskets full of warm round loaves marked with the eight-spoked Wheel of the Year on their crusts.

They went with butter, cheese, fresh salads—everyone gorged on greens this time of year—glazed hams, a great cold roast beef, fried chicken, a noble dish of Sam's apple-cured bacon with wild chanterelle mushrooms, steamed vegetables, a huge pot of baked beans with bits of fat pork standing amid the crumbling brown crust, and for dessert, cream with the first peaches and berries and bowls of dark red Mona cherries, and honey for dipping. Jugs of cold water, milk, Dennie's home brew, cider and wine and chilled herbal tea went down on the planks.

Juniper was suddenly conscious of how ravenous she was, and how good the salty brown smell of the ham was, and that the first new potatoes were waiting, steaming gently as the lids of the pots were removed, beside deep royal purple baby beets . . .

And I'm aware of the fact that I intend to not *worry about anything for the rest of the day, starting with letters from the Protector and the negotiations. Work drives out care, but so does sheer willpower.*

Everyone waited politely while the Lopez family said their grace, then started passing plates. Juniper took a sampling of side dishes around a slab of the ham, added a dab of the strong homemade mustard before she began to eat, and noticed Nigel Loring dipping a spoon into a crock of equally strong homemade creamy horseradish to put beside thin-sliced rare roast beef.

"Careful," she said. "It's good, but Melissa makes it hot enough to jump over for luck like a Beltane bonfire."

"All the better," he said, nodding up the table.

Melissa sat at the head of the trestle table, with Sam Aylward at her right and an improvised cradle of sheaves and blankets on her left. There was a tender fondness in Loring's face as he saw the other man raising his infant daughter in both hands, chuckling when she grabbed at his face and tiny pink fingers closed on one nostril.

"I always thought Aylward would be a good father," he said; the buzz of conversation was loud enough that privacy was possible, even in the open air, if you leaned close. "I'm very glad to see him settled. *He* claimed he was married to the SAS, of course, and that *'roots are for ruddy turnips, sir.'* "

"That's hard to imagine, after all these years. Sam seems like a butte or some other natural feature—anything solid and strong—and about as rooted as a man can be and not sprout leaves like the Jack-in-the-Green," Juniper said.

Then she paused to cut one of the new potatoes across, add a pat of butter and chew blissfully. When she had swallowed: "Of course, the time before the Change seems . . . unreal a good part of the time."

"Except when you wake and everything *since* the Change seems like a fading dream, and in a minute you'll hear autos and aircraft and the television," Loring said quietly.

Juniper nodded. "Less and less often, but it still happens," she said. "And will until the last of us who were old enough to remember the time before pass on."

Then she shrugged and smiled. "As for Sam, not a day's gone by since I found him in April of the first Change Year that I haven't thanked Cernunnos for him."

Loring coughed slightly. Juniper grinned at his blush and went on: "Yes, I'm quite serious about it," she said. "Really I am, all the way through. Though I'm told I can be surprisingly rational most of the time . . ."

It's true that most stereotypes have a core of fact in 'em, she thought with amusement. *So some Englishmen really do dread embarrassment more than they do fire and sword! I think before the Change the Lorings were very, very old-fashioned. Now they may be back in fashion . . . who knows? He doesn't talk much about his past, or hasn't until just recently.*

Nigel cleared his throat. "We have . . . they have traditions much like this back in England," he said. "The harvest supper and even the corn-straw figurines. Done with an Anglican emphasis, of course. The king encouraged it; for that matter, so did I, before we had our little falling-out."

"You mean before he tried to kill you?" Juniper chuckled and filled her mug with Dennie's brew, then held the tall pitcher over his. "More? Here you go then. I'm not surprised some of it's familiar: Who do you think you Christians stole it all from originally? Or to put it another way, we modern Witches reconstructed—plundered, stole and copied, some say—from the same sources."

"Pass those creamed potatoes, would you? Ah, reconstruction is one thing, but I don't doubt the whole affair feels a little different since the Change, eh? More serious for most? And we're none of us really *modern* anymore, are we?"

Juniper gave him a considering look. "Well, you're not just a pretty face, are you then?" she said, and enjoyed his blush again. "Or just a strong sword arm. Yes, it's . . . different now. I suppose you were always Church of England yourself?"

"Nominally, for tradition's sake." He smiled at himself. "I was a choirboy, if you can believe it."

They chatted and ate as the sky darkened and the last of sunset's gold faded from the stooked grain and turned ruddy on the mountaintops eastward. Lamps were hung from the branches of the oak tree, and eventually the youngsters down at the foot of the table began a round of songs. Someone brought Juniper her fiddle case; she spent a moment tuning, then joined in as one tune after another was called.

At last something unfamiliar came, and she cocked her head, listening:

> *"We'll run the course*
> *From Stonehenge up to Uffington!*
> *On a white chalk horse we'll ride . . ."*

Hordle's deep bass and Alleyne's firm baritone sounded through the warm darkness, as everyone listened to catch the unfamiliar words. Sir Nigel unexpectedly joined in, his voice a little rougher than his son's:

> *"Within the wood where Robin Hood once made his secret den*
> *We'll play a song and sing along with all his merry men*
> *And tell a tale with fine-brewed ale and friends from long ago*
> *And tread the miles of Robin's cross—"*

She caught the lilt and whistled softly, nodding her head to the beat as she memorized the words, then struck up her fiddle to follow along. Not long after yawns said it was time to go, after a long day of heavy work and a full meal; a good many of the children were already asleep on blankets, and scarcely stirred as they were lifted into the wagons for the short trip home. Their older siblings helped the adults stow the rest of the gear and the remains of the feast, and hitch the reapers for towing. Juniper walked alongside one cart where Tamar and Rudi, Mathilda and young Edain Aylward all lay tumbled amid blankets and straw like exhausted puppies, stirring a little when the vehicle jounced.

The farm lane twisted away eastward like silk ribbon in the night, field and forest murmurous on either side. Ahead she could see the outline of Dun Fairfax's walls, and lights behind them; a few hundred yards to her right Artemis Creek chuckled over its bed, and the roadway beside it was white beneath stars and moon, next to the dark riverside trees.

Nigel Loring was not far away, she noticed, and he'd slung on the heater-shaped shield with the five roses, and his sword. Along with the loose robe, it gave him an oddly Biblical look, or perhaps that of some warrior monk of the Crusades.

Although I doubt he'd do well at Mt. Angel, she thought whimsically. *Abbot Dmowski is a good enough man, but sadly lacking in a sense of humor, I think. There's a good deal of quiet humor in this man, when he isn't sad.*

Alleyne Loring was on the other side of the wagon, also armed and unobtrusively alert. Near him were Astrid Larsson and Eilir, both looking as if they were trying to crowd next to him without making it too obvious.

Not obvious to anyone who's blind, perhaps, she thought, and suppressed a grin. It wasn't that she didn't sympathize with both girls, but . . . *The Foam-Born will have their little jokes, and oh, how the young suffer! What storms and stress and follies! And how they hate it when anyone laughs!*

John Hordle was not far away, whistling the old tune softly in the mild summer night. *He* didn't have the same air of hidden tension as the others; more one of alert patience, if she read him aright—and she had some confidence in her skill at that. They bid farewell to the Dun Fairfax folk at their own gate and turned north through the winding track that climbed the densely wooded hillside. Within it light vanished save for a few lanterns hooked over spearheads, casting flickering illumination upward into the branches, and once glinting suddenly from eyes beside the trail—a fox or coyote, from their green flash and the swift flight.

Then they came through onto the benchland that held Dun Juniper; stars and moon were almost painfully bright for an instant, silvering the waterfall to her right and the tall white walls of the Mackenzie citadel. The wind blew in her face, cooler now and fir-scented. The horses snorted, knowing their stalls were close; a sentry hailed them quietly, out among the stock in the fenced paddocks. The gates swung open with a groan, and suddenly there was light from the windows of homes and Hall, and hands to help.

Mom? Eilir signed.

Juniper started from a reverie. *My heart?*

Astrid and I thought we might take some of the Dunedain . . . and Alleyne and his friend . . . up through the woods after Lughnassadh, she said, and nodded eastward and north. *These are some boar that have been sniffing around the gardens, and . . . well, just in case anyone was nosing around who shouldn't.* Her eyes flicked to Mathilda Arminger.

Good idea, Juniper said. *The crew working on Dun Laurel could use some feeding, if Cernunnos favors you.*

Then on impulse, looking down at her son: "Nigel, give me a hand with these two, would you?" Not even the rocking passage through the woods had woken the two nine-year-olds.

"My pleasure," he said, and seemed to mean it.

"It seems a shame to wake them at all," Juniper said softly.

"Then don't," Nigel replied unexpectedly. "They grow so quickly, and very soon they'll be too old to be carried to bed anymore."

They lifted carefully; Mathilda was considerable weight in her arms, but the Englishman bore her son's solid sixty pounds without evidence of strain. The big loft room was dark but welcoming, warm from the heat soaked into the brick chimney that ran through it from the hearth below, scented with flower sachet, wool and wood and wax; neither child did more than stir and mutter as they were undressed and tucked into the blankets on their futon beds. Nigel Loring paused for a moment, looking down at Rudi Mackenzie. His sword-callused fingers brushed back a lock of tousled hair the color of raw gold.

"I envy you," he murmured softly. At her look he went on: "Alleyne has grown to be a man any father would be proud of, but sometimes I still miss the boy he was. There was so little time, and I was often away, as a soldier had to be then. Maude and I wanted more children, but—ah, well, forgive an old man's foolishness."

He looked up and smiled at her, blinking in the darkness. Suddenly the thought rammed home in her: *I want this man.*

Less a thought than knowledge, felt with heart and belly and loins as much as brain, but that too. *I have been too long alone; and this man is the one I want—the one She sent to me. Fierce and tender, terrible and gentle. And I will bring out that quiet laughter, and make him whole again.*

He rose and bowed slightly. After his footsteps had faded on the treads of the stairs, her smile remained.

I will have him. So mote it be!

CHAPTER TWENTY

Mithrilwood, Willamette Valley, Oregon
August 10th, 2007 AD—Change Year Nine

These foothills the Dunedain Rangers had christened
Mithrilwood were a day's journey north and a little east of
Dun Juniper; the area was a mix of tall Douglas fir and
overgrown fields and abandoned clear-cuts, ideal for game;
more steep rugged hills than true mountains and surrounded by empty ex-farmland on three sides. Outside this
canyon you could see the snow peaks eastward—Mount
Washington best of all, and sometimes Mount Hood tiny to
the north—but down here where the stream had cut its
way into walls of basalt the world closed in, with rock walls,
falling water, and dense growth. The light filtered through
conifer needles and big-leaf maple into a thick umbrous
green shadow, like being underwater; moss dripped from
tree limbs, and mushrooms grew thick beneath them. Behind him the stream chuckled over polished water-
rounded rocks and poured down a basalt ledge in a torrent
of spray.

Alleyne Loring waited, alert, the boar spear gripped in
his hands. The scrub ahead of him shook, amid an enraged
squealing. He smelled a new scent under the green sappi-
ness of bruised vegetation; something hard and rank with
musk. They hadn't seen anyone in a week save one pair of
Mackenzie hunters. Nothing human, at least . . .

Astrid's weapon came up to his right; the head was
broader than a war spear's blade, and had a steel crossbar

welded to the base. Dogs barked farther into the brush that crowded from the cliff face up to the edge of the old trail, and the beaters made noise of their own; the wind was from the north, in his face. Fairly soon those pigs would discover they'd been tricked . . . There was a series of deep snuffling grunts, then an enraged squeal, loud and shrill.

"Jesus!" he shouted as he saw what came out of the woods, on the heels of Hordle's *"Bugger me!"*

Wild boar were increasingly common in England; they'd been reintroduced just before the Change in game parks, and enough had hidden successfully from the clumsy attentions of urban refugees. The survivors bred fast afterward, spreading through the burgeoning wilderness. He knew from experience they could be dangerous, but most of the people here had talked about feral swine, and he'd been expecting something more like a barnyard pig gone wrong.

This one was five hundred pounds if it was an ounce, a black low-slung torpedo of muscle and bone and little clever hating eyes, tusks like daggers on either side of its bristling snout, heavy shoulders and hump armoring its vitals. *Someone* had brought the real wild-boar article from Europe in days long past, and those genes had been doing very well indeed.

The boar hesitated when it saw the line of humans, its hindquarters switching from side to side in a rush of fallen leaves and duff while its heavier forequarters pivoted in place. Other shapes were moving beneath the trees, but he ignored them as he crouched and flourished the spear, drawing the beast's attention. He could see it taking him in as it turned its head to get a view from either eye as slobber drooled from its champing jaws and every coarse needlelike hair bristled erect; then the hindquarters hunched and it sprang. For an instant he could swear it was off the earth, and then all four split hooves were churning the forest floor like tank treads, throwing twigs and leaves head-high as it hurtled at him as fast as a good horse.

The boar's shoulders were sheathed in gristle, and it held its massive dished head low to protect its neck and set itself for the upward rip with its tusks. Alleyne skipped a half pace to the side just before it struck, going down on one knee and ramming the butt of the spear into the earth. The broad sharp head knifed in, and then there was a shock like being thrown headfirst into a stone wall. He skidded backward as the spear butt dug a trough through the earth, and the crossbar below the blade fulfilled its ancient function: keeping the self-impaled boar from shoving itself up the shaft of the spear to savage him in a dying frenzy.

Eeeeeeeeeeee—

The squealing was loud enough to hurt his ears, and the spear shaft jerked like a monstrous fishing rod in his hands with Leviathan on the hook as the boar twisted and heaved against the palm-wide foot of steel, trying to thrash him against the unyielding ground. Blood sprayed out over Alleyne's boots as he jerked his feet aside and tried to set them, and a four-inch spike of ivory missed the soles by a fractional inch.

"A Elbereth Gilthoniel!"

The words were a hawk screech as a spear lunged at the boar's flank, with Astrid's white-blond mane trailing behind. Eilir's struck an instant later from the other side, and the boar went to its knees with blood pouring down from its mouth mixed with slaver. Then it surged erect again, impossibly moving against the weight of three strong humans bearing down on the shafts that impaled it, its long grisly head tossed high in agony and rage. Alleyne went down again, kicking a heel against its snout as the beast lunged to try to grab his foot in its jaws.

"Out of my bloody way!" Hordle bellowed.

All three of them rolled aside. The big man's sword swung, a yard and a half of steel with both hands on the long hilt. It struck the boar's neck just before the shoulder hump with a hard *crack* as if the edge had hammered into an oak. The squealing was cut off instantly, and the great beast slumped to the ground. Alleyne lay panting for an instant before he climbed to his feet. The four of them stood looking at each other, the sweat of fear and utmost effort running down their faces, and then they began to grin. Arms went about shoulders in a momentary grip, and then they broke apart, laughing.

"Anyone hurt?" Astrid called.

Voices answered; Alleyne saw that the others had made kills as well, mostly beasts *much* smaller and younger. One young man loosed a shaft from his longbow as he watched, and a retreating squeal was abruptly cut off.

Eilir's hands moved. Alleyne followed it without difficulty: the Rangers used sign as much as speech, and the summer had been an education in it—the last fortnight a lesson by total immersion. The main alternative was Sindarin, not English.

Julie's sept totem is Boar, she signed. *She should do the honors.*

Astrid nodded and called. A girl in her late teens with black braids under her Scots bonnet came up.

"Wow!" she said, looking at the boar while she stabbed her spear into the earth to clean the blade. "I just got a little yearling! Man, that one looks mean! Must be ten feet long."

That yearling will taste a lot better, Eilir signed. *But this was their chief.*

The girl nodded and went down on one knee, leaning on her spear shaft as she touched a finger to the blood and marked her forehead.

"Go in peace to the Summerlands, brother boar," she said solemnly. "You fought well for your kin. We honor your courage, and we thank you for your gift of life."

Eilir raised her hands to the forest, then signed in a way that was half a dance:

Take this warrior's spirit home to rest, Lord Cernunnos of the Woods, Horned Master of the Beasts. Our thanks to You for Your bounty to us, who are Your people. We take in need, not wantonness, knowing we too shall walk with You the shadowed road, in our appointed hour. Let this brave boar be reborn through the Cauldron of the Goddess, the source of all things. So mote it be!

"OK, let's get to work," Astrid added. "The meat won't keep at all if we don't drain them fast. Hey, Crystal!"

A girl in her midteens brought up the packhorses; she was the Rangers' junior probationary member, and beaming with pride at being able to help with the chores. The beaters came down through the last of the brush, making a lot less noise than they had when they were driving the sounder of swine, and the dogs with them set up a joyful wuffing and leaping, roughly translatable from canine as: *We killed something, hot damn, boss, that smells good, let's eat!*

"Can I have the tusks?" black-haired Julie asked Alleyne. "I know that they're yours, you're the first spear, but seeing as it's my totem and all . . ."

Alleyne nodded, a bit bemused. *It would all seem a bit put-on, if I hadn't spent the past decade playing at knights-in-armor,* he thought. Then: *Well, no. I* played *at it before the Change, with lath swords and careful rules. With edged steel, it's all too real . . . and these Rangers are all younger than I.*

He'd noticed that in England, too. Alleyne had been twenty when the Change struck; a young adult, but adult. Those who'd been in their early teens when the world went mad were different; almost as different as men his age or Hordle's were from his father's generation.

And I suppose children born since will be more different still.

He was working as he thought. They lashed the hogs' hind legs to sticks, tied ropes to those and then over convenient branches, hoisting the carcasses to drain and for ease of access. Besides the monster boar there was another of about two hundred pounds, a young sow of the same age, and half a dozen others down to near suckling size. Gutting and skinning were messy and smelly tasks, but familiar enough. The way the Rangers stripped to the buff to avoid getting blood on their clothes wasn't, but he had to admit it was practical—if a bit distracting at times. People in Britain had gotten a little more straitlaced since the Change; evidently things had gone the other way in this particular part of Oregon.

"I hate to lose the heads and guts," a red-haired boy said. "Wasting all that headcheese and sausage casing, it's not right."

"Be thankful we can salvage most of the meat, this time of year," Astrid said. It was mildly warm, in the seventies,

Alleyne estimated. "Lucky none of them are wormy. Besides, the coyotes and crows and ants have to eat, too. It'll cool well in the springhouse, though, and be all the better for hanging a little when we get it to Dun Laurel."

"Do you get many boar that size?" Alleyne asked, whetting a curve-bladed skinning knife on a pocket hone; the others were using their *sgian dubh,* and there were hatchets and saws with the packhorses.

"Christ, I hope not," Hordle added, as he slung the animal's head—minus the tusks—aside; half a dozen hounds squabbled a little over precedence; then the victors settled in for concentrated gnawing while the others went for lesser prizes. "This one was more excitement than I like when I'm standing up."

There are more and more of them every year, Eilir signed, pausing with the hilt of the knife in her teeth before she made the first anus-to-throat cut on one of the sows. *And the big ones get bigger and bigger. There were so many hunters in the old days, with guns, that they could keep them down. We can't.*

"Pigs like brushy country, right enough, after oak or beechwood," Hordle said, hauling the boar up hand-over-hand without perceptible strain; the huge muscles bunched and coiled under the pale skin of his shoulders and back. "Lots of roots and such. They're a bloody menace back in Blighty these days and getting worse. Not enough people to keep them down there either."

Eilir nodded; this time she stuck the knife into the tree trunk to speak for an instant—you had to be careful about the uncooked blood and flesh of pigs.

The things are getting to be a real pest here in the Valley too, and there's all the camas root and abandoned farmland for them. Nothing short of a tiger will tackle a grown boar, or a sounder of sows with piglets, and what they do to a garden or vineyard is just enough to make you cry, not to mention the way they rip up the woods. And they breed like rabbits.

"They might as well be people," Astrid said dryly, to general laughter; Eilir laughed too, a silent mirth with a toss of her head that made Alleyne chuckle himself.

They loaded the carcasses on the packhorses—the boar was quartered first, since it would be unfair to make any one horse carry quite that much. The canyon path ran beside a waterfall; then *behind* the falling water. A deep pool lay below; they all slid down a rope secured to a steel piton driven into the living rock and dove and swam in it, or stood under the fringes—but only the fringes, since the stream was narrow but the water fell from nearly two hundred feet above. After a moment—it was *cold* water—they hauled themselves out on the rocks and spread towels to dry off.

And I'm just as glad that it's cold water, Alleyne thought. *Given the scenery, one doesn't wish to make one's interest too clear, eh? Free and easy is one thing, rampant another.*

Astrid leaned back on her palms and looked up at the water falling down the green-mantled black rock, seeming to drift as it launched itself free from the cliff and then turning to swift-plunging silver lace farther down. She signed instead of speaking, clearer under the toning roar of the falls: *That's why we call this area Mithrilwood. In the winter, when the mist freezes on everything it's like a world of silver.*

I'd like to see it then, he replied. *But not to wash in.*

She laughed at his shiver, and then looked away with a flush that spread down from face to breasts.

Eilir leapt up: *Let's get home!*

Home in Mithrilwood had turned out to be, somewhat to his surprise, a log-cabin lodge with a stone kitchen attached, built in the 1930s by the CCC. Whoever that acronym belonged to had had high standards of craftsmanship. The low building was better than a hundred feet long and nearly forty wide, with a great fieldstone hearth set in one wall. The high-peaked shingle roofs were green with moss save where the Rangers had made repairs in recent years; outbuildings of the same construction were sleeping quarters, stables, storehouses, and a springhouse—diverting a cool stream through it provided a semblance of refrigeration, enough to keep meat and milk fresh a bit longer. The works of man hugged the earth amid tall Douglas firs, maples and oaks, scattered through a stretch of rolling hilly land; brush and saplings were reclaiming the road that had led here before the Change, save for a narrow path kept open by axes and hooves.

Once the meat was stowed and the horses stabled, the Rangers set to practice for the rest of the afternoon, except for a pair whose turn it was to cook. Alleyne saw Hordle's eyebrows rise as they shot at the mark; every one of them was a good archer, and some were very good even by the exacting standards Nigel Loring had set for the regulars. They joined in for the unarmed-combat practice, recognizing Sam Aylward's eclectic freeform, and then for sword drill . . .

"Give it a go?" Astrid asked.

"Ah . . . certainly," Alleyne said.

I'll have to be careful not to hurt her feelings, he reminded himself.

He had his own heater-shaped shield along, and there were plenty of the alderwood practice blades much like the longsword he customarily used; he took stance with his left foot advanced, shield up under his eyes and his sword over his head, hilt towards her. The protective bars across the face of the drill helmet they found for him might well be an advantage, since he was used to wearing a visored sallet rather than the open-faced helms favored in western Oregon. Astrid was using Bearkiller gear—a round shield two feet in diameter, and a long single-edged sword with a basket hilt, much like a Renaissance schiavone or a claymore.

"Kumite!" said the Ranger acting as referee. *Fight!*

The point of Astrid's sword flicked out at his eyes, seeming to float and then blur like a frog's tongue after a fly. *Fast,* he thought admiringly, and smacked it aside with a two-inch movement of his shield, whipping the longsword down in an overarm cut.

Crack!

The hard polished leather of the targe shed the edge, precisely angled to throw him off-balance and jar every bone in his body down to the small of his back. He recovered with a skipping hop like a child jumping rope as her blade hissed in from the side in a hocking cut at the side of his knee; she blocked his counterthrust with an upward flick of the practice blade, striking from the wrist . . .

Just under ten minutes later they stepped back by unspoken mutual agreement, both breathing deep and quick, sweat soaking their gambesons in huge fresh patches and making runnels down face and neck. A circle of Rangers gave an admiring cheer, and several of them clapped him on the back.

"That's a lot longer than any of us has ever gone with Astrid without her getting a touch home," someone said. "Except Eilir, of course."

Remind me not to think bloody nonsense, Alleyne thought, bringing his blade up in salute with a wry grin.

Astrid's face had been inhumanly calm during the bout, except for a disconcerting small smile. Now she grinned back, then quickly looked aside, her eyes fluttering unconsciously.

That's a good sign, Alleyne thought. *Except that it might not be . . .*

"Hey, let me try," a brash youngster named Kevin said. "Let's see how you handle short sword and buckler."

After a more few bouts of his own Alleyne found himself watching Eilir working with Crystal, the newcomer, who was grimly determined as she hefted the practice blade of alderwood, double the weight of the real thing.

No, Eilir signed, stepping back after a brief slow-time passage and letting her practice blade swing on its wrist-thong for a moment. *Remember, keep the buckler towards me, not swinging behind you, slightly ahead of your sword point.*

"Whenever I try to think of what I'm doing with it, I lose track!" Crystal grumbled.

Everyone starts that way. That's why we do it slow to start with. You practice until you don't have to think about it. Once more. You attack.

Crystal did, bringing the short broad-bladed sword up in a stab towards Eilir's stomach. The deaf girl's buckler came down in a sweep that knocked it out of line. In the same motion she stepped forward and continued the arc, ending up with the bowl-shaped boss of the little shield in front of Crystal's nose. Then she stepped back again.

You can punch the buckler, or strike with the edge of it. It's a weapon too—believe me, when you've whacked some-one hard in the face with a two-pound steel weight, they lose all interest in hitting you. And don't block the opposing sword directly—bat it away as if the buckler were an exten-sion of your hand. It's not like a man-at-arm's shield, or even a Bearkiller targe, it's supposed to redirect force, not absorb it. Now back to the basic position—crouch a little, left foot forward and knee bent. Sword . . . buckler . . . sword. One-two-three! Let's go!

They engaged again; even in slow motion, Eilir's darting grace was impressive. So was the gentle patience she showed in the face of the girl's clumsiness. He guessed that that was why Astrid worked with the more advanced stu-dents.

Better! Eilir signed, stepping back again when Crystal had turned puffing and red and the weapons started to quiver in her hands.

A dozen yards behind her Astrid smiled as she took a dare and went to one knee, her eyes closed; then they flared open as she rose, twisting and drawing and striking in a blur of speed. Her long blade hissed in a horizontal streak and she was extended in an impeccable follow-through. The severed dragonfly dropped, spiraling towards the ground in neat halves.

Alleyne caught it out of the corner of his eye. *She's not human,* he thought, with a slight inward quiver.

"This is a lot harder work than I thought it would be!" Crystal said to Eilir. "I thought I was *used* to hard work since I was a little girl!"

There's nothing harder than sword work, Eilir signed sympathetically. *It uses different muscles from almost any-thing else. Let's go try you on the pells again. You've got to go full-out to build speed, and get used to the shock of hit-ting something. Remember, most of the people you fight will be stronger than you are. You have to be quicker, and you build speed like you build muscle.*

A rock-fringed natural swimming pool not far from the

buildings had been reconditioned—diverted stream water in at one end and out the other replacing the chlorine cycle. Nobody minded a few floating leaves anymore. Alleyne ambled down a flagstone path towards it, with the clatter and bang of combat fading behind him, stripped and dove in; the other Englishman joined him. Alleyne rested against the steps and spoke low-voiced to Hordle: "Having a good time, Little John?"

"Well, I'm not the one with the two best-looking girls panting after him," the big man said, grinning. "Seriously, I know you're the one who looks like a prince, and I make people think of *fee fi fo fum* and grinding the bones of an Englishman. Which is a bit hard, innit, seeing as I *am* an Englishman?"

"Luckily, women aren't as fixated on looks as we males," Alleyne pointed out.

Hordle's grin got wider. "No, but looking good doesn't hurt much, does it? Still, I reckon my charm and wit will win out in the end."

They both laughed; Hordle's voice was like a monstrous frog croaking. "That was quite a display you put on with little Astrid."

"Christ! But it's not that which makes me hesitate."

"Her relatives?"

"No . . . no. I like her brother-in-law and most of the others seem good sorts at heart, though Signe Havel is just a trifle too carnivorous for my taste; and that man Hutton is a magician with horses. Nor am I so noble and pure as to spurn the thought of being related to the local royalty. And she's good company, we've got a good many common interests, she's clever, and a stunner . . . well, you've got eyes, don't you, man?"

"She's not pretty, sir. Eilir is pretty, pretty as a man could want. Astrid is like something you'd see in a painting, the type you're not allowed to get close to because your breath might pollute it."

He ducked and came up blowing and rubbing at his thatch of dark red-brown hair. "Let me guess. It's the fact that she's bloody barking mad that's giving you the collywobbles?"

Alleyne made a gesture, and tried to keep the defensive tone out of his voice: "She's not mad. She couldn't have put this Ranger thing together if she was mad. She doesn't *actually* think she's living in the Third Age of Middle Earth, or that she's a warrior elf-maid fighting the Dark Lord, though when you think of what that man Arminger is like . . . But she is . . . obsessed. The problem is that I share her obsession . . . in a very, very much less intense fashion. And seeing how it *might* flower into full-blown form *is* rather frightening." He sighed. "I meet a beautiful American heiress, I like her, she likes me . . . and then she turns out to be a fundamentalist with a more literal interpretation of scripture than I feel comfortable with. Only our bible was written by an Oxford don about sixty years ago."

Hordle thought for a moment, his heavy brows knotted in thought. Alleyne waited; one of the advantages Little John Hordle had in life was the way people assumed his massive size and strength meant he was stupid. It wasn't so.

"Well, I wouldn't be quite so frightened as all that, if I were you. I would if this were the old world, but it isn't."

Alleyne's fair eyebrows went up further. "What difference does that make?"

"Look at it this way, Mr. Loring. If this were the time before the Change, what use would it be to be obsessed with horses, and swords, and bows, and living in the woods like a poncing elf and fighting bandits and man-eating beasts and evil kings? As opposed to here and now, where she can actually *do* all those things—*has* to do most of them, in fact."

Alleyne opened his mouth, then closed it again; it was his turn to frown. "You know, Sergeant, that is a very acute observation. If it's madness, it's a very practical form of insanity. Now that I think of it, even if she's living a fantasy she's gone about it in a very practical way."

Hordle shrugged. "Think nothing of it. Sergeants are supposed to figure things out and let officers take the credit."

"Of course, the fact that if I were to make a play for Astrid, her friend might have time to think about someone else has *no* bearing on your advice."

Hordle rolled his eyes upward and put his hands together in an attitude of prayer: "Of *course* not, Mr. Loring! I deny everything! How could you think such a thing?" He clutched at his chest. "I'm wounded, wounded, I tell you!"

Alleyne laughed. "We'll see what develops. What do you think of settling here? Father's giving it serious consideration."

"And I know why," Hordle said with a wink. At Alleyne's blank look he chuckled and went on: "Seriously, it's pretty country, right enough, nice climate—a lot like Hampshire, only better—there's plenty of land for the asking, and the hunting's good. I could get myself a bit of a farm, or even a farm *and* a pub. Incidentally, they're not bad, themselves, this Ranger lot, even the girls. I thought they were a bit, *mmmm* . . . informal-like, but they know what they're doing and they don't waste time talking when it's important."

"Not surprising, when you consider that Sam had a say in training them early on. Not to mention Mr. Havel. *And* they've had real work to do here, with bandits and raiders and the prospects of a pukka war hanging over them. More than we did in England, when we weren't sent abroad. Being in the regulars back home was too much like being a policeman at times for my taste, this last little while."

"Right. Never did want to be a copper. Still, at first I thought . . ."

Alleyne grinned at him. "Thought they were too given to playing dress-up here, like me, eh?"

Hordle shrugged his massive shoulders. "I deny everything!"

That evening was pleasantly cool, enough for the fire they lit in the big fireplace to be welcome for more than the leaping flames. Dinner was a whole young pig just past weaning, butterflied and grilled with a hot sauce, potatoes roasted in the ashes, and a heaping salad of wild greens. The interior of the lodge was big enough for the full score of Rangers; everyone lay around on cushions after the meal, facing the fire and sipping at wine or cider, singing and talking as the flames illuminated the corners of the room with flickering ruddy light. The warmth of the flames brought out the spicy scent of the heavy myrtlewood furniture.

A chorus ended:

> *"I watch the deer and geese go by, fox-foot in the snow;*
> *Climb the peak of Washington mountain,*
> *looking to the valley below—"*

"Hey, people," Astrid said when the tune died down. "Business for a minute. Look, we've been using this place for years, but only on and off. What the Dunedain need is a base. Someplace we can train new members, store our goods, an armory, have a few people always on hand. I've talked to Lord Bear about it . . ."

And I've spoken to Lady Juniper, Eilir added. *She thinks it's a good idea.*

"We could claim this whole area—the old state park, and say another ten thousand acres around it, and manage the woods. Nobody's using it much and we did run those bandits out of here; Mark got killed doing it. And it's such a good hideout more would be sure to come here if we didn't patrol."

The Rangers looked at each other. The redhead—*Kevin,* Alleyne thought. *The one with the medical training*—raised a hand. "How would we live?" he said.

Partly by hunting, Eilir said. *That's good here even in winter—animals come down from the high country. We could swap the surplus for things, and eventually sell some timber, and things like nuts. And we wouldn't be here all the time, not all of us. Plus we could contract for special jobs. We already get paid for tracking down man-eaters, and we could do more guarding caravans south past Eugene, or out east over-mountain. We already get top rate for road-guard work, a lot better than the scruffy thugs who usually get hired. They'd know we wouldn't rob them.*

"And since what we do here in the Valley helps everyone, I think we can get a contribution from the Mackenzies and the Bearkillers both," Astrid said. "Maybe from Corvallis and Mt. Angel, too. You know, flour and cloth and spuds, horses, some cash, too, that's only fair. There's enough meadow near here for our horses, and we could have a few milch cows and a garden, if there were someone here to keep an eye on things. Shall we try it?"

The youngsters looked at each other. "Beats spending all your time farming," one said meditatively. "Beats it all to hell and gone."

"Rangering's the most fun I've ever done," another said, winding a braid around her finger. "It would be nice not to have to give it up. But what about kids and stuff?"

"Well, the original Dunedain were Rangers for generation after generation," Astrid pointed out. "It ran in families . . . I mean, most jobs do, these days, don't they? There's plenty of places like this we could have bases—call them Ranger-steadings, say. Like the hidden city of Gondolin, or Thingol's hidden kingdom, but on a smaller scale."

Like Imladris, Eilir signed.

The discussion went on into the night. The proposal passed on a show of hands; then Astrid went and stood by the mantelpiece with its load of books.

"What'll it be tonight?" she went on brightly. *"Silmarillion, Book of Lost Tales, History of Middle-Earth,* the *Bestiary,* or the trilogy itself?"

And here I was going to suggest a walk in the moonlight, Alleyne thought. Then he saw Eilir glancing at him. *Of course, I hadn't quite decided whom to ask.*

Dun Laurel, Willamette Valley, Oregon
August 14th, 2007 AD—Change Year Nine

"Eilir!" Juniper Mackenzie called, waving broadly. "Astrid! Over here!"

The site of Dun-Laurel-to-be was swarming with workers under the bright August sun, filled with wagons, teams of oxen and horses, heaps of logs, timber, cement, and wheelbarrows, and loud with the sounds of saws and axes, shovels and hammers and ratcheting winches. Laurel Wilson's people were there, all eighty-nine of them, plus another forty who'd decided to join the new settlement, and a good three hundred from elsewhere in the Clan's territory, plus quite a few wanderers and gangrels come in to earn a little by casual labor. Three sides of the palisade were up, with blockhouses at the corners—a new refinement—and the rest of the great logs were ready, left down to make access easier for the work going on apace within. One old farmhouse was already there, now repaired and made weathertight again, and other buildings were already frames or sheathed in planks; houses, a meeting-hall-cum-bad-weather-covenstead, barns and sheds and smithy, weaving shops and granary. Enough space was left for small gardens, herbs and flowers; outside, below where the little creek broadened out into a pool, pegs marked out truck allotments.

Most of the fields about were shaggy-overgrown, or grew nothing but tents and temporary paddocks, but a start had been made on clearing a few, and they showed as neat squares of brown tilth, plowed and harrowed.

Near Juniper, Laurel Wilson, Alex Barstow and Nigel Loring bent over a table crowded with drawings, and weighted down with slide rules, compasses and set squares. Laurel frowned and hitched at her plaid as Nigel traced a line with one finger.

"And once the windmill has pumped the well water there, Ms. Wilson, you can lead it by gravity to all the houses and to your livestock as well. Then waste drains into this artificial-swamp system; first these covered pits full of chopped bark and sawdust—or straw and leaves, anything like that will do—to take the raw waste, then through the reed-bed, into the pond with willows around it, and at the downstream end of that you've got clean potable water you can use for stock, or irrigating your truck gardens. The reeds are very useful, the composting pits give you fertilizer when you dig them out every few months, and you can raise fish in the pond, as well."

"You'll be the envy of the Clan with that," Juniper put in. "We're putting one in at Dun Juniper ourselves, and it's a lot better than what we had. Sir Nigel gave us the idea."

"Not mine, not mine," he said modestly, smoothing his mustache with one finger. "His Majesty has a system like this at his country estate, Highgrove. I've overseen building dozens of them in England. All you need is a head of water for the flow."

Tom Brannigan of Sutterdown was there as well; a large contingent of the volunteers was from his settlement, with the experience of putting up their own town wall fresh in their minds and hands.

"Could we hire you to put one in for us?" he said hopefully. "Our present system is expensive as hell, and we're running out of those treatment chemicals."

"Possibly," Nigel Loring said, starting a little as Juniper trod on his foot.

"Don't do it for free!" she whispered in his ear. *"Laurel needs all the help she can get without adding to her folk's debts, but Brannigan can afford to pay."*

"Ah, perhaps we could discuss it later," he said. "At this horse fair you were telling me about, perhaps?"

The mayor of Sutterdown nodded. Just then Eilir and Astrid pushed through the crowd, blinking at the worksite, followed by the two young Englishmen.

Aha, thought Juniper, reading the signs. *You could tune a harp to the tension there. No resolution to* that *little problem, yet.*

Astrid whistled. "Lady bless, but you've made a *lot* of progress on that!"

Eilir nodded emphatically. *What's with, excellent Mom? You've got twice as much up as I thought you would! At this rate, we'll be able to break a lot of land for the Dun Laurel folks before everyone has to go home to get their own crop in.*

"Nigel here has been a wonderful help," Juniper said, squeezing his arm. "With tricks of the trade, and organizing."

Nigel Loring shrugged. "Experience, don't you know. Glad to be a bit of help. And I had basic engineering training."

"Speaking of helping," Astrid said, and pointed.

The Rangers were coming down the road, striding out beside a long train of horses with packsaddles loaded high.

We've got half a ton of meat, Eilir amplified. *Wild hog, mostly, and some deer, and a feral cow. I don't suppose you could use any of it, Tom?*

Tom Brannigan grinned; he was in charge of feeding the workforce. In theory it went towards the debts Dun Juniper would owe the Clan as a whole, but it would be years before those tallies were paid in full. Even if the first draft was Dun Laurel folk helping harvest his vineyard that Mabon season, and prune it over the winter.

"I'll say!" he said, enthusiastically. "Thanks for the contribution, Rangers."

Eilir put a hand on Astrid's sleeve and raised an eyebrow at Sutterdown's Mayor, High Priest and wealthiest resident.

Brannigan sighed and nodded. "OK, I'll throw in one hundred-gallon barrel . . . OK, *two* hundred-gallon barrels of the Special for your Rangers." A silence dragged. "OK, some wine too, and two hundred pounds of barreled salt pork this Yule, and sixty bushels of flour when you want to draw on the town mill. That enough?"

"We're both making goodwill gifts," Astrid said sweetly. "You'll have to be the judge of that."

Sutterdown, Willamette Valley, Oregon
August 21st, 2007 AD—Change Year Nine

"I can't *tell* you how much help this has been, Nigel," Juniper said.

"Oh, you've got some very capable chappies," the elder Loring said, self-depreciatingly. "You've accomplished a great deal. I've just given them a few ideas."

They sat their horses just east of Sutterdown; he nodded towards the tall walls that surrounded the town, shining in their white stucco.

"Those are quite remarkable. I'd never have thought of using the old *Murus Gallicus*, and me with the remnants of a classical education, at that."

"We've got a fair number of craftsmen and builders," she said. "And we've done larger projects mostly by brute force and rule of thumb. I never suspected how useful it would be to have someone who could *calculate* things."

She nodded towards the water-race before them. "This,

for example," she said, and grinned. "I'd have missed some of the implications, if you hadn't pointed them out."

Sutterdown had tall hills just north of it, outliers of the Cascade foothills. The Sutter River ran south of town, but the pioneers who'd founded the settlement had dug a mile-long canal to take water from the river higher up. Now it provided power again; besides the tannery half a mile away—that was a smelly business—a big four-stone grist-mill stood by the canal just outside the town, wood-built on a stone foundation, with its twenty-foot overshot wheel turning briskly and water pouring off it in white foam. A wagon left as she watched, piled high with sacks and barrels of whole meal, and another sent bags of wheat up a rope hoist to the second story; under the creak of wood and rush of water went a burring rumble as the granite millstones worked.

The men walking towards the Mackenzie chieftain had more uses for the water in mind: Tom Brannigan, and two others in the brown jean trousers and four-pocket wool jackets common among the well-to-do in Corvallis, with businesslike short swords by their sides and broad-brimmed hats on their heads. One was a short, stocky dark man, and the other a tall lanky woman with her barley-colored hair gathered in a ponytail. They were sweating a little in the warm late-August sun; Juniper nodded politely, but kept to her saddle.

Height as a psychological advantage is not to be despised, she thought. *And as one shorter than most for most of my life, don't I know it!*

"You don't like them, do you?" Loring murmured.

She shot him a glance. *Perceptive of you, Nigel,* she thought. *I'm not an easy person to read, when I don't wish to be.* Aloud: "Not much, but we can do business with them, perhaps. Tom Brannigan likes to do well out of a bargain, which I don't grudge him. Those two might as well be adding machines in human form, and that I do not like. Besides which, they're also leaders of the faction in Corvallis that thinks it can do business with the Portland Protective Association. The which I do not like or sympathize with or agree with at all, so."

The Corvallis men cut the pleasantries shorter than most Mackenzies would have considered polite, and came to business sooner:

"It's a viable proposition," one said; his name was Turner, and he was as close as the Willamette Valley came to a banker these days, as well as half-owner of a big metalworking shop and foundry. "Provided the contract is reasonable. Obviously, a project this big requires long-term guarantees for the amount of capital we'll have tied up. It's not like selling a load of anvils or sledgehammers."

"My thought exactly, Mr. Turner," she said. "And your papers were quite detailed. Ms. Kowalski, we've done business before."

She cast a sidelong glance at Nigel before she went on: "That's why I'm inclined to reject the deal as it stands. Or to recommend to the town's assembly that it be rejected, that is. Of course, if you can persuade them better than me, or refer it to the Clan as a whole . . ."

Turner's eyes went wide; Brannigan's closed in a wince. The chance of Dun Sutterdown's adults voting the two-thirds majority required to override the Chief was somewhere between nil and nothing. Even a simple majority would be vanishingly unlikely without Lady Juniper's agreement.

"Why?" the Corvallan said. "Lady Juniper, breaking and scutching flax and slubbing and carding raw wool by hand are a *lot* of work, but they're easy and simple to do with powered machinery. Granted there isn't the market or population to support a full-blown mechanized spinning and weaving industry yet, but we could make a start. Cloth's getting more and more expensive."

Juniper nodded, smiling sweetly. "Yes, both those are sort of labor-intensive. I've done both myself, on many a long winter's day. And everyone needs to make more cloth, now that we're finally running out of the last of what was left from before the Change."

"Well, then," Turner said. "This is a perfect location for a slubbing and scutching mill. And there's plenty of wool and flax available, and more wool from the CORA country over the mountains."

"Processing it here makes sense—it cuts down on transport costs," Agnes Kowalski added. "The finished goods are a *hell* of a lot less bulky to ship. Particularly getting the fiber out of the raw flax, that's *got* to be done close to the point of production."

They'd known each other—slightly—before the Change; Kowalski had made and sold handlooms to hobbyist weavers like Juniper. After things stabilized in the Corvallis area, she'd taken up the trade again, then to renting looms to those who couldn't afford to buy them, buying wool as well in bulk, doling it out on credit to the weavers using her looms and taking the output in payment at a fixed, usually low, price. These days she had a dozen workmen building and repairing looms, and several score weavers and spinsters in and around Corvallis working for her on contract.

Ken Larsson had told Juniper once that had been known as the "putting-out system" in Europe in the old days, and Juniper disliked both it and the woman who'd reinvented the idea all on her own.

"Yes," Juniper said patiently once more. "But you two had best understand that we're not interested in a wonderful mill the wonderfulness of which benefits only *you.* Corvallis, in my opinion, is too given to falling in love with toys for their own sake. And you, Tom, but it's mostly Mr. Turner and Ms. Kowalski I'm concerned with. You see, most of the flax-breaking and wool-carding gets done in the winter, as I've said, when our crofters have little else to do, particularly now that most of our duns have threshing machines and they don't need to beat the grain out with flails in the off-season. If the slubbing and scutching's to be done in a mill instead, then the crofters have to sell their raw flax and wool, and buy them back for spinning and weaving."

"If it's still cheaper—" Kowalski said.

"Then yes, they'll benefit, because they can spin and weave the more, or make shoes, or whatever takes their fancy and suits their skills. But that depends on how much of their produce they have to pay to the owners of the mill for the processing of their materials, doesn't it?"

Turner closed his mouth with a comment unspoken. *Didn't think I'd understand that, did you?* Juniper thought. *And thanks to Nigel I know just how much of the added productivity you were planning on keeping for yourselves.*

"What's your objection to the contract, Lady Juniper?" he said.

"That you plan on *renting* us the millwork," she said. "And we end up paying you for it forever, the more so as you seem to feel we should take all responsibility for breakage, wear and replacement as needed. I've no objection to paying you a fair price for your contributions. Mr. Turner, you've got forges that can do castings on that scale and we don't and it would be expensive for us to duplicate them, and Ms. Kowalski, you've got useful outlets for our produce. That doesn't mean we're going to be your tenants. At seventh and last, we can do without you more easily than you can without us. You'd have built these mills in Corvallis territory if you could get the water-power as cheaply and a location as good, and that's just the start of why you want to locate here."

Turner was a short stocky man, with burn scars on the spade-shaped hands below his embroidered shirt cuffs. He took off his felt hat and slapped it against his thigh.

"What's your counteroffer, my lady?" he said, his voice clipped.

"Oh, it's not my place to tell Sutterdown and its people what to do with their own," Juniper said lightly, and watched Turner surreptitiously grind his teeth. "I would *suggest* to them that they keep full ownership, with a phased purchase arrangement . . ."

When the talk was over the short muscular Turner and his tall lanky companion walked away towards their tethered horses to give the matter *further consideration.*

Which means they'll take our terms, in the end, more or less, Juniper mused with satisfaction. *I thought so.*

"OK," Brannigan said. "I got too hungry and jumped at the fly without looking at the hook."

"Let that be a lesson to you, Tom," she said. "And thank Sir Nigel here, too. I smelled a rat, but it was he skinned the beast for me and read its entrails, sure."

When the mayor had gone, she let her hand rest on the pommel of her saddle and looked at the town, the checkerboard of small farms about it, and the tents and rope corrals of the folk arriving for the horse fair.

"This is what I should be doing, if I have to be Chief," she said after a moment, surprised at the passion in her own voice. "Helping my people better their lives! Instead I have to spend most of my time thinking about wars and threats. I hate it!"

"You should," Nigel Loring replied. "God preserve me from a leader who *likes* to fight; that's tolerable in a soldier, bad in an officer, and a disaster in a ruler. But it's all part of what a Chief has to do as well, and you know it." He nodded down the valley. "You're keeping their homes from the torch and their children from death."

"Thank you, Nigel," she said. "You understand."

His hand rested on hers; she turned her fingers and clasped his for an instant, worn and strong like her own. Then he cleared his throat and looked down at the town.

"I suppose we should go find ourselves some lunch."

"That we should," Juniper said, smiling as she neck-reined her horse about.

Sutterdown's horse fair had started modestly in Change Year Two with a group of ranchers bringing surplus stock over the mountains to swap, cutting down on the expense of guards and the risk of bandits by driving their herds together. Then it made sense for folk from other parts of the Willamette to come and buy horses here as well, this being the slack season after the grain harvest and Sutterdown being very well placed. Once the habit was established, it was also a fine chance for anyone with *anything* to sell to meet potential customers, which made a fine market for food and drink, so crofters from all over the Clan's territories brought their surpluses here.

"So you see, it's very much to our Clan's benefit, because it's to everyone else's as well," Juniper said to Eilir and Rudi. "People meet and exchange ideas and plans and news as well as goods and stock."

Astrid was walking with their party as well, Sam and his

lady and their daughter Fand in a backpack, and the Lorings and Little John Hordle. They were all working on ice-cream cones; it was a fine bright late-summer day, comfortable shirtsleeve weather without being hot, and the morning sun shone from a sky azure from horizon to horizon.

"Beneficial even in small things," Juniper went on. "For instance, the stockbreeders need to rent pasture. Farmers for miles around get a fee for it—and also manure for the fields they plan to plow and plant this fall."

Rudi nodded gravely, but Mathilda wrinkled her nose. "Manure!" she muttered.

"Manure grew the fodder for the cow that made that ice cream and fertilized the beets that gave us the sugar, my girl," Juniper said sternly. "Earth must be fed or we all go hungry."

A horse fair was necessarily a sprawling affair; tents were pitched for miles in every direction, over pastures and harvested grain fields and in orchards still heavy with fruit. There were jugglers and singers as well, and vendors of everything from taffy to toasted nuts, and food stands, and sellers of salvaged books and silverware and jewelry—some new-made, these days—and traveling sword masters showing off their style and taking on all comers for a bet, and wrestlers and martial artists doing likewise, and games where you threw balls to win a prize, and even a few carousels and miniature Ferris wheels, all horse- or ox-powered, of course. The children were goggle-eyed, and Astrid and Eilir and the young Englishmen were enjoying themselves as well; you didn't see many strangers day-to-day in these years, or hear such a babble of voices talking and shouting and singing, or the mixture of music and neighs and shouts—there was even a table with a woman shifting a pea between three cups.

They came to a big paddock set up with a six-rail fence; there seemed to be a commotion there, and then Juniper saw a horse rearing and bugling its battle call, hooves flailing. "Make way, there!" she said quietly; she knew the difference between a horse venting and one in genuine fear and anger. *I won't have cruelty here.*

Sam filled his lungs and shouted: "*Make way for the Chief!*"

People did a double-take and let her and hers through to the fence. For a moment everyone was spellbound, watching tense black loveliness canter around the enclosure, forgetting even the bleeding groom being helped through the gate as hooves seemed to barely touch the ground beneath floating grace. The mare arched her neck and dodged back and forth as she saw the staring mass of humanity, then did another circuit, wedge-shaped head high and high-held tail streaming.

"Oh, my goodness," Nigel murmured. "Sixteen hands, would you say, Alleyne?"

"And a fraction. Warmblood with a fair bit of Arab folded into its family tree," he replied. "Looks a little like a hunter, but faster, I'd say. Fit for a destrier of the best. Have to see how her wind holds up over a long course, but I'd wager she'll run most things on four feet into the ground."

The horse chose that moment to hop in place, lashing out with its hooves behind in case anyone should be sneaking up in its blind spot, then landed and took up its canter without missing a beat.

"*Look* at her motion, would you, Father? That one has dressage in her genes," said Alleyne. "What a *horse!*"

Rudi wiggled forward and sprang onto the fence, standing on a rung and resting his hands on the top rail, his face shining. Nobody paid him mind; across the paddock was the party from Larsdalen, Mike Havel at their center. The murmuring died down until it was a background hum, quieter than the drum of shod hooves on packed dirt.

In the quiet, the voices of the men were easy to make out; and the desperation in the voice of the ranch-country wrangler talking to the Bearkiller bossman.

"My lord, you aren't going to see a better horse than Donner here. She's worth every penny of three hundred new silver dollars, but for you, I'll take two seventy-five."

Mike Havel's slanted eyes looked at him coldly; that was a *lot* of money in terms of the ninth Change Year in central Oregon, where barter was still more common than coin; easily twenty times the price of a good-quality riding horse.

Then he handed his sword to his wife and vaulted over the tall fence with fluid grace, approaching the horse slowly, speaking softly and soothingly. That turned to a curse and a catlike leap backward as it reared and milled its forefeet like lethal steelshod clubs, and then stood with its head cocked and ears forward, nostrils flaring red pits as it snorted warning and wrath.

"You'll never see a more intelligent four-year-old mare," the wrangler said. "See how she's looking at us right now, thinking!"

Havel gave a snort of laughter, almost as loud as the horse. "Mister, she's not looking at us that way because she loves us, and that's a fact, by Christ Jesus."

"You could easily train this one to rear up in battle and strike at the enemy!"

"Well, shit, yeah, and have her get a spear in her belly and leave me standing in front of someone's lance point with my thumb up my ass," Havel said dryly.

"Lord Bear, I've been raising horses all my life and—"

The man stumbled to a stop at a cold gray-eyed gaze. Havel spoke over his shoulder. "Will, how long have you been wrangling?"

The middle-aged ex-Texan had been watching, squinteyed. Now he spat into the dirt of the corral and scratched the back of his neck.

"Since my daddy put me on an old cow-pony, when my momma was still changing my diapers," he said. "I've seen that look in a horse's eye before. Back when I was riding roughstock."

Then he slipped between the bars and tried in his turn. "Whoa there, girl. Whoa, there, Donner. Easy, girl, easy, I don't mean you any harm 'tall."

He got two paces closer than Havel had, and had to dodge teeth after a warning snort; Hutton went forward, into the space by its shoulder where a horse has trouble kicking, then backpedaled as it turned and struck with its head extended like a snake.

"That horse is a man-killer!" he swore.

Hutton backed for a moment to be sure the horse wouldn't charge, but it seemed satisfied to have driven him off. Then he turned to the Bear Lord, keeping a weather eye cocked on the mare.

"Mike, this man's right. That's a fine horse; don't think I've ever seen a better, for a war mount; good legs, short back, deep chest; she'll go like a jackrabbit with those haunches and she moves right pretty, as pretty as sun on water. Only you'd have to say it *was* a good horse, before this damn fool ruint it, tryin' to break her spirit. Look there, see? She's been whipped up under the belly. He's got her afraid of her own shadow, and killing mad at the whole human race besides. This shitheel ain't fit to break a pig's head in with a hammer, much less wrangle a horse."

"My lord, for you, two hundred—"

He stopped and winced as Havel poked a finger like a steel rod into his chest; it hurt even through the leather jacket.

"Mister, I wouldn't get on that horse if *you* paid *me* to do it. When I go into a fight, I've got the enemy trying to kill me—I can't afford to worry about my own damn horse trying it too. I might give you fifty for her as breeding stock—no, I'm not going to risk my farm staff getting kicked into next Thursday. Not a penny, unless you want to trade a side of bacon for the hide and hooves."

He turned away. The wrangler took off his battered Stetson and threw it down and stamped his riding boot on it, then glared murder at the horse. It was easy enough to see his thought; any likelihood of a sale had just publicly evaporated, and he wasn't going to go to the trouble and danger of taking her back east over the mountains.

Rudi murmured, just loud enough for his mother to hear: "He'll *kill* her! Kill her and feed her to his dogs!" Then, aloud, calm and happy: "What a waste!"

Rudi's clear young voice sounded like a bell of crystal, cutting through the murmur of the crowd; kilted Mackenzies and leather-clad ranchers and Bearkiller A-listers alike fell silent. A few of the Corvallans and traders from the Protectorate pointed and told each other who he was.

"A horse in a million, going to waste, Uncle Mike! All she needs is the right hand!"

Havel turned back, grinning across the paddock at the

boy with his face. Will Hutton smiled too, at the boy's display of spirit. The Bearkiller lord laughed and waved, ignoring the fresh hopeful babbling of the wrangler.

"She's a good horse, all right, but she's spoiled, Rudi," he called.

"I could ride her! Like an eagle on the wind!"

"Kid, if you can convince your mother to buy that horse, go ahead!" he called again, his voice warm and friendly. "I'll go halves on the price for a colt of hers, if Juney can magic her into not being crazy-mean."

Signe Havel's voice was coolly neutral as she called: "I'll pay the man's price myself and give her to you if you *can* ride her, Rudi!"

The boy was off the fence and out in the middle of the corral before Juniper's astonishment-slowed grab was halfway to his plaid. The crowd was shocked into silence.

Mike Havel's voice was soft and commanding, a controlled contrast to the throttled fury and fear in his eyes: "*Get* out of there, Rudi. Back off to the fence. Do it now."

The boy laughed. "Don't worry, Uncle," he said. "She knows me, you see."

"Rudi," Juniper called, her voice tight with urgency. "Do what Mike says. That's an order. I promise I won't be mad, just *do* it."

"It's all right, Mom," he said cheerfully, not three paces from half a ton of wild anger and lethal strength. "Really. Epona won't hurt me."

Behind Juniper Sam Aylward and John Hordle and Eilir strung their bows and nocked arrows with quick sure movements. The rest of the party used ruthless elbows and shoulders to give them a clear field of fire, and Astrid and the Lorings poised to leap the fence. Astrid slipped her sword free of its belt and unbuckled, wrapping a length of it around her right hand so that she could snap it like a whip in the mare's face to drive her back.

Juniper swallowed, watching the horse shake its head and stare at the small form before it. Time seemed to slow, as if the air was become thick amber honey and she imprisoned in it like an unwary insect. Her own breath roared in her ears, and her heartbeat was like a great slow Lambeg drum beating beneath her throat, and every particle of dust was crystal clear and etched in memory. Her mouth opened to call the archers to shoot the horse down, but a hand closed about it, vast and impalpable. Instead she spoke in a flat tone of command:

"Wait. Wait and watch. Don't let anyone startle the beast."

She could feel their incredulity, but the moment stretched, tighter and tighter like a rope hauling up some great weight, the only sound the very faint creak of the bowstaves. The honed razor edge of the broadheads glinted at the corner of her vision, etched with death.

"Epona," Rudi said, and his voice was like the wind itself. "Epona."

The horse shifted slightly, turning its head to watch him, small and unthreatening.

"Epona, you know me, my lady. You've always known me. From the days when we ran together in the country where the forever trees grow. I'm Artos."

Juniper felt a small electric jolt, flaring through the power points of her body. *That's his Craft name!* she thought; her own interior voice was infinitely distant, as if she was disconnected from her body, but she could feel everything so immediately, even the slight prickle of the plaid's wool against her neck above the brooch. Sweat ran down her flanks and slid into her eyes, although the day wasn't hot.

I haven't even told him *his Craft name! Who did? Chuck heard at the Wiccanning, but he wouldn't tell—*

"We know each other, lady. No fear, ever again. You know me."

Rudi took a single slow step forward, speaking in the voice of a harp, his small hands stroking the air to either side. Juniper felt as if those moments stretched into infinity, full of visions of the hooves hammering down on the small body, of the great square teeth sinking in and lifting him and shaking him like a rat. But the fear that choked her throat was nothing beside the greater power that held her motionless, as if a voice with the weight of worlds in it commanded.

Rudi spoke again: "Epona. We're together again, and it's all right."

The proud neck arched, the mare snuffling at his face and hair. Rudi stroked her nose, then ran a hand down her neck, eased the bit out of her mouth. He made a slight disgusted sound as he threw it down—it was a chain-curb with a barbed lever to press within—and breathed into her nose, urging her around until she was facing the sun over the Cascades.

Then he grabbed a handful of mane and vaulted onto the great animal's back, his legs clamping down on her barrel. The horse reared again, bugling a neigh, then came down with its forefeet stamping in the dust, raising puffs that drifted away like yellow-brown clouds.

"You're Epona!" Rudi said, and this time his voice sounded the way a trumpet might, if it was young and happy. "Epona and Artos. We run, but we don't run away 'cause we're scared. Wait!"

There was a single moment of electric tension, and then he clapped his heels to the mare's ribs and leaned forward over her neck. She shot ahead as if launched from a catapult, and the crowd at the corral's gate flung themselves flat. That was needless; the mare's hooves would have cleared their heads if they stood on tiptoe. She landed like dandelion fluff and pivoted down a lane between two paddocks full of draft oxen in the same motion, scattering folk to either side, and disappeared into the open fields beyond to the west, lifting over a hedge like a great black eagle. Boy and horse dwindled as he flew down the long meadows beside the Sutter River; from here they could see for miles into the valley, and they became a speck and then invisible faster than seemed possible.

Signe Havel came up beside her, milk white and trembling. "Oh, God, Juney, I'm so sorry, I don't know what came over me—"

She jarred to a halt as Juniper touched her on the sleeve and gave her one quick glance. "I don't have time to be angry now, Signe. And besides . . . I think I *do* know what came over you. Us."

The blond woman clasped a hand over her own mouth.

The crowd waited, spilling into the corral but leaving a space near the gate where Mike Havel stood like a statue.

When Rudi returned he sat with back erect and one hand on his hip, the other resting lightly on the curve of the arched neck; Epona's hooves struck the ground with a ringing sound, like the cymbals of a conqueror. She stood silently as Rudi flung a leg over her neck and slid to the ground and into Mike Havel's arms.

The Bear Lord was weeping. His voice was hoarse as he folded the boy into an embrace and spoke: "My son, my son!"

And everyone heard that, too, she thought. *Oh, Powers, what have You done to us?* After a moment: *And what song is it that You are playing this time, with us as Your instruments?*

"OK, this time *you* fucked up, Signe. Bad. Really, really bad."

Signe's face was still pale under its honey tan, and she was silent for long moments.

The guesthouse had been a bed-and-breakfast before the Change; even within the new wall, Sutterdown still had plenty of room, and the four-poster bed and flock wallpaper were pretty enough. There wasn't room enough to pace, though, so he went and looked out the window ahead. There was plenty of light in the crowded streets below, even though it was an hour after the late summer sunset—lantern- and candlelight from windows, torches, and southward, on its hilltop, the balefire boomed and danced behind the black outlines of the covenstead's pillars, and he could see figures dance about it under a thutter of drums.

"Mike . . . Juney said . . ."

He turned. "Yeah. *She* thinks Big JuJu made you do it, though only because you wanted to at some level anyway. But you know something, Signe? Smart as she is other times, when that subject comes up Juney is fucking *crazy.* Like you hadn't noticed? I seem to remember you saying so yourself. And second thing, I don't believe in Big JuJu."

"I'm sorry," she said, in a small voice.

"*Sorry* doesn't cut it. You tried to kill a kid—my kid, specifically, but there's a matter of principle involved, and you should have noticed *that* too. I'm telling you now, Signe, that if you want us to stay together, you never, ever try anything even remotely like this again. Got it?"

She nodded, and he went on: "It's late. Let's sleep." A wry quirk of the lips. "The Protector's man is arriving tomorrow, to talk about *Arminger's* kid."

CHAPTER TWENTY-ONE

Juniper received the Protector's ambassador in Sutterdown's town hall, which had once—long before the
Change—been a church; the broad high-ceilinged room
that had been the nave was usually used for public meetings these days, plus dances and sundry social events; banners and wheat sheaves and horns-of-plenty on the walls
remained from the last such. His party carried a flag of
truce, and in any event the horse fair itself was peace-holy,
sacred to Epona and sanctuary for all but those formally
outlawed.

Which Eddie Liu should *be. And we're in for a blizzard
of formality,* Juniper thought. Then: *Sacred to Epona . . .*

She shivered slightly at that thought and instead
watched Eddie Liu approach, the boots of his party sounding hollow on the hardwood floorboards. Mackenzies with
bows across their backs and spears grounded before them
waited silent and motionless along either side of the aisle,
looking a little strange in the Victorian-era room with its
plastered roof and tall arched windows, and a mixed crowd
waited behind them. Tom Brannigan sat beside her, and
Sam Aylward on the other side; Mike and Signe Havel
were at one end of the table, Mathilda Arminger at the
other, and the Clan's banner of antlers and moon hung on
the wall behind. Conspicuously, the Clan's Bearkiller allies
had their sheathed swords lying on the table before them;

equally, the ambassadors were unarmed—even Mack, Liu's giant two-legged Doberman, though he could probably pluck a normal man apart. From the crowd behind the Clan's spearmen, she could see Little John Hordle giving the massive figure of the bodyguard a considering glance.

Juniper glanced at the half-dozen following Liu and Mack, tramping stolidly in a column of twos. They were supposedly servants, clerks and attendants, but they all had the broad-shouldered, thick-wristed build of men who swung swords for hours every day, and from their slightly rolling walk they rode just as often. Hard-faced young men, wary and silent, their eyes flicking across the faces around them in unfriendly appraisal. She was reminded of nothing so much as a group of large, silent, hungry and not-very-sweet-natured cats.

Protectorate knights, she thought. *Too young to have been among the SCA re-creationists or gangbangers or university students who'd made up Arminger's earliest cadre, but certainly their younger siblings, and those of their friends and retainers.*

And more dangerous than the first set, this younger generation. They're not just *thugs. Which doesn't mean they aren't thugs, too.*

"Lady Juniper, my master Norman Arminger, the Lord Protector of the Portland Protective Association and liege lord of its dependencies, sends his greetings," Eddie Liu said formally. That sort of thing always sounded a little strange in his Brooklyn accent. "I speak in his name and with his voice."

Equally formally, he went to one knee, removed his silver-banded hat and bowed his head, and so did his followers, in unservantlike unison. Several of them also made an unconscious gesture with their left hand and foot, to move nonexistent sword sheaths out of the way. Kneeling was Protectorate protocol, and they had to show the same respect for a foreign head of state that he would for a public audience with the Lord Protector.

"As I speak for the Clan Mackenzie, being Chief of the Clan by the Clan's choice, and I send my greetings to him through you, Baron Liu," Juniper said coldly.

I'd really like to send a spear through the both of you, you little weasel, she thought, but did not let it show.

"I acknowledge you as his ambassador. So long as you and yours don't break my peace, you are safe." She allowed herself a chilly smile. "And if you do break it, I will kill you." Then she leaned forward a little. "All right, my lord of Gervais, what is your message?"

"The Lord Protector wants his daughter back, of course," Liu said. "He sent me because you didn't answer your mail. And he wants me to check on her."

"Returning her is going to take more than a request," Juniper said dryly. The girl's face was white and strained.

"The Lord Protector protests at your breaking the laws of war, and the truce agreed in Change Year Four," Liu went on doggedly.

He ignored the snicker of laughter from the audience, and Havel's audible snort. So did Juniper.

"I've protested border violations by Protectorate nobles and border commanders rather frequently," she said, and paused for a second to let *Not least by you, Eddie Liu, Marchwarden and Baron Gervais* come through without the need for words. "But that's ground we've covered before."

To her surprise, Liu nodded. "Yeah, Lady Juniper, the Protector thought you might see it that way. He also wants me to check that Princess Mathilda's all right—that you're treating her right—and to bring some of her stuff. If you're not treating her right, he wants me to warn you that he threatens war."

"He threatens war every time he notices we're still breathing and not taking orders from him," Juniper said. "But despite that, we're still breathing—and still free."

Liu's hand clenched on an absent sword hilt, which was an indication of how long it had been since the Change in itself. Juniper held up a hand to silence the baying laughter of her people, and then indicated Mathilda with it.

"You can see the girl's in good health—we don't harm children. As for how she's treated, she's sleeping in the same room as me and my son, eating at the same table, and not doing anything my son doesn't."

Liu's lips thinned. That wasn't how she was treated at home, of course, but he could scarcely complain now, after the Mackenzie chieftain proclaimed that Mathilda was being handled like her own child.

He ducked his head. "I'd like to talk to the princess myself," he said. "And I've brought some of her things—her favorite horse, some clothes, her cat, and a lady-in-waiting. The Protector won't begin serious negotiations unless you allow her to have her belongings."

Juniper's eyebrows went up, as Mathilda gave a little bounce of glee.

I wonder if that's for the horse, the cat, or the nanny? she wondered. But . . . that implied he *would* negotiate seriously if she *did* allow it.

If only his word were good, we might get a nonaggression treaty useful as something besides toilet paper out of this. Unfortunately, his word isn't *good the minute you're not holding something over his head. I don't know what we're going to do with Mathilda, really . . .*

"That at least seems reasonable, Lord Gervais," she said cautiously. "Let's arrange it."

"Hi, kid," the Marchwarden said. "You OK, Princess?"

Mathilda smiled broadly and hugged him. "Sure, Eddie," she replied. "I'm fine—but I miss Mom and Dad."

"Yeah, they miss you too," the blue-eyed man with the Asian face said. "Your goddamn cat missed you plenty, going by the way he's been yelling his head off all the way here."

Odd, Juniper thought, watching with her arms crossed on her chest; she and Astrid were alone with Liu and Arminger's heir in an office room, bare now save for a table and chair. Astrid stood in a corner, with her long single-edged sword drawn, the point resting at her feet, her strange silver-streaked eyes chilly in their focus on Liu.

Juniper wouldn't have wanted to be the object of that gaze; you could forget what else Astrid was, if you thought only of her eccentricities or her loopy charm. It was wise to remember what happened when she used that sword. Movement like moonlight flickering on water as it tumbled over rapids, a beautiful smiling image of inescapable death.

All the more terrifying to see, because you know what she's *seeing is ancient glories and heroes out of song and story.* Even when shrieking ruin kicked its heels and loosened its bowels in a last rattle at her feet.

Sam Aylward might have been a better choice in the unlikely event something went violently wrong, but possibly not, and he was off organizing the trip back to Dun Juniper. Liu ignored Astrid as if she were a wall ornament; but then, there had never been any doubt about his nerve, and he knew her safe-conduct was good.

It was disorienting to see a child beaming at him, though. *Hard it is to think of anyone actually* liking *Eddie Liu . . . I suppose some people must, though. His mother, perhaps; and he has a wife and children of his own. And it would serve his ends to have Mathilda his friend from childhood, which he's smart enough to recognize.*

Mathilda was indifferent to the boxes of clothing, but she gave a cry of delight when the carrying case with the airholes was opened. A mewling growl came from within; she lifted out a large, black, very unhappy cat and cried: "Saladin!"

They don't travel well, Juniper thought, watching the beast's mad lemon yellow eyes and noting its ruffled fur and bottled tail. *Particularly in a box strapped to a pack-saddle.*

"That tom is fixed, isn't he?" she asked.

It was unlikely to be much happier in Dun Juniper, away from its territory and forced into association with a half-dozen strange felines. Spraying was something she didn't need. What had Mike called cats once? *Little furry Republicans.*

"Oh, yes," Mathilda said, lifting it up under the forelimbs, which made its hind pair splay open. "And he's a *good* cat. Well, he likes to break things and claws furniture sometimes and he'll bite if he doesn't like the way anyone but me pets him, and he sort of hates other cats, but apart from *that* he's a good cat."

He's a cat with murder on his mind, Juniper thought, amused, noting ears laid back and whiskers bristling and claws slipping out of their sheaths. *Even if he lets you hold him like that normally, he's not in the mood right now, by the cats who draw Freya's chariot!*

"Better put him back in the box for now," she said.

"The other Kat's waiting," Liu said, with a hint of a nasty edge to his smile.

Mathilda's brows went up. "Dad sent Katrina?" she said, surprise in her voice. "Oh, that's OK," she said, turning to Juniper. "She's one of my tutors. Not my nanny, though. But Nan's sort of old, she's over *forty*, so I suppose they didn't want her taking a rough trip."

Juniper nodded, slightly surprised that either of the Armingers would show a servant that much consideration, and made a gesture of assent. Liu bowed and went to open the door. A woman came through: youngish, of medium height, with hair cropped to a halo of black curls, a rather hard good-looking face, and impassive blue eyes. She was dressed in practical traveling garb, not the trailing dresses upper-crust females in the Protectorate usually affected.

"Lady Katrina," Liu said, inclining his head.

"My lord," she replied distantly, returning the gesture. Then a genuine smile for Mathilda: "Hi, sprout! You OK?"

"Why does everyone keep *asking* me that?" Mathilda said, a little of the old waspish note in her voice. "Sure. You, Kat?"

"You bet, sprout, except that we're both in bad company here."

"Oh, they're not so bad, for rebels," Mathilda said generously. "Sort of weird, but OK. Did you hear about Rudi and the horse nobody else could ride?"

"Yes. Did you see it?"

"No." Mathilda pouted slightly and kicked at the floor. "I was watching this guy with a dog that climbed up a ladder." More brightly: "But Rudi showed me the horse later. Hey, it's a *real* pretty horse!"

"That's good; I've got Lion with me for you to ride, by the way. Everyone's been treating you properly?"

"Well, not properly like Mom and the people back home do. But nobody's been mean to me at all and sometimes things are fun. I just miss home and Mom and Dad and everyone."

Katrina bent the knee to Juniper. "Katrina Georges, Lady Juniper," she said.

Juniper cocked an eye at the way the young woman moved. "Pleased to meet you," she said, and extended a hand.

Georges looked uncertain for a moment whether Juniper expected a handshake or a suppliant's kiss on the fingers, then took it in a quick firm clasp. There was a ring of callus around the forefinger and thumb of her right hand, and the grip was very strong when Juniper squeezed a little. Some things just couldn't be disguised.

Aha, she thought; then aloud: "What exactly do you tutor Mathilda in, Ms. Georges?"

"Ah . . . I'm the physical-education tutor, Lady Juniper. And the riding instructor. But I'm also qualified to teach the princess in most subjects for a while at least."

Probably true, since she knows I can check, Juniper thought. *Does Arminger think I'm going to underestimate her because she's a woman, the way one of his testosterone-poisoned barons might? Or is he just taking out insurance, as I would if Rudi were being held hostage, sending someone like Astrid or Sam to look after him?*

"She can attend our school at Dun Juniper with my son, if we haven't come to an arrangement with her parents before then," Juniper said coolly; the term started in September, roughly when the fall rains came, and ran until March.

Georges nodded. "I have the princess's personal schoolbooks, and copies of some of her favorite reading," she said.

"I'd best have a look at that."

The tutor unslung a small leather trunk from her back and put it on the table. The trunk was newish, and also very well made—the combination bespoke great wealth these days, the ability to command the services of the rare skilled artisans. The surface was tooled around every edge in Greek keys, the corners were wrought brass, and the lock was a silver saint's face. When it opened, the interior was lined with fine linen, a contrast to the fairly shabby look of most of the volumes within. There were a couple of classic children's books—*Pooh,* for starters—readers and grammars, arithmetic primers, a geography text and an atlas. And a number of paperbacks . . .

"Is this something you know about, Astrid dear?" Juniper asked, reaching in and picking one out. There hadn't been many things to smile about this day . . .

She held up a slim volume with a bluish cover, showing an erupting volcano and someone riding a very stylized pig. Astrid's eyes narrowed, and she came out of the almost hieratic trance of watchfulness. Juniper smiled as the young woman fumed wordlessly, feeling very slightly ashamed. Then she felt much worse, as she saw from the narrowing of Eddie Liu's eyes that he was sharing the amusement.

Suddenly that ran out of his face, leaving total blankness. "Lady Katrina, where did you get that book?" he said.

The tutor looked at him, puzzled. "It was on the list and I brought it from . . . no, wait, I lie. I forgot that one in Portland and got a copy in Gervais when we were staying over at the castle. Your house steward got it for me. Any problem?"

Liu's face stayed blank, but Juniper had the impression it suddenly required an immense effort of will to keep it that way as he shook his head.

I wonder what that was about? she thought. *But anyway . . .*

"This interview was supposed to be short, Baron Gervais," she pointed out. "If you're finished."

"Yeah. I mean, yes, of course, Lady Juniper."

"You'd do best to leave immediately, then," Juniper went on.

She more than half expected Liu to protest and demand quarters for the night; the day was half gone, and he'd have to camp out at least once in unsettled country. Instead he bowed again and left.

Juniper fixed Katrina Georges with a steady eye: "Let's understand each other, Ms. Georges. I don't trust anyone who works for your employer. You'll be watched. Don't make me do anything Mathilda would regret."

That went over the girl's head, but the tutor caught it: *She might regret it if you ended up with half a dozen arrows through you but I wouldn't.* That wasn't strictly true: Juniper never liked killing anything, and human beings in particular. *Which doesn't mean I won't, if I have to.*

"We'll be leaving tomorrow morning early," she said. "Please be ready."

Mathilda gave her an abstracted nod; she'd settled down near the cat's box with her book and was reading bits of it under her voice, giggling as she did so. The tutor's face was unrecognizable.

Outside in the corridor three Clan warriors stood guard. "Shaun, get me—" *No, Sam headed back yesterday to make sure Dun Juniper was safe.* "Get me Rowan of Dun Carson, if he hasn't left town yet."

The Larsdalen contingent had tactfully headed back for Bearkiller territory. That had seemed advisable at the time, but . . .

Best to get back home quickly.

Between Sutterdown and Dun Juniper,
Willamette Valley, Oregon
August 25th, 2007 AD—Change Year Nine

"What on earth?" Astrid said, then repeated it with Sign.

The little clump of woods was too dark for easy lipreading. They'd picked it because it was convenient and had good water, shelter and firewood. Once inside the outer ring of thick brush, the ground under the tall firs and alders and oaks made it plain someone else had been there, and not too long ago.

Horse traders from Sutterdown? Eilir said, glancing around at the ground.

Someone made a torch from fallen branches and set it on fire with their lighter. Astrid looked around, raising it above her head so that it wouldn't dazzle her eyes, but instead cast light to let her see. The hoofmarks were many and deep; so were piles of dung, where the mounts had been tethered to a picket line strung between two young trees. The bark bore the scars of the rope, and there was sap to make a finger sticky when she touched it, the balsamlike scent of Douglas fir.

There's an awful lot of them. And why would they be headed southeast? There's nothing that way but Dun Carson and Dun Juniper, unless you go all the way south to Peoria and then up to Corvallis.

Eilir cast about, going to one knee occasionally, sometimes sniffing at a horse apple. *A day old, but some's fresh; oat-fed horses, too—see, there's some grain that spilled from a feed bag. They were here during the last of the horse fair and left only an hour or two ago. They didn't let their horses graze, either.*

That was odd; the fields about were Mackenzie land, of course, but unclaimed by any dun, and they were tall with grass. Why waste feed?

Bandits? Eilir asked. *Waiting to jump people coming back from the fair?*

That was why they'd gone on a scout-about after the fair, rather than riding straight back to Dun Juniper or west to Larsdalen. Astrid did more of her own looking. *No. All big horses, well-shod. Men in boots with built-up heels, wearing armor, from the way they sank in.*

Another of the Dunedain waved from deeper within the woods, where a small creek ran in a hollow. *Campfires,* he signed in broad form. *Forty, fifty men and more horses.*

Definitely not bandits, Eilir signed. *Too well ordered.*

Yrch! Astrid replied. *Servants of the Lidless Eye.*

Eilir nodded, her face tight with worry. Then: *Look!*

A hazelnut bush that fronted the edge of the woods had been turned into a blind; someone had put a blanket down, a ragged tattered one, and not bothered to take it up again. Astrid crawled through, wrinkling her nose at the sweat smell . . . and whoever it was hadn't bothered to go far when he pissed, either. That gave her a view of the white ribbon of road ahead, over the scrub-grown field. The road to Dun Juniper, which Lady Juniper's party would have taken a few hours ago; unlikely they'd try to push through to home, that would mean traveling long after dark. More probably they'd camp out—

This was an ambush party, she signed. Eilir gasped, and Astrid went on: *Too many men for spies. They probably came in disguised as horse traders and then hid here. And then followed.*

Eilir's face firmed. *Anamchara, you go for Lord Bear. He's only a few hours away, there and back—he was heading for the southern crossing to Corvallis.*

We'll send one of the others.

No! It has to be you. He'll listen. We'll follow the enemy directly.

But you've only got six Rangers here!

There's better than thirty warriors with Mom. We'll do what we can . . . but get them here, and hurry! They've got something worse than just an attack planned.

The dark was dense when Mathilda Arminger awoke in her tent. The night was just a little too cool to be comfortable on top of the bedding, but her blanket and the warm curled lump of Saladin made it cozy. She stirred and yawned, wiggling for a more comfortable position— Saladin just didn't move when *he* was comfortable, and that was that. That was one reason she'd been happy enough when Lady Katrina had insisted she have a tent of her own, separate from the one Lady Juniper and Rudi had. Then Rudi had said he intended to sleep by the side of his new horse, and there had been an argument . . . although Katrina had seemed to get along well with the young guard assigned to her.

"Mmmm?" she said drowsily, realizing that a noise outside the tent had woken her.

Now the flap opened, letting in a slight wash of starlight, bright by comparison to the utter blackness a moment earlier. Katrina was there, but when she came to kneel by the cot Mathilda could see that she wore a mail vest and had her hair tucked under a light helmet. A crossbow was cradled in her hands.

Mathilda shot upright, excitement making her blood race. "What's up, Kat?" she said.

"We're taking you home, Princess," she replied, speaking quietly. "Get up and get dressed. Quickly now. Don't make any noise."

She scurried to obey. *A rescue, like the stories!*

Another figure knelt at the opening of the tent and whispered. Mathilda recognized Baron Liu's voice, and the edge of his heavy sword glittered slightly. He was in armor, too, a laced-together cuirass of finger-sized lamellar steel plates and mail sleeves and leggings, and a darkened helmet; the harness gave off a muted sound as he moved, a low sibilant rustling.

"Any problem with the guard?" he said softly.

"No," Kat answered. "Everyone knew he was with me, and he was asleep when I made sure of him. The perimeter?"

"They heard the little glass balls tinkle, and then they *all* went sleepy-byes," Liu said. "This is good stuff."

Abruptly, Mathilda recognized the smell from Katrina's right sleeve: it was blood. Surprise rocked her silent for an instant, and then Kat's hand went over her mouth.

"These are your father's enemies, Princess. Now hold still for a moment."

She pulled out a small leather case and opened it. Starlight gleamed on a set of hypodermics; the woman lifted one and tapped it, letting a bead of clear liquid trickle down the needle. There was a slight sting in the girl's arm, and the plunger went home. The spot itched and burned, and then a rush of faintness overtook her for a moment, as if the fire were spreading throughout her body.

"What *is*—" she began, then gave a muffled squawk of indignation as Katrina clamped her hand back across her mouth.

"Princess, I have your parents' permission to tie you up and gag you if I have to. Now are you going to come along like a good girl?" Mathilda nodded, and her tutor went on: "That was to keep you safe. I took some myself and the feeling goes away in a few minutes. Now let's get ready to go."

She turned in surprise as Liu crawled into the tent, then hissed: "What are you *doing*, you idiot?"

Liu was upending the leather case that held her books and papers. "Where is it?" he said. "Where *is* it?"

"Where's *what*? We've got the princess; let's go before the kilties catch on!"

"Fuck the kilties; that's why we've got the gas! You think the Protector wants us to scoot and go with a chance like this? And *where's the book*?"

"The *book*?" Katrina's face went fluid with shock.

"Yeah, bitch, the book you took from my castle at Gervais," Liu said tightly. His hand moved, and the heavy sword twitched; it was suddenly under Katrina's chin. "And don't ask why. Just don't. *Get* it!"

Katrina's hand had left Mathilda's mouth as she made an abortive grab at the hilt of the long dagger at her belt.

Mathilda spoke, in a small, quiet voice with a shiver in it, younger than her years. "I loaned it to Rudi," she said. "I'd told him about it. That's why I said to bring it."

Eddie Liu began to swear, softly and venomously. Mathilda swallowed; she knew what most of the words meant, but she also knew there was something very wrong if Baron Liu was talking that way to her.

"Where is the little shit?"

"Eddie!" she whispered. "You're scaring me!"

"Where is he?"

"And here I thought you were a man of initiative," Juniper said, leaning her chin on one palm. "Tsk, tsk. I go to all the trouble of getting my son his own tent—"

On the other side of the table, Nigel Loring laughed softly. "And I thought, dear lady, that it was simply that he *must* have one if young Miss Arminger had her own."

"*He* certainly thought so."

His smile died slightly. "Are you quite sure?" he said.

"Quite. As if a little bird had whispered in my ear." *Or Herself.*

He moved the lamp to the other side of the camp table and reached out both hands; she took them in hers. "I'm a bit older than you—ten years—"

"Oh, hush, Nigel; I discovered my first gray hair some time ago. We're neither of us teenagers in lust. We're middle-aged, and friends. Let's see where that takes us." An impish smile. "And I do covet that fair body of yours, you know."

"Which I assure you is mutual."

They were leaning towards each other when the first shout sounded outside.

Rudi Mackenzie bolted upright at the soft *thud* of steel in flesh. He made an instinctive grab for the book that slid off his chest, then reached for the knob on the lantern beside his cot. Then he froze; the starlight was just enough for him to see the glitter of cold steel at the entrance to the tent. A huge gauntlet clamped on his ankle with bruising force and yanked him through the entrance and onto the turf beyond in a single motion; behind him the lantern toppled sideways, and there was a rush of flame as the glass shattered and burning wood alcohol rushed out across canvas and cloth.

"Got him, boss!" a voice like gravel dropping into a steel bucket said, and a huge armored figure loomed over him.

"The book, you fuckhead, the book!"

A smaller figure darted through and scooped up the paperback, stuffing it hastily into a pouch at his belt. He swore in relief and then clamped a hand on the back of Rudi's neck.

"Kat, you got the princess? Sorry I was rough, Princess; business. All right—"

Juniper Mackenzie had her sword in her hand as she dashed out into the dark; that was a measure of what she felt, because running around in the dark with two feet of pointed, edged metal in your hand wasn't something you did casually. Light flared up a second later, as someone threw dry wood on the low-burning campfires; the wagons were strung out in a pasture alongside the road, and the tents behind them, with the picket line for the horses beyond that. She squinted . . .

Rowan was there, panting, his ax in his hands. "Sentries dead on the north end—not a mark on them."

"Damn the man!" Nigel Loring said. "He was talking about launching it with crossbows. Stonebow type, to throw little thin glass containers of it, like pebbles. There would be enough in the carboy of the real thing for some of those."

Juniper felt her mind whirl. "Mathilda!" she said. "That must be it, why he sent that lady in so-called waiting!"

She whirled; Nigel's hand fell on her shoulder. He'd managed to get most of his armor on, somehow.

"They may still have some of it left," he said. "Don't go running in blind."

More and more of her folk were boiling out of their tents. "Rudi," she snapped; that was in the same direction anyway. "Now!"

A dozen of them formed up on her, and they trotted forward. Her back was to the campfires, but there was light ahead too, a sullen red glow mingled with black smoke that smelled rank and hot; burning canvas. Horses neighed, stark fear in the night, and her heart hammered at her ribs.

Then a great calm descended as she saw that it was Rudi's tent that burned. Katrina Georges was there, armed, with Mathilda against her side. The towering form of Mack, several of the knights she'd seen in Sutterdown, out of their disguises now and back in their hauberks . . . and Eddie Liu, with her son's neck in his hand, and the other gripping some sort of pistollike contraption . . . no, more like an old-fashioned water pistol but heavy and bulky. The boy's hands were bound behind his back, and there was a rising bruise on the side of his face.

"Hold!" Juniper cried. "Hold, everyone!"

Liu's smile was white in the dimness, framed by his darkened helmet. "Yeah, Ms. Witch, hold it. 'Cause I brought some Raid on this raid." He flourished the pistollike apparatus. "We've all got the antidote. But funny, we didn't give any to Junior here. So if I start spraying this stuff, chances are he may catch some. And it doesn't take much, you know? I got some friends arriving soon, like in minutes, and then we'll all take a ride. And you can send an ambassador to see how *your* kid is getting on, hey?"

Juniper cast desperate eyes aside at Nigel Loring. He spoke without moving his lips. "Probably not. There wasn't much of the real agent left. But he *may* have it in that."

But Arminger would never let my child go, no matter what I did. And he would torment him from spite.

Rudi's eyes met hers; there was no fear in them, only a clear anger, his lips braced tight. Eddie Liu grinned at her.

"*Told* you I'd make you pay, bitch," he said softly. "Do you like your choices now?"

Hooves sounded in the night, galloping horses pressed to desperate haste. One of the Protectorate knights stooped to take a burning tent pole from the ruins of Rudi's tent, waving it aloft in signal.

Whatever he expected, it wasn't the shaft that hissed out of the night and struck him full in the chest, sinking through the mail and halfway to the feathers. The others shouted and jumped to surround their leaders and the children, raising their shields in a protective fence; Mack swept out the huge blade of his greatsword and poised, growling. Firelight shone on the edges of the hungry swords; then she saw Eilir sitting her Arab behind the attackers, and more of her Dunedain on either side.

Liu jerked Rudi closer and poised the water gun. "One more arrow and he dies!"

"You won't harm my son," Juniper said, amazed at the calm strength of her own voice. "You know what would happen to you if you did."

"If I go down, I take your kid with me," Liu said. "I figure that'll hurt you worse than killing *you* would, and bitch, I've wanted to do that for a *long* time."

Juniper sheathed her sword and raised her hands, and her voice tolled in the flame-shot night: "Eddie Liu, Katrina Georges. I curse you, now; in the name of the Dark Goddess, by the power of the Dread Lord. I curse you in their names and mine, and that curse is this: Death not long delayed. So mote it be!"

Rudi's eyes went wide. One of the knights licked his lips and his sword moved as he crossed himself, but Liu bared his teeth again. "Sorry, Witch Queen, that mojo only works on people stupid enough to believe it. Now we're going to back away, real careful, and if any of your folks get in our way . . . well, I've got me a *real* good shield, right here."

More hooves moved in the darkness, not close, but moving fast; Liu grinned. Then it died as there was a sudden ringing clash of steel, a brabble of voices, a stamping and thudding and iron clangor.

"Hakkaa paalle!"

Liu looked over his shoulder. "OK, those are big boys, and they can take care of themselves. Let's go!"

Please, Mother-of-All, Juniper thought, drawing a great breath. *Hear me, for I'm a mother too. Not him! Anyone, but not him!*

Then, in a high clear shout: *"Take them!"*

Hanging back was the hardest thing she had ever forced herself to do, but she was no more than a middling hand with a sword, and this was far too dangerous for bows. All she could do would be get in the way of those who *might* save her son. Liu's hand moved, and a stream struck Rudi's neck and the side of his face; he cried out and twisted in the man's hands. Liu shot again, quick as a striking snake, and droplets of the same heavy, oily liquid landed on her face; it had a nasty chemical stink, and the drops itched and burned . . . and the night did not darken, and her chest continued to pump in hard quick breaths. Then he screamed a curse and used the heavy glass-and-metal pistol to club Rudi down; the boy went to the ground, writhing.

"A Loring! A Loring!" Nigel shouted as he went forward with darting speed.

Not quite in time, for Mack's first stroke was straight down at Rudi's young body. A desperate leap put Nigel's shield above the boy, but the four-foot blade of the greatsword cut three-quarters of the way through the tough laminate of wood and metal, and broke the arm below it. Mack's steel-splinted boot stamped on the blade of the Englishman's sword and snapped it across, and the next blow sent his sallet helm spinning off into the darkness. Nigel Loring slumped backward, blood running from nose and eyes and mouth, motionless.

The Mackenzies were throwing themselves desperately at the ring of swords now, shrieking and sheerly mad, but many hadn't had time to don their brigandines, and the knights were sheathed in mail and splints of hard metal from ankle to head, armored cap-a-pie. Arminger's men stood shield-to-shield and cast back their rush. Rowan led the next, making for the Marchwarden's giant bodyguard, his long ax spinning, crashing at head and hip and leg.

Crack. The greatsword struck the tough ashwood and broke it in half. The head flipped up into its master's face and laid it open to the bone; he staggered, blinded by his own blood, blinking it clear just in time to see the second stroke that took him between neck and shoulder.

"Father!" Alleyne Loring cried.

"No! *Mine!*" a deep bass voice bellowed, and John Hordle's bastard sword hammered its way past a shield and sent a man reeling, then turned the stroke of Mack's blade with a grunt of effort, a harsh clangor in the night and a stream of sparks. Alleyne tried to use the moment to take the troll-man from behind, but Katrina Georges was suddenly between them, a sword in one hand, a long knife in the other. The circle of shields was breaking up into combats that raged through the flame-shot darkness, two against one, a pair against three.

Eilir was there too, light glittering from eyes gone huge in a face bone-white pale, shining ruddy-bright on teeth bared in a silent gape as she turned the stroke of Liu's *bao* on her buckler and struck, struck . . .

Juniper ignored all of it. Instead she saw her moment and darted in, dragging her son free of the melee. His face was a mask of blood, but it was the wound under his short ribs that pulsed red, where the tip of the greatsword had passed after it punched through Nigel's shield. She staunched it with her hands, leaning to put pressure on it.

"Healer!" she shouted. "A healer here! *Now!*"

Her eyes swiveled, through chaos and death. Glimpses struck her vision and slid from the focus of her mind: Mack sinking to his knees, with Alleyne's sword and a spear through his gut, and Little John Hordle's sword sweeping through a horizontal arc towards his neck; Eddie Liu shrieking as Eilir's short sword punched up under the skirt of his mail and sank home; the lance points of Bear-killer A-listers flickering as they rode into the circle of firelight.

Suddenly Kevin of the Rangers threw himself on his

knees beside her. "Let me see . . . Oh, sweet Goddess, there's too much blood lost—"

He shouted, and the sound carried; battle was dying down, save for someone who shrieked for his mother in a long gurgle that cut off sharply. "I need a donor here! Emergency!"

Shadows fell across them. Juniper looked up, with her son's lifeblood on her hands. Mike Havel stood there, blood on his sword and his face twisted with raging grief; Astrid, supporting Alleyne Loring as he slumped with both hands clapped to a wounded face. And Signe Havel, calm as she stripped the vambrace of her right forearm and pushed the mail sleeve of her hauberk back, lying down beside the wounded boy.

"I'm type O," she said. "Universal donor. As much as he needs, Juney. As much as he needs."

Mathilda Arminger had to call her name several times before Juniper Mackenzie heard the words. The cold light of dawn made the tumbled filth of the battlefield bleaker and more lost; somewhere a raven croaked, and tatters of mist lay along the ground. She could taste something old and dead in her mouth as she leaned back against the wagon wheel, but it was too distant to make her move her hand towards the water bottle someone had put there.

I should sleep. Fear and grief and raw magic have hollowed me, and I should sleep.

"Lady Juniper?"

Juniper looked up; tears made runnels down the girl's face, melting a track through a spray of dried blood.

"Will Rudi be OK? Please, can't you, I don't know, make magic about it?"

"I have, girl. I don't know if he'll be all right. He's lost a very great deal of blood, and they're doing what they can. He may get well."

"I'm so sorry. It's because of me."

I should tell her it isn't, but I'm too tired, the Chief of the Mackenzies thought.

"It's because I lent Rudi the book," Mathilda sobbed. "I

lent him the book and Baron Liu went to get it. Katrina didn't want him to but he wouldn't leave without the book!"

That pierced the gray chill that swaddled her mind. "Your book, child?"

A shaking hand held a blue-tinted paperback. "I got it out of Baron Liu's belt pouch after he . . . when I could. It's not my copy. Kat said she got it at Castle Gervais, and the baron got so angry, and he went for it—"

Memory stabbed her. Eddie Liu's face in that room at Sutterdown . . . *Goddess gentle and* strong, *was it only yesterday?*

"Altendorf substitution codes," she whispered, looking northward—to where Arminger brewed his plots.

She rose. Eilir was close, and she looked up sharply, a tentative wisp of smile curling her lips at the sight of her mother moving.

Get me Mike Havel, she signed. *Now, girl! Run!*

To herself: *The Protector wants war. He'll have it, and not only with the Mackenzies . . . but we'll need more than talk to do it. When his plans are laid bare . . . but we'll have to do it at the right time and place. A meeting of all the communities, yes, but not at Larsdalen or Dun Juniper or Mt. Angel. It will have to be a blow to the heart—the heart of the Valley. A meeting at Corvallis.*

"Goddess of the raven wings," she whispered, gathering herself. "Strong avenger, give me Your strength."

EPILOGUE

The path that led upward from Dun Juniper to the mountainside *nemed* was steep; it wove back and forth beneath tall trees, turning on itself like a serpent in a bed of reeds or the words of an oracle. She had walked it in daylight under summer leaves, and when moonlight shone on snow white as salt beneath stars uncountable. Today gray skies pressed down like the grief of gods, hiding the mountain peaks eastward and the valley to the west alike, and sending drifts of mist through the tops of the great dark-green firs. A wet wind tossed their limbs with an edge of ice; the air soughed around them with the prickling smell of cold snow heavy in it, and the darkness was coming before the cusp of day and night.

Juniper shivered a little, despite the heavy wool of her black ritual robe; the hood was drawn forward shadowing her face and the crescent moon on her brows. It was her folk's custom to sing as they walked to the sacred Wood, but today . . .

She stilled her mind and raised her voice:

> "As the sun bleeds through the murk
> 'tis the last day we shall work
> For the Veil is thin and the spirit wild
> And the Crone is carrying Harvest's child!"

The Initiates and Dedicants were robed as she, though only the High Priests and Priestesses wore the tricolored

cord belts. Many were masked on this day; some danced
with spears flashing dully in the gray light, enacting the
Wild Hunt. A harp played, and a flute, and the eerie sweetness of the Uilleann pipes; the beat of the bodhran was like
the pulse of blood in her ears. Threescore voices rose in the
chorus:

> "Samhain!
> *Turn away*
> *Run ye back to the light of day*
> Samhain!
> *Hope and pray*
> *All ye meet are the gentle Fae."*

Leaves from oak and maple blew past in a cloud of old
gold and dark crimson.

> *"Burn the fields and dry the corn*
> *Feel the breath of winter born*
> *Stow the grain 'gainst season's flood*
> *Spill the last of the livestock's blood!"*

They came to the Wood, with its great circle of oaks. The
trunks were closely placed on a nearly level knee that
thrust out from the mountainside; each tree was forty feet
and more to the first branch, candle-straight, thicker
through than her body. Her great-uncle had planted many
trees on his land, three generations ago. What had
prompted him to plant *this* he had never said, but she could
guess.

> *"Let the feasting now begin*
> *Careful who you welcome in*
> *The table's set with a stranger's place*
> *Don't stare openly at his face!"*

Iceplant still grew beside the spring that bubbled outside the circle. Juniper led the weaving passage around it,
as the song went through heart and bone:

"Stranger, do you have a name?
Tell us all from whence you came
You seem more like god than man
Has curse or blessing come to this clan?"

Then all together, gathering strength:

"Samhain!
Turn away
Run ye back to the light of day
Samhain!
Hope and pray
All ye meet are the gentle Fae."

And one last great shout:

"SAMHAIN!"

Silence fell as she approached the opening in the northeast corner of the *nemed* to begin the ritual. Motion and word flowed through her as she cut with the sword to close the Circle. Leafless with new-come winter, twigs grated and squeaked as they swayed and rubbed eighty feet above; the fire that boomed and crackled in the stone-lined pit in the center of the sacred space seemed as if it were the only color and warmth left in the world. Winter was coming early to the high Cascades this year, and the edge of its cloak brushed them here.

Robed in black, the coven of the Singing Moon waited while the High Priestess turned at last to the black veil that today covered the Eastern gate. Behind her on the shaped boulder that made the Altar of Earth were the cauldron and sword, dish of salt, censer, incense . . . and today, a skull for the Aspect that was called.

The ceremony made its way, and as Juniper faced the Veil of Death she chanted:

"The Year dies, as all things must. The Moon Herself wanes—mourning—in the sign of the Sacrificial Bull. Samhain comes and we greet our beloved dead! Great

One, I now call upon Thee to put on Thy dark cloak. I invoke the Utter Night!"

She raised the athame: "Akare Bal Krithe! The Circle is cast. The Altar is made. Way has been prepared for the coming of the Dark Lady and Dark Lord. In the name of our dead sent untimely to You, we invoke Your power as your people march to war . . ."

The world faded from around her, even as her body moved through ritual. She had experienced such before, as a communion with a universe of singing light, when all creation swirled around her and she was dancer and the dance, the singer and the song. Now she was . . . nowhere. Now she spoke, but not in words. Somehow she knew that later there would be words in her memories, but for now there was only Meaning, stripped of symbol.

Do you ask? Something asked of her. *Beloved daughter, do you ask this of Us?*

Her mind creaked beneath the weight of the contact, struggling to turn away from the task her will compelled; it was like gasping for breath at an effort beyond you yet utterly needful, or like the day when you first felt how tiny the span of your life was in the depths of time. She remembered that day, holding the lump of rock with the fossil shell, and *knowing* . . .

For if you ask, daughter, it will be given.

Why do You question me? Isn't this the road that You have laid before me, step by step, whether I will or no?

Images cascaded through her mind; a wheel of fire in darkness, like a galaxy turning through a billion years against a well of night; a man cloaked in blue; a spear, a horse and a single eye; a woman with many arms who danced creation and destruction across the dust of stars beneath her feet; the tormented birth of suns and the death of worlds that foundered in slow fire; ash leaves blowing across a heath; a ship built of bones and dead men's nails on a frozen sea.

There is Fate, and yet there is also Choice. We will not end untimely the tale We sing through you.

Like a flash of fire it went through her.

Then give me my desire, Victory-Father, Dreadful Bride!

Be with me, become me now. Enter, where I have opened the Door, and do all Your will!

And as suddenly she was within the sunless circle again, her skin roughening beneath the coarse fabric of her robe. A raven flew about the tall trees, deasil, and departed northward, its voice a harsh *gruk-gruk-gruk* in the gathering night.

"So mote it be," she whispered.

IN HARDCOVER FROM Roc

S. M.
STIRLING

NATIONAL BESTSELLING AUTHOR OF *THE PROTECTOR'S WAR*

A MEETING AT
CORVALLIS

0-451-46111-8

Roc Science Fiction & Fantasy
Available September 2006

FIRESTORM:
Book Five of
The Weather Warden

by Rachel Caine

0-451-46104-5

Putting aside the personal chaos that has
plagued her, rogue Weather Warden Joanne
Baldwin must rally the remnants of the
Weather Warden corps against a double
threat—the Djinn who have broken free from
Warden control, and a cranky Mother Earth
who's about to unleash her full fury against
the entire world.

Available wherever books are sold or at
penguin.com

THE ULTIMATE IN
SCIENCE FICTION AND FANTASY!

From magical tales of distant worlds to stories of
technological advances beyond the grasp of man, Penguin has
everything you need to stretch your imagination to its limits.

penguin.com

ACE
Get the latest information on favorites like
William Gibson, T.A. Barron, Brian Jacques,
Ursula Le Guin, Sharon Shinn, and Charlaine Harris,
as well as updates on the best new authors.

ROC
Escape with Harry Turtledove, Anne Bishop,
S.M. Stirling, Simon Green, Chris Bunch, Jim Butcher, E.E.
Knight, and many others—plus news on the
latest and hottest in science fiction and fantasy.

DAW
Mercedes Lackey, Kristen Britain, Tanya Huff,
Tad Williams, C.J. Cherryh, and many more—
DAW has something to satisfy the cravings of any
science fiction and fantasy lover.
Also visit dawbooks.com.

*Get the best of science fiction and fantasy
at your fingertips!*